as an intense and inventive literary form'
Library Journal

'With its stopwatch timing, locked-room murder and perplexing abundance of alibis ... Readers are in store for plenty of surprises'
Wall Street Journal

BY KEIGO HIGASHINO

THE DETECTIVE GALILEO MYSTERIES

The Devotion of Suspect X
Salvation of a Saint
A Midsummer's Equation
Silent Parade

THE KYOICHIRO KAGA MYSTERIES

Malice
Newcomer

Under the Midnight Sun

SILENT PARADE

KEIGO HIGASHINO

ABACUS

Originally published in Japanese as *Chinmoku no paredo* by Bungeishunju, Ltd.
First published in the United States in 2021 by Minotaur Books
First published in the United Kingdom in 2021 by Little, Brown
This paperback edition published in 2022 by Abacus

13 5 7 9 10 8 6 4 2

A CIP catalogue record for this book
is available from the British Library.

ISBN 978-0-3491-4502-0

Designed by Gabriel Guma
Printed and bound in Great Britain by Clays Ltd, Elcograf S.p.A.

Papers used by Abacus are from well-managed forests
and other responsible sources.

Abacus
An imprint of
Little, Brown Book Group
Carmelite House
50 Victoria Embankment
London EC4Y 0DZ

An Hachette UK Company
www.hachette.co.uk

www.littlebrown.co.uk

Professor Manabu Yukawa (aka "Detective Galileo"): Professor of physics and occasional unofficial consultant to the Tokyo Metropolitan Police Department

TOKYO METROPOLITAN POLICE DEPARTMENT

Director Mamiya: Head of the Homicide Division

Detective Chief Inspector Kusanagi: Leads the investigation, college friend of Professor Yukawa

Detective Inspector Kishitani: Part of Kusanagi's team

Detective Sergeant Kaoru Utsumi: Part of Kusanagi's team and a friend of Professor Yukawa

Detective Inspector Muto: Detective, Kikuno precinct

KIKUNO AREA RESIDENTS

Yutaro Namiki: Co-owner of Namiki-ya restaurant, father of Saori Namiki

Machiko Namiki: Co-owner of Namiki-ya, mother of Saori Namiki

Natsumi Namiki: Younger daughter of Yutaro and Machiko, sister of Saori

Saori Namiki: Eldest daughter of Yutaro and Machiko

Naoki Niikura: Music impresario

Rumi Niikura: Wife of Naoki

Shusaku Tojima: Owner of local food-processing company. Childhood friend of Yutaro Namiki

Maya Miyazawa: Owner of local bookstore and head of the Kikuno parade team

Tomoya Takagaki: Boyfriend of Saori Namiki

Eiji Masumura: Former coworker and roommate of Kanichi Hasunuma

Yuna Motohashi: Twelve-year-old girl, believed to have been murdered by Kanichi Hasunuma twenty-three years ago

Kanichi Hasunuma: Suspected murderer, never convicted

NOTE

One million yen is approximately equal to 9,000 U.S. dollars.

PART ONE

I regret to say I was the very last person to notice what was going on.

—JOHN DICKSON CARR, *SHE DIED A LADY*

1

Glancing up at the wall clock, he saw that there were only twenty minutes to go until ten o'clock. *Think I'll call it a night.* Yutaro Namiki looked around the restaurant. It was almost empty—only a couple middle-aged women were left. When they came in, one of them had said something about how nice it was to be back. Yutaro Namiki sneaked a peek at her. The woman was certainly not one of their regulars. He had a vague sense that he recognized her but he could just be imagining things.

Right about then, the woman announced that she wanted to pay her check. "Coming," called out Machiko, Yutaro's wife, who was standing beside him, washing dishes.

Yutaro heard the woman say, "Thank you. That was quite delicious."

"Thank you for coming," Machiko replied. "I hope you'll come again."

"I'm sure we'll be back soon. Actually, I've been here before. It was quite a long time ago—maybe five or six years ago."

"Oh, really?"

"There was this amazingly pretty waitress. We ended up chatting and she told me she was the owner's daughter. I seem to remember that she was still in high school. Is she well?"

Yutaro was busy in the kitchen, putting away the knives, but his hand stopped in midair. He knew that hearing his wife's response to the offhand inquiry would only cause him pain, but he couldn't help straining to listen.

"That was my daughter. She's doing fine." Machiko sounded perfectly relaxed. She was keeping her feelings well hidden.

"Oh, good. Does she still live at home?"

"No, she's moved out."

"Really? She seemed such a well-adjusted kid. Not like mine. They're getting older but they still look to us for everything. I'm getting sick and tired of it."

"Oh, I don't know. That has its own charms."

"'Lucky the house with a child to spoil,' you mean?"

"Exactly."

He heard Machiko and the woman heading for the exit. There was a rattling sound as someone pulled the sliding door open. "Thank you very much. Good night," he heard his wife say.

Putting down the knife he was holding, Yutaro walked around the counter and out into the restaurant. Machiko had taken down the *noren* curtain over the front door and just come back inside.

Their eyes met and she cocked her head slightly. "Something wrong?"

"No. I just couldn't help overhearing." Yutaro scratched the back of his head. "You really kept your cool. I know it can't be easy."

"It's no big deal. I've been dealing with customers for years. That's the business we're in, after all."

"I know, but still . . ."

Machiko leaned the curtain pole up against the wall and turned to her husband. A petite woman with a small face, she'd always had a penetrating gaze, even as a young woman. It was hard not to flinch when she made eye contact.

"Haven't you accepted it yet?"

"Accepted what?"

"The fact that Saori has gone. I've come to terms with it. Since you spend all your time in the kitchen, you may not realize it, but people talking about Saori the way that woman did—it happens all the time. It's the same for Natsumi. She never makes a fuss about it because she's come to terms with it, too."

Natsumi was the younger of the Namikis' two daughters. She was a sophomore in college and helped out at the restaurant when she had the time.

Yutaro stood there, saying nothing.

"Look, I'm not saying that there's anything wrong with you holding on like you do. I'm just saying that you don't need to worry about me."

"Yeah, okay."

"Can you tidy up the kitchen? There's something I've got to do upstairs." Machiko pointed up at the ceiling. The family lived on the second floor above the restaurant.

"Sure, no problem."

"See you later, then." Machiko started climbing the stairs in the back corner of the restaurant.

Yutaro shook his head feebly. He wasn't in the mood to go straight back to work, so he pulled up a chair and sat down. He could feel his back rounding into a slouch. *Women are so much stronger than us!* It was something he felt acutely now—and had felt countless times in the past.

Saori had been their firstborn. A big-eyed baby with glowing pink skin. Yutaro had long been convinced that he wanted his first child to be a boy, but that particular prejudice evaporated the instant Saori was born. She was the apple of his eye. No, she was more than that: He was ready to lay down his life for her.

Machiko was an integral part of running Namiki-ya, as their restaurant was called, so the restaurant became Saori's nursery. When the restaurant was busy, the regulars would often pick up Saori and bounce her on their knees.

Saori had been a healthy child and adored by everybody. All sorts of people from the neighborhood would greet her on her way to kindergarten. She would always return their greetings in her piping voice. Yutaro felt a surge of pride every time someone congratulated him on Saori's good manners.

Saori had been popular at elementary school and junior high school. When her homeroom teacher came to visit Machiko, she had said that "what made Ms. Namiki special was that she was nice to everyone, cheerful, and never made a fuss even when things got difficult."

Saori's test scores were not that good, but neither Yutaro nor Machiko were overly concerned. Saori was basically a serious and kind person who almost never caused them any grief or worry. She was also a lovely big sister who liked taking care of Natsumi, who was three years her junior.

Outside of school, Saori had one shining talent: She could sing. She'd liked singing as a very young child, but as the years went on, she started to display signs of exceptional talent. No matter how difficult a song was, she only needed to hear it once to memorize it, and she was never out of tune. That was when Yutaro first heard the phrase *perfect pitch*. Saori, people told him, had it.

Saori got to display her talent at the neighborhood street festival that was held every autumn. While the main event was a grand parade with costumes and floats, there was also a singing contest, which the locals all looked forward to. Saori first took part as a fourth grader when her rendition of "My Heart Will Go On," the theme song of the movie *Titanic*, had amazed the audience. It was the first time he had seen his daughter really perform.

After that she was roped into performing at every autumn festival, becoming something of a local celebrity. The singing contest always attracted a good crowd, with plenty of people there specifically to hear Saori.

As she got older, Saori started helping out in the restaurant during the summer holidays.

Some of the more cynical customers would ask her what she was doing, helping out in a fusty old place like Namiki-ya. Didn't she know that a beautiful girl like her could make a lot of money working in a hostess club in central Tokyo? Even her parents had to admit that she had grown into a beautiful woman. She was like a flower in bloom; her presence alone was enough to transform and brighten the atmosphere of the restaurant. She attracted more and more customers to the place as people associated Namiki-ya with her.

When Saori was about fourteen, a man named Naoki Niikura came to the restaurant. His family, who were very well-off, were well-known in the neighborhood. As a young man, he had attempted a career as a musician, he explained. While that never quite panned out, he had plenty of connections in the music business. He switched his focus to the business side and now he owned several music studios in central Tokyo and was always looking for fresh talent. He went on to list a few of the singers he had discovered.

"Your daughter has what it takes to be a professional singer. I'd like you to let me manage her," Naoki Niikura said to Yutaro and Machiko.

Although Yutaro was aware that Saori enjoyed singing, the idea of her becoming a professional singer had never occurred to him. The offer came as something of a bolt from the blue. He was rather flummoxed and Machiko, his wife, seemed to feel the same way.

After he left, the two of them discussed Niikura's proposal. They both wanted Saori to have a "normal" life, but they agreed that they should ask Saori her opinion.

As soon as Saori heard Niikura's proposal, she announced that she would love to take a stab at becoming a pro. She had kept her ambitions to herself because she thought her parents would be opposed to the idea.

If it was what she wanted, then that was the end of the matter. As far as Yutaro was concerned, they should encourage her to follow her dream, and they agreed to let Niikura manage her. If it didn't work out, then it didn't work out. They could regroup when the time came. Even if Saori failed to break through, the experience would stand her in good stead for whatever she decided to do next.

Natsumi, their younger daughter, was thrilled. Just the thought of Saori performing in front of a big audience was enough to get her excited.

Saori started taking lessons from Niikura while continuing to attend high school. Luckily for the family, her tuition was completely free of charge.

"Oh, don't worry about paying me for the lessons. After we've launched Saori's career and she's become a big star, I'll just charge her a hefty management fee," was what Naoki Niikura said whenever the subject of money came up. A fan of John Lennon, Naoki cultivated the same trademark look: long, lank hair and little pebble glasses. He was a warm, good-natured soul and not in the least snobbish about his privileged background.

He was, however, a stern taskmaster. "I do my best in the lessons, but Mr. Niikura never says anything nice about me," Saori often grumbled. Niikura wasn't shy about setting strict rules for his protégée, either. "You don't need that smartphone of yours. It will just get in the way of your singing career," was a warning he never tired of giving her. Hearing that convinced Yutaro that he had made the right decision in putting his daughter into Niikura's hands. Niikura was telling her the same home truths he believed himself.

Saori eventually graduated from high school.

"I think now's the right time to get Saori to sing for this producer guy I know," Niikura announced cheerfully, when he turned up at the restaurant just after the turn of the year. Saori was nineteen years old at the time.

It was just two weeks later that it happened. Saori went out in the early evening and didn't come home even as it got later and later. Becoming increasingly anxious, her parents made repeated calls to her cell phone. No one picked up.

The Namikis contacted everyone they could think of, starting with the Niikuras, but no one had any idea where their daughter was. By the time it was after midnight, they could no longer bear the anxiety and contacted the police.

The police moved into action the next morning. They initiated a neighborhood-wide search and reviewed the footage from all the local security cameras.

CCTV footage from a camera outside the local convenience store showed Saori walking along the street. She was alone and holding her phone up to her ear, suggesting that she was talking to somebody.

The police got her call history from the cell phone company. At the time of the footage, no outgoing call was being made from Saori's phone. In other words, Saori had received a call from someone else. Unfortunately, her cell phone company didn't charge for incoming calls and didn't keep a record of them.

Worried that Saori might have been the victim of foul play, the police did everything they could; they even dragged all the local rivers.

They didn't find Saori. It was as if she had vanished in a puff of smoke.

Yutaro, Machiko, and Natsumi put up missing person flyers around the neighborhood. Other local shopkeepers and the regular patrons of Namiki-ya also pitched in. But all their efforts came to nothing.

The stress was too much for Machiko. She had a breakdown and took to her bed. Natsumi's eyes were swollen from crying day in, day out, and she began skipping school. Knowing what was happening, none of their regular patrons grumbled about the increasing frequency with which the restaurant was closed.

Eventually, the police asked the family to provide an item containing their daughter's DNA. *They must want it so that they can do DNA analysis when an unidentified body turns up* was what the family assumed. All three of them felt as if they had been flung down into a deep, dark hole.

They heard nothing more from the police after that. Yutaro

was increasingly unsure how he should feel about that. If the police called now, it would be because they found her body. At this point, his daughter had to be dead. As much as he didn't want to hear that, he desperately wanted them to find her body so that he could lay her to rest with all the proper rites.

The month before last had marked three years since Saori's disappearance. Even though he knew he was wasting his time, Yutaro had handed out leaflets on the anniversary of her disappearance, appealing to the public for information, just as he had done the year before, and the year before that. As expected, they yielded no results. No matter. The act itself had become almost a ritual by now.

Yutaro consulted his watch. It was half past ten. Had he been daydreaming for so long? He pulled himself to his feet and shook himself to wake up. Perhaps he, too, should come to terms with what had happened. If he fell into a funk every time he thought about Saori, he would never get his life back.

He was heading to the kitchen when the restaurant telephone rang. Who could be calling at this time of night?

He picked up the receiver. "Good evening, Namiki-ya restaurant," he said.

"Am I speaking to a Mr. Yutaro Namiki?" inquired a soft male voice.

"That's right. Who is this?"

"I'm with the Shizuoka Prefectural Police," the man said.

2

He took a deep breath, then knocked on the meeting room door. "Who's there?" barked a gruff voice.

"It's Kusanagi."

"Come in."

He opened the door, ducked his head in greeting, then looked up. Director Mamiya was sitting on the far side of the big table. He had his jacket off and his shirtsleeves rolled up. The table was littered with documents and files.

Kusanagi was feeling nervous but it had nothing to do with Mamiya, the former chief of his team, and everything to do with the man who was standing by the window with his back to him. Kusanagi recognized him by his extraordinary head of slicked-back silver hair.

Mamiya looked over Kusanagi's shoulder and grinned. "I see you've brought your shadow along with you."

"She was the only person who was free." Kusanagi grimaced. Kaoru Utsumi, one of the detectives on his team, was standing behind him looking rather uncomfortable.

"I know that your hands must be full with that robbery-murder case and I apologize for calling you in like this." Mamiya waved his palm at the seat across from him. "Come on. Sit."

"Yes, sir," Kusanagi said, but found himself unable to pull out a chair. He was still staring at the man by the window.

"Commissioner," said Mamiya, slightly raising his voice. "Chief Inspector Kusanagi is here."

The silver-haired figure swung around and lowered himself into a nearby chair without uttering a word. It was Tatara, Mamiya's predecessor, who had just been promoted to commissioner of the Tokyo Metropolitan Police Department.

With a look, Mamiya indicated for Kusanagi to sit down. He pulled out a chair. His female companion, however, stayed on her feet.

"Detective Utsumi, why not grab a seat, too?" Tatara finally broke his silence, with a voice so deep that Kusanagi could feel it rumble in his guts.

"Oh, I'm fine here, I don't—"

"This will probably take a while," Mamiya interrupted. "If you insist on standing, all you'll do is make the rest of us uncomfortable. Sit down."

"Yes, sir." Utsumi sat down beside her superior officer.

"Okay," said Mamiya, looking directly at Kusanagi. "Chief Inspector, we know that you and your team are busy with another case. Still, there's a case we want you—you, specifically—and your team to handle."

Kusanagi tensed. This had to be something major. Normally, when a crime occurred, it automatically became the responsibility of whichever team was on duty at the Tokyo Metropolitan Police Department headquarters. Approaching a team that was already part of an active investigation was highly unusual.

"I'll explain why we chose you later. First, just listen."

Mamiya picked up the file closest to him on the desk and launched in.

"Two weeks ago, there was a fire in a small town in Shizuoka prefecture. The fire destroyed one of those so-called trash houses—a house so overflowing with junk that it becomes a local landmark and eyesore. The cause of the fire remains unknown. It was speculated that one of the neighbors, fed up with all the mess, started it; that, however, wasn't why it has become a big news story.

"After the fire was extinguished, an inspection of the ruined building turned up human remains. There were, in fact, two bodies. Neither of which were recently deceased.

"One of the bodies appeared to belong to the old woman who had lived alone in the filthy house; the identity of the other one was a mystery.

"Based on the height of the corpse and the accessories that had survived the fire, the Shizuoka Prefectural Police guessed that the body might be that of a young woman. They sent out an inquiry to the regional police forces all around Japan and they got one promising response: information about a young woman who had gone missing three years ago in Kikuno, a suburb of Tokyo. Because the cross pendant that she had been wearing at the time of her disappearance bore a resemblance to one found in the ashes of the building, they conducted a DNA test. The upshot was that the young woman in the fire and the young woman from Kikuno were unquestionably the same person. There was, however, no connection whatsoever between the girl and the burned-down house. According to the girl's family, she never even set foot in Shizuoka prefecture when she was alive."

Mamiya placed a document with a photograph clipped to it on the desk in front of Kusanagi. It listed the girl's name, address, date of birth, and other details.

"The young woman's name is Saori Namiki. She was nineteen years old when she went missing."

Kusanagi picked up the document. The photograph showed a teenage girl smiling as she held up two fingers in the V peace sign. Her eyes were big and bright, her chin elegantly sculpted, and her lips a little on the fleshy, sensuous side.

"She's very pretty," Utsumi murmured, as she scrutinized the picture. "Looks like a singer from a girl group."

"You're right on the money there." Mamiya shot a grave look at Utsumi. "Apparently, she was trying to become a professional singer."

Kusanagi gave a grunt of surprise. From what Mamiya had said, he could tell that this case was going to be a tricky one. Why wouldn't the bosses ever give him something nice and easy?

"What about the other set of bones?" Kusanagi asked. "How sure are we that they belonged to the house's occupant?"

"They compared the DNA from the bones with DNA found on clothing and other items retrieved from the burned house. The answer is a definite yes. The people living nearby said that none of them had seen the occupant of the house for six years. Since she didn't have regular social contact with any of them, none of them gave it a second thought. According to the family register in the local municipal office, six years ago, she was already north of eighty. The Shizuoka Prefectural Police are sure that she died of natural causes, probably not long after she was last seen. She was old and she died alone—one of those 'lonely deaths' you hear about nowadays."

"Six years ago?" Kusanagi jabbed a finger at the photograph of the teenage girl. "Meaning that the old woman had nothing to do with the death of our aspiring singer here?"

"It seems not, no."

"Do we have a cause of death for Saori Namiki?"

Mamiya sucked air through his closed teeth with a hissing sound.

"An examination of the bones established depressed skull fracture as the cause of death." Mamiya solemnly crossed his arms on his chest before going on. "We don't know how the skull was fractured. All we know is that doesn't seem to have been caused by the fire."

"So what you're saying," said Kusanagi, looking hard at his superior, "is that we currently have no evidence that she was murdered."

"For now at least, no," said Mamiya, glancing at Tatara beside him.

"I know what you're thinking: that you're being landed with a lousy and rather problematic case." Tatara's eyes glinted behind his metal-rimmed glasses. To the casual observer, he looked sophisticated, even gentlemanly. Back when he was much younger and working the street, though, he was known as a tough guy with a hair-trigger temper.

"No, I . . . uhm . . . I don't—"

"Don't try and give me the runaround. It's written all over your face." Tatara smiled maliciously. "If we assume that we are dealing with murder here, then the crime has to have taken place a little over three years ago. Finding witnesses will be all but impossible. Ditto with the physical evidence. On top of that, the place where the body was concealed has been almost completely destroyed by fire. How are you supposed to conduct a serious investigation in circumstances like that? I really don't know. Whoever gets put in charge will have drawn the shortest of short straws; they'll have every right to feel pissed off."

Kusanagi looked down at the table and said nothing. Tatara had summed up the situation perfectly.

"However—" the commissioner went on. "Kusanagi, look at me when I'm talking to you."

Kusanagi turned toward Tatara and looked into his eyes. "Yes, sir."

"I absolutely insist that you—by which I mean you, Director Mamiya, and you, Chief Inspector Kusanagi—work this case."

"'This case' being what exactly . . . ?" said Mamiya.

Tatara stared back at Mamiya and gave a crisp nod.

"The old woman who lived in the trash-infested house wasn't completely without family. She actually had a son. If anyone was going to sneak into her house after her death, the chances are that it was him."

Mamiya leaned forward in his chair.

"Do we know where the son is?"

"He renewed his driver's license a couple of years ago. The address on it is in Edogawa Ward, and he's still living there. Before moving there, though, he had an apartment in the south of Kikuno. Around a mile from the victim's house, as the crow flies. One day, he suddenly quits his job at a junk removal and recycling company and moves out of his apartment. That was right after Saori Namiki vanished."

Kusanagi heaved a sigh of relief. Finally, a glimmer of light.

Mamiya picked up another sheet of paper, which he deposited in front of Kusanagi. "This is the man. Take a good look at him."

It was an enlarged photocopy of a driver's license. Kusanagi gave a start the moment he saw the man's face. He'd seen him somewhere before. . . . No, that was wrong. He'd actually *met* him face-to-face. When he caught sight of the name on the license, Kusanagi's heart skipped a beat. He felt hot all over.

The typewritten name was Kanichi Hasunuma.

Kusanagi's eyes opened wide and he looked from one to the other in turn. "Is it . . . *that* Hasunuma?"

"Yes, it is. It's *that* Hasunuma," Mamiya replied solemnly. "The defendant in the Yuna Motohashi case."

So many thoughts flooded into Kusanagi's mind that he was left quite speechless. He could feel one of his cheeks twitching uncontrollably.

He took a second look at the photograph. Hasunuma was older than when their paths had last crossed, but the coldness behind the eyes was exactly the same.

"Let me refresh your memory about another important matter." Mamiya showed him another photograph. "This is the trash house that was destroyed in the fire. Someone from the local municipality took this picture a few years ago. Look familiar to you?"

Kusanagi picked up the picture. At first, all he could see was an enormous heap of garbage. When he looked carefully, however, he managed to detect the outline of a roof and something resembling a small front gate.

Kusanagi burrowed deep into his memory. A sudden realization hit him.

"It was Shizuoka prefecture, wasn't it? Are you telling me . . . that this is the house where we seized that refrigerator?"

"Indeed I am." Mamiya was jabbing a finger at Kusanagi's face. "You went to this house with me. The two of us. Nineteen years ago. Of course, it wasn't completely buried in trash back then."

"It's the same house?"

"I imagine you've finally realized why I want you and your team to handle this case, Chief Inspector Kusanagi," Tatara said. "I've already made my position known to the heads of CID and Homicide—or would you prefer that I put someone else in charge?"

"No, sir." Kusanagi clenched his hands into fists on the tabletop. "I completely understand. Please put me in charge of the case."

Tatara nodded rather smugly.

"Sorry," Utsumi broke in, "but I'm a little lost. What was the Yuna Motohashi case?"

"I'll bring you up to speed later," said Kusanagi.

Tatara had apparently said all he was going to say. Without a further word, Tatara rose to his feet. Kusanagi and Utsumi jumped to their feet and stood at attention. The commissioner stalked out of the room with long strides. Mamiya was following in his wake, when he stopped abruptly and turned back to them.

"We're setting up a joint investigation task force with Shizuoka Prefectural Police at the Kikuno Police Station. Turn over your current case and let others tie up any remaining loose ends. What I want you to do is to switch over to this investigation as fast as you can."

"Yes, sir," Kusanagi said with great emphasis.

As the door slammed shut behind Mamiya, Kusanagi swung around to Utsumi. "Contact everyone on the team. Tell them to assemble at TMPD headquarters right now."

"Yes, sir."

3

Yuna Motohashi went missing twenty-three years ago. She was twelve years old at the time. She went out one afternoon to meet a friend in the local park. The park was near her house and was along the route the local students would walk to school. Because of this, Yuna's mother wasn't concerned about her. When dinnertime came and Yuna was still not home, her mother went to the park to fetch her. Yuna, however, was nowhere to be seen. When the mother went to the friend's house to ask after her daughter, the friend said they had parted hours ago.

Starting to feel uneasy, the mother contacted her husband. The two of them visited every place they thought Yuna might be. When that yielded no results, they reported her as missing to the police.

Given the circumstances, the police immediately launched a full-scale search but they found no clues to the missing girl's whereabouts. In those days there were far fewer security cameras and CCTV than there are now.

The only significant lead they uncovered was a statement from someone who had seen a girl who resembled Yuna walking alongside a man dressed in pale-blue work overalls. Because the witness—a housewife—had only seen them from behind, she had no idea what the man looked like. She described him as being of average height, neither fat nor thin; she hadn't noticed anything peculiar about the girl's appearance or behavior.

The workers at the factory, which Seiji Motohashi, Yuna's father, owned and managed, all wore a uniform of that color. When they showed a set of the company overalls to the housewife, she confirmed that yes, they were similar to the ones she had seen the man wearing.

The factory had a staff of around thirty. Investigators visited and interviewed them all. The majority allowed the investigators to look around their apartments. Those who refused seemed to have plausible reasons for doing so and gave no grounds for suspicion.

Kanichi Hasunuma was one of the factory's employees. He was thirty years old and lived alone. According to the investigation notes, a detective had visited Hasunuma three days after Yuna went missing and inspected his apartment. Nothing suspicious had been found.

Despite everyone's efforts, Yuna wasn't found. The case remained open and was classified as ongoing, but without any leads, the police had to move on. One month after Yuna went missing, her mother committed suicide. In her note, she apologized to Yuna and to her husband. She also blamed herself for letting the girl out to play too late. Convinced that her daughter was dead, she'd lost all hope.

About four years later, the case took an unexpected turn. A hiker trekking deep in the mountains to the west of Tokyo reported seeing what looked like human bones. The local police hurried to the site and exhumed a number of dismembered bones. Careful analysis confirmed that they were definitely human and, based on size and length, belonged to a child.

Since the skull was still intact, the crime laboratory was able to produce a possible likeness. When they sent the facial reconstruction to regional police forces all over Japan, word came back that it might be Yuna Motohashi. DNA test results confirmed their suspicions.

An investigation task force was established and it was Tatara who headed the team, with Mamiya as his second-in-command. At the time, Kusanagi was an up-and-coming young detective recently assigned to the Homicide Division.

Outside of the dismembered body itself, there was an almost complete lack of clues. There was one unusual thing about Yuna's remains: not only had the bones been dismembered, chopped up, and buried, the body had been burned first. The focus of the investigation therefore shifted to finding places near the last sighting of Yuna Motohashi where it was possible to cremate a body. An incinerator seemed the most plausible solution. Not only did the police carefully check all the incinerators in the neighborhood, they also took a second look at workers at the Motohashi factory to see if any of them lived close to an incinerator.

It was then that Kusanagi set his sights on Kanichi Hasunuma. Hasunuma had by now quit his job at the Motohashi factory, but the HR department still had his résumé on file. It revealed that he had previously worked at a company specializing in personal and industrial waste disposal, and that firm had multiple incinerators.

When Kusanagi interviewed Hasunuma's former boss, he learned one noteworthy piece of information. Four years ago, Hasunuma had phoned the man; he had something he needed to dispose of, he said. Could he possibly use one of the company's incinerators that weekend? When the boss inquired what exactly he was planning to burn, Hasunuma had explained that he had a number of dead animals that he intended to cremate. He hinted that he'd set himself up as a sort of pet undertaker for friends and neighbors to earn a little cash on the side. Since the company was used to cremating dead dogs and cats along with regular household rubbish, his boss gave his okay, as long as Hasunuma left the place nice and tidy.

When Kusanagi checked the precise dates, he found that Hasunuma's use of the incinerator coincided with Yuna Motohashi's disappearance. It was at this point that Kanichi Hasunuma became the prime suspect.

Kusanagi immediately started investigating Hasunuma's past. Many of the details of his life were fuzzy. All Kusanagi managed to ascertain was that Hasunuma had been born in Shizuoka prefecture and that he changed jobs frequently.

When Mamiya announced that he wanted to have a face-to-face meeting with the guy, Kusanagi asked if he could tag along, and the two detectives went directly to his apartment to interview him.

Hasunuma had small, narrow eyes and a blank, inexpressive face. The skin of his sunken cheeks barely moved even when he spoke.

Mamiya got the ball rolling by asking Hasunuma for the names of the people whose pets he had disposed of at the incinerator. With a list of names, it would be easy for them to check whether his pet-undertaker story was true or not.

Hasunuma, however, said that he couldn't give them any names "because he had promised the owners confidentiality."

Mamiya followed up by asking what kind of animals the pets were, how many of them there were, and how much he had charged his friends. Hasunuma answered none of these questions, either. "Is it a crime if I refuse to reply?" he finally asked. Kusanagi could still remember the tone of his voice: quiet and utterly devoid of emotion.

Hasunuma's refusal to cooperate only deepened their suspicions. In addition, he was of middling height and neither fat nor thin— exactly as the eyewitness had described the man she'd seen walking with the murdered girl.

What followed was a series of misfires. They spoke to a wide range of people—starting with Seiji Motohashi, the abducted girl's father—in an effort to establish a link between Hasunuma and Yuna. But apart from the fact that Yuna was the daughter of the owner of the factory where Hasunuma worked, they turned up nothing. Nor was there any history of bad blood between Hasunuma and his employer.

As all this was going on, one particular photograph from the case file caught Kusanagi's attention. The detective who had visited Hasunuma four years earlier had taken one of the interior of his apartment.

While Mamiya interviewed Hasunuma, Kusanagi was looking over the place rather than listening to their conversation. Kusanagi wanted to see if there was anywhere one could easily hide a body. After all, Hasunuma must have hidden the body somewhere before getting access to the incinerator. Somewhere the original detective wouldn't have thought to inspect.

Hasunuma's apartment was modest: just two small rooms with a tiny kitchen area. The only places one could conceivably hide a body were the futon cupboard and inside the ceiling. But what caught Kusanagi's attention was the refrigerator. It was small, like the minifridges you see in hotel rooms.

The refrigerator in the photograph from four years ago had been bigger, he remembered. Although not quite as large as a standard family refrigerator, it had been at least waist-high.

Sometime over the past four years, Hasunuma had replaced his refrigerator. Why had he done so?

Assuming that Hasunuma had burned the body in the incinerator, then in the interim he would have had to keep the body in his apartment. The best way to retard decomposition was to put the body in a refrigerator. Then, once he had buried Yuna's incinerated remains deep in the mountains, he would have gotten rid of the refrigerator itself. That would make sense.

If this hypothesis was right, then the original refrigerator should contain some trace of the girl's body.

Back at headquarters, Kusanagi showed the photograph to Mamiya and Tatara and explained his theory. While they both agreed that the young detective might be onto something, their faces hardly lit up. Locating the refrigerator was clearly going to be a challenge; for all they knew, it might no longer exist.

The three men tried to imagine what Hasunuma would have done with the refrigerator. He would be keen to dispose of it discreetly. Hasunuma probably couldn't have carted the refrigerator out on his own. It was too big. He would need someone to help him.

Hasunuma didn't have an extensive circle of friends. One of the few they came up with was one of his mahjong buddies who was also the owner of a minitruck.

The truck owner admitted it the instant they confronted him. Around four years ago, he had helped Hasunuma transport his old refrigerator, he said. They had taken it to the Hasunuma family home. Hasunuma had told him that he was going to give his old refrigerator to his mother.

Kusanagi and Mamiya promptly went to check out the place. Yoshie, Hasunuma's mother, was short and stooped and looked considerably older than she really was. As soon as she realized that the two unfamiliar men who had suddenly appeared on her doorstep were from the police, she was gripped by fear. "I haven't done anything wrong," she kept muttering, as if chanting a magic spell.

Yoshie Hasunuma's jaw dropped when Mamiya said that they only wanted to ask her a few questions about a refrigerator. She didn't seem to know what they were talking about. Understanding only dawned when Mamiya continued, "We believe your son brought you a refrigerator around four years ago."

"That thing? Never used it. He just came and dumped it on me. It just gets in the way," she replied, the furrows on her brow deepening.

"Where is it?" they asked.

"In the tatami room at the back of the house," she said, leading them inside. Kusanagi was dumbfounded: The place was about as far as you could get from a traditional serene Japanese room; it was more like a storeroom crammed from floor to ceiling with stuff. Right at the back of it all was a refrigerator. And it was definitely the one from the photograph.

They immediately impounded it and sent the refrigerator to the crime lab for analysis. Minute flecks of blood and pieces of flesh were found, and using DNA analysis, it was determined that Yuna Motohashi was the source of both. When the news was announced, the whole investigation task force broke into a cheer.

Kusanagi wanted to beat his chest and say, *Look at me. A newbie in Homicide and I've already got a scalp on my belt.*

Things, however, didn't develop as expected.

Kanichi Hasunuma denied any involvement in the crime.

When they pressed him about blood and tissue residue from Yuna Motohashi being found in his refrigerator, he simply said, "No idea how it got there." When they pressed him about his reasons for getting a new refrigerator, he simply said that the other one had gotten old.

Tatara went ahead and ordered Hasunuma's arrest, despite his stonewalling. They were confident that with him in custody, extracting a confession would only be a matter of time.

Normally, they would have arrested him on several charges, including the unlawful disposal of a corpse or for mutilating a dead body, while they tried to get a confession. But not in this case. The statute of limitations, which was three years for both crimes, had already run out. The only charge they could arrest him on was murder.

But Hasunuma didn't capitulate or confess. No matter how much they blustered and threatened, he refused to say anything.

"Do whatever it takes. Just get me the evidence I need," thundered Tatara. His subordinates redoubled their efforts.

Through diligent sleuthing, Kusanagi and his colleagues turned up several new pieces of evidence suggestive of Hasunuma's guilt. For instance, Hasunuma had rented a car two days after making use of the industrial incinerator. The distance on the odometer was almost exactly equivalent to the return trip from his home to the place where the remains had been found. When they searched Hasunuma's apartment, the investigators discovered an old shovel wrapped up in newspaper. Analysis of the soil stuck to the shovel's blade revealed that it had the same characteristics as the soil where the bones had been found.

They found more new information. But all of it was circumstantial evidence, no single piece of it providing decisive confirmation of Hasunuma's guilt.

Some members of the task force suggested a compromise. How about getting Hasunuma to accept a charge of manslaughter—or even the lighter charge of involuntary manslaughter—instead of murder?

The idea infuriated Tatara, who was violently opposed to offering deals to criminals. He rejected it out of hand. "The fact that Hasunuma refuses to say anything is tantamount to an admission of guilt. We've absolutely got to indict him on a murder charge," Tatara said.

In the end, they sent the case to the public prosecutor without managing to find a single piece of conclusive physical evidence. It was up to the prosecutor's office to decide what to do next.

The prosecutor decided to go for an indictment. They probably assumed that the sheer volume of circumstantial evidence guaranteed that he would be convicted.

But the trial didn't go as expected.

On his first day in court, Hasunuma denied the charges. His denials were the first and last words of any significance that he uttered throughout the trial. Thereafter, he stayed resolutely silent. Whatever the prosecutor asked him, his only response was: "I have nothing to say."

As the trial went on, Kusanagi began to hear whisperings that Hasunuma might be found innocent.

I just can't believe it, Kusanagi thought. *Sure, the evidence is circumstantial, but with so much of it, you can't tell me there isn't enough to convict.*

The trial focused on two issues. First, was Yuna Motohashi's death the result of murder? And second, could a charge of murder be proven through the accumulation of circumstantial evidence, even though neither the motive nor the method of the murder was known?

Hasunuma had burned the girl's corpse and buried what was left. Any normal person could see that he must have murdered her—but that wasn't, apparently, how the justice system operated. If there was even the tiniest possibility that Hasunuma hadn't killed the girl, then the murder charge would no longer stand up.

The day when the verdict was announced was bitterly cold. Kusanagi was at a local police station when he heard the outcome.

The verdict? Not guilty.

4

Kusanagi shook his head as he contemplated the burned-out ruin. "Hard to believe this was once a house."

"Very hard, sir," said Detective Utsumi, who was standing beside him.

The place looked less like a burned-out house than a refuse incineration plant. A vast jumble of wood, metal, and plastic had been charred and fused together. The fire probably released not only a cloud of filthy smoke but also a lot of toxic gas. Kusanagi pitied the firefighters who been sent in to extinguish the blaze.

Kusanagi and Utsumi came to inspect the site along with the prefectural police before he took control of the joint investigation task force.

"I've driven by this place more times than I can count. Unless you knew, you'd never have guessed that there was a house behind all the garbage." The speaker was Detective Ueno. He was there as their guide. He looked young—he was probably in his early thirties—and was built like an ox.

"Was it that bad?" Kusanagi asked.

The young policeman nodded.

"The garden was packed with piles of random trash: broken TVs and radios, bits of furniture, mattresses, quilts, you name it. Plus, bundles of newspapers and books—hundreds of the damn things. My guess is that people took to dumping their trash here rather than having it hauled away."

"Why would anyone want to do that?" Utsumi asked.

"Search me." Ueno tilted his head to one side. "When we interviewed the local people, they told us it had been in that state for a decade or so before the fire. The woman wasn't interested in getting on with her neighbors: When they complained about the smell, she simply ignored them. When the municipal authorities offered to help her dispose of the stuff, if it was all proving a bit too much for her, she sent them packing. 'This is my property and I don't feel like throwing it away. Just leave me in peace.'"

Listening to Detective Ueno's explanation, Kusanagi tried to recall the face of Yoshie Hasunuma from nineteen years before. She was something of an oddball even then but had only become more idiosyncratic with the passing of time, apparently. He wondered if her son's arrest might have had something to do with it.

"According to the report, no one remembers seeing Yoshie Hasunuma for roughly six years. Didn't anyone think that was odd?" Kusanagi asked.

"They discussed it, but it never went much beyond, 'You don't see that Mrs. Hasunuma around much lately.' I imagine no one wanted to get involved."

"What about the utilities: the water and the electricity?"

"The bills were all paid on time. The old woman's bank account remained open and the charges were automatically deducted. Since she wasn't actually using any water or electricity, the charges were minimal."

"And her pension? Was that still being paid?"

"It seems it was. That's why her account never ran out of money."

"What about payments into or out of any other accounts?"

"We're looking into that right now," Ueno said.

Placing his hands on his hips, Kusanagi took another look at the site of the burned-out house.

"The report said that the two bodies were found in different places."

"That's right. The first set of remains was found in the tatami room on the first floor. Bundled up in a burned-up quilt. They found the second body under where the floor would have been."

"And that was Saori Namiki?"

"Correct."

Kusanagi was convinced that Yoshie Hasunuma had died from natural causes six years ago. Someone else hid Saori Namiki's corpse beneath the floor three years after that.

"How much do we know about Yoshie Hasunuma's family?" Kusanagi asked.

Ueno frowned.

"Very little, to be honest. There were some distant relatives, but she doesn't seem to have been in touch with them. She had lost her husband some twenty-five years before she died. Her family basically consisted of a single son, Kanichi Hasunuma. He was actually her husband's son by a previous marriage, not her biological son. Yoshie was his stepmother."

"This isn't the house where Kanichi Hasunuma was born and raised, then?"

"No, it's not." Ueno pulled out a small notebook. "The Hasunumas moved here thirty-five years ago. When the family came here, Kanichi Hasunuma moved out on his own."

Kusanagi reflexively clicked his tongue. "I see . . ."

The Shizuoka Prefectural Police had recently called Kanichi Hasunuma in for an interview. In the transcript, Hasunuma claimed that he had neither contacted nor seen his stepmother for years; that he knew nothing about all the trash around the house; and that the house itself had nothing to do with him. He also stated that he had no idea where the bodies in it had come from. Although the fact that he deigned to answer their questions at all was a slight improvement over his last police interview nineteen years ago, there was little change in his overall uncooperative demeanor.

Kusanagi got Ueno to drop them off at the station, where they caught the next bullet train for Tokyo. Sitting beside Utsumi, Kusanagi swallowed a mouthful of can coffee.

"Can we assume that Hasunuma is the person who hid Saori Namiki's corpse in the trash house?" Detective Utsumi asked him.

"Probably, yes. For starters, Yoshie Hasunuma died six years ago, and her body was wrapped up in a quilt. Whoever hid Saori Namiki's body must have known that. They must have thought, 'Look at this place. Three years, and no one even suspects the old lady's dead. This place is perfect for hiding a body.' And why didn't that person report Yoshie Hasunuma's death, even though they knew about it?"

Utsumi cocked her head slightly. "Presumably because it worked out better for them to have people think she was still alive."

"Precisely. Can you think of a reason why?"

Utsumi frowned. "Maybe her pension?" she said tentatively.

Kusanagi grunted. The girl was sharp.

"I think so, too. The scheme was to pretend that she was still alive to get continued access to her pension. There's only one person who could cook up something like that: someone who knew where Mrs. Hasunuma had her bank accounts and what the PIN numbers for them were—it's got to be Kanichi Hasunuma, her stepson."

"So he was stealing her pension benefits."

"The fact that the place was a trash house proved an unexpected boon when it came to concealing her body. We can't be sure until the prefectural police have checked Yoshie Hasunuma's bank statements, but I'm pretty sure about the pension thing."

Utsumi blinked and nodded gravely.

"As a theory, it makes plenty of sense. The first thing we have to do, then, is to prove that Hasunuma hid Saori's body."

"Yes. For starters."

That was only the starting point. Kusanagi was determined not to repeat the mistakes of nineteen years ago. They had to prove Hasunuma was involved in Saori Namiki's death.

Kusanagi glanced out of the train window as he sipped his coffee. He didn't even notice the view; all he could see was the distant past.

The profound sense of defeat he felt then hadn't weakened with the passing years.

The defendant is found not guilty—

The verdict had turned the whole world on its head for the young detective.

Ultimately, Kusanagi just couldn't accept it. He read through the text of the ruling over and over again. The judge stated that the likelihood of Hasunuma being involved in the death of Yuna Motohashi was extremely high. Despite that, none of the abundant circumstantial evidence was sufficient to confirm the defendant's intention to kill. Other than a certain number of adult videos in the defendant's apartment, there was no solid basis for the argument that Hasunuma had first sexually assaulted Yuna Motohashi, then murdered her when she fought back. The judge dismissed this argument, which he characterized as "unconvincing."

Kusanagi's memories of the press conference given by Seiji Motohashi, Yuna's father, after the publication of the verdict, were also crystal clear. Despite his best efforts to stay composed in front of the television cameras, he had been unable to prevent his voice from cracking and his body trembling with rage.

"I never imagined that the court would find Hasunuma not guilty. What does it mean? That anyone can get away with anything, provided they remain silent? I just can't accept that. I intend to keep fighting. Whatever it takes, I want the prosecutor and the police to uncover the truth and bring my daughter's killer to justice."

Sure enough, the prosecutor appealed. However, when the court of appeals published its ruling, it only served to plunge the victim's family deeper into despair.

The appeals court judge used even more forceful language than his predecessor. "There is a very strong probability indeed that the defendant caused the death of Yuna Motohashi." He said that it was hard to see the new evidence put forward by the prosecutor as "constituting adequate proof that the defendant intentionally caused the death of the victim." He dismissed the appeal and handed down another not-guilty verdict.

There was considerable public interest in how the prosecutor would respond to this second setback. In the end, however, the prosecutor's office decided against an appeal to the supreme court, because a detailed analysis of the verdict showed that it was in line with both precedent and the constitution, meaning they had no grounds for a fresh appeal. The look of frustration on the deputy chief prosecutor's face when he made the announcement was something Kusanagi would never forget.

"The biggest mistake that was made nineteen years ago was to believe that Hasunuma would break and confess," said Kusanagi, still gazing out the train window. "It's not fair to blame the people heading the investigation for thinking like that. Biological evidence was found proving that a body had been in the refrigerator. No one could reasonably expect anyone to be able to talk their way out of that."

"I agree, sir."

"It turned out, however, that there was another escape route," sighed Kusanagi.

"You mean remaining silent?"

Kusanagi gave a curt nod, then finished off the last of his coffee. As he crushed the empty can in his fist, he chewed his lip.

"Not many people knew about the right to remain silent in those days. Most defendants still felt that if they were asked a question, they were obliged to give some sort of answer. Hasunuma, however, just kept his mouth shut. It didn't matter whether they were asking him questions about the case or simply making chitchat; he was completely unresponsive. And he maintained the same attitude throughout his two trials. I feel a bit odd saying this, but I was sort of impressed by his strength of character."

"I wonder if he'll use the same technique this time."

"If he's guilty, I'm sure he will."

Utsumi pulled out her phone. She must have gotten a call. "Excuse me one second, sir." She stood up and walked off along the aisle between the seats.

Kusanagi stuffed the empty can into the seat-back pocket in front of him, and, after glancing over his shoulder to check there was no one sitting behind him, he reclined his seat and half closed his eyes. But with the case preying on his mind, he knew there was little chance of falling asleep.

One of the problems they were facing was the same one as nineteen years ago: Arresting Hasunuma for the unlawful disposal of a body was impossible. It was three years and two months since Saori Namiki had disappeared, and the statute of limitations had already expired.

So what sort of evidence would they need to assemble to arrest Hasunuma for murder? The child's bones in the house had included a caved-in skull. This suggested that the killing had involved a violent blow with an instrument of some kind. If they searched Hasunuma's apartment and found the murder weapon, they'd be home and dry—

"Chief," he heard Utsumi saying, "are you taking a nap?"

Kusanagi opened his eyes. "Who was it on the phone?"

"It was Inspector Kishitani. The deputy commander of local police asked him to confirm the overall thrust of the Saori Namiki investigation."

Inspector Kishitani and the rest of the TMPD team were already at the joint task force headquarters, sharing information with the local detectives.

"Okay. Tell them that we will go straight to the investigation headquarters in Kikuno as soon as we get back to Tokyo."

"I guessed you'd say that, so that's what I said we'd do," said Utsumi matter-of-factly, dropping into her seat.

"Kikuno, huh? It's part of Tokyo, but I know hardly anything—no, scratch that—I know absolutely nothing about the place."

Kusanagi knew that Kikuno was somewhere in the west of Tokyo. He had driven through it, but never got out of the car to look around.

"From what I can see, it's pretty nondescript," said Utsumi, looking it up on her phone. "Hang on a second. There is one thing the place is famous for: its parade."

"Parade?"

Utsumi started tapping away on her phone.

"Here we go. This is it: the Kikuno Story Parade."

She held up the phone. On it was a photograph of someone dressed as Momotaro, the Peach Boy, with other people in ogre costumes.

"What is it? Some kind of fancy-dress parade?"

"Apparently, it used to be called the 'Kikuno High Street Autumn Parade.' Then it opened itself up to cosplay enthusiasts from all around Japan so they could take part. When that wasn't exciting enough, they turned it into a team competition."

"A team competition?"

"A group of people get dressed up and re-create a scene from a famous story. That might mean something like a man and a woman dressing up as Urashima Taro and Princess Otohime and having a feast, while their teammates, togged out in sea bream and flounder costumes, dance around them."

"Sounds difficult to do while marching in a parade."

"There's a variety of gimmicks. Some of the teams use floats, apparently. There seem to be all sorts of rules about what you can and can't do, if you're using a large set."

"You said people come from all over Japan? So is it a big event?"

"They get so many applications they have to hold an elimination round. All the teams are asked to send in a homemade video; the executive committee uses them to make their selections. It says here that nearly one hundred videos were submitted last year and that the overall level was so high, they struggled to whittle down the numbers."

"From what you're telling me, it sounds like a major event."

"A friend of mine goes every year. She says it gets bigger every year."

"When's it held?"

"October."

"I see."

Kusanagi was relieved. That was more than six months from now, so there shouldn't be a problem. They should be finished with the investigation by then.

"Oh, that reminds me," piped up Utsumi as she put her phone away. "Isn't our mutual friend in Kikuno right now?"

"Our mutual friend?"

"Professor Yukawa. He sent me an email at the end of last year."

It had been a long time since Kusanagi last heard that name. Manabu Yukawa was a friend of his from his university days. Although he was a physicist, Yukawa possessed extraordinary powers of deduction, and Kusanagi had sought his help with more than a few investigations. They hadn't seen each other for several years now.

"Didn't Yukawa go to America? I haven't heard from him since he left Japan."

"He came back last year. That's what the email he sent me was about. I thought he'd have contacted you, too."

"Not a word. Guy's got no manners."

"He probably thought he didn't need to email you because I'd tell you he was back. That's how his mind works; he's a rationalist."

"He's lazy, you mean. Anyway, what's he doing in Kikuno?"

"He said that he was going to be working for a new research institute that had just opened up there. He didn't say what kind of research he'd be doing."

Probably thought you wouldn't understand his explanation. Kusanagi suddenly remembered Yukawa's habit of pushing his spectacles higher up on his nose with the tip of one finger.

"So he's in Kikuno, eh . . . ?"

Kusanagi decided to contact Yukawa once he'd cleared up this case. Hell, it would be fun: to hear what he had to say about life in America as they drank their whiskey and sodas (made, of course, with high-end whiskey). The only problem was what it would take to sort out this challenging case.

5

The day after the joint investigation task force was set up, Kusanagi decided to go to Namiki-ya and meet with the family. Since the local police force had all the records related to Saori Namiki's disappearance, Kusanagi had a general grasp of the case; as the officer in charge of the investigation, however, he wanted to speak directly to the girl's family. He had Kaoru Utsumi arrange the meeting and join him.

Namiki-ya was located on Kikuno Avenue, one of the streets on the route of the area's annual parade. The restaurant was an unpretentious place, with a traditional exterior sheathed in vertical wooden slats. Inside, there were four tables for six, and two tables for four. Kusanagi and Utsumi were sitting on one side of one of the six-person tables in the middle of the restaurant, with the three members of the Namiki family on the other side: Yutaro, the father; Machiko, the mother; and the surviving daughter, Natsumi.

With his high forehead and elegantly arched eyebrows, Yutaro Namiki looked like a stand-up guy. On the thin side, he sat bolt upright in his chair and radiated a quiet dignity. His wife, Machiko, was a beautiful woman with strikingly large eyes. Kusanagi recalled the pictures he had seen of Saori Namiki. She had obviously taken after her mother. The features of Natsumi, the sister, were nice and regular, but she was of a different type to her mother and elder sister.

"We've got no idea what's going on. Is there any chance you could fill us in?" Yutaro asked, before he had even put Kusanagi's business card down on the table. "The Shizuoka Prefectural Police called us out of the blue. They said they believed they'd found the remains of our daughter and wanted to do a DNA test. We told them that we provided a sample when Saori disappeared and gave our consent for them to proceed. They got back to us a few days later saying that it was a match and we should come collect her remains. We went, of course, but we're baffled. We had never heard of the place. That's what we want to know: Why in God's name was Saori's body found all the way out there in Shizuoka?"

Kusanagi nodded twice, slowly and deeply.

"I understand how you must be feeling. For our part, we're very conscious that this case comes with a lot of questions. And our investigation will address precisely that point: Why was the body found where it was?"

"Saori . . . ," began Machiko Namiki. "She was murdered, wasn't she?" Her voice was faint and had a slight quaver.

"That is a possibility," replied Kusanagi in a somber tone. "I hope that our investigation will uncover the truth of what happened."

Machiko's eyebrows shot up.

"What else could it be, if not murder? You're not seriously going to tell me that—what?—she went to some stranger's house in Shizuoka, got sick, and died there?" She was speaking with such fervor that spittle was flying from her lips.

"Come on," Yutaro chided her. "Calm down."

Machiko glared at her husband, then silently dropped her eyes. She was breathing so hard that her shoulders were heaving.

"You're quite right, Mrs. Namiki." Kusanagi did his best to sound conciliatory. "The circumstances suggest with a high level of possibility that Saori was the victim of some sort of crime. That's why I would like to ask you whether you noticed anything unusual before your daughter went missing. Did she get any strange phone calls? Did you see anyone suspicious hanging around the house?"

The couple looked at each other. Yutaro then turned to Kusanagi and tilted his head to one side.

"The police asked us the same questions when she went missing. Nothing came to mind then, either. We saw no sign of her associating with bad people; she seemed to be living a completely normal, ordinary life. . . ."

"Did she have a boyfriend?"

Machiko frowned thoughtfully, then looked over at Natsumi, who was sitting beside her.

"My sister asked me to keep it a secret," began Natsumi, speaking with reluctance, "but she was actually going out with one of the restaurant customers.

"His name was Tomoya Takagaki," Natsumi said. "He was a little older than Saori, about five years, and he had some sort of an office job. Saori was convinced that our parents would disapprove of her dating a customer, so she didn't tell anyone about it, except me."

"Does he still come to the restaurant?"

"Oh, I don't think he's been here for about a year now. He used to pop in from time to time after Saori went missing."

"Do you happen to have his contact details?"

Machiko glanced over at her daughter.

"I can tell you where he works," said Natsumi. It turned out to be a printing company, not far from the station, four stops along the line.

"Was there anyone else with whom Saori was especially close? Male, female, it doesn't matter."

"I can think of several people: school friends and the like. She had an address book. Shall I fetch it for you?" Machiko replied, getting to her feet.

"You can get it for us another time. There is something I would like you all to take a look at now," said Kusanagi, giving Utsumi a meaningful look.

The female detective slid a photograph out of her bag and laid it flat on the table. It was actually an enlarged color copy of the driver's license photo for Kanichi Hasunuma. The three members of the Namiki family all craned forward for a closer look.

Machiko was the first to react. She gasped and her big eyes widened further.

"Does the picture mean anything to you?" Kusanagi asked.

Machiko picked up the photograph, scrutinized it closely, then nodded.

"I recognize him. I recognize this man," she said and handed the photograph to her husband.

Yutaro looked grim. There was an extraordinary intensity in his eyes as he contemplated the picture.

"Yeah, I remember him. It's that fellow." He spat the words.

"Who is he?" Natsumi asked innocently. Unlike her parents, she didn't seem to recognize the man.

"He used to come here a lot. Always on his own and always

grumpy. . . . He was a weirdo." Machiko thrust the picture back at Kusanagi. "So, was it him? Did he murder our Saori?"

"We don't yet know. All I can say is that we think he may have a connection to the case." Kusanagi reached out and took the photograph from Machiko's hand. He held it up so that both the parents could see it. "Clearly, neither of you have very positive feelings toward this man. Did you have some sort of run-in with him?"

"Not exactly a run-in." Machiko looked to her husband for support.

"We banned him," Yutaro said.

"You mean, from the restaurant?"

"Yes," Yutaro said. "The way he behaved—it was intolerable."

"Why? What did he do?"

"He kept trying to get Saori to pour his drinks for him."

"Pour his drinks?"

"That's right." Yutaro pulled his chin into his neck with an air of distaste. "We're a small restaurant, so we have lots of regular customers who are more like family friends, really. Saori was very relaxed and comfortable with people like that; she was happy to top off their glasses from the bottle on their table." Yutaro paused briefly, glared at the photograph in Kusanagi's hands, then went on. "When *he* saw her doing that for other people, he was like, 'Come on, give me a top-off. Oh and come here and sit down next to me.' He was a customer, so Saori reluctantly did what he asked. And then it went on, the same thing, gradually getting worse and worse. What he said to her, how he treated her, it was uncomfortable . . . inappropriate. In the end, I had to take a stand. 'We're a restaurant, not a hostess bar. We don't like the way you're carrying on, so please leave and don't come back again.' If I remember right, I didn't charge him for that final evening."

"Did he say anything?"

"No, he left without a word."

"What about after that?"

"After that?" said Yutaro, twisting around to face his wife. "He didn't come back, did he?"

"No, he never came back." Machiko shook her head.

"And roughly when did these incidents take place?"

"When would it have been?" Yutaro cocked his head to one side. "Oh, yes. The first time he asked Saori to pour his drinks for him was the day of the big local parade. It went on for more than a month afterward. . . . So that would take us to December, a little over three years ago, I guess."

"Not long before Saori disappeared," whispered Natsumi.

"Thank you." Kusanagi handed the photograph back to Utsumi.

"Who is that guy?" asked Yutaro. His voice had an edge to it. "He came here often enough, but I never knew the first thing about him."

Kusanagi gave him a conciliatory smile. "I'm very sorry. I can't share any information with you yet."

"Can't you at least tell us his name?" Machiko had a beseeching look in her eyes.

"Please, try and understand. The investigation is only just getting underway. I promise to be back in touch as soon as we have anything to tell you."

Kusanagi glanced over at Utsumi, then got to his feet and faced the Namikis.

"Thank you all for your help today. We are completely committed to finding out what happened. I sincerely hope that we can count on your support. Thank you and goodbye." As he said this, he gave a deep bow. Beside him, Detective Utsumi did the same thing.

None of the three members of the Namiki family said so much as a word.

6

He adjusted the color balance, closed his eyes, waited a few seconds, then opened them again and looked back at the computer monitor. Without doing a conscious "self-reboot" like this, he found it hard to judge whether the design had improved or not.

Not bad, thought Tomoya Takagaki, examining his own handiwork. The image on the monitor was of a room in a rather upscale retirement home. Tomoya was selecting photographs for the retirement home's brochure and the client had asked him to make sure the whole thing felt bright and cheerful.

Tomoya was wondering how to enhance the sunlight streaming in through the window, when the phone on his desk lit up with an incoming call. He picked up; it was the woman at reception.

"Mr. Takagaki, I have a lady here who says she wants to see you. A Ms. Utsumi."

"Ms. Utsumi? Where's she from?"

"She says she's from the Kikuno shopping district."

"From Kikuno?"

He knew Kikuno well. Recently, however, he had been giving the shopping district a wide berth. He had his reasons.

"What do you want me to do? I can tell her you're too busy to see her."

"No, it's fine. I'm on my way down." Curious to know what she's here for, Tomoya got to his feet.

Waiting for him in the reception area was a woman in a black pantsuit with long hair tied back. She was in her early thirties, possibly a bit older.

"Mr. Takagaki?" she inquired, walking toward him.

"Yes, that's me," he said. The woman drew a step closer. She glanced discreetly back at the reception desk, then extracted something from the inside pocket of her jacket. "This is who I am," she said, deliberately keeping her voice low.

He didn't immediately grasp what she was showing him. It was only after a few seconds that he realized it was a police badge. Tomoya blinked and stared into her face.

The woman looked straight back at him. He thought he detected a hint of confrontation in her eyes. "It would be nice if we could find a quiet place to talk."

"There's a meeting room. Would that be all right? It's a bit on the small side."

"Thank you. That'll be fine."

Tomoya was relieved. Her courteous manner suggested that she wasn't going to accuse him of committing a crime. He couldn't recall the last time he'd had anything to do with the police. Pulling out her business card, the woman introduced herself formally. She was Kaoru Utsumi from the Homicide Division of the Tokyo Metropolitan Police Department.

"I know you must be busy, so let's get straight down to business. I believe you know this woman?"

As she said this, she produced a photograph. Tomoya swallowed at the sight of it. He hadn't forgotten that face—couldn't have forgotten it even if he had wanted to.

"It's . . . uh . . . Saori Namiki," he replied, gazing at the photograph. In it, Saori was smiling and making the peace sign.

"What was the nature of your relationship?"

He swallowed again, then said: "We were going out together. That is . . . three years ago we were. What is it, Sergeant Utsumi? Are you here to tell me that Saori has . . . ?"

Tomoya couldn't finish his question.

Utsumi frowned slightly and gave a gentle nod.

"Saori's body was recently discovered in a burned-out house in Shizuoka prefecture."

"*In Shizuoka?*"

"However, we believe that she actually died a long time ago. Perhaps immediately after she went missing."

It was a physical sensation, as if part of his body had hollowed out and vanished. *That's it. She's dead.*

In his heart, he had always thought so. Still, to be told like this was a big shock.

Tomoya caught his breath, then he looked at Utsumi. "Why Shizuoka?"

"We don't yet know. It's one of the things we are currently looking into. Can you shed any light on the subject, Mr. Takagaki? When Saori was alive, for example, did she ever mention Shizuoka to you?"

"Never." Tomoya spoke with conviction. "I don't think she'd ever even been there."

"Her parents told me exactly the same thing," said Utsumi, nodding. Then she gave Tomoya a piercing look. "How close was your relationship with Saori?"

"How close? I suppose I'd say our relationship was, you know, normal," replied Tomoya, scratching his head. "To call it 'official' sounds a bit weird, but the first time we officially went out on a date was around the time Saori graduated high school. I was in my second year at work, I'd got a handle on my job, and I was just starting to have a bit more time for myself outside my job. Until then, I just talked to her when I went to Namiki-ya for dinner, so we were hardly close."

"And how often did you go out together?"

"Once every week or two, I guess. We were both quite busy."

"Where did you go on these dates, if you don't mind me asking?"

"We mostly went into the center of Tokyo. We didn't do anything special, just wandered around, went shopping, stuff like that."

Tomoya wondered if Utsumi was expecting him to reveal whether or not their relationship was physical. Sure, she was the police, but did she have the right to intrude on a person's privacy like that?

But Utsumi didn't ask any more intrusive questions. Instead, she switched her focus to the big issue. "Could you tell me in as much detail as you can about the time when Saori went missing?" she asked.

Tomoya dug into his memory.

"I only found out she was missing several days after it happened. It was funny, I was sending her texts, which I could see weren't being read; she wasn't picking up my calls, either. I thought I'd drop into Namiki-ya on my way home from work, and I found the place closed. I realized something serious must have happened. That was when Natsumi contacted me and I finally found out what was going on."

"Did the police ever contact you?"

"No, they didn't. Natsumi was the only one who knew about my relationship with Saori, and I guess she didn't mention it to the police. Later on, she told me that she didn't want me to get caught up in all the trouble."

Talking about it brought back vivid memories.

Tomoya often went to Namiki-ya after being told about Saori's disappearance. But the place was always closed. Although he was desperate to know what was going on, he kept telling himself that Saori's family were suffering even more than he was himself.

"I'm going to ask you point-blank." Utsumi looked him in the eye. "Can you think of any reason for Saori Namiki to disappear?"

Tomoya shook his head in puzzlement.

"I really have no idea. I mean, how should I know? She just disappeared one day—and then she stayed missing."

"We believe it is highly likely that Saori Namiki was the victim of some sort of crime. What's your opinion? Do you agree?"

"Of course, I do." Now Tomoya's head was bobbing up and down. "I think somebody murdered her."

"And have you any idea who that somebody might be?" Utsumi asked, her gaze intense.

A thought flitted through his mind. It was the matter of a moment, but enough to perceptibly delay his answer. "No, no idea," he said.

"You paused for a moment there," Utsumi said. "Are you quite sure you didn't think of something?"

"No, I . . . uh . . . ," mumbled Tomoya incoherently.

"Mr. Takagaki," said Utsumi, smiling and speaking more gently. "There's only me here and I'm not even taking notes. If there's something you want to say, you should go ahead and say it. You don't need to tie yourself in knots worrying about sharing what may be nothing more than a groundless hunch with the police. It's our job to extract the truth by sifting through a jumble of information. Please, work with me here." She bowed curtly.

Tomoya's lips were dry. He licked them. The woman was disquietingly perceptive. She seemed to know exactly what he was thinking.

"I've no real grounds for what I'm about to say. It's just a feeling."

"That's not a problem." Utsumi lifted her face. He noticed the gleam in her almond-shaped eyes.

Tomoya coughed once, then began to speak.

"I think it started in the autumn of the year Saori graduated high school. I remember her telling me about this creepy guy who'd started coming to Namiki-ya. He was always ogling her, getting her to pour his beer for him, stuff like that. Apparently, he used to come in late, which is why I hadn't met him. Anyway, there was this one time when I did end up staying later than usual and he turned up. Just like Saori had told me, he made her fill his glass; he even tried to force her to sit down next to him. On that occasion, Saori managed to come up with some excuse and fled upstairs. It didn't make any difference, though; the guy kept on coming to the restaurant after that. I was worried, but Saori told me everything was fine. In the end, her father threw the fellow out and he did stop coming. But . . ."

He hesitated.

"But what?" Utsumi had no intention of letting Tomoya off the hook.

"But Saori told me she used to bump into the guy in the street now and then. There were several occasions when suddenly he was right there, right next to her. One time, when he got too close, she just took off and ran."

"Did he run after her?"

"I don't know. Saori said she might be imagining things."

"Is there anything else you can tell me about this man? His name, perhaps? His job?"

Tomoya shook his head. "I don't know anything about him. He was a Namiki-ya customer, but where he lived, I've no idea."

"This is the first time you've mentioned him to the police?"

"Yes, it is. I mean . . . this happened a little while before Saori went missing. I didn't speak to the police at the time and I didn't make the connection right away. It was months later, as I was mulling things over, that it occurred to me that perhaps the guy had something to do with her disappearance. . . ."

Utsumi sat in silence for a while, then she opened her bag.

"Is the man here?" she asked, arranging five photographs on the table. They all looked like pictures from driver's licenses or mug shots.

Tomoya gave a start when he looked at the picture second from the end on the left. He remembered those sunken cheeks, those deep, dark eyes.

"This is him." Tomoya jabbed a finger at the picture.

"Is it, now?" The woman's expression was quite blank. With quick, deft movements, she replaced the photographs in her bag.

"I was right, then. It is him, isn't it?" Tomoya said. "If you're walking around with a picture of the guy, that's got to mean the police have got their eye on him. Are you going to arrest him?"

Utsumi gave him a bland smile. "We're pursuing multiple lines of inquiry. This man is by no means our only suspect."

"Okay, but . . . can't you at least tell me his name? *Who is he?*"

"I am very sorry, Mr. Takagaki. Sharing that information with you at this point wouldn't help our investigation."

"It wouldn't hurt it, though, would it?"

"If you mentioned his name to someone else and the information got out there, there's every chance that it could impact negatively on our investigation."

"I won't tell a soul. I promise."

"It's less risky if I simply don't tell you. I hope you can understand our position on this."

Tomoya bit his lip at the brush-off. He felt thwarted; at the same time, the detective had a valid point.

Utsumi looked down at her watch.

"You've been most helpful. I really appreciate it." She rose to her feet and gave him a little nod of gratitude.

Tomoya accompanied her to the lobby to see her out, then returned to his desk. Concentrating on his work proved almost impossible. Before he was even aware of what he was doing, he had his smartphone out and had started scouring the internet. Inputting "Saori Namiki" produced no results. That suggested that the police hadn't yet released her name to the media.

Putting his phone aside, Tomoya leaned back in his chair and absentmindedly contemplated his desk. It was the same desk they had given him when he had joined the firm. The memories from that time came back to him.

April, five years ago. That was when he had first eaten his dinner at Namiki-ya. He lived with his mother, Rie, who was a nurse. She had had a night shift that night. She had always made Tomoya's dinner before she headed out to the hospital, but now that he had a job of his own, Tomoya had decided that he ought to start feeding himself. Not only was Namiki-ya conveniently situated halfway between the station and his house, it looked like a nice place, and he had always fancied trying it out.

On the evening of the first visit, Saori was working at the restaurant. With her small face and big eyes, she looked more like a show business personality than a waitress and Tomoya couldn't help noticing her. What he found most attractive about her was the expressiveness of her face. He was delighted when she treated him—a first-time visitor—with as much friendliness as a regular.

It didn't take long for Tomoya to become a regular. In no time at all, he was going to Namiki-ya once a week. Even when his mother wasn't on the night shift, he would text her to say that he was going to grab a bite on the way home from work and would go to Namiki-ya. Although the food was undeniably good, his real goal was to see Saori.

Tomoya was in no hurry to tell Saori how he felt about her. What guarantee was there that Saori felt the same way about him? As his visits to the restaurant became more frequent, he began to get the sense that she liked him; at the same time, he worried that he might be reading into the situation what he wanted to be true.

From listening to Saori's mother chatting with the customers, he had learned that Saori didn't have a boyfriend. He was also aware that there were quite a few people who went to the restaurant specifically to see her. The presence of other young male customers put him on edge, since he was convinced that they must have her in their sights, too. The fact that Saori was equally nice to all of them made him uneasy.

Before Tomoya knew it, almost a year had gone by. One evening in March, he deliberately went to Namiki-ya at a time when he knew it would be empty and presented Saori with a gift "to celebrate her graduation." It was a golden hair slide in the shape of a butterfly.

Saori's eyes lit up and she immediately put it on. Since there was no mirror at hand, Tomoya took a picture of the back of her head with his phone to show her what the slide looked like.

"Oh, it's so cute!" Saori gushed when she saw it. Tomoya was sure her reaction was genuine. "I want to go out with this on just as soon as I can. Where shall I go?" she said, tugging at the clasp. She looked straight at Tomoya. "What about you, Mr. Takagaki? Will you take me out somewhere?"

Tomoya was shocked. That was the last thing he had expected her to say.

"Uhm, shall we go and see a movie?"

Saori was less than delighted with Tomoya's hasty suggestion. What would be the point of going somewhere dark?

That was how they ended up going to Tokyo Disneyland for their first date. Every time Saori came across a mirror, she would turn around and look at her reflection with the hair slide and comment on how nice it looked.

They started to go out on a regular basis after that. The more time they spent together, the more Tomoya grew to like Saori. She was a gentle, thoughtful person.

He told no one that they were going out except for his mother, Rie. She promptly declared that she would like to meet Saori, so Tomoya brought her home with him. Rie took to her at first sight. "A beautiful girl like that is way out of your league," she even said to her son.

Saori was only nineteen but she had ambitions. She was with a producer and wanted to become a professional singer. Tomoya felt duty bound to help her make her dreams come true.

But all that had been taken away from him in an instant. The three years since Saori had disappeared had been a living hell. Internally, he was a writhing mass of pain and anguish. He had continued going to Namiki-ya for a while with the hope of hearing some news about Saori, but eventually he stopped. The reason was simple: He had given up hope.

7

Two detectives came to Naoki Niikura's house: Inspector Kishitani of the Tokyo Metropolitan Police and a junior detective from the Kikuno Police Station. Kishitani was a man of forty or so with an intelligent face and a mild manner.

Naoki Niikura had expected the police to show up at some point. Yutaro Namiki had phoned him that Saori had been found.

Inspector Kishitani's questions focused on three areas: Could the Niikuras tell him anything about what was going on with Saori at the time of her disappearance? Did they know anything about her personal relationships? And finally, did they have any ideas about why she might have been targeted?

Naoki was eager to provide as much information as he could. However, he had no answers for them. Ultimately, all he could muster was a furrowed brow and a head tilted quizzically to one side. It was pathetic, but that was the reality of it. Had he known anything useful, he would have shared it with the police three years ago.

Kishitani and the junior detective nonetheless thanked Naoki and his wife for their help, as they got to their feet at the end of the interview. As Naoki accompanied them back to the doorstep, he felt acutely conscious of his own powerlessness.

He and his wife went back into the living room. Two cups of green tea, which the detectives hadn't touched, stood on the coffee table in the middle of the room.

"Shall I make us some coffee?" Rumi asked, as she tidied away the detectives' cups.

"That would be nice. I'd love a cup." Naoki dropped down onto the sofa. He sighed as he picked up the business card that Kishitani had left for him.

If the Niikuras hadn't been able to provide the police with any worthwhile information, they also hadn't been able to extract anything worthwhile from them, either. The police hadn't even told them where in Shizuoka Saori's remains had been found.

The only concrete thing that came out of their meeting was the photograph they were shown to see if they recognized the man. Yutaro Namiki had said something about being shown a photo by the police. It was probably of the same person. According to Yutaro, the man in the photo had been a regular customer and had treated Saori outrageously. Naoki, however, had never met the man and knew nothing about him.

Was he responsible for Saori's murder? He certainly looked wicked enough. *Maybe he tried to assault her and when she resisted, he killed her.* If so, it was just too senseless.

It had been a long time since Naoki had met anyone with the raw natural talent of Saori Namiki.

He had heard all the chitter-chatter about the brilliant girl singer from the Kikuno shopping district. So many people wanted to hear her perform that the annual singing contest was always packed. Naoki, however, refused to take the rumors seriously. *It's just some stupid local singing competition. Along comes some girl who can sing a little better than the average, and all the adults get carried away. Big deal!*

But at some point a friend in the music business pulled him aside, showed him a brochure, and said, "You really should give this girl a listen." The brochure was for the annual festival of the local high school, which included a performance by the school band with the local "girl genius" on vocals.

Since Naoki's schedule was clear that day, he decided to go and take his wife, Rumi, along with him. Their expectations were rock-bottom. They steeled themselves to endure a series of cheesy rock covers.

They couldn't have been more wrong. Saori Namiki and the band played jazz and blues, and they performed a few standards as well as songs that only the most committed music fans would be familiar with. Saori had a distinctive voice with a deep timbre reminiscent of a woodwind instrument. She also had an extraordinary musical instinct. She seemed to grasp the meaning of each song at the deepest level. Her abilities far outstripped those of any normal high school girl.

Without intending to, the Niikuras stayed through until the end of the concert.

Naoki and Rumi were in a state of excitement. They both felt the same way: *Leaving that extraordinary talent undeveloped was simply not an option.*

As soon as they could, they went to Saori's house to meet her parents. Although the Namikis knew that their daughter was talented, it had never occurred to them that she could turn professional. It was only when Naoki started making the case with audible passion in his voice that they finally seemed able to treat the issue as a real-world problem. They would ask Saori how she felt, they said.

Our daughter wants to give it a go. The Niikuras were overjoyed when Yutaro Namiki called back the next day with the news.

And that was how Naoki Niikura secured Saori Namiki. She was a diamond, but still a diamond in the rough; she would need polishing if she was really going to shine. Using his network of contacts, Naoki found Saori a top-notch voice trainer. The Niikuras had a soundproof room in their mansion and Naoki arranged for her to take lessons there.

I'm going to do whatever it takes to make Saori's talent blossom, he thought. *The girl could be a star in Japan—no, a worldwide superstar. I'm going to throw everything I've got at this.*

The Niikuras were all doctors, going back generations. The family owned several hospitals, which Naoki's two older brothers managed. At university, Niikura was accepted into the medical program. The plan had always been for him to become a doctor, too, but the direction of his life changed when he started playing in a band. Naoki had always liked music; he had started taking piano lessons at age five and gone on to develop an interest in composition at junior high school. His secret dream had always been to become a musician rather than a doctor.

Naoki's family and friends were all opposed when he announced his decision to drop out of school, but when they saw how committed he was to his music, more and more of them began to come around to his side. His two brothers were particularly supportive, telling him not to worry; they would look after the family hospitals so he could do what he loved. It was thanks to his brothers' generosity that Naoki also managed to avoid any financial hardship.

At a relatively early stage, however, Naoki realized that he didn't have any great talents of his own. Instead, the idea of scouting and training up young talent started to appeal more. Running a music school and a clutch of rehearsal studios would give him the opportunity to do that. He had already discovered several successful artists over the years. Saori, however, was in a completely different league.

Saori's progress was rapid. At the rate she was going, she could easily make her mark in the music world on a global scale. Then, just when his belief in her had reached its peak, the unthinkable happened. *His most precious treasure disappeared.*

Even in his worst nightmares, Naoki had never imagined such a scenario. Had she been involved in an accident or just fallen sick, he might have been better able to come to terms with his loss. What, though, was he supposed to do when she just vanished one day? When he heard the news of her disappearance, he raged against the Namikis, all the time knowing it was unfair. *Why didn't they keep a closer eye on their daughter?*

Saori's disappearance upended Naoki's whole existence. He lost his enthusiasm for life and spent his days in a stupor. He became an empty shell of a man.

A fragrant aroma brought Naoki back to himself. Rumi was in the room with a tray laden with coffee cups.

"Black, right?"

"Please." Stretching out a hand, he took a cup. He took a swig, but the flavor hardly registered. Even his taste buds had dulled. Thoughts of Saori monopolized all his faculties.

"Hey," said Rumi. "Do you think the man in the photo is the killer?"

"Don't know . . . but it seems probable."

"He'll get the death sentence if he is."

Naoki cocked his head.

"Don't be too sure about that. Murdering one person isn't always enough to get you the death sentence."

"Seriously?" Rumi's eyes widened in surprise.

"Definitely. The sentence is more like ten-something years in jail, I think." Naoki put his cup down and gazed off into space. "If I could get away with it, though, I'd kill the guy myself."

8

A week had passed since the establishment of the task force. Director Mamiya, who had just received an update from Detective Kusanagi, was looking gloomy. And no wonder. They had uncovered next to nothing.

"As things stand, this pension thing is our only angle of attack," Mamiya said. He was sitting down and leafing through a written report.

"Whether he was stealing from her pension or not, we still need to prove that Hasunuma used to visit his stepmother's house," said Kusanagi, who was standing in front of him.

"Any results from canvassing the neighborhood?"

"So far, nothing."

Mamiya scowled and groaned.

Over the past week, the joint investigation task force had been looking for evidence that Kanichi Hasunuma had visited his stepmother over the past six years. If they could find even a single instance of him having done so, Mamiya and Kusanagi believed they could use that to prove that he knew his stepmother was dead.

The Shizuoka Prefectural Police had found something important: Someone had been using an ATM card to periodically withdraw money from her bank account. In fact, just recently, almost all the money in the account had been withdrawn at an ATM in central Tokyo. When they reviewed the security-camera footage, they found a man who resembled Hasunuma. Perhaps, when he heard about his stepmother's body being found, he'd decided to withdraw all the money he could before the account was frozen.

This was what Kusanagi had been hoping for. If they could find evidence suggesting that Hasunuma knew his stepmother was dead all along, then they could arrest him on a charge of fraud.

Even though a large number of detectives were interviewing people, so far they had nothing to show for their pains.

They had looked into arresting Hasunuma for illegal disposal of a dead body. Here, too, they confronted the same problem: They couldn't indict him unless they could prove that he had actually been to the house. The statute of limitations was another stumbling block.

"Has Hasunuma made a move?" Mamiya asked.

"No. Same old, same old."

They had been keeping Hasunuma under twenty-four-hour surveillance ever since the two bodies had been found. Unfortunately, his visit to the ATM happened before the team was in place. According to the surveillance team, Hasunuma spent most of his time in his Edogawa Ward apartment, with occasional forays outside to shop or to play pachinko. The scrap iron merchant where he had been working until a month before had gone bust, leaving him with no visible source of income.

Frustratingly, Hasunuma knew full well that he was being watched.

Mamiya crossed his arms and sighed heavily. "I don't think we're yet at the stage when we can ask him to voluntarily present himself at the station."

"He'd probably claim that the body we found in his stepmother's house has nothing to do with him."

"Probably would," grunted Mamiya sourly. "Thanks for the update. Keep at it."

Kusanagi went back to his desk. He was looking through some files when Inspector Kishitani came rushing over.

"Chief, I've figured out what vehicle Hasunuma was making the most frequent use of three years ago. It was his employer's minivan." Kishitani presented Kusanagi with a printout of a small white van. "It was the same make as this."

Kusanagi took the piece of paper, had a look, and grunted approvingly.

If Hasunuma had moved Saori Namiki's body, then it would have required a vehicle to do so.

"At the time, Hasunuma was the only person using this vehicle; none of the other employees did. I went through the company's vehicle use log."

"Good work." Kusanagi looked at the printout of the van with renewed interest.

"We found something else interesting," Kishitani said.

"What?"

"The last known sighting of Saori Namiki on the security camera of a convenience store. We looked through the footage very carefully." Kishitani placed two printouts on Kusanagi's desk. One showed Saori Namiki walking along the street with her phone held up to her ear. The other a white minivan.

"Wha—? Is that . . . ?" Kusanagi looked at the time stamp. The interval between the two pictures was less than one minute.

"This minivan drives by almost immediately after Saori Namiki has passed the convenience store. It's not much of a stretch to assume it was following her."

"Got the license number of the van?"

"Sure, we do."

"Check it against the N-System data. Liaise with the Shizuoka Prefectural Police."

"Yes, sir," replied Kishitani, his tone buoyant. "Oh, and there's one more thing." He raised his index finger. "One of the recycling company employees told me something interesting: Over the last three years, Hasunuma would occasionally call him but the calls always came from pay phones."

"From pay phones?"

"And they were always about the same thing. Hasunuma would ask whether the police had been there. That was his biggest worry. The calls were frequent in the first few months, he said, but they gradually tailed off, and he hasn't heard from him in the last year."

Kusanagi grunted his acknowledgement of Kishitani's hard work.

"Hasunuma probably wanted to check that he wasn't a suspect in the Saori Namiki missing-person case. He didn't update his details on the official residents' register for a while after moving out of his apartment. He was probably being careful, taking steps to prepare for the police coming after him. That would also explain why he used pay phones. When he decided that the coast was clear, he updated his entry in the residents' register, and got his driving license renewed."

"I think you're right, sir," Kishitani said.

It was yet another piece of evidence that made the cloud of suspicion surrounding Hasunuma even darker. But it, too, was only circumstantial.

Soon after that, the search results from N-System came back. A little over three years ago, the white minivan of Hasunuma's employer had departed Kikuno, got onto the expressway at the nearest interchange and headed toward Shizuoka; about two hours later it reappeared, driving in the opposite direction. The timing corresponded perfectly with Saori Namiki's disappearance.

Kusanagi decided it was time to order a search of Hasunuma's apartment and to get him to come to the station for an interview.

Kusanagi chose to conduct the interview himself.

The Hasunuma sitting across from him in the interview room today was considerably thinner than the Hasunuma of nineteen years ago. His cheeks were hollower, his face more wrinkled, and his eyes sunk deeper into their sockets. Only the deadness of his eyes and the blank, inexpressive quality of the face were the same.

Hasunuma didn't react when Kusanagi introduced himself. *He's probably forgotten all about that low-ranking detective from nineteen years ago,* Kusanagi thought.

He felt a degree of relief when Hasunuma volunteered his name and his address when he asked for them. Hasunuma wasn't going to opt for the silent route right from the get-go.

Kusanagi decided to play his first card. "Is this you?" he asked, placing a printout in front of Hasunuma. It was a photograph showing him withdrawing money from an ATM.

Hasunuma shot him a cold glance. "I don't know," he said in a flat voice.

"A sum of money was withdrawn from the bank account of Yoshie Hasunuma on this day. Now, if this person is *not* you, that would mean that someone has stolen your stepmother's cash card and managed to find out what her PIN number is. We would have to investigate this as a case of theft and we would, of course, have to ask you, as a member of the victim's family, to help us with our inquiries. Would you be prepared to help us?"

Hasunuma looked directly at Kusanagi. He noticed how much white was visible under his irises. Hasunuma sniffed loudly, pulled his wallet out of his jacket, and extracted a card from it. A cash card. He placed it on the table.

"May I have a look?"

Hasunuma slowly closed his eyes to indicate yes.

The name YOSHIE HASUNUMA was embossed on the card. It was one of the old-fashioned ATM cards without a built-in fingerprint reader.

"Why are you in possession of this card?" Kusanagi asked, handing it back.

"Oh, I have my reasons." Hasunuma took the card.

"Those reasons being?"

Hasunuma gave a modest shrug. "It's private. I'd rather not say."

"In your interview with Shizuoka Prefectural Police, you stated that you hadn't been in contact with or seen Yoshie Hasunuma, your stepmother, for many years. When was the last time you saw her?"

"It's so long ago, I've forgotten."

"A rough date will be fine."

"I wouldn't want to say anything vague or imprecise." Hasunuma pressed his lips together. Kusanagi got the impression he was stifling a laugh.

Now he's starting to show his true colors. Kusanagi steeled himself.

Kusanagi shifted to a different angle of attack.

"Where were you living three years ago?"

Hasunuma tilted his head to one side. "I can't remember. I'm always drifting from one place to another."

"You were renting an apartment in south Kikuno in Kikuno City. There are records of these things."

"There are?" Hasunuma was completely impassive.

"Why did you move out?"

"I dunno. Can't remember."

"You also quit your job. Why? Did you have a reason for that? Something serious?"

"Uhm, no," said Hasunuma listlessly. "I really don't remember. I mean, whatever. I'm always changing jobs."

Whatever the question, apparently his strategy was to play dumb.

"What did you do for dinner in those days? Cook at home? Eat out?"

"Me? Sometimes fixed my own meals, sometimes went out, I guess."

"Did you ever go to a local eatery called Namiki-ya?"

The shadow of a grin appeared on Hasunuma's lips.

"Oh, I went to all sorts of places. I can't remember them all."

"The daughter of the couple who run the restaurant was called

Saori Namiki. She's the girl whose body was found in your stepmother's house after it burned down. Does that bring anything to mind?"

Slowly shutting his eyes, Hasunuma started to shake his head robotically from side to side. "No. I have nothing to say."

Kusanagi glowered at Hasunuma whose face was as blank as a Noh mask. He sat there limp, immobile, and indifferent.

"A little over three years ago, you used one of the company minivans to drive from your apartment to the house of your stepmother, Yoshie Hasunuma, and back, didn't you? The journey was recorded on the N-System."

This was a partial bluff on Kusanagi's part. They hadn't yet checked the journey to that precise level of detail.

Nothing changed in Hasunuma's expression. "I don't recall," he replied flatly. Something in his manner suggested that he found the whole idea of making such a claim based on N-System data faintly ridiculous.

That'll do for today, Kusanagi thought to himself.

"I think we're good. Thank you for coming in."

Getting languidly to his feet, Hasunuma headed to the door, which the junior detective, who had been taking notes during the interview, was holding open for him. He stopped halfway and looked back at Kusanagi.

"How's this going to play out, Detective Kusanagi?" He was almost smiling.

"I'm sorry?"

"Mamiya—wasn't that his name? I bet he's quite the big shot, too, now, eh?"

The snide remark left Kusanagi speechless.

So Hasunuma did remember. He had known all along that his interviewer was the junior detective who had visited him in his apartment nineteen years ago.

With a final sneer, Hasunuma left the room.

About two weeks after this interview, an important development took place. Among the articles seized during the search of Hasunuma's apartment were his work overalls from when he worked at the recycling company. Even though the overalls appeared to have been washed, there were faint traces of what looked like blood.

The overalls were immediately sent to the crime lab. Both the blood type and the DNA turned out to be a match for Saori Namiki.

Should they arrest Kanichi Hasunuma? Kusanagi discussed it with Director Mamiya and Commissioner Tatara. The whole situation was strikingly similar to what had happened nineteen years ago. They could prove that Hasunuma had handled and unlawfully disposed of Saori Namiki's corpse; but proving that he had killed her was a different matter entirely. They had no direct, physical evidence.

After talking it over, the three men concluded that going ahead was a viable option. This time the body had a depressed skull fracture. That was different from nineteen years ago when specifying the cause of death had been impossible to determine. Someone had struck Saori with sufficient force to stave in the cranium; one couldn't argue that there was no intent to kill.

The moment they arrested Hasunuma, he started behaving exactly as he had nineteen years before. Throughout his time in detention, he remained resolutely silent. Apparently, he did the same thing when questioned by the prosecutor.

Kusanagi and the rest of his team were not surprised. It was what they had anticipated. They had arrested Hasunuma on the assumption that he could still be indicted even if they didn't manage to get him to confess.

The prosecutor took a different view of the matter. Just before the end of the legal detention period, when they had to charge him or release him, the prosecutor reached his decision: They would defer prosecution until there was more evidence.

Possibly forever.

Kanichi Hasunuma was released.

9

The Kikuno train station was an elegant little four-story structure. He passed through the turnstile and emerged into a shopping mall. The coffee shop was right in front of him.

Kusanagi went in and looked around. The person he was looking for was over by the window, reading a magazine. There was already a cup of coffee on the table in front of him.

Kusanagi wandered over and looked down at his old friend. "Hey."

Manabu Yukawa looked up. A smile played around his lips. "How many years has it been?"

"Four. You could at least have got in touch when you got back to Japan." Kusanagi dropped into the chair opposite.

"I told Kaoru Utsumi."

"Well, she didn't tell me."

"I'm not here to listen to your gripes about the indolence of your subordinates."

An ironic smile flashed across Kusanagi's face. "Always ready with a wisecrack. Nothing changes."

When the waitress brought him a glass of water, he ordered a coffee. Then he cast an appraising look at his old friend.

Yukawa was hard and lean rather than thin. No change there. Subtle though they were, there were definite hints of gray in his hair.

"You look well," said Kusanagi. "How was America?"

Yukawa shrugged and picked up his cup.

"Stimulating enough, I would say. My research went well, so all in all, it wasn't bad."

"Utsumi told me you're a full professor now."

Yukawa extracted a business card from the inside pocket of his jacket and placed it flat on the table in front of Kusanagi. "My contact details have changed."

Kusanagi picked up the card. Sure enough, Yukawa's job title was now professor.

"Congratulations," Kusanagi said.

Yukawa radiated indifference as he tipped his head slightly to one side. "Nothing to congratulate me about."

"Oh, come off it. Surely it means there's no one above you to stop you doing what you want."

"Even when I was an associate professor, my superiors didn't restrict my activities much. I had the freedom to research whatever I was interested in. It doesn't work like that when you're a full professor. Whatever you want to do, you always have to think about *this*." Yukawa made a ring with his thumb and forefinger, the Japanese sign for money. "My main job now is to find sponsors. I make presentations about the value of our research and then solicit donations from them. I'm no longer a researcher myself; I'm more like a producer."

"That's what you're doing, is it? Doesn't seem very *you*."

"Whatever the field, the old generation always has to make way for the new. The time has come for me to help smooth the path for the next generation. I've got to accept that reality and deal with it," Yukawa said somewhat sardonically, then looked over at Kusanagi. "I imagine things have changed for you, too?"

"Utsumi told you?"

"No, I'm just guessing."

Now Kusanagi produced his business card. Yukawa took it and raised an eyebrow.

"Dare I hope that means one more trustworthy chief inspector at the Tokyo Metropolitan Police Department?"

"Nice of you to say so, but I'm sure there are plenty of people who think I'm useless."

Kusanagi's coffee arrived. He added milk, stirred it, and drank a mouthful.

"You look a bit glum." Yukawa looked at him appraisingly with his scientist's eyes. "Oh, that reminds me, something in your email has been bugging me. You said you wanted to see me, if I had the time, because you had some 'unpleasant business' that was going to take you to the Kikuno shopping district?"

"Something exasperating has happened." Kusanagi shrugged his shoulders. "It's a frustrating and, frankly, rather pitiful story."

"Has your investigation hit rough waters?"

"Not so much hit rough waters as run aground."

"That sounds interesting." Yukawa leaned forward, put his hands on the table, and laced his fingers together. "I'm happy to listen, if you're prepared to share the details with a civilian."

"You are? I couldn't tell just any old civilian, but you, you're different." Kusanagi frowned, interrupting himself and waving his right hand, palm outward, in a dismissive gesture. "No, I really shouldn't. Here we are, meeting after such a long time. Why talk about my miserable police work? Tell me what you got up to in America. I want to know."

"Research. That's all I did over there. Do you really want to hear about whether the magnetic monopole search connects to the grand unified theory? Do you?"

Kusanagi grimaced. "You can't have only done research. What about your days off?"

"I took it easy," Yukawa replied tartly. "I rested so I could fully concentrate on my research when the working week started again. I was over in the States for a fixed period of time; I didn't want to waste even a single day."

Kusanagi suddenly felt tired. Yukawa's manner was lighthearted enough, but he was probably being serious. Kusanagi had trouble imagining his friend playing a round of golf or going out for a drive in his free time.

"What's the problem? Tell me your troubles. Tell me everything that's gone wrong with this investigation." Yukawa raised his hands high and drew them toward himself in a grand gesture of solicitation.

"America's changed you. You used to say that police investigations didn't interest you."

"That was only because every time you came to me with one, it always involved a really convoluted problem. Someone's head had suddenly spontaneously combusted. A dodgy cult leader had attacked someone using his telekinetic powers. Stuff like that. You'd always come running to me to work out how it had been done. I don't think I need to worry about that this time, though."

Kusanagi gave a derisive snort.

"Oh, I get it. You're quite happy to hear about my case, provided you can just stay on the sidelines. Fine. Well, I don't know if you'll enjoy this story." Kusanagi ran his eye swiftly around the café. The other customers didn't appear to have any interest in them.

Kusanagi began by giving an overview of the case. A girl who had gone missing a little over three years ago had recently been found dead; they had arrested the man they believed responsible for her death; and he had been released because the prosecutor declined to indict him—technically a deferment of dispensation.

"That's got to be annoying for the police. Still, someone being released due to lack of evidence—that has to be pretty rare?"

"It is. It's very rare indeed," said Kusanagi. "If the suspect was a normal person, the prosecutors would probably have gone after him hard—but that's not what happened."

Yukawa jerked his chin and used the tip of one finger to adjust his spectacles on his nose. It was a habit, an unconscious gesture he made when something aroused his interest.

"What makes the defendant so abnormal?"

"He's a silent man."

"A silent man?"

"It's a long story. It goes back about twenty years."

Kusanagi then gave Yukawa a brief account of the Yuna Moto-hashi murder case, before going into the details of the two trials.

Yukawa couldn't suppress a groan.

"So the defendant was found not guilty, even though you had as-sembled all that circumstantial evidence. It sounds unreasonable—but in a way that's what the court system is all about. What's the connection between that case and the present case?"

"Believe it or not, but the suspect is the same."

Yukawa's temples twitched.

"Now, that is interesting. Hence you describing him as 'the silent man.'"

"And the case I'm working on now has several striking similarities to the Yuna Motohashi case. The fact that the statute of limitations has expired for unlawful disposal and mutilation of a corpse; the fact that there is no physical evidence that he committed the murder. The only difference this time is the presence of the depressed skull fracture. We have pinpointed that as the cause of death, which in turn leads to the method of killing. . . ."

"But the prosecutor didn't see it like that?"

Kusanagi pulled a face and nodded his head.

"He apparently thought that still wasn't enough. The depression of the skull was all very well, he said, but one couldn't tell whether she had been struck with a weapon or if the injury was the result of some kind of accident. Worse yet, he said, one couldn't even be certain that it was the cause of death."

"When you put it like that, I suppose he's right."

"With any other suspect, I don't think the prosecutor would have thought twice about indicting him. But from what I heard, Hasunuma was completely relaxed when the prosecutor questioned him."

"Because he was confident that he could win the case just by keeping his mouth shut."

"Correct."

"But he would still be kept in detention until the trial was over. Surely he wouldn't want that?"

"That guy probably just sees detention as another chance to make money."

"Make money?" Yukawa frowned dubiously. "What do you mean?"

"After he was found not guilty in the Yuna Motohashi trial, he immediately claimed police reparations and trial costs. I heard he got over ten million yen all told."

"Impressive. The guy's got guts." Yukawa let his eyes wander around the room for a moment, then he pointed a finger at Kusanagi. "From what you've told me, it sounds like he's got a pretty high IQ."

"You're right about that. The police had investigated Kanichi Hasunuma in considerable detail. He was an only child; his parents were divorced when he was ten, with his father getting custody. When he was thirteen, his father remarried, and Yoshie became his stepmother. Around then, he began hanging out with a bad crowd and his behavior became problematic. He left home immediately after graduating high school. In fact, his father kicked him out of the house, sick of the embarrassment he was causing the family. The father worked"—Kusanagi paused a moment—"as a police officer."

Yukawa jerked upright in his chair. "Ha! This is getting more interesting by the minute."

"It's hard not to think that his dislike of his father translated into a generalized animosity toward the police."

"That interpretation strikes me as a little oversentimental. I'd argue that he probably saw what his father was doing and made up his mind to do the polar opposite."

"You mean he took his father as an example of what *not* to do? What aspect of him in particular?"

Yukawa tilted his head to an angle. "It wasn't his father who provided him with something to react against; I think it was the suspects his father dealt with. Think about those days: back then, the police were free to do whatever they wanted. They could arrest someone based solely on circumstantial evidence, then coerce a confession out of them. They would just wear the suspect down and as soon as he'd signed a written statement cooked up for him, it was game over. Confessions nearly always resulted in a guilty verdict. If we assume that the father was in the habit of bragging about this rather convenient system at home, then what do you think the son, his captive audience, made of it?"

Kusanagi saw what Yukawa was getting at. "That if you did something wrong and were unlucky enough to be caught, confessing was absolutely the worst thing you could do."

"Put it another way: that provided you didn't confess, you stood a chance of winning. I think that's the lesson he learned."

Kusanagi rested his chin on his hands and sighed. "I hadn't thought about it like that. . . ."

"If I'm right, then it's the Japanese police force that's the begetter of this monster Hasunuma."

Yukawa's face wore an expression of studied neutrality. Kusanagi scowled at him.

"Sometimes you do come up with the most unwelcome ideas."

"Come on, I said it was only a theory. There's no reason to get upset." Yukawa glanced at his watch and gulped down what was left of his coffee. "Time for me to get back to work. I'm glad I got to hear about this interesting case. I'd like to hear more. Next time, let's make sure we have more time."

"Do you come to Kikuno every day?" Kusanagi asked.

"Two or three days a week, usually."

"You commute?"

"As a rule, yes. Sometimes I stay the night here. There's a place to sleep on campus. We're pretty far from central Tokyo."

As Yukawa reached for the bill, Kusanagi managed to swoop in and grab it. "Today's on me. You've had me over for coffee in your office often enough."

"Only instant coffee. And served in a rather unsightly mug, too! You should come over for another sometime," said Yukawa, getting to his feet. "Right, I'll say goodbye."

He must have remembered something, as he promptly sat back down again.

"There's one crucial thing I forgot to ask. That 'unpleasant business' you mentioned earlier—what was it? I presume that's the reason you got in touch with me?"

"Yes," Kusanagi said. He knew his face had fallen. "I have to go and see the victim's family and explain to them why the suspect was released. It's not something I would normally handle myself, but there's nothing normal about this case."

"You're going to see the family? A restaurant in the Kikuno shopping district, you said. What's the place's name?"

"Namiki-ya," said Kusanagi, after a moment's hesitation. He was dealing with Yukawa here; making a fuss about invasion of privacy would be stupid.

"Have you eaten there?"

"No, I haven't," said Kusanagi. "But it's a nice, unpretentious place. Very friendly."

"I'll keep it in mind." Yukawa got back to his feet. "See you around," he said and headed for the exit.

Kusanagi reached for his cup. The small amount of coffee left in it had gone cold, so he waved at the waitress and ordered a fresh cup.

He then took out his notebook and reviewed a number of details. He could already see the Namikis and the repressed rage on their faces in his mind's eye. *What happened? Why weren't you able to indict Hasunuma despite all the evidence you had?* They were definitely going to give him a hard time and would have trouble accepting the outcome. No surprise there; he couldn't accept it himself. That's why he had prepared a little speech.

Hard though it is, you must do your best not to lose hope. I assure you, we have no intention of backing off.

She slid open the lattice door and went outside to slot the *noren* curtain into position. After raining all day, the weather had cleared up. It felt nice: a crisp breeze and no sticky, oppressive heat.

I wonder if autumn proper is finally here, thought Natsumi Namiki. Although it was nearly October, they were still getting plenty of humid days; it annoyed her that she couldn't switch to her autumn wardrobe.

She went back into the restaurant. She was busy setting the tables when there was the rattle of the front door being pushed open.

A face like a craggy piece of rock appeared. Natsumi knew its owner well. He wore industrial overalls over a shirt and tie.

"Oh, Mr. Tojima." Natsumi's eyes sparkled. "What's up? Why are you here so early today?"

"You know how it is. Things happen." Shusaku Tojima pulled out a chair at a four-person table near the door.

Natsumi darted toward the back of the restaurant. "Dad, Mr. Tojima's here," she yelled in the direction of the kitchen.

"Shusaku?" Yutaro Namiki looked up from his cooking. "How come?"

"I think something happened."

"Don't worry, don't worry. It wasn't anything serious." Tojima was waving his hand from side to side in an extravagant gesture of depreciation. "You don't need to pass on everything I tell you to your dad, Natsumi. The important thing is to bring me a bottle of beer."

"Coming right up," said Natsumi, taking a bottle out of the re-frigerator.

"What was the problem, then?" Yutaro Namiki shouted from the kitchen.

"Oh, nothing serious." Toshima waved his hand again. "A piece of machinery was acting up. We couldn't do our jobs, so I closed up shop early."

"Acting up?"

"One of the food freezers. It broke down."

"A freezer? Again? Didn't you tell me about one of the employees getting injured when one of your freezers broke down a few months ago?"

"It was a different freezer this time. We got in touch with the manufacturer; they said they can't do anything till tomorrow. It's a disaster. This is a busy time of year for us."

Yutaro liked to describe Tojima as his "best bad friend." Smoking, drinking, betting—the two of them had done all sorts of "bad" things together, going all the way back to elementary school. In high school, they had regularly ditched school to go to pachinko parlors.

Like Yutaro Namiki, Tojima had also taken over the family business. In his case, it was a food-processing business.

Tojima was in the habit of dropping into Namiki-ya for a bottled beer and a snack on his way back from work. He typically showed up at around eight o'clock.

Natsumi brought the beer, a glass, and an appetizer to Tojima's table.

"As long as it's only from time to time, it may be good for you. Overworking's unhealthy." Natsumi poured Tojima his beer.

Tojima grinned as he picked up his glass.

"Natsumi, my dear, only you would say that. My wife is more like, 'You said you were busy, so what are you coming home for?'"

Natsumi laughed.

"She's not joking. She's deadly serious. I ask you, is that how a woman should treat her lord and master?" Tojima picked up a piece of the burdock root with his chopsticks. He caught sight of something and his eyes focused. "Ah, I see the poster's ready."

Natsumi turned to the wall behind her. "Yes, Ms. Maya delivered it yesterday."

On the wall was an advertising poster for the local autumn festival, which was due to take place any day now. It was a photograph from the previous year's parade showing a cluster of people dressed up as characters from fairy tales and children's stories marching cheerfully along the street. The Kikuno Story Parade was now a popular event, and people traveled a long way to see it.

Ms. Maya was Maya Miyazawa. She was the daughter of the family who owned Miyazawa Books, Kikuno's biggest and best bookstore. She was a director of the local neighborhood association and the chair of the parade's executive committee.

"I can't believe it's been a year. Time really does fly," said Tojima solemnly.

"I'm excited about it. Apparently, they've come up with a new gimmick specially for this year. The preparations are even more difficult than usual, Maya says."

"Are you lending a hand, Natsumi?"

"Maya asked me to come and help, but only when I have the time for it. Last year, I was doing face painting for the kids, stuff like that."

"You just help out? You don't take part in the parade?"

While most of the participants in the parade were cosplayers from all around Japan who had gone through the official application process, a team from the Kikuno shopping district had the automatic right to take part. Last year, they had performed a tableau from the tale of Princess Kaguya. They had done a great job re-creating different scenes from the story: the princess being discovered inside a shining stalk of bamboo as a baby; the five princes who come to ask her for her hand in marriage; and her climbing into the moon envoy's palanquin to leave Earth for good. Much to their relief, they were awarded third place. Since they represented the host district, everyone involved was determined to place in at least the top five.

"I'm not so keen on performance," Natsumi said.

"Why not? You'd enjoy it. You young people have got to take part. Besides, Natsumi, we need a pretty girl like you to boost the beauty quotient. There was this fantastic performance some years ago. There was this enormous conch shell and halfway through the parade, it opens up and out pop all these mermaids. It was sensational—" Suddenly, Tojima broke off. He froze, his mouth hanging open and eyes darting to and fro. He realized he'd said something quite unpardonable.

Thank goodness for that, Natsumi thought. She had been wondering how to get Tojima to shut up. Pretending not to have noticed anything, she applied herself to rearranging the bottles in the refrigerator. When she glanced back at Tojima, he was drinking his beer and looking rather shamefaced.

A moment later, there was the sound of footsteps on the staircase and Machiko appeared in the restaurant.

"Oh, good evening, Mr. Tojima. You're here early."

"Yes, I knocked off early. A man's got to play hooky now and again."

"Well, you just relax now," Machiko said, and headed for the kitchen. Looking at her as she walked off, Natsumi wondered whether her mother had overheard Tojima from the top of the stairs. She had probably waited for him to stop talking before coming down.

Natsumi had very clear memories of the parade Tojima had been talking about. It was the parade of four years ago. Natsumi, too, had been surprised when the mermaids suddenly emerged from inside the shell.

Saori had been so beautiful that Natsumi could hardly recognize her own sister.

A little before half past six, there was a clattering sound as the door opened and a customer stepped in. Even though Natsumi had her back to the door, she had a pretty good idea of who it was. There was one customer who always came at this particular time on this particular day of the week.

She turned around to see the person she'd expected settling down at the end of an empty six-person table.

Natsumi took him a cool towel to wipe his hands. "Good evening."

"Good evening," said the man, smiling and nodding. He had on a pair of rimless glasses. With his lean, hard physique, he looked younger than his fortysomething years.

"Would you like a beer to start?"

"Sure. And the usual after that."

"The *takiawase*. Very good."

Natsumi went back to the kitchen to relay his order. Then, she placed a bottle of beer, a glass, and an appetizer plate on a tray, and took it all back to where the customer was waiting.

He had taken off his jacket and was reading a magazine. There were some gorgeous 3D patterns on the page he was looking at. "Oh, they're lovely," gushed Natsumi as she put the beer bottle and the glass on the table.

"Aren't they just?" The man looked rather pleased with himself as he held the magazine out for Natsumi to look at. "What do you think these are?"

"They look like pieces of paper folded into complicated shapes."

"Good guess. It's origami. The idea is to take one large sheet of paper and fold it with maximum efficiency into the smallest possible shape. It's important that the process not just of folding it up but of opening it back out should be as simple as possible. Why do you think that is? The materials you're looking at here are not paper; they're solar panels for use in outer space. You load them onto a rocket in their folded-up state, shoot them into space, and then unfold and make use of them there. The Japanese art of origami inspired this technology." After delivering this enthusiastic speech, the man looked at Natsumi to gauge her reaction.

Pressing the tray flat against her chest, Natsumi gave a dutiful smile. "Is this what you're researching at the university, Professor?"

The man frowned, then pushed the bridge of his glasses higher up on his nose using the tip of one finger.

"Sadly, what I'm doing is neither as elegant nor as attractive." With a sigh, he shut the magazine and crammed it into the bag beside him. "I get asked that a lot: What practical benefits does your research have? Will it make my life more convenient? Is it as cool as smartphones?" He picked up his beer bottle and filled his glass. "Unfortunately, I can't really provide a satisfactory answer to questions like that. Science is just one word, but it can mean a multitude of things. Most academic research will never have even the smallest impact on the lives of the majority. The research I'm doing probably falls into that camp." He raised his glass, took a swig of beer, and used his free hand to wipe the froth off his lips. "If you're still curious, I'm quite happy to tell you about my research theme."

"I think I'll take a rain check."

"That's probably better for both of us! Now, I have a question of my own. Can anyone go to that event?" he asked, pointing at the poster on the restaurant wall.

"The parade? Of course, they can. The only thing is, there's such a crush of people that you won't see very much if you're standing toward the back."

"Aren't there any seats?"

"Some, but they're only for the parade organizers and special guests. You can get one if you've got the right connections."

"Connections? Well, that's no good to me."

"In that case, you need to get up early and secure a good spot. If you're interested, just let me know. I can show you a good place."

"Thanks, I'll bear that in mind." The man nodded several times. "Good to know. Thanks a lot."

"Don't mention it. Enjoy," said Natsumi, and left him.

The customer in question was Manabu Yukawa, a physics professor.

He had first visited the restaurant in early May at the end of the Golden Week holiday. It had been around seven o'clock, when the restaurant was at its most crowded, so there were no empty tables. When Natsumi had inquired if he would be okay sharing a table, he said he was fine with that, so she had asked a couple of the regulars who were sitting at a six-person table if Yukawa could join them.

Many of the Namiki-ya regulars felt so at home there that they were quite uninhibited. The two men at the table were like that. They chatted with each other for a while, but eventually they found themselves unable to ignore the stranger sitting by himself at their table. Finding some pretext, they started peppering him with questions: Did he live nearby? What was his job?

Natsumi looked on nervously. She was worried that they might rub this first-time customer the wrong way.

The man wasn't in the least put out. He was explaining in an easygoing way that he taught physics at Teito University and came to Kikuno several times a week to work out of the new research facility here. He went on to ask the two regulars to give him their recommendations from the menu.

With food as the topic of conversation, the regulars were completely in their element and they started to lecture him, almost spluttering with enthusiasm. If he was looking for a snack to go with a drink, then the regular omelet was good, but the omelet in broth was even better; he should definitely order the yakitori chicken skewers with both plain salt and *tare* sauce; not to try the restaurant's vegetable *takiawase* would be the height of folly. Far from getting annoyed, the man nodded along, noting down their comments and ordering several of their recommendations. He ordered a few other dishes of his own choosing and nodded contentedly as he munched through them all.

The two regulars were clearly delighted and, as was only to be expected, introduced themselves. Natsumi had overheard that exchange, too.

Since that day, Yukawa had made repeated visits to Namiki-ya. He invariably came by himself, so he often ended up sharing a table. The regulars would always engage him in conversation and, as far as Natsumi could judge, Yukawa enjoyed the whole experience.

After several months, Yukawa had joined the ranks of Namiki-ya regulars. Customers who knew him called him simply "Professor." Natsumi had recently started doing so herself.

At a certain point, Yukawa had begun arriving a little before six. He must have realized that the place tended to fill up after six and decided to get there early to secure his favorite spot.

That certainly held true this evening. By a little after six o'clock, the customers appeared in waves, almost as if they had coordinated their arrivals.

Then, just a little after half past six—

Natsumi heard the clatter of the front door opening. She said an automatic, "Good evening," then looked over to the restaurant entrance.

A man was standing there. A chill ran down Natsumi's spine the moment she saw him. There was something odd about him. He was wearing a black windbreaker with the hood up. He was probably in his fifties, but perhaps because of his sunburn, his face appeared unusually lined. His black eyes were deep-set and his cheeks hollow.

I've seen that face before somewhere. No sooner had Natsumi thought that than she remembered him. She felt paralyzed. She had no idea what to do.

It's . . . It's . . .

It was the man from the photograph. The photograph that Chief Inspector Kusanagi had shown them. It was the man her father had banned from the restaurant several years ago. It wasn't long after that Saori had gone missing. Chief Inspector Kusanagi had arrested him on suspicion of murder. That was when Natsumi and her parents had first heard the name *Kanichi Hasunuma.*

What was that man *doing here?*

Hasunuma turned to Natsumi. His face was expressionless. After looking slowly around the restaurant, he pointed to a nearby table. "All right if I sit myself down here?"

It was a six-person table. Yukawa was sitting at one end of it.

"Be my guest," replied the professor, who was eating sashimi with one hand while holding a magazine with the other. He didn't seem particularly interested. He must have assumed that the newcomer was just an ordinary customer with whom he would share his table, the way he always did.

Hasunuma pulled out a chair and sat down. His hood was still up. He turned to Natsumi and brusquely ordered a beer.

"Yes, sir," Natsumi replied. Her mind had gone blank and she was quite unable to think straight. She mechanically opened the refrigerated cabinet and extracted a bottle of beer.

She was walking toward the kitchen to pick up an appetizer for the new customer, when she stopped in her tracks. Yutaro had a savage expression on his face. Machiko was standing right behind him. They were both glaring out into the restaurant.

"What should I do, Dad?" asked Natsumi quietly.

Yutaro said nothing. He came out of the kitchen, tore off his half apron, and marched over to Hasunuma.

"What are you doing here?" he asked, looming over Hasunuma. He was obviously struggling to keep his emotions in check.

Hasunuma's shoulders twitched. "This is a restaurant, right? You serve food and drink here," he said, cocking his head and giving Natsumi a look. "So where's my beer, then?"

"There's no beer for you here," Yutaro said. "No food, either. Go on, get out."

Hasunuma raised his chin and glared up at Yutaro.

"Hey, you." Tojima, who was seated some distance away and had been quiet up to that point, was pointing a finger at Hasunuma. "I thought something was upsetting Natsumi. Now I see that it was you. You've got some nerve, showing your face in here."

"Shut up, Shusaku," barked Yutaro, swiveling around briefly before turning back to Hasunuma. "I don't know why you're here, but you're not welcome."

"Oh yeah?" Hasunuma scratched one side of his nose. "Why not?"

"It's pretty darn obvious: You're bothering our other customers. Come on, scram." Turning smartly on his heel, Yutaro headed back to the kitchen.

"I think you've got your wires crossed, Mr. Namiki."

Yutaro stopped in his tracks. "My wires crossed?"

"Yeah," said Hasunuma, his jaw hanging open. "I don't know what you all think, but as far as I'm concerned, *I'm* the victim here. I was treated like a criminal because of you all. I lost my job. I lost my credibility. How are you going to make that good?"

"*Treated* like a criminal? You're guilty. I know you are."

Hasunuma emitted a derisive snort.

"If I'm guilty, how come I'm here and not in jail?"

"It's only a matter of time," Yutaro said. "The police haven't given up yet. It won't be long before they come and rearrest you."

"I wonder . . ." A smile played about Hasunuma's lips. "Anyway, you haven't answered my question. How do you plan to compensate me for what I suffered?"

"Compensate you? What d'you mean?"

"I'm talking about financial damages. You're the guy who shopped me to the police, aren't you? You cooked up a bunch of half-truths to get me arrested. I'm right, aren't I?"

"I just told the police the truth."

"*Bullshit.* I know exactly what you told the police. And I'll tell you why: because of what they asked me in my interrogation. That is why I've got every justification in the world to be here. I want to negotiate my compensation with you."

Yutaro took a step forward. Thinking her father was about to take a swing at Hasunuma, Natsumi held her breath.

"If that's what this is about, then come back when the restaurant's closed," said Yutaro. His voice was soft but full of suppressed rage.

"I'll come here whenever I want to. But for today at least"— Hasunuma got to his feet—"I'll do you a favor and leave. Besides, you probably need a while to adjust your attitude. Just remember one thing, though: I'm not being indicted. The prosecutor is talking some crap about 'deferment of dispensation'; basically what that means is I'm off the hook, scot-free. You've got no grounds for bad-mouthing me; no grounds for kicking me out of this restaurant. *I'm* the victim here; *I'm* the injured party who was falsely accused by you all. What I deserve from you is pity."

After this brazen declaration, Hasunuma looked around the restaurant. The customers' faces expressed a combination of perplexity, shock, and distaste. Hasunuma's mouth twisted into a smug smile, and he left the restaurant, roughly pulling the door shut behind him.

"Machiko," Yutaro shouted. "Bring me salt. A whole bag of the stuff."

Machiko came out of the kitchen, holding a plastic bag of salt with both hands. "Give that here," said Yutaro, grabbing it from her. He headed for the door, which he slid open before starting to scatter fistfuls of salt in the street.

11

Kusanagi was at the Fukagawa Police Station when he got the news. It came via a phone call from Inspector Muto at Kikuno Police Station who was in charge of the continuing investigation into the unnatural death of Saori Namiki.

"Chief Inspector, I know that you're working on another case and must be extremely busy. Still, I felt I had to let you know about this." Muto spoke in a subdued tone.

Kanichi Hasunuma had moved out of his apartment in the Edogawa Ward the previous day, Muto said. The reason was simple enough: His lease had run up.

"We knew the cutoff date was imminent, so we asked the landlord if he planned to renew the lease. Having heard about this case, he wasn't wild about having someone who'd been arrested for murder staying in his building. He cooked up some plausible excuse for not rolling over the tenancy agreement and we watched Hasunuma after he moved out to see where he went."

Hasunuma, Muto went on, had made a beeline for Kikuno. That was already startling enough, but from Kikuno station he went straight to Namiki-ya.

"Hasunuma? Went to Namiki-ya? What the hell for?"

"He didn't stay long. One of our investigators went into the place to find out what had happened. He spoke to Yutaro Namiki and some of the customers. Apparently, Hasunuma was raging about the way he'd been treated as a criminal and is set on getting compensation from Namiki. The term he used was 'damages.'"

"Damages . . ."

It was absurd. Kusanagi had never heard anything like it. But given the kind of man Hasunuma was, it sounded like something he would try. He'd won reparations from the police in the Yuna Motohashi case. Since he hadn't even been indicted this time, perhaps he was planning to extort money from the people whose cooperation had led to his arrest instead.

"And his final destination? Do you know where it was?"

"We do. It's a warehouse. It belongs to the recycling company where he used to work."

"A warehouse?"

"Not exactly. It's a small office that's part of a warehouse. The warehouse itself is hardly used anymore, so the company converted the office into a living space four years ago and one of the company employees now lives there. He's particularly close to Hasunuma and is someone that our investigators have spoken to multiple times. Hasunuma was in touch with him from time to time after he stopped working at the place."

Kusanagi burrowed into his memory. This must be the fellow Hasunuma used to call from pay phones to check whether the police were showing any interest in him.

"The man's name is Masumura; he's around seventy," Muto continued. "I sent an investigator to the recycling company today. He spoke to Masumura who confirmed that Hasunuma had called him a few days ago. He asked if he could stay at his place while he looked for a new place to live."

"Masumura said yes?"

"No reason to turn him down, he said. We had put a watch on the place last night. It was quite the party. They must have been celebrating their reunion—they were up till all hours drinking."

Kusanagi sighed. If there was someone who could be friends with a monster like Hasunuma, then it really was true that it took all types to make a world.

"I made a few inquiries about this Masumura fellow. He's been inside." Muto had lowered his voice. "Manslaughter. Forty-plus years ago."

Kusanagi emitted a noncommittal grunt. They sounded like birds of a feather.

"How are you planning to proceed with the continuing investigation?"

Kusanagi's question elicited a pained groan.

"The only thing we can do is gather eyewitness testimony. Honestly, I feel like we've already done everything we can."

"Will you maintain surveillance on Hasunuma?"

"We'll check on his whereabouts at regular intervals, but, no, we don't think he merits round-the-clock surveillance. We see no risk of him destroying evidence or trying to escape."

"Right."

The decision seemed reasonable enough to Kusanagi. It was hard to believe that Hasunuma would make a blunder at this late stage. The normal practice in a case like the Saori Namiki murder was to arrest the suspect on a different charge, keep him in detention, and interview him until you got a confession. With a person like Hasunuma, however—someone who didn't object to being locked up for long periods and was capable of remaining silent—it wasn't going to work.

"I just wanted to keep you in the loop, sir," said Muto, then hung up. Kusanagi put down his phone. He felt bitter, fed up. Overcome with a sense of his own powerlessness, he didn't have the energy to get to his feet.

Kusanagi had approached the prosecutor immediately after Hasunuma's release to ask what kind of evidence he needed to indict Hasunuma.

The prosecutor said they needed a minimum of two things to proceed to indictment. First, they needed proof that the victim hadn't died an accidental or natural death. Second, they needed incontrovertible proof that Hasunuma—and no one else—had committed the crime. Even then, precedent suggested that the chances of him being found not guilty were extremely high.

"What makes this case so damn awkward is the fact that we can't argue in court that Hasunuma transported Saori's body to Shizuoka, because the only basis we have for that claim is N-System data, not eyewitness testimony."

There was nothing Kusanagi could say. Currently, the police had an unspoken rule that they would never put forward data from N-System as evidence in court. Doing so would compel them to go on record with details of how N-System worked and where its surveillance points were located. The policy of the National Police Agency had been to keep that information secret.

Even though the prosecutor had set a high bar, Kusanagi was determined to find evidence that met his conditions. He wanted to show the Namiki family that he'd meant what he said about never giving up.

Despite trying everything he could think of, he'd failed to turn up the evidence needed. All the forensic medicine experts he'd spoken to had told him, given the state of the skeletal remains, determining the cause of death was impossible. He needed to solve that impossible problem before he could make a single step of progress.

At the same time, other criminals were out there committing equally atrocious crimes on an almost daily basis. The reality was that he couldn't keep obsessing over this case forever. Sure enough, it wasn't long before Kusanagi's team was assigned a new robbery-murder in eastern Tokyo.

Fortunately, the investigation was going well. An acquaintance of the victim had confessed to the crime in the most matter-of-fact way. They then found a kitchen knife with traces of the victim's blood on it exactly where the acquaintance told them he had disposed of it. They were steadily assembling everything they needed to send the case to the prosecutor. With this case, at least, the prosecutor would have nothing to complain about.

Nonetheless, Kanichi Hasunuma was always in the back of his mind. On the one hand, it seemed as if the moment to solve the case had already passed; on the other hand, he couldn't allow it to end like this.

12

The warehouse was near a small river, away from the residential part of town. There was a hut next to the warehouse. This, apparently, was the former office.

Sitting in the passenger seat, Naoki Niikura held the binoculars to his eyes and adjusted the focus. The lights were off and there was something inside blocking the window, so he couldn't see inside.

"See anything?" asked Shusaku Tojima from the driver's seat.

"No. Nothing." Naoki Niikura lowered the binoculars. "Is *he* really in there?"

"He should be," Tojima replied. "I saw him walking out of there yesterday."

Tojima started the car and Niikura stared at the window of the hut as they drove past the warehouse. He still couldn't tell if there was anyone inside.

They went to a nearby diner and sat at a table in the back, far away from the other customers.

"I had to pull out all the stops to find that place. There's a guy of around seventy who lives in there by himself," Tojima said.

"And is *he* in there with him?"

"Yes," Tojima replied, speaking softly. "Hasunuma's living there now."

Niikura shook his head listlessly. "I just can't believe it."

"Disgusting, isn't it?"

"I could understand if he'd gone into hiding, but to return to the place where he committed a murder—it just beggars belief, the brazenness of it. What's wrong with the man?" Niikura clenched his right hand into a fist and thumped the table.

Tojima had called Niikura earlier that afternoon and told him that Hasunuma was back in Kikuno. Niikura and Tojima had met indirectly through Saori, when Yutaro Namiki had invited Tojima to one of her performances. Since then, the two men always said hello when they bumped into each other at the restaurant.

"Like I told you on the phone, Hasunuma showed up at Namiki-ya last week."

"Shocked is too weak a word for what I feel," said Naoki, sighing heavily. "I'm just glad I wasn't there. In my fury, God only knows what I might have done. I just can't understand what the guy's—"

"It's harassment, pure and simple," said Tojima, with venom in his voice. "The man was arrested based on the testimony of local residents, especially everyone at Namiki-ya. He holds a serious grudge against us for that and he's rubbing our noses in the fact that he's been released."

"That's outrageous."

"The police are hopeless. I don't care about insufficient evidence or whatever it is—they should never have let someone like him back out on the streets. They should just lock him up and throw away the key."

"I agree, but that isn't going to happen, is it?"

Tojima nodded. There was a sour expression on his face.

"I don't think we should expect too much of the police. Apparently, their hands are tied. That doesn't mean *we* have to accept the way things are. When I think about Yutaro—no, when I think about how everyone at Namiki-ya must be feeling, it's just unbearable. Do you know what I mean?"

"Of course, I do," Naoki said warmly. "What the Namiki family must be going through! It makes me mad. If I could get away with it, I'd finish off that bastard myself."

"I'm sure you would." Tojima was nodding his head vigorously up and down. That was exactly the kind of response he wanted. "You discovered her abilities, you trained her, you were making a professional singer of her. You've got plenty to hate the guy for. And it's because I know how you feel—" Tojima quickly looked around, then resumed, his voice slightly lower than before. "Because I know how you feel, that I wanted to talk to you about this plan of mine."

"Plan?" Niikura drew himself upright in his seat. "What plan is that?"

Tojima once again glanced around the diner to check that no one was in earshot, then leaned over the table.

"We can't expect anything from the police. The courts won't punish the guy. The way I see it, the only option we've got left is for us to do it ourselves."

The proposal was so unexpected that Niikura gave a start of surprise. "Do it . . . ? Do what?"

"Punish the guy. *Him.* Kanichi Hasunuma." There was a purposeful gleam in Tojima's eye. Obviously, he was serious.

Niikura was at a momentary loss for words. He reached for his glass and gulped down some water.

"Punish him . . . ? What sort of punishment?"

"A punishment befitting his crime," said Tojima. "It wasn't actually me who came up with this plan. You can probably guess who did."

"Was it . . . Yutaro?"

Tojima nodded a couple of times.

"Yutaro and me are childhood friends, friends through thick and thin. We played together, we got up to all sorts of mischief together, and when we got found out, we got hauled over the coals together. That's the kind of friendship we have." As he reminisced, the scowl on Tojima's face briefly softened. "When my best friend said that he wanted a once-in-a-lifetime favor, how could I turn my back on him? Especially, when it involved Saori's murder."

Naoki took another swig of water. He still had some coffee in his cup, but his mouth was too parched for that. He needed something else.

"I, uh, find it hard to believe . . . that Namiki . . ." Naoki struggled to find the right words. "You're saying he wants retribution . . . that he wants to avenge his daughter's death?"

"It's only natural for a father to feel that way. I've got two kids of my own. If something like that happened to them, I know I'd feel the same."

"Well, uh . . ." Niikura wasn't sure how to respond. He knew he ought to disagree, but that wasn't what he really felt. He made a first step toward agreeing. "I can understand that."

"Of course, you can. I mean just now, you said something about wanting to finish the bastard off yourself."

"No, but—" Niikura put out a hand as if to restrain Tojima. "I also said, 'If I could get away with it.' Vendettas aren't allowed in today's society."

"Are you just going to give up then?" Tojima's eyes seemed to be staring directly into Naoki's heart. "Are you willing to sit by and let that scumbag get away with this?"

Naoki clenched his right hand and thumped the table a second time.

"It's maddening. Of course, I don't want to. The thing is, it's simply not realistic. I don't know what you've got in mind, but you can be damn sure that if anything happens to Hasunuma, the police will be all over it. Just because the guy *deserves* to die doesn't mean the police won't investigate his death. And Namiki and his family would be the logical suspects. But—" Niikura's eyes widened suddenly as he stumbled onto the answer to his own half-finished question. "Oh, I get it. If he can avenge his daughter's death, Yutaro doesn't mind being arrested. And he won't tell on anyone who helps him. He's that committed. Am I right?"

Tojima frowned and placed a finger to his lips. "You're talking too loudly."

"Sorry." Naoki placed his hand over his mouth. He hadn't realized how loud he was being.

"Mr. Niikura," said Tojima quietly, drawing himself upright. "You've got it exactly right. Yutaro Namiki has made up his mind to go ahead with it. He told me, 'If it comes to that, I'm not afraid to go to jail.'"

"And it may very well come to that."

"Hold on a minute. I haven't finished yet. Like I told you, Yutaro and me are tight, tight since childhood. Do you seriously think I'd be prepared to let someone I've known my whole life go to jail?"

Niikura was confused.

"What are you trying to tell me?"

"That Yutaro *won't* get arrested. Not him, and not anyone else, either. And we're going to teach that Hasunuma a serious lesson. We've come up with a plan and we want you to be part of it. Let me be clear about one thing: that even if the whole scheme is uncovered, you won't be charged with a crime."

"Is that possible?"

"It is—provided we all work together."

There was a sly glint in Tojima's eyes.

13

As he read the text message, Tomoya Takagaki felt slightly dazed. *This must be some kind of joke*, he thought. Then, when he saw who it was from, he realized that it wasn't.

The sender was Natsumi Namiki. They had exchanged contact details six months ago, when Tomoya had visited Namiki-ya for the first time in ages.

He went there after Detective Sergeant Utsumi had told him about Saori's body being found. He hadn't seen any of the Namiki family for around a year at that point. When he wished them good evening and again expressed his condolences, he couldn't hold back his tears. Saori's parents wept, too.

Tomoya had started going to Namiki-ya again. Every time he went, he would ask the family how the investigation was coming along, but they never had any news to share. Even though Chief Inspector Kusanagi often came to see them, all he said was the boilerplate: "We are doing all we can to arrest the person responsible."

The police, however, did notify the family when Kanichi Hasunuma was arrested. When Tomoya got a text from Natsumi telling him the news, his grip tightened on his phone, while his other hand bunched into a fist. *Finally*, he thought. *Finally! Now we can learn the truth, and Saori will be avenged.*

That evening, Tomoya went straight to Namiki-ya from work. The place was heaving; many of the regulars were there, including Naoki Niikura, Saori's mentor. There was general jubilation at Hasunuma's arrest. The Namikis wept tears of joy and Tomoya wept with them. As the tears coursed down his cheeks, it struck home that he'd not been able to forget Saori.

The way things developed after that wasn't at all what Tomoya had expected.

He was wondering what was going on with the case, when he got the shocking message from Natsumi. *Hasunuma has been released!* How could that even be possible?

Tomoya called Natsumi immediately. "We've no idea," she said. Detective Kusanagi had come to Namiki-ya to explain that the prosecutor had decided that there was insufficient evidence to indict.

"Do you seriously expect us to buy that?" Namiki had snapped at Kusanagi. "Are you just giving up?" Kusanagi had protested that, far from giving up, the police intended to work closely with the prosecutor to collect the necessary evidence.

Several months had passed since then and Kusanagi's promise still remained unfulfilled. So what were the police doing? Tomoya was ignorant about what was going on and Natsumi stopped texting him.

Tomoya eventually tried texting her. *How have you all been? Is everyone at Namiki-ya well?* was all his message said.

It took Natsumi a while to text him back and when she did, he was horrified. *Hasunuma showed up at Namiki-ya about ten days ago*, Natsumi said. It was such a shock that they closed the restaurant for several days. They only reopened three days ago.

From the moment he read her text, Tomoya was incapable of focusing on his work. Why had Hasunuma gone to Namiki-ya? What was he planning to do?

As soon as it was quitting time, Tomoya collected his stuff and left the office. Hurrying to the station, he called Rie, his mother, to say he wouldn't be home for dinner.

"Has something happened?" Rie asked anxiously.

"Sort of."

"Saori?"

"Yeah."

"What? Did they finally charge the guy?"

"If only. No, he's turned up in Kikuno again."

"What are you talking about?"

"I don't know much. I'll tell you more when I get home." Tomoya ended the call and started walking even faster.

He'd discussed the case with his mother after Saori's body had been discovered. She'd been delighted at the news of Hasunuma's arrest and indignant at his release.

Recently, though, her attitude had begun to change. She started saying things like, "Hasn't the time come to put this behind you?" and "It doesn't matter. Nothing will bring Saori back to life."

All she wanted was for Tomoya to forget about this gruesome episode as fast as he could and find himself another girl.

Though it probably was the right thing to do, Tomoya couldn't bring himself to take even the first step down that road. His feelings for Saori were worth more than that.

It wasn't yet six by the time he got to Namiki-ya. He assumed the restaurant would be empty, so he got a surprise when he slid open the door. Every single table was occupied.

As Tomoya stood there waiting, Natsumi bustled up from the back. "Oh, hi. Sorry. This group here will be leaving any minute."

"Excuse us," said a woman sitting at a table in the middle of the restaurant. Tomoya had met her a few times in the restaurant. It was Maya Miyazawa. She ran the biggest bookshop in the neighborhood. She was tall, quite muscular, and she exuded an air of reliability, like everyone's dependable big sister.

Maya Miyazawa had a notebook open on the table in front of her. It took Tomoya a minute to realize that all the fifteen or so people in the restaurant were facing her. Then the penny dropped. Of course, it was a preparatory meeting for the annual parade! Maya Miyazawa was in charge of the local team this year.

A couple of people sitting at a four-person table moved up and offered Tomoya a seat. Grateful for their kindness, he sat down.

"Here's a final checklist," said Miyazawa, rising to her feet with a notebook in her hand. "Group A should finalize the costumes and the props. Group B are responsible for editing the music and checking the sound equipment. Group C, I want you to coordinate the final rehearsal and check the giant inflatable. That's everything, I think. Any questions?"

"People keep asking me what the theme of our performance will be this year," said a young man in a bandanna. "Are we supposed to keep it secret until the big day?"

"Absolutely, you must," said Maya Miyazawa. "I say the same thing every year: Surprise is a big part of the entertainment. Please remember that. Anything else?"

There was silence. "Okay, then," said Maya Miyazawa, shutting her notebook. "That's enough for today. Only a few days until the big day. Let's do a great job, everyone."

"Yes, ma'am," came the cheerful reply, as the whole group started getting to their feet.

Natsumi brought a cold towel to Tomoya. "Sorry for the delay."

"No problem. Tell me, is it really true? That Hasunuma came here?"

Natsumi's face clouded over instantly. She gave a curt nod.

"What does the guy think he's even doing?" chimed in Maya Miyazawa, as she got ready to leave. "I couldn't believe it when I heard. That man is guilty, plain and simple. And still he shows up here—I mean, what was that all about?"

"He said he wanted us to pay him damages and that he'd keep coming until he got them."

Tomoya was confused. "Damages?"

"He was like, 'It's your fault that I was treated like a common criminal, so I want compensation.'"

"What sort of nonsense is that?" Maya Miyazawa spat out the words. "Is the bastard completely crazy? And what about the police?"

"A detective showed up a few minutes after Hasunuma left here. That probably means they've got him under surveillance. He asked us if Hasunuma had caused any trouble."

"I heard he's still in the neighborhood," said the young man in the bandanna.

"Seriously?" Maya Miyazawa's eyes bulged in their sockets.

"There's stuff on social media. A friend told me."

Maya Miyazawa clicked her tongue. "I wonder how long he's planning to stay here in Kikuno. And do you think he's serious about that damages thing?"

The young man with the bandanna twisted his neck awkwardly as if to say, *Don't ask me.*

Tomoya got to his feet, cleared his throat, and looked across at the young man with the bandanna.

"Did your friend know anything about where Hasunuma's staying?"

The young man, starting to look a little out of his depth, shook his head. "No, the post he saw didn't go into that much detail."

"Natsumi!" someone shouted, before Tomoya could respond. It was Yutaro Namiki. He had emerged from the kitchen. "Natsumi, what are you doing? Have you taken Tomoya's drink order?"

"Oh . . . I was just about to . . ."

"And *we're* just about to get really busy. Now's not the time to go dopey on me. I'm very sorry, Tomoya." Yutaro Namiki nodded apologetically.

"No worries," Tomoya said. He sat back down and looked up at Natsumi. "Could I possibly get a beer?"

"Coming up," said Natsumi, heading for the back of the restaurant.

Maya Miyazawa turned to Yutaro. "If there's anything we can do to help, Mr. Namiki, you only need to ask. If you want to keep Hasunuma away from here, I'm sure we can figure out a way to make that happen."

With the merest hint of a smile, Yutaro whispered, "Thank you."

"Right, we'll be on our way," said Maya Miyazawa.

She and her group left the restaurant.

Natsumi brought a tray with a bottle of beer, a glass, and an appetizer to Tomoya's table. "If you don't mind?" said Yutaro, sitting down across from Tomoya and pouring his beer for him. "Was it Natsumi who told you that Hasunuma had been here?"

"Yes, earlier today."

Yutaro clicked his tongue disapprovingly and turned to confront his daughter. "You really shouldn't bother people when they're at work."

"Yes, but—" Natsumi pouted and hung her head.

Yutaro turned back to Tomoya. "We're all very grateful that you still care about our dear Saori. Still, you've got your own life and your own future to worry about. The time's coming when you will need to move on."

Tomoya put down the glass of beer he was carrying to his lips.

"Are you telling me to forget about Saori and what happened to her?"

"I don't expect you'll ever manage to forget her completely. I just think that holding on to her memory probably won't be good for you in the long term. As a family, we can never get away from what happened to her. That's enough victims for one tragedy. We don't want our problems to bring other people down."

"Problem? It's not a problem," replied Tomoya forcefully. "As Ms. Miyazawa said, I want to support you any way I can. I just can't understand how *that man* was released."

"I appreciate your kind words. As far as I'm concerned, knowing that you feel that way is enough for me. There is one thing I have to say to you. If you do decide to move on and put this whole sad business behind you, I won't hold it against you. I know you're not a cold- or hard-hearted man."

"Put it behind me? What do you mean?"

"Nothing mysterious. Just what I said. Have a nice evening," said Yutaro. He rose to his feet and headed back into the kitchen.

Tomoya watched him walk away with mixed feelings. He couldn't understand what Yutaro was trying to say.

There was the clatter as the door slid open. A new customer had arrived. Tomoya looked up. It was Yukawa, though everyone just called him "professor."

The professor recognized Tomoya and gave him a friendly nod.

Natsumi brought Yukawa a cool towel. "Good evening. Will you have the usual?"

"Yes, the usual. And a beer."

"Coming up," replied Natsumi, who went to the back of the restaurant.

As Tomoya ate his dinner by himself, he wondered why Yutaro had said what he said. He couldn't help but feel there was some deeper meaning to his words.

Beside him, Yukawa was chatting away to Natsumi about the Kikuno parade. She reminded him that he would need to arrive at least an hour before it started to secure a good place.

Tomoya left the restaurant a little after seven. His emotions in turmoil, he dragged his feet as he walked.

He had barely taken more than a few steps, when someone hissed his name, "Takagaki." He stopped and looked around.

"Over here," came the voice for a second time.

It was coming from a sedan parked on the far side of the road. The person in the driver's seat was Tojima, one of the regulars at Namiki-ya.

"What's up?" he asked.

"Got a moment? I need to talk to you."

"About what?"

"What do you think?" Tojima moistened his lips, shot a nervous glance back at Namiki-ya, then looked up at Tomoya. "It's about Hasunuma. But only if you still feel something for Saori."

Tomoya inhaled deeply. "I'm all ears."

"Okay, slide in on the other side."

Tomoya's heart was pounding as he went around to the other side of the car.

It was nearly eleven o'clock by the time he got home. Rie, his mother, was sitting on the living room sofa watching television. The instant Tomoya appeared, she reached for the remote and switched it off. "You're very late."

"Yeah. Well, we had a lot to talk about."

"What kind of thing?"

"You know, thing things. Lots of the regulars were there."

"What's going to happen with the guy who did it? What's he doing here in Kikuno anyway?"

"I don't know. But everyone's furious about it."

His mother shouted after him as he got up to go to his room.

"Remember, Saori's not coming back."

"What's that supposed to mean?"

"Have you thought about not going to Namiki-ya anymore? You're only bringing back painful memories."

Tomoya left the living room without a word. Once in his own room, he tore off his suit and tie and lay down on his bed. He pondered his conversation with Tojima. What Tojima was proposing was nothing if not surprising. His mother would be violently opposed, if she ever heard about it. She'd beg him to stay well away.

Now he understood why Yutaro Namiki had spoken to him as he did. Namiki knew that Tojima was going to ask him for his help, and he was signaling to Tomoya that he was free to turn down the request, that he—Namiki—wouldn't think any the less of him if he did so.

Tomoya, however, had given his answer to Tojima right then and there. He would love to be part of it.

He knew that if he missed this chance, he would regret it for the rest of his life.

PART TWO

It is a capital mistake to theorize before one has data. Insensibly one begins to twist facts to suit theories, instead of theories to suit facts.

—Arthur Conan Doyle, "A Scandal in Bohemia"

14

That Sunday was a special day for the Kikuno shopping district. When Natsumi looked out, the street was heaving with people walking in every direction. It was early—only just after eleven—and there was still an hour until the parade got underway. They must all be hunting for the best place to watch it from.

"Thank goodness the weather's nice," came Machiko's voice from behind her.

"Quite." Natsumi turned and nodded. "It's awful when it rains after everybody's put in all that hard work."

"Isn't it?" said Machiko, before heading into the kitchen to help Yutaro, who was already busy cooking. While they were only open in the evenings during the week, on weekends they opened for lunch as well.

Natsumi saw a shadow on the sliding door. The door slid open noisily, revealing the person she'd been expecting.

"The rail company is just too stupid," said Professor Yukawa with irritation. "They should run more trains on a big day like today."

"Was the train very crowded?"

Yukawa pulled his chin into his neck and looked thoroughly fed up.

"Like sardines. It wasn't so much that you couldn't get a seat, you couldn't even stand without getting bent out of shape."

Natsumi laughed. "Sounds awful."

"The parade route is busier than I was expecting. Everyone's trying to claim the best spots along the route."

"You're probably right. We should get going, Professor." Getting to her feet, Natsumi pulled on a parka, which was hanging over the back of a nearby chair. "Mom, we're leaving."

Machiko's face appeared above the kitchen counter. "See you later, then. Have fun, Professor Yukawa."

"Thanks very much. I'll be back this evening," said Yukawa, turning toward the kitchen with a big grin.

A couple of folding wooden stools were leaning against the wall. Natsumi held one out to Yukawa. "Here, take this."

Taking the stool, Yukawa nodded sagely. "What a good idea. It'll be great to sit down and watch the show."

"Sadly, life isn't quite that easy."

Yukawa frowned inquiringly. "Meaning?"

"You'll see soon enough. Come along, let's go." Natsumi picked up the second stool.

As they emerged from the restaurant, they almost collided with a man holding a camera. A crowd was forming at the edge of the road, so there was very little room on the already narrow sidewalk.

"It really is carnival time here," grumbled Yukawa, as they walked along the street. "If everywhere's as crowded as it is here, all the good places will be gone already."

"This parade gets more and more popular every year. People post tons of pictures on social media and they do it in real time, while the parade's going on. Some people probably camped out all night to get the best spot for taking pictures."

"Seriously? Takes all sorts to make a world."

"The pictures are well worth it. You'll understand when you see the parade, Professor."

"Well, I'm looking forward to it."

They kept moving, pushing their way through the crowd until they reached a large intersection. The road perpendicular to the one they were on was also closed to traffic for the day.

Walking right up to the exterior wall of the building on the street corner, Natsumi unfolded her stool.

"Professor, put your stool here, next to mine."

"Is here okay?"

Natsumi watched as Yukawa opened out his stool. "Good," she said and sat down on hers.

"Will we be able to see anything from here?" Yukawa asked doubtfully, as he settled himself on his stool. "I mean, just look at all the number of people walking here in front of us. There'll only be more of them once the parade gets going. We won't see a thing unless they squat down."

"The people in the front might crouch, if you asked them, but the ones at the back definitely won't. If anything, they'll all be standing on tiptoe."

"That's bad news for us."

"Don't worry about it. Trust me."

As time went by, the crowd continued to grow. Plenty of them were dressed in costumes themselves. The parade's official home page said that cosplayers were welcome, and the ones in more elaborate costumes were holding impromptu photo shoots.

"I know this isn't the best time, but did that man ever come back again?" Yukawa asked Natsumi.

"That man?"

"The one who barged into Namiki-ya—I'm not quite sure when it was. The man suspected of murdering your sister."

"Ah . . ."

"Your father threw him out, but he threatened to come back. Did he?"

"We've not seen him since, no."

"Glad to hear it. Seeing him must have brought back horrible memories."

"No." Natsumi could feel her jaw clenching even as she shook her head.

The truth was that the mere thought of Hasunuma was enough to make her miserable. Now that he was somewhere in the neighborhood, fear rather than hatred was her dominant emotion; fear that perhaps he'd come back for revenge. Machiko, her mother, probably felt the same way, as she had advised Natsumi to go out by herself as little as possible. If Hasunuma was going to target anyone, she thought, he would target her.

Natsumi had no idea why Hasunuma was released instead of sent to jail. The anger and the loathing she felt for him hadn't weakened, but chafing against the injustice and unfairness of it all was starting to wear her down. If the law couldn't punish him—if that was an immutable matter of fact—then it would make more sense, and be less painful, to accept it and try to look to the future rather than looking back to the past.

If he wasn't going to be punished, then at the very least she wanted him to go somewhere far away. She wanted to be able to forget that a man called Hasunuma had ever existed.

The report of a starting pistol brought her back to herself. The

parade was about to start. There was a crush of people around them
and they could barely move.

Eventually, they heard the distant sound of music. That had to
be the first of the teams approaching. Everyone stood on tiptoe and
craned their necks for a look.

Natsumi got up off the stool and tapped Yukawa smartly on the
shoulder. "Professor, stand up." She climbed onto her stool without
removing her shoes.

Yukawa quickly did the same thing. "Using a stool as a steplad-
der: Now that's a smart idea. This is great. I can see everything."

He looked up the road over the heads of the people. A color-
fully costumed group was slowly coming toward them, marching in
time with the music. Natsumi pulled out a folded-up flyer from the
pocket of her jeans. It was the program of the parade and gave the
teams' order of appearance.

"This must be the team from Kobe," said Natsumi. "They came
in second last year. Their theme was the Arabian Nights. This year
it's Beauty and the Beast."

The team came close to their side of the road. First to parade
by were the attendants, decked out as items of cutlery, crockery,
and furniture. It was obvious that money had been spent on their
outfits. The two main characters followed in the attendants' wake.
The costume of the Beast was magnificent. As for Beauty, not only
was her ball gown splendid, but the young girl in the part was quite
beautiful.

Up to this point, the performers had just been marching along
and waving to the spectators. When they got to the center of the intersection, however, Beauty and the Beast started dancing together,
while the household-item attendants started playing on their instruments. It was a famous scene from the film, and a cheer went up
from the crowd.

"Fabulous," exclaimed Yukawa beside Natsumi. "This is much
more fun than I expected."

"You see."

"There's just one thing, though."

"What?"

"Copyright. This Beauty and the Beast has a striking resemblance to the Disney movie. I'm wondering if they got the proper
permissions."

"Really? That's what occurs to you right now?"

Yukawa turned toward her, a puzzled look on his face. "What do you mean?"

"Well, timing aside, it is a serious issue. The performance this team put on last year, Arabian Nights, was an exact copy of Disney's *Aladdin*, right down to the music. As far as I know, they didn't get permission."

"Did they get away with it?"

"It's complicated." Natsumi waggled her head. "The issue gets debated from time to time. Most people think that, strictly speaking, it's piracy and it's not allowed. On the other hand, this isn't a commercial event, and this sort of thing is often permitted at Halloween. The municipal organizers decided to leave it up to the individual teams."

"How does Kikuno itself deal with the problem? They've got their own local team, haven't they?"

"Team Kikuno only puts on performances where copyright isn't an issue—old legends, fairy tales, stuff like that. Or else things where the author's been dead for decades and the copyright's expired. Last year, they did Princess Kaguya."

"And this year?"

Natsumi consulted the program. "This year it's Treasure Island."

"Robert Louis Stevenson, eh? That should be good. I wonder when they'll be by."

"Team Kikuno always brings up the rear of the parade. That's the rule. The program says they'll step off at around two this afternoon."

"Two o'clock? Am I meant to perch up here till then?"

"You're welcome to sit down and take a rest, if you get tired. After all, that's what stools are for in the first place."

"Indeed, it is."

A series of teams then passed by. Many of the performances were based on popular cartoon characters and looked likely to run afoul of copyright law, just as Yukawa had said. Natsumi, however, preferred to believe that the original creators would just smile and let it go. The presentation of all the teams was polished and their enthusiasm tangible.

Natsumi felt her phone vibrating. It was her mother calling. Natsumi was startled when she saw the time. It was past midday.

"Sorry, Professor. I need to pop back to the restaurant," Natsumi said. She had to shout because of the noise coming from an approaching sound truck. "I'll be back here before two."

Yukawa nodded and Natsumi climbed down from her stool.

There were already three groups of customers at Namiki-ya by the time she got there. Machiko, who was looking after them, frowned at her daughter, rolling her shoulders and sticking out her tongue in mock indignation.

The sound of up-tempo music filtered in from the street. There was a variety of tracks: theme songs from animated movies, nursery rhymes, classical music.

The customers came in an uninterrupted stream. From what Natsumi could make out of their conversations, all of them seemed to have a favorite team and only came to grab lunch after their favorite had passed by.

Natsumi was hoping to go and rejoin Yukawa around one thirty, which was the cutoff time for ordering lunch, but a customer came in just a moment before half past. She was a plumpish, middle-aged woman and seemed to be on her own.

"Are you still open?"

"You're welcome to come in, but it's already last order."

"Don't worry. I'll make up my mind quickly."

The woman sat down and immediately ordered fried oysters and a few other dishes. The way she rattled off her order without even needing to look at the menu suggested she'd been there many times, although Natsumi couldn't recall seeing her before.

Natsumi relayed the woman's order to the kitchen, then told her mother. "Right. I'm going to rejoin the professor."

The parade was approaching its climax. Watching a group of popular cartoon robots striding along out of the corner of her eye, Natsumi headed for the intersection where Yukawa was waiting.

The professor was standing on the stool, taking photos with his phone. His expression was so grave that it was almost comical.

"You look like you're having fun," said Natsumi, clambering up onto the stool beside him.

"Not so much having fun as learning a lot." Yukawa pushed his spectacles higher on his nose. "All the teams are re-creating famous scenes from well-known stories. Naturally, though, everyone has different ideas about what the best and most famous scenes are. A few minutes ago, there were a couple of teams who had both taken the same animated movie as their subject but who performed two completely different scenes. It was really fun."

Natsumi looked at the physicist with amazement. "That's your idea of fun?"

Several more teams marched past. When the parade first started, there had been fewer teams and their costumes had been less elaborate. Now, with every passing year, there were more teams and their costumes were ever more magnificent and extravagant.

"The next team's the last one. It's time for Team Kikuno!" said Natsumi, after consulting the program.

They could hear music in the distance. The applause and cheers seemed to be even louder than before.

It wasn't long before they caught sight of a large object coming toward them. Straining for a look, Natsumi was startled to see a ship—or rather, a large float decked out to look like an old wooden sailing ship. A number of pirates stood on the deck.

The ship was followed by a giant map showing the location of the hidden treasure, and the map was followed in turn by a number of treasure chests. The lids of the chests had been flung open and they were overflowing with jewels and gold coins. People in pirate costumes were by turns pushing the treasure chests and dancing around them.

No sooner had the ship come to a stop in the middle of the intersection than the pirates started fighting one another, both on and around it. They must have rehearsed exhaustively, because the whole thing went like clockwork. The noise of the treasure chests crashing against one another was tremendous.

Once the skirmish was over, the pirates resumed the parade. Some of them were clearly out of breath.

After the pirates passed by, an enormous blue inflatable appeared to the accompaniment of music. It was the theme song of the parade, and the composer was none other than Naoki Niikura.

"What the heck is that?" Yukawa asked. "That monster frog thing?"

Natsumi bristled. The professor was referring to the giant inflatable.

"It may look like a frog, but it's actually an imaginary creature. The things that look like eyeballs are its ears, while the things that look like nostrils are its eyes. It's a PR mascot specially created for this parade. Its name is Kikunon. For the last four years, it's been the grand finale of the parade."

"Huh. Kikunon, you said? Inflating that must be quite a task," Yukawa said, sounding rather unimpressed.

The inflatable was about thirty feet in length. Since it was full of helium, it was lighter than air. Several people were marching underneath, holding guy ropes attached to its body to prevent it from floating away.

"Well, that's it for this year." Natsumi climbed down from her stool, keeping her eyes on the inflatable as it disappeared into the distance. When she checked the time on the screen of her phone, she saw it was a little after three.

"It will be about two hours before they announce the results. I wonder who'll win this year. You saw all the floats, Professor. Which one did you like best?"

Yukawa started fiddling with his phone. Natsumi guessed he was looking over the video footage he had taken.

"They were all great. For me, personally, I liked Heidi, a Girl of the Alps best."

"Heidi, a Girl of the Alps? A team did that?"

"They'd made this giant swing. I was impressed. I mean, you need guts to climb on something like that."

Natsumi frowned and tilted her head to one side. She couldn't really picture it.

She was about to ask the professor for a better description, when her phone started to vibrate. The number of Namiki-ya's landline appeared on the screen.

"Hello," she said.

"Natsumi, where are you? Right now, I mean?" Machiko asked.

"Let me see . . . We're at the intersection on Fourth. The parade's just finished."

"In that case, can you get back here as fast as you can? We're in trouble."

"Why? What's happened?" Natsumi felt a sudden surge of fear.

"One of our customers has been taken ill." Machiko's reply took her completely by surprise.

"A customer?"

"Yes, that lady who came in at the last minute. The plump one."

Natsumi remembered her. "Oh, the woman who ordered the fried oysters?"

"That's the one. She had her lunch, went to the bathroom—and then didn't come out for ages. When she did, she said she had an awful stomachache."

"You think she got a bad oyster?"

"They'd all been properly cooked, so, no, I don't think it was that. Anyway, we thought she should go to the hospital. Your father drove her there."

"How terrible."

"Can you get back as fast as you can? I want to go to the hospital to see how she's getting on, but there's a stew I need to slow-cook on the stove for this evening."

"Okay."

Natsumi ended the call and explained the situation to Yukawa. He blinked behind his glasses.

"That's not good. You'd better get going. I'll bring both stools around to the restaurant later."

"Really? Thanks, that's so kind of you. Catch you later, then." Natsumi dashed off.

Machiko was ready to leave by the time Natsumi got to the restaurant. "Any new developments?" Natsumi asked.

"I've no idea," said her mother, "but I'm going to go to the hospital, anyway. The gas is on, so just leave the casserole in, okay? Oh and, sorry, but while you're at it, could you finish the washing up?"

Then she left.

There was a big pile of dirty dishes and cooking utensils in the kitchen. Natsumi sighed and reached for her apron, which was hanging on the wall.

Two hours later, Yutaro and Machiko returned. They both looked rather gloomy, so Natsumi assumed the news was bad. When she inquired, however, Machiko told her that it hadn't been anything serious.

"The lady was moaning and groaning all the time your father was driving her to the hospital, but she started to feel better soon after. By the time I got to the hospital, she'd already seen the doctor and was quite relaxed about the whole thing. She just felt out of sorts, that's all. She apologized for the trouble she caused us."

"Well, that's good news. I was worried it might be food poisoning."

"Tell me about it. I wonder what was wrong with her, though." Machiko waggled her head from side to side.

"I didn't recognize her face. Does she come here often?"

"No," said Machiko, shaking her head. "I think it was her first time here. Your father says he hasn't seen her before, either."

"What's her name?"

"Yamada, she said," murmured Yutaro. "Anyway, thank goodness it was nothing serious." He went into the kitchen. The whole episode must have been pretty nerve-racking for him. He seemed quite shattered.

A text came to Natsumi's phone. It was from Yukawa. He was asking how things were.

She sent him a reply: *Everything's fine.*

They opened the restaurant at half past five. Natsumi was just switching the sign around from CLOSED to OPEN, when she heard a voice behind her. "Perhaps I'm a bit too early?" Yukawa was standing there, holding the two stools.

"Your timing's perfect. Thanks for bringing back the stools." She slid open the door and gestured for Yukawa to go in. "After you."

"Good to hear that your customer was okay in the end," he said, as he sat himself down.

"Oh, tell me about it. I was terrified that the health and safety people were going to be jumping all over us."

"Food poisoning is a matter of life and death for a restaurant," Yukawa said, then he raised a finger. "I'll start with a beer. Then I'll have—"

"The *takiawase*, right? Got it." Natsumi placed a cool towel on the table in front of him and went into the back of the restaurant.

A little after six o'clock, the regulars began to arrive in dribs and drabs: Tojima, the Niikuras, Tomoya Takagaki. Everyone was enthusiastically discussing the parade. Heidi, a Girl of the Alps had been proclaimed this year's winner. Natsumi exchanged a look with Yukawa as he contentedly drank his beer.

Maya Miyazawa arrived with two young men in tow. They were going out for a celebratory bar crawl later, she explained, but they thought they'd line their stomachs here first. They were slightly disappointed that Team Kikuno had only placed fourth this year.

"You were fantastic," said Natsumi, as she delivered them their food. "The ship looked so authentic; the pirates really looked the part, too."

"Yes, a great job, really impressive," chimed in Tojima, who was sitting some distance away but had overheard the exchange. Everyone else then joined in with praise.

"Thank you very much. It's very nice of you to say so. How about a toast," said Miyazawa. "Cheers!" The three of them clinked their glasses.

After a while, another member of Team Kikuno came into the restaurant. There was a strained, anxious look on his face. He scuttled over to Maya Miyazawa's table.

"What took you so long? Where've you been?" asked Miyazawa, pouring him a glass of beer.

"There was something I had to do. I went to the neighboring district. On the way back, there were all these police cars, so I stopped to see what was going on," the young man replied, his untouched beer glass in his hand. "It was by the river where all the warehouses are. I found out that—"

He lowered his voice at this point and Natsumi could no longer hear what he was saying.

"I can't believe it," exclaimed Maya Miyazawa. "Really?"

"Yes, really. I overheard one of the police officers."

Maya Miyazawa looked at Natsumi. Natsumi wondered why she was looking at her. There was a moment's awkward silence.

"Apparently Hasunuma's dead," Maya Miyazawa said.

15

He couldn't believe his ears. Then again, Director Mamiya would never joke about something this serious.

"It's definitely Hasunuma? You're sure of that?" asked Kusanagi, gripping his phone tightly.

"Yes, the Kikuno police have confirmed his identity. They don't yet know whether it was murder."

"Where did it happen?"

"At an old colleague's place."

"Oh, right," Kusanagi said. "I heard that Hasunuma got kicked out of his own apartment and was crashing with some old workmate."

"Exactly. It was that old workmate who found the body."

"I see, sir. Okay, I'll head over to the scene right now."

Kusanagi got up from his dining table, a half-eaten plate of pasta in front of him. "If it turns out to be murder, please put me in charge of the case. You'll do that, won't you, sir?"

"That's why I called. However"—Kusanagi heard Mamiya exhale—"I need you to proceed with great care."

"Yes, sir."

He put down the phone, picked up his plate of pasta, went into the kitchen, and threw the leftovers into the trash.

Outside, he hailed a taxi and headed for Kikuno. On the way, he phoned his junior officers, Detective Inspector Kishitani and Detective Sergeant Utsumi, to give them the news. Utsumi asked if she could join him at the crime scene, to which he replied that she was welcome, if that's what she wanted to do.

He then gave Inspector Muto of Kikuno Police Station a call. When he picked up, Muto's first words were, "Did you hear about Hasunuma?"

"I did. I can't believe it."

"Me, either. It's crazy."

"I'm on my way there now. Could you meet me there?"

"Not a problem. I'm there now. As soon as Forensics have done their thing, I'll give you a guided tour."

When the cab got close to the address, they saw the flashing red lights of police cars, several of which were parked in a cluster.

Kusanagi got out and headed for the crime scene, looking around him as he walked. There was a long stretch of warehouses and workshops, but he couldn't see any private houses or shops. They'd probably mobilized everyone at Kikuno Police Station for a house-to-house, but getting useful eyewitness testimony in an area like this wouldn't be easy, thought Kusanagi.

The warehouse was cordoned off with tape and a number of uni-formed policemen were standing guard. Kusanagi showed his badge to one of them.

"Is Inspector Muto around?" he asked.

"Just a minute, sir."

The young policeman spoke into his transceiver. "He says to please wait here," he told Kusanagi.

There was a second smaller structure beside the warehouse. Kusanagi guessed that was where Hasunuma had been living. People in forensics coveralls were going in and out of it.

After a while, Inspector Muto emerged. After the briefest of greetings, the two men got down to business.

"The body's been taken away and Forensics is wrapping up. Would you like to see the crime scene?"

"Absolutely."

"Fine. Follow me. You may be disappointed."

"How so?"

"You'll see what I mean soon enough."

Kusanagi followed Muto to the little hut. The door was wide open and there was a light on inside.

Kusanagi peered in. The floor was made of wooden slats. There was a space just inside the door for putting on and taking off your shoes. Kusanagi took off his shoes and followed Muto into the room, pulling on a pair of gloves as he did so.

The converted office was small, maybe roughly one hundred square feet. There was a single bed in one corner, and a kitchen area with a small sink, a small refrigerator, and some shelves with plates on them.

Otherwise, there was a small table and a television. There was no chest of drawers, but a few wire hangers hung from nails that had been hammered into the walls. Beneath these were a few cardboard boxes. Kusanagi looked inside; the boxes contained clothes, crammed in any old how.

Kusanagi noticed a sliding door at the far end of the room. The door was open. "Is there a second room back there?" he asked.

"Yes. Whether it deserves to be called a room is another question," Muto said. "Hasunuma's body was found in there."

Muto walked to the far end of the room. Kusanagi followed him.

They stood in the doorway and looked in. The floor area was less than fifty square feet and the ceiling was low enough that Kusanagi could touch it. The room had no windows and no storage of any kind. The parquet floor was grubby.

"Apparently, this used to be a storeroom," Muto said.

"Makes sense," Kusanagi replied. "There's nothing in here. Did Forensics take everything away?"

"They did—though there wasn't actually much here to start with." Muto tapped his phone a few times, then showed the screen to Kusanagi. "This is what the place looked like when we found him."

Hasunuma, wearing a gray sweat suit, lay sprawled faceup on a quilt-covered mattress. The floor was covered with a ground sheet. To one side of Hasunuma were his clothes and a bag.

"I can't see any obvious cause of death."

"No. When the occupant of the room returned, he found Hasunuma like this; he wasn't breathing. He called an ambulance and the paramedics contacted the police after they had confirmed that Hasunuma was dead. There were no visible external injuries and no signs of strangulation on his neck. Nor was there any evidence of a struggle. The paramedics estimate he died somewhere between thirty minutes and two hours before he was found." Muto slipped his phone back into his pocket.

Hasunuma had been found at five thirty. If he had already been dead between half an hour and two hours, that put the time of death somewhere between 3:30 and 5:00 P.M.

"By the occupant, you mean Hasunuma's colleague, don't you? Let's see . . ." Kusanagi reached for his notebook.

"His name's Masumura."

"Could I speak to this Mr. Masumura?"

"He's currently being interviewed at the police station. They've arranged for him to spend the night at a business hotel near the railway station. If you want to speak to him directly, though, I can set that up."

"Please do. I'd really appreciate it."

"No problem, sir."

Muto pulled out his phone and made a call.

Kusanagi ran his eye around the small former storeroom again. What sort of schemes had Hasunuma been cooking up in this cramped little space? One of the first things he'd done was go back to Namiki-ya. Why was he so keen to provoke the victim's family?

The room had a sliding door with a hasp for a padlock on the outside. Kusanagi guessed it was there for security purposes, back when it was a storeroom.

Muto ended his call.

"They've already finished interviewing Masumura. I've asked them to bring him here on the way to the hotel."

"That's very helpful. It'll be easier to get him to explain things here."

"You don't mind if I sit in?"

"Not at all," Kusanagi replied.

They heard a noise at the door of the hut and they both turned around. Detective Kaoru Utsumi was peering in.

"Is it all right if I come in?"

"Come on in," said Muto. He turned to Kusanagi. "I assume that Detective Utsumi is here because the Tokyo Metropolitan Police think this might be a murder?"

"What's the view of the Kikuno precinct?"

"Murder is definitely a possibility. There's no lack of reasons why someone would want to kill him. Our investigators have already gone to make inquiries"—Muto paused a moment—"at Namiki-ya."

Kusanagi nodded wordlessly. Anyone who had worked on the Saori Namiki case would have thought the same.

"Can I go and join them? Would that be okay?" Utsumi asked.

"Better not," Kusanagi replied. "Kikuno precinct hasn't yet officially contacted the TMPD to ask for help. Don't be pushy."

Utsumi squared her shoulders and looked momentarily disgruntled. "Understood, sir," she replied.

"You said there were no noticeable abnormalities on the body.

What about the rest of the crime scene? Did Forensics have anything interesting to say?" Kusanagi asked Muto.

"Nothing stood out. Nothing obviously disturbed, no sign of anyone having wiped away fingerprints, or anything like that."

"Okay."

Kusanagi sighed. Right now, there was no reason to designate this a murder. They would have to wait for the results of the autopsy. If it was murder, the absence of external injuries made it likely that poison had been used.

There hadn't been a cup or mug anywhere near Hasunuma in the photo Muto had shown him. If that was how the killer got Hasunuma to ingest poison, then he must have taken it with him when he left.

In his mind's eye, Kusanagi saw Yutaro Namiki. If this was murder, then Namiki would be the prime suspect. He had a motive in spades.

But . . .

Kusanagi ran his eyes around the little room. He found it difficult to imagine Namiki and Hasunuma facing off within this confined space. Had Namiki forced his way in, Hasunuma would have been on his guard. The idea that he would willingly have drunk anything laced with poison made no sense.

Muto pulled out his phone to take an incoming call.

"We're inside. Come on in." He ended the call and looked over at Kusanagi and Utsumi. "Masumura has arrived."

There were voices outside and Kusanagi's eyes went to the door.

A uniformed policeman ushered a small man in a windbreaker into the room.

16

The precinct detectives arrived at Namiki-ya just as it was about to close, waited for the last customers to leave, and then interviewed the members of the family separately.

Natsumi was questioned in a patrol car parked outside the restaurant. Most of the questions were about what she had been doing all day: Where had she been? What had she been doing between such and such time and such and such time? Who had she been with? Had she received any calls; if so, when and from whom? Had she made any calls? If so, when, to whom, and what were they about?

Natsumi answered all the questions with absolute honesty. She didn't find the experience particularly pleasant; it was clear that the detective was checking to see if she had an alibi.

After the detectives had left, Natsumi talked to her parents. They, too, were questioned with equal persistence.

"Did they tell you how Hasunuma died?" Yutaro looked first at Machiko, then at Natsumi.

Machiko tilted her head to one side and said nothing.

"They didn't tell me, either," Natsumi replied. "They just kept asking me an endless series of questions. I never got the chance to ask them anything. What about you, Daddy?"

"I asked them, but they wouldn't tell me. No, that's not quite right. My impression was that the detective didn't actually know. Still, the fact they were asking us about where we were at various times suggests they think he was killed."

"After all, if Hasunuma was murdered, we'd be logical suspects," Machiko said.

"I think they could tell we were telling the truth," said Natsumi.

Her mother and father exchanged a look.

"I suppose so," said Yutaro, scratching the back of one ear.

A cell phone started to ring. Yutaro walked over to the counter and picked up his phone.

"It's from Shusaku," he said, swiping to answer the call.

"Yeah, hi, it's me. . . . Yeah, they left literally one minute ago. Yeah, Machiko and Natsumi as well. Detectives questioned them both separately. . . . To make sure we weren't coordinating our stories, I suppose. . . . That's what it was about." Yutaro went into the kitchen, still talking on the phone.

"Natsumi, I'm going to turn off the light." Machiko flicked the wall switch.

"Okay." Natsumi took off her shoes and went upstairs.

Alone in her room, she checked her phone. She had a text from Tomoya. He wanted to know what was going on.

She decided to call him. It was faster and he was probably still awake.

He picked up immediately. "Yes? Is that you, Natsumi?"

"Hi, Tomoya. Can you talk?"

"Sure. What happened after I left?"

Bedlam had broken out at Namiki-ya after Maya Miyazawa announced Hasunuma's death. The customers were regulars and they all knew who Hasunuma was. They were all talking over one another, wondering how he had died.

After a while, the hubbub died down and they all fell silent. With no information, they must have realized that speculation was a waste of time.

That was when Yutaro came out of the kitchen. "We'll get to hear the details soon enough. In the meantime, let's keep calm, wait, and see how things play out," he said. His remarks were met with silent nods of agreement.

When Maya Miyazawa and her companions headed out for their cast revel, that triggered a mass exodus. Before he left, Tomoya had whispered to Natsumi, "If anything happens, let me know."

Natsumi told Tomoya about the detectives who had come and questioned her and her parents.

"I'm not surprised. You and your family are the prime suspects."

"That's what my mother said. I mean, we hated the guy." Natsumi was being brutally honest. "Still, all three of us told them in great detail what we were doing all day. I don't think they can suspect us anymore."

"You mean you've all got alibis?" blurted out Tomoya.

"Well, my parents do, at least. They were in the restaurant until the end of lunch service and then they went to the hospital."

"To the hospital?"

"That's right. One of the customers got sick while she was here—"

Natsumi told Tomoya about the woman and the oysters.

"Wow. I didn't know."

"When you think about it, it was a stroke of good luck. Normally, once they stop serving lunch, my parents are here by themselves until we reopen for dinner. If any of us has a problem with their alibi, it's me, because I was here minding the fort alone."

"I don't think anyone would seriously suspect *you*."

"Anyway, that's about all I've got to report. I've no idea what's going to happen next."

"No, I know. As the boss said, all we can do is sit tight and wait."

"I'll let you know if I hear anything. Thanks for your concern."

"It bothers me, too, you know. . . ." Tomoya was mumbling and Natsumi couldn't make out what he was saying.

"What?"

"I'm just saying that, I can't stop thinking about who killed Hasunuma, if he was murdered."

Natsumi didn't know how to respond. She felt vaguely uncomfortable.

"As far as I know, the police don't yet know if he was killed or just died suddenly."

"Hmm." Tomoya grunted ambiguously. "Still, to keel over and die suddenly like that isn't exactly normal, is it?"

Natsumi could only respond with a noncommittal grunt of her own.

"No point in agonizing about it, I guess. Good night."

"Good night."

Natsumi pressed the button to end the call and plugged her phone into the charger. She was just about to change into her pajamas, when she remembered something.

If he was murdered, Tomoya had said. *Who killed Hasunuma, if he was murdered?*

Did that mean he thought someone in her family had murdered him?

Well, I think we all know it's not such an unreasonable idea, is it?

Natsumi sighed to herself.

17

Kusanagi woke up, got out of bed, and went to brush his teeth. Kusanagi looked at his face in the mirror. *No two ways about it. You're getting older.* The sagginess of his face couldn't all be blamed on the stark white lighting.

He took a shower to clear his head and emerged from the bathroom rubbing his wet hair with a towel.

The hotel room was small and smelled, faintly, of disinfectant. The only places you could relax were the bed or a small chair and you had to twist your body into an acrobatic pose to open the closet door. Kusanagi suspected that a cabin on the Orient Express, the train from Agatha Christie's famous novel, would probably be more comfortable than his room. Nonetheless, the hotel had been full on Saturday night because of all the people in Kikuno for the parade.

Kusanagi had opted to spend the night in Kikuno to be closer to the precinct as information came in. Detective Sergeant Utsumi had wanted to stay, too, but he persuaded her to go home instead. She'd be there soon enough if they were brought in officially.

Eiji Masumura was being put up at the same hotel. While his place was potentially a crime scene, Masumura would be living in the hotel. Maybe he was happy that he got to stay at a business hotel, albeit a modest one, at the police's expense. In their interview, Kusanagi didn't get the impression that Masumura was unduly upset by Hasunuma's death. That probably showed how close the two men had—or hadn't—been.

Kusanagi tugged his notebook out of his jacket pocket, sat down on the bed, and started working through what Masumura had told him the night before.

He had first met Hasunuma around four years ago, when Masumura started working at the recycling plant where he was still employed. They had ended up becoming friends.

"He approached me first. Someone had told him I'd been in prison, and he started pestering me, asking me what I'd done."

Hasunuma vanished about a year later. It wasn't long, though, that Hasunuma got back in touch. That's when he started calling Masumura to see if the police had shown up.

"I asked him if he'd done something wrong, but he would just hem and haw. He never gave me a straight answer. Then, about a year ago, he stopped calling completely."

This wasn't the first time Kusanagi had heard this story. Inspector Kishitani had told him the same thing.

Around two weeks ago, Hasunuma got back in touch. Hasunuma explained that he was being forced to vacate his present apartment and asked if could he stay with Masumura until he found a new place.

"He offered to pay half the rent, so it wasn't a bad deal for me. 'You don't mind the room being so tiny?' I asked and he said, 'No,' all he needed was a place to crash. Two men living together has its downsides, but it's always good to have a drinking buddy close by."

Inspector Muto had told Kusanagi about Hasunuma's first night as Masumura's lodger. According to the cop who'd been on surveillance duty that night, the two of them had been boozing it up until the small hours.

Kusanagi asked how Hasunuma spent his time.

"Search me." Masumura cocked his head to one side. "He would drink with me in the evenings, but I've no idea what he got up to in the daytime. Probably just hung around here or went out and played pachinko—you know, stuff like that."

Had Hasunuma been trying to find a new job? Once again, a rather bored-sounding "Search me" was all the response he got. Did Hasunuma ever have any visitors? "How should I know?" Masumura replied.

Then it was time for the crucial questions. Kusanagi asked Masumura to run through his movements for the day. "I've already gone through this hundreds of times at the police station," Masumura said. He looked rather grumpy as he gave his explanation.

"I was at home all morning, then I went out a bit after midday to get a bite to eat. But that thing was on—you know what I'm talking about—that parade thing. Because of the parade, all the restaurants were jam-packed so I walked over to the next ward. I signed up for this internet café there recently. It's nine hundred yen for three hours, with free manga to read and free showers, too. I picked up a bento-box lunch at the convenience store and then I went there to read manga and watch TV. I left at five."

Masumura got home around five thirty. Finding the door to the back room open, he had peered in and saw Hasunuma lying on his futon. *Sleeping like a baby*, he initially thought, but then, when he saw how motionless he was, he put his hand over his mouth and found that he wasn't breathing. At that point, he got scared and called the emergency number.

When Masumura left the apartment, Hasunuma had been watching television. Masumura had asked him if he wanted to go out to lunch with him, but Hasunuma had said he wasn't hungry yet.

No, said Masumura, he didn't think he'd locked the front door behind him.

Kusanagi snapped his notebook shut. He didn't think that Masumura was lying. What he'd said about going to the internet café was probably true. Anyway, places like that always had CCTV. If Masumura was lying, it wouldn't take long to find out.

Kusanagi picked up his phone. He was about to send a text to Inspector Muto when he noticed that he'd gotten one. It was from an unlikely sender: Manabu Yukawa.

He was even more surprised when he read the text. *I want to talk to you about Hasunuma's death. Get in touch when you have time*, it said. The text had been sent a bit just after seven that morning, or a little more than an hour ago.

When he called, Yukawa picked up almost instantly. Skipping the niceties, he simply said, "So you got my message?"

"How do you even know?" Kusanagi said, getting straight to the point. "That Hasunuma's dead, I mean."

"I was at Namiki-ya last night. Some guy overheard the police talking about it over near the crime scene. He came straight over to the restaurant to report the news."

"Okay, but what were *you* doing in Namiki-ya to start with?"

"I was there for dinner. What else? Come on, it was you who told me about the place."

"Go there often?"

"I'm not quite sure what level of frequency the word 'often' denotes. I probably go there about twice a week."

That made him the most regular of regular customers.

"Why do you want to talk to me about Hasunuma's death?"

"Because the proprietor of my favorite restaurant and his family could be suspects in a murder case. It's hard for me not to care."

Kusanagi snorted. "That's an unusually human thing for you to say. Your time in America has turned you into a softy."

"That's nonsense. Come on, just tell me what you know."

"Sadly, I don't have any information to share."

"Meaning it's information that you can't share with an ordinary civilian?"

"You know you're not an ordinary civilian. That's not the problem. We really don't know much. The cause of death is still unknown, so we can't yet determine whether or not it was murder."

"Oh, I see. I guess I'll have to be content with that for now. Thanks for calling me so early like this. I appreciate it."

Yukawa sounded as though he was about to hang up. "Wait," Kusanagi said hastily to stop him doing so. "You were in Namiki-ya last night, you said. There are a few questions I'd like to ask you. Have you got the time to get together today?"

"I'm free this morning. I haven't the time to travel into central Tokyo, though."

"Central Tokyo? So where are you?"

"I'm staying in the staff accommodation at our Kikuno research institute."

"Why didn't you say so? Had breakfast?"

"No, not yet."

"Good," said Kusanagi. "Then have it with me. My treat."

About thirty minutes later, Kusanagi was sitting across from Yukawa at the train station coffee shop. It was the same place they got together the last time.

"I never expected to see you again here like this," Kusanagi said.

"You chose the place."

"Because it's easy to find. Anyway, that's not what I meant. What I meant is that I didn't expect to see you here as part of an investigation."

"Am I part of an investigation?" Yukawa raised his eyebrows.

"No, uh . . ." Kusanagi faltered. "We can't refer to it as an investigation since we don't know yet if a crime occurred."

Kusanagi briefly ran through the facts: how Hasunuma was staying in the room of his one-time coworker; what the crime scene looked like.

"You said the cause of death was unclear."

"There were no external injuries and no marks of strangulation on the neck."

"Did Hasunuma have any preexisting conditions? Heart disease, for example?"

"Not that I've heard—though he certainly was a hard-hearted bastard."

"I wasn't talking about metaphorical hearts. Either way, there's a low likelihood of disease being the cause of death. Do you think that some kind of drug could have been used?"

"We don't know yet. Personally, I think that's the likeliest—"

The waitress came to the table and Kusanagi broke off with a dry cough. They both watched in silence as she put the dishes down in front of them.

"The problem is getting him to ingest the stuff," said Yukawa, reaching for his coffee cup after the waitress had gone. "The poison, I mean."

"Exactly. Hasunuma was no fool. Not the kind of person to swill down a suspicious drink without even a second thought."

"By 'suspicious drink,' you mean one prepared by a person with the intention of killing him?"

Taking a bite of his sandwich, Kusanagi nodded as he chewed and swallowed.

"Let's get down to business. That's precisely what I wanted to talk to you about. You were at Namiki-ya last night, right? Tell me how the people there were behaving. How did they react when they got the news of his death?"

Yukawa stuffed what was left of his sandwich into his mouth and looked thoughtfully upward and off to the side. Kusanagi guessed that he was trying to picture the scene in the restaurant on the previous night.

"In a nutshell, there was general surprise."

"General?"

"Everyone at the restaurant. Last night, all the customers were regulars, so they all knew who Hasunuma was."

"I'm only interested in the ones with murderous intent. I don't care about the rest of the regular customers."

"That doesn't make any sense." Yukawa placed his hands flat on the table and looked intently at Kusanagi. "How are we meant to separate people who have murder on their mind from people who don't? It's not possible. The best you can do is to pinpoint the people who *might* have such an intention toward Hasunuma. If we're only talking about a matter of possibility, then that group will end up being everyone who knew about Hasunuma."

Kusanagi frowned and scratched the side of his nose. Yukawa had a good point.

"Okay, I'm sorry. It was a poorly phrased question. What I want to know is how the Namiki family reacted; Yutaro Namiki, the father, in particular. How did he respond?"

Yukawa grunted and crossed his arms on his chest.

"There was uproar when the regulars heard that Hasunuma was dead. At that point, Yutaro Namiki and his wife were in the kitchen, so I didn't see how they reacted. After a few minutes, the customers quieted down. That was when Namiki came out and said something like, 'Let's just wait and see how this turns out.' He was calm and I didn't detect anything strained or unnatural in his behavior. I can't tell you about his wife because she didn't come out of the kitchen. As for Natsumi . . . well . . . she looked stunned. That's all I can tell you about the family."

"Okay . . . And what's your personal opinion?"

Yukawa wrinkled his brow slightly as if he hadn't understood the question.

"Do you think those three have got anything to do with Hasunuma's death?"

"If you're asking, do I think they killed him, I'd say no, they couldn't have. The police interviewed them and said that each of them had a solid alibi for the rough time of death. I imagine the detectives have already verified the details."

Yukawa then explained that he had spent the afternoon of the previous day watching the parade with Natsumi until she had to go cover for her parents, who were taking a customer to the hospital.

"From what I know, both Yutaro and Machiko Namiki have almost flawless alibis and while it's true that Natsumi was alone for a certain amount of time, that was in response to an unanticipated event. She couldn't have committed the murder."

Kusanagi groaned softly. "It sounds like they're above suspicion, then."

Yukawa put down his salad fork. "We can safely put to rest the question of whether they killed Hasunuma themselves. That still leaves us your original question: Do I think that the three of them had anything to do with Hasunuma's death? My only answer to that is, I don't know. We have a man on a murder charge, almost certainly guilty, who's been released because of insufficient evidence, who then dies mysteriously during a parade that's held only once a year. We have the family of the murder victim, each with fortuitous, ironclad alibis. I'm not able to ascribe all that to coincidence."

"You think there's something behind their alibis?"

Yukawa grunted and tipped his head pensively to one side. "At present, I really can't say—hence my saying that I don't know." He picked up his fork and started to eat his salad.

Kusanagi pondered the implications of the physicist's gnomic remark. He was about to finish the remains of his sandwich, when his phone started buzzing. He glanced at the screen; it was Inspector Muto.

He stood up and walked over to a corner of the café to take the call. "Kusanagi here."

"Muto. Can you talk?"

"Yes. What's up?"

"We've got partial results from the autopsy. They haven't yet managed to identify the cause of death, but they have found petechiae on the body."

"Petechiae . . . Meaning there's a strong possibility of asphyxiation?"

When a person experiences breathing difficulties, the movement of the diaphragm affects the heart, which in turn chokes off the blood flow. With nowhere to go, the blood in the veins breaks through the capillaries and leaks out into the skin. The process is known as extravasation of the blood, while the visible clusters of spots are called petechiae.

"Correct. The petechiae aren't pronounced enough for manual strangulation or ligature strangulation. And there aren't any marks where the throat was compressed. There are no abnormalities in the bones or joints of the neck, either."

"Hmm. That's unusual."

"There was one more thing. Some of the blood work came back. They found some of the ingredients of sleeping medication."

Kusanagi's grip on his phone tightened. "Are they sure about that?"

"Apparently, yes. And no sleeping medication was found among Hasunuma's personal effects."

Kusanagi exhaled loudly and made an effort to tamp down his excitement. "Was it a normal sedative, or could it have been some kind of poison?"

"No, they don't think so."

"Okay. And so what's next?"

"The precinct commander and the head of CID are currently having a meeting. I think they'll probably call in the Tokyo Metropolitan Police Department."

"Great. Thanks for letting me know. I will drop by the station later."

Kusanagi ended the call and returned to the table. Yukawa, who had finished his food, was drinking his coffee.

Kusanagi summarized what Muto had said. Amazingly, the professor was unfamiliar with the term *petechiae*.

"So can we sum it up like this, then?" said Yukawa. "Someone induced sleep in Hasunuma by getting him to ingest a sedative and then asphyxiated him somehow."

"Sounds about right. It's the 'how' that's the problem. Even if he'd been given a regular sleeping pill, he'd have woken up if he was having trouble breathing. If anyone had been physically covering his nose and mouth, he'd have fought back."

"How about if his wrists and ankles were tied? If he'd been restrained not with rope, but with gum tape wound around his clothes, that wouldn't have left any marks on his skin."

"If he was thrashing around like crazy, his clothing would have left abrasion marks. The medical examiner wouldn't miss something like that," Kusanagi said.

"When you put it like that, I have to agree with you," Yukawa said, backing down, not something he often did. "In that case, it's the killing method that is the big problem. Do tell me if you manage to figure out how he was asphyxiated."

Kusanagi pointed at Yukawa with his fork. "When it comes to unraveling impossible crimes, you're the master. It's time for Detective Galileo to stand up."

Kusanagi was expecting Yukawa to pull a sour face and turn him down flat. To his surprise, he complied meekly.

"Why not? Let me think about it when I have the time."

Kusanagi stared at Yukawa in astonishment.

"What is it? Is something wrong?" Yukawa asked.

"No, nothing. Thank you. I'd appreciate that."

"I'll need to see the crime scene. Can you arrange that?"

"Shouldn't be a problem. I'll take you as soon as the local police have filed an official request for TMPD support and my team is put in charge."

"Great. I'll wait to hear from you." Yukawa looked at his watch. "I've got to get going. Do you mind?" He picked up the check.

"Hang on. I said *I* was paying."

"I got a lot more information from you than you got from me. And besides, you paid last time. I like to keep my accounts in balance. I'll see you."

Yukawa lifted the hand with the bill in a gesture of farewell and headed for the cash register.

Kusanagi remembered his friend's words as he watched him go. *We have a man on a murder charge who's been released because of insufficient evidence, who then dies mysteriously during a parade that's held only once a year. We have the family of the murder victim, each with fortuitous, ironclad alibis. I'm not able to ascribe all that to coincidence.*

From Kusanagi's point of view, there was one more coincidence at play: the fact that Yukawa got himself involved.

18

He realized that his fingers had stopped moving and he was just staring at the computer monitor. The deadline was tomorrow and he wasn't making any headway at all. When he glanced at his watch, it was almost four in the afternoon.

Tomoya got to his feet, intending to get himself a coffee. He had only taken a couple of steps when his cell phone started ringing. He didn't recognize the number but decided to take it, anyway.

"Yes?"

"Am I speaking to Mr. Tomoya Takagaki?" inquired a woman's voice.

"Yes, that's me."

"Sorry to call you at work. This is Detective Sergeant Utsumi of the Tokyo Metropolitan Police Department's Homicide Division."

"Ah," Tomoya murmured. He didn't know what to say.

"There's something I want to talk to you about," Utsumi continued. "Could you spare the time?"

"That's not a problem. Um, when did you have in mind?"

"The sooner, the better. In fact, right now would be good. I'm actually outside your office right now."

Tomoya gave a little gasp of surprise. With his phone pressed to his ear, he went to a nearby window and peered down but couldn't see Detective Utsumi in the street.

"Well, Mr. Takagaki?"

"Um, yes, fine. Come on up, then."

"Thank you very much."

"See you in a minute."

As soon as he ended the call, his mind started racing. It had been six months since he'd seen Detective Utsumi. He'd given her his business card but she'd never contacted him before, so why was she here now?

It's blindingly obvious. It's to do with Hasunuma's death. She must suspect me of being involved. I must be very careful.

He took a deep breath.

He was waiting in front of the reception desk when Utsumi walked in. Her long hair was tied behind her head and she was wearing a dark-blue pantsuit. She radiated competence, as she walked toward him with long, brisk strides.

When she reached him, she nodded her head in greeting. "I apologize for turning up suddenly like this."

"It's not a problem. . . . Would the same meeting room we used last time be all right?"

"That'll be fine, yes."

They sat facing each other in the cramped room. Utsumi placed both hands on her knees and drew herself upright in her chair.

"Let me start by thanking you for your help with our previous investigation."

"Was I any help?"

"The information you provided was invaluable. In fact, it was thanks to you that we were able to make an arrest." Utsumi looked at Tomoya intently. "I imagine you heard, Mr. Takagaki, that the case didn't make it to trial. The prosecutor decided on a deferment of dispensation, so the suspect was released." She was scrutinizing his face. Tomoya got the sense that she was watching for even the tiniest reaction.

He said nothing, so she followed up with, "But, of course, you were aware of that?"

"Yes, I'd heard."

"Who told you?"

"Saori's—Saori Namiki's family. To be precise, I heard it from Natsumi, Saori's sister," Tomoya replied. He wondered why Utsumi was interested in that now specifically.

"How did you feel when you heard the news?"

"How did I feel? I thought it was weird. There was loads of evidence against the guy, right? It makes no sense for him to be let off scot-free."

"I can see why you might feel like that. What did you decide to do about it?"

"Huh?" Tomoya was thrown off-balance. "Decide to do? . . . What do you mean?"

"If you don't mind my asking, do you know what deferment of dispensation means?"

"Uhm, to be quite honest, no, I'm not sure I do. Natsumi said something about there not being enough evidence. So, I figured it meant something like 'get off unpunished.'"

"It doesn't necessarily mean that, no. It does involve deferral, so there is a good chance that the suspect will not be indicted. And if the suspect's not indicted, then obviously he won't be punished, either. Were you happy with that outcome?"

"No, uhm, what I mean is . . ." Tomoya was shaking his head furiously. "Of course, I wasn't happy with that. It's intolerable. I was hoping the police and the prosecutor would go the extra mile. I wanted them to get to the truth."

He had spoken with a lot of feeling, but Utsumi was seemingly unmoved. If anything, there was a coldness in the look she gave him.

"If a decision was taken not to punish the suspect—I mean, if it was decided not to indict him, what would you do then?" Utsumi asked.

"You mean, if the case against him was dismissed?" Tomoya knew that his eyes were swimming about shiftily. "I did my best not to think about it. I prayed that it wouldn't turn out like that." After a pause, he added, "Prayed from the bottom of my heart."

Utsumi didn't respond. Tomoya started feeling uncomfortable.

"Let me ask you frankly. Were you thinking of appealing to the Prosecutorial Review Commission, if the case against him was dropped?"

"The prosecutorial what?"

"The Prosecutorial Review Commission. It's a commission with the power to review prosecutors' decisions not to bring charges against suspects in a criminal case. The only people who can appeal to it are the plaintiff, the accuser, or the victim's family. Given that you were on such friendly terms with Saori's family, Mr. Takagaki, I thought that you might have proposed or discussed an appeal with them. That's why I'm asking you about it now. From your reaction, I assume that you didn't?"

Utsumi's businesslike explanation only served to make Tomoya more flustered.

"No, it never occurred to me. I don't know anything about the law. . . ."

"A moment ago, you said that you were praying that the charges against Hasunuma wouldn't be dropped. Did you think that if the charges against him were dropped and he wasn't indicted, that then there would be nothing you could do, that you would have no more recourse under the law?"

"Yeah, I guess so. . . . I guess I thought that. Rather fuzzily, though."

Utsumi nodded curtly and jotted something down in her notebook. Tomoya was curious but there was no point in asking her what she was writing. She would never tell him.

"Uhm, that Prosecutorial . . ."

Utsumi looked up. "The Prosecutorial Review Commission, you mean?"

"Yes. What would happen if we did appeal to the Prosecutorial Review Commission?"

"They would deliberate the reasoning of the prosecutor's decision not to indict. Were they to conclude that the wrong decision had been made, the prosecutor would then have to review the case. Were he to decide not to charge the case for a second time, then, depending on circumstances, a second Prosecutorial Review Commission could be convoked. The whole process can take a surprisingly long time."

"You're telling me that the prosecutor's decision can be reversed? Does this commission often recommend that the prosecutor go ahead with a case?"

"Honestly, no, that's very rare—but it's not nonexistent. In a murder case where the suspect hasn't been indicted, an appeal to the Prosecutorial Review Commission represents the last recourse for the victim's family."

"I had no idea."

Tomoya wondered if the Namiki family were any better informed than he was. Natsumi had certainly never mentioned the commission to him.

"Let me change my line of questioning," Utsumi said drily. "The man who was arrested on suspicion of murdering Saori Namiki—I would like you to tell me what you know about him and his recent activities. In as much detail as possible, please."

"About Hasunuma, you mean?"

"That's right." Utsumi nodded and gave him a wan smile.

Tomoya realized that she hadn't uttered the man's name. Was that deliberate?

"Whatever I know about him is stuff I heard from Natsumi or the people at Namiki-ya."

"That's fine. Fire away." Utsumi's pen was poised above her notebook.

Tomoya told Utsumi about the night Hasunuma showed up at Namiki-ya; about him living in an old warehouse office in Kikuno; and finally that he had died the day before. He also told her where he'd gotten the information in each case.

Utsumi's pen stopped moving across the page. She looked hard at Tomoya.

"Do you know where Hasunuma was living before he moved back to Kikuno?"

"No."

"Did you ever try to find out?"

"No. Why would I?"

"When you heard the news that this man—a man you felt deserved to be punished—had been released, didn't that make you curious? Didn't you want to see what kind of life he was leading?"

Tomoya blinked and shook his head. "It never occurred to me, no."

Utsumi pulled her chin back. Her mouth was relaxed, but her eyes were as sharp as ever.

"How did you feel when you heard about Hasunuma's death?"

"Surprised. Shocked." Tomoya's eyes widened. "I thought that something must have happened."

"What did you think caused it? Accident? Illness?"

I must be careful what I say here, Tomoya told himself. He took a deep, slow breath. "I didn't hear anything about Hasunuma being sick, so it didn't occur to me that it could be that. But I didn't assume it was an accident, either. I just had a vague notion that . . . that he'd been caught up in some kind of trouble; yes, caught up in some kind of trouble. With someone like him, it's only to be expected."

"Someone like him?"

"Someone who can happily kill another human being."

"We don't officially know that he killed her."

"He's guilty. He murdered Saori. I'm sure of it."

Tomoya was getting annoyed and he scowled at Utsumi. Her face showed only the most complete indifference.

"You used the word 'trouble'? Are you implying that he was murdered?"

"I hadn't really thought it through. A brawl, maybe, something that got out of hand . . ."

"Do you think he could have been murdered?" He thought he detected a gleam in the woman's eyes.

"Well—" he said, moistening his lips with the tip of his tongue. He knew he had to avoid any kind of verbal slipup here. "I honestly have no idea. At the same time, I don't think it would be *that* extraordinary if he had been. There were loads of people with reason to hate him. Like, uhm . . ." He thought hard before he continued. "Like, if you were to tell me that one of the Namikis had killed him, I'd be surprised—but on the other hand I'd also think, 'Of course they did.'"

Utsumi nodded her head several times. "And what if it was you?" she asked, pointing at Tomoya with the tip of her ball pen. "If your friends knew that you were the one who had killed him, how do you think they would take it?"

"*Me? Killed him?*" The unexpected question threw Tomoya off-balance. He could feel the blood rushing to his face.

"It's common knowledge that you and Saori Namiki were in a relationship. No one would be shocked to hear that Yutaro, Saori's father, was the killer. By the same token, no one would be surprised to hear that you had done it, either. That's all I'm saying."

What was the detective getting at? What was the right way to answer her question?

"Well, I, uh, don't know what to say. Maybe you're right. Maybe some of my friends wouldn't be all that surprised. But it would be a different story with anyone who knew me well: I'm a total coward. You need guts to take revenge. . . ."

"Are you saying you hadn't even *thought* about it?"

Tomoya felt the sweat dripping down his temples. He took his handkerchief out of his pocket and wiped it away.

"I fantasized about taking revenge," he replied candidly. "But that's only fantasy. I'm not so dumb that I don't know what the consequences would be."

"Thank you," Utsumi said, looking pleased. "Now for my last question. I'd like you to talk me through what you did all day yesterday in as much detail as possible. It would really help to know where you were."

She was checking his alibi. Tomoya had been expecting this.

He launched into an account of the day. After spending the morning at home with his mother, Rie, he'd gone out just before midday to watch the parade. He got together with two of his younger coworkers, one of whom was a young woman who had only joined the firm this year. He had offered to act as their guide, since neither of them had been to the parade before.

"Where did you watch it from?" Utsumi asked.

"Near the finish. A lot of the teams keep their best gimmicks and performances for the end."

"Did you watch the parade right through?"

"We did, yes. It finished sometime after three P.M. After that, we split up for a while."

"Split up?"

"Both my colleagues had things they wanted to do. We decided to separate and do our own thing for a while. We agreed to rendezvous at this bar near the train station at four, then went our different ways."

This was something that Tomoya hadn't really wanted to tell the detective. However, since she could check his story just by asking his two colleagues, it made more sense to be up-front with her from the start.

"Where did you go, Mr. Takagaki?" Although her expression and tone hadn't changed, Tomoya got the sense that she felt she was onto something.

"I went to this area just past the finish line to say hi to the members of the local team, Team Kikuno, who had just finished their performance—Maya Miyazawa and the rest of the bunch."

"Who is this Ms. Miyazawa?"

"She's the leader of the team and the manager of Miyazawa Books. I'm not sure I have her contact details. . . ."

"Not to worry. Who else did you talk to?"

"Some people I bump into at Namiki-ya from time to time. Sorry, I don't know their names."

"And after that?"

"It was almost time, so I headed to the bar and met up with my two coworkers. We had a few beers and left the place at around six thirty, I think."

After that, he told her, he went to Namiki-ya. It was there that he heard the news of Hasunuma's death.

After listening to his account, Utsumi asked him to furnish her with the names and contact details of the two coworkers and unable to think of a reason not to, he did.

"Thank you. This is all very useful. I may need to ask you a few more questions, so I may get in touch again." Utsumi shut her little notebook and nodded her thanks.

"You won't be sharing any information with me today, either, then?"

"Huh?" was all the reply Toyoma got.

"Any information about the case. It's just like last time: You get to ask all the questions. You haven't even told me whether Hasunuma was murdered."

"I think I explained my position at our last meeting."

"Yes, I know, but . . ."

"Then thank you for your understanding," said Utsumi, getting briskly to her feet.

"The truth is," she said, looking Tomoya in the eyes, "there isn't actually all that much I can tell you."

"Which means what?"

"Which means we haven't yet pinpointed the cause of death."

"Oh, really?" Tomoya blinked.

Utsumi nodded discreetly. "Thank you for your help," she said, and opened the door.

19

The Prosecutorial Review Commission? Yes, of course." Naoki Niikura nodded his head. "Of course, it had occurred to me."

"So you knew about it? Most people have never even heard of it." Inspector Kishitani's eyes widened. The man's got a surprisingly genial face for a detective, thought Niikura. He had a glass mug of tea in his hand.

"I only heard of it recently. When I heard the news about that guy's release, I wondered what on earth 'deferment of dispensation' actually meant, so I started looking into it."

"Did you manage to figure it out?"

"I guess." Niikura shrugged. "To be frank, I thought it was a pretty half-assed rule. No, I mean, legally-speaking, it's not even official."

"You're right. The police send a case to the prosecutor. The prosecutor has to decide whether or not to prosecute within a fixed time period. All they're doing is postponing that decision."

"I tried to find out if there was any way to appeal the decision to defer. That's what led me to the Prosecutorial Review Commission. I realized that you can only lodge an appeal after the final decision has been made. We were still at the deferment of dispensation stage, so we weren't there yet. On top of that, the only people who can lodge an appeal are the plaintiff, the accuser, or the victim's family."

Inspector Kishitani took an appreciative sip of his herbal tea, then placed his teacup on the table. There was a faint smile on his lips. "You've certainly done your homework."

"The only thing we could do was wait—right?" Niikura looked over at Rumi, his wife, for confirmation. She was sitting in a dining chair, a tray clutched in her hands.

She nodded silently.

"How did you see the case going? Did you expect Hasunuma to be indicted in the end?" Smile or no smile, Inspector Kishitani's eyes were dead serious.

"Well, I, uhm . . ." Niikura mumbled something incoherent.

He would be lying if he said that he believed Hasunuma would be indicted. He had spent days agonizing at the thought that nothing would be done; that the man would be able to go about his life completely unpunished.

"Would you have filed an appeal if the prosecutor had decided not to prosecute?"

"Probably. Rather, I'd probably have advised the Namikis to do so. They couldn't possibly accept such a decision."

"So you hadn't yet discussed the matter with them?"

"That's right. Lately, when my wife and I meet the Namikis, we seldom discuss Saori. It's just too painful for both sides."

"And that was the case even after Hasunuma reappeared in Kikuno?" Kishitani asked, inspecting Niikura with his eyes.

Aware that he needed to be careful, Niikura tried to focus. "I didn't actually know anything about that."

"Sorry, 'that'?"

"'That' being the fact that Hasunuma was back here in Kikuno; or rather, that he was back in Kikuno and had showed up at Namiki-ya. The first I heard of it was last night; the other customers at Namiki-ya told me about it after we got the news of Hasunuma's death. I'd not actually been to Namiki-ya for quite a while, you see."

Naoki Niikura hadn't actually known that Hasunuma was back in Kikuno until Tojima alerted him. No one else had mentioned it to him since then. His story would be inconsistent if he said that he knew anything about it before the fuss at Namiki-ya last night.

"Aha. I see."

Kishitani's lips parted in surprise and he started writing in his notebook. He seemed like a genial fellow, but from certain angles his face could also look quite sly. Niikura couldn't tell if Kishitani believed him.

His pen stopped moving across the page. Kishitani looked up.

"Could you tell me how you feel now? What were your emotions when you heard that Hasunuma was dead? Be honest."

"How do I feel now?" Niikura paused and looked down. His mind was racing. What was the most appropriate response in this situation? He looked up at Kishitani. "How I feel would depend on how he died."

"What do you mean?"

"If Hasunuma was murdered, then I'd say the bugger got what he deserved. I'd like to thank the killer for taking revenge on our behalf. If it was disease or some kind of accident, if Hasunuma died just like any other normal person, then I'd feel a bit . . . no, I'd feel *very* bitter and angry. I'd have to try and think of it as divine retribution."

Kishitani gave a grunt, then turned his attention to Rumi. "And you, Mrs. Niikura? How do you feel?"

"Me, too . . . uhm . . . let me see. I've not fully processed it yet. The whole thing's a bit bewildering. . . ." Her words just petered out.

"Tell me, Detective." Niikura looked hard at Kishitani. "What did actually happen? Was Hasunuma murdered? I'm guessing he was, otherwise a detective from the Tokyo Metropolitan Police Department would hardly be on the case, would he."

Kishitani listened stone-faced, then grinned at them both.

"We're still in the middle of our investigation. Now, there's something else I need to ask you." He picked up his pen. "Where were you yesterday?"

Here we go. Naoki Niikura steeled himself. *Time to confirm our alibis.*

"We both went to the parade. It only comes around once a year."

"If possible, I'd appreciate as much detail as possible. Try and break things down for me: where you were, what you were doing, who you were with. Oh, and give me times."

"The precise times?"

"As precise as memory permits." Kishitani smiled self-deprecatingly. "It's just one of those bureaucratic hoops we detectives have to jump through."

"We were here at home all morning. We left the house at—" Niikura looked over at Rumi. "Was it after midday?"

"I'm not quite sure. All I know is that the Heidi, a Girl of the Alps float went past the minute we got there."

"So it did."

"Where did you watch the parade from?"

"Just a little bit past the start. There's this raised section in front of the post office and you get a good view from there."

"Did you watch the whole parade from there?"

"No, not the whole thing. We moved a few times, but we couldn't find anywhere else as good, so we eventually went back."

"Did you run into anyone you know?"

"Oh yes. Quite a lot of people."

"Who were they? I'd like you to tell me their names, if you can." Kishitani held his ball pen poised above his notebook.

"I'm afraid I don't recall the exact times and places."

"That doesn't matter. We'll check the details."

To Niikura that sounded like: *We'll know if you're lying to us.*

Niikura listed several names. They were all people he and his wife had actually bumped into. Kikuno wasn't a big place and Niikura knew everyone. People were always coming up to say hello.

The last name he gave was that of Maya Miyazawa.

"Miyazawa's the leader of Team Kikuno. I'm involved with the performance, so I went to wish her luck and have a last-minute chat before the team set off."

"What's the nature of your involvement?"

"I'm the music supervisor for their songs. I help them avoid any copyright problems and I composed the theme song for the local mascot that comes after them in the parade."

"I see. Most impressive," Kishitani said with slightly insincere admiration. "Where did you go after the parade?"

"We went to Kikuno Park where they hold the singing contest. Rumi and I are on the judging panel. The contest probably wrapped around six, after which we went to Namiki-ya. We were completely stunned by the news of Hasunuma's death, but we still ate our dinner and left around eight or so, then came back here. That's the whole day," Niikura said, rounding things off.

Kishitani muttered to himself as he stared down at his notebook. Niikura wondered if he was reading his notes back to himself. He shut the notebook with a snap.

"That's all very nice and clear. Thank you for making the time to speak to me." Kishitani got to his feet and put his notebook and pen into his bag.

Niikura accompanied the detective to the front door and saw

him off. When he got back to the living room, Rumi hadn't moved. She was pale and staring intently at the dining table.

"Any problems?"

"What?" She looked up at her husband.

"The answers I gave the detective. Did I do okay? I didn't screw up?"

Rumi looked uncomfortable as she tilted her head to one side. "You did okay . . . I think."

"I think I did, too."

Niikura was heading for the sofa when he noticed Rumi's hands. He came to a stop.

It was very subtle, but they were trembling.

He went and placed his hands on her shoulders.

"It's all right. There's nothing to be frightened about."

Rumi looked up at him. Her eyes were bloodshot.

"Hasunuma killed Saori," Niikura said. "He deserved to be punished. No one would ever blame us, if they found out what we did."

20

"You should come out with us just once in a while," one of her girlfriends had said. Tonight, apparently, there was a big party. *A change of pace might be just the thing to cheer me up*, Natsumi thought. In the end, she turned her friend down, making an apologetic gesture as she did so. "I'm sorry, I just can't." Her mother took over front-of-house duties at the restaurant whenever she took time off, but Natsumi knew it wasn't easy for her. On top of that, the news of Hasunuma's death was still a weight on her mind. She wondered if the police were making any progress.

It was after five when she got home. Her parents were already hard at work in the kitchen. She dashed up the stairs and got changed. The stylish clothes she wore to university weren't suitable for waitressing.

Back downstairs, she gave the dining area a good cleaning, then hung the *noren* curtain over the front door on the stroke of five thirty.

She was sitting on one of the chairs in the restaurant playing with her phone, when the door slid open. The first customer of the day was someone she had seen only the day before.

"Good evening," said Manabu Yukawa, as he stepped inside.

"Good evening. Yesterday was fun."

Natsumi went to the back of the restaurant and returned with a rolled-up cool towel on a little tray. "What would you like to drink?"

"Beer. Then the usual."

"Coming right up."

She relayed the order to the kitchen, extracted a bottle of beer from the refrigerator, and took it to his table, together with a glass and the appetizer. Today's appetizer was boiled and half-dried bonito simmered in soy sauce.

"Thank you." Yukawa poured beer into his glass. "I got a visit from a detective today. To grill me about my movements yesterday."

"A detective went to see *you*? I wonder why."

"He asked me when we were together—from what time until what time—and then when we were apart. He didn't say why he was asking. My impression was that he was less interested in my movements than in verifying your statement."

"Oh . . . really?"

"I knew you had nothing to hide, so I just told him the facts. He pressed me to be as precise as possible about times. I explained that my memory was a bit hazy and he should take my answers with a pinch of salt. If I did get anything wrong, there may be some small discrepancies in our statements. I just wanted to say sorry in advance."

"I should apologize to you for the police bothering you like that."

"No need, you're the ones who have suffered. Of course, taking a purely objective view, the police have every reason to be suspicious of you and your family."

"That's true, but I think we'll be okay. My mom and dad have both got perfect alibis."

"They took a customer who wasn't feeling well to the hospital, I heard?"

"That's right."

"Do they know the woman's identity? I imagine the police will want to speak to her."

"I'm not sure."

Natsumi hadn't thought about that.

"Natsumi," came Yutaro's voice from the kitchen. The *takiawase* Yukawa had ordered was ready.

As she was picking up the dish from the kitchen, Natsumi asked her father if he knew who the woman customer was.

"No, not really. All I know is that her family name is Yamada," replied Yutaro, busily cooking something.

Natsumi brought the dish of *takiawase* to Yukawa and told him the woman's name.

"Yesterday was a Sunday, so there can't have been all that many patients in the emergency room. If the police know her name, it will be easy enough to get the rest of her details from the hospital. They may not even need to go that far. The nurses can testify that your parents were at the hospital, can't they?"

"Yes, they can." Natsumi found Yukawa's cool and reasonable tone comforting.

For a while, no more customers came in, not even customers who were usually there, day in, day out. *Was this because of Hasunuma's death?* Natsumi wondered. Perhaps the locals had decided that the Namikis had something to do with it. Natsumi remembered her phone conversation with Tomoya Takagaki the night before. He certainly seemed to think that. At that moment, who should appear but Tomoya himself.

"Evening," Natsumi said.

Tomoya looked around the restaurant. He was obviously unsure where to sit.

"Why not this one?" Yukawa motioned to the seat opposite his. "Fancy sharing?"

"May I?"

"Of course. You're very welcome."

"I'll take you up on that." Tomoya sat down in the seat Yukawa had indicated.

It was a novel sight. Since both men were regulars, Natsumi had often seen them exchange the odd word now and again, but she'd never seen them sitting at the same table.

"Did you a get a visit from a detective?" Yukawa asked, pouring beer into Tomoya's glass.

"How did you know?"

"It's not hard to guess. You're like the Namiki family. From the police point of view, your position is a sensitive one." Putting the beer bottle down on the table, Yukawa picked up his own glass. "You're on their list of suspects."

"The detective who came to see me in my office today is the same one who came to see me after Saori's body was found," said Tomoya. "She asked me for my alibi."

"A woman detective, eh? Does your alibi hold up?"

"It ought to. I was with a couple of friends from work during and after the parade."

"Then you've got nothing to worry about," Yukawa said. "What else did she ask you?"

"She asked me if I'd heard of something called the Prosecutorial Review Commission."

"The Prosecutorial . . . Oh, of course." Yukawa's eyes blinked behind his glasses as if he'd just realized something.

"What is it—the Prosecutorial Review Commission?" Natsumi asked the two men.

Yukawa looked up at her.

"It's a panel that reviews and rules on the rightness of a prosecutor's decision when he decides not to indict a suspect. If anyone disagrees with the prosecutor's decision, there can be an appeal. The people on the commission are ordinary members of the public. They've got to be over twenty and they are chosen by lot."

"You're very well informed, Professor," Tomoya said.

"One of my friends was selected," said Yukawa offhandedly.

"Well, I'd never heard of it. To be honest, today I finally understood the difference between deferment of dispensation and simply dropping charges. . . . I don't quite know why she was asking me questions about that, though."

"Probably because the police believe that no one familiar with the workings of the Prosecutorial Review Commission would murder Hasunuma at this stage of the legal process. Even if the prosecutor did formally decide not to indict, there would still be the opportunity to lodge an appeal against the decision. There was no need for anyone to do anything as extreme as to take revenge into their own hands."

"I see. Well, I didn't know about the commission, so I could still be a suspect." Tomoya sighed and picked up his beer glass. "The detective asked me another odd question. Had I tried to find out where Hasunuma lived before he moved back to Kikuno? I told her no, I hadn't. It never even occurred to me to do so."

"The police must be working on the assumption that whoever killed Hasunuma started plotting their revenge as soon as the prosecutor released him. Finding out where he lived would have been part of that."

"You think that's why she asked me? If I were the killer—I'm just speaking hypothetically here—I would hardly give her an honest answer." Tomoya stuck out his lips in a pout. "I don't know why she even bothered asking."

"Because she thought she'd be able to tell if you were lying." Something in Yukawa's tone suggested that he knew the detective.

"Maybe you're right. She's quite an attractive woman, but she's got eyes like razors." Tomoya grimaced and took a swig of beer.

Customers started floating in in dribs and drabs. None of them were the usual familiar faces.

After finishing his dinner, Tomoya left. The professor, who said he was going to stay, insisted on paying for his drinks. It was unusual for Yukawa to hang out in the restaurant for such a long time.

Niikura and Tojima came in together not long after. They had each decided to go to the restaurant and had just bumped into each other on their way there, they explained. They both sat down at Yukawa's table, where Tomoya had been.

Although Natsumi never heard the three men mention Hasunuma by name, she did catch the occasional phrase like "that bastard" and "divine punishment."

Niikura was the one who brought up the subject of the Prosecutorial Review Commission. Yukawa mentioned that Tomoya Takagaki had been talking about the same thing. Tojima hadn't yet been visited by the police, but he was listening intently to this part of the conversation.

Natsumi looked into the kitchen. She guessed that the conversation was probably inaudible to Yutaro and Machiko. At the same time, she got the impression that the two of them were silently focusing on cooking as part of a deliberate effort *not* to hear what was being said.

21

Someone made a noise and he awakened. When he opened his eyes and saw the white wall and fluorescent lighting, it took him a second or two to remember where he was. He blinked, looked around, and finally realized he was in one of the meeting rooms in the Kikuno Police Station.

"Sorry. I seem to have woken you up," said a voice from behind him. Swiveling around in his chair, he saw Detective Kaoru Utsumi standing near the door.

Kusanagi plucked at the blanket, which was draped over his shoulders. "You do this?"

"Yes," replied Utsumi. "We don't want our chief catching cold, do we?"

With a sardonic smile, Kusanagi dumped the blanket on the chair beside him. "Must have dozed off for a while."

He looked at his watch. It was a little after 11 P.M.

"It's late. Why are you still here?"

"I've been verifying Tomoya Takagaki's alibi. I went to speak to his two colleagues, the ones he went to the parade with."

"How was it?"

Utsumi advanced farther into the room.

"For the most part, their statements tallied with his. They seem to have been together for most of the time."

"In your earlier report, you mentioned that they'd split up and done their own thing."

"Yes, for about forty minutes, plus after subtracting time needed for walking."

"Forty minutes?" Crossing his arms on his chest, Kusanagi noticed that Utsumi was holding up a white convenience store plastic bag. "What have you got in there?"

"Two cans of beer and some snacks," Utsumi replied. "I thought you might enjoy a bit of a break, sir."

"Out with it, then. Chop-chop." Kusanagi pointed at the table-top.

Keeping one eye on Utsumi as she extracted the beer and snacks from the bag, Kusanagi looked down at the report that he was working on.

He had compiled a list of bullet points, but it wasn't good enough yet to show to Director Mamiya and the rest of the top brass.

The Kikuno local police had filed an official request for support of the Tokyo Metropolitan Police Department. In line with the original plan, Kusanagi's team was sent to Kikuno but the head of the Homicide Division wanted to hold off on setting up an investigation task force.

"We're not yet sure it was murder," Mamiya had explained. "The executive team has agreed to adopt a wait-and-see attitude at least until we have a clear cause of death. On the other hand, there's a risk of falling behind if we don't start gathering information until we know that for sure. We want you to get started with the understanding that an investigation task force will be set up soon."

Kusanagi summoned his team and held a meeting with the detectives of the Kikuno precinct. Even if this wasn't yet officially a murder case, they were going to treat it like one.

The first thing Kusanagi wanted to get a handle on were the alibis of the Namiki family, in particular Yutaro, the father. It turned out that the Kikuno investigators had interviewed all three of them the night before.

What they'd found tallied with what Kusanagi had heard that morning from Yukawa. Just as the restaurant was about to stop serving lunch, a female customer had complained about feeling unwell. Yutaro Namiki had driven her to the hospital; his wife, Machiko, joined him not long after. The two of them had waited in the ER until a doctor was able to see the woman. There turned out to be nothing seriously wrong with her, so the Namikis left the hospital at about four thirty and headed home. They went straight into the kitchen and got everything ready before opening up the restaurant as usual at five thirty. Yukawa, one of their regular customers, showed up soon after—

Another local policeman had gone to the hospital this morning to verify the Namikis' story. He got corroboration from the receptionist in the ER who remembered the Namikis hanging around anxiously in the waiting area.

There was a hiss as Utsumi pulled the tab on one of the beer cans. "Here you go, sir," she said, placing the beer in front of Kusanagi.

"Cheers." Kusanagi lifted the can in a gesture of thanks, then took a swig. As the slightly bitter liquid flowed over his tongue, he felt the tiredness of a long day being transformed into a sensation of mild pleasure. He sighed heavily.

"My impression is that Tomoya Takagaki's innocent," said Kaoru Utsumi, tearing open a bag of *kakinotane* spicy baked chips.

"Appearances can be deceiving." Kusanagi stretched a hand into the bag and crammed chips and peanuts into his mouth. "You're a detective. How often do I have to remind you of that?"

"Yes, I know." Utsumi picked up her beer can. "But he was just too panicky."

"Too panicky?"

"I asked him this question: 'If your friends knew that you were the one who had killed him, how do you think they would take it?'"

"What was his reply?"

"That no one who knew me well would believe it, because they all know he's a coward at heart."

"Sounds like a pretty standard response. What about it?"

"I got the impression that he was extremely on edge before he came out with his answer. Like it had never occurred to him that people who knew him might see him in those terms. I don't think he'd have been so openly flustered if he was the killer."

Kusanagi grunted ambiguously and took a swig of beer.

There was some truth to what Utsumi was saying. If Takagaki was the killer, he'd have anticipated the kinds of questions he was likely to be asked by the police and been prepared not to display any nervousness.

"Tomoya Takagaki said he was away from his workmates for forty minutes. What's he saying he did in that time?"

Utsumi took her notebook out of her bag and opened it up.

"He went to the end point of the parade to say hi to the Team Kikuno performers."

"Have you confirmed that?"

"I spoke to Maya Miyazawa, the woman who manages the team.

According to her, yes, Takagaki came by to say hi to them all right after the parade ended. But—" At this point, Utsumi broke off in a rather histrionic fashion. "Despite what he said about talking to the team, he barely exchanged more than a few words with them. 'Nice work. Great job.' That was about it. Probably took him all of thirty seconds."

"Could you confirm the exact time?"

"Miyazawa couldn't remember. That's legitimate enough; we know it was right after the parade ended. Besides, as team leader, Miyazawa probably had a thousand and one things to do."

"Let me see if I've got this right. At just after three, immediately after the parade ended, Tomoya Takagaki was in the vicinity of the finish line. We know that for a fact. But he has no alibi for the next forty minutes, until he joined his friends at the beer bar."

"Correct."

"Roughly how far is it from the parade finish to Hasunuma's place?"

"Something over a mile," Utsumi answered promptly.

Let's say roughly three miles there and back, then. Kusanagi did some rapid mental arithmetic. *Assuming that Tomoya Takagaki used a car traveling at an average of twenty miles per hour, the return journey would take him ten minutes. He'd need some extra time for things like getting to the car, finding a parking space, and so on, leaving him with only around twenty minutes for everything else. Could he really accomplish everything required to kill Hasunuma in such a short amount of time? Plus, an average speed of twenty is probably unrealistic in an area like Kikuno.*

"There's no way he could have knocked Hasunuma out with sleeping medication and then asphyxiated him," sighed Kusanagi. "Tomoya Takagaki cannot have carried out the murder."

"My opinion, too, sir. In addition, we have no indication that he knew where Hasunuma lived, now or before he moved back into the area. When I asked Takagaki about that, he said the thought had never even crossed his mind. I don't think he was lying."

"Okay, so what do we have? The Namiki family are in the clear and Tomoya Takagaki is in the clear, too?" Kusanagi looked down at his half-written report.

"Inspector Kishitani went to interview the Niikuras, didn't he?" said Utsumi. "What was his impression?"

"Fishy," he said.

"How so?"

"Naoki Niikura claimed not to be aware that Hasunuma was back in Kikuno. He says that the first he heard of it was last night at Namiki-ya, when some of the regulars there told him. It's true that he hasn't been going to Namiki-ya much recently; even so Kishitani thinks that the idea that no one would have told him strains credulity."

"Very perceptive. I think he's right."

"However," Kusanagi continued, "Kishitani can't see Naoki Niikura as the kind of person who would murder anybody as an act of revenge, even if that person has killed his favorite pupil. And Kishitani is a good judge of people."

"What did the Niikuras have to say about the Prosecutorial Review Commission?"

"They knew what it was. And speaking hypothetically, they said that they would probably have teamed up with the Namiki family to figure out a legal strategy, had the prosecutor ultimately decided against indicting Hasunuma."

"Sounds very reasonable."

"Yes, as far as we know."

When Kusanagi had sent Utsumi and Kishitani to interview the persons of interest in the case, he had them find out if the interviewees were familiar with the Prosecutorial Review Commission. Anyone who was would be less likely to murder Hasunuma at this particular point in time.

"What about the Niikuras' alibis?"

"A little wobbly," answered Kusanagi, looking down at his report. "They claim to have gone to watch the parade and to have bumped into a number of people they know in the course of it, but no one else was with them for the duration of the event. After the parade, they went to judge the singing contest. There is a brief period that's unaccounted for between the two events."

Utsumi put her beer can down on the table and cradled her chin in her hands.

"Since we don't know how long it took to murder Hasunuma, it's difficult to interpret these gaps in time. Of course, that's assuming that it *was* a homicide in the first place."

"That's the problem!" Kusanagi scratched his head and frowned. "There are clusters of petechiae on the body. That means that death by asphyxiation is a high probability. Against that, there are no marks on the body suggestive of manual or ligature strangulation; plus, the petechiae would be much more pronounced, if he'd been strangled."

"What if he was asphyxiated without any pressure on his neck? By occlusion of the nose and mouth, I mean."

"Then why didn't the victim resist? Yes, some sleeping medication was detected in his system, but not large quantities of the stuff."

Kusanagi smiled at the sight of Detective Utsumi plunged in thought. "What is it?" asked Utsumi testily.

"I met with Yukawa this morning. Turns out he's a person of interest, too."

Kusanagi told Utsumi about his conversation with Manabu Yukawa.

"Professor Yukawa's a regular at Namiki-ya? That's a surprise."

"If Hasunuma *was* murdered, then how was it done? I suggested to Yukawa that he might apply his famous powers of deduction to answering that question. Somewhat to my amazement, he said yes. He asked to look at the crime scene, so I'm planning to take him there soon. There's a good chance he of all people will notice something that everyone else has overlooked."

"That sounds promising." Kaoru Utsumi cocked her head to one side. "But it's still a surprise."

"What?"

"From what I hear, Namiki-ya is a very casual and friendly place that's kept in business by a faithful cohort of regulars. It's hard to see Professor Yukawa going there on a regular basis. He's someone who actively dislikes ties of any kind."

"I see what you mean," Kusanagi said. "I think he changed a bit after going to America. You should go and visit him. You'll see."

"I will. Soon." Utsumi smiled and drank another mouthful of beer from the can.

22

The young uniformed policeman who was standing in front of the hut where Eiji Masumura lived was looking thoroughly bored. He stifled a yawn. *No one's going to break into a place like this*, his fed-up expression seemed to say.

His expression changed as Kusanagi and his companion approached the hut. His eyes brightened and his whole face perked up.

Kusanagi pulled out his badge. "Kusanagi, TMPD."

The young policeman saluted him. "I was told you were coming, sir. It's good to see you." He spun on his heel, and briskly unlocked the door of the hut. "There you go, sir."

Kusanagi extracted a couple pairs of latex gloves from his pocket and passed one back to Yukawa. Yukawa took them without a word.

It was day three since Kusanagi's team had officially joined the investigation. No progress had been made in determining the cause of Hasunuma's death, which left the investigation at a standstill. In an attempt to break the logjam, Kusanagi got permission to show Yukawa the crime scene.

Turning the knob with his gloved hand, Kusanagi opened the door of the hut. Forensics must have been in and out of the place countless times, but the interior looked exactly the same as when he was last there.

He removed his shoes and climbed onto the duckboard floor. "This is a modest little place," said Yukawa, following his example.

Kusanagi strode directly to the far end of the room and came to a stop in front of the back room. The sliding door was open.

"So this is the room." Yukawa came and stood beside him. "It's tiny. It would be unbearable for anyone with claustrophobia."

"It's all a question of mindset," Kusanagi said. "Some people actually *enjoy* staying in capsule hotels. Hasunuma seems to have been comfortable enough. He spread out a ground sheet, then put a mattress and a quilt on top."

"You're the one who described him as a hard-hearted bugger."

"Exactly."

"Can I go in?"

"Be my guest."

Yukawa went inside, took up a position in the center of the room and slowly looked around. After a while, his gaze came to rest on the sliding door.

"Have you noticed something?"

Pulling the door part of the way shut, Yukawa started fiddling with the door hasp to which a padlock could be attached.

"This room can be locked from the outside."

"Probably because it used to be a storeroom. The lock was to keep whatever was inside safe."

"What about the padlock? Did Forensics take it away?"

"Nobody said anything about a padlock, but I'll ask."

The next thing Yukawa turned his attention to was the door handle. He looked at the handles on both sides of the door.

"Could I send the officer on sentry duty to go buy something?" Yukawa asked.

"Buy something?"

"Yes, I want him to get me a set of screwdrivers."

"Screwdrivers? Why?"

"Just something I need to check. If he can't go, I'll do it myself." Yukawa's gaze was still fixed on the metal door handle. In profile, he looked every inch the scientist.

"Fine. I'll tell him."

Kusanagi went outside and had a word with the policeman who was a little puzzled but agreed to go. When Kusanagi came back inside, he found Yukawa sitting on the bed, sunk in silent thought.

"He'll be right back with what you need."

"Very good of him," said Yukawa, not opening his eyes. "There was no evidence of resistance, was there?"

"I'm sorry?"

"Hasunuma. There were no indications of him having struggled or fought back?"

"No, none. He was just lying on top of his quilt. His clothes weren't even disheveled."

Yukawa opened his eyes, rose to his feet, pushed the sliding door shut, then ran his eyes around the whole doorframe.

"What are you checking for?"

"Airtightness. I'm trying to see how much air can get in and out when the door's fully closed." Yukawa slid the door back open. "Even when you push it shut as hard as you can, there are still lots of gaps between the door and the frame. It's not remotely airtight. It would be different if you sealed it up with duct tape."

"And if there was a high level of airtightness?"

"If you could make the room fully airtight, then all you'd need to do would be to shut and lock the door while Hasunuma was asleep inside. With no oxygen going in, the room would fill up with carbon dioxide and he would eventually suffocate."

"I see." Kusanagi cocked his head to one side. "But wouldn't he wake up if he was having trouble breathing?"

"Yes, he'd definitely regain consciousness," said Yukawa, po-faced. "The room is small, but not so small that you would suddenly run out of oxygen. Hasunuma would still be capable of moving, so he would do his best to open the door. If he found it locked, he would try to smash it down."

"That theory's no good. It doesn't fit with the facts."

Yukawa was wagging a finger in front of Kusanagi's face.

"You're getting ahead of yourself as usual. There's an order for doing things. All I did was propose the simplest possible solution first. Now I'm going to gradually build on that to develop new ideas. We know that simply sealing the door shut isn't going to produce a sudden oxygen deficit. How to produce that is the next question we need to consider."

"So how do you do it?"

Yukawa frowned. "Aren't you tempted to try and figure it out for yourself?"

"What do you think I brought you here for?"

Yukawa shook his head in a theatrical display of disappointment. "What about getting Hasunuma to take a sleeping draught? Have you had any thoughts about that?"

"No, I'm stumped there, too." Kusanagi held both hands out, palms upward. "I have no idea when, where, or how he was fed the stuff."

Yukawa pointed to one corner of the room where there was a small refrigerator. "Did you check the contents?"

"Of course. Forensics removed and examined everything that was inside it. They didn't find anything suspicious."

The only drinks they had found in the refrigerator were an open bottle of oolong tea and an open bottle of water. Neither of them contained any sleeping medication.

"Still, there is one thing that's bothering me," Kusanagi said. "According to the pathologist, it's highly likely that Hasunuma was drinking beer. His blood alcohol was a little on the high side. We know that Hasunuma was quite a drinker, so if someone offered him a beer, chances are he would drink it. To some extent, it would depend on who offered it to him."

"What about the occupant of the apartment? It would be easy enough for him to get Hasunuma to ingest something laced with a sedative."

"True, but he has no motive," Kusanagi replied smartly. He had already thought that possibility through. "There is no connection whatsoever linking Eiji Masumura and Saori Namiki. Masumura and Hasunuma actually met almost a year *before* Saori was murdered. I trawled through his past and couldn't find any kind of link."

"What if the killer bribed Masumura to spike his drink . . . or would that be too risky?"

"Too risky. Masumura could blow the whistle anytime he chose. And even if he didn't say anything, he could always ask for more money."

"That's true," Yukawa murmured, resuming his inspection of the little room.

A moment later, the young policeman popped his head around the door. "I'm back. This is what I got. Will it be okay?"

He held out a plastic case containing multiple varieties of screwdrivers. "That's more than good enough. Thank you," said Yukawa, taking it from him.

Yukawa sat on the floor by the sliding door of the storeroom and used one of the screwdrivers to loosen the screws that held the door handle in place. He was a scientist and obviously used to working with his hands.

"What are you doing?"

"Wait and see."

Yukawa needed only two or three minutes to detach the handle fittings from both sides of the door, exposing a square hole in the wood beneath.

"As I thought." Yukawa smiled complacently as he put his eye to the hole.

"What's this all about? Come on, tell me."

"It's so blindingly obvious, I really shouldn't need to."

Yukawa had slithered off to one side, so Kusanagi crouched down and peered through the hole. He could see to the far back wall of the small room.

"I can see right through it."

"Indeed, you can. When carpenters fit handles to doors, they seldom drill a hole right through. This door, however, is on the thin side, so they did."

"I can see that, but what's your point?"

"Do you know the mystery novel *The Judas Window* by John Dickson Carr?"

"Never heard of it."

"Why am I not surprised?" said Yukawa, shaking his head. "What I'm saying is that this door contains a little secret window." Yukawa pulled the door shut. "Even if you shut the door like this, you can exploit this window to do something to the person inside."

"What can you do with a hole this small?"

"I told you a minute ago. It's about causing a sudden oxygen deficit. I can think of several ways to do it, using this hole."

"For example?"

"For example, by sucking out the oxygen through it."

"*Huh?*"

"You could use an aspirator of the kind found in vacuum cleaners. You couldn't make a perfect vacuum, but I suspect you could probably make the air very thin indeed."

"For God's sake, Yukawa?" Kusanagi peered into the professor's eyes behind the rimless spectacles. "Are you serious?"

"I haven't got the time to fool around."

"Do you think that method could work?"

"Probably not. If that level of thinness of air was enough to cause asphyxiation, then all the world's mountain climbers would probably be dead."

Kusanagi felt himself go weak at the knees with disappointment. He braced himself. If he got upset by this sort of thing, he should stay away from Yukawa altogether. "And what's your next idea?"

"Since the aim is to reduce the amount of oxygen, another thing you could do is to make the room smaller. To put that in the terms a physicist would use, you need to reduce the room's volumetric capacity."

"Using this hole here? How?"

"First, you seal up any gaps around the door, then you introduce some object or objects into the room through this hole. The volume of the room will diminish in proportion to the volume of the object introduced, driving the air out. If you persist, the room volume will eventually diminish to the point that an oxygen deficit can easily occur."

Yukawa delivered this speech with great solemnity. Kusanagi looked at him and then pointed at the square hole. "And what sort of object can you introduce through this hole? It's only big enough for a glass bead. Yes, the room is small, but you'd still need tens of thousands—no, hundreds of thousands—of the things."

"That's true, if we're talking about objects that don't change shape. How about, though, if you used, say, balloons?"

"Balloons. How?"

"You stuff an uninflated balloon through the hole keeping the mouth of the balloon on the outside of the door. You then start to inflate it with air from this side. Once the balloon has expanded to a sufficiently large size, you knot the mouth and let it go. As I explained a minute ago, the volume of the room will shrink in proportion to the cubic volume of the balloons. Provided you use balloons that can be blown up to a large size, it should be a highly efficient method."

Kusanagi pictured the interior of the room filling up with more and more balloons. How many would you need to fill up fifty square feet?

"That's certainly a novel idea—but it doesn't seem altogether realistic."

"Doesn't find favor with you? Killing someone by burying them in a welter of colorful balloons strikes me as a surrealistic, humorous, and rather delightful trick."

"I'll allow you the surrealistic part. A couple of problems remain, though. First, the victim wouldn't asphyxiate rapidly, and second, he would come to when he had trouble breathing. Once he realizes that his problem is being trapped in a small room with a whole load of balloons, then all he needs to do is to start popping the things."

"Perhaps you're right. Okay, what if the balloons weren't filled with air?"

"What are you getting at?"

Yukawa smiled meaningfully, then laughed under his breath.

"If you didn't use air, I suppose you wouldn't need balloons in the first place."

23

Detective Sergeant Utsumi opened her almond-shaped eyes wide. "Helium?"

"Yes. You shut the sliding door, lock it, and pump helium gas from a tank in through this little square hole. Helium's lighter than air, so it stays in the upper part of the room. As more and more helium is pumped in, the air is pushed out of the room through gaps around the door. Hasunuma may be lying on his mattress down on the floor, but the overall concentration of oxygen in the room is still going down. If he realizes something funny's happening halfway through and gets to his feet, there's even less oxygen in the upper part of the room than the lower part. He tries desperately to breathe, but now he's inhaling helium and not air, so he loses consciousness instantly. If his unconscious state persists, he will inevitably lapse into anoxia." Kusanagi fidgeted with his empty paper coffee cup as he looked up at his team.

They were in one of the meeting rooms at the Kikuno precinct station. Kusanagi had been relaying a hypothetical scenario from Yukawa to Detectives Utsumi, Kishitani, and Muto.

"Vintage Detective Galileo!" said Kishitani with a sigh. "I'd never have thought of anything like that."

"I discussed it with Forensics. They thought it plausible enough. Sudden loss of consciousness would explain why there were no signs of a struggle in the room or of Hasunuma having flailed around. I also talked to the pathologist who conducted the autopsy. He said that there's nothing incongruous about helium causing anoxia. In fact, helium would actually help explain why the petechiae is so much less pronounced than it would be with strangulation."

"In that case, the problem we need to figure out is where the perpetrator got the helium," Muto said.

"Professor Yukawa had some interesting ideas about that, too. Inspector Muto, you may be familiar with this creature." Kusanagi pulled up a photo on his phone and showed the display to the three detectives.

"What is it?" Utsumi frowned as she looked at the screen.

"Is it a . . . frog?" Kishitani tipped his head quizzically.

"That's what everyone says," Muto exclaimed. "That's what I thought when I first saw it."

"It is the local parade mascot. It's called Kikunon, apparently," explained Kusanagi to his subordinates. "It always brings up the rear of the parade. As you can see, it's an enormous inflatable. Since it's around thirty feet long, it needs a very large amount of helium gas to inflate it. Obviously, it depends on their size, but Yukawa reckons that you need more than a couple of large high-pressure cylinders to get the job done."

"You think one of those cylinders might have been used in the murder?"

"I think it's definitely worth exploring."

"Fine. I'll send someone to investigate immediately," said Kishitani. He turned on his heel and left the room.

"If that's your opinion, Chief, shouldn't we be looking elsewhere, too?" Muto asked.

"What do you mean?"

"Kikunon is the only giant inflatable in the parade, but the teams often make use of smaller balloons as props. I didn't watch this year's parade, but I imagine it was the same as previous years. Free balloons are also handed out to kids at several locations along the route. They must have had tanks of helium, too."

"That makes sense. . . ."

A parade is like a traditional Japanese *matsuri* festival—and no *matsuri* is complete without balloons.

"If helium was used for the crime," Muto continued, with a degree of hesitancy, "I think it's highly probable that the gas cylinder wasn't stolen."

"Why do you say that?"

"Helium is actually very easy to buy. When my kids were small, we often got balloons for their birthday parties. My wife would buy helium for them online."

"Same with a friend of mine," Utsumi chimed in. "I went to her house and she had all these balloons floating around from her daughter's birthday party. She'd also bought a little tank of helium to inflate them."

"Huh." Kusanagi looked at Utsumi. Given her age, most of her female friends probably already had kids. He kept the thought safely to himself.

"The tanks are disposable. You don't need to return them after use. They only cost about five thousand yen each," Muto said.

"Five thousand yen? That's really cheap."

"If we assume that this crime wasn't a spur-of-the-moment thing, then the perpetrator would buy the helium in advance, wouldn't they?"

"I suppose so. It might be difficult to trace the purchase." After a moment's thought, Kusanagi had an idea. "Wait a minute. If you don't have to return the helium tanks after use, then how would the perpetrator get rid of them?"

"The tanks are bulky and heavy, too. The killer would want to get away from the crime scene as fast as possible; having to lug a gas canister around would really slow him down." Muto seemed to have grasped the implications of Kusanagi's remark. He got to his feet. "Let's round up everyone who's free and get them to search the vicinity of the crime scene," he said, and dashed out of the room.

Utsumi gave a curt bow and made as if to leave the room. Just before reaching the door, she stopped and turned around. Something was obviously on her mind.

"What's the problem?" Kusanagi asked.

"Why opt for such a complicated method?" asked Utsumi, a disgruntled look on her face. "First knock him out by getting him to ingest sleeping medication, then asphyxiate him by pumping helium into a sealed room. Isn't the whole thing a bit convoluted, a bit grandiose?"

"What?" Kusanagi looked at Utsumi with open surprise. "That's not like you. Have you got your doubts about Yukawa's theory?"

"It's not so much that. It's more that I can't see what the perpetrator was trying to accomplish."

"My guess is that he wanted to make it hard for us to pinpoint the cause of death. Hasunuma's preliminary death certificate says that the 'possibility of cardiac failure of unknown origin cannot be ruled out.' Because we haven't got proof that it was a murder, we haven't been allowed to set up a proper investigation task force."

"If we were talking about anyone else, I might be able to accept that. But this is *Hasunuma* we're dealing with! The dead man is the one and only Kanichi Hasunuma."

"What are you trying to say?"

"That unless the killer was hopelessly naive, he would expect the police to launch a murder investigation, whether or not they could identify the cause. Given that, why not opt for a simpler murder method?"

Kusanagi had no answer. Detective Utsumi's argument was logical and cogent.

"You think that the elaborateness of the killing method may imply something else?"

"I think it's possible."

"Okay," Kusanagi said. "I'll be sure to keep that in mind."

Utsumi bowed briskly and left the room.

About two hours later, Kishitani returned to the meeting room. He looked rather downcast and the news he gave Kusanagi was disappointing.

None of the helium cylinders used to inflate the giant mascot were missing.

"It took four seven-thousand-liter cylinders to inflate the Kikunon balloon. The empty cylinders were collected by the gas merchant the day after the parade, the same as they are every year."

"Could somebody have stolen one of the cylinders and then replaced it later?"

Kishitani shook his head. "The person responsible for Kikunon was at his post all day."

"I see." Kusanagi clicked his tongue in frustration.

Maybe Muto was right, he thought. *Maybe buying gas is easier than stealing it; it's certainly less risky.*

"Get in touch with any businesses that sell helium. See if anyone's bought any recently under a false name."

"Yes, sir," Kishitani said. He was about to leave the room, when the door burst open and Muto came rushing in, his face slightly flushed.

"Chief Inspector, I found it."

"Found what?"

"The tank. I found the helium tank."

24

Behind the counter, the silver-haired bartender was solemnly polishing glasses as he stood in front of a wall covered with an array of different bottles: whiskey, brandy, vodka, and tequila. Kusanagi should be able to enjoy a variety of good, strong tipples.

It was nearly 11 P.M. A couple had just left a moment ago and now he was the only customer in the bar.

He was inspecting the old film posters on the walls and was about halfway through his pint of Guinness, when the street door creaked slowly open and Yukawa strolled in.

Kusanagi waved.

Yukawa ran his eyes around the bar with evident curiosity, before making his way to the small table where Kusanagi was sitting.

"I would never have expected to find a trendy place like this here in Kikuno," said Kusanagi, as Yukawa himself sat down opposite him. "I asked one of the guys at the police station if there was anywhere good for a quiet drink that stayed open late, and this was the place he recommended. They have got all sorts of different brands."

If you go a few times and the bartender gets a sense of what you like, he'll probably create a special, original cocktail just for you, Muto had said when describing the place to Kusanagi.

Yukawa inspected all the various bottles lined up on the shelves behind the bar before making his order: "Ardbeg and soda, please."

The silver-haired bartender narrowed his eyes approvingly. "Very good, sir," he said.

"Were you doing your research this late at night? You're seriously busy," Kusanagi said.

"Not really. At the moment, I'm getting my assistants to conduct this experiment for me. It's been dogged with problems and it failed to produce any of the data I was expecting to spend today checking. Since I had nothing to do, I just played chess against my office computer. My opponent was only a first-generation program, but my record was still dismal: played three, lost three. It's not easy for an amateur to win against AI." Yukawa shrugged and sighed.

"A hard day at the office, then."

"Speak for yourself. Anyway, what are you doing in Kikuno at this time of night? Are you staying here now?"

"Yes. Looks like I'll be staying here for a while."

Yukawa blinked uncomprehendingly.

"The text you sent me said you wanted to thank me in connection with the investigation and that I should get in touch, if I was here in Kikuno. Was my advice some use to you, then?"

"Extremely useful." Kusanagi pointed a finger at Yukawa's chest. "Good old Detective Galileo. You're just as perceptive as ever. Your theory was about half right."

"Only half?" Yukawa knit his brows doubtfully. "Then I was wrong about something?"

"You were right about the use of helium. We found the tank. It wasn't one of the large high-pressure cylinders used for the giant inflatable." Kusanagi pulled his phone out and pulled up a photograph. "There's a river running behind the warehouse where the crime scene is located. The investigators from the Kikuno Police Station found it. It had been dumped in a patch of weeds on the riverbank about sixty feet from the warehouse."

The photo showed a small tank about fifteen inches high and twelves inches wide. Someone had put a beer can next to it to give a sense of scale.

"The tank was empty. All the helium in it had been used. There were several sets of fingerprints on it. We're in the process of getting them checked."

"This thing?" Yukawa was looking at the picture with his head tilted to one side. "How many of them?"

"How many what?"

"Tanks. How many tanks like this did you find?"

"Just the one. Should there be several of the things?"

"*One?* That simply makes no sense," Yukawa said forcefully, just as the bartender came gliding over. He slipped a coaster onto the table and placed a tumbler on top of it. Fine bubbles danced in the amber liquid.

Yukawa took a sip. A benign expression spread across his face. He looked up at the bartender. "Delicious. You got the proportions just right."

The bartender smiled happily and went back behind the counter.

Yukawa put the tumbler down and pointed at the phone on the table. "I'm just asking this to be sure. What's the capacity of that tank?"

Kusanagi took his notebook out of his pocket. "It weighs roughly six and a half pounds. A full new tank contains around four hundred liters."

Yukawa gave a derisive snort. "Ridiculous. That's impossible."

"How so?"

"We need to start by calculating the volume of the small room at the crime scene. Let's say that it's about eight feet wide, six and a half feet deep, and six and a half feet high. That would come to a volume of ten thousand liters. Would pumping in a paltry four hundred liters of helium cause death from oxygen deficiency? Hardly. To kill someone, you would need to use high-pressure, industrial-use helium cylinders. They would be difficult to purchase under a false name. That's why I suggested that the killer might have 'borrowed' a gas cylinder from the giant inflatable." Yukawa was speaking rather faster than usual. Kusanagi wondered if he was annoyed.

"Yes, I remember. But I've not yet told you the most important thing." Kusanagi took his smartphone off the table and put it back in the inside pocket of his jacket. "I told you we had found a gas tank. I didn't tell you that it wasn't just lying there; it was inside a forty-five-liter garbage bag."

"A garbage bag?" Incredulity was etched onto Yukawa's face.

"We checked the inside of the bag very carefully and found something else." Kusanagi didn't think the bartender was interested, but he still lowered his voice. "Hair. Just two strands of it, but still enough for analysis."

"Hair?"

"We thought it might be Hasunuma's hair and the results of the analysis confirm it."

Yukawa scowled ferociously, muttered under his breath, then nodded slowly. "Oh, I get it. So that's what this is all about."

"Have you figured it out?"

"The killer slipped the garbage bag over Hasunuma's head while he was asleep, pulled it tight around his neck, then opened it just enough to pump the helium in—"

"Exactly." Kusanagi rapped the table with his knuckles. "Hasunuma would lose consciousness in ten seconds and die pretty soon thereafter. The pathologist confirmed our theory."

Yukawa picked up his tumbler and took a sip of his whiskey and soda. He was gazing off into the middle distance.

"What's wrong?" asked Kusanagi. "You don't look happy. Is there something wrong scientifically?"

"No." Kusanagi shook his head gently. "Scientifically, I have no problem with the theory. It's just that I don't understand what the murderer's intentions were, why he would use that method. . . ."

"If you're going to go down that road, remember you were the one who deduced this method in the first place. Utsumi actually felt the same. 'What's the point of using such a grandiose and convoluted method to kill a person?'"

"The killing method I proposed was laden with significance. It was based on the hypothesis that the murder was an act of revenge by someone with a grudge against Hasunuma."

"And what was its significance?"

"It implied an act of execution. I believe that the killer wanted to take the place of the state and to execute Hasunuma. There are different ways of executing people. In Japan, we use hanging. In America, they've got a long history with the electric chair, even if lethal injection is much more common now. There were also some states that until recently used the gas chamber. It's a method of execution which involves confining a person in a small room and killing them by filling it with hydrocyanic acid gas."

"'Confining a person in a small room . . .'" A vivid image of Hasunuma lying dead in the tiny converted storeroom came to Kusanagi. "You think that the killer wanted to carry out the death sentence using the gas-chamber method?"

"It's pure speculation on my part. Then again, as a method of killing, it has a second benefit."

"What's that?"

"The killer doesn't need to lay so much as a finger on Hasunuma. With the door of the room locked and Hasunuma shut up inside, it's possible to follow through with the murder even if he regains consciousness halfway through. Oh, and that reminds me, slipping a garbage bag over Hasunuma's head and pumping helium into the bag is a very risky method, because there's the danger of Hasunuma waking up and fighting back. If, however, he was sleeping so deeply that you didn't need to worry about him waking up, then why use helium at all? Why not just tie up his wrists and ankles while he was unconscious and strangle him or stab him? Don't you agree?"

Kusanagi groaned. Yukawa's arguments were typically logical and persuasive.

"To be quite frank, I've no idea what the killer's purpose was," Kusanagi admitted reluctantly. "No doubt there was a reason why he adopted this particular method, but I don't think we need to worry about that right now. Isn't it better if we catch the guy and get *him* to tell *us*?"

Yukawa nodded simply. "That's the most rational and reliable thing to do."

"What's important is that we now know that we can classify Hasunuma's death as a murder. I told you I'd be staying here in Kikuno for a while. The decision has been made to set up an investigation task force at the Kikuno Police Station. Starting tomorrow, things are going to ratchet up a notch. I invited you out this evening because we'll probably have fewer opportunities to discuss things in the days ahead."

That makes sense, thought Yukawa, his expression softening. He picked up his tumbler. "At any rate, you're now the bigwig chief inspector at Homicide."

Kusanagi winced. "Please don't call me that."

"Here's to solving the case." Yukawa lifted up his tumbler.

As he reached for his glass to join in the toast, Kusanagi discovered he had finished his Guinness. He called out to the bartender to bring him another.

25

It was the day after Kusanagi met for drinks with Yukawa that the police managed to identify the fingerprints on the helium gas tank.

The fingerprints belonged to a man by the name of Morimoto. He was the owner of an auto repair business in North Kikuno.

Kusanagi got one of the investigators to look into Morimoto. He couldn't find any link between Morimoto and Hasunuma; nor could he find any point of contact between Morimoto and Saori Namiki or anyone else in the Namiki family.

He did, however, uncover one very interesting fact. As a director of the North Kikuno Neighborhood Association, Morimoto helped run the festival singing contest on the day of the parade, and free balloons had been handed out to children at the contest venue.

Kusanagi decided that they needed to bring Morimoto in for questioning. He was willing to believe that Morimoto had nothing to do with the killing but his fingerprints were on the "murder weapon." Kusanagi sent a few officers to pick Morimoto up in case he tried to make a run for it.

That proved unnecessary as Morimoto, although confused, came along quietly.

Kusanagi assigned Kishitani to question Morimoto. While that interview was in progress, he joined Utsumi and Muto in the conference room to prep for their first big investigation meeting.

"It doesn't look as if we'll get much joy from the security cameras near the crime scene," said Muto, despondently. "We found one in a metered parking lot nearby, but there were no suspicious vehicles in the footage."

Kusanagi groaned and looked at Utsumi, who was sitting beside him. "What about the 'likely suspects'? Did you manage to track their movements on security-camera footage?"

"Partly, yes." Utsumi swiveled her laptop around so that Kusanagi could see the screen.

It was a still image from an outdoor security camera that showed a large number of pedestrians walking in opposing directions.

"This particular camera is near the end point of the parade. I believe that this man in the navy-blue jacket is Tomoya Takagaki." Utsumi pointed at a section of the screen.

Although Kusanagi had only ever seen a photograph of Tomoya Takagaki and the resolution of the CCTV image was on the low side, he was pretty sure that Utsumi's identification of him was correct. He was looking off to the side onto the street, rather than in front of him, which suggested that he was walking and watching the parade at the same time. The time stamp was just after two in the afternoon.

"The young man and woman we see here walking alongside Tomoya Takagaki must be his colleagues from work. The video footage shows them chatting to one another. Do you want to watch it?"

"No need. Have you got any later footage of them?"

"I've asked our local precinct colleagues to look. They haven't found any yet."

"Okay," replied Kusanagi, resuming his scrutiny of the image.

Tomoya Takagaki didn't have a backpack or any other item of baggage. Nor did his male companion, though the girl did have a small shoulder bag.

A few days ago, Utsumi reported that Tomoya Takagaki had no alibi for between three thirty and four in the afternoon. The problem was, what could he actually *achieve* in such a short period of time?

"And the other avengers?" Kusanagi asked.

Kusanagi had come up with the "avengers" nickname for the group of people he thought likeliest to have killed Hasunuma. That meant all three members of the Namiki family; Saori's boyfriend, Tomoya Takagaki; and Naoki Niikura, Saori's manager.

Tapping a few more keys, Utsumi pulled up a different image. It was a different location this time with what looked like the entrance to a post office on the right-hand side.

"This is the Niikuras."

Utsumi pointed to a man in late middle age wearing a brown bomber jacket and a woman in a violet cardigan. They were standing side by side and looking out toward the road. Neither of them was holding or carrying anything and Kusanagi couldn't see any baggage at their feet, either. The time stamp said 2:25 P.M.

"This would be exactly when Team Kikuno started marching," Utsumi said. "That's probably why the Niikuras start moving soon after. They were probably following Team Kikuno. Since that was bringing up the rear, plenty of other people decided to do the same thing."

"There should be more security cameras on this stretch of road," Muto chimed in. "If we examine the footage from them, we should be able to track the Niikuras' subsequent movements. Let's get anyone on the team who's free to trawl through the footage for them."

"Good idea," Kusanagi agreed, with the briefest hint of a smile. His expression tensed the moment he returned his eyes to the screen.

The fact that neither Takagaki Tomoya nor the Niikuras were carrying any baggage bugged him. The murder of Hasunuma required at least one tank of helium, and a gas tank that was close to sixteen inches high and twelve inches wide would require a very large bag or backpack.

Of course, the killer could always have stashed the tank somewhere in advance and picked it up later. In that case, though, where could it have been hidden?

Kusanagi called Muto over. "Inspector Muto, I need you to go through this video footage and check for anyone with a large item of luggage. We're looking for something big enough to hold that helium tank we found."

"Yes, sir," said Muto, grasping what his superior wanted. His eyes gleaming with enthusiasm, he left the room.

Kusanagi and Utsumi then started compiling the documentation they needed for the investigation meeting. They were still at it when Kishitani came into the room, having finished interviewing Morimoto.

"We'll need confirmation but my impression is that Mr. Morimoto is clean. According to Forensics, all of the fingerprints on the helium tank belong to him. That tells us something important." There was a glint of smugness in Kishitani's eyes. "The gas tank was stolen."

"How did you work that out?"

"On the day of the parade, Morimoto was distributing balloons to children in the park where the singing contest was held. He started at three thirty P.M. He had about one hundred balloons and three tanks of helium. As one tank is enough for around forty balloons, he had slightly more gas than he needed. When I showed him the tank we found in the weeds, he confirmed that it was the same type."

Kishitani looked down at his notes, then went on with his report.

As a director of the neighborhood association, Morimoto had a range of tasks to perform. These tasks often took him away from his post. Since he had no one helping him with the balloons, when he went on an errand, he would take the uninflated balloons with him, but leave the gas tanks behind.

The first time he left his station was at about 4:30 P.M. When he got back around fifteen minutes later, he was about to start distributing more balloons, when he realized something wasn't quite right. Despite him having only just switched out the gas tanks, there was no helium coming out of the new one. When he took a closer look, he discovered that the tank was the first out of the three, which was already empty. *That's a bit odd*, he thought, but he switched to a new tank and went on filling and handing out balloons. In the end, he handed out around sixty balloons in total. He had enough gas and didn't experience any difficulties.

"Morimoto realized that the second canister had been stolen while he was away from his station. Since he didn't run out of helium and wasn't too keen to alert people to his own negligence, he didn't mention the theft of the tank to anyone else." Kishitani looked up from his notes. "When I spoke to him, I found him quite credible."

"That would mean that the gas tank was stolen between four thirty and four forty-five P.M. Remind me, what's the distance between the park where the singing contest was held and the crime scene?"

"Approximately two miles," replied Kishitani promptly. He had obviously anticipated Kusanagi's question. "Hasunuma's body was discovered at five thirty. A car would be essential to travel between the two locations in that time frame."

"I see . . ."

This cleared Tomoya Takagaki of any suspicion. By 4 P.M., Tomoya Takagaki was already in the beer bar with his coworkers.

And then—

It also cleared the Niikuras. They were both judges for the singing contest, which had started at 5 P.M. Even if they had used a car, they couldn't have committed the murder.

"The first thing we've got to do is look for witnesses. Ideally, we want someone who saw the tank being stolen; failing that, someone who saw a person carrying an item of suspicious-looking luggage. Someone lugging around a large piece of baggage would stick out like a sore thumb at a singing contest! Next, we need to check the footage on any security cameras in or around the park. The metered parking lots will all have cameras, so why not start with those? If you find anyone suspicious, try and figure out who they are. Let's be systematic about this."

"Yes, sir." Kishitani picked up his notebook.

"Got any ideas, Utsumi?" Kusanagi asked, turning to his subordinate sitting next to him.

"Traffic restrictions were being enforced on the main roads because of the parade," said Utsumi calmly. "And there were lots of pedestrians. The number of viable routes from the park to the crime scene was probably limited. It's possible that a vehicle got picked up on the N-System somewhere along the way."

"Great idea. Work with the Kikuno Police Station guys. Check every vehicle that was logged on N-System in the vicinity of the crime scene in the half hour between four thirty and five on the day of the incident." There was a note of excitement in Kusanagi's voice.

"Yes, sir," Utsumi said. Her tone was lukewarm and her mind seemed to be elsewhere.

"What's wrong? Something bothering you?"

"Well . . . uhm . . . yes. I still don't understand why the perpetrator choose such a convoluted method of killing?"

"That again?" Kusanagi grimaced. "Who cares? We'll find out soon enough when the killer confesses. Even Yukawa's accepted that."

"Professor Yukawa?"

"I saw him last night."

Kusanagi told Utsumi about meeting with Yukawa at the trendy local bar.

"Now that we've found physical evidence, we need to push things forward hard and fast. I intend to throw all the manpower we've got

at this problem. We'll do whatever it takes to find the person who
transported the helium tank from the park to the crime scene."

After delivering this rousing speech, Kusanagi consulted his
watch. Now that the investigation task force was officially up and
running, Director Mamiya was supposed to put in an appearance.

*We need to be able to report some progress. Otherwise I won't be able to
look him in the eye*, he thought to himself.

26

Detective Sergeant Utsumi took a deep breath as she looked up at the imposing gray building. She didn't know why she was feeling so nervous. Even when she interrogated the toughest of criminals, she was never this anxious.

As she walked up to the front entrance, her eyes were drawn to the metal plaque on the wall: TEITO UNIVERSITY METALS MATERIALS RESEARCH INSTITUTE. The sans serif font felt cold and aloof. To her, it seemed to be looking down on the visitors.

She went in. There was a small office on the right, with a gray-haired guard sitting inside. She filled out the form he handed her and slipped a lanyard and visitor pass over her head. When she asked for directions, the reply was terse and ungracious: "Third floor, far end," the guard said.

She rode the elevator to the third floor and made her way down the long corridor. There was a whole series of doors. On one of them was a sign that read MAGNETISM RESEARCH SECTION, and beneath that RESEARCH LABORATORY 1 and RESEARCH LABORATORY 2. Kaoru was supposed to go to the Magnetism Research Section: Chief Research Officer's Room.

Utsumi took another deep breath and knocked on the door.

"Come in." Utsumi felt a twinge of nostalgia when she heard the resonant voice.

"Hello?" She pushed the door open. In front of her was some armchairs and beyond that, a desk. The person sitting at the desk spun briskly around in his chair. "Very nice to see you."

There was a moment's silence. "It's been a long time," Utsumi said with a little bow.

Manabu Yukawa rose slowly to his feet.

"I wasn't expecting you to get in touch. With the task force up and running, I thought you'd be too busy."

"You're right. As I said in my message, my visit today is much more than a simple courtesy call."

"Let's get straight down to business, then." Yukawa dropped into one of the armchairs and motioned with his open palm for her to sit in the one opposite.

"Thank you," said Kaoru, sitting down. "Has our unit chief explained to you how Kanichi Hasunuma was killed?"

"When you use terminology like 'unit chief,' I'm not quite sure who you're talking about." Yukawa narrowed his eyes behind his lenses. "Yes, Kusanagi told me: the combination of helium gas and a plastic bag."

"What do you think?"

"Think? If you mean, do I think it's scientifically plausible? Then yes, I do."

"It was slightly different from your own theory, Professor."

"There's nothing odd about that. In science, we create hundreds of hypotheses, most of which end up being proved wrong."

"Don't you have any doubts about it?"

"Doubts? In what way?"

"Doubts about that method."

Yukawa's jaw twitched and his eyes became cold and rational. He looked hard and appraisingly at Utsumi.

"What is it?"

"Kusanagi told me. That you were critical of the method of killing. That you couldn't understand the point of anything so grandiose and convoluted."

"Yes, but I was prepared to accept it after Chief Kusanagi explained the theory to me in greater detail. The method of killing you deduced, Professor, came with real advantages for the killer. As for the deduction that the small room where the crime took place was a substitute gas chamber—that is the sort of idea that only you could have come up with."

"Nonetheless, ingenious though my deductions were, they were also wrong, so they mean nothing."

"Wrong? . . . Do you really think so? I'm inclined to think you were right, Professor."

Yukawa was breathing hard and his chest was visibly rising and falling. He fixed his eyes on Kaoru. "Why do you say that?"

"First, there's the issue of the nature and quantity of the sleeping medication. Based on the traces that were found in Hasunuma's bloodstream, the sleeping medication he took wasn't very powerful; nor did he take it in any significant quantity. If he was asleep, his state was far from comatose. He would probably have woken up if anybody had touched him. In terms of making sure that he wouldn't wake up while the crime was in progress, the method you proposed seems far likelier to succeed. I even think that the killer might have deliberately made a lot of noise *specifically* in order to wake Hasunuma up after locking the sliding door."

"Deliberately woken him up?" Yukawa frowned. "What for?"

"To frighten him."

"To frighten him." Yukawa gazed at Utsumi admiringly and straightened himself against the back of his chair. "That's certainly novel."

"I was working on the hypothesis that the motive in the Hasunuma killing was revenge. I tried to imagine how I would take revenge if someone had murdered a member of my family. I certainly wouldn't slip a plastic bag over anyone's head and use helium to kill them through oxygen deficiency. And the reason is not because it's too convoluted or troublesome. Why do you think it is?"

Yukawa shook his head. "I don't know."

"There've been a lot of articles on the internet recently about using helium to commit suicide. Do you know why?"

Yukawa thought for a moment. "Perhaps," he murmured, "because you can die . . . comfortably?"

"Correct." Utsumi gave a crisp nod. "If helium works fast, you can lose consciousness with your first breath and then go on to die from there. You barely suffer. But would anyone deliberately select a method like that to kill someone whom they *hated*? If it was me, I'd choose a method that caused maximum pain and fear."

"There's some truth—" said Yukawa, crossing his long legs. "No, I think there's a great deal of truth in what you're saying. It's highly logical and persuasive."

"That's why I think your theory is right: The killer deliberately wakes Hasunuma up and only then does he start pumping the helium into the room. The oxygen concentration gradually goes down. Hasunuma starts to feel nauseous and gets a headache. He's trapped. He's got to be feeling intensely afraid."

"In other words, it's the perfect way to execute a cold-blooded killer. It's a very original idea, but it does have one problem: the very large amount of helium required."

"That's what I thought, too." Kaoru bit her lip. "Nobody helped themselves to one of the gas cylinders used for the giant inflatable mascot, and if the killer had bought a high-pressure cylinder, there'd be some trace of the purchase. . . ."

Yukawa broke into a beatific smile.

"Is something wrong, Professor?"

"No, no. It's just been a long time, so I'm feeling a bit sentimental. Here I am with a beautiful young lady detective theorizing her heart out in front of me."

"I'm hardly young anymore."

"But you'll accept the beautiful label?"

Kaoru scowled at her old friend. "If you're going to make fun of me, I'll just leave."

"What have you learned about the helium tank that was found?" asked Yukawa, ignoring her threat.

"We know that it was being used in Kikuno Park on the day of the parade and we know what time it was stolen. The man who was looking after it had an alibi."

"That sounds like a bounteous harvest to me. You don't think so?"

Utsumi couldn't suppress a sigh.

"Is there a witness who saw the tank being stolen? Are there any reports of a suspicious-looking person carrying a package or luggage big enough to hold the helium tank? Is there any useful footage on any of the nearby security cameras? I've been running around like mad since yesterday hunting for answers to all those questions. That's what I've been doing since early this morning, too—with absolutely *nothing* to show for it."

"I'm sorry to hear that. People started piling into the area early in the morning on the day of the parade to secure a good spot; the sidewalks were absolutely heaving. It'll be like looking for the proverbial needle in a haystack," Yukawa said.

"If that helium tank played a part in the crime, timing issues mean that the killer must have made use of a vehicle. There's a major road he would have to cross to get from the park to the crime scene. There's an N-System monitoring device on that particular intersection, so we've managed to identify all the vehicles that passed that way in the relevant time period, but . . ."

"You can't find anyone who's linked to the case?"

"Exactly. You talked about a 'bounteous harvest,' but I have the opposite impression. As far as I can see, finding that helium tank only served to knock the whole investigation off course."

Yukawa crossed his arms on his chest and leaned back in his armchair. "That's a serious allegation."

"You think? Anyway, shall we keep it between the two of us?" said Utsumi, lowering her voice. "Did Kusanagi tell you where the helium tank was found?"

"He said something about a patch of weeds."

"Yes, a patch of weeds only about sixty-five feet from the crime scene. Close enough to be within the radius of any police search. That helium tank was literally crying out to be found. *Plus*, there was Hasunuma's hair. *Plus*, the tank had fingerprints on it that made it easy to work out when and where it was stolen. The whole thing strikes me as just a little too convenient. We then use this piece of physical evidence to work out the killer's movements, and what do we end up with? The most likely suspects now have alibis that hold up perfectly."

"I agree about keeping this between ourselves. I'm planning to drop in to Namiki-ya any day now."

"Oh, sorry, Professor. The chief told me you're one of the regulars there."

"The vegetable *takiawase* is a culinary masterpiece," Yukawa said. A dreamy look flitted across his face, then he was all business again. "What you're saying is that the helium tank the police found was nothing more than a decoy designed to confuse the investigation?"

"I think it's a very real possibility. My theory is that a different helium tank was in fact used, which was then disposed of somewhere else. But"—Utsumi cocked her head—"I still have my doubts about the method of killing. Why should the perpetrator be so obsessed with helium? What's the point of such a fixation?"

"You're wondering why he fetishized helium?" said Yukawa. Suddenly, he drew a breath sharply, then frowned, gazed off into the middle distance for a while, and finally expelled all the air in his lungs, slowly and loudly.

"Had an idea?" Utsumi asked.

"At the crime scene, there was a sheet on the floor with a mattress and a quilt on top. That's where Hasunuma was lying."

"I believe that's right, yes. Does it mean something to you?"

Yukawa didn't answer right away. He was looking down, deep in thought.

"Professor?" Utsumi said.

"Just wait a moment." The physicist hushed her by holding up his hand, palm out.

After a minute or so, Yukawa looked up again.

"There's something I want you to look into for me. Ask Forensics; they should be able to do it."

"What is it?" Utsumi reached hastily for her notebook.

"It's several things, in fact. I'll go through them with you later. There's something else I want to deal with first. Now, am I right in thinking that Kusanagi has made up his mind that the Hasunuma case is connected with Saori Namiki's unnatural death and that he isn't pursuing any other lines of inquiry?"

"Such as what?"

"Well, there've got to be other people who bore Hasunuma ill will. Take Kusanagi as an example: He's got his own special feelings for Hasunuma."

Utsumi realized what Yukawa was getting at.

"Because of the other unresolved case from twenty-three years ago . . . Let me have a look." She flipped opened her notebook and found the victim's name. "You're talking about the family of Yuna Motohashi?"

"They're a possibility."

"Possible—but unlikely."

"Why so?"

"Simple. Too much time has passed. Yes, the case was brutal and the court's verdict was unconscionable. Her family had every right to feel embittered. But that strikes me as a very good reason for why, if they were planning to take revenge, they would have done so earlier. Why should they suddenly pick now as the right time for retribution?"

"We'd need to ask them that. They could have their reasons. Either way, I don't think it's smart to reject the possibility out of hand. Will you be informing Kusanagi of your visit here today?"

"Yes," Utsumi replied. "I don't want him to think I'm trying to keep it secret."

"In that case, could you give him a message? Even if he doesn't have much faith in my hunch, he should take a look at the victim's family and any other people of interest in the Yuna Motohashi murder case. He may find a link to the present case. No, I *guarantee* that he will."

Yukawa spoke with such force that Utsumi felt almost uncomfortable.

"Where does your sense of conviction come from, Professor Yukawa? How can you be so unequivocal?"

"The reason is—" Yukawa held up his index finger. "If my latest hypothesis is correct, then as things stand now, we're only missing a single piece to complete the puzzle. And that piece must exist in the past."

27

Hearing the sound of raucous laughter, Natsumi looked away from her phone and up at the television. A popular comedian was swimming in a dirty river. Natsumi had heard that this show, which featured different television personalities tackling a range of challenges, was very popular. She'd tuned in for the first time tonight, but it quickly bored her and she'd switched her attention to social media.

Glancing up at the clock, she saw that it was just before 8 P.M. At Namiki-ya, it was a time-hallowed custom to keep the television on even when the restaurant was empty. They didn't want potential customers who looked in to get the impression that the place was lifeless. Typically, at this time of night, they would have the channel set to NHK, the national broadcaster. Now, because they didn't want to watch the news, it was set to another channel. Crimes and disasters, even ones that didn't involve them directly, were the last thing they wanted to hear about.

Customers had noticeably declined since Hasunuma's death. A few people would wander in around seven o'clock, but otherwise the place was deserted. In the eyes of the public, the restaurant was run by murder suspects and people wanted to give it a wide berth. The Namikis could hardly put up a sign out front that said: EVERYONE HERE HAS AN ALIBI.

Natsumi saw a silhouette from the outside of the sliding glass door. She was on her feet before the door even opened.

It was Yukawa who walked in. "Welcome," said Natsumi with studied cheerfulness.

Yukawa looked around the restaurant and selected a four-person table.

"Beer and the *takiawase*. Then I'll have the miso-simmered mackerel," Yukawa said, as he wiped his hands on the wet towel Natsumi had handed him.

She went back to the kitchen and relayed the order to Yutaro, then returned, carrying a tray with a bottle of beer, a glass, and the day's appetizer to Yukawa's table. The appetizer of the day was spicy *konnyaku.*

"This is unusual timing for you."

"Someone I'd not seen for years dropped by to see me and we got to talking."

"Oh, that's what happened. I suppose the people who drop in to see you are all physicists?"

"No, it was the antithesis of a physicist." Taking off his glasses, Yukawa began wiping the lenses with a cloth. "In fact, it was a detective."

"What? . . . Another detective came to see you?"

"This was a different detective, one I've known for a long time."

"Oh really?"

A physicist and a detective—what can the link between them be? Natsumi wondered.

"By the way, has Mr. Tojima been in yet?" asked Yukawa, putting his spectacles back on his nose.

"Tojima? Not yet, but he'll be here soon enough. Have you arranged to meet him?"

"No. I just thought it'd be nice to have someone to chat to. He's about the only regular I know who's always here at this time."

"You're right about that."

Even after Hasunuma's death, her father's childhood friend Tojima was still coming to the restaurant regularly, and would make a point of asking Natsumi if everything was all right. He would never get too specific, but it was obvious that, in his own way, he was worried about her and her parents. Natsumi was grateful.

Yukawa had nearly finished his dinner by the time the man in question appeared. "Evening all. Hey there, Professor. Okay if I sit with you?" said Tojima, already pulling out a chair for himself on the opposite side of the table.

"Go ahead," conceded Yukawa with a smile.

Tojima ordered his usual beer.

"The professor was waiting for you to show up. Said he wanted somebody to talk to."

Tojima grinned.

"I'm honored. If you're okay with an old geezer like me, I'm happy to have a drink with you anytime. I should warn that I don't have a whole lot to talk about. I'm not a betting man and I don't have any interesting hobbies."

"Perhaps your work is your hobby?"

"That's a nice way to put it, but yes, I suppose it is." Tojima patted his hair, which was combed straight back from his forehead.

When Natsumi brought him a bottle of beer, he filled his glass and clinked glasses with Yukawa.

"Shall we talk about your work, then?" Yukawa said. "Now, if I remember right, the firm you manage is a food processor. What's your big product?"

"You really want to know?" Tojima sipped his beer appreciatively. "Well, our biggest earner right now is boil-in-the bag foods. They can be stored at room temperature, which makes them very popular these days, when e-commerce is such a big thing. And actually, they don't taste half bad. You wouldn't want to compare them with the food you get here at Namiki-ya, but they can certainly hold their own against your average restaurant."

"Interesting. How about frozen food?"

"Of course, we handle that, too," Tojima said. "It's a key product line, up there with boil-in-the-bag. The big sellers are fried rice dishes and *gyoza* dumplings."

"What kind of freezers do you use?"

"Huh—? Freezers? When you say what type . . . ?"

"There are different types of freezers: screw compressor, reciprocating compressor, and so on. What type do you use at your factory?"

Tojima laughed and threw himself back in his chair.

"The things you academics are interested in! Not like ordinary people. Do you really care?"

"I'm sorry. People often tell me I'm weird."

"I think it's great. What was the question again?"

"About the freezers you use."

"Oh, of course. We mainly use the screw-compressor type."

"You said mainly. Have you got some other ones, too?"

"Yes, for very specific purposes . . ."

"The cell walls of food suffer less damage if food is frozen very fast, don't they? I assume you use a special quick freezer for the more delicate foods?"

"I'll be damned. You really know your stuff." Tojima sounded rather less enthusiastic than before.

There was the rattle of the sliding door. Looking toward the entrance, Natsumi saw a middle-aged woman walk in. She wasn't a regular, although she did come in from time to time. She held up four fingers. "Party of four?" she said.

"Yes, no problem. Please, come in." Natsumi led the group to a table for six.

After that group, a second group—three women of around the same age as the first group—came in. As they settled down, Natsumi handed them their cold rolled towels and took their orders. She got the impression from the way they spoke to one another that they were old friends. They had just been to see a play and were all chattering away at the top of their voices.

As she moved back and forth between their table and the kitchen, Natsumi could no longer keep tabs on Yukawa and Tojima's conversation. Things seemed to be going less than swimmingly. The expression on Tojima's face was getting grimmer by the minute.

Yukawa eventually raised his hand and summoned Natsumi over to the table. "Could I get the check, please?" he asked.

He settled up. "That was most informative. Thanks very much," he said to Tojima and left the restaurant.

Tojima then asked for his check. Natsumi worked out what he owed and brought the check to his seat.

"What time did the professor get here tonight?" Tojima inquired in a low voice, as he dug a handful of thousand yen notes out of his wallet.

"About eight, I think."

"Doesn't he normally come earlier?"

"Yes, he does. He was catching up with an old friend. That's why he was later than usual today." Perhaps influenced by Tojima, Natsumi also lowered her voice. "His friend is a detective."

"A detective?" Tojima's eyebrows shot up. "What business does an academic have with a detective?"

"I didn't ask. . . ."

Tojima looked preoccupied and said nothing.

When Natsumi returned with his change, Tojima put it in his wallet without checking it and without a word of thanks. He marched to the back of the restaurant and said a few words to Yutaro in the kitchen. Eventually, he turned away from the counter and headed for the door. "Thank you very much. Good night," he said to Natsumi and went out.

Natsumi peered into the kitchen. Yutaro was busy at the fryer.

"Daddy, what did old Tojima say to you?"

"Nothing much. Just some neighborhood gossip," Yutaro replied, without leaving off his work.

Natsumi's and Machiko's eyes met. Her mother, who was standing farther back in the kitchen, had her head cocked slightly to one side. Natsumi guessed that she hadn't heard what the two men had been talking about, either.

"What are you doing staring into space like that?" Yutaro said to Machiko. "Get a move on or the food will get cold."

"Oh . . . ah . . . sorry." She quickly put a rolled omelet onto a plate.

"There, I'm done. Natsumi, serve this, would you?" said Yutaro testily, as he dumped a plate heaped with fried mackerel on the counter.

28

He went to his room to change into his sweatpants. When he got back to the dining room, dinner was neatly arranged on the table. There was a big dish of grilled ginger pork and a smaller dish of spinach salad, along with miso soup with lumps of tofu in it. It was a classic family meal.

Tomoya Takagaki sat down, put his phone on the table, and placed his hands together in a gesture of gratitude. "This looks delicious."

"You deserve it," said Rie, his mother, placing a small bowl heaped with rice in front of him. "It's not like you to be back so late."

"I was nearly done for the day, when my section chief had a sudden change of heart. 'Sorry, Takagaki, but I'm going to need these designs ready first thing tomorrow morning.' I get that he wants to please the client, but he should think a bit about us, too."

With a sigh, he reached out with his chopsticks to help himself to some grilled ginger pork. By the clock on the wall, it was nearly 10 P.M. Tomoya had never done more than two hours of overtime before in his life.

Poor old you.

Since she had already finished her meal, Rie walked over to the sink and started doing the washing up. Tomoya looked at her from behind. She had turned fifty the month before. She definitely seemed to have more gray hair than before; or perhaps she was just too busy to go to the hairdresser.

Rie was an excellent cook. The taste of the grilled ginger pork was a little more intense than usual tonight, but when you mixed in the generous helpings of shredded cabbage she served with it, the flavors balanced out perfectly.

He had just polished off the last grain of rice in his bowl, when his phone started to vibrate. He blanched when he saw the incoming caller's name: it was Tojima.

He got to his feet, grabbed his phone, and went out into the hall.

"Takagaki here," he whispered.

"It's me, Tojima. Can you talk now?" Tojima's voice was so low that Tomoya immediately started feeling nervous.

"Yes. What's the problem?"

"Has anything odd happened since we last met? Have any more detectives been around to see you?"

"No, nothing I can think of . . ."

"That's good."

"Why? Has . . . uhm . . . something happened?"

"Yeah." There was a brief pause. "It's that professor fellow," Tojima said.

"Sorry? Professor?"

"Professor Yukawa. You see him all the time at Namiki-ya."

"Oh, him." Tomoya was puzzled. It wasn't a name he'd been expecting to hear. He knew Yukawa quite well. Although something of an oddball, the professor was very knowledgeable and well worth talking to. "What's he done?"

"You need to watch out for him."

"Wha—? Watch out? Why?"

"Because it looks like he's poking around the Hasunuma business. Plus, I heard that he's pals with a detective. He may have been asked to spy on us."

"*Him?*"

In his mind's eye, Tomoya pictured Yukawa. He really didn't strike him as the spying kind.

"Planning to pop into Namiki-ya anytime soon?"

"Namiki-ya? No plans to go, no."

"Best hold off on it for a while, then. That fellow—the professor—if you bump into him, he might start asking you all sorts of questions. I thought we were talking about something completely different, but he suddenly starts asking me all these really on-the-nose questions, as if it were the most natural thing in the world. He even asked me to account for my movements on the day of the parade, for God's sake!"

"He asked you that?"

"Yeah. Caught me completely off guard and I panicked. What

surprised me even more was when he suddenly brought up, you know—I mean, when he starts asking me about my freezer systems."

"How could he even—?"

"Search me. Anyway, that's what happened, so I'm advising you to stay well away from the guy. If he phones you and asks to meet, make up an excuse."

"Got it. I'll be on my guard."

"Good. Bye, then."

Tojima was about to hang up, so Tomoya hastily blurted out, "Oh, uh, Mr. Tojima, wait. I . . . uh . . . something's really bugging me."

"What?"

"What actually happened. And who did what."

He heard a heavy sigh.

"Haven't I told you a thousand times? The less you know, the better."

"But—"

"All right, Takagaki," Tojima interrupted. "It's like I said at the start of this. Tell the truth, if you absolutely have to. You don't have to lie and you don't need to hide anything. Again, the less you know, the better off you'll be. Got that? I'm going to hang up now."

Tomoya couldn't accept what Tojima was telling him. At the same time, he didn't know how to express his reservations. He knew that Tojima was thinking about what was best for him.

Before he could say another word, the phone went dead. He could imagine Tojima wincing at his whining.

Feeling dejected, he went back into the dining room. Seated at the far side of the table, Rie was looking at him intently. He started.

"You've finished the dishes?" Tomoya said, sitting down and picking up his chopsticks.

"Who was it?" Rie asked.

"A colleague from work. The section chief's demanding the impossible from him, too."

"Why are you lying to me?" Rie was leaning forward and peering up into his face.

"I'm not lying." Tomoya looked away.

"You said 'Namiki-ya.' I heard you."

A wave of anger coursed through him. He felt hot all over.

"Then you heard wrong. Why would I be talking to him about Namiki-ya?"

"Well, what did you say? Tell me."

"Oh, just shut up," snapped Tomoya, unable to meet her gaze. "It's nothing to do with you. Just back off."

"If my son's mixed up in any funny business, I've no intention of backing off."

"'Funny business'? What are you talking about?" Tomoya lifted his face and looked at his mother. He recoiled. Her eyes were red and tearful.

"That's what *I* want to know. What have you done? What have you got yourself involved in?" Rie's voice was shaking. "I heard you saying something about being on your guard. On your guard against what?"

Tomoya looked away again. "It's nothing you need to worry about, Mom."

"Then tell me. Tell me the truth. Please."

Tomoya put down his chopsticks. "Thanks for dinner," he said and got to his feet. He no longer had any appetite.

"Just tell me this one thing," said Rie, in a pleading voice. "That incident a little while ago—you know, when the man who murdered Saori died—you weren't involved with that, were you?"

"Of course I wasn't."

Tomoya again thanked his mother for dinner and turned on his heel. As he headed for his room, there was a welter of confused emotions in his chest.

Then tell me. Tell me the truth. Please. His mother's words echoed in his brain.

Tomoya knew exactly how she was feeling.

29

Naoki Niikura was sitting on the sofa in his living room talking on his cell phone. Tojima was on the other end of the line.

From her husband's expression, Rumi could tell the call wasn't going well.

"By professor, you mean *that* professor? That Yukawa chap? Why should he be asking questions about things like that . . . ?" Niikura scowled.

Rumi had no idea what the two men were talking about. Yukawa, she supposed, must be the academic chap she saw from time to time at Namiki-ya. But what had he done? The expression on her husband's face was unrelentingly grim.

Unable to bear the sight of him looking so miserable, Rumi went out to the kitchen. She decided to prepare for the worst by making herself a nice cup of jasmine tea. It would help calm her nerves.

She switched on the kettle and placed the glass teapot and a teacup on the counter nearby. There was a wide range of different teas lined up in cans on the shelf. She took down her favorite variety of jasmine and was trying to open the lid, when her hand slipped. The can tipped sideways, and the tea leaves scattered over the floor.

She felt a sense of existential misery as she contemplated the mess. She couldn't be bothered to tidy it up and just stood there indecisively, doing nothing.

Why have I ended up like this? Life used to be so good, just one wonderful day after another.

Rumi didn't come from a well-to-do family. Her father, a taxi driver, was a luckless fellow who, according to her mother, said, "Specialized in driving around in circles in the parts of town where no one needed a cab." When Rumi got to the last year of primary school, her mother announced that she would have to start working, too, so she got herself a part-time job at the local supermarket.

When she was on her own, Rumi spent a lot of time listening to music. The high school girl who lived in the apartment next door would give her any CDs she was bored with. Rumi was thrilled, even if the songs weren't the latest hits. She would listen to the albums over and over again until she knew all the melodies and lyrics by heart. The portable CD player that she had begged her mother to get for her was her most prized possession. She would put it in her bag and take it with her whenever she left the house.

While she was in junior high, she made friends with a girl named Kumiko. Kumiko played the piano. They were discussing their favorite songs one day, when out of the blue Kumiko suggested that they go to the karaoke parlor. Rumi was a little startled. Her parents had taken her to karaoke often, but she didn't really think that children were supposed to visit karaoke parlors by themselves.

"It's fine. And the daytime rate's cheaper." Kumiko was clearly an old hand at karaoke.

Early one Saturday afternoon, the two of them went to a parlor near the station. Kumiko insisted that Rumi go first, so, after a little bashful hesitation, she sang one of her favorite songs. It was the first time Rumi had sung in front of anyone other than her parents.

Kumiko's eyes lit up and she clapped along with the music. When the song was over, she declared that Rumi was "incredibly talented." Although Rumi assumed her friend was just being nice, the expression on Kumiko's face was deadly serious when she asked Rumi what other songs she knew and begged her to sing some more.

Everybody likes to be praised. And Rumi enjoyed singing, anyway. She was wondering what song to sing next, when Kumiko picked out a song for her. "Can you sing this one?" A recent hit, it was a difficult song with plenty of high notes.

Rumi hadn't sung it before, but was prepared to give it a go. It felt good when she started to sing along with the backing track. The way she synchronized with the music, it was almost a physical sensation.

Kumiko applauded at the end. "You're better than good, Rumi; you're professional level. You could definitely make it as a singer," she said. It was what she went on to say after that changed Rumi's life. "Let's start a band. I've been looking for someone like you."

Rumi was a little taken aback. She liked to sing, but she'd never thought doing anything with it. As Kumiko poured out her heart and the two of them discussed her idea of starting a band, singing was transformed into a beautiful but realizable dream for Rumi.

They started out as just piano and vocals. They called themselves Milk, a name made by combining some of the syllables in both their names. They began by performing cover versions in amateur competitions but once they realized that was hardly the high road to success, they started to write their own songs. Kumiko handled the composition, while Rumi added lyrics to the finished melodies. She just cobbled words together so they'd be as singable as possible.

When they got to tenth grade, the two of them went to different high schools. Milk, however, continued. It was only in their final year of high school that Kumiko suggested pausing the band so they could focus on their university entrance exams. Rumi was stunned. The two of them had always talked about becoming professional musicians. The idea of going to university had never crossed her mind.

"If you can make it as a professional, the more power to you. In case you can't, you always need a backup plan."

Kumiko's own backup plan was to become a teacher, which was why she was applying for the education department at university.

Kumiko was a logical, dispassionate person. In her mind, dreams were dreams and reality was reality and a clear line divided the two. Rumi was different. She felt that her best friend had drifted away from her and that she had been left all on her own.

When she sat down to discuss her future with her parents, neither of them was especially keen for her to go to university. Since her school grades were rather mediocre, they couldn't see much point in sending her to an expensive private university. Rumi felt the same: Music was all she was interested in doing.

It was at that moment that a club where she'd performed got in touch. Someone had approached them for Milk's contact details. Was it okay for them to give them out? The someone was a musician who was trying to recruit a young female vocalist.

Her interest piqued; Rumi said yes. And that was how she met Naoki Niikura.

Niikura played the synthesizer in several bands as well as composing music and lyrics for other artists. Rumi discovered later that he was well-known in the music world.

Niikura had actually seen Milk perform live on several occasions. That was why when someone floated the idea of putting together a new band, he thought of adding her in on vocals.

When Rumi explained all this to Kumiko, her friend was thrilled. The chance to team up with a group of real professionals was the luckiest of lucky breaks for Rumi. Kumiko was also relieved. She'd been feeling guilty because she'd decided not to restart Milk after its current pause.

Niikura didn't hold back. He promised Rumi he would make her into a star, a household name in Japan. Rumi found his extravagant praise intensely motivating, that only she had the talent necessary to sing the songs he wrote.

After around a year of rehearsals, their band made its debut on a major record label. The first CD they released garnered little attention, but the single they put out afterward was used in the credit sequence of an anime and became a respectable hit.

Rumi started to dream big. *Maybe we can make it.* Rapturously, she imagined herself performing in an arena in front of tens of thousands of fans.

Sadly, real life is seldom so sweet. The new songs they put out got no traction at all, their concert tickets went unsold, and sales of their CDs drifted downward.

They battled on with limpet-like persistence. Niikura was convinced that Rumi's talents would be recognized somewhere down the line.

"You've got something, Rumi. People can't overlook you forever. It's simply can't be," he used to say when he was drunk.

The band stuck together for exactly ten years. Niikura then made a couple of proposals to Rumi, who was on the eve of turning thirty. The first of these was to retire from performing.

"I wasn't able to bring out your full talent. That's my fault. Sadly, I think we've missed our moment as a band. If you want to find someone else to work with, I won't stop you. I can help you if you need an introduction. For myself, though, I plan to retire from on-stage performance."

Rumi accepted what Niikura was saying, but that didn't make her feel any less sad. She felt even worse that he was tying himself up in knots for her sake. He insisted that he was to blame, but Rumi knew full well that wasn't true. It was down to deficiencies in her that the wonderful songs composed by Niikura had failed to get the recognition they deserved.

"I'm so sorry," said Rumi, bursting into tears. "I let you down. I'm sorry. I can't imagine working with anyone else. If you're going to retire, then I'll retire, too."

That was when Niikura made his second proposal. It concerned their shared future. Would Rumi marry him?

Until then, their relationship hadn't been romantic. Despite admiring Niikura and harboring feelings for him, Rumi had worked hard to conceal them. Niikura didn't approve of romantic entanglements between band members.

On the one hand, she was sorry to retire from performing. On the other hand, the joy she felt at Niikura's second proposal was more than enough to compensate. She accepted his proposal on the spot.

From that day on, she and Niikura became a tight-knit team. Niikura moved into the business of finding and nurturing young talent. Making money was never his primary goal—and his family was sufficiently well-off that he could safely take that approach. Rumi worked behind the scenes to support her husband. The second phase of their life was by no means a disappointment. Their inability to have children was the only thing that didn't go according to plan. When, however, they sent the young artists they had discovered out into the world, they got a sense of quasi-parental satisfaction from watching their "children" making their own way.

Time passed. Eventually, they stumbled upon an extraordinary raw talent: Saori Namiki. Rumi would never forget the thrill of hearing Saori sing for the first time.

The glory of her voice and her technical skill as a singer were both overpowering. *This girl's talent is of a completely different order to mine. She is a born singer,* Rumi told herself. At the same time, she was further excited by the enthusiasm she could feel coming off Niikura, who was sitting beside her.

"I want to manage that girl," Niikura said, as they made their way home from the cultural festival where they had seen Saori perform. He spoke in a monotone, but Rumi could feel the extraordinary conviction behind what he was saying.

The passion Niikura devoted to training Saori was astonishing. Eager to elevate his new protégée's abilities to the highest possible level, he put everything he had on the line for her. Inevitably, Rumi saw echoes of the past, when Niikura had been guiding her career. It was obvious that he was taking a second run at the dream that he had failed to realize with her.

Naturally, Rumi gave him her full support. She and Niikura were spending less time together, but that was only to be expected. Her husband's single-minded obsession with Saori caused Rumi no unease. There was no reason for jealousy.

Under Niikura's direction, Saori made steady progress. Her ability to learn was quite extraordinary. She could pick up techniques quickly that an ordinary person would need months to master. *This is what genius looks like*, thought Rumi in amazement.

They were almost there.

The gateway to success was right in front of them. All they had to do was push it open and a bright, shining road into the future would stretch out before them. They just needed to stay on track and single-mindedly put one foot in front of the other.

But, all of a sudden, their personal treasure was torn away from them. The road to the future was cut off. When Rumi recalled her sense of despair, even now she would start trembling uncontrollably. It was that bad—

"What's wrong?" asked a voice.

The question brought Rumi back to herself. She found herself squatting down on the kitchen floor, the tin of jasmine tea still in her hand.

Niikura was standing over her with an anxious look on his face. "Are you all right?"

"Uh . . . I'm fine." Rumi started sweeping up the tea leaves from the floor. "Finished your call?"

"Uh-huh." There was something ominous in the brevity of his answer. "I got some slightly—no, some very worrying—news."

"What is it?"

"You know that Yukawa guy? The one we've met a few times at Namiki-ya?"

Rumi stopped her sweeping and looked up at her husband. "Yes, I know who you mean."

"He was at Namiki-ya tonight and he was asking Tojima all kinds of questions."

"Him? But why?"

"Apparently, he's got a friend on the police force."

Rumi gasped.

"Tojima thinks the police may have seen through the trick with the helium tank and figured out how Hasunuma was really killed."

Rumi swallowed and put her right hand to her chest. Her heart was beating painfully fast.

Niikura walked over to her. Rumi buried her head in his chest.

"It'll be all right," the husband said to the wife. "There's no need to worry."

30

When you revisit a street that you frequented as a child, it is often far smaller and narrower than you remembered it. This probably comes down to the change in one's physical size. Typically, when, after the interval of a few years, you revisit a street you first saw as an adult, the impression hardly changes.

However, as Kusanagi walked along this particular street after almost two decades, it felt a great deal more cramped than he remembered. As he walked along and looked around him, he finally realized why.

Several big apartment blocks had been built where there had once been low-rise workshops and storehouses. They blocked the view, creating the sense that the already-narrow street had gotten even narrower.

Kusanagi came to a halt before a house. Back when it was surrounded by old, traditional Japanese houses, it had stood out for its elegance with its white façade and Western architecture. Now that it was surrounded by contemporary buildings, it felt more like an anachronism.

"This seems to be the place," Utsumi said. She was standing beside him, looking at the engraved stone nameplate on the front gate. The name was Sawauchi. Nineteen years ago, it had been Motohashi.

"No doubt about it."

Utsumi pressed the button on the intercom.

"Yes," a woman's voice answered almost immediately.

"This is Detective Sergeant Kaoru Utsumi. We spoke on the phone this morning."

"Of course."

Up at the far end of a little path, the front door of the house opened. A little woman with spectacles and silver hair came out. Kusanagi's first impression was of dourness, so he was relieved to see the shadow of a smile playing around her lips.

The woman's name was Sachie Sawauchi and she was the younger sister of Seiji Motohashi. Seiji Motohashi was fifty-two when his daughter Yuna's remains were found. If he were still alive, he would be seventy-one.

Kusanagi got Utsumi to follow up and she found out that Seiji Motohashi had died six years ago. The family firm was now being run by a hired manager, and his sister and her husband had moved into the old Motohashi house over a decade ago.

Sachie Sawauchi showed Kusanagi and Utsumi into a living room furnished with a big leather sofa and armchairs.

Before sitting down, they presented the old woman with the box of candies they had brought for her. Motohashi. She waved her hands in a gesture of deprecation.

"You really shouldn't have."

"We are the ones dropping in on you out of the blue."

"I really don't mind. Anyway, thank you." With a demure little bow, Sachie Sawauchi took the box.

"I'm going to make some tea. Won't you have a seat?"

"There's no need. This is a work visit."

"To be honest, I'd like some for myself. It's not often I get the chance to have a nice cup of tea with visitors." Sachie Sawauchi smiled and left the room.

Kusanagi took a deep breath and turned to his female colleague. "Shall we sit down then?"

"Let's," Utsumi replied.

They sat down on the sofa next to each other. Kusanagi ran his eyes around the room. There were some heavy-looking bookshelves filled with hardbacks, including a number of English books, and some framed paintings of flowers on the walls. Were they the work of a well-known artist? he wondered.

"How does it feel, Chief?" Utsumi asked. "Is it different to when you were here all those years ago?"

"Yes," Kusanagi replied, glancing around the room for a second time. "Completely different, frankly."

"Oh yes?"

"Everything was different then. There'd been a family—a mother, a father, and a daughter. The daughter disappeared at the age of twelve. The mother took her own life soon after. Then, four years after that, the daughter's remains were found in the mountains. That's when I was here. Seiji Motohashi was living on his own, sure, but do you think he'd put away his wife's things and his girl's toys?"

Utsumi sighed sympathetically. "The opposite, I imagine. He probably wanted to keep their things around to remember them."

"Exactly. Everything connected to Yuna was left exactly as it was when she disappeared." Kusanagi pointed at the bookshelf. "There was an upright piano over there with a family portrait on top of it. The room still felt like the living room of a family with a young daughter. Time had stopped for Seiji Motohashi."

Kusanagi remembered being ushered into this room nineteen years ago. He was with Mamiya; they had come to announce the arrest of Hasunuma to Motohashi. "We should be able to crush him with the full might of the law," Mamiya had said confidently.

Kusanagi had never dreamed that he would be back, let alone under these circumstances. The whole experience of the Yuna case had been painful and frustrating, but—assuming that it was all in the past—he had done his best to let go.

He wasn't surprised when Utsumi told him about going to see Professor Yukawa. The two of them were old friends, after all. Their shared interest in Hasunuma's unnatural death was further motivation. Without Yukawa's theories, figuring out how the murder was committed would have taken far more time and trouble.

If he was honest with himself, though, Kusanagi was puzzled when Utsumi had passed on Yukawa's advice about looking into the people connected with what was a twenty-three-year-old case. No doubt, some of the people with links to Yuna Motohashi's murder might still be nursing a grudge against Hasunuma. But why act on it now?

But Yukawa, Utsumi said, had been emphatic that the one missing piece of the puzzle was to be found in the past. When she followed up by asking him what sort of thing to look for, he'd simply said, "Relationships."

"I don't want to plant any preconceptions in your heads. I'll just say this: There's a link of some kind between that old case and the present case. And that link is a person."

As perverse as Yukawa was, though, Kusanagi knew that his powers of deduction were quite extraordinary.

So what was Yukawa's new hypothesis? Kusanagi was eager to know. Their investigation centered around the helium tank found in the clump of weeds was going nowhere fast.

There were multiple security cameras in and around Kikuno Park and they had yielded a considerable amount of footage, even for the fifteen-minute period that was their focus. The task of reviewing it had been divided between many investigators but they had failed to find anyone carrying a case, bag, or box big enough to accommodate the helium tank. The team's current thinking was that the killer must have known where the cameras were located and exited the park via a blind spot.

They imagined that the perpetrator's next move would have been to travel by vehicle from the park to the crime scene. They had, therefore, analyzed the N-System data for the area around the local main road. This, too, had failed to produce any results, despite the traffic restrictions having greatly reduced the number of cars on the road that day.

Another possibility was that the killer had used a bicycle, rather than a car. They started checking footage from the security cameras over an expanded area. They failed to find any suspicious bicycles.

The investigation hit a brick wall. That was when Kusanagi remembered the opinion that Detective Utsumi had so hesitantly proffered: that the helium tank they had found was nothing more than a decoy designed to throw the investigation off track. Yukawa felt the same way.

The main reason that Kusanagi had taken Yukawa's advice and was talking to people associated with the twenty-three-year-old Yuna Motohashi case was that the investigation was flailing and he had no other options.

Sachie Sawauchi came in, pushing a trolley. On it was a hot water dispenser, a Japanese teapot, and three Japanese teacups. She had clearly meant what she said about enjoying teatime with her visitors.

Sachie Sawauchi sat down opposite the two detectives. She briskly poured some boiling water into the teapot, then filled the three cups with green tea.

"Here you go," she said, placing a white teacup in front of Kusanagi.

"Thank you," he said, and took a sip.

"I heard that he's dead," said Sachie Sawauchi, placing another teacup in front of Utsumi. "That Hasunuma fellow; the one they found not guilty in Yuna's case."

"You knew?" Kusanagi asked.

"Yes," she replied softly. "I seldom watch television and I don't do the internet, whatever that is. One of my neighbors told me the news. Even though it all happened twenty years ago, there are always good-natured people who are keen to help." She put sarcastic emphasis on the word *good-natured*. "As soon as you said you were from the Tokyo Metropolitan Police Department on the phone this morning, I knew you'd be coming around to see me."

"We're very sorry for the inconvenience," Utsumi said.

Hasunuma's death had been a major news story over the past few days. The whole world and his dog seemed to know that he had been arrested several months earlier in a murder investigation, then released due to a lack of physical evidence.

"How did you feel when you heard that Hasunuma was dead?" Kusanagi asked.

Sachie Sawauchi looked at him blankly.

"I didn't think or feel anything. Perhaps it's because I never wanted to have to think about that man, ever. Whether he's alive or dead, it makes no difference. All I wanted was never to have to think about him again. How many people suffered because of him? How many people's lives destroyed?" Her face was reddening and her voice rising. She must have realized, because she looked down at the floor and apologized, her voice little more than a whisper. "I'm sorry."

"Your brother . . . Seiji Motohashi . . . he passed away six years ago now?"

"That's right," the silver-haired lady replied. "Cancer of the esophagus. By the end of his life, he was like a chicken, just skin and bone. . . . I think death was probably a release for him. He always said his life was empty of happiness."

The phrase landed like a heavy blow to Kusanagi's gut. "I see . . ."

Sachie Sawauchi ran her eyes briskly around the room.

"My brother lost everything because of what happened to Yuna. He lived a lonely life for years and years, all by himself in this big house. When he got to sixty, he retired from managing the firm and moved into an apartment complex for seniors. He couldn't bear to sell off this piece of land—it's been in our family for generations—so he asked me and my husband to live here. That's why we moved in. We had always lived in a rented apartment before; my husband prefers that. Our only child, a boy, had just left home and we had been talking about moving out of Tokyo and out into the country, anyway. My husband passed away two years ago, so I'm alone here now. It makes me realize just how lonely my poor brother must have been, though. Of course, he suffered in ways I can't even imagine."

"Your brother . . . did you ever talk to him about the case?"

"We discussed it right after the not-guilty verdict came out. We were thinking about gathering signatures for a petition and demanding a retrial. It never happened. Our supporters gradually drifted away. My brother had his company to run and I started getting the sense that he didn't want me bringing it up. He'd certainly never broach the subject himself."

"How about when he was dying?"

"I don't know." Sachie Sawauchi tilted her head to one side. "He must have looked back over his life, I suppose. My guess is that he thought about Yuna's death every day. He never spoke about it in front of us, though. He probably thought it would only make us even more unhappy."

Listening to her, Kusanagi felt a weight in his belly if he had ingested a lump of lead. He couldn't imagine how Seiji Motohashi must have felt. Not only had he lost his whole family but no one had been punished and the truth never brought to light.

"I'm just going to ask you this straight." Kusanagi looked the old woman in the eye. "Did your brother ever think of taking the law into his own hands?"

Sachie Sawauchi's eyes opened wide behind her spectacles. The question had taken her by surprise. She blinked, then said, "You mean avenge Yuna by killing that Hasunuma fellow?"

"Yes."

Sachie Sawauchi cocked her head and looked slantwise down at the floor. After a moment or two, she lifted her face and looked at Kusanagi. "'I'd like to kill the guy'—I certainly heard him say that on a number of occasions. I don't think he actually meant to do it. You only *say* you want to kill someone when you know you can't really *do* it."

"That makes sense. Can you think of someone who's the opposite? Someone who wouldn't *say* anything but might actually *do* something?"

"Someone who would actually take revenge? Oh no, I really don't know." Sachie Sawauchi tilted her head even farther to one side, then began shaking it from side to side. "I can't think of anybody, no. People were angry, but why would anyone who wasn't directly involved go so far?"

She's got a point, thought Kusanagi. *No one would avenge the death of someone else's child.*

"May I?" Utsumi piped up from where she was sitting on the sofa next to Kusanagi. Apparently, she was asking permission to ask a question. He grunted his agreement.

Utsumi turned to Sachie Sawauchi.

"Have you had any reason to think about the Yuna case recently? Has somebody said something to you about it? Asked you something about it?"

Sachie Sawauchi was waving her hand from side to side in a deprecating gesture before Utsumi had even got to the end of her question.

"As I told you, yesterday one of my neighbors told me that Hasunuma was dead. That brought back all sorts of horrible old memories. That aside, no, no one's mentioned it to me for years."

"Do you ever talk about it with your relatives?"

"It happened twenty years ago. There aren't that many people around who still remember those days. My son was still very young then. He doesn't even remember his cousin Yuna."

"Is there anyone who was particularly fond of Yuna who is still alive?"

"I think that would be me," said Sachie Sawauchi, breaking into a grin. "I lived here with the family until Yuna was two. As far as my brother's wife Yumiko was concerned, I was the annoying sister-in-law who was taking far too long to get married! I'm sorry, I really can't think of anyone else. After all, her father and mother are both dead."

"Of course," Utsumi said, then she nodded at Kusanagi.

"What about Yumiko's family?" Kusanagi asked. "They must have adored Yuna."

"No." Sachie Sawauchi was waving her hand again. "Yumiko didn't have any family."

His phone vibrated inside his jacket. He pulled out the cell and saw that it was Kishitani. "Excuse me," he said, turning away from Sachie Sawauchi to take the call. "Yes, what is it?"

"I looked through all the old case files. I couldn't find anyone who looks as though they could be involved in our current case," Kishitani said.

"Okay. Well, thank the guys at the Adachi Police Station and get back to Kikuno," said Kusanagi and hung up. He'd ordered Kishitani to go and review the documentation of the Yuna Motohashi case at the Adachi Police Station. It had apparently been another dead end.

"Would you like another cup of tea?" Sachie Sawauchi gestured toward Kusanagi's teacup with her open hand. His cup was empty, though he had no recollection of drinking anything.

"Thank you, I'm fine. Could you tell me what you did with your brother Seiji's effects?"

"I threw most of them away. There are a few things I didn't know what to do with. They're still stored here."

"Could we see them?"

"Certainly, but I'll need your help. They're a bit on the heavy side."

"Of course," Utsumi said, springing to her feet.

The cardboard box the two detectives carried back into the living room was jam-packed with old photo albums and letters. They pulled on latex gloves, determined to look through everything.

Kusanagi dealt with the photo albums. Whenever he came across a photograph of Yuna with another person, he would ask Sachie Sawauchi who the other person was. The Motohashis had obviously been over the moon when their daughter was born. There were reams and reams of pictures of her.

Once Yuna started going to school, there were more and more people Sachie Sawauchi didn't know in the photographs. Some of them were Yuna's friends, some were the friends' parents, and others looked like teachers. Kusanagi found it hard to believe that any of Yuna's classmates—no matter how close they had been as children—would wait twenty years to plot revenge after a twenty-year interval. Anyone prepared to do something like that would have to be more intimately connected to her.

It took Kusanagi almost two hours to go through all the photographs. Utsumi had finished reviewing all the letters. Neither of them found any leads.

Sachie Sawauchi, who had popped out of the room, reappeared, this time with coffee.

"Oh, that's too kind. Here we are, already taking up so much of your precious time." Kusanagi felt embarrassed.

"Please, don't worry about it. Looking through all those old photos for the first time in years was fun," she said, before adding, "though it had its painful side."

"What about this album?" Utsumi picked up an old photo album with an expensive-looking leather cover that lay in the bottom of the cardboard box.

"Mrs. Sawauchi says that all the pictures in it are from before Yuna was born," answered Kusanagi.

"Oh, yes?" said Utsumi. She flipped the album over and started leafing through it backward. She apparently wanted to see the pictures with the chronology reversed.

"Yumiko, you said her name was? Yuna's mother was beautiful."

"She was young and bursting with energy," said Sachie Sawauchi. "The whole house was so bright and cheerful after she became part of the family. Our mother was still alive back then. You hear a lot about young wives always being at daggers drawn with their mothers-in-law, but there was none of that here. Yumiko was a great daughter-in-law and a fabulous mother for Yuna, too. . . . That's why she was so hard on herself when Yuna went missing. It was painful to see. She killed herself by jumping off a building not far from here. My brother said she'd been behaving a bit strangely."

Kusanagi felt even more gloomy. He found himself thinking about "cycles of misfortune."

He heard a little gasp of appreciation. Peering across at the album that Utsumi was examining, Kusanagi saw a picture of Yumiko in her wedding dress and Seiji Motohashi in his tuxedo. They were both beaming with happiness.

"Seiji was always going to take over running the family firm from our father, but as a young man he spent a couple of years working for this big manufacturer. That was when he met Yumiko. My brother was thirty-three when they got married. Yumiko must have been twenty-three or twenty-four."

Kusanagi looked at the wedding photograph again. Yumiko was all alone in the world with no family at the time. . . .

"When did Yumiko lose her parents?"

"Her father died in an accident when she was little more than a baby. As for her mother, she died just after Yumiko started high school."

"Was she sent to an orphanage?"

"She never mentioned anything like that. She said something about boarding school."

"With both her parents dead, who was her legal guardian?"

Sachie Sawauchi looked perplexed.

"I don't know much about it. I didn't want to pry."

"I can understand that. . . ."

Utsumi, who was now sitting next to Sachie Sawauchi, was leafing through the album. As she went further back into the past, the pictures became all of Seiji Motohashi by himself, and there were none of Yumiko. By the time she had gone from his university days all the way to his primary school years, the pictures were all in black and white.

Kusanagi checked the inside of the cardboard box. There were no more albums in it.

"Yumiko didn't bring along any photographs of her own when she married your brother?" he asked Sachie Sawauchi.

"Apparently not. I was struck by that, when I was tidying her things. . . ."

Kusanagi turned his attention back to the album. Utsumi was flicking through the pages faster now. The picture on the frontispiece was of a baby: presumably, the infant Seiji Motohashi.

"That's odd," Kusanagi muttered. "Yumiko's mother only passed away when her daughter was already at high school. It's hard to believe she *never* took any pictures of her daughter at all. If there were any family photos, she would have brought them with her here, when she got married. So, where have those photos gotten to? Do you think Seiji threw them out?"

"Strikes me as unlikely," said Utsumi.

"Me, too."

Kusanagi pondered for a moment. Yuna Motohashi wasn't the only victim in the crime from twenty-three years ago. Yumiko Motohashi was a victim, too. The idea that someone would want to avenge her was by no means unthinkable. Could that be the missing piece of the puzzle Yukawa had mentioned?

"Detective Utsumi," he called peremptorily. "I want you to check the family register for Yumiko Motohashi— No, check for Yumiko *Fujiwara*, her maiden name. Draw up a comprehensive list of her immediate family and her relatives."

"Yes, sir," Utsumi promptly replied.

31

The man sitting opposite him in the interview room looked like a completely different person compared to the last time they met. There was nothing ingratiating in his attitude, and his face was as expressionless as a mask. *He's ready for the worst*, Kusanagi thought. *He's probably just starting to figure out why he's been asked to come in for questioning. I mustn't make any mistakes.*

"What's your name?"

The man only smiled faintly. "You know my name."

"I need you to state your name."

The man's face went blank again. "My name is Eiji Masumura."

"And what about the name of your father?"

At the word *father*, Masumura caught his breath. Then he said, "I don't have a father."

"I don't think so." Kusanagi looked down at a sheet of paper he had in his hand, then looked back at Masumura's expressionless face. "Your parents were properly married. You should know your own father's name."

"It was Isamu. Or was it Osamu? I don't remember much about my old man. He walked out on us when I was a kid."

"His name was Isamu Okano. Your parents got divorced when you were six."

Masumura snorted. "Why bother asking, if you know already?"

"I told you. Because I want to hear you say it. What was your mother's name?"

"Kimiko."

"And her family name?"

"Masumura."

"That's not true." Kusanagi jabbed his finger at the sheet of paper he was holding. "Tell me the truth."

"I've forgotten her name," Masumura said morosely. "It's all so long ago. Besides, it's got nothing to do with anything."

"Your mother's family name was Fujiwara. She remarried when you were eight. Her second husband was a man called Yasuaki Fujiwara, but you were never enrolled in his family register."

The name *Fujiwara* elicited a wan smile from Masumura.

"That's it. Fujiwara. God, I've not heard that name for years."

"You never used the Fujiwara name?"

"Not that I recall."

"You can still use your father's family name, even if you're not officially adopted. I know you were born in Yamanashi prefecture. If I want to, I can easily find out which schools you went to and the name you used there."

Masumura sank into a sullen silence. His body language seemed to say: *Go on. Do your worst.*

"Yasuaki Fujiwara died five years after he married your mother," Kusanagi said, looking down at the piece of paper, before returning his gaze to Masumura. "That's very tragic. Your mother—Kimiko Fujiwara—she must have been crushed by that."

Masumura frowned and looked uncomfortable.

"What's the point of digging up the past like this? If there's something you want to say, Detective, just come out and say it."

"You're in a better position than anyone to know what we should really be talking about today. I don't want to tell you anything; I want to ask you something—and please, don't make me repeat myself. How did your widowed mother make a living?"

Averting his eyes, Masumura scratched one of his eyebrows with the tip of a finger.

"Don't remember. A bit of this and a bit of that, I guess."

"Like working in bars and nightclubs?"

"Yeah, that's about right."

"It must have been hard for her. I mean, she had two children. And her second child was only four years old when her husband died."

Kusanagi noticed that Masumura's cheek was twitching.

"Ms. Yumiko Fujiwara. Yumiko is your little sister's name, isn't it?"

"Yeah, something like that. Sure."

"Your fathers were different. That's why your baby sister was nine years younger than you. I bet she was adorable. I bet you doted on her."

Masumura exhaled loudly and tilted his head to one side. "There was a big age gap between us. Like you say, we had different dads. My parents told me Yumiko was my baby sister, but I never really believed them. To me she felt more like, I don't know, the neighbors' kid. She wasn't especially attached to me and I didn't have much to do with her. I stayed away."

"But you must have done some babysitting?"

"Babysitting?"

"Yes, with your mother out working in those clubs and bars. You must have taken care of your sister when she was out of the house at night?"

Masumura rubbed the bottom of his nose. "I dunno. Don't remember."

Kusanagi shuffled the pieces of paper he was holding, moving the bottom one to the top. On the second sheet, there were edited excerpts from the records of Masumura's manslaughter trial.

"Talk me through your job history after you left junior high school."

"My job history?"

"You didn't go to high school, did you?"

"Uhm . . . no, I got a job with an electronics manufacturer in Kanagawa prefecture."

"How long did you work there?"

"I dunno . . . twelve years, give or take."

"And why did you quit?"

"I had no choice. I was fired. You really want to go there?"

"You were found guilty of manslaughter. Sentenced to three years."

"Yes," growled Masumura.

Kusanagi looked carefully at the paper in his hand.

Masumura had just moved into a new apartment. There was friction between him and one of the residents on the floor below, who thought he made too much noise.

The downstairs neighbor showed up at his door one night, roaring drunk and holding a beer bottle. Yelling incoherent insults, he threw himself at Masumura and began raining punches on him. The bottle he was holding hit something and broke. There was glass everywhere, but the neighbor didn't slow his assault.

There was a kitchen knife on the drainage board by the sink

in Masumura's apartment. Instinctively, Masumura grabbed it. He only meant to use it to threaten the other man, but when the neighbor came at him in a frenzy, he stabbed him without really knowing he was doing so.

The knife buried itself deep in the other man's belly. Vast quantities of blood poured out of him. He crashed to the floor.

Although Masumura called an ambulance, the man was past saving.

Those were the bare facts of the case.

"It was the middle of Japan's high-economic-growth period at the time. The production line of the factory where you worked was running twenty-four hours a day. One of your coworkers made the following statement about you at your trial. 'For us, Saturday is a workday like any other day. There are three shifts a day, every day. We do day shifts for two weeks, followed by a week of night shifts. In the course of that one week, we all lose weight—about four to five pounds—which we put back on while we're doing the day shift. Swings and roundabouts. Many of the guys try to get away with doing as little as possible, but Masumura is serious: He works hard, never complains, never slacks off. He was sending most of what he earned to his family—it can't have been easy for him.'"

Masumura gave a dry cough. "That's all old news. I'd rather not think about it."

"You'd been on the job about ten years, when Kimiko, your mother, died from a subarachnoid hemorrhage. Your little sister, Yumiko, was still in ninth grade. So what did you do?"

Masumura said nothing. He knew that Kusanagi would see through any lies he told immediately.

"You sent Yumiko to a girls' boarding school." Kusanagi was reading from the document in his hand. "You paid for her tuition fees, living expenses, room and board, everything. According to the trial record, on your salary, the money left over was barely enough for you to scrape by on. Yumiko provided testimony to the same effect. 'My brother was willing to sacrifice his quality of life to protect mine,' is what she said."

Masumura snorted. "That's just tactics."

"Tactics?"

"The lawyer was trying to plead extenuating circumstances. It was one of the tricks he came up with. Yes, I looked after Yumiko until she graduated high school, but that was all I did. After that, I'd had enough of caring for her, so we broke off contact."

"After high school, Yumiko got a job with an auto manufacturer in Chiba. At the trial, however, she testified that you always used to tell her she was smart and should go to college."

"Yeah, because that—" Masumura's voice was getting louder. "Because that was my lawyer's strategy. He wanted to work the whole sob-story angle as hard as he could."

"You're saying that Yumiko provided false testimony to the court as part of that strategy?"

"That's exactly what I'm saying. That's what trials are all about. That shows you what trials are worth."

"Yumiko must have adored you if she was willing to perjure herself for you."

Masumura grunted. He groped around for a reply and, when that proved hopeless, he waved his hand dismissively from side to side. "That's not how it was," he finally said. "She did it for herself. Having a murderer in the family can seriously fuck up your life. She thought that getting a lighter sentence for me would help make things easier for her. That's all it was."

"Did Yumiko visit you in jail?"

"No, she didn't. Why should she? After going to jail, I never saw Yumiko again. She never contacted me, either. It's only natural. I mean, who wants to fraternize with a jailbird?"

"Did you tell her not to come? Refuse her visits?"

"That's bullshit. It wasn't like that. I'd completely broken off contact with her. I had no idea what she was doing with her life. She didn't know anything about mine. That's how it was." He delivered this speech so forcefully, it was clear that he would never give ground on this point.

"Were you aware that Yumiko is dead?"

"*What? You're serious?*" Masumura's eyes widened. "I'd no idea. When did it happen? Did she get sick?"

"No, she committed suicide. Over twenty years ago, in fact."

Shocked, Masumura exhaled long and loudly. "I can't believe it. I really had no idea. We weren't in touch."

At this point, Kusanagi realized that Masumura was committed to a strategy of all-out lying.

Did he know that Yumiko had a daughter called Yuna? Did he

know that a man by the name of Hasunuma had been arrested for Yuna's murder? Did he know that ultimately Hasunuma was found not guilty? Kusanagi had a whole series of questions he wanted to ask Masumura, but he decided against it. He would never get the truth from him at this rate.

Kusanagi put down his papers and looked at the small man sitting in front of him. His perceptions had been flipped on their head.

Masumura was doing his best to come across as a tough guy. In reality, he was a good man who'd been prepared to go to any lengths to take care of his little sister. Kusanagi was ready to believe that the positive character testimony at his trial was probably all true. Yes, he had been declared guilty, but the manslaughter itself was an unavoidable accident.

A man like this would never be able to sit quietly on the sidelines when someone had driven his darling baby sister to suicide. It wasn't difficult to imagine him nursing his hatred for almost twenty years. And there was something almost surreal in the fact that he should have a connection to the current case. Kusanagi was now convinced that the stone-faced man in front of him was the person Yukawa had directed Utsumi to look for: the hinge between the old case and the current case.

"How's life in the business hotel?"

The question caught Masumura briefly off guard. His expression softened and he grunted, "Pretty darn good. I'd like to stay on, if I could."

"I think we'll be sending you back to your own place very soon. We need to do a search first and may confiscate some of your things. I hope that's okay," Kusanagi said, looking Masumura right in the eye. "We'll do a very thorough search. We'll be looking for photographs of the people you care about most."

Masumura's face stiffened. There was a determined glint in his eye.

"Be my guest," he said. "There's no one I care about and I don't have even one photograph. You go ahead and search all you damn well want."

32

He was so sure of himself. I can't believe he was bluffing. My guess is that he really doesn't have any photos," Utsumi said.

The red Kilchoman Distillery box that Utsumi had brought with her stood on Yukawa's desk. Kusanagi had asked her to get Yukawa a nice bottle of Scotch to thank him for his brilliant deduction.

Utsumi was in Yukawa's office to update him on the interview with Eiji Masumura, which had taken place earlier that day. While Kusanagi had asked the questions, Utsumi had been sitting next to him, taking notes.

"It sounds like we've got a formidable opponent on our hands." A paper cup in each hand, Yukawa made his way back to his armchair. Putting both cups on the low table, he asked Utsumi if she took milk.

"I'm fine without. You don't believe in mugs?"

"As you can see, this room doesn't have a sink. It's not very eco-logically sound, but there you go. It's paper cups or nothing."

"Thanks," Kaoru said, sipping from the paper cup. It should have tasted the same as any other instant coffee, but for some reason it always tasted just a bit special when it was brewed by this particular physicist.

She put her cup back on the table and looked up at Yukawa. "Why do you call him formidable?"

"It would be different if Masumura was telling the truth: that after he went to jail, he and his sister really had broken off all com-munication and had nothing to do with one another. But that's not what you think happened, is it?"

"No. The chief and I agree on that point. At the cost of making dramatic economies in his own life, he somehow drummed up the money for Yumiko's school fees and living expenses. He wouldn't have done that unless he loved her. As for Yumiko herself, she testified about the debt of gratitude she owed him. Ultimately, the manslaughter thing was just a silly squabble that spiraled out of control. I don't think he would have cut off the relationship. Still, it's always possible that Masumura tried to break off with his sister because he loved her and was worried about her future. They've got different family names, and there's no mention of a stepbrother in Yumiko's family register. My guess is that Masumura thought no one would ever know that she had a convicted felon in the family, provided they both kept quiet about it. And sure enough, she married a well-established man from a good family. I'm sure it wasn't easy for Yumiko, but I think she saw complying with Masumura's request to keep his existence secret as a way to repay him for his kindness."

"That would explain why she didn't bring any family photos with her to her new husband's house."

"Yes."

Yukawa resettled himself in his chair, took a sip of his coffee, then put his coffee cup down on the table.

"What do you think happened to those photographs? Do you think Yumiko threw them out before her marriage?"

"I don't think she'd do that. My guess is that she gave them to Masumura for him to take care of."

"I agree. The pictures were probably Masumura's most prized possession. I can imagine him keeping a couple of them in his wallet and taking good care of the others, taking them with him as he moved from place to place. If anything, his photo collection probably grew after Yumiko got married."

Utsumi understood what Yukawa was implying.

"You think Masumura and Yumiko stayed in contact and met in secret."

"Masumura lived for his little sister's happiness. When Yuna was born, I think she became a source of joy for him. I can easily imagine Yumiko bringing baby Yuna with her to their secret rendezvous."

"They may even have taken photos. The three of them together."

"Lots of them, I bet. But Masumura is adamant that no such photos exist and is quite happy for you to knock yourselves out looking for them. Why do you think that is?"

"Because he chucked them all out?"

"That's right." Yukawa gave an emphatic nod. "I suspect that he got rid of them all in advance, so that even if the police did find out that Yuna Motohashi's mother was Masumura's little sister, he could counter that, no, they had broken off all contact and he didn't even know she was dead. He probably burned them to prevent us finding even a scrap. Those pictures were an irreplaceable treasure for him. The fact that he destroyed them shows just how committed he is. That's why I described him as a formidable opponent."

Utsumi nodded and sighed. She remembered Masumura fearlessly facing down Kusanagi's searing scrutiny. Throughout the interview, he'd radiated a sense of passionate conviction.

"The other day, Professor, you said we were missing only a single piece to complete the puzzle, and that that piece existed in the past. Did you know that Masumura was the missing piece?"

"Of course I did," Yukawa replied. "I knew that if my process of deduction was right, it had to be him."

"Why didn't you just say so?"

Yukawa raised an eyebrow and grinned at her.

"You mean the investigation would have been easier for you if you'd known it was him from the get-go?"

"I don't know about it being easy but it would have been more efficient."

"Oh . . . *efficient*?" A smile played around the corners of Yukawa's mouth. "The reason I didn't hand you our missing puzzle piece on a plate was because I wanted to make sure that the answers you came up with were all objective."

"What do you mean?"

"Let's say I had told you that Masumura was the missing piece. What would have happened then? Most likely, you would have gone through Masumura's past with a fine-tooth comb, searching for his connection to the abduction and murder of Yuna Motohashi twenty-three years ago."

"Well, yes." Utsumi couldn't deny it. "I sure would."

"If that process had led you to the right answer, then all well and good. But there was every reason to think you might go off track and end up with the wrong answer. The Yuna incident took place in Adachi Ward, didn't it? What if, purely by coincidence, Masumura had once had a job in that part of Tokyo? You'd have been in ecstasies; you'd probably have started investigating all his friends and associates from that time. The only way to find out that Masumura had a stepsister was to check his mother's family register—but would you have gone that far? I think you'd have started believing that all sorts of irrelevant details were important clues, got sidetracked, and ended up taking an enormous detour. Or do you disagree?"

Kaoru bit her lip. Mortifying though it was to admit, Yukawa probably had a valid point.

"Who knows . . . perhaps, you're right."

"It's something I see all the time when my students do experiments," Yukawa said. "They usually know what the result of the experiment is supposed to be. Because of that, they conduct the experiment specifically to produce the desired result. They do things like deliberately misreading the numeric display on the measuring apparatus, either on the high or the low side. They're happy to end up with a result close to what they wanted and they don't even realize that they're guilty of committing a very basic error. If you want to conduct an experiment properly, you're much better off not knowing what sort of result it's going to produce. That's why I thought it was better for me not to reveal the last piece of the puzzle. I was ensuring the objectivity of your answers."

Yukawa often likened police investigations to scientific experiments, but this time the comparison felt particularly compelling.

"I see. I'll relay your explanation to the chief—though I doubt I'll be as eloquent as you, Professor."

"Give it your best shot."

"I have one more question. Why did you think that Masumura might have some kind of link to that murder case from twenty-three years ago?"

"That's easy enough to answer. Masumura had to be involved in Hasunuma's murder for my hypothesis to hold up. I'm referring to my hypothesis about the killer transforming the little room into a gas chamber for an execution. A number of conditions had to be in place for the hypothesis to work. Let me tell you about three of them."

"Just a moment." Kaoru pulled a notebook from her bag and readied herself to take notes. "Go on, please."

Yukawa took a sip of coffee, then raised an index finger.

"First, the killer had to get Hasunuma to take some sleeping medication. Second, Hasunuma had to fall asleep specifically inside the little storeroom. Third, the killer had to be aware that the little room could be locked from the outside. Those are my three conditions."

Yukawa had rattled them off and Utsumi was having trouble keeping up. "Okay. And?"

"Masumura was the only person who fulfilled all three conditions. It was easy for him to get Hasunuma to drop his guard and to slip sleeping medication into his drink. Since they lived together, Masumura obviously knew where Hasunuma slept. The most crucial condition is number three. Unless you actually lived in the hut, you would never know that the sliding door could be locked shut."

Utsumi raised her eyes from the scrawl in her notebook and looked thoughtfully at the physicist.

"It seems so obvious when you explain it."

"You think I'm right?"

"So obvious, I'm almost disappointed."

Yukawa frowned. "I disappointed you?"

"No, I disappointed myself. I mean, why couldn't I figure out something so simple? The chief will be annoyed with himself, too."

"It's because both of you had made up your minds that Masumura had no connection to the case. Hasunuma went to live in Masumura's place of his own volition; the two men met long before the death of Saori Namiki; and, to top it all, Masumura had an alibi. He was one of the first people to be struck from the suspect list."

"But that's not how you looked at it, Professor."

"No. Kusanagi told me that there was no point of contact between Masumura and the Namiki family. In that case, Masumura's motive had to predate Saori's death. Could something have happened when the two men were working at the recycling firm where Masumura is still employed? Hardly. If there had been friction between them, Hasunuma would not have gone to live in Masumura's spare room later, would he? That was when I tried flipping the problem." Yukawa turned his hand palm upward to illustrate his point. "The question became had Masumura met Hasunuma completely randomly, or did Masumura actively seek him out? Once Masumura managed to track him down, did he insinuate himself into the same workplace, befriend Hasunuma, and wait for an opportunity to take his revenge? Hasunuma, however, quit his job and moved on before Masumura could execute his plan. A few years later, the opportunity to do so presented itself in an unexpected fashion. This time, it was Hasunuma who approached Masumura. And, this time, Masumura was determined to settle his decades-old score. Okay, if we assume that all that was indeed the case, then what was this old grudge of Masumura's?"

"That's when you realized that Masumura might have a connection to the Yuna case."

"Yes, if my hypothesis was correct, he had to." Yukawa swallowed a mouthful of coffee with an air of smug composure.

"What about Masumura's alibi?"

"I don't think he's lying about that. Masumura is just an accomplice. He didn't do the deed himself."

"You think someone else is the principal?"

"I suppose I must." Yukawa put down his cup with a sigh. "This problem is not a simple one. To be honest with you, my hypothesis remains something of a work in progress. I still haven't solved the mystery central to the whole thing."

"What do you mean? Is it something to do with the method that was used?"

"No, I think I've got that covered." Yukawa sounded confident.

"The idea of converting the little room into a gas chamber?"

"Yes."

"What should we be thinking about the helium issue? You were the one who said that a huge amount of helium would be needed."

"I'd like to hear the results of that thing, before I go into that. You know, that thing I asked you to get Forensics to check up on? Did they get back to you?"

"They gave me a written report. I've brought the results with me." Utsumi extracted several folded sheets of paper from inside her bag and placed them on the table.

After adjusting his glasses, Yukawa picked up the report.

"How is it?" Kaoru asked somewhat timidly. "The guy in charge at Forensics was actually rather skeptical. 'Why does Professor Yukawa care about something like that?'"

Yukawa's mouth, which had been a stern straight line, suddenly creased into a smile. His eyes twinkled.

"This is fantastic," the physicist said. "Now I think we need Forensics to conduct a little experiment for us. Naturally, I'll have to be there myself."

33

The young technician from Forensics was down on one knee in front of the sliding door, using a screwdriver to loosen the screws that kept the door handle in place.

Having removed all the screws, the technician detached the handles from both sides of the door, revealing what Yukawa had referred to as the Judas Window.

Utsumi peered over the technician's shoulder. "It's true. It goes right through."

"That's absolutely key," said Yukawa, who was standing next to Kusanagi behind Utsumi. "What can you get through a small square hole of this size is the crucial question."

"A hole this size is fine," said Shimaoka, the director of Forensics. He was there to both direct and observe the test.

They were about to conduct an experiment in Eiji Masumura's small apartment. Kusanagi, Utsumi, and Yukawa were the only non-technicians there. They planned to photograph every stage of the experiment using multiple cameras and report back to Director Mamiya and the other top brass.

The young technician had moved away from the sliding door, so Kusanagi peered into the little room, which was the actual crime scene. Inside, everything was ready.

A ground sheet had been laid over the parquet floor and a mattress and quilt placed on top of it. A mannequin lay on the mattress. It was a crash test dummy but had the same weight, articulation, and size as a real person.

"We've tried to re-create the scene exactly as it was when the body was found. The mattress and the quilt are identical," Shimaoka said. "The victim's actual bedding is not available, so we'll be using a brand-new quilt and mattress. Is that all right, Professor Yukawa?"

"You know their weight?"

"Yes, we've already weighed them."

"That'll be fine then. Thanks very much."

Kusanagi examined the little room. Cameras had been set up in two locations and several square devices eight inches high were dotted around the room. One of them was very close to the dummy.

"What are those machines?" Kusanagi asked Shimaoka.

"Oxygen densitometers. Obviously, we can't have an observer inside the room, so we've set it up so we can monitor the video feed and the densitometer readings from out here." As he said this, Shimaoka pointed at a folding table that had been erected to one side of the sliding door. On it were two laptops.

The forensic technician who had removed the door handles came back in and said something to Shimaoka. Shimaoka nodded and turned to Kusanagi.

"Everything's ready. We can start whenever you like."

Kusanagi looked at Yukawa. Yukawa nodded. "Go ahead," Kusanagi said to Shimaoka.

Two more technicians came in carrying a cylindrical tank with handles on either side. It was about two feet in height and one foot in diameter with a rubber bulb and special hose on the top. They carefully placed the cylinder on the floor in the middle of the room.

"We need to keep the room well ventilated. Let's have the front door and the window open," Yukawa said.

The technicians opened the door and the window as directed. Shimaoka then pulled the sliding door of the small room shut. "Okay, are we ready?"

"Before we start the experiment proper, could you discharge a small amount onto the floor here?" Yukawa said.

"Here in this room?" Shimaoka asked, just to make sure.

"Yes," replied Yukawa. "I'd like to give Detectives Kusanagi and Utsumi the chance to witness this phenomenon directly."

"Fine," said Shimaoka. He nodded to his subordinates.

Leaving the hose dangling onto the floor, the technicians turned several valves and squeezed the rubber bulb on top of the tank until it was flat. A mixture of white vapor and liquid spouted out of the hose and onto the floor.

The liquid disappeared instantaneously, meaning that the floor didn't get wet.

"What we have here is liquid nitrogen," Yukawa said. "It has a boiling point of minus one hundred and ninety-six degrees Celsius. Pouring it onto the floor is like dripping waterdrops into a hot frying pan. It vaporizes instantaneously, as you can see. So, what will happen if we take this liquid nitrogen and"—here, he pointed at the sliding door—"we feed it in large quantities into the closed-up small room via the Judas Window?"

"What does happen?" Kusanagi asked.

"That's what we are going to put to the test right now."

"Proceed," Yukawa said to Shimaoka.

Shimaoka gave the word and the forensic technicians got to work. One of them carried the tank up to the sliding door and fed the hose through the square aperture. The other turned on the two laptops. One of the monitors displayed the room's interior, the other displayed various numeric readouts and graphs.

Yukawa had taken up position behind the technician who was monitoring the computers. Kusanagi and Utsumi followed suit.

"Let's go," Shimaoka said.

Just as he had done a minute or two before, the technician squeezed the bulb at the top of the gas cylinder several times. Immediately, a change was visible in the interior of the room on the computer display.

It was filling up with a white mist. The ground sheet, the mattress, and the quilt were only dimly visible through a haze.

"The liquid nitrogen cools the water vapor in the air, condensing it into small gloating droplets of water. You might say we've created a cloud inside the room," Yukawa explained.

"The door cracks . . . It's coming through . . . ," Utsumi murmured.

Kusanagi looked up. Sure enough, white smoke was seeping through whatever gaps there were, though it quickly vanished. When Kusanagi commented on it, Yukawa snapped back, "The temperature's warm in here, so it's reverting to water vapor. How's the concentration of oxygen?" Yukawa asked the technician seated at the table.

"Almost unchanged in the upper part of the room. In the vicinity of the mannequin, it dropped below eighteen percent very rapidly. It's about to go below seventeen," the technician replied.

"When the oxygen concentration gets to sixteen percent, you get subjective symptoms like headache and nausea," Shimaoka said, keeping an eye on the monitors. "Once you go below twelve percent, you start to feel dizzy. And once you go through ten percent, mental functions are impaired."

Ten minutes later, the oxygen densitometer nearest the dummy was giving a reading of just six percent.

"Six is the level where you experience respiratory arrest. What's the capacity of the tank?" Yukawa asked Shimaoka.

"Twenty liters. It was almost full when we started. We'll weigh it when we've finished, of course. I don't think there'll be much left."

Yukawa nodded and turned to Kusanagi and Utsumi.

"When liquid nitrogen vaporizes, its volume increases by around seven hundred times. In other words, a twenty-liter tank like this produces fourteen thousand liters. The cubic capacity of that room is around ten thousand liters. Any excess gets pushed out here through the gaps around the door. Since the original air inside and the vaporized nitrogen don't instantaneously mix, the oxygen concentration is different in different parts of the room. As you can see from this experiment, the oxygen thins out in the lower part of the room first. For anyone asleep inside, there's a high likelihood of getting oxygen deficiency culminating in respiratory arrest, even if the person were to get to their feet halfway through the process."

"You're saying that the murder weapon wasn't helium after all?" Kusanagi said.

"The helium tank we found was a decoy. It was designed to throw us off track. I owe you an apology there. I was the one to suggest that helium might have been used."

"Where did you get the idea of liquid nitrogen?"

"I asked myself why the killer had to opt for helium rather than anything else and what he really used for this murder. That's when it came to me. Perhaps the killer actually *wanted* the police to think that helium was the murder weapon. Now, if we start looking for a substitute for helium, then what have we got?" Yukawa smiled and pointed at the liquid nitrogen tank. "An inert gas that's the most abundant element in the atmosphere. And nitrogen is its name. If you use it in liquefied form, all you need is a paltry twenty liters," said Yukawa, then turned and looked at Utsumi. "I asked Detective Utsumi to check one thing to help me verify my hypothesis."

"What was that?" Kusanagi asked his female colleague.

"The quantity of moisture in the mattress and quilt when Hasunuma's body was found," Utsumi replied.

Kusanagi frowned. "The quantity of moisture?"

"You saw the video feed from inside the room, didn't you?" said Yukawa. "When liquid nitrogen is pumped into the room, the water vapor in the air turns into a floating white mist. If the temperature in the room goes up, the mist dissolves into the air. If, however, liquid nitrogen keeps on being pumped in, then the temperature in the room does not rise. The room becomes something like the inside of a cloud. It's an environment where condensation forms very easily. What do you think would happen to a quilt and mattress in a place like that?"

"They would absorb a lot of moisture?"

"When Forensics checked, they found that they were damper than under a normal-usage scenario," Utsumi said. "In fact, they contained a large amount of moisture; equivalent to about half a cup of excess water."

"Director Shimaoka," said Yukawa. "Could we have a look at the interior of the room?"

"Of course. For safety reasons, I'd like you to stand back a little."

The three of them did as they were told and stepped away from the door. One of the technicians slid the door open but didn't go in. The oxygen level was still too low.

Cold air came wafting toward them. They gasped and shivered.

"Oh, it's chilly—no, more like downright cold," Utsumi said.

"No surprise there. Twenty liters of liquid nitrogen at a temperature of minus one hundred and ninety-six degrees has just vaporized," Yukawa said. "Quite a long time ago, this really heartbreaking accident took place in a research facility up in Hokkaido. The temperature in the low-temperature testing room started rising because the temperature-control machinery had broken down. The staff poured large quantities of liquid nitrogen onto the floor in an effort to get the temperature back down as fast as they could. They must have panicked, as they completely forgot to ventilate the room properly. In the end, they were all asphyxiated."

"I hadn't heard about that," Kusanagi said.

"Something similar must have happened when Masumura opened the sliding door after getting back from wherever he had been. Since he was aware of the dangers of liquid nitrogen, I suppose he didn't go directly inside."

The technician at the computer said, "Oxygen concentration is now above twenty percent."

Shimaoka nodded to Yukawa. "Go ahead, Professor."

Yukawa went inside. Kusanagi followed him.

The interior of the room didn't appear to have changed. The white mist had already dispersed.

Yukawa, who was looking down at the floor near his feet, stopped and extracted a pair of leather gloves from his pocket. He pulled them on, squatted down, and picked something up off the floor.

"What have you got there?" Kusanagi asked.

Yukawa opened the palm of his gloved hand to reveal something that looked like a small, thin rice cracker.

"The liquid nitrogen was all pumped into a single spot in the room. That area was supercooled in a very extreme fashion. The carbon dioxide in the air got frozen as well as the water vapor. This here is dry ice."

"Forensics didn't report finding any."

"Of course they didn't. Masumura would have got rid of it."

"Oh, right . . ."

Still clutching the little piece of dry ice, Yukawa started touching the walls, before crouching down to scrutinize the ground sheet.

"What is it?" Kusanagi asked. "Have you noticed something else?"

Yukawa pulled himself to his feet and adjusted his spectacles on his nose.

"I know that I'm repeating myself, but the key thing is what happens to the water vapor in the atmosphere. It will vary depending on the conditions—the temperature, the humidity, the degree of air-tightness, and so on—but I thought it possible we might find some waterdrops on the ground sheet. As far as I can see, though, there aren't any. There is a certain amount of moisture on the walls, but nothing one could describe as abnormal. Anyway, the walls would have dried somewhat, or possibly even reverted to their original state by the time the crime scene was inspected. What do you think, Director?"

Shimaoka and his crew of technicians were busy rolling up the mattress and quilt and tying them with string in preparation for attaching them to a suspension weighing scale.

"The pre-experiment weight of mattress and quilt was thirteen point eight pounds. According to the digital readout here, that's now increased to fourteen point one pounds. A weight gain of roughly three and a half ounces."

"Which is the equivalent of half a cup's worth of water. That tallies perfectly with the condition of the mattress and quilt found at the scene," said Yukawa. He turned to Kusanagi. "We seem to be one step closer toward proving my hypothesis."

34

A search and seizure warrant was issued for Tojima-ya Foods, the company owned and managed by Shusaku Tojima, the day after they ran the liquid nitrogen experiment. Kusanagi, who took personal charge of the search, went to the managing director's office with Detective Sergeant Utsumi and Detective Inspector Kishitani.

Tojima recoiled at the sight of the warrant. "What is the meaning of this?" he protested. "Are you trying to say that my company's got something to do with your murder investigation? We're just a food-processing company! We're not doing anything illegal here!"

"In that case, you've got nothing to worry about. Kindly cooperate with the search," Kusanagi said, returning the warrant to his chest pocket.

It was something that Yukawa had said to him after the liquid nitrogen experiment that inspired him to order the search.

"When I realized that liquid nitrogen had probably been used and not helium," the professor had told him, "I realized something else, something important: Someone very close to the Namiki family could get his hands on liquid nitrogen with ease. Shusaku Tojima, the childhood friend of Yutaro Namiki, runs his family company, which handles frozen food. You can use a whole range of machines to freeze food, but flash-freezing systems rely on liquid nitrogen."

Yukawa went on to explain that he'd already spoken to Tojima in order to confirm his hunch.

"It was after Detective Utsumi came to visit me at the university research center. I went to Namiki-ya specifically at a time I knew Tojima would be there, too. I managed to share a table with him, so I got the chance to ask him what freezer systems he used. As I'd expected, Tojima-ya Foods did use liquid-nitrogen-based freezer systems. Chiefly for desserts, he said. I questioned Tojima pretty persistently, so I may have aroused his suspicions."

This was important. Kusanagi had no excuse for dillydallying. He quickly pushed through the necessary paperwork to execute a search of Tojima's company premises.

Some eight hours after the search of Tojima-ya Foods had ended, Kusanagi was in the meeting room at the Kikuno precinct station with Utsumi and Kishitani, giving an update to Director Mamiya.

"From interviews we have conducted, we have learned that this March there was an accident involving liquid nitrogen at Tojima-ya Foods," said Kusanagi, referring to his notes. "Instead of using an automatic freezer, one of the workers was manually spraying some food products with liquid nitrogen, when he lost consciousness and collapsed. The cause of the accident was poor ventilation. The worker's condition wasn't life-threatening or even especially serious, but further missteps could have resulted in death."

"And you think that the accident gave Tojima the idea for the murder?" Mamiya asked.

"We don't know whether it was Tojima himself who had the idea or someone he mentioned the accident to," Kusanagi replied circumspectly. "Detective Utsumi!" His tone was suddenly peremptory.

Utsumi tapped a few strokes on the keyboard, then swiveled her laptop around so that it faced Mamiya. On this display was the entrance of the Tojima-ya Foods factory.

"This footage comes from the security camera at the entrance to the Tojima-ya Foods factory. It's from the day of the parade and, as you can see from the time stamp, it's from around one o'clock. As it's a Sunday, you'd expect the whole place to be closed, but the shutter on the loading dock is up."

Utsumi tapped her keyboard and the video started to play. A minivan drove up to the loading dock. Mamiya gasped.

"I'm now going to jump a few minutes forward." She fast-forwarded the video to 1:20. The minivan was driving away from the loading dock.

"Can we see the driver's face?" he asked.

"With this particular footage, we can't. But there is some from another camera." Kusanagi shot a glance at Utsumi.

Utsumi pulled up another video. It showed a line of minivans parked in a row.

"This is the parking lot for commercial vehicles at Tojima-ya Foods," Utsumi explained. "The time's slightly earlier than the other video. See. The time stamp is 12:56."

She started the video. A few seconds later, a plump man in a bomber jacket appeared in the left-hand corner of the screen. He clambered into one of the vans and drove off.

Utsumi rewound the footage slightly, froze a frame, and enlarged the man's face.

Kusanagi had brought a copy of the photograph from Shusaku Tojima's driver's license. He showed it to Mamiya. "We think it's the same person."

Mamiya narrowed his eyes and scrutinized the picture. "Tojima procured the liquid nitrogen from his own factory?"

"We think it probable, yes."

"Any evidence?"

"The quantity of liquid nitrogen in the factory's storage tank is monitored on a daily basis. Between the Friday and the Monday, it decreased by roughly twenty liters. With liquid nitrogen, there's always going to be a small percentage that evaporates. The tank manager, however, was adamant that it had never gone down so much before."

"I see. Still, that's hardly decisive," Mamiya said grumpily. "Did you manage to track the minivan's movements?"

"He handled that," Kusanagi said, with a jerk of the chin in Kishitani's direction.

"We went through the footage from the security cameras in the vicinity of the factory. So far, we've not been able to find the minivan in question," Kishitani said to Mamiya. "N-System didn't catch it on the main road, either."

"Is there a way to get from the factory to the crime scene while avoiding N-System?"

"It's possible, but it involves such a major detour that no one would ever decide to go that way. You've got to remember that ordinary civilians have no idea where the N-System monitoring points are located," Kishitani said.

"Moving on," said Utsumi. Tapping her keyboard, she pulled up an image of the parking lot. The minivan drove back in and a man resembling Tojima climbed out and walked off.

"The time stamp says 1:51. Since we know Tojima left the factory at 1:20, that gives him roughly half an hour. Even by the shortest route, it still takes over ten minutes to get to the crime scene. He certainly wouldn't have taken a roundabout route."

Mamiya crossed his arms on his chest and turned to Kusanagi. "Has Tojima got an alibi?"

"Yes, he has," Kusanagi shot back. "He was with his friends at the neighborhood association from around three P.M. He did step outside occasionally, but never for very long. He stayed with them until early evening, when he went to Namiki-ya. His alibi checks out."

"In other words," muttered Mamiya, "Tojima isn't the principal."

"No, I don't think he is," Kusanagi said. "We should probably think of it in these terms. Tojima used the minivan to take the liquid nitrogen out of the factory and deposit it somewhere, before driving back. Somebody else—not him—then took the liquid nitrogen from there to the crime scene."

"And that somebody else is the principal. But who is it?"

"We don't know. Our prime suspect is Yutaro Namiki, but, as you know, he has an alibi. The same's true for Masumura."

Mamiya groaned softly, knitted his fingers behind his head, and leaned back in his chair.

"That fellow . . . Detective Galileo . . . what does he have to say? Hasn't he been able to come up with one of his beautiful theories?"

"He has come up with what he calls a 'for-the-time-being solution.'"

"What's that supposed to mean?"

"I should warn you, it's an outlandish theory. . . ."

It was a theory Yukawa had unveiled after he'd come to the same conclusion: that Tojima wasn't the principal.

"Masumura is one accomplice and Tojima is probably another. But are they the only accomplices who took part in the crime? Take Tomoya Takagaki, for example. While he *appears* to have an alibi, there's also a roughly thirty-minute chunk of time that's unaccounted for. What was he doing in that time? In addition, if the helium tank we found in the clump of weeds was only a decoy, that makes it possible that the murder was committed *before* the helium was stolen at 4:30 P.M.—something that undermines the perfect alibi of the Niikuras. Taken all together, do these facts amount to anything significant?"

Yukawa's theory had hit him like a bombshell, Kusanagi went on.

The physicist was proposing that a large number of people might have been involved in committing the crime.

Yukawa had emphasized that what he was putting forward was "no more than a for-the-time-being solution."

"Up to a point, at least, I know all the people involved. They're all good, decent, ordinary folk. I know that they loved Saori Namiki and probably hated Hasunuma. At the same time, I just can't see them taking part in a murder. Just because there are, say, ten accomplices doesn't mean that each of them only suffers one-tenth of the normal pangs of conscience. That's why my hypothesis remains incomplete."

Yukawa had delivered this speech with a melancholy expression on his face. Kusanagi understood Yukawa's point: It was hard to believe that so many people would participate in a murder plot.

Seeing that Kusanagi had finished, Mamiya weighed in. "I agree with that last point of Yukawa's," he said. "The multiple-accomplice theory is certainly an interesting one, but with a crime as atrocious as murder, it's difficult for a lot of people to preserve a united front. More people just multiplies the risk, especially when the crime is detected."

"Still, sir, it looks like Masumura and Tojima are definitely. And since there's got to be something to connect the two of them, it's hard to think that the connecting link would be anyone other than Namiki. . . ."

"Yet Namiki, the crucial figure, has an alibi." Mamiya crossed his arms. "Which means we end up going around in circles."

"This is what we need to look at, if we want to break the logjam." Kusanagi pointed at the computer display, which was showing a still of the minivan parked in the Tojima-ya Foods lot. "Our experiment proved that roughly twenty liters of liquid nitrogen were needed for the crime. A standard tank for liquid nitrogen is around two feet high, around a foot in diameter, and weighs around fifty-five pounds when full. The question we have to answer is, once Tojima took it out of the factory, how did a second person transport it to the crime scene?"

"Okay, so the helium tank has now become a tank of liquid nitrogen. Regardless which gas it was, the perpetrator still had to transport something very large. We haven't yet found any such a person, have we?"

"Our focus until now has been the security cameras in the vicinity of the park from which the helium tank was stolen. We also focused on a time period after four thirty, when the theft of the tank took place. What we need to do now is to conduct interviews and analyze the security camera footage over an enlarged area and a longer time frame."

Although Kusanagi's tone was confident, in his heart of hearts he still felt uneasy. Not even Professor Yukawa had managed to put together a complete hypothesis. He had no faith that the investigation was proceeding along the right track.

PART THREE

"As you yourself have said, what other explanation can there be?"
Poirot stared straight ahead of him.
"That is what I ask myself," he said.
—AGATHA CHRISTIE, *MURDER ON THE ORIENT EXPRESS*

35

The bar was located about a ten minutes' walk from Kikuno station. It was on a narrow side street in a small modern building. Standing at a certain remove from the busy shopping district, it didn't seem an ideal location but as the place had been in business for years, it probably benefited, like Namiki-ya, from a core of regular customers.

Utsumi pushed open the door and stepped inside. From behind the counter on her right, a gray-haired bartender—the owner, she assumed—wished her a good evening. A wide array of glass bottles was arranged on shelves behind him.

All the tables were occupied by couples and there was another couple sitting at the counter. At a certain distance from them, right at the back, sat the person Utsumi had arranged to meet.

"I hope you've not been waiting long?" Utsumi said, speaking quietly as she sat down on the seat next to Yukawa.

Yukawa slipped his phone into his inside jacket pocket and reached for his tumbler. "I only just got here myself."

The bartender came over to them. Utsumi ordered a Virgin Moscow Mule.

"Planning to head back to the station afterward?"

"Yes. I've got a report to write."

"Hard life, eh?" It looked as though Yukawa was drinking a highball. "Investigation hit a brick wall?"

"Nothing gets past you, does it?"

"You invited me for a drink, but I see no sign of a gift."

"Sorry about that." Utsumi sighed and let her head droop to one side. "I don't think that the investigation's actually on the wrong track."

"What did Tojima have to say for himself? Kusanagi told me about the drop in the volume of liquid nitrogen in the company storage tank."

"Tojima's saying he doesn't know how it happened. He's admitted that he did drive one of the company's minivans on the day of the parade. He checked up on the freezers at the factory, then set out for the parade venue, he says. Worried that he wouldn't find a place to park the van, he ended up driving back. We have a statement from a witness who saw a Tojima-ya Foods vehicle very close to the starting point of the parade."

Yukawa exhaled loudly. "As excuses go, it's plausible."

"It doesn't feel quite right to me. He's the boss. He can always get one of his employees to inspect the freezers. Plus, why do that sort of thing on a Sunday in the first place?"

"He can just say, 'It's my decision and it's nothing to do with you.'"

"Yes, I know but . . ." mumbled Utsumi.

The bartender placed a tumbler in front of Utsumi. There was a half slice of lime floating in it. When she took a sip, a fresh, tart fragrance perfumed the air.

"Is Masumura still refusing to say anything?"

Utsumi nodded listlessly.

"He says that he got the job at the recycling company because he'd heard that the place welcomed ex-cons on its workforce; that he had no idea Hasunuma worked there; and that he knew nothing about Yuna Motohashi's murder."

"Did you check with Masumura's previous employer?"

"I sent an investigator to talk to them. They're a construction subcontractor. The place has such a high level of employee turnover that almost nobody there remembered Masumura."

"I can believe it." Yukawa sounded quite unfazed. "If there was any weakness in that part of their plan, the whole thing would disintegrate. Whatever happens, Masumura has to keep denying any link between himself and what happened twenty-three years ago."

"You said 'their plan'—but who exactly is 'they'? Masumura and Tojima, all three members of the Namiki family, Tomoya Takagaki, both the Niikuras—do you regard them all as suspicious?"

"It would be illogical not to do so."

"Yes, but all three members of the Namiki family have alibis. We have located the Takagaki and the Niikuras in CCTV footage from the parade and we know that none of them was carrying any bulky items. Based on how long Tojima was away from his factory in the minivan, the furthest he could have transported the liquid nitrogen—assuming he did so—would be to the starting point of the parade. So who transported it from there to the crime scene and how did they do it?"

"Isn't answering questions like that meant to be your job?"

"We're doing our best. Have you heard of utility wagons, Professor?"

"Utility wagons? It sounds faintly Wild West."

"They're trolley-mounted square boxes covered in plastic sheeting. Delivery company drivers use them. They stick the packages they're delivering in the box and push them to their destination. The sheeting keeps the packages dry when it's raining and stops them falling off the trolley. You must have seen them around?"

"Oh, yes. I know exactly what you mean." Yukawa was nodding enthusiastically. "I see them all the time."

"Deliveries were still being made in Kikuno on the day of the parade. These utility wagons pop up from time to time on the security-camera footage. In every case, we've contacted the delivery company and are checking to see that the deliveries actually arrived. We thought that the perpetrator could have disguised himself as a deliveryman and transported the liquid nitrogen that way."

"Interesting. Was it Kusanagi who gave that order?"

"Yes, it was."

Yukawa smiled and drained his highball. "He's shaping up to be a pretty good chief inspector."

"Shall I tell him you said that?"

"There's no need."

"That gives you an idea of how thorough we're being. From reviewing the footage of security cameras in every possible location, I've got a good grasp of how the spectators were behaving, how they moved around. Despite all our efforts, we still can't figure out how the perpetrator transported the liquid nitrogen. That's why I've come here to see you tonight."

"You want me to figure it out?"

Utsumi placed both her hands on her knees and turned in her seat to look directly at Yukawa. "Professor, I'm sure you can solve the mystery."

"Now you're just being illogical," said Yukawa. He called the bartender over and, pointing to his tumbler, asked for a refill.

Utsumi scratched the top of her head. "Are we missing something?"

"Perhaps you are. No, make that a probably. At times like this, it's always a good idea to look at things from a different point of view."

"A different point of view, huh." Utsumi took a sip of her cocktail, then rested her chin on her interwoven fingers and watched the deft movements of the bartender's hands as he made a whiskey and soda. Her gaze wandered across to the bottles arrayed behind him. A small frog-shaped knickknack at the corner of the bottom shelf caught her eye.

What on earth is that frog doing here? she wondered. She soon realized what it was and her mouth creased into a spontaneous smile.

"What is it?" Yukawa asked.

"That thing there." Utsumi pointed to the knickknack. "You know its name?"

Yukawa took a look, then snorted. "It's Kikunon. The mascot of the parade."

"I'm not a big fan of the design. Just looks like an ordinary frog to me."

The bartender placed a new highball in front of Yukawa. "One of the customers left it behind."

"That explains it," said Yukawa, sounding relieved. "It doesn't really match the rest of the decor."

"I can't just throw the thing away. It's a bore. I wish they'd hurry up and come and collect it," said the bartender before walking off.

Utsumi stared at the miniature Kikunon. The giant inflatable version of it had been the last attraction in the parade. The thing required several high-pressure cylinders' worth of helium.

"Ah!" Utsumi exclaimed loudly.

"What is it now?"

"Nothing. Nothing." Utsumi flapped a hand from side to side. "I thought I'd had an inspiration. . . . Sorry. It was stupid."

"What was stupid?"

"My bright idea. It was totally stupid. Far-fetched. Impossible. Forget about it."

Yukawa returned his tumbler to the coaster.

"You shouldn't be the one to decide if your idea is stupid or not.

And you certainly don't want to rush to judgment about something being impossible. Buried inside a crazy idea, you can often find useful hints for solving problems. You should come out and say it, and see what a third party has to say."

"I don't need to. If I told you, Professor, you'd just laugh. And if you didn't laugh, you'd be horrified."

"Now I *really* want to hear your idea!" This time, it was Yukawa who swiveled around on his seat to face Utsumi. The expression on his face was deadly earnest. "Go on. Tell me."

Utsumi exhaled slowly. *I should never have told him that I'd had a brainstorm.* She was kicking herself.

"I thought that . . . perhaps the perpetrators used the gas from that thing," she said, pointing at the miniature mascot on the shelf.

"From *that*?" Yukawa drew his brows together skeptically.

"Yes, the gas from the giant Kikunon inflatable. It contains a lot of helium. They could have drained the helium from it when the parade was over and then transported it to the crime scene. That way they could have asphyxiated Hasunuma using the first method you proposed." At that point, Utsumi's self-confidence collapsed. "Look, please just forget about it. After all, it was liquid nitrogen, not helium, that was used for the murder, anyway."

Yukawa wasn't laughing. Nor was there an expression of horror on his face. "Interesting," he simply said, while looking pensively at the Kikunon mascot on the shelf. "With that method, the perpetrators wouldn't actually need to do anything between the starting point of the parade to the finishing point of the parade, because the members of Team Kikuno would transport the balloon and the gas inside it for them."

"That's what I thought. And that's why I thought—for about a microsecond—that it was a good idea. But it's impossible, isn't it? To extract the helium from the balloon, I mean."

"Extracting the gas from the balloon isn't difficult. It's getting it back into the cylinders that would be a mind-boggling challenge."

"Of course. So, yes, just forget about it. At least you didn't laugh at me." Relieved, Utsumi took a sip of her Moscow Mule.

"I'm very far indeed from laughing at you." Yukawa took his smartphone out of his inside jacket pocket. "I think you may have hit upon the mother of all solutions."

"Really? Explain."

Yukawa thumbed the screen of his phone.

"A few minutes ago, you said that you'd examined the footage from all the security cameras along the parade route and had got a good grasp of how the crowd moved and behaved."

"That's right."

"I rather doubt that you paid much attention to the movements of this particular group." As Yukawa said this, he turned the display of his phone toward Utsumi.

On it were the pirates in the parade.

36

At three stories high, Miyazawa Books was large for a bookstore. On the first floor, they actually sold music, DVDs, and computer games. Books were on the second floor, while the third floor was the company office.

Maya Miyazawa had a firm, straight mouth that suggested strength of will. Clearly, she also had a certain charisma since she was a director of the neighborhood association and the leader of Kikuno's official parade team.

She had looked askance at Kusanagi when he showed her his police badge, but when he asked if he could see the props for the parade, she looked daggers at him.

"What's the problem with our props?"

"We just need to check something. Where are they kept?"

"They're in the parade committee's storeroom."

"Where is that? Is the place staffed?"

"It's just up the road. No, normally there's no one there. Uh . . . do you want to see the props right now?"

Kusanagi bowed curtly while maintaining eye contact. "Yes, if we could."

"Fine," said Maya Miyazawa. She opened a drawer in a nearby desk and pulled out a bunch of keys.

She took them to the parade committee building herself. It was a modest, two-story structure, located a little ways from the shopping district. The first floor was a storeroom, while the committee's offices were upstairs.

"In December, all the shops have their end-of-year sales. Team Kikuno always does a special performance, and we store the costumes and props here. We dismantled the float after the parade, because we don't use that in December," Miyazawa said, as she pressed the switch to open the storeroom's electric shutter.

The storeroom itself was full of piles of cardboard boxes and clothes cases, along with wooden boards, bits of lumber, and metal sheeting.

"So what is it you want to see?" asked Miyazawa, turning to Kusanagi.

Kusanagi gestured to Utsumi who was standing just behind him. He had also brought several junior officers along with them, to handle any physical work.

Utsumi deftly thumbed her phone, then showed the display to Maya Miyazawa. "These things."

Kusanagi scrutinized the young bookstore owner's face. He didn't want to miss even the subtlest change in her expression.

He thought he saw a slight twitch in one of her cheeks. He had no way of parsing her reaction to what Utsumi had shown her. Had she been shocked and dismayed? Or was she expecting it?

"You mean . . . the treasure chests?"

"Correct," Kusanagi replied. "I heard from people who saw the parade that there were several of them."

"Yes, we made five."

"Are they here?"

"They're here." Maya Miyazawa ran her eye around the storeroom. "But they've been disassembled."

"That's not a problem. If you show my men how to do it, they can put them back together again."

"Fine. What color chest do you want to start with?"

"How many colors are there?"

"They're all different. We've got gold, silver, copper, red, and blue. They're all the same size and shape."

"In that case, any color will do."

Maya Miyazawa nodded. "Follow me," she said and headed for the back of the storeroom. With a jerk of his head, Kusanagi indicated for the junior officers to follow her.

As he watched them putting together the chest under Maya Miyazawa's guidance, Kusanagi took out an e-cigarette and started vaping. He had given up traditional cigarettes three years before.

"Do you smoke that thing when you're with Professor Yukawa?" Utsumi asked, walking over to him.

"Never. If he knew I smoked this thing, he'd tease me, I know. He'd say that I was illogical—I was giving up smoking without really giving it up."

"I happen to agree with him."

"Oh, shut up and leave me alone. They're my damn lungs."

While they were chatting, the young officers had finished assembling the treasure chest.

The base resembled a large handcart. The treasure chest, which was about three feet high, had its lid up, and was overflowing with gold and jewels. When Kusanagi touched the "treasure," it turned out to be a sheet of carved polystyrene that was glued into place.

"It's pretty tacky when seen up close, isn't it?" said Maya Miyazawa self-mockingly in a bid to preempt any criticism. "The chest itself is made of plywood." She rapped the side of the chest with her knuckles. It made a flimsy, hollow sound.

"Can you shut the lid?" Kusanagi asked.

"No, you can't. It's fixed open like this."

"What about the inside?"

"What about it? The treasure part is just a shelf, like a false bottom. There's nothing under it."

Kusanagi grabbed the handle part of the trolley with both hands and gave it a shove. It moved much more easily than he had expected. When he pushed down gently on the handle, the front wheels of the trolley rose off the ground.

Kusanagi exchanged a look with Utsumi. She gave a discreet nod, as if to say, *Just as Professor Yukawa predicted.*

"Is there anything else?" Maya Miyazawa asked.

"We'll get back to you. So this treasure chest here is complete?"

"Yes."

"And it was used in the parade just like this?"

"Yes . . ."

Kusanagi detected a suggestion of wariness on Maya Miyazawa's face.

"Detective Utsumi, show Ms. Miyazawa that video."

"Yes, sir," said Utsumi, thumbing her phone again.

"This video was taken by one of the spectators on the day of the parade," said Utsumi, showing the screen of her phone to Miyazawa Maya. "There are people dressed in pirate costumes dashing around and pushing the treasure chests."

"So what?"

"They're performing little stunts. Sometimes they stand on the backs of the trolleys, but the front wheels don't lift off the ground. We consulted an expert and he said that would only be possible if the treasure chests were weighted down in some way."

Maya Miyazawa nodded and moistened her lips with her tongue. "Oh, is that what this is about?"

"Did you do something to make the chests heavier?" Kusanagi asked.

"Yes, we added ballast. Sorry. I forgot to mention that."

Did she really forget? Kusanagi wasn't inclined to believe her. "Tell us about this ballast then."

"When the chest is like this, its balance is hopeless. The lid is open, right? That gives the chest a very high center of gravity. Unless you're very careful, the whole thing will just topple over. We put ballast in the bottom of the chest to add stability. We actually killed two birds with one stone that way. You need to be a good actor to make it look like you're pushing something heavy when you're actually pushing something that doesn't weigh much. That's too much for amateurs."

"Our expert reckons that the overall weight, chest included, would have to be around ninety pounds," Utsumi said.

"That's probably about what we had."

"What did you use for ballast?"

"Bottles of tea and water. We stuck a couple of cardboard boxes—each of them holding six two-liter plastic bottles—into each of the chests. When we'd finished marching in the parade, we gave the drinks away."

Kusanagi did some quick mental arithmetic. That would be fifty-three pounds per chest.

"How did you get the boxes in and out?"

"That's not especially difficult. In fact, it's easy." Maya Miyazawa undid a couple of metal clips at either end of the chest. The front and both side panels swung down and open, exposing the interior. A couple of straps were bolted to the bottom of the empty chest. "You stick the boxes in here, fix them in place with these straps, and then put the sides back up."

It certainly was very simple. You could probably do it in less than three minutes.

"When did you put the ballast in the chests?"

"When we assembled them. On the morning of the parade."

"Where did you do it?"

"At a sports ground near the starting point of the parade. It was the designated place for the teams to prepare."

"Your team was the last team in the parade. Were the treasure chests in the sports ground the whole time you were waiting?"

"Yes. Does that matter?"

"There are more and more teams taking part in the parade every year. Isn't there a risk of mix-ups with so many people milling around in one place?"

"To an extent, yes," conceded Maya Miyazawa. "That's why we get there early. We want to be sure we've got more than enough time to make our preparations."

"With the place being so crowded, would you notice if someone tampered with your props?"

Maya Miyazawa's face clouded over. "Tampered? What do you mean?"

"It might, for example, be possible for someone to surreptitiously replace the ballast in the chest with something else."

Maya Miyazawa looked puzzled. "Why on earth would anyone want to do a thing like that? Still, I suppose that, yes, someone could probably do it, if they wanted to."

"What did you do with the chests when you got to the end of the parade?"

"We stored them in the yard of the nearby elementary school. Just temporarily."

"Temporarily meaning how long?"

"Until the results were announced. If you make the top three, you get to do an encore. Sadly, we finished fourth."

"How long did you have to wait for the announcement?"

"About two hours."

"I know I'm repeating myself, but were the treasure chests in the schoolyard throughout those two hours?"

"They were," replied Maya Miyazawa, looking rather fed up. She flung out her right hand, palm facing outward, as if to parry Kusanagi's next question.

"Don't! I know what you're going to ask me. Would I have noticed if someone had tampered with them there? The answer is, no, probably not. Are you happy now?"

"Thank you very much," said Kusanagi. "Who was responsible for assembling and disassembling the chests?"

"The props team."

"Did you get any feedback from them? Any reports of anything untoward happening with the chests?"

"No, not so much as a peep." Maya Miyazawa shook her head.

"Okay. Could I get the names and contact details for everyone on the props team?"

"Sure. I'll email you a list later."

Kusanagi peered into the back of the storeroom. "Oh, that reminds me. Would I be right in thinking that the themes of the performances are kept secret until the day of the parade?"

"Absolutely. We never tell anyone the theme unless they're directly connected to the team."

"Meaning who exactly?"

"The members of the team and our supporters."

"Your supporters?"

"Our sponsors, I mean. The money we get from the local authority doesn't come near to covering our expenses. My bookstore makes a contribution, for example."

"How about Tojima-ya Foods?"

Maya Miyazawa seemed to catch her breath. She nodded feebly.

"Tojima-ya Foods is one of the bigger local businesses. Yes, they support us, too."

"You seem to be on friendly terms with Shusaku Tojima, the firm's managing director. Would he have known the theme of this year's performance in advance?"

"Probably."

"Would he have known about the treasure chests?"

"I'm not sure." Maya Miyazawa tilted her head to one side. "Some of the sponsors drop in on us to see how we're getting on with our preparations. He could have come by when I wasn't here. But if he did, someone would have shown him what we were doing."

"You don't recall showing him yourself?"

"I don't remember doing so. I can't be sure. Maybe it's slipped my mind."

Maya Miyazawa was choosing her words with care. One got the impression she was doing her best to avoid any inconsistencies finding their way into her story.

Kusanagi opted for a change of tack.

"You saw the Niikuras at the starting line before the parade got underway, didn't you?"

"Uh-huh . . ." There was a look of vague distrust on Maya Miyazawa's face. "They help out with the music and they did a last-minute sound check for us. I've already discussed this with another detective."

Kishitani had interviewed Maya Miyazawa to confirm the Niikuras' alibi. At the time, they had regarded her as a third party with no direct connection to the case.

"How long did you chat to the Niikuras for?"

"Oh, I don't know: ten, possibly fifteen minutes." Maya Miyazawa's head was at an angle of forty-five degrees and she was looking off into the middle distance.

"Did you speak to Tomoya Takagaki when you got to the finish?"

"I did, yes."

"You just said hello and nothing more than that. Is that right?"

"Uh-huh, right."

Kusanagi was about to ask another question when Maya Miyazawa said, "Detective, could I ask you a question?"

"What?"

"I'm familiar with the concept of perjury, but what about remaining silent? Is that also a crime?"

"Remaining silent?"

"Yes. Not lying, but not answering any questions, either. Does that count as a crime, too?"

Kusanagi gave a small shake of the head. "No, it doesn't."

"I thought as much. There is such a thing as the right to remain silent."

"What are you trying to say, Ms. Miyazawa?"

Maya Miyazawa inhaled deeply. "I'm not going to inquire why you're so interested in these treasure chests. At the same time, I don't want to make any careless remarks involving people who are my customers and whose patronage I value."

"Customers. Who do you mean?"

"Everybody who lives around here. No, I'll rephrase that. By customers, I mean not just the people who live in this neighborhood but anyone who could come into my bookstore. I don't want to do anything that might be prejudicial to any of them. So, if you're planning to come and see me again to ask me about my customers, let me just tell you up front that you'll probably be wasting your time."

"You mean to cover for them?"

"I mean to keep my mouth shut. I have the right to remain silent if I want," said Maya Miyazawa with a smile. She turned around and looked at the treasure chest. "If you've finished what you came for, I'd appreciate it if you tidied up after yourselves."

Kusanagi glanced over at the junior officers. "Give the woman a hand," he said, with a jerk of his chin.

37

Feeling a light tap on his shoulder, Tomoya Takagaki turned around. Tsukamoto, his section chief, was standing close behind him. Although he was a good-natured fellow, he looked unusually tense. "You got a minute?"

"Sure."

"Okay." Tsukamoto pointed in the direction of the door and marched off toward it. That must mean *Follow me*. Tomoya scrambled to his feet.

It was only when they were sitting across from each other in the meeting room that Tsukamoto began to speak.

"Tanaka told me something bizarre. About a detective coming to his apartment the other day. A woman."

Tomoya gasped.

"I'm guessing from your reaction that you know what this is about," Tsukamoto said. His voice was low and tense, and his eyes, behind the lenses of his glasses, were stern. "Tanaka told me that the same detective also went to see Ms. Sato. Sato was asking him for his advice."

Tanaka was one of Tomoya's colleagues, and a little younger than he was. Sato was a brand-new hire. Tomoya had taken both of them to see the parade.

"What sort of questions did she ask them?"

"About the day of the parade in Kikuno. You took them, didn't you?"

"Yes."

"She interviewed them in great detail about their movements that day. They both said that the detective was particularly persistent about confirming the precise time when the three of you split up to do your own thing."

Tomoya pictured Detective Utsumi's intelligent face. When she had the bit between her teeth, she wouldn't care how irritating she was.

"What the hell is this all about, Takagaki? Have you done something wrong?"

"Me? No, nothing," he replied reflexively. He had a sudden spasm of blinking.

"Then why are the police investigating your every move? It's not exactly normal."

"It's because—" Tomoya's voice broke. "It's because the guy who murdered my girlfriend was found dead. . . ."

"*What?*" Tsukamoto glared at him.

"And I seem to be a suspect. He died on the day of the parade. That's the reason they wanted to verify my alibi."

The blood drained from Tsukamoto's face, and the skin of his cheeks visibly tautened.

"Just a minute. This guy who killed your girlfriend, didn't they arrest him?"

"He was arrested, then released due to lack of evidence."

Tsukamoto's face was a picture of amazement.

"That's a serious crime you're connected to. . . . Why didn't you tell me?"

"It's a personal matter. Besides, I didn't want to inconvenience the firm. . . ."

"It's all very well you saying that, but it seems to me the inconvenience has already happened! Tanaka and Sato are both rattled."

"I'm very sorry."

Tsukamoto was jiggling his legs nervously up and down. It was obvious that he was annoyed and was having trouble getting his thoughts in order. His eyes swam around the room before finally coming to rest on Tomoya.

"Are we really okay here?"

"Is what okay?"

"I mean *you*: You didn't have anything to do with this incident, did you? Well?"

"No . . . I . . . uh . . . didn't."

He knew he should have put more oomph into his answer. He had sounded awkward and clumsy. Maybe that was why Tsukamoto still looked less than satisfied.

"Okay, fine. But I want you to let me know if there are any developments. You understand?"

"Yes, sir. I'm very sorry." Tomoya bowed his head apologetically.

Tsukamoto rose to his feet and opened the meeting-room door. He turned around as he was about to leave the room. "And I don't want you giving Tanaka and Sato any blowback."

"I understand, sir."

Tsukamoto went out into the hallway and slammed the door behind him.

Tomoya waited a moment, then headed back to his desk. Tanaka's desk was in the corner of the same room. Their eyes happened to meet. Tanaka looked desperately embarrassed. Tomoya, meanwhile, produced his best forced smile.

When the end of the working day arrived, he hurriedly tidied up his desk, then left the office. There was still work he had to do, but today he couldn't bear to stay in the office even a minute longer.

He was on his way to the station when he heard someone calling his name. He started. He recognized that voice.

He stopped and looked around. He was right. It was her—and she was walking toward him.

"Good evening. I see you're done for the day," said Utsumi, by way of a greeting.

"Not again?"

"I'm afraid so. I've got lots of questions I want to ask you."

"Lots?"

The female detective took a step closer. "So, if you don't mind, I'd like you to accompany me to the Kikuno Police Station. It shouldn't take long and I can drive you home afterward."

"Accompany you . . . ?" murmured Tomoya in a stupor. He looked past Utsumi and realized that, at some point, several men in suits had surrounded him.

"If you don't mind?" Utsumi bobbed her head. Tomoya couldn't muster a reply.

There was a black car parked nearby. He was ordered to get in. When he looked out of the car window, he got a shock.

Tsukamoto, his section chief, was standing on the sidewalk, rooted to the spot in amazement.

Tomoya, who had never been in an interview room in a police station before in his life, found himself sitting opposite a man by the name of Kusanagi. He reminded him of a recently retired athlete. Kusanagi started by telling Tomoya his name and rank, but Tomoya wasn't listening. The knowledge that Kusanagi was a battle-hardened detective was enough to make him shrivel up inside.

Tomoya's heart was still pounding even though it had been several minutes since he had been brought into the station. And shivers were running up his spine, despite his temperature having spiked from all the excitement.

"You look pretty nervous," Kusanagi said, as if he could read Tomoya's emotions like a book. "Just relax. As long as you answer my questions, this will be over and done with in no time."

What kind of questions are you planning on asking me? Tomoya wanted to say, but his lips wouldn't cooperate.

"There's just one thing I want you to tell me." Kusanagi held up the index finger of one hand. "Your movements on the day of the parade. That's all."

Tomoya finally managed to speak.

"But I've already . . ."

"Yes, I know, you've already told Detective Utsumi. She reports to me." Kusanagi glanced to the side, where Utsumi was sitting with her laptop, then returned his gaze to Tomoya. "A couple of your colleagues . . . Let's see." He picked up a sheaf of documents from the table. "Ah, here we go. You watched the parade with a Mr. Tanaka and a Ms. Sato. There was, however, a stretch of time when you separated; from a little after three P.M. to four P.M. It's that hiatus I want to ask you about. We know that you went to say hello to Ms. Maya Miyazawa, the owner of Miyazawa Books, at the finish area—but what were you doing for the rest of the time?"

"What was I doing? I don't know. Nothing special . . . Just walking around the place."

"The place being—where exactly?"

"The shopping district."

"That's funny." Kusanagi dropped the sheaf of documents onto the table and crossed his arms. "We've reviewed all the footage of all the security cameras in the shopping district, but we can't find you on any of them for that whole hour, even though we did find your friends Tanaka and Sato in multiple locations. So where were you all that time?"

Tomoya lowered his eyes. His heart was beating even faster. He could feel the sweat beading on his temples.

Tomoya knew better than to make anything up on the fly. He had no idea where the damn security cameras in the shopping district were located.

"I don't remember," he said weakly. It was the best he could do in the circumstances.

"Mr. Takagaki," Kusanagi said to him. "Mr. Takagaki, look at me."

Tomoya timidly looked up. Kusanagi placed a single photograph on the desk. When Tomoya saw what it was, his heart started pounding even faster.

"You know what this is?"

"A treasure chest . . ."

"That's right. It's one of the props Team Kikuno used in the parade. Now, we know something interesting about these treasure chests. They were loaded with bottles of oolong tea and water as ballast to stabilize them. Once the parade was finished, the drinks were distributed to the staff—but that was when something odd happened. With this one chest, the original oolong tea had disappeared, while the number of bottles of water had increased! Everyone assumed that the guy in charge of the props had just made a mistake. He is adamant that he didn't. I wonder what really happened?" Kusanagi was speaking softly, but every word he uttered was boring a hole into Tomoya's guts.

"We believe that this strange episode of the treasure chest is intimately connected with Kanichi Hasunuma, the suspect in a murder, who died that day. Through our investigative work, we've identified your actions as a key issue—particularly that unaccounted-for gap of thirty or forty minutes. That's why we must find out what you were doing in that time."

Tomoya lowered his eyes again. He couldn't maintain eye contact with Kusanagi.

Suddenly, Tojima's voice was echoing around his head. It was something he had said to him on the phone the other day.

Tell the truth, if you absolutely have to. You don't have to lie and you don't need to hide anything—

Is now that time? he wondered. *But if I come out and tell the truth, what will that mean for everyone else? Won't they be charged with a crime? I can't let that happen. A man died!*

"There were five treasure chests," Kusanagi continued. "We're currently checking them all for fingerprints, paying particular attention to the metal clasps on the side panels."

I'm okay there, thought Tomoya. *I had gloves on.*

"Of course, fingerprints aren't the only thing we'll be checking for. There's also DNA. The science is now so advanced that we can analyze the tiniest amount of anything: sebaceous matter, sweat, dandruff. Unless you wear a full face mask, it's almost impossible to prevent crap like that falling off your head and sticking to things. We'll also be checking for hair. Oh, and, last but not least, glove prints."

Tomoya was horrified and his shoulders spasmed.

"Something wrong?" asked Kusanagi, who had noticed his reactions. "Haven't you heard about glove prints? They're marks that are left when you touch something wearing gloves. We can work out what kind of gloves a person was wearing. Cotton work gloves leave behind fibers that we can identify. Which reminds me—" Kusanagi paused a moment, then went on. "Forensics have found glove prints on one of the chests. Leather gloves, they tell me. The thing with leather gloves is that leather has a distinct grain, meaning every pair is different. Once we've checked the glove prints properly, we'll be able to identify the gloves that were used."

Cold sweat was oozing from Tomoya's armpits. He could feel his ears reddening, but his body was beyond his control.

"Mr. Takagaki," Kusanagi repeated. "I'm sure that you own at least one pair of leather gloves. I just need to put through a little paperwork, then we'll have the right to go and look around your house. It's something called a domiciliary search. If we find any leather gloves, we'll test them to see if they're a match for the prints on the treasure chest. If we don't find any gloves at your house, then we'll go to your office. We will dig around everywhere: your desk, your locker, you name it. Is that what you want?"

"Of course it isn't," continued Kusanagi, answering his own question. "It will be a nasty surprise for your mother. Worse than a surprise. She'll be so worried about what her little boy's gone and done that she'll probably get stomach cramps. It'll be the same with the people at work: your bosses, your coworkers—they'll all start looking at you differently. That's got to be something you want to avoid?

"To be frank, it's not how we want to proceed, either. We'd like to get the job done without having to go so far. That's why we're offering you a way out. This thirty- or forty-minute-long gap on the day of the parade—just tell us what you were doing, and we can all spare ourselves a great deal of unpleasantness. Well? Are you tempted? Or do you prefer the other path where you break your mother's heart and get shunned by your workmates?"

Kusanagi was a veteran detective who had locked horns with the wiliest of criminals over his career. He had driven Tomoya into a corner. In his mind's eye, the young man could see his mother, Rie, brooding and fearful, and his boss, Tsukamoto, bitter and aggrieved.

"*Mr. Takagaki.*" Kusanagi was almost shouting as he smacked the table hard. Tomoya's head jerked up in shock.

"This is your last chance. Tell me about that thirty- or forty-minute gap. If you choose not to answer, it's no skin off my nose. But, if that's what you opt to do, we will keep you here in the station overnight. And as soon as we release you, I will be applying for a search warrant. If you change your mind then, I'm afraid it will be too late. *What do you want to do?*" Kusanagi was speaking fast in an effort to bulldoze Tomoya into submission.

Tomoya felt lost. He buried his head in his hands. In front of him, he seemed to see a deep, dark abyss.

When he glanced off to the side, his eyes met Utsumi's. She nodded tenderly, giving him a look that seemed to say, *I know exactly how you feel.* He had always thought of her as coldhearted and hardheaded; now, however, she could have been the Virgin Mary.

Tomoya drew himself up and looked Kusanagi in the eye.

"You promise you'll keep this secret from my mother and my colleagues at work?"

"I promise," Kusanagi replied emphatically.

38

Tomoya Takagaki's statement went something like this.

One evening, a few days before the parade, he had just left Namiki-ya, when Tojima called out to him from his car. "I've got something important I need to talk with you about." They drove a certain distance away, at which point Tojima made his surprising pitch. He wanted to strike Hasunuma a hammerblow, and he needed Tomoya's help.

"We're not going to kill the guy," Tojima said. "But we are going to punish him—sanction him, if you like."

Tojima didn't go into any detail of how Hasunuma was going to be punished. "It's better that you don't know," was all he said. "If everything ends up going according to plan, then I'll tell you. Until then, I want you to act in good faith and accept being kept at arm's length. Everyone's agreed to those terms."

Tojima couldn't reveal who "everyone" was, he explained.

"If you insist that I reveal their names, then that's it. If that's what you want, you should get out of this car right now and go home. And this little talk we're having now, it never happened."

Tomoya could guess easily enough: It had to be Yutaro Namiki and Naoki Niikura.

"Can I decide after you've told me what it is you want me to do?" Tomoya asked.

"Of course you can," Tojima replied.

What Tojima went on to say was nothing like what Tomoya had been expecting. On the day of the parade, Tojima wanted him to transport an item hidden inside one of Team Kikuno's props from one place to another.

"When I say prop, I mean it's a treasure chest. The theme of this year's performance is Treasure Island, so it's going to feature five treasure chests. They're all different colors; the item we need will be hidden inside the silver chest. Once Team Kikuno gets to the finish line, we need you to remove the item from the chest, transport it somewhere in a truck, then return the truck to its original location. That's all you have to do." Tojima paused. "If you agree to do the job, I can share a few more details with you."

From Tojima's description, the job didn't sound especially difficult. Tojima offered him a day to consider, but Tomoya felt that dithering would be an insult to Saori's memory.

"I'm in," he said.

Come the actual day, Tomoya watched the parade with his two coworkers. They briefly went their separate ways just after 3 p.m., when the parade ended. It was Tomoya himself who suggested that they do so.

He went to the finish line and looked for Maya Miyazawa. Tojima had advised him to go and say hello to her, so he'd have an alibi.

Having found and exchanged a few words with her, Tomoya headed for Yamabe Shoten, a rice shop about one hundred feet farther along the road. The shop was closed for the day. A minitruck was in the parking lot to one side of it. On the flatbed of the truck were a trolley, two cardboard boxes, and a white plastic bag. Each of the cardboard boxes contained six two-liter bottles of water, while the plastic bag contained one of the official staff jackets worn by volunteers helping with the parade.

Tomoya slipped on the jacket, loaded the two cardboard boxes onto the trolley, and headed for the nearby elementary school. The area was full of people bustling about wearing the same jacket he had on. Nobody gave him a second glance.

He went to the schoolyard and looked around for the silver chest. It didn't take him long to find it. There was no one nearby.

As he walked up to the chest, he slipped on the leather gloves he had in his pocket, then, after checking that no one was watching, he opened the side panels of the chest as Tojima had taught him to do.

Inside, he found a large cardboard box held in place with two straps. When he slid it out and put it to one side, he was surprised at how much it weighed.

Tojima had told him that the box contained liquid nitrogen. (Tojima hadn't wanted to reveal the contents to Tomoya, but he was worried that keeping him in the dark could be dangerous.)

"The cardboard box is not hermetically sealed. A sealed box would swell and burst because liquid nitrogen is gasifying all the time. Be sure to wear leather gloves when you carry the thing. That's not just to avoid leaving fingerprints; it's also a precaution against getting any liquid nitrogen on your hands, should the container topple over inside the box. Cotton or cloth gloves aren't good enough; liquid nitrogen will penetrate them and give you frostbite."

The leather gloves he used had been a Christmas present from his mother.

He put the two boxes full of bottled water into the chest, retied the straps, and put the side panels back in place. Then he lifted the cardboard box he had removed from the chest onto the trolley and went back the way he had come. No one paid him any attention. After looking around to check that no one was watching, he took off the staff jacket.

When he got back to the rice merchant's, he loaded the cardboard box onto the flatbed of the truck, then went to check the front number plate. The car key was stuck to the back of it with tape, just as Tojima had said it would be. He fired up the minitruck and headed for the hut where Hasunuma lived. When he got there, he dumped the box outside the door, got back into the minitruck, and returned to the rice shop. He put the key back behind the license plate and set out for the place where he had agreed to rendezvous with his friends, clutching a plastic bag with the staff jacket inside. On the way, he shoved the bag into the basket of an abandoned bike.

After spending a certain amount of time at the beer bar with his coworkers, he then headed off to Namiki-ya by himself. He wanted to find out what had happened. Had Hasunuma's punishment gone to plan?

A couple of the regular customers showed up after he got there, followed by Tojima, then the Niikuras. None of them would tell him anything.

Eventually, a friend of Maya Miyazawa's came into the restaurant. He looked rather shell-shocked. He gave Miyazawa a shocking piece of news: *Hasunuma was dead.*

Tomoya looked at Tojima.

Tojima refused to make eye contact.

Tomoya still had no idea what had happened that day and who— other than himself—had done what. Now that he had made his confession, he was eager to learn the whole truth as soon as possible.

39

When he had finished reading the statement, Director Mamiya looked up at Kusanagi. The crotchety expression on his face turned into a smile as he dropped the document onto his desk. "Good job."

"Thank you, sir." Kusanagi nodded.

"Utsumi told me that you called Takagaki's bluff big-time."

"Oh, the business with the leather gloves?"

"Yes. She told me Forensics hadn't actually reported finding any glove prints."

"I was using something I'd picked up from Yukawa. If liquid nitrogen was used in the crime, he said, whoever handled it would have to have worn leather gloves. Takagaki's expression changed when I brought up the subject of glove prints, so I thought, maybe I'm onto something."

"Nice." Mamiya picked the statement off the desk. "The way they transported the liquid nitrogen—that was a surprise."

"Honestly, I was skeptical when Utsumi first told me about Yukawa's theory. It was only after we went to see Maya Miyazawa that I started thinking he might be onto something."

Yukawa had theorized that the liquid nitrogen had been transported concealed inside one of the treasure chests. Still, the idea that all the members of Team Kikuno were in on it hardly seemed plausible. It seemed more likely that Maya Miyazawa, the team leader, was the only one involved. Even she probably had no idea how dangerous the cargo was and probably took no direct part in the loading and unloading of the chest. The person who handled that task had to be someone more intimately associated with Saori Namiki.

That was when they thought of Tomoya Takagaki. Suddenly, the fact that he had talked to Maya Miyazawa after the parade and that unexplained gap of thirty or forty minutes felt very suspicious.

"By that time, we had already reviewed all the security-camera footage in an effort to find someone with a large piece of baggage. What we had failed to scrutinize were the start and the end points of the parade. The performers were carrying large props and pieces of scenery around in those areas, but we didn't see that as problematic, as long as they stayed in those two areas.

"Did Takagaki remove the item from the treasure chest at the end of the parade? When we started asking that question, we realized something else: There had to be another person who had put the item *into* the treasure chest at the start of the parade.

"We assumed that this individual would be as close to—or possibly even closer to—Saori Namiki than Takagaki. That left us with a short list of candidates. We asked those people to come in for questioning and Inspector Kishitani and his team are currently interviewing them."

Mamiya nodded. He seemed pleased.

"Do you think that there were more accomplices?"

"Perhaps. But the functions of the different individuals all had a different level of importance. Take Takagaki as an example. Although he knew that the plan was to punish Hasunuma, no one filled him in on the details. There may be other people who played their part knowing even less than he did. This morning, I sent an investigator to Yamabe Shoten, the rice merchant, to speak to the proprietor there. He admitted lending his minitruck and a trolley to Tojima, as well as buying some bottled water for him. Tojima gave him the staff jacket in advance and told him to put it together with the other things. The explanation Tojima gave was that he'd been asked to help out with the parade at the last minute."

Mamiya stroked his chin. "Do you think Tojima masterminded it all?"

"I'm pretty sure he did. What I can't get my head around, though, is the way none of the Namikis seem to be tied in. If the goal was to avenge Saori, then it is weird for the Namiki family not to be involved."

Mamiya said nothing. Kusanagi interpreted his silence as agreement.

One of the junior detectives sidled over. "Excuse me, sir?"

"What is it?" Kusanagi asked.

"Shusaku Tojima is here, sir."

Kusanagi and Mamiya exchanged a look.

"The eagle has landed," Mamiya said.

"I'll go and look in on him." Kusanagi saluted the director, turned smartly on his heel, and marched off.

Shusaku Tojima was waiting in the interview room, his shoulders slumping with an air of slighted virtue. Kusanagi exchanged a look with Detective Utsumi, who was once again going to be taking notes, and sat down. "Thanks for coming in."

"Not at all," said Tojima, with a curt nod.

His salt-and-pepper hair was cut close to his scalp. His face rugged and tough-looking. He certainly wasn't most people's idea of what a successful businessman should look like, but he must have excellent people skills to have expanded a modest family business to its present size. With an opponent like this, things wouldn't be as easy as they had been with Tomoya Takagaki, Kusanagi thought.

"Has Mr. Takagaki been in touch with you?"

"Mr. Takagaki? Oh, you mean young Tomoya? No. Why?"

Although Kusanagi thought it highly unlikely that Tomoya Takagaki hadn't phoned Tojima after getting home from the police station the night before, he never expected Tojima to admit it.

"We heard that you and Mr. Takagaki had a very private conversation just a few days before the parade."

"When exactly?" Tojima tilted his head to one side. "I'm always bumping into that guy. At Namiki-ya and elsewhere."

"This was outside Namiki-ya. You were sitting in your car and called out to Mr. Takagaki after he left the restaurant. 'There's something I need to talk to you about,' you said. Jog your memory?"

"Ah." Tojima's jaw slackened a little and he jerked his chin. "*That* day."

"What did you talk about?"

After calmly looking at each of his interviewers in turn, his questioning eyes came to rest on Kusanagi. "What did he tell you?"

"We do the asking here." Kusanagi smiled sourly. "Just answer the question. What did you talk about?"

"A private matter."

"Takagaki told us everything."

Tojima nodded and stretched.

"If he's already told you, then you're all right, aren't you? You can take what he said on trust."

"Should we?"

"That's up to you, Officer."

"'Help me punish Hasunuma,'" said Kusanagi, looking the other man right in the eye. "That's what Takagaki told us you said to him."

Nothing changed in Tojima's face. If anything, he appeared to relax a little.

"If that's what he says, then maybe it's true."

"Are you denying it?"

"I'm not denying anything, Detective." Tojima grimaced. "I said maybe it's true."

He's a sly old bugger, this one, thought Kusanagi.

"A certain item was necessary for that punishment. You needed that item delivered to the hut where Hasunuma was living. That's what Takagaki says you asked him to do. Is that true?"

"Well, if that's what he says—"

"I am asking *you*," Kusanagi interrupted. "Did you ask Takagaki to do that?"

Tojima wasn't going to cede an inch. "I'll leave that to your imagination."

Kusanagi half rose from his chair and leaned over the table toward Tojima.

"What was that item? What did you ask Takagaki to deliver for you?"

"Is it a crime," Tojima said, glaring right back at him, "if I refuse to answer?"

"What's your reason for not answering?"

"I don't want to."

Keeping his eyes firmly on Tojima and the butter-wouldn't-melt-in-my-mouth expression on his face, Kusanagi pulled his chair in closer.

"As things stand, Mr. Takagaki's statement will be used as evidence in court. Doesn't that bother you?"

"Court? I don't know what you're talking about." Tojima shrugged demurely. "Anyway, there's nothing I can do."

Kusanagi put his clasped hands on the table.

"When we arrested Hasunuma several months ago, I was put in charge of the investigation. Did you know that?"

"Uh-huh." Tojima gave a curt nod. "Yutaro told me."

"Yutaro . . . Still on first-name terms at your age—isn't that sweet? That's friendship for you. And I bet you adored his daughter Saori, too."

"I used to change her diapers on the tables in Namiki-ya," Tojima said, grinning.

"Believe me, I understand why you loathed Hasunuma. We felt frustrated, too, not being able to get him off the streets."

"You felt frustrated? You can't compare your frustration to ours," Tojima said. He was still smiling, but there was a fierce light in his eyes. "Ours was of a different dimension, a different level."

"You don't mind if we make a record of that?"

"Be my guest," said Tojima. "If it's speeches about my loathing for Hasunuma you want to hear, I can keep going all day."

"What we want you to tell us is what you did *because* of your loathing him."

"I'll leave that to your imagination."

"Would you be prepared to sign a statement we come up with based on us letting our imaginations run wild?"

Tojima snorted derisively. "Of course not. But if you do produce one, I'd be happy to read it. I'm curious what you think I did."

"You want us to give free rein to our imaginations? Okay, then. I bet that when Takagaki phoned you last night, you were even more spooked than when we searched your factory. I bet that you never expected us to figure out the liquid nitrogen thing, let alone the treasure chest ploy, too. Some people have exceptional powers of imagination."

A shadow flitted behind Tojima's eyes. It was the first sign of insecurity he had shown so far.

"Are you talking about that . . . that university professor? That Yukawa fellow . . . ?"

"Yes, what about him?"

"If I'm wrong, fine." Tojima waved a hand. "Just forget about it."

"Which is why, Mr. Tojima"—Kusanagi stared at the other man with renewed intensity—"it's only a matter of time before we figure out how all of you worked together to do what you did. Tell us everything now and the penalty you face will be that much lighter. Do you get that, Mr. Tojima? Maybe Hasunuma was a brute and maybe he didn't deserve to live—but killing him is still a crime. Only the judiciary has the right to sentence a man to death."

Tojima remained stone-faced. The twinge of alarm he had shown at the mention of Yukawa's name was gone.

"Except that they couldn't," said Tojima with open scorn. "The judiciary couldn't do it. They couldn't even bring the guy to trial."

"So you banded together and bumped him off for the family?"

Tojima endured Kusanagi's stare impassively and in silence. The silence lasted until there was a knock on the door.

"Come," Kusanagi said. The door opened. Inspector Kishitani stuck his head in.

"Excuse me one second," Kusanagi said to Tojima, getting to his feet.

He exited the interview room and shut the door behind him. "What's up? Has one of them cracked?"

Kusanagi had put Kishitani and his team in charge of interviewing Naoki Niikura and Rumi Niikura. Separately, of course.

"We've got a problem," Kishitani said quietly and with a look of dismay on his face. "The wife collapsed in the middle of the interview."

40

After seeing off the last of the customers, Natsumi went out to take down the *noren* curtain from above the entrance of the restaurant. It was about ten past ten at night. Namiki-ya had been busy for the first time in long time.

She was taking the curtain back inside, when she heard a male voice behind her. "Good evening." She recognized the voice.

"Professor . . . what are you doing here at this time of night? We're closed."

"I can see that. I'm here not as a customer, but as a friend. There's something important I need to discuss with your father." His eyes were grave even if his mouth was smiling. *He's different from normal*, Natsumi thought.

"Just a minute, Professor."

She went back into the restaurant and explained the situation to her parents, who were busy tidying things up in the kitchen. "That fellow?" Yutaro said, looking skeptical. He thought for a moment. "Fine, show him in," he said.

Natsumi went back outside and invited Yukawa in.

Yutaro and Machiko had come out of the kitchen. They both looked tense.

"Good evening. I'm sorry to barge in on you so late." Yukawa ducked his head apologetically at each of them in turn.

"What's this important thing you want to talk about?" Yutaro asked, not bothering to sit down.

"It's a little complicated. It involves the unnatural death of Kanichi Hasunuma."

"You're just an academic. His death's got nothing to do with you."

"Yes, I am an outsider—and that's an advantage here. When you know people on the police force, there's always a certain amount of information that leaks." Yukawa glanced briefly at Natsumi, before returning his gaze to Yutaro. "I have a friend who's a police officer. This friend of mine is actually in charge of the Hasunuma case. He doesn't *officially* know that I am here now."

Apparently, this meant that he did, in fact, know.

"I see," Yutaro said. He turned to Natsumi. "You, go upstairs."

"No. I want to hear this, too."

"*Natsumi.*"

"If it's okay with you," Yukawa broke in, "I'd like Natsumi to hear what I have to say as well."

Her father looked pained but said nothing, so Natsumi sat down.

"Professor, please, take a seat," Machiko said to Yukawa, pulling out a chair for herself. Yutaro also sat down, albeit with bad grace.

Natsumi bunched her hands into fists on her knees. She knew that whatever Yukawa had to say, it was going to be something extraordinary.

If she was honest with herself, both her parents had been behaving a bit strangely. It started late the night before when Yutaro got a phone call. Natsumi didn't know for sure who'd called him, but she guessed that it was Tojima.

"The police are learning more and more about Kanichi Hasunuma's unnatural death," Yukawa began, his tone bland and uninflected. "They are aware that multiple people were involved in the crime and they have already secured a statement from one of those people. I suspect, Mr. Namiki, that you were already aware of that. The person in question is Tomoya Takagaki, a frequent customer here at Namiki-ya."

How was Tomoya involved? Natsumi wondered.

"Takagaki said that he did what he did because Tojima asked him to. 'We want to inflict a hammerblow on Kanichi Hasunuma. Can you give me a hand?' The police believe that Tojima made a similar request to quite a few people and that ultimately a large group of people collaborated on Kanichi Hasunuma's punishment. I think their theory is correct. However, I cannot believe that Mr. Tojima would embark on something like this without your blessing. Would I be right in thinking that you were cognizant of the plan?" Yukawa was looking directly at Yutaro Namiki.

Yutaro cocked his head and emitted something halfway between a grunt and a sigh. "I'm not sure what you're getting at."

"As a thought experiment, I tried putting myself in your shoes," Yukawa continued in a matter-of-fact tone. "First, I imagined there was someone that I loathed with a complete and absolute hatred. Then I imagined myself wanting to get revenge on this person. I knew that if I killed him, suspicion would immediately fall on me. At that point, a close friend of mine proposed killing the man on my behalf. 'I'll deal with him,' he says. 'You focus on creating the perfect alibi for yourself.' I'm grateful, naturally, but would I actually agree to his proposal? Any slipups and my dear friend could go to jail. Personally, I wouldn't accept it. I wouldn't agree to such a proposal. And I don't think that you, Mr. Namiki, would do so, either. Well?"

Aghast, Natsumi listened to Yukawa's fluent little speech. Had all this been happening on the day of the parade without her knowledge?

"That's a complete and utter fairy tale. I don't know what else to say," Yutaro replied, his voice a lifeless monotone. "And even if it were true, I'd never have agreed to it."

"I think you're telling me the truth. Which means that, as I suspected, Mr. Tojima acted of his own volition and without your permission. When the police and the prosecutor have a clearer idea of how the murder was committed, they'll have to assemble a narrative of the crime in which has Shusaku Tojima as the mastermind and you having nothing to do with it. However, unnatural that particular version of events may feel, that's what they'll have to do. Because that's the way trials work. Will you be able to live with that, Mr. Namiki?"

Yutaro lowered his eyes. Machiko anxiously scrutinized his profile.

"Personally, I think that an accident occurred," Yukawa said. "On the day of the parade, a customer became sick. That threw everything out of whack. Not just for you but for Tojima and his associates, too. The police suspected that the whole indigestion episode might be an exercise in alibi creation, but it wasn't. After all, if you needed an alibi, you could have easily gotten your wife here to pretend to be sick and taken her to the hospital. What happened with the customer really was something that came out of left field.

Someone who'd eaten at your restaurant was feeling unwell. You couldn't just ignore the woman. Taking what must have been a very difficult decision, you drove her to the hospital. But what would have happened if that accident hadn't occurred? What role were you assigned in the original plan?"

Yukawa, who had delivered this speech with great energy, paused and sighed.

"I believe that you will regret it for the rest of your life if you have to sit by and watch Tojima and his associates being punished while that particular question remains unanswered. I believe you will end up blaming yourself for what happens to them. That's what I came here to say."

"Is it true, Dad?" Natsumi broke in. "What's going on, Mom? Tell me."

"Keep your mouth shut," Yutaro bellowed.

"I'm not going to—"

Yutaro gave the table a resounding smack before Natsumi could finish.

The silence lasted for a few seconds. Yutaro cleared his throat and looked at Yukawa.

"I appreciate your tact, Professor. What you say is right. Speaking as one man to another, you're right. Assuming your theory is correct, of course."

"But there's nothing you want to say?"

"I'm sorry," Yutaro said gloomily. "Now is not the right time for me to say anything. The others are all sticking to their guns and staying silent. How could I face them, if I talked?"

"Is that how you feel?" Yukawa broke into a smile. "Then there's nothing I can do. I'll stop interfering."

Yutaro bowed his head in silence.

"I'll be on my way," Yukawa said. As he got to his feet, his phone started buzzing in his inside jacket pocket. He pulled it out and looked at the display. "Excuse me a second," he said, turning away. Lifting the phone to his ear, he opened the sliding door and went out into the street.

Natsumi looked at her parents. Yutaro got up and made for the kitchen in a bid to avoid his daughter's gaze. Machiko stared broodily down at the floor.

"Mom—" Natsumi began. The sliding door opened, cutting her off. Yukawa stepped back inside, his face slightly flushed.

"There's been an important development. I may be divulging more of the investigation's secrets, but this is something I feel I absolutely I must tell you."

Yutaro came out of the kitchen. "Why? What's happened?"

"Naoki Niikura has confessed. He's saying that *he* was responsible for the death of Kanichi Hasunuma."

41

Chief Inspector Kusanagi and Eiji Masumura were once again facing each other in the interview room. When Kusanagi told Masumura that Niikura had confessed, the old man's shoulders slumped and he sighed loudly.

"He confessed, did he? Well, if he's admitted it, then that's that, I guess. That guy was probably in the tightest corner of all of us."

"That guy?" Kusanagi repeated. The phrase struck him as odd.

"Yeah, I've never met him. This Niikura guy. I'd never even heard his name before today."

Kusanagi exchanged a glance with Utsumi, who was sitting beside him taking notes on her laptop, then turned his attention back to Masumura.

"What do you mean? I need the full story."

Masumura groaned feebly. "Where should I start?"

"How about twenty-three years ago—with the Yuna Motohashi case?"

"No," said Masumura, tilting his head to one side. "I'll need to go further back than that for you to really understand things."

"Further back is fine."

"This'll be a long story. Very long."

"That's not a problem," Kusanagi said. He spread his arms in a gesture of invitation. "Please. Go ahead."

Masumura resettled himself in his chair and cleared his throat. He started to talk.

And his story really was a long story.

Masumura's main concern after his arrest for manslaughter was the negative impact it was likely to have on Yumiko's future.

Masumura adored his little stepsister, who was nine years younger than him. It was his determination to save her from the sort of hardships he had experienced that inspired him to work so hard, to send her money, and to then keep looking after every aspect of her life after their mother's sudden death, including arranging for her to attend an all-girls boarding school.

Masumura was keen for Yumiko to go to university. She had excellent grades. But after finishing high school, Yumiko, who was adamant that her brother had already done more than enough for her, got a job at a car manufacturer. She worked in a factory in Chiba and lived in an employee dormitory.

Convinced that he could at last put a difficult period of his life behind him, Masumura moved into a new apartment. The manslaughter incident occurred almost immediately after the move. When Yumiko came to visit him in the detention center, Masumura told her to stop visiting him.

"We should break off all contact. We're lucky. We've got different names. Even if people check your family register, they won't find out that we're related."

"Do you honestly think I could do that?" Yumiko protested through her tears.

She appeared as a character witness at his trial. Masumura couldn't hold back the tears when he listened to her heartfelt testimony about how much she owed her big brother and what a compassionate person he was.

She wrote to him often while he was serving his sentence. Her letters were a source of both comfort and concern to Masumura. He couldn't stop worrying that his life might have a baneful influence on her future.

A little before he was due to be released, a letter came from Yumiko in which she revealed that she had a new boyfriend. The man in question worked at the same firm as her and was on the management fast track. He was the son of the head of one of the company's subsidiaries and had been sent to Yumiko's factory for training.

Masumura lost no time in replying. She must never tell her boyfriend that she had a brother who'd been in jail and they should stop writing to each other immediately, he told her.

Yumiko, however, disobeyed, sending him another letter in which she begged him to contact her when he got out of jail.

The day of his release finally arrived. He called Yumiko with considerable trepidation. He hadn't heard her voice for a long time. She sounded well. As they chatted, they both became tearful.

Yumiko told him that she wanted to see him. He felt a hot surge in his chest. Unable to refuse, he agreed to meet her the very next day.

When he went to the agreed-upon place, he discovered that his baby sister, Yumiko, had grown into a woman. He couldn't find the words, even though there was so much that he wanted to say. It didn't matter. He was content just to look at the woman his sister had become.

"There's someone I want you to meet," Yumiko said.

A young man walked over to them. He was polite and sincere.

It was Seiji Motohashi—Yumiko's boyfriend.

Masumura was taken aback. He thought that his sister had kept his existence a secret.

"I told him about you because I knew he would understand," Yumiko said, looking at her boyfriend.

The two men started talking. Masumura learned that Moto-hashi's father's company was based in Adachi Ward and that Moto-hashi, who was then twenty-eight years old, would be moving back to the family firm in a few years' time.

When Motohashi went on to make a formal bow and ask for permission to marry his sister, Masumura was flabbergasted. He had never expected anyone to care how he felt.

"I'm wholeheartedly in favor of the marriage. What about you, though? Are you okay having me in your family?"

"That is a problem." Motohashi's face was drawn.

What he went on to say was pragmatic and down-to-earth.

He was in love with Yumiko and he trusted her implicitly. If she felt respect and a sense of indebtedness toward Masumura, then, for his part, he was prepared to overlook the fact that he'd been in jail. From what Yumiko had told him, it sounded as though the episode was more a matter of extreme bad luck than anything else.

The trouble was that other people weren't necessarily going to see it like that. He expected both his immediate and his extended family to oppose the marriage, Motohashi said.

That was why Motohashi wanted to keep Masumura's existence a secret, at least for a while. Yumiko, who was listening in silence, looked increasingly uncomfortable.

"No. That's not good enough," Masumura said. Both Moto-hashi and Yumiko flinched. "A while is not good enough. It's got to be permanent. You've got to keep me a secret permanently. If word gets out about me, Yumiko will be the one to suffer. Promise me that you'll never tell anyone in your family about me. Unless you make that promise, I'll withhold my consent. I won't permit the marriage."

Tears coursed down Yumiko's cheeks. Seiji Motohashi bowed his head. There was a pained expression on his face.

And that was how the two of them got married. It was the autumn of Yumiko's twenty-fourth year. Masumura gave her the family's old photo album as a wedding present. He had never showed it to anybody else.

Although the newlyweds never breathed a word about Masumura to anyone, Yumiko didn't break off contact with him. Brother and sister continued to meet, albeit at irregular intervals. Whenever they met, Yumiko would bring the baby Yuna with her. Since her husband was the only person who knew what she was doing, Masumura couldn't object.

Once Yuna started becoming aware of her surroundings, Yumiko stopped bringing her along. It was too risky; she might mention Masumura to someone else. Masumura, who missed his niece, had to content himself with photographs. Every time he met his sister, his stock of pictures of Yuna grew. They were a treasure more valuable than life itself.

More than ten years passed in this way. Yuna was twelve years old when the calamity occurred. One day, she just vanished. In a frenzy of anxiety, Masumura went to see Yumiko.

She was haggard. An empty shell. Completely. He was terrified she might do something rash.

His sense of foreboding proved prescient. Yumiko jumped to her death from the roof of a nearby building one month after Yuna's disappearance. In the suicide note she left behind, she apologized for being a bad mother.

Masumura wept inconsolably when he got the news from his brother-in-law.

His memory of the next few years was unclear. He lived in a daze, his life empty and devoid of purpose.

The discovery of Yuna's body brought him back to earth with a jolt. He learned about it from a random newspaper article that happened to catch his eye. He had lost touch with Seiji Motohashi.

He thought he had steeled himself but having to confront the fact of her dead body being found was still a shock. The profound despair that overwhelmed him was reinforced by a second wave of grief at the loss of his sister.

Who could have committed such an atrocious act? he wondered. Several years had already passed and Masumura wasn't hopeful that the killer would ever be found.

He turned out to be wrong. Soon after, the perpetrator was caught. A man by the name of Kanichi Hasunuma.

Masumura couldn't help himself. Full of trepidation, he reached out to his brother-in-law.

When Seiji Motohashi answered the phone, he sounded utterly dejected. Was it because the arrest of the perpetrator would still not bring Yuna and Yumiko back to life?

No.

Motohashi explained that the arrested man was refusing to say anything. This was preventing the police from getting any closer to the truth of what had happened.

"That's just a temporary thing. It won't last," Masumura said. "I've got firsthand experience, so I know what I'm talking about. Your brain shuts down when you're arrested. Often, even if you want to say something, your mouth can't get the words out. You're terrified that you might say something stupid that you can't ever take back. Don't worry. Detectives know how to get people to talk; it's their job. Just hang in there a little longer, the guy's sure to confess."

"I hope so . . . ," Motohashi muttered gloomily. The police had already briefed him, so he knew that Hasunuma was probably keeping quiet as part of a strategy to get maximum leverage from his right to silence.

Masumura was more optimistic. Now that the perpetrator had been arrested, he would have to go on trial at some point. The man hadn't just murdered a child, he had also driven her mother to suicide. He deserved the death penalty.

Masumura was expecting the day the verdict was announced to be the day when the spirits of Yuna and Yumiko could finally attain their eternal rest. As the day approached, he started to think that perhaps it was time for him to make a fresh start in life, too.

The reality turned out very different. As he read about the trial verdict in the newspaper, he was incredulous. Was this even possible? *Not guilty?* He read and reread the article. Was the journalist talking about some other case? No, there was her name—Yuna Motohashi—in black and white.

Masumura immediately phoned Motohashi. "What the hell's going on?" he asked, knowing the question was futile.

"It was a matter of . . . insufficient evidence. I don't know what went wrong. All we can do is trust the prosecutor."

The pain in Motohashi's voice made Masumura acutely conscious of his own powerlessness. *There was nothing he could do*—and he despised himself for it.

All he could do was pray; pray they would win the appeal. If Hasunuma managed a second not-guilty verdict, he would know that there was no God.

But the second trial likewise failed to produce a guilty verdict. This time, Masumura saw it on the television news. His legs turned to water and he couldn't stand up for several minutes. The whole thing seemed like a terrible dream.

On this one occasion, he didn't call his brother-in-law. He knew that Motohashi would be as devastated—no, perhaps even more devastated—than he was.

He wondered if Motohashi was thinking of taking justice into his own hands when the courts failed. If he was, then he wanted to help. He hoped that Motohashi would contact him. He waited and waited—but the call never came. There was nothing on the news about Motohashi having taken revenge on Hasunuma. On reflection, that only made sense. After all, the man was the director of a company; many people depended on him.

Masumura realized that if anyone was going to act as the instrument of divine justice, it would have to be him. From that point on, revenge became the whole purpose of his life. *He would find Kanichi Hasunuma and he would kill him. If he ended up in prison for his pains, then so be it.*

Accomplishing that plan proved remarkably difficult. After the two trials, Hasunuma vanished. Masumura, who didn't have a wide circle of friends in the first place, had no way of tracking down someone who had deliberately dropped off the map.

Long years passed during which he achieved nothing. He needed to work to make a living, but, as an ex-con, finding a steady job was always a challenge. He seemed to spend too much of his time in a desperate search for work. While the intensity of his hatred for Hasunuma remained the same, he had half given up on his plan. He felt the same about life in general: It meant nothing to him anymore.

That was brought to an end by someone's chance remark.

The someone was a man he had met on a building site where he was working as a day laborer. When Masumura explained how being an ex-con made finding work difficult, his friend said that he knew the perfect company for him in Kikuno, a Tokyo suburb.

"The boss is a real character. He has this policy of hiring ex-cons. His theory is that they work harder than regular people, if you give them a second chance."

The company specialized in junk removal and recycling, he continued, and he'd been working there himself until recently.

"There's this one amazing guy there. Not an ex-con, but he was arrested for murder and managed to secure a not-guilty verdict by keeping his mouth zipped shut throughout his trial."

Masumura's ears pricked up when he heard the words *murder* and *not guilty*. What was the man's name? he asked. "Hasunuma," came the answer.

The blood rushed to Masumura's head and he began to tremble all over. "Tell me more," he demanded. Puzzled by Masumura's sudden display of excitement, his friend explained that what he knew about Hasunuma was from listening to his coworkers' gossip; he'd never spoken to the man himself.

Masumura found the recycling company online. One phrase on the page for recruitment caught his eye: *We welcome applications from seniors*, it said.

Masumura didn't waste any time. He phoned the HR department. When they asked him why he was interested in a job, he explained that he'd been in prison. The HR guy seemed happy with that.

The next day, Masumura went to the company office, armed with his résumé, for a one-on-one meeting with the boss. He spoke candidly about the episode that had led to his manslaughter conviction. "You caught a bad break," the boss commented, before offering him a job on the spot.

Did he have a place to live? the boss then inquired. When Masumura said that he was going to start looking right away, the boss countered that he happened to have the perfect place.

It was the office part of an old warehouse that was barely used anymore. It had a sink and a toilet, if not a bath. The boss arranged for someone to show him the place. Since it wasn't too decrepit or dirty, Masumura was happy to take it.

He had hardly almost no stuff of his own, so moving was easy. Masumura started his new job the following week.

A wide range of people worked at the company: Some of them smelled like trouble while others seemed quite good-natured.

It was his third day there that he found the man he was looking for. A group of men were smoking in the designated smoking area; one of them wore a nameplate saying HASUNUMA.

Masumura had never seen Hasunuma before. His deep-set eyes, thin lips, and pointed chin all radiated coldness. He was smoking at a slight remove from the rest of the group. Perhaps he liked to keep his distance from people.

That's the man who murdered Yuna and drove Yumiko to suicide!

Masumura was tempted to grab a knife and go for him right there—but he fought down the impulse.

Simply killing him isn't enough, he thought. *Before I do that, I want to hear the truth from his lips.*

To do that, he would have to become friends with Hasunuma, though it was the last thing he wanted to do. He needed to find an opportunity to get close to the man.

The opportunity came knocking in an unexpected form a few days later. Masumura was enjoying a cigarette in the smoking area, when Hasunuma came up and asked him for a light.

"Heard you're an ex-con?" said Hasunuma, blowing out smoke.

"Yeah, well. It's something that happened a long time ago." Masumura was surprised at how calm he sounded.

"What were you in for? Robbery?"

"Not even close."

Masumura told Hasunuma about the manslaughter incident, keeping nothing back. Telling him the unadorned truth, he believed, was the best way to win Hasunuma's trust.

After hearing his account, Hasunuma shrugged his shoulders. "All I can say is, you were pretty darn stupid."

"It was all over in a second. I was out of my mind. I thought the guy was going to kill me."

Hasunuma shook his head.

"I wasn't talking about you stabbing the guy. I'm saying, why'd you go and spill your guts to the police like that?"

Not quite understanding what the other man was getting at, Masumura said nothing.

Hasunuma went on: "You should have said that you didn't remember stabbing the guy; that he reached for the knife before you, that you tried to take it off him and he was down on the floor bleeding out before you even knew what was going on—something like that."

Masumura shook his head. "I couldn't have done that."

"Why not?"

"The police can tell if you're lying. They ask you a ton of questions at the crime scene reenactment. Say even one thing that doesn't tally and your whole explanation is shot."

"You're too honest for your own good. You've got to brazen it out with 'I don't remember anything' and 'I'm not sure about that.' Your story doesn't have to hang together. That doesn't matter. It's not your responsibility. Maybe you were the person who ended up with the knife, but they can't *definitively* say that the other guy didn't have it before you. Your fingerprints could have got on top of his and erased them. Believe me, if you'd made a statement like that, you'd probably have been found not guilty."

Masumura looked on dumbfounded as Hasunuma expounded with absolute self-assurance.

Maybe Hasunuma was right. Maybe his trial would have ended in a different verdict if he had made a statement like that after his arrest, taking a complete what-the-fuck-do-I-know-or-care attitude to any inconsistencies in his story.

In reality, that had been beyond his powers. Stared down by hard-faced detectives and pressured to tell the truth in the interview room, he wouldn't have been able to come up with any off-the-cuff lies or equivocations. Even if he had, the detectives would probably have seen through him, forcing a confession out of him anyway.

But this man—this Hasunuma—he was different. He'd only needed to hear the bare outlines of Masumura's story to come up with a strategy for evading punishment. He seemed to be uniquely quick-witted when it came to acts of criminality. And he had nerves of steel. He was quite comfortable defying the authorities and refusing to answer any questions he couldn't answer.

Masumura felt that he had gotten a glimpse into the evil recesses of the mind that had killed Yuna.

"You really know your stuff," said Masumura, stifling the anger that was rising in his gorge. "Speaking from experience?"

Masumura was hoping to get Hasunuma to say something about Yuna's murder. He just grinned and sidestepped the question with a noncommittal "Who knows?"

After that, the two men took to exchanging a word or two whenever their paths crossed. Hasunuma was standoffish with all the other employees, but with Masumura, for some reason, he lowered his guard. Perhaps spending time with someone who'd ended up in jail out of sheer dumb honesty gave him a renewed appreciation for his own ingenuity and sense of superiority. Although this only served to fan the flames of Masumura's hatred of Hasunuma, he worked hard to hide his true feelings. He focused instead on getting friendlier with Hasunuma. The ultimate goal was to get him to open up about Yuna's murder.

After around six months, the two men started going drinking together. Although Hasunuma seldom spoke directly about himself, he did let slip the occasional detail about his background.

Apparently, he loathed his father, who'd been a police officer.

"My dad despised ordinary civilians. He was quite open about it. He was the original fuck-you cop. When he snapped his fingers, he expected everyone to jump to it. The guy was a moron."

Hasunuma went on.

"When he got hammered at home, he liked to brag to me. 'Today, I got this guy to spill his guts. We knew he was guilty, but we had no evidence; we were stumped. So what do we do? We arrest him on another charge, stick him in the interview room, give him the third degree, and get a confession out of him that way.' My dad always used to say: 'Confessions are the king of evidence. I extract the confessions, so *I* matter more than any damn prosecutor.' You know what that made me think? That if I ever got investigated by this bunch of clowns, I'd rather die than say a single word to them."

So that's what this is all about. Everything began to make sense. Hasunuma's father had given him the speech about confessions being the king of evidence one too many times. From it, he had learned that silence and dogged denial would see you safely through. And he had put that knowledge to work when he was arrested.

It wasn't long after that that Masumura got Hasunuma to say something definitive. They were having a drink when the subject of detention centers happened to come up.

"Those places are awful. Tiny cells. Boiling in summer, freezing in winter. What the hell right have the cops got to treat people like that?"

Masumura's response was reflexive. "What did you do?"

"What?"

"You were in the detention center? So what did they arrest you for?"

Hasunuma had never spoken about his own arrest before.

He seemed to hesitate a moment, then said "murder" in a quiet voice. "Like you, it's ancient history."

"So who'd you kill?"

Hasunuma didn't answer the question right away. With a self-important air, he deliberately poured some sake into his little sake cup, which he drained in one gulp. Only then did he continue.

"The factory I worked at—the boss's daughter went missing. They found her remains a few years later. They arrested me on suspicion of murder."

"Did you kill her?" Masumura's heart was beating rapidly in his chest. "Did you?"

Hasunuma shot Masumura a sideways glance, then looked off into the middle distance.

"I was indicted and sent to trial. But I never said a word more than I had to. My lawyer said that was fine. We went through the motions and—long story short—I was found not guilty."

"That's good news for you. But what really happened? Did you do it? I won't blab. You can tell me about it," wheedled Masumura, working hard to stifle his rage.

Hasunuma leered. He started to chuckle, his shoulders moving up and down.

"You want the truth? What does true even mean? I was declared not guilty by a court of law. That's all you need to know. They even paid me compensation for the time I spent in detention!"

He made a gesture as if zipping his lips shut. "That's all I'm going to say about that," he said.

Thereafter, no matter how much Masumura tried, Hasunuma wouldn't be drawn out on the subject. "Just give it a rest, okay?" he would say with a scowl. Eventually, Masumura gave up asking. The last thing he wanted was to needle Hasunuma to the point of driving him away.

He'd managed to get results already. Hasunuma had spoken about the Yuna Motohashi case for the first time. As long as Masumura stayed on this same path, he should get the truth from him at some point.

However, that plan got thrown off course. Hasunuma abruptly stopped coming to work one day. He called the boss to say that he was quitting. When Masumura went around to his apartment, it had already been cleared out. When he tried calling his cell, he couldn't get through because his phone contract had been canceled.

Masumura asked around, but none of his coworkers knew where Hasunuma had gone. He hadn't given any reason for quitting to the boss, either.

Masumura was completely nonplussed. If he'd known that this was going to happen, he'd have taken his revenge sooner. He felt faint with regret at the thought of the opportunity he'd allowed to slip through his fingers.

A few days later, he got a call on his cell. It was from a pay phone. When he picked up, he was surprised to hear Hasunuma's voice at the other end of the line.

"What happened to you? Disappearing like that."

"I've got my reasons. Any cops show up at work?"

"Cops? No, not that I've heard."

"Good to hear."

"What's going on? What have you done?"

Hasunuma snickered.

"Nothing much. Let's leave it there."

Hasunuma sounded as though he was about to hang up.

"Just a minute," Masumura said hastily. "Where are you?"

"Can't tell you that right now. Be in touch. Bye," said Hasunuma. He ended the call.

Hasunuma phoned Masumura on multiple occasions after that. He always used a pay phone and the first question he asked was always whether anything "funny" had happened at the firm.

The calls became less and less frequent over time. And the intervals between them went from a few days, to a few weeks, and finally to several months. Masumura was worried about losing track of Hasunuma entirely. He was still using pay phones and hadn't yet revealed where he was living.

Three years went by, then, one day, when Masumura went into work, a couple of men were waiting for him. They were detectives. They showed him a mug shot. Did he know this man? they asked. It was Hasunuma.

When he said that, yes, he knew him, they bombarded him with questions.

Their questions mainly focused on the time when Hasunuma quit his job and disappeared. What had he talked about? Was there anything unusual about him? Had he been in touch since then? After a certain amount of hemming and hawing, Masumura came clean and told them about the sporadic phone calls he was getting.

The detectives seemed to be pleased. They thanked him for his help and went on their way without ever revealing what crime they were investigating.

He found out soon enough when the case became a major news item. The remains of a girl had been found in the ruins of a burned-out house in Shizuoka prefecture. One of Masumura's coworkers had heard that the girl's family ran a restaurant in Kikuno.

So that's what this is all about. It all started to fall into place. Hasunuma had occasionally mentioned the 'cute little sexpot' who worked in a restaurant he sometimes went to. He must have attacked her, killed her, hidden the body, and then gone AWOL to avoid being caught. He'd been calling Masumura to find out what the police were up to.

Not long after that, Masumura heard the news that Hasunuma had been arrested.

He felt mixed emotions. Surely this time—*this time*—Hasunuma wouldn't get away with it. Surely this time he would get the punishment he deserved. Whatever punishment he got, though, it wouldn't be for the crime of killing Yuna. And if he ended up in jail, he would be out of Masumura's reach.

That wasn't how things played out. With his route to revenge cut off, he was at a loss what to do: Sticking with his present job was futile, but he had nowhere else to go. One day, to his surprise, he got a call from Hasunuma.

"You? I thought you were under arrest?"

"I was. But they let me go."

"Let you go . . . ?"

"It's like I told you. The confession is the king of evidence. And without the king, the cops can't do a thing."

Masumura was dumbstruck. Had Hasunuma used his strategy of remaining silent to elude justice for a second time?

"You still living in Kikuno?" Hasunuma asked, when Masumura said nothing.

"I am, yeah . . ."

"In that case, I may drop by to see you any day now. Look forward to it."

"Uh, okay."

Hasunuma hung up. Masumura stared at his phone, stupefied.

He couldn't believe it. Hasunuma had now killed two people—and was still not going to be brought to justice?

He didn't know the Namikis, but his heart ached at the thought of the pain they must be going through. *None of this would have happened if I had killed Hasunuma earlier.*

Sometime later, Masumura went around to have a look at the restaurant. It was closed. You could hardly expect the family to keep operating their restaurant at a time like this.

Masumura racked his brains. What should he do? He couldn't let things go on as they were. He had to make sure that Hasunuma got the punishment he deserved. But he had no idea how to proceed.

In this impotent state, every day was torture. The more time that passed, the more desperate he became.

One day, he got a call from a number he didn't recognize. It was Hasunuma. It was almost three months since he had last called.

"I've got a favor I want to ask," Hasunuma said. "Can I crash at your place for a while?"

"My place? Why?"

"My bastard landlord didn't renew my contract. I kind of expected it. No big surprise. I thought maybe you could put me up at yours. I'll pay a decent rate."

"What are you planning to do?"

"Going to take my time finding myself a new place. Anyway, how about it? Can I come stay?"

It was a one-in-a-million chance. If Masumura wanted his revenge, he was going to have to seize it right now and with both hands.

"Uh, yeah, sure you can. It'll be cramped, though."

"No problem. As long as there's enough space to lie down."

Hasunuma came by soon after. They hadn't seen each other for a long time. Hasunuma's face was as cruel and brutal as ever.

"This area's not changed a bit," said Hasunuma, kicking off his shoes and sitting down cross-legged on the floor. "The shopping district's still a total shithole. God, what a dump."

Hasunuma snickered quietly.

"What's the joke?"

"Just that I popped in to pay my respects—to the victim's family."

"You *what*? The victim's family? You mean—?"

"That Namiki-ya place. I went and put the screws to the owner. 'You're the reason I got arrested. It's your fault no one trusts me anymore. I want compensation.'"

"What did he say about that?"

"Some bs. The guy's a loser. I was like 'screw you' and I walked out."

As he looked at the triumphant expression on Hasunuma's face, Masumura tried to imagine how the Namiki family must be feeling. Gloom swallowed him up. *This man isn't even human; he's a devil in human skin*, he thought.

Nonetheless, Masumura donned the mask of an old friend and spent the evening drinking with Hasunuma to celebrate their reunion. Hasunuma, who was in high spirits, made endless gibes about the police and the prosecutor.

What did he plan to do if the indictment went ahead? Masumura asked.

"I'll think about it, when the time comes," Hasunuma said nonchalantly. "I'll do the exact same thing I did before. It'll mean spending a year or more in detention, which is a bummer, but then I'll have the compensation payment to look forward to for my trouble. Overall, not a bad deal."

"What if you're found guilty?"

"Ain't gonna happen," Hasunuma fired back. "I was found not guilty in the previous case and there's even less circumstantial evidence this time around. No, provided I keep my mouth shut, the prosecutor can't do jack."

"About the previous case . . . ," said Masumura. "Why did you kill the girl? You've got your not-guilty verdict, so there's no danger in coming clean. Come on, tell me."

Hasunuma's drunken face contorted into the most hideous expression Masumura had ever seen: a smile charged with malevolence.

"I didn't mean to kill her," he said, holding his teacup full of *shochu*. "It's like, there was this cute kitten; I tried to give it a stroke; it bit back; I taught it a lesson and the silly thing went and died on me. I couldn't leave the thing like that, so I burned the body, said a few words, and buried what was left. End of story."

Masumura could almost hear the blood draining out of his body. *Hasunuma had come out and admitted to murdering Yuna Motohashi. And to add insult to injury, he had likened her to an animal.*

"Humph. So that's what happened, is it?" Masumura responded. His voice was flat and affectless. He wasn't playacting. When the shock to the emotions is too great, he realized, people can no longer show their reactions.

That night, Masumura was unable to sleep. He could hear Hasunuma, wrapped up in his blanket, breathing in his sleep in the next room over. His breathing sounded unsuspecting, unguarded. *I could easily kill the guy now*, Masumura thought.

He got up and picked up the kitchen knife from inside the sink. He glared down disgustedly at Hasunuma's sleeping face. He raised the knife high above his head.

But he didn't deliver the fatal blow.

He had realized something: He wasn't the only person who wanted revenge.

42

It was three days after Yutaro Namiki heard about Naoki Niikura confessing that a couple of detectives turned up at Namiki-ya and asked him to accompany them to the station for questioning. Namiki was busy cooking for that evening, but the detectives assured him that, if all went well, he would be back in time to open the restaurant. What exactly did "if all went well" mean? Presumably it meant them not finding any grounds to arrest him. *In that case, maybe I won't make it home tonight*, he thought.

Machiko and Natsumi both looked on anxiously as he was escorted off the premises. He was expecting them to be summoned to the station at some point, too. He'd already told them the truth.

Nothing was going according to plan, Namiki thought. Things hadn't just gone slightly awry, they had veered wildly off course—and destroyed Naoki Niikura's life in the process. You could argue that it was Niikura who had made the fatal choice, but Namiki was the one who had put him in a position to do so.

It had all started that night. The night when Hasunuma suddenly showed up at Namiki-ya.

They were just starting to see a glimmer of light at the end of the tunnel.

When Kanichi Hasunuma was released, the Namiki family felt as though they had been plunged into a deep, dark abyss. Kusanagi, the detective heading up the investigation, came personally to explain the situation. It made no difference: They couldn't accept what had happened.

The only scrap of hope that the Namiki family had to hold on to was what Kusanagi had said about his commitment to finding a decisive piece of evidence that would make it possible to take the case to trial.

After that, with every passing day, Namiki's pessimism intensified. He was doing his utmost not to think about the case. Saori's death was a horrific event, but the past was the past; nothing they could do was going to bring her back.

Namiki started to think that he had to get on with life. He never put the thought into words, but it somehow transmitted itself to his wife and daughter. He could see that by the way the smiles gradually began returning to their faces. It was a slow process, but the Namikis began to recover some of their old cheerfulness.

Kanichi Hasunuma's appearance in the restaurant pitched them back into the deepest despair. Their hatred for the man, which had ebbed ever so slightly, flared up again, becoming even more intense than before.

That night, Namiki couldn't sleep a wink. And it was the same for Machiko. Namiki could feel her tossing and turning until all hours. They didn't speak to each other. Their grief was so raw it robbed them of the words to express their anger and hatred.

The following day, they decided not to open the restaurant. They simply didn't have the energy. Natsumi managed to drag herself off to the university, but Machiko never even got out of bed.

Namiki went down to the restaurant and started drinking at lunchtime.

A little after five in the afternoon, he heard the sound of someone tapping on the slats of the front door. Looking up, he noticed someone standing on the street outside. *That's odd*, he thought. *I'm sure I put out the sign saying we're closed for the day.*

He unlocked the door and slid it open. A small, gray-haired man was standing there. He was wearing a face mask that concealed most of his face. He was dressed in a grubby jacket and trousers that bagged at the knees.

"We're closed today."

The man started waving his hand from side to side.

"I've got something important I need to talk to you about. . . . It's about Hasunuma."

Namiki started. "Who the hell are you?"

"It will take a while to explain. Can I come in?"

There was stubbornness in the man's eyes. Namiki nodded and motioned him into the restaurant.

Once inside, he took off his mask. The deep lines etched into his face testified to a life that had been far from easy.

The old man introduced himself. The name *Eiji Masumura* was

new to Namiki, but it was what he said next that really took his
breath away.

"You probably know that Hasunuma was found not guilty in a
murder trial about twenty years ago. The victim, Yuna Motohashi—
she was my niece."

Namiki gestured for the old man to sit down. He deserved to be
heard out.

What Masumura then went on to say was even more startling. In
a calm and steady tone, he explained how revenge had been the sole
purpose of his life for the past two decades; how he'd finally tracked
down and befriended Hasunuma; how he'd managed to worm his
way into his confidence.

"Hasunuma was here yesterday, wasn't he? He was boasting about
it when he got back to my place. He's human scum, that guy! Last
night, I almost killed him. I had the knife in my hand. I was ready
to strike. The only reason I didn't go through with it was because
I thought of you. If *I* killed him, I'd be denying you the chance of
becoming spiritually whole. I realized that just like me, you must
want to take revenge."

Masumura looked probingly at Namiki. "Well?"

"You're right," said Namiki. "I'd like to kill the man myself."

Masumura gave an emphatic nod.

"Just as I thought. How about it, Mr. Namiki? Shall we join
forces and give him the punishment he deserves? He's living in a
little fifty-square-foot room at the back of my place. It used to be
a storeroom, so it's got no windows and you can't see in from the
street. We could take our time killing him and no one could do a
thing about it."

Namiki found the offer appealing.

*If the state won't bring him to justice, then I'll just have to do it my-
self.* He had thought so countless times—but never progressed from
thought to action.

When Namiki remained silent, Masumura asked if he was afraid
of being sent to jail.

"No, I'm prepared for that. . . ."

"But you're also worried about your family," Masumura said, putting his finger on Namiki's biggest concern.

Namiki nodded feebly. "There's my daughter's future, too."

"You've got nothing to worry about. If things don't work out, I'll turn myself in." Masumura slapped his chest with one hand. "I'll say that I did it."

"You can't do that. It's not fair if I'm the only who gets away with it. . . . Besides, there's something I want to do before I avenge my daughter."

"What's that?"

"To find out the truth. Why did Hasunuma have to kill Saori? That's what I want to know. They released Hasunuma because he kept his mouth shut. But even if they indict him and find him guilty, I still won't feel any better until he comes clean about what happened. The first thing I want to do is to get him to tell the truth. I'll decide whether to take my revenge after that."

Masumura frowned and narrowed his eyes in sympathy. "I understand how you must feel."

"Could you give me some more time?" Namiki said. "I need to think about this. Let's talk again once I've thought things through."

"Fine," Masumura said. "Hasunuma will be at my place for a while. Take all the time you need."

They exchanged contact details. "Look forward to hearing from you," said Masumura and went on his way.

Namiki watched the small figure of the old man recede into the distance. Turning around, he was astonished to find Machiko right behind him.

"Oh . . . you decided to get up?"

"I felt like a cold drink."

"Right."

Namiki started tidying up the tables in the restaurant.

"So what do you plan to do?" Machiko asked.

"I'm sorry?" Namiki looked at his wife. Her eyes were hard, brooding.

"How are you going to get him to tell you the truth?"

Namiki ran his tongue nervously over his lips. "You were listening?"

"Yes, from the top of the stairs. I was curious."

"He's the uncle of Hasunuma's previous victim."

"I heard that. Anyway, what are you going to do?"

Namiki pulled out a chair and sat down. "I wonder . . ." He poured some sake from a big *ishobin* bottle into a cup that he had intended to tidy away.

Machiko fetched herself a cup and sat down across from him. She had apparently decided to have a drink, too. Namiki filled a cup for her.

Machiko tossed off her sake in one go, then let the breath out of her lungs loudly. She stared at the bottom of her empty cup. "You don't need to worry about us," she said. "You don't need to worry about Natsumi and me."

Namiki looked at Machiko in astonishment. Her bloodshot eyes had a glazed look. *That's about more than one little cup of sake*, Namiki thought.

"We'll go along with whatever you decide to do. Whatever it takes to avenge Saori. Natsumi would agree, I'm sure."

Namiki shook his head, took a swig of sake, and wiped his mouth with the back of his hand.

"I don't want you two involved. Whatever has to be done, it'll be me who does it."

"Yutaro . . ."

"Except that, right now, I've got no idea what to do. You got any good ideas?"

"Of how to get Hasunuma to come clean?"

"Uh-huh."

Machiko put down her cup and tilted her head to one side. "That's a tough one."

"Tell me about it. It's something neither the police nor the prosecutor managed to do."

"In the old days, they would have just tortured him. You can't get away with that nowadays."

It was just a throwaway comment, but it lodged in Namiki's mind. *Torture?*

Now that was something worth thinking about. When it came to interrogating suspects, there were strict new rules to prevent the police from being overly aggressive. But if they were the ones doing the interrogating, they could use all the unlawful techniques they wanted.

Intimidation alone wouldn't be enough. If the best Namiki could do was to brandish a knife, Hasunuma would laugh in his face. And if it came to a hand-to-hand fight, he stood no chance of winning. He would probably be the one who ended up getting stabbed.

How about drugging him with sleeping medication, tying him

up, and *then* threatening him with a knife or something? With Masumura's help, that could be doable.

But when he ran the idea by Machiko, her reaction was less than positive. Hasunuma, she felt, was hardly the sort of person to be cowed by something like that.

"'You want to stab me, go ahead and stab me; you want to kill me, go ahead and kill me.' That's probably how he'd come back at you," she said.

Namiki agreed. *She's definitely right*, he thought. He also knew in his bones that he wouldn't be able to follow through and kill Hasunuma, no matter how much he taunted him.

He was checking the food in the restaurant freezer the next morning when he remembered something Shusaku Tojima had told him: an episode when one of his workers who'd been handling the liquid nitrogen in a small and badly ventilated room had almost suffocated.

According to the man's own account of the experience, his head had started to hurt, he felt dizzy, and fell to the floor. But the real terror only came after that, when he found himself unable to move, despite knowing the danger he was in.

Sounds good to me, Namiki thought. Masumura had mentioned that Hasunuma lived in a small room with no windows. They could lock him in, then pump the liquid nitrogen in, little by little, through an aperture. As his discomfort increased, Hasunuma would realize that they were not making empty threats. Once he was in terror of his life, he would have to tell them the truth about Saori's murder when they pressed him for it.

Namiki quickly contacted Masumura and shared his plan with him.

"I like it." Masumura was enthusiastic. "Poison-gas torture. I think it could do it. Getting hold of liquid nitrogen isn't that easy, though."

"Any idea how we could get some?"

The two men discussed the plan in great detail. They examined Hasunuma's room while he was out. They initially thought they would need to drill a hole in the sliding door to pump in the liquid nitrogen, but when they removed the metal door handles, behind them they discovered a square hole that went right through the door.

"We'll need a funnel that's exactly the same size as this hole,"

Masumura said. "A bit of nosing around and I should find one easily enough."

They had settled on the method they were going to use. The next problem was getting hold of the liquid nitrogen.

Namiki got Tojima to join him for a drink at one of their favorite bars to discuss the problem. When Tojima asked what Namiki wanted the liquid nitrogen for, he didn't believe Namiki's explanation about "one of my nephews needing it for a home science experiment."

"You may not know it yourself, Yutaro, but your eyes are all bloodshot and you look like a total wreck. I know you're planning something."

"No . . ."

"You can't pull the wool over my eyes. We're old friends." Tojima lowered his voice. "Are you planning to bump off Hasunuma?"

Before Namiki could even formulate a reply, Tojima plowed ahead. "That's what I thought. You've got to let me help you. I won't do a thing unless you're completely up front with me. Well?"

Namiki shook his head.

"I'm not planning to kill the guy. And I don't want to involve anyone who's not connected to Saori."

"Not connected?" Tojima raised an eyebrow. "You want me to thump you, Yutaro?"

With a sigh, Namiki told his old friend about the plan that he and Masumura had devised together.

"Sounds rather complicated," said Tojima, slightly dismayed. "Still, I think it's basically a sound plan. You've got to do something pretty brutal to get a man like Hasunuma to confess."

"Can you provide the liquid nitrogen?"

"Leave it to me. From what you've told me, twenty liters should be enough. With the right kind of container, you can transport it by car." Tojima paused and a thoughtful expression came over his face. "There's one thing I have to ask you. What are you going to do with the guy *after* you've got his confession? You said you weren't going to kill him. What, so you're going to terrorize him till he comes clean, then leave him with his life?"

"I . . . I really don't know. We'll just have to see how it goes on the day. It depends on what Hasunuma says, I suppose."

Namiki was just being honest. He genuinely had no idea what he might do. If anger took over, then perhaps he would keep going until he'd killed Hasunuma. Perhaps reason would intervene and stop him from going too far. Either scenario was plausible.

"Listen, Yutaro," said Tojima. "I'm quite happy to kill him. The thought of a scumbag like that simply being alive is enough to poison my life. I *want* to kill him. I do mind you doing it. I don't want you to go to jail."

"Believe me, I don't want to go to jail. We need to be careful not to overreact, whatever Hasunuma says."

Tojima looked angry.

"That's not what I meant. Feel free to overreact and kill the guy. That's not a problem. It's natural. What I'm saying is that if you do end up doing that, then I don't want you to go to jail for it. Oh, and one more thing: Hasunuma may well die even if you don't intend to kill him."

"What do you mean?"

"That liquid nitrogen is quite hard to handle."

Tojima spelled out the risks: how a small amount of liquid nitrogen vaporizes into an enormous quantity of gas; that breathing it in directly causes rapid oxygen deficiency; that people who transport the stuff never travel in the same elevator with it, because it's continuously vaporizing even when stored in a special container, and so on and so forth.

"What I'm trying to say is this: While you may plan to pump just enough liquid nitrogen into the room to scare the living daylights out of Hasunuma, the tiniest error in quantity could easily kill him."

Namiki's anxiety returned when he heard that.

"What's wrong? Have you lost your nerve?" Tojima asked. "Do you want to pull out?"

"Absolutely not." Namiki shook his head. "I'm more committed than ever. I intend to go through with this."

"Now you're talking." Tojima grinned, before his expression relapsed into seriousness. "There's something else I want to make clear. Regardless of whether we intentionally kill Hasunuma or just cause his death by mistake, the police will launch an investigation when they find his body. They may well figure out that liquid nitrogen was used, so we need to take steps to preempt that."

"How?"

"When Hasunuma's body is found, the first person that the police will suspect is you. You don't have easy access to liquid nitrogen, so they'll start sniffing around my factory. The factory has security cameras. If they find any footage of me driving out of the place, they'll assume I'm transporting the liquid nitrogen cylinder."

"That's no good," Namiki said. "I don't want you getting in trouble, Shusaku. I'll transport the liquid nitrogen myself."

"Are you a total idiot?" Tojima spat out the words. "I'm the boss of the damn company. What's the problem with me going to my own factory? *There isn't one.* I can cook up a thousand reasons for being there. You do it and you might as well shout from the rooftops, 'Hey, it's me. I did it. Arrest me.'"

"Okay. But you can't go directly from your factory to Hasunuma's place, either. There are security cameras all over town. You only need to get caught on one of those and it's all over for you."

"You're right. Security cameras are a major pain in the ass. The special twenty-liter container for the liquid nitrogen will be big and heavy. We'll need a vehicle to transport it. We should expect the police to review all the local security-camera footage to find the vehicle we use. I've also heard rumors about this recent innovation—something called N-System. The police can use it to track vehicles in the most incredible detail—car type, the routes they take. . . ."

"Then I should be the one who transports the stuff. I'll take care not to kill Hasunuma; and if I do slip up and accidentally cause his death, I'll do the right thing and turn myself in."

Tojima clicked his tongue loudly.

"Didn't you listen to a word I said? *I don't want you to go to jail. And regardless of how careful you are, whether or not he dies may be beyond your control.*"

"Maybe . . ."

"We need to use our brains. Let's assume that the police do figure out that we used liquid nitrogen. Okay. We need to anticipate their thought processes and outsmart them."

"Outsmart them? How?"

"Give me a day." Tojima held up a finger. "I'll come up with something."

The two men met the following day. Tojima was looking rather jaunty.

"The police are sure to think that whoever did it used a vehicle.

We want to outsmart them, so—" Tojima paused for dramatic effect. "We need to transport the liquid nitrogen without using a vehicle."

Namiki's eyes widened.

"You said the container was big and heavy? So how are we supposed to move it? If we push it around on a handcart, every man and their dog will see it."

"That's why neither of us can do that particular job."

Namiki swallowed. "You want to involve more people?"

"There are plenty of people who are more than happy to help. We need only ask. I'm sure you can think of a couple yourself."

Namiki knew Tojima was right. The Niikuras and Tomoya Takagaki appeared in his mind's eye.

"Provided we make it crystal clear that we don't intend to kill the guy, they'll be happy to help us. I'll speak to them, Yutaro. You don't need to do a thing. All you need to do is get yourself over to Hasunuma's place on the actual day."

"What are you going to do? What's the plan?"

"The less you know, the better. All I'll tell you is: We'll do it on the day of the parade."

Yutaro was stunned.

"The day of the parade? Why choose a day when there are so many people around . . . ?"

"That's what makes it such a good day for it. There's one thing I need to ask you. This guy Masumura—what does he want to do?"

"He says he wants to be with me. Wants to be there when I interrogate Hasunuma."

Tojima shook his head. "That's not an option," he said. "If Hasunuma dies, the police are sure to suspect foul play. And if they detect the sleeping medication in his system, they'll start wondering who got Hasunuma to take the stuff and they'll start looking into Masumura's background. I know it's unlikely, but *if* the investigation leads back to Masumura's connection to Yuna Motohashi, the police will leave no stone unturned. We need to prevent that by creating an alibi for Masumura. I'm not talking about a false alibi. I mean a genuine, perfect one."

Namiki saw that what Tojima was saying made sense. If the police made up their minds that Masumura had nothing at all to do with the crime, their investigation would never make any progress.

Despite feeling a little guilty about it, Tojima relayed their decision to Masumura. He was half expecting him to get angry, protest that it wasn't fair, and say that if that was what they were planning, he'd have been better off acting alone.

Masumura, however, was very amenable.

"That's fine with me," he said. "I don't care if they send me to jail, but that doesn't give me the right to force the same thing on Mr. Namiki. I fully understand that preventing suspicion from falling on me is crucial to this plan. I'll create an alibi by going somewhere public while you put the screws on Hasunuma.

"But I do have one condition," continued Masumura.

"At present, you don't plan to kill Hasunuma. If you still feel that way after going through with the plan, can you leave the sliding door latched shut when you leave the scene? I want to be free to do what I want to do after that."

With the latch down, Hasunuma wouldn't be able to open the door. Weakened by oxygen deficiency, he probably wouldn't have the strength to break it down, either. He would be trapped inside.

Tojima didn't need to ask what "doing what I want to do" meant.

"I'll stab him to death. Then I'll turn myself in to the police. The investigation won't go anywhere near Mr. Namiki. The whole thing will be nice, neat, and wrapped up with a ribbon." As Masumura said this, there was a fresh, eager look on his face.

That was how the plan came together. All that was left to do now was to wait for the day of the parade.

Namiki was ignorant of the plan's ins and outs. Tojima was the only person with a grasp of the plan in its entirety. Namiki had some vague idea of who might be helping, but he couldn't be sure.

He suspected that Tomoya Takagaki was one of their accomplices. There was little chance that Tojima hadn't approached him.

When Namiki looked at the young man and saw his face, which still had all the simplicity and candor of a child, he felt guilty about getting him to participate in an act of cruelty. Takagaki probably felt that he had to help because of Saori. In his heart of hearts, though, he probably wanted nothing to do with the plan. It was that realization that prompted Namiki to tell Tomoya that it was okay for him to forget about Saori and that he wouldn't regard him as coldhearted for doing so.

Namiki wanted to say something similar to the Niikuras, but he never got the chance.

The day of the parade arrived. Namiki was on edge from the moment he woke up. "I'm going to go to Hasunuma's place this afternoon. I'm not going to kill him, just get him to tell me the truth," he told Machiko. He didn't go into any detail about the plan. He would tell her what he'd done when it was all over.

Tojima had told him that 4 P.M. would be the moment of truth.

"I'll phone you when everything's ready. Use the Yamabe Shoten's minitruck. I've cleared it with them so it won't be a problem. When you get to the hut where Hasunuma lives, you'll find a cardboard box containing you-know-what outside the front door. Take it in with you, then do everything as we discussed."

Tojima didn't tell Namiki who would be delivering the cardboard box to the hut.

Despite his anxiety, Namiki went to work in the restaurant kitchen at Namiki-ya, as if it were a normal day.

The phone rang a little before two. It was Tojima.

Masumura had called. He had successfully slipped some sleeping medication into the beer can Hasunuma was drinking from. Hasunuma had already been looking very sleepy when he left the hut. He should be out cold for the next two or three hours, provided no one woke him.

Masumura went on to add something.

"Niikura wants to be there when you interrogate Hasunuma."

"*Niikura?*"

"I can understand how the guy feels. I told him to talk to you directly. He'll be waiting in the Yamabe Shoten parking lot. If you don't want him there with you, just tell him no."

"Okay."

Namiki saw no reason to rebuff Niikura. If he was honest with himself, it would be good to have someone to consult if things went somehow awry.

Namiki's anxiety ratcheted up a notch. *Any minute now, I'll have to make my decision and go through with what I decide,* he thought.

But something unexpected got in the way. The restaurant was about to close for the afternoon, when a customer, who'd been shut up in the restroom for a long time, finally staggered out. She looked limp and was complaining about a stomachache.

They couldn't just ignore her. Machiko didn't have a driver's license. Namiki had no choice; he'd have to take the woman to the hospital.

After dropping her off at the emergency room, Namiki called Tojima to explain what was going on.

"Everything's ready and I was about to call you. God, why did this have to happen today of all days?" The disappointment in Tojima's voice was palpable.

"I'm sorry. There's nothing I can do about it."

"You don't need to apologize. It's okay. I'll work something out. We'll get another crack at the guy. I'll contact the others." Namiki was heartened by Tojima's adaptability.

But once he got off the phone, all the strength seemed to drain out of his body. He could barely think straight. When Machiko arrived at the hospital, he was just standing around in the waiting room in a daze. When he explained the situation to her, the expression on her face was one of mingled disappointment and relief. Namiki realized that she'd been afraid of what he might do.

It turned out that there was nothing seriously wrong with their customer. She came out and apologized to them both for the trouble she had caused them. Since she was well enough to make her own way home, they parted just outside the hospital.

That should have been the end of it all. *Nothing's going to happen today*, he was thinking—until he got a phone call from Tojima that plunged him into confusion.

"Things have taken an unexpected turn. I'll call you tonight with the details. I'll be dropping in at the restaurant a bit later. I want you to make out like nothing's happened."

"What *has* happened?" Namiki asked.

"Haven't the time to go into it," Tojima said. The phone went dead.

At five thirty, Namiki opened the restaurant just the same as usual. The regular customers started showing up. Tojima came in with the Niikuras. Tojima's behavior was the same as usual. Thinking back on it later, Namiki could only marvel at his friend's acting skills. He didn't get a good look at the faces of the Niikuras. Had he done so, he might have detected something out of the ordinary there.

Namiki heard the news of Hasunuma's death via one of the members of Team Kikuno. He glanced at Tojima, and their eyes locked just for an instant.

This, he realized, was the "unexpected turn of events."

Tojima called him later that night. "Who did it?" Namiki asked.
"Well, I didn't do it. Nor did Tomoya Takagaki. So, go figure."
"Was it Niikura?"
"It was," Tojima replied.

43

Shusaku Tojima called me one week before the parade. "There's something I want to discuss with you, Mr. Niikura," he said. He went on to tell me that Hasunuma was back in Kikuno and had even shown up at Namiki-ya. I was incredulous.

Tojima drove me to have a look at the hut where Hasunuma was living.

Then he made a proposal—something completely unexpected—to me at a diner nearby.

"We've got a plan to punish Kanichi Hasunuma and we'd like you to lend a hand," he said. That was when I discovered that the plan had originated with Yutaro Namiki.

I was taken aback. On the one hand, I loathed Hasunuma enough to *want* to kill him; on the other, I had never imagined actually *doing* it. I knew that if I did the police would swing into action. There's no such thing as the perfect crime—a crime that's undetectable.

I wondered if Namiki was willing to get arrested. Was he prepared to shoulder all the blame himself, even if some of us helped him?

Apparently not. "I won't let my dear childhood friend go to jail," Tojima told me. "We can find a way to deliver a hammerblow to Hasunuma without anyone getting arrested."

Was it possible to do both those things? I had my doubts, but I changed my mind after Tojima explained the ingenious method they were planning to use. Locking Hasunuma in his room and terrorizing him with liquid nitrogen until he told the truth struck me as startlingly original. In terms of the penal code, Tojima said it would count as "aggravated assault with intent to cause bodily harm." The idea, however, was that Hasunuma wouldn't file a complaint, meaning that no one would get arrested.

What Tojima asked me to do was to hide the container of liquid nitrogen inside one of the Team Kikuno treasure chests. To be honest, it was a bit of a letdown. I was hoping to be assigned a more important role. Still, I agreed on the spot.

I didn't breathe a word about the plan to my wife, Rumi. Knowing that her husband was going to do something borderline criminal would have upset her. She is not the most robust person, either mentally or physically. And I didn't want to burden her with an important secret, either.

As the big day came closer, I was increasingly on edge. Just imagining what Hasunuma would say was exciting.

Eventually, I realized that I needed to be there myself. *I wanted to see Hasunuma suffer.*

I decided to ask Tojima if that would be okay. He said he would propose it to Yutaro on the day based on his assessment of the situation.

Come the day of the parade, Rumi and I left our house a little after midday. We watched most of the parade, bumping into people we knew from time to time, then headed over to say hello to Maya Miyazawa before Team Kikuno got started. I had to confirm a few details about the music with her, but Tojima had also advised me that I needed to establish my alibi, just in case.

After chatting with Miyazawa, I told Rumi that I'd just got an urgent text from a colleague and told her to go and watch the parade by herself for a while. I let her get a certain distance away, then hurried toward the municipal sports ground. A Tojima-ya Foods minivan was parked in one of the nearby streets with Mr. Tojima sitting in the driver's seat. When he saw me, he got out of the van and unloaded a trolley and a large cardboard box from the van's flatbed. He handed me a parade staff jacket.

I put the jacket on, lifted the cardboard box onto the trolley, and headed for the municipal sports ground. It didn't take me long to locate the silver treasure chest. There were two cardboard boxes inside it. One contained six plastic bottles of water, the other the same number of bottles of oolong tea. I took both boxes out and replaced them with the one big cardboard box I had brought with me, which I fixed in place with the straps. The whole operation took me less than ten minutes. Then I pushed the trolley loaded with the two boxes of drinks back to where Tojima was waiting and returned the staff jacket to him.

Mr. Tojima told me that if I wanted to be present at Hasunuma's interrogation, I should wait in the parking lot of Yamabe Shoten. Apparently, he'd already communicated my request to Mr. Namiki.

For the time being, I went to rejoin my wife and resumed watching the parade.

It wasn't long before Team Kikuno stepped off. We walked alongside their float.

When they eventually got to the end of the parade route, I told Rumi to go on to the singing contest venue by herself, because there was something I needed to take care of. She set off. I don't think she suspected anything.

I went to Yamabe Shoten and waited for Namiki in the parking lot. Four o'clock came and went with no sign of him. That's odd, I was thinking, when I got a call from Tojima. There had been an accident, he said, and the plan was called off. He told me to get into the minitruck and go and retrieve the cardboard box from where it was in front of the hut.

Having been raring to go, all of a sudden I felt quite deflated. The whole plan was a nonstarter and I just had to let it go. I did what I was told and drove the minitruck to the hut where Hasunuma was.

Sure enough, there was the cardboard box just outside the front door, where someone had put it. I thought I'd try the door to the hut before loading the box back onto the truck. It was unlocked.

I looked to the far end of the hut where the little room was. The sliding door was pulled shut and the latch was down. The metal door handle had been removed, as I'd been told it would be, and where it had been there was a square hole that went right through to the other side.

I took my shoes off and walked over to the sliding door, taking care to be as quiet as I could. I was halfway there, when the sound of a loud snore made me start. I froze.

Hasunuma didn't wake up. I went right up to the sliding door and peered through the square hole into the room.

I could see Hasunuma's face. He lay sprawled out on his mattress, drooling and grunting. The sight of that face ignited a fierce surge of rage in me.

That was the man who had killed our darling Saori? Why, for God's sake? What happened between the two of them? How had she died?

I had to have answers, right then and there. This was our only chance to get Hasunuma to tell the truth. What if I stepped in and took over Namiki's role in the plan?

I lugged the cardboard box into the hut and unpacked it. One of the things inside the box was a special funnel and the first thing I did was stick it into the hole in the door. I then removed the cover plug from the liquid nitrogen container. After that, I started thumping the sliding door and shouting Hasunuma's name.

He woke up. "Who's that?" he yelled. He must have got to his feet, because he tried to open the sliding door. Since it was on the latch, it remained firmly shut.

I lifted up the container, carried it over to the door and started tipping the liquid nitrogen into the mouth of the funnel. Hasunuma was quite taken aback. "What is this stuff?" he shouted.

"Liquid nitrogen," I said. "The more I pour in, the thinner the oxygen in there will get—and you will die."

Hasunuma started yelling wildly: "Stop it"; "I'll kill you"; stuff like that. Worried he might try to break the door down, I leaned against it with my full weight, still holding the container. Nothing like that happened. I can only assume that he was trying to keep his distance from the liquid nitrogen as it poured out of the spout of the funnel and into the room.

It wasn't long before Hasunuma started complaining about the physical effects of the gas: his head hurt, he was feeling nauseous. "Tell me the truth, if you want to get out of there alive. Tell me what you did to Saori Namiki," I told him.

"Just open the door," Hasunuma said. "Let me out of here and I'll tell you." It was obvious he was lying. "First, tell me everything and *then* I'll let you out," I replied. I continued pouring the liquid nitrogen.

A little later, I heard screaming from inside the room. "Okay, okay, I'll talk. Please just stop!" I stopped pouring the liquid nitrogen.

"I always fancied having a go at the girl from Namiki-ya," Hasunuma began. Basically, what he said was that he had had his eye on Saori for quite a while. He was furious when the restaurant banned him and he resolved to get back at them by assaulting the girl. One evening, he spotted her from his car. She was alone. He followed her to a small park and assaulted her there. The park was being refurbished, so there was nobody around. He tried to drag her back to his car. She resisted. He shoved her to the ground. She suddenly went all quiet on him. Wondering what was going on, he knelt down for a closer look. For whatever reason, the girl was dead. *This is a disaster,* he thought to himself. In a panic, he stuffed the body into his car. As he was wondering where he could get rid of the girl, he remembered the house with his mother's undiscovered corpse inside. This was what Hasunuma told me, gasping for breath the whole time.

I felt a renewed surge of fury. *Why didn't you hand yourself in to the police?* I asked him.

What do you think the bastard said to that? "Why would I do anything dumb like that? If I hide her corpse, then I have the advantage." That's what he said.

I resumed pouring the liquid nitrogen into the room and I commanded him to make an apology. "Say you're sorry to the dead Saori. Beg for her forgiveness! Beg from the bottom of your heart!" He did say something, but it didn't sound much like an apology to me, so I just kept on pouring.

At a certain point, I realized that the room had gone silent. The liquid nitrogen container was almost empty. I plucked the funnel out of the hole and peered into the room.

Hasunuma had fallen to the floor. He was lying there, completely motionless. *I've screwed up!* I thought to myself. I unhooked the latch and slid open the door. I knew it was dangerous to go in right away, so I waited a minute or two before stepping inside.

Hasunuma's heart had stopped and he wasn't breathing. I tried CPR, but he showed no sign of coming back to life. I placed the funnel and the liquid nitrogen container in the cardboard box and carried it out of the hut.

I loaded the box on the bed of the minitruck and drove back to Yamabe Shoten. On my way, I called Tojima to tell him what had happened.

For a few moments, Tojima was dumbstruck. Then he really showed his mettle. "You just stick to the plan," he said. "I'll take care of the rest."

I did what he said. I parked the minitruck in its original spot, then went to the park to rejoin Rumi. I was hardly in the mood for a singing contest; having to be all cheerful and upbeat as a member of the judging panel was a struggle.

After the singing contest was over, I bumped into Tojima. Since Rumi was there, he kept his mouth shut.

The three of us went to Namiki-ya. It was there that we heard the news of Hasunuma's death, together with all the other custom-ers. Maintaining the pretense of calm until then hadn't been easy.

Tojima called me later that night. He had already told Masumura and Namiki what had happened, he said.

"Yutaro feels terrible about having put you in such a difficult po-sition," Tojima said. "'I was the one who had this crazy idea in the first place—then I went and off-loaded all the responsibility onto his shoulders.'" Those, apparently, were Namiki's exact words.

Tojima promised to take care of things. "Relax," he went on. "As long as we all keep our mouths shut, the police won't be able to fig-ure out what happened."

But the police zeroed in on the truth much faster than we'd imagined. When Tojima told me that they had worked out that the helium tank was only a decoy and that liquid nitrogen had been used in the actual crime—that was the worst. Everything went black for me. I was pretty sure that Professor Yukawa must have had a hand in it. I'd never expected him to get involved.

When I heard that you'd discovered Masumura's true identity and that Tomoya Takagaki had confessed to his role, I knew in my bones that it was just a matter of time. When the police asked me and my wife to come down to the station for questioning, I was al-ready prepared for the worst.

We were interviewed separately. I stuck to my story of know-ing nothing and having nothing to do with the murder. For all my stonewalling, though, inside I was worried sick about Rumi. Al-though she had no knowledge of the plan, I think she had guessed quite early on that I was involved. Her anxiety came to a head when the police called us in.

When they told me that Rumi had collapsed in the middle of her interview and been taken to the hospital, I wasn't surprised. I rushed to her bedside.

She had hyperventilation syndrome. The doctor asked me if she'd ever had such an attack before and I told him that she'd shown mild symptoms many times.

The doctor had given Rumi something and she was sleeping in her room. I sat down by her bed and squeezed her hand. As I looked at her peaceful, sleeping face, I knew that I had to get her out of the situation I had put her in.

44

The door at the far end of the corridor was wide open. A man in work overalls came out just as Utsumi reached it. He was pushing a large cardboard box on a handcart. Utsumi had a flashback to Tomoya Takagaki's statement: the part where he talked about transporting the liquid nitrogen.

Utsumi popped her head into the room. Yukawa was standing there with his hands on his hips, his jacket off, and his sleeves rolled up. When he noticed Utsumi, he jerked his chin in her direction.

Utsumi watched the man in overalls move off down the corridor, then she went into Yukawa's office. She looked around. The room was quite different from her previous visit. The bookshelves were empty of files and the top of the desk free of clutter.

"My research has reached the stage where I no longer need to be here," Yukawa said, making for his desk. The hot water dispenser, jar of instant coffee, and paper cups were still there.

"That's good timing."

"What do you mean?"

"The case has also got to a decisive point. There are only a few odds and ends that still need to be taken care of—tracking down corroborative evidence, stuff like that."

Yukawa was quietly making instant coffee. Despite him having his back to her, Utsumi sensed that he had something important to tell her.

"Did Chief Kusanagi fill you in on the developments?"

Yukawa turned and walked back toward her, holding two paper cups.

"Yes, he gave me a rundown on the phone. Turns out a lot of people were involved, which is what I expected."

"Director Mamiya was singing your praises, too. 'All Detective Galileo's theories were right. That man has extraordinary powers of insight.'"

Not happy at Utsumi's use of his Tokyo Metropolitan Police Department nickname, Yukawa arched one eyebrow and shot her a grumpy look. He placed the two paper cups on the table and sat on an armchair. Utsumi also sat down.

Yukawa crossed his legs and reached for one of the cups. "Can I get the full story from you?"

"That's why I'm here." Utsumi took a file out of her bag. "First, though, I've got to give you a message from the chief. He wants to thank you in person at your earliest convenience, so if there's any particular restaurant or bar you fancy going to, do please let him know."

"I'll give it a think."

Utsumi nodded and flipped the file open. She had edited together statements from multiple people to make a summary of the case. After hearing that Naoki Niikura had confessed, even Tojima, who had refused to cooperate for so long, had finally and reluctantly provided a statement.

As she slowly leafed through the file, Utsumi reviewed the case in her own mind.

It had been a genuinely complex case. The whole thing had been motivated by the failure of the legal system to bring Hasunuma—a vile and diabolical man—to justice. It was all too easy to sympathize with Naoki Niikura, who did the deed; Yutaro Namiki, who devised the plan; and Shusaku Tojima, who managed it. But feeling sympathetic didn't alter the fact that no human being has the right to take the life of another human being, despicable or not. Under Kusanagi's guidance, their next task was to prove that the crime had been reprehensible and unjustifiable. The thought of that final task was enough to make Utsumi depressed.

"Naoki Niikura called Shusaku Tojima to let him know that Hasunuma was dead. The first thing Tojima then did was to call Masumura to tell him what had happened. He also directed him to pluck a few strands of hair from Hasunuma's head. The next day, Tojima collected the strands of hair from Masumura and stuffed them, along with the helium tank, into a garbage bag. (He'd hidden the stolen tank in the park where the singing contest was held.) He then dumped the bag in a clump of weeds about sixty-five feet from the crime scene."

"Was it Tojima who stole the tank of helium?"

"When the man handing out the free balloons vacated his post briefly, no one thought twice about it when Shusaku Tojima took his place. Tojima wrapped the helium tank in a piece of green cloth and hid it in the undergrowth behind the public restroom. The color made for good camouflage, which is why no one noticed it."

"Was Shusaku Tojima expecting Namiki to kill Hasunuma?"

"He thought he *might* do so. His position was that Namiki had every right to kill him and that he would do his best to get him off the hook if he did. That was what inspired him to come up with the whole helium tank decoy strategy."

Yukawa shrugged. "That's what friends are for," he murmured.

"Moving on," said Utsumi, consulting her file again. "Maya Miyazawa, the owner of Miyazawa Books, continues to deny any involvement in the plot. For his part, Shusaku Tojima claims not to have spoken to her about it. Working against that is something we heard from Team Kikuno's props team, who were responsible for the treasure chests among other things. Apparently, Miyazawa summoned them for confabs both before and after the parade, even though she had nothing important to say to them. Our theory is that she just wanted to draw them away from the treasure chests. All that notwithstanding, it's debatable how much she knew about the plan. Tojima could well have asked her to help in the most vague and roundabout terms. When you think of the vigor with which the pirates manhandled the treasure chests in the parade, it seems likely that she didn't know that one of them contained liquid nitrogen." Having reached the end of the file, Utsumi dropped it on the table and reached for her cup. "That's everything. What do you think?"

Yukawa only spoke after staring silently into the bottom of his paper cup for a while. "I don't see any glaring contradictions. Everything seems to line up quite nicely."

"That's what we think, too. There's probably the occasional small lapse of memory, but we don't see any major or deliberate falsehoods."

"Is that the story you'll be sending to the prosecutor?"

"That's what we mean to do, yes. . . ."

Yukawa's use of the word *story* bothered Utsumi.

"If you don't mind my asking, on what charges will the prosecutor indict the different individuals involved?"

"That's rather complicated." Utsumi picked up the file again. "If we take Naoki Niikura's statement at face value, he didn't intend to kill Hasunuma. That means we will have to go with a charge of manslaughter for him. Meanwhile, at the end of the day, Yutaro Namiki didn't participate in the crime at all. Since he originated the idea, we could charge him as an accomplice, though the charge would only be one of bodily harm. As for Tomoya Takagaki, he'd only been told that they were going to 'punish' Hasunuma and didn't know how the liquid nitrogen was going to be used. If we try to charge him as an accomplice, the chances are the case against him won't stick. The problem is Shusaku Tojima. In his case, the charge of accomplice in bodily harm would definitely stand up; in addition, he took measures in anticipation of Hasunuma's death by devising the helium tank alibi. There are issues of legal interpretation, but willful negligence leading to murder might be the most suitable charge to bring against him. At the same time, that charge seems unlikely to stick since it wasn't Tojima, but Niikura, who took the final decision about whether Hasunuma should live or die. As for Rumi Niikura, we suspect that she was aware of the plan, but whether that constitutes grounds for charging her is another matter."

Utsumi looked at Yukawa. "And that's everything."

"What about Hasunuma?"

"Huh?"

"How will you deal with Hasunuma? Is it a case of 'suspect deceased, prosecution abandoned'?"

"Ah . . ." Utsumi had been caught off guard. She hadn't thought about that. "I suppose so."

"What's Kusanagi's take on that? The reality is that it was Masumura who uncovered the truth of Yuna Motohashi's murder and Niikura who did the same for Saori's death."

"Kusanagi says it's complicated. On the one hand, it's a good thing that the truth came to light. On the other hand, he'd prefer it if we had solved both cases ourselves."

"That's more or less what I was expecting . . . ," murmured Yukawa, gulping down the last of his coffee. He replaced the now-empty cup on the table.

"Have you located the park?"

"What park?"

"You know, the one that appears in Niikura's statement. He says that Hasunuma assaulted Saori in a little park."

"Ah-ah," gurgled Utsumi vaguely, as she nodded and reached for her notebook.

"We did locate it, yes. Niikura mentioned something about construction work being underway. That proved a useful clue. We think it was probably West Kikuno Children's Park. It's about a ten minutes' walk from Namiki-ya. It was undergoing refurbishment three years ago, when Saori was murdered. Anyway, what about it?"

Yukawa, who was plunged in thought, didn't answer the question. Utsumi knew better than to press him at a time like this. What was on his mind? she wondered.

"Utsumi." Yukawa looked at her intently. "There are a couple of things I need you to look into for me. Do you mind?"

Utsumi took a ball pen out of her bag, opened her notebook, and hunched forward. "Fire away."

"A word of warning before I start. I need you to keep this secret from Kusanagi. I also would appreciate if you don't ask me why I am getting you to make these inquiries. Unless you're willing to accept these two conditions, I won't go on."

Utsumi looked at her old friend the physicist. The brooding expression on his face was atypical.

"Could I ask you one thing?"

"What?"

"Do you accept the version of events that I presented as true and correct? Or do you still have some doubts?"

Yukawa breathed out loudly, crossed his arms, then put his left hand to his chin with the thumb, index finger, and middle finger extended. His face was pensive, but when Utsumi saw the position of his fingers, she was reminded of something—something she thought she had learned in physics class.

By the time she finally remembered what it was—Fleming's left-hand rule for motors—Yukawa had relaxed somewhat.

"Do I accept your version of events? I can't yet answer that question. Which is why I'm asking you this favor."

"Fine," Utsumi replied promptly. "Tell me what you want me to do. I won't ask you why."

45

When she opened the front door and went outside, her neck and shoulders shuddered as the chilly air enveloped them. It was already November. Winter was definitely on its way.

Rumi walked around the house and into the back garden. She'd taken up gardening and tending to her flowers as one of her daily tasks.

She contemplated her flowers before getting down to work.

The youth-and-old-age zinnias—as the name suggests—stayed in flower for a long time. They were in full bloom, but probably didn't have long to go. The pale pink salvia was still in flower and looked to have plenty of life in it yet. Although it was a perennial, it couldn't make it through the winter unless it was pruned and brought indoors.

How will the garden fare this year? Rumi wondered. Maybe it was hopeless. It wasn't just the salvia, but the other flowers, too: Unless someone took care of them, they would wither and die.

The sasanqua camellia hedge wasn't yet in bloom. It shouldn't be long now, but would she get the chance to enjoy its beauty?

As she examined the buds, she could see the street through gaps in the hedge. A black car was parked on the side of the road. Recently, it was there all the time. The back windows were tinted, so she couldn't see inside.

One time, when Rumi was collecting her mail from the mailbox, she caught sight of a man in a dark suit leaning against the car having a smoke. He'd quickly clambered back inside, looking rather agitated.

The memory depressed her. They were police and were keeping an eye on her. That much was obvious.

She suddenly lost all interest in tending her flowers. While none of the nearby houses overlooked the garden, there were several big apartment blocks a certain way away. For all she knew, they could be spying on her from a high floor using a telephoto lens.

Pulling off her gardening gloves, she went back around to the front of the house. She had just reached the path leading to the front door, when she noticed someone standing on the far side of the garden gate. *Not another damn detective,* she thought. But it wasn't. The instant she saw the man's face, her heart started racing. It was someone she knew; someone she had often seen at Namiki-ya: Yukawa, the university professor.

Yukawa seemed to have noticed her, too. He smiled and bowed.

Feeling very wary, Rumi walked up to the gate. She remembered what her husband had told her. *He's not just your regular academic; he's chummy with the lead detectives and closely connected to the police.*

She pushed the gate open. "What do you want here?" she asked.

"I'd very much like to talk to you," said Yukawa, a kindly expression on his face. "It's about the case."

Rumi was too unsettled to know how to respond.

"Nothing I tell you is supposed to work to your disadvantage," went on Yukawa, who seemed to have anticipated Rumi's discomfiture. "I'm just here to tell you that you have a choice."

"A choice?"

"Yes." Yukawa nodded, looking straight at her.

Those eyes! Rumi got the impression they could see right through her.

She didn't know what to do. The only reason she invited him into the house was to get away from the scrutiny of the police she knew were watching them.

Rumi ushered Yukawa into the living room, then made some tea in the kitchen. She chose Earl Grey, her favorite. She had the vague sense that this might be her last chance to enjoy a nice cup of tea for a while.

When she returned to the living room, carrying a tray with teacups and a little jug of milk, Yukawa was standing near the row of acoustic guitars hanging on the wall.

"Are you interested in guitars?" Rumi asked, as she put the tray down on the coffee table.

"I dabbled as a student. This one's a Gibson; a vintage Gibson, if I'm not mistaken."

"I don't know much about guitars. My husband collects them."

"Would you mind if I had a little play?"

Bemused at the academic's request, Rumi agreed. "Sure, go ahead."

Yukawa took the Gibson down off the wall, pulling out a nearby chair and sitting down. He picked out a few notes, then started to play a slow tune.

Rumi gave a start. It was a song Niikura had composed many years ago. It was one of her favorites. A pastiche of the folk songs of the 1970s, it had been a complete commercial flop.

Yukawa stopped in the middle of the song. "It's a nice-sounding instrument," he said as he put the guitar back on the wall.

"You're good. Keep playing, if you want to."

"No, I think that's enough for today. Any more and my lack of practice will start shining through," said Yukawa, grinning as he made his way back to the sofa.

Lack of practice? Had he been rehearsing for today's little performance? Had her husband told him they had acoustic guitars in the house?

"Please, help yourself," said Rumi, gesturing at the tea tray. Yukawa sat down on the sofa, thanked her, picked up one of the teacups, brought the cup to his nose to savor the aroma, then added a dash of milk from the jug.

"Did Saori Namiki used to practice in this room?"

"Oh, no. Never." Rumi smiled. "The neighbors would complain. We have a soundproof room. She used to practice there."

"You got complaints? But I heard that her voice was beautiful."

"It was, when she was performing. When she was rehearsing, it was more like noise."

"That's a little harsh." Yukawa sipped his tea. "I wish I could hear it—the voice of your brilliant diva. I did a search in YouTube, but I couldn't find her."

"Would you like to hear one of her songs?"

Yukawa blinked. "Can I?"

"Of course," said Rumi. She pulled out a remote-control unit from a rack by her feet and switched on a high-tech sound system, which ran along one side of the room. She then picked up her phone and opened up a music app. She had hundreds of her favorite tracks on her phone.

From the speakers came the sound of the overture. Yukawa, who must have recognized the song, was nodding his head approvingly. It was "Time to Say Goodbye," the song made famous by Sarah Brightman.

A voice slid in on top of the music. Although little above a whisper, it was by no means weak. It was extraordinary: It seemed not so much to enter through the ears as to resonate throughout one's body. Yukawa's eyes suddenly widened. The music was affecting him.

As the song neared its climax, Saori's astonishing talents came even more strikingly to the fore. The sustained high notes seemed to penetrate the heart and the brain, while the heavier low notes lodged in the pit of the stomach. This wasn't a talented teenage girl self-consciously performing an exercise; it was more like a gift straight from the laps of the music gods.

The song ended, leaving a sweet afterglow in its wake.

Yukawa shook his head appreciatively from side to side and clapped his hands. "That was magnificent. I wouldn't have imagined."

"Would you like to hear another?"

"Thank you. I think that's enough for now. Much as I'd like to, it will only make it harder for me to broach the matter at hand."

Rumi breathed in deeply, then took a sip of tea. "You said you wanted to talk about the case?"

"Yes," said Yukawa, "but before I talk about the death of Kanichi Hasunuma, I'd like to go back to when this all began."

"When is that?"

"About six months ago. When Kanichi Hasunuma was arrested on suspicion of Saori's murder. Are you familiar with the details?"

"Shizuoka prefecture, wasn't it?" Rumi put a hand to her cheek. "They discovered Saori's body in an old house there. . . . I think that's how it started."

"That's right. To be precise, two bodies were found in the burned-out remains of a private residence that had degenerated into what's popularly called a trash house. One of the bodies belonged to the occupant of the house—she's believed to have died several years earlier—while DNA analysis showed the other body to be Saori

Namiki. Among the female occupant's family, friends, and associates, the name *Kanichi Hasunuma* jumped out at the investigators. Which brings me to my first question." Yukawa raised one finger. "Why should this trash house, which had been abandoned for years, all of a sudden go up in flames? I asked someone I know in the police to look into this for me, but they have yet to pinpoint the cause of the fire. They suspect arson, but they can't find any evidence of who the arsonist was."

This wasn't what Rumi had been expecting and she felt perplexed. She genuinely had no idea where Yukawa was going with this.

"The investigation team had its suspicions about Hasunuma, so they started looking for links between him and Saori Namiki. Those links didn't take long to find. Hasunuma had been a regular customer at her family's restaurant, Namiki-ya, three years earlier. They also heard that his feelings for Saori were less than wholesome. They concluded that there was a high probability of Saori having been murdered by Hasunuma. They needed to find physical evidence to back that up. They looked everywhere until they did. They found Hasunuma's company overalls from his former employer. The overalls had bloodstains—very small bloodstains, admittedly—on them. Analysis showed the blood to be Saori's. As far as the investigation team was concerned, this constituted decisive evidence and they proceeded to arrest Hasunuma.

"Now that brings me to my second question," said Yukawa, unfurling a second finger.

"Something about this version of events puzzled me from the first time I heard it. Why should Kanichi Hasunuma have hung on to those old overalls so fanatically? Don't you think that any normal person would have chucked them out after quitting their job and moving to a new part of town? Perhaps you could argue he forgot or just never got around to it, but I still don't get it."

"Why are you telling me all this, Professor?" Rumi interrupted. "I'm sure it all makes very good sense, but I'm not competent to answer questions like this."

Yukawa leaned forward and looked at Rumi as if he could see right into her soul. "Are you quite sure about that?"

"Sure? Why should . . . ?"

"Are you really sure? What if you really do know the answers but you just don't know that you do?"

Rumi was thoroughly discombobulated. She had no idea what Yukawa was getting at.

"Let's push on," said Yukawa. He drew back so he was sitting normally again and raised a third finger.

"The third question. This is the most important one. After Kanichi Hasunuma was arrested for Saori's murder, he never wavered. He resolutely maintained his silence, exactly as he had done nineteen years earlier. He'd pulled off something similar before so was probably confident that staying silent would be enough for him to avoid being charged. But the police and the prosecutor certainly weren't going to give up without a fight. There was always the possibility of them coming up with some very powerful piece of evidence. So how did Hasunuma manage to be so laid-back the whole time he was in custody? We know that after his release he bragged to a friend of his that 'a police confession was the king of evidence and that he'd be fine as long as the king wasn't around.' In other words, he was one hundred percent certain that no evidence would be found to prove his guilt. *Why was that?*"

Lowering the hand with the three raised fingers, Yukawa picked up his teacup, took a sip of tea, and looked at Rumi.

"Well? You're not going to tell me that you can't answer my third question, either, are you?"

Rumi felt something give way inside her. It was as if some key part of a foundation had given way. With that having crumbled, the whole superstructure was destined to come crashing down. Yukawa had seen through everything.

"How could Hasunuma be so confident that he would never be charged? Deduction has led me to the only possible answer: *It's because he didn't kill Saori.* More than that, Hasunuma knew who had killed her. Knowing that meant he had the option to make that information public, if he ever found himself well and truly cornered. That's why he was able to remain silent the whole time."

Rumi could feel the blood draining from her cheeks. Her whole body went limp. It was a struggle to remain upright in her chair.

"May I continue?" Yukawa asked, sounding rather anxious.

"Yes, go ahead." Rumi could barely form the words. Her heart was racing, and she was out of breath.

"The question now becomes why Hasunuma did what he did," Yukawa went on. "I don't just mean him knowing who really killed

Saori and keeping quiet about it. He did something else that is very hard to explain before that. He concealed Saori's body in a trash house in Shizuoka prefecture. Taken together, these actions make him an accomplice to the actual killer—and a very loyal one at that. But who would Hasunuma be so loyal to?" Yukawa slowly shook his head. "So far, the investigation has failed to find any such person. If it wasn't loyalty, then what was Hasunuma's motivation? Only one thing comes to mind: money. He helped the actual killer for the sake of money."

"No, no, you're wrong," Rumi spluttered. "There's no way you can call anything he did 'help.'"

"I know what you're trying to say," Yukawa said. He restrained Rumi by raising his right hand.

"The actual killer didn't ask Hasunuma for his help. My theory is that Hasunuma stepped in without being asked. What do I mean by that? I mean that he took Saori's body and concealed it in the trash house after the actual killer had left the crime scene. Saori's disappearance caused a lot of pain to a lot of people, but it was no less disturbing to the killer. They had no idea what had happened to the body. Hasunuma subsequently left Kikuno. He kept a watchful eye on the progress of the police investigation to make sure that he wasn't a suspect. Then he kept a low profile and just waited. For three years—until the statute of limitations for the crime of illegal disposal of a dead body was up."

Rumi was unable to speak. She needed all her energy simply to breathe. She wanted to run away but her body seemed to be frozen in place.

"Only one person in the whole world knew that the young girl's corpse was hidden in an eyesore trash house in rural Shizuoka, along with the dead body of the house's former occupant, an old woman. That person was Hasunuma. The actual killer had no idea. Maybe as time passes, the killer started to forget about Saori—" Having got that far, Yukawa paused and shook his head. "No, that's not what happened, is it? Let me rephrase that. Her memory never stopped weighing on them."

You're right about that, Rumi thought to herself. She hadn't forgotten about Saori once, even for a minute.

"Once three years had passed, Hasunuma swung into action. The first thing he did was to expose the fact that Saori Namiki had been murdered. How did he do that? You know how. Think of my first question: Why did the trash house burn down? *Because Hasunuma deliberately set it on fire.* That's the only possible answer."

Yukawa's soft voice resonated deep inside Rumi's head. She experienced a moment of revelation. *So that's what happened!* She had never given it a moment's thought before now.

"If Hasunuma had killed Saori, would he ever have done anything that resulted in her body being found? By that logic, he wasn't the arsonist if he was the killer. The Shizuoka Prefectural Police never moved beyond that interpretation of events. However, if instead you posit that Hasunuma set the fire *specifically* so that the body *would* be found, you get an answer to the second question: Why did he hang on to the clothing that was stained with Saori's blood? That, too, was something that he did intentionally. What I am trying to say is that Hasunuma arranged everything in order to be arrested. What does that tell us? Personally, I see the whole series of actions he took as a message to the real killer, that message being: 'I know what really happened to Saori.' But if he did know, then why didn't he come out and say so? Presumably, because he knew that his unusual way of behaving would pile enormous psychological pressure on the actual killer. He was as cunning as he was bold, but he wouldn't have acted as he did unless he knew that he couldn't be charged for the crime. He had an ace up his sleeve: He knew the real killer's identity. Plus, he was emboldened by his successful use of the tactic of silence two decades ago."

Every word Yukawa uttered in his matter-of-fact way was like an individual piece in a jigsaw puzzle. One after another, he was slotting the pieces into place and they all fit perfectly. Even the gaps, which Rumi herself had never fully understood, were now being filled in.

"I don't think that Hasunuma was expected to be released under deferment of dispensation. I think he was ready to spend two years in custody until the courts handed him another not-guilty verdict. He wouldn't have minded. When he got out, he could have demanded compensation, like he did the last time. That could well have been part of his motivation for getting himself arrested. When, rather to his own surprise, he was released, Hasunuma decided to accelerate his plan. How, I am not quite sure, but he contacted the real killer to propose a deal, demanding money in return for not revealing the truth. Deal's the wrong word; it was more like blackmail."

Yukawa paused, took a sip of his tea, then returned his cup on its saucer. His cup was empty.

Would you like another? The phrase drifted across Rumi's mind, but she couldn't articulate it.

"I don't know how or why the real killer killed Saori. I imagine that the whole thing was a sudden and unlucky accident, almost as much for the killer as for the victim. If the killer had contacted the police at the time, the problem could have been sorted out without ballooning to its current dimensions. There must, I suppose, have been a reason why the killer couldn't do that. That would also explain why the killer couldn't hold out against Hasunuma's blackmail efforts. It was pretty clear that his demands for money were never going to be a one-off. The awareness that he was going to be hounding them forever provoked the most profound feelings of despair in the killer. It's heart-wrenching just to imagine their psychological state."

At some point, Yukawa's manner had changed. He had gone from pontificating like an academic in a lecture theater to speaking directly to Rumi in a gentler and kindlier tone.

"At that point, the killer got wind of something extraordinary—Yutaro Namiki's plan to imprison Hasunuma in his room and force the truth out of him. That must have come as a big shock. If the plan succeeded, Hasunuma would reveal the truth. The killers were prepared to do whatever was necessary to prevent that outcome. They devised their own counterplan; they thought it was a silver bullet. The idea was to tie Namiki down with something, then step in and kill Hasunuma themselves. The woman customer who was suddenly taken ill at Namiki-ya—her name was Yamada, wasn't it?" Yukawa looked hard at Rumi. "Who was she?"

The question, which seemed to have come from nowhere, pierced Rumi like a sharp arrow. It was the final blow. The equilibrium she had only managed to maintain with such difficulty finally broke, and such support mechanisms as she had came crashing down.

"Mrs. Niikura! Mrs. Niikura!" A voice was calling her name. Her eyes snapped open. She had no idea what had happened.

She had slipped off the armchair down onto the floor. She realized that she must have momentarily lost consciousness. Yukawa was down on one knee beside her, looking anxiously into her face. "Are you all right?"

"Oh, yes . . ." Rumi pulled herself upright and placed a hand on her chest. Her heart was pounding.

"I'm sorry," Yukawa said. "I got carried away. I talked too much. You need a little rest."

"No, I'm fine. I need to go to the next room for a moment. I should take my pills."

"Of course. Take your time."

Rumi grabbed hold of the armchair and pulled herself to her feet. Tottering slightly, she left the living room and made for the bathroom. The pills the doctor had prescribed were in her sponge bag.

She swallowed a pill and gazed into the mirror above the sink. What she saw was the face of an utterly worn-out middle-aged woman. Her complexion was bad and her skin was sagging.

He wouldn't like other people to see me looking like this— The thought rekindled her anxiety and she reached again for her toiletry bag.

When Rumi got back to the living room, Yukawa was standing in front of something that was hanging in a frame on the wall. It was a single page of sheet music.

"That's our debut song," Rumi said, "from ages ago. We released it just after I became the singer in Niikura's band. It was our first single after we got picked up by a major label. Sadly, it didn't sell at all."

"An important first step in your career," said Yukawa. He turned to Rumi and his eyes widened in surprise. "I don't know what medicine you took, but it certainly works fast! All the color's come back to your face. You look quite different."

Rumi managed a rueful smile.

"All I did was fix my makeup. When you're looking in the mirror to do your face, your mind goes completely blank. It's good therapy. Probably works better than any stupid drug."

"It certainly looks like that," Yukawa agreed.

"How about some more tea? I'll make a fresh pot."

"I'd love some."

"When I bring the tea"—Rumi looked straight into Yukawa's eyes—"it's your turn to listen to me, okay?"

Yukawa blinked with embarrassment, then smiled broadly. "If you're happy with me as your audience."

Rumi grinned back at him, then headed for the kitchen. Halfway across the room, she stopped and turned around.

"Are you interested in the language of flowers? Tea is a flowering plant, so it has its own meaning."

"Really? No, I didn't know. What does it mean?"

"Tea signifies remembrance and also pure love."

Yukawa looked slightly nonplussed.

"I'll just be a couple of minutes," Rumi said. She went out to the kitchen.

46

Everything was going well. Their darling—the treasure that the gods of music had bestowed upon them—was about to set the world alight. As the moment came ever closer, Rumi was savoring every minute of every day. Contemplating her husband—his eyes shining like an enthusiastic teenager's whenever he spoke about Saori—she felt a happiness that was almost tangible.

There was just one shadow on her life: Tomoya Takagaki.

She had seen him a few times at Namiki-ya, where he seemed to be one of the regulars. Eventually, they had exchanged a few words of chitchat. He was a polite and handsome young man.

What bothered Rumi was the way he looked at Saori. On second thought, no, perhaps that wasn't the problem. Given Saori's looks, men couldn't help finding her attractive.

The problem was more on Saori's side. She gave every indication of being in love with Tomoya Takagaki. Even if no one else had noticed, Rumi was certain of it. She couldn't pinpoint why she was so sure; perhaps it was just women's intuition.

Now of all times, she thought bitterly. Plenty of people in the creative arts like to maintain that there's nothing like falling in love for boosting one's powers of expression. The reality is rather more nuanced than that. As often as not, infatuation means a much-reduced level of commitment. Because Saori's talent was still a work in progress, the Niikuras had always managed her life quite strictly. They wanted to keep her focused on her training and stop her attention being diverted into other channels.

Things now seemed to be moving in the direction that Rumi most dreaded. Something had changed in Saori soon after her high school graduation. Rumi had guessed that Saori was going out with

Tomoya Takagaki, even though Saori hadn't said a word to any-body.

Rumi couldn't bring herself to tell her husband. He had no idea what was going on, and finding out would be a shock. As far as he was concerned, his darling pupil's sole interest was singing—and absolutely nothing outside that.

For a long time, she was uncertain what to do. Eventually, she decided to put Saori on the spot. When Rumi asked her if she was in a relationship with Tomoya Takagaki, the girl admitted it im-mediately. "Oh, you could tell, could you?" Sticking out her tongue playfully, Saori failed to show any sign of guilt.

"This is a crucial moment in your life. I need you to show a little self-restraint," Rumi said. "I'm not ordering you to break up with him. Make your professional debut and develop some momentum. Once that's safely out of the way, then whatever happens after-ward— Well, it's your life and you can do as you please. For the time being at least, focus on your singing lessons. You want to make it as a pro, don't you?"

Saori nodded miserably and said that yes, she did. Rumi was wor-ried: She didn't believe Saori was being sincere. For all she knew, Saori was just kicking herself for not concealing the relationship better.

Rumi's guess proved right. One day, when an errand took her to Shibuya, she spotted Saori walking happily arm in arm with Tomoya Takagaki. The problem was that Saori had canceled her voice lesson that day, on the pretext of having to visit a friend in the hospital.

Rumi confronted Saori the very next day. Was she serious about wanting to become a pro?

The response Rumi got wasn't what she had been expecting. "As far I'm concerned, the time I spend with Tomoya matters every bit as much as my dreams of becoming a singer," Saori said. "Why do we all work so hard to realize our dreams? Because we think our dreams are going to make us happy. For me, though, right now, all I need to be happy is to be with Tomoya. What's the point of me sacrificing my happiness now just to get my hands on some other form of happiness in the future?"

Rumi was blindsided. She felt dizzy. Saori's relationship was nothing more than a silly little fling with an immature boy. How could she compare anything so trivial to their grand project of achieving global success? It was a dream that meant everything to Naoki. Rumi felt that Saori was trampling his feelings underfoot.

She and Naoki had the highest opinion of Saori's talents, Rumi said. All they wanted was for Saori to fulfill her own natural potential. She was almost begging now.

Saori said that she'd gotten the message. But had she?

After that, Rumi was more worried than ever about what was going on in Saori's private life. She would interrogate her when she failed to show up for practice. She would ask her where she was going whenever she went out.

Soon after the turn of the year, Niikura remarked that there was something "not quite right" about Saori. She didn't seem completely serious about her lessons.

"We're almost ready to launch Saori's career, but I don't think that her heart's in it like before. Still, I always thought she'd go through a phase like this. I should probably give her a good talking to."

Rumi felt a surge of irritation. What was he saying? Managing Saori's personal life was *her* responsibility.

And then that day—

It was late in the afternoon when she called Saori to arrange a meeting. She only said that "there was something important they needed to discuss," but Saori seemed to know instinctively what it was about. From the tone of her voice, Rumi could imagine the sulky look on her face.

Rumi wasn't sure where the best place for their heart-to-heart would be. She didn't want anyone eavesdropping on them. Saori said that she'd rather meet outdoors than indoors, so they settled on a little out-of-the-way park.

When Rumi got there, the park was deserted, perhaps because of the ongoing construction work. There were no houses in the vicinity. The whole area was silent, lifeless.

The two women sat down side by side on a bench and Rumi got straight to business. Niikura had finally twigged that something was going on. Saori needed to start seeing less of her boyfriend.

Saori said nothing and just stared at the ground for a while. Then she raised her head and looked at Rumi. The intensity of her gaze made Rumi almost flinch. She felt a heavy sense of foreboding.

"I just . . . I'm going to give it up," Saori said.

Niikura didn't understand what she meant. "Give it up? . . . Give what up?"

"Trying to be a singer." Saori moistened her lips with the tip of her tongue. "I give up. I quit."

It took a while to register. Although she had heard the words, on an intuitive level she refused to understanding their meaning.

"What are you talking about?" Rumi's voice was shaking. Her whole world had been turned upside down. "Quit? You've got to be joking."

Saori shook her head. Her face was serene.

"I mean it. I've had enough. I want to take another path."

"Another path? Apart from singing, what other path is there for you?"

Saori smiled tenderly. What she said next was a complete bolt from the blue.

"I'm going to be a mother. I'm going to have a baby and start a beautiful family."

"A *baby*?" Rumi looked at Saori's belly. "You're not saying . . . ?"

"Yes, I did a test this morning. It was positive. I haven't told To-moya yet. I'm sure he'll be thrilled; he's been after me to marry him."

Saori spoke with vivacity, but what Rumi saw was a demented person. *What was the stupid little girl saying?*

"Hang on a minute, Saori. You need to think this through. Do you know what you're saying? A baby . . . at a time like this . . . Why? You're about to make your professional debut. This is the most important moment of your career. . . ."

"Don't you get it? I won't be making any debut. You're the one who doesn't know what they're talking about."

Saori giggled. Being laughed at only made Rumi angrier.

"Do you seriously . . . do you seriously think we'll let you do that? Have you no idea of what we've done for you? Everything humanly possible to turn you into a top-level singer—that's what we've done. My husband sacrificed everything for you. . . . Do you really think he'll just roll over and abandon his dreams? Have you no respect for our hard work?"

Seeing that Rumi was genuinely angry, Saori apologized.

"I'm sorry. And thank you. I am grateful to both of you. I'm sure I can put this experience to use in other aspects of my life in the future."

"I don't care about your life or your future. What's going to happen to *our* dreams? We're the ones who took a chance on you. . . ."

Saori frowned. "Isn't that a bit weird?" she asked, tilting her head to one side.

"Weird? What is?"

"Why am *I* supposed to realize *your* dreams for you? Mr. Niikura is always telling me that I'll succeed where you couldn't. But I never signed up to provide a happy ending for your life story. I just wanted to sing, in my way and without any baggage. I think I've got every right to change course, if my own dreams change."

Rumi glared at Saori. "You ungrateful little bitch, how could you . . . ?"

"Fine," said Saori, an icy expression on her face. "I'll have a frank talk with Mr. Niikura. I'll apologize to him. Or are you going to tell me to have an abortion? I'm warning you, that's something I'll never do."

Rumi panicked when she saw Saori pulling out her phone. "What are you doing?"

"Like I said, I'm going to call Mr. Niikura. I'll be completely upfront. I'll tell him everything."

"Wait, just hang on a minute."

She made a grab for Saori's phone. She didn't want Niikura to have to hear this. She had to do something—

"Don't do this. Please, let's work something out. There's got to be a way. Go ahead. Have the baby. Enjoy motherhood. Just, please, please, don't give up singing."

"Please, shut up! I'm not quitting singing because I have to. I'm quitting to follow another path that will make me happy. Stop shoving *your* dreams down my throat. Why should I have to work through your hang-ups for you? It creeps me out."

They had both risen to their feet as they fought for the phone.

"Creeps you out?" Rumi's eyes were wide open. "What do you mean . . . ?"

"Exactly what I said. I feel like I can't breathe. It's like having a couple of stalkers watching every move I make."

It was at this point that Rumi lost her capacity for rational thought. *All the work that the two of them had put into the girl and she compared them to—of all things—stalkers!*

"How dare you!" She shoved Saori backward as hard as she could.

The girl's heel must have snagged on something, because she just keeled over. Rumi heard a muffled thunk.

Expecting Saori to get back up, Rumi drew her hand back in readiness to fetch her an almighty slap on the cheek. That was how angry she was.

But Saori didn't move. She just stayed on the ground, flat on her back, arms and legs splayed. Rumi called her name, peered into her face. Her eyes were half-open, but she didn't respond, even when Rumi shook her. *Oh God, no!* she thought. She held her hand a little above Saori's mouth. *She wasn't breathing.*

At that moment, she realized what she had done.

She had caused Saori's death. She had killed her—

Her mind went blank, then plunged into violent confusion. Barely aware of what she was doing, she ran away from the park. Her capacity for rational thought had deserted her; the only thing she could think about was how on earth she was going to explain what had happened to her husband.

Her despair only deepened, as she wandered aimlessly around. The police would probably arrest her. Niikura's life would be thrown into disruption. Worst of all, she could never justify having taken the life of his protégée, the girl who made his life worth living.

I should kill myself. It's the only way to make amends. How shall I do it? Where? Jumping off a building is probably easiest.

She was just wondering if there were any tall buildings nearby, when she heard the sound of an ambulance siren in the distance. Had someone found Saori's body? Were they taking her to the hospital? The park was probably crawling with people by now.

Next thing she knew, she was walking back toward the park. In her mind's eye, she pictured a cluster of parked police cars. The police would have no trouble identifying her as the killer. *I must kill myself before they get around to it*, Rumi thought.

When she got close to the park, there was no commotion of any kind, nor were there any police cars. The ambulance she had heard, she realized, had nothing to do with her.

Full of apprehension, she made her way to where she had pushed Saori to the ground. Her legs were trembling uncontrollably. Awareness of the enormity of what she had done made it hard to breathe.

However—

Saori's body was no longer there. Had she got the place wrong? She looked around. It was nowhere to be seen.

Rumi was mystified. What the hell was going on? Where had Saori's body got to?

She was looking down when she noticed something glinting on the ground. She picked it up. It was a gold hair slide in the shape of a butterfly. She remembered that Saori had been wearing it. It must have come off when she fell over.

What if I was too quick to decide Saori was dead? Perhaps she was just unconscious. Perhaps she came to, got up, and has walked off somewhere. If anyone had found her, the police would definitely be here.

The more Rumi thought about it, the more plausible it felt. She called Saori on her cell. She had to apologize for lashing out like that. But she couldn't get through. She wondered if Saori had switched off her phone on purpose.

Unsure what to think, Rumi started walking home. Saori had a singing lesson scheduled for the next day. Maybe she wouldn't show. Maybe Niikura would get annoyed. That was the last thing she cared about now. All that mattered was to establish that Saori was safe and well as fast as possible.

Niikura got back home late that night. A good meeting about Saori's imminent debut had left him in high spirits. Rumi's heart ached at the sight of him. She couldn't bring herself to tell him that Saori had decided to abandon her dreams of becoming a singer.

Her anguish then was nothing compared to what came later. She shuddered with horror when her husband got a call from Yutaro Namiki late that night. "Saori went out this evening and isn't back yet," Niikura told her after hanging up.

Rumi fell into a full-blown panic. She was completely bewildered. Seeing the state she was in, Niikura thought that concern for Saori's welfare was behind it. "There's no need to worry," he said to comfort her. "She'll turn up right as rain, I'm sure."

When the next day came and Saori was still missing, the police launched a proper investigation into her whereabouts. Rumi knew that she ought to tell the police about what had happened, but she couldn't bring herself to do so. It was just too painful to have to tell Niikura about Saori's change of heart—and she wanted to keep her own bad behavior secret. She kept assuring herself that there was no link between what she'd done and Saori's disappearance.

That was how Saori vanished. Rumi never knew what had happened to her. The sight of her husband—who had lost the great dream and purpose of his life—was a torment to her, but she kept her mouth shut. She persuaded herself that saying nothing about what had happened that night was better.

More than three years went by. With the passing of time, Rumi's memories of the event became hazier. While she never forgot what had happened between her and Saori, she began to feel that it wasn't quite real; that something from a dream had got mixed up with reality.

About six months ago, her worst nightmare was proven to be true. Saori was indeed dead. Her body had been found—and in a most unlikely place: a burned-out trash house in a small town in Shizuoka.

With no idea what was going on, Rumi and her husband just looked on as events unfolded. The police soon arrested a man by the name of Hasunuma. They were almost certain that he was the killer.

Rumi cast her mind back to that. *What on earth had happened after she pushed Saori to the ground and left the park?*

No further information came to light. Throughout his time in custody, Hasunuma remained doggedly silent. In the end, the police just let him go. At the news of his release, Niikura exploded with rage. "I want to kill the guy myself," became a verbal tic with him.

Rumi found the whole thing baffling. If the police had bothered to arrest Hasunuma in the first place, they must have had evidence. So why had they subsequently let him go?

A phone call Rumi received not long after rendered all those questions moot. The caller was a man who introduced himself as her "savior."

He sounded like a creep. Rumi was about to hang up, but the caller must have sensed that. "Cut me off and things could get very awkward for you. I know what you did to Saori Namiki on that night three years ago," he said.

"You've probably heard my name, if nothing else," he continued. "I'm Kanichi Hasunuma. I was accused of murder. My reputation was destroyed. And I almost got sent to jail. When it should have been you."

Rumi was dumbstruck. Hasunuma snickered under his breath.

"Shocked? I know. I bet you thought the whole business was over and you were done with it. You thought it had all been laid to rest. Well, that's not how it is. You're still the star of this show. Or maybe it's more like your star turn is only just getting started: your performance in the role of Saori Namiki's murderer. Don't tell me that it slipped your mind. You knocked the girl down and killed her right there. I was—ha, ha, ha—watching. The whole thing. Including the bit where you ran away. I didn't report you to the police. What *do* you think I did? I took the body away. I took it and I stashed it some place where no one was ever going to find it. It's thanks to me that the police haven't come knocking on your door. They never suspected you—*because I kept my mouth shut*. I think I've said enough for you to get what happened."

"But why? . . . Why did you hide the body?"

"Huh? You'd have preferred if I didn't? You'd have liked it better if the body had been found, and you'd been arrested for murder? You think I should have minded my own business? What I saw that night was a business opportunity that I wasn't willing to let pass by."

"A business opportunity?"

"That's right, business. Come on. Don't tell me you thought I got rid of the body and kept my mouth shut out of the pure goodness of my heart? No one's that stupid. I did what I did because I saw money in it."

Every word he uttered was like a fragment of darkness that stuck to her body. If it went on, she'd be reduced to a black lump.

"Which is why you'll be fine," said Hasunuma in a chirpy tone that was the antithesis of Rumi's own despair. "The police aren't going to arrest you. No one knows the truth. The girl's family, the general public—they'll all keep right on thinking that I'm the one who offed her. As long as you accept my deal, that is. Still, I'm hardly expecting you to turn me down."

As Hasunuma went on, Rumi finally realized what he was after.

"Me . . . uh . . . what do you want me to do?"

Hasunuma snickered quietly. "Something ever so easy. For you, at least."

Rumi had chosen Darjeeling for their second cup of tea. Its strong aroma would give her a psychological boost, she felt. She took it straight with no milk or lemon. She emptied her cup to the last drop and returned it to the saucer.

"He demanded a payment of one million yen," Rumi said. "He instructed me to open a new account under my own name, transfer the money to it, then post him the ATM card and the PIN code."

"One million yen," echoed Yukawa. "It's an odd sum to ask for. I feel bad saying this, but wasn't it rather less than you'd expected?"

"Yes, it was. I'd been expecting a demand of ten or twenty million, perhaps even in the hundreds of millions."

"If he'd come straight out and demanded one hundred million, what would you have done?"

Rumi cocked her head to one side. "I couldn't have paid."

"Would you have told your husband?"

"Perhaps. Or perhaps I'd have just thrown in the towel and turned myself in to the police. No, that's wrong. Most likely—" Rumi drew in a breath, then went on. "Most likely, I'd have killed myself."

"I believe you. Either way, there was no advantage there for Hasunuma. A million yen was a different story, though. He probably thought that a million was the kind of sum that a woman who belonged to a wealthy family could raise with relative ease. He saw it as a sum you'd be happy to pay as a stopgap, even if the whole blackmail thing was unsettling."

Yukawa had guessed right. Not knowing how to respond to him, Rumi just hung her head in silence.

"So you gave him what he wanted?"

"Yes." Her voice was weak and hoarse.

"Did he make a second demand?"

"He did. About one month later. And for the same amount: one million yen."

"And you paid that, too?"

"Yes. I was too much of a coward to go to the police or to talk to my husband. I just kept procrastinating, even though I knew I couldn't keep that up indefinitely. I felt more dead than alive—particularly after Hasunuma moved back to Kikuno."

"Did Hasunuma contact you by phone? Or did you sometimes meet face-to-face?"

Rumi hesitated. "Just the one time. When he asked me for something else. Not cash."

"Something other than cash?" Her meaning dawned on Yukawa as he repeated what she had said. "Oh, I see. Well, we don't need to go into that."

"Thank you," Rumi replied.

It had happened shortly before Hasunuma moved back to Kikuno. He told Rumi that he needed to talk to her in person, so they arranged a meeting in central Tokyo.

"You and me, we're coconspirators. It's a bond we have in common. I really think we should get to know each other better." As Hasunuma said this, there was something vile and clammy not just in his voice but in his eyes, which ran over Rumi's body as if licking her all over. "You're not going to say no, are you?"

About one hour later, in a cheap hotel room, Rumi surrendered herself to the vilest man in the world. She did her utmost to keep her mind a blank and just waited for the experience to end.

When they finally parted, as she fled from Hasunuma as fast as she could, his words still rang in her ears: *Not bad for a woman on the wrong side of forty.* She seriously started thinking about killing herself again.

"I was desperate when—just as you described, Professor—my husband came to me with that unexpected proposal. I got goose bumps when he told me about Tojima's plan. My whole life would be destroyed if Hasunuma ever told the truth. And it wasn't just my life—my husband's life would be wrecked, too. He must have noticed I was behaving strangely, because he asked me what was wrong. I was in two minds, but eventually I realized I couldn't keep my secret to myself anymore. I told him everything."

47

He'd found no mention of what he was looking for despite having read through the entire newspaper. The incident had taken place in Kikuno, an insignificant place that most people had never even heard of. The headline MURDER SUSPECT IS HIMSELF MURDERED had briefly trended on the internet, but public attention was fickle and quick to move on.

That's something to be grateful for, thought Naoki Niikura. He didn't want anyone to be interested in his case. Anyway, he could sum the whole thing up more succinctly: *Musician manqué targets suspect in killing of protégée—and ends up killing him.*

He neatly folded the newspaper he had finished reading and laid it on the carpeted floor. The free newspapers were one nice thing about the detention center.

He sat down, leaned his back against the wall, and reached for the digital music player beside him. It was a present from Rumi. He slipped on the headphones and switched the player on. He looked over toward the door. When he was sitting, he could avoid making eye contact with anyone else thanks to the opaque cover on the little window by the cell door. His room was eighty square feet in size, and, fortunately for him, he was the only detainee in it. He had expected to have to share his cell with several other people. Finding himself alone like this had been a great relief.

He knew the song he was listening to well: "I Will Always Love You." It had started as a country song and gone on to become a worldwide megahit for Whitney Houston.

But it was Rumi who was singing the version in Niikura's headphones. She had recorded it when she was still in her twenties.

Her voice had a wonderful purity and she knew how to sustain a note. Even if Saori had been a musical genius, Rumi's talents were hardly inferior. It was *his* lack of ability that had been the problem; he had failed to foster her talent to its full potential.

Closing his eyes, he tried to remember the days when he and Rumi had been battling to make their names in the music world. Instead, all that came back to him was that one episode on that one particular day: the time when Rumi told him the truth about Saori's death.

As he listened to Rumi's tearful account, Niikura experienced a strange sensation. He felt that somewhere off to one side, a second self was watching the scene—of an oblivious, carefree husband absorbing his wife's shocking confession—with complete detachment. *This must be what depersonalization disorder is all about*, he was thinking in one corner of his mind.

Reflecting on it later, he understood that the whole situation had been so brutal that he had been psychologically incapable of accepting it.

Rumi's story was hard to believe and hard to come to terms with. He could feel himself blinking incredulously throughout her account. He wanted to believe that the whole story was no more than a fantasy that his wife had invented to give him a nasty shock, but her racking sobs showed that she wasn't playacting.

After she finished, he was unable to speak for a while. He had the sensation that the whole world had been turned on its head, pitching him into some deep, dark hole.

"I'm so sorry, so sorry," Rumi kept repeating, her voice weak through her tears. Niikura stared at her in blank amazement—while his second self calmly looked on.

"Why did you do it?"

That idiotic question was the first thing that came out of his mouth when he finally recovered the power of speech. But hadn't Rumi just painstakingly explained the reason why? She had done it because she wanted to keep Saori on her current career path. Why did she want that? Because she believed that making a global singing sensation of Saori was their—no, was *her beloved husband*'s dearest wish and the whole goal of his life.

"Darling?" Rumi raised her head. Her eyes were bloodshot, their rims red and puffy. Her cheeks were damp with tears. "What should I do? Should I turn myself in?"

Although that was exactly what he thought she should do, Nii-kura couldn't bring himself to say it. Besides, he could never accept his wife being arrested for Saori's murder. Kanichi Hasunuma was the sole culprit. That was what everyone else believed. And that was why they had all banded together to give him the punishment he deserved.

That was when Niikura had an idea.

He knew that Yutaro Namiki was planning to extract the truth from Hasunuma. What if he stymied that plan and killed Hasunuma instead? Namiki and the others would all be surprised and shocked. That was unavoidable. Still, thought Niikura, if he said that he had felt compelled to avenge Saori, they would probably come around to his side.

On the other hand, if Hasunuma managed to make it through the whole ordeal—standing firm against Namiki's threats and not revealing the truth about Saori—then he would just go back to blackmailing Rumi. Whichever way you looked at it, Hasunuma was a problem he had to deal with once and for all.

If the police found out that he'd killed Hasunuma—then so be it. It was highly unlikely and besides, this was a crime he wouldn't really mind being arrested for. Public opinion would probably be with him. No, the only thing that mattered was concealing the fact that Rumi had caused Saori's death.

Deep inside his eardrums, Rumi was singing "I Will Always Love You." *I will always love you*: That was how he felt about her, too.

His mind was made up. He would protect Rumi, come what may.

48

Tojima talked my husband through his plan. It was complicated, with a large number of people each playing a small part in the crime. Yutaro Namiki was supposed to be on his own when he interrogated Hasunuma, trapped in his little room. My husband's idea was to engineer a situation where he got to take over from Namiki." Noticing that Yukawa's cup was empty, Rumi paused. "Would you like some more tea?" Yukawa guessed that she could be calm and rational now because, having made up her mind what to do, she was under less psychological pressure than before.

"No, thanks. I'm okay." Yukawa waved his hand over his cup. "Please, go on."

"A few minutes ago, you mentioned the trick he came up with. He was quite sure that Namiki wouldn't be able to turn down a sick customer who begged to be taken to the hospital."

"Which is where Mrs. Yamada comes in." There was a glint in Yukawa's eyes. "Who was she?"

"To be honest," Rumi said, "we don't know her real name."

"I'm sorry?" Yukawa's eyes widened behind his spectacles.

"We got her through one of those rent-a-family agencies."

Yukawa knitted his brows. "What on earth's that?"

"They're sometimes called family rental or proxy family agencies. What they do, basically, is to provide actors to perform whatever family roles a client might need. Like, if for some reason you can't take get your real parents to meet your girlfriend or boyfriend, they'll arrange for a couple of actors to play the part of your mom and dad."

"What a business model . . . Amazing!"

"They don't just supply family members. They can provide

people who perform all sorts of roles: posing as your boss when you have to visit a client to formally apologize for some work-related mistake; phony audience members for an author's book signing. The list goes on."

"And Mrs. Yamada was an actor from an agency like that?"

"Yes. The story we fed her was that we were doing a surprise inspection of the crisis-management capacity of restaurants in the Kikuno shopping district."

"That's pretty plausible. Good thinking on your part."

"The plan went off even better than we expected. Hasunuma was asleep by the time my husband got to the hut. What he said about making a racket and shouting to wake him up—that was just a lie. He just went straight ahead and started tipping the liquid nitrogen into the room. The liquid nitrogen turned out to be a far deadlier weapon than he thought. He didn't hear a sound from inside the room; no groans, no cries, nothing. When he had tipped the whole container into the room, he opened the door. Hasunuma was already in a state of cardiac arrest."

"If he was already asleep when the liquid nitrogen started coming into the room, he probably never woke up."

Rumi took a deep breath. She seemed quite reinvigorated.

"That's all I can tell you. Sorry, my explanation was probably all over the place."

"Not at all. You've been a model of clarity."

"I hope I can do a better job," Rumi said, "when I go to the police. I want to be clear about a few points—like how everything my husband did, he did for me."

Yukawa's face clouded. "Are you planning to turn yourself in?"

"Isn't that why you're here? To make me?"

"Far from it," said Yukawa, with a shake of his head. He spoke with startling emphasis.

"I'm not a detective. I've got no legal authority to take a statement from you. I made that clear right from the start: that I didn't want you to say anything that works to your disadvantage. I told you that you had a choice."

"Will you tell the police what I . . . ?"

"I have no intention of telling the police anything. My sense is that, as long as I don't say anything, they'll struggle to work out the truth. Perhaps, though, I'm just being conceited."

Rumi ran her tongue over her lips. "You mean you'll keep quiet about me?" she said.

"The idea of people I like all being sent to jail doesn't appeal to me. As things stand, Mr. Niikura will get a sentence of at least three years for manslaughter. Considering who the victim was, that seems reasonable to me."

Yukawa looked away for a moment. Then he went on: "Something like this happened to me once before and it wasn't a pleasant experience. There was this man who took on the responsibility for a murder committed by the woman he was in love with. When I revealed the truth of what he'd done, the woman's conscience got the better of her, which undermined the man's acts of self-sacrifice. Frankly, I have no desire to go through anything like that again."

Yukawa's expression, as he delivered this explanation, was grave. Abruptly, he broke into a self-deprecating laugh and began to shake his head.

"You're probably wondering why I bothered coming. If I'm not here to encourage you to turn yourself in, then what need do I have to ascertain the truth? I should just keep my thoughts to myself. That's fine, but there is something I absolutely have to share with you—a crucial piece of information that I'm aware of and you're not."

Uncertain what the professor was going to say next, Rumi frowned and tilted her head quizzically to one side. "What might that be?"

"I need to ask you a question first," said Yukawa. "In your account, you mentioned that Saori had a hair clip, a hair clip in the shape of a golden butterfly. . . ."

"You mean the hair slide?"

"Yes. You said you found it on the ground near where Saori fell. Have you got it here in the house?"

"I do, but . . ."

"Could I see it?"

"The hair slide?"

"Yes," replied Yukawa.

Rumi got to her feet. She had no idea where this line of inquiry was going. "Wait a minute," she said.

She went into the master bedroom and walked over to the dresser. She opened the bottommost drawer and extracted a small box that was shoved right to the back. She hadn't opened the box even once in the past three years. She had no idea what to do with the thing, but she couldn't even think of getting rid of it.

She took it back to the living room. "Here it is," she said. When she handed it to Yukawa, she was startled to see that he had put on white gloves.

"Let's have a good look." Yukawa took off the lid and plucked the hair slide out of the box. The gold had lost none of its shine over the past three years.

Yukawa inspected the hair slide with great care. He then put it back in the box and replaced the lid on the box. As he pulled off his gloves, he turned to Rumi with a satisfied look on his face. "I was right."

"Right about what?"

"Your account of events was one hundred percent true. Not a single falsehood in it."

"Of course there wasn't. Why would I be lying at this stage?"

"The important thing is this: What you *believe* to be the truth and the *actual* truth are not necessarily the same thing. Until you know the difference, you can't make the choice that will decide your fate." Laying his white gloves on the table, Yukawa used the tip of one finger to adjust the position of his glasses on his nose, then looked directly at Rumi. "I will tell you the real truth: the truth as I deduced it."

49

When he opened the door, Yukawa was sitting at the far end of the counter, chatting with the gray-haired bartender. Both men turned to look at Kusanagi. "Good evening, sir," the bartender said.

Apart from a couple seated at a table, there were no other customers. Kusanagi walked over, sat down next to Yukawa, and ordered a Wild Turkey on the rocks.

"Got something to celebrate?" Yukawa asked. "Well, as long as you're not drinking to drown your sorrows, it's all good."

"I'm somewhere between the two poles." Kusanagi took a long rectangular package out of his bag and put it on the counter in front of Yukawa. "First things first. I want to give you this."

"What's this? From the shape, I'd have to say a bottle of wine."

"It's one I've been meaning—and failing—to give you for years now."

"Opus One? Oh, very nice. Received with thanks." Yukawa took the box and put it into the bag on the seat beside him.

A lowball glass arrived in front of Kusanagi. He picked it up and Yukawa lifted his tumbler. The two men gently clinked glasses.

Kusanagi took a sip of his bourbon on the rocks. He felt it burn his tongue, then his throat before the aroma burst in his nose. "Naoki Niikura retracted his statement."

"Really? How did that happen?"

"You don't sound very surprised."

"Should I be?"

Kusanagi snorted. "I got a report yesterday from the investigators who are surveilling the Niikuras' place. A guest showed up there. The investigators sent me a photo. It was you. You were in there, talking to the wife, for over an hour, they said. This morning, Rumi Niikura came to the Kikuno Police Station to see her husband. 'Five minutes is all I need. Just let me speak to my husband alone,' she said. Normally the custodial officer has to be in the room during visits, but given that Niikura had already made a full and frank confession, he went to have a word with the station commander who agreed to bend the rules. Because of that, we have no idea what passed between the two of them in that room. The upshot was that at his next interview, Naoki Niikura came out and said that all the testimony he had provided us with so far was false. He hadn't killed Hasunuma accidentally; he had murdered him, and he had done so intentionally. Cue general consternation. It's common enough for a suspect who's admitted to murder to deny having the intent to kill, but the opposite—that's something I've never encountered before."

"His motive for the murder?"

"To protect his wife. 'Ask her, if you want to know more,' he said."

"And did you?"

"You bet we did. We summoned Rumi Niikura to the station immediately. She was quite calm. When we informed her that her husband had changed his statement, she briefly appeared saddened, but she soon started talking, very much as if she'd made up her mind to do so. I was surprised at how coherent her explanation was. As for the content, I found it downright astonishing."

Rumi Niikura's account completely upended the police's previous understanding of the case. From Saori Namiki's unnatural death onward, the truth was very far from anything that Kusanagi and his team had imagined.

Rumi Niikura's story contained no contradictions or inconsistencies. If anything, her account actually helped clear up many trivial questions the investigation team had.

"What a disaster!" said Kusanagi, raising his glass. "We all started wondering ourselves what the hell we'd been doing these last few months. That's why I said I was halfway between celebrating and drowning my sorrows. I believe we've now solved the case. I have absolutely no sense of victory. Our strategy was completely off target. We won only because our opponent gifted us a goal."

"Who cares? A win's a win."

"It's not quite that simple. There are still a few loose ends we need to tidy up. The thing I find puzzling is why the Niikuras decided to tell the truth *at this particular moment*. It's obvious enough that their meeting at the police station this morning was extremely significant. Unfortunately, neither the husband nor the wife are willing to tell us what they discussed, citing their right to privacy.

"That was when I realized that my only option was to ask you." Kusanagi twisted around to look at Yukawa. "What was it that Rumi Niikura went to tell her husband? What did she say to him that made him decide to retract his statement? *I know you know.* No, let me rephrase that. You masterminded this whole thing. It's you who got the two of them to change their minds. Am I right?"

Yukawa took a sip of whiskey and shook his head. "I did no such thing."

"Liar."

"I'm not lying. It's certainly true that yesterday I told Mrs. Niikura my theories about the truth of the case. My goal was neither to condemn them nor to inspire them to turn themselves in. I just wanted to let them know the truth about something that I was pretty sure they didn't know."

"And what particular truth was that?"

Yukawa took a couple of deep breaths to settle himself. "It was something to do with Saori Namiki's death."

Kusanagi pulled a sour face. "You're not going to tell me that Rumi Niikura's statement was false, are you?"

"Her testimony covered only what she *knew*. That doesn't necessarily imply that it was all *true*."

It was a comment that Kusanagi had to take seriously. He looked around the bar. "Shall we go somewhere else?"

"Here'll be fine. No one's listening."

Kusanagi moved his face closer to Yukawa's. "Go on, then. Tell me."

"The question is," Yukawa began, "when did the bleeding occur?"

"The bleeding?"

"You decided to arrest Hasunuma after finding traces of Saori's blood on his old work overalls. Now, in a bad case of a depressed skull fracture like this, significant blood loss is par for the course. Okay then, shouldn't blood have been found at the crime scene? The day after Saori disappeared, the local police conducted a search over a wide area. They would have taken the discovery of any blood on the ground very seriously indeed. I got Utsumi to check the records. The police did examine the little park, but in the record there was no mention of them finding any bloodstains. Then there's Rumi's own testimony to consider. In a state of shock from having caused Saori's death, she absconded from the crime scene for a period. After going back there, she was unsure where the body had been until she came across the hair slide. Both these pieces of information tend to suggest that there was no blood on the ground, don't they?"

"There was no blood—which means that . . ." Kusanagi had seen what Yukawa was trying to suggest. "Which means that Saori's body wasn't bleeding when Hasunuma removed it from the park."

"You said 'body.' I wonder if that's the appropriate word."

"Saori wasn't yet dead; she was still breathing—you think that's a possibility?"

"No, I think it's an *extremely high* possibility. People can die instantly when they're shoved to the ground—but it's not very likely. The same is true for a depressed skull fracture—is the human skull really quite so fragile? Is such an injury likely from merely being pushed over? Rumi Niikura told us that Saori wasn't breathing. I think it's highly probable that in her distress she just imagined that she wasn't."

"Which would mean that the person who really killed Saori . . ."

"Hasunuma may well have thought that she was dead, too. To start with, at least. But what if Saori regained consciousness while Hasunuma had her in his car? His whole ingenious plan would be wrecked. And he wouldn't want her making a noise and attracting attention, either."

"So he finishes her off by striking her on the back of her head," said Kusanagi. "And you think that's when the bleeding occurred?"

"As a theory, it's not inconceivable"

"It's not inconceivable at all. . . . God, this is just too horrible." Kusanagi felt the heat surging through his body in a wave.

"If I were Rumi Niikura's lawyer, I'd definitely produce the hair slide as evidence in her favor," Yukawa said.

"Sorry, what hair slide?"

"There was a gold hair slide at the crime scene. If Saori was bleeding after she hit the ground, the hair slide ought to have traces of blood on it. If analysis failed to detect any blood, then the lawyer could argue that someone else must have dealt the fatal blow."

"Right, I see . . ."

Kusanagi consulted his watch. It wasn't yet midnight. Reaching into his jacket pocket for his phone, he started to get to his feet. Yukawa grabbed Kusanagi's arm to stop him.

"Not at this time of night! Come on, let your people have a decent night's sleep. The hair slide isn't going anywhere. Rumi's got it safe."

"I guess you're right," conceded Kusanagi, lowering himself back into his chair. He knocked back what remained of his bourbon and ordered another from the bartender.

"What you mentioned earlier—the truth that even the Niikuras didn't know. Was that it?"

"Yes," Yukawa said. "Whether or not they come clean about their actions is their choice to make. But that choice is meaningless unless they know the *real* truth. That's why I went to tell Rumi Niikura."

"And you guessed that Rumi Niikura would want to talk to her husband about it. Sure enough, off she goes to see him this morning. . . ."

"Rumi was conflicted. As things stood, her husband was only going to be charged with manslaughter. Telling the truth results in that charge being bumped up to murder and in Rumi being charged, too. But if they both kept quiet, then no one would ever know what Hasunuma did. My impression is that they're actually willing to pay the price for the crimes they've committed. That's what matters to them right now."

A fresh glass appeared in front of Kusanagi. He jabbed a finger at the ice. It made a tinkling sound.

EPILOGUE

50

She hung the *noren* curtain over the front door and flipped the wooden sign over from CLOSED to OPEN. Natsumi felt that she had accomplished something meaningful.

She heard a woman's voice behind her. "Ah, so you're reopening, then?" When she turned around, she saw the woman from the local tofu shop. She was on the plump side and her dark-purple cardigan was clearly rather a tight fit.

"We are, yes. I hope you'll come in for a meal."

"Best of luck. I'm rooting for you." The lady smiled warmly. "I'll drop in very soon. Promise."

"Thank you very much. Look forward to seeing you." Natsumi clasped her hands at her waist and bobbed her head politely.

"See you later," the woman said and went on her way. Watching her waddle off, Natsumi let out sigh of relief.

Namiki-ya had been closed for a long time because of the frequency with which Yutaro was being summoned to the police station for questioning. It got to the point that the family started worrying about having to shut down for good. The restaurant could hardly keep going if the owner was arrested and sent to jail.

The police were questioning Yutaro in connection with two crimes: acting as an accomplice and conspiracy to murder. He ended up not being charged with the former, as he couldn't be expected to have foreseen what Niikura ended up doing. That left conspiracy to murder.

The facts were these: Yutaro has asked Tojima to procure and put in place the liquid nitrogen, which was used in Hasunuma's murder. His plan had been to use the liquid nitrogen to frighten Hasunuma. He hadn't made a final decision on whether or not to kill him. He intended to make that decision only after hearing what Hasunuma had to say.

The problem was, would anyone accept such a rationalization? The police thought that Namiki had made up his mind in advance that Hasunuma had murdered Saori; he simply wanted to get him to admit his guilt before he went on to kill him.

When the detective responsible for interviewing him pressed him on this issue, Yutaro had the following to say.

"I can see why you might see it like that. The truth is, though, that when I asked Shusaku to get me the liquid nitrogen, I hadn't yet made up my mind. I never really felt that I would be capable of committing a dreadful act like murder. . . . At the same time, I thought I might suddenly feel the compulsion to kill him when that monster . . . that Hasunuma told me how he killed Saori."

Whatever anyone else might think about his explanation, Natsumi, at least, was convinced that her father wasn't lying. At bottom, he was mild-mannered, even timid. She knew that he was mortified at his own spinelessness, when he'd failed to grab a knife and launch himself at his daughter's murderer when the man had been right there in front of him.

The detective interviewing Namiki seemed to have formed the same impression. Ultimately, the police decided not to charge him with conspiracy to commit murder. And that was how the restaurant was able to open up again for the first time in a while.

If the rumors were to be believed, Tojima wasn't going to be charged with anything serious, either. At the end of the day, he had only tried to help Yutaro Namiki; he hadn't procured the liquid nitrogen for Naoki Niikura. His use of the helium tank to create a false alibi remained problematic. Since, however, he had done so without knowing what had really happened, the police expected this issue to settle down with no legal sanctions.

Tojima would probably show up at some point, when word reached him that Namiki-ya had reopened. He'd probably carry on as if nothing had happened. Natsumi looked forward to seeing him being his old generous and openhearted self.

The whole thing had been a dreadful experience.

Following Naoki Niikura's confession, a series of astonishing revelations had come to light. Natsumi had no idea what had really happened and who was or wasn't telling the truth.

That was when Yutaro finally decided to tell his wife and daughter the truth. Although her mother seemed to have some knowledge of the plan, she hadn't been given the full picture.

Natsumi was astonished at the notion of using liquid nitrogen to terrify Hasunuma into telling the truth. She was even more astonished when Yutaro explained all the different tricks that he and his fellow conspirators had deployed. *Wow! All that was going on at the same time as the parade*, she thought.

That wasn't how things turned out. The case took off in a new and wholly unexpected direction, which started with the arrest of Rumi Niikura—a person everybody had assumed had nothing to do with the case. When the Niikuras' statements were made public, Natsumi was astonished. Naoki Niikura confessed to having killed Hasunuma intentionally, motivated by the blackmailing of his wife.

Natsumi found it hard to believe. Rumi Niikura had always struck her as a kind and friendly person. Could she really have killed Saori? Of course, had she not done so, she wouldn't have been vulnerable to blackmail.

Natsumi was mystified. Like her mother and father, her days were anxious and her nights sleepless. After a certain amount of time, Chief Inspector Kusanagi came to visit them.

"My being here today is a breach of the most basic police regulations. Nonetheless, I felt that forcing you to wait until the trial was over would be just too cruel."

Kusanagi stressed that they should not share what he was about to tell them with anybody else.

Although Kusanagi's tone was very matter-of-fact, Natsumi found everything he said astonishing. The fact that Saori intended to abandon her dream of becoming a professional singer was already a major surprise, but when she heard why—because Saori was pregnant with Tomoya Takagaki's child—Natsumi simply couldn't believe her ears. Her parents seemed to feel the same; they just kept repeating, "Is that true? Are you sure that's true?"

Kusanagi always gave the same reply. He didn't believe that Rumi Niikura was making things up.

Keeping his eyes fixed on his notebook and his voice heavy with suppressed emotion, he outlined what had happened in the park. When he got to the point where the enraged Rumi shoved Saori to the ground, he spoke a little faster as if he wanted to get it over with as quickly as possible.

After dealing with Hasunuma's blackmailing of Rumi, Kusanagi then switched over to Naoki Niikura's testimony. He read them the part in which Niikura made up his mind to kill Hasunuma, after Rumi had confessed what she had done to Saori.

"Everything from that point on, we uncovered in our original investigation." Kusanagi closed his notebook. "Do you have any questions?"

Natsumi couldn't think of any. She looked at her parents. The sheer volume of unexpected news seemed to have left them unable to think straight.

"There is one more thing that I should mention," Kusanagi went on, somewhat stiffly. "We got the results from an item of evidence, which we sent for analysis."

The item in question was the hair slide. Kusanagi explained what the implications would be if blood was—or wasn't—found on it.

"The bottom line is this," he went on. "There was no blood on the hair slide. DNA testing of trace amounts of sebaceous matter and skin on the slide has enabled us to confirm that it is definitely the hair slide that Saori was wearing."

"What does that mean? That Saori lost consciousness when she was pushed to the ground by Rumi Niikura, but that Hasunuma was the one who actually killed her?" Yutaro asked.

"We can't definitively reach that conclusion," Kusanagi said, weighing every word with care. "Nonetheless, I would certainly expect her lawyers to present it as a possibility in court."

Natsumi felt a sense of relief. She had no desire to see Rumi Niikura as an enemy.

"We've got to draw a line under this," Yutaro announced after Kusanagi had left. "We can't go on agonizing about this forever. We'll end up going crazy. We should let the police and the prosecutor do their jobs, while we concentrate on getting the restaurant up and running again. Are you both okay with that?"

Machiko nodded her head in silent agreement and Natsumi did the same. Her father was probably right.

I must do my best, she thought, as she remembered that day. She ran her hand down the freshly laundered *noren* curtain.

She had opened the door and was about to step back into the

restaurant, when, out of the corner of her eye, she noticed someone walking hurriedly toward her. She looked up and gave a start.

It was Tomoya Takagaki. How long was it since they had last met?

"Reopening on schedule, I'm glad to see," Tomoya said, his eye on the *noren* curtain.

Natsumi had sent him a text the day before to let him know that they were planning to open today. He had texted her back right away. *I'm pleased to hear it. Wishing you the best of luck.* Natsumi had detected a hint of something standoffish in his language.

"Tomoya . . . I thought we wouldn't be seeing you here again."

Tomoya's gaze shifted from the *noren* to Natsumi. "Why?"

"Coming here must awaken so many painful memories. . . ."

Tomoya gave a curt nod and his face darkened.

"You're right. It will take me years to forget. I'll always be mulling things over, you know: 'What if Saori were still alive today?' 'What would our baby be like?'"

Shocked, Natsumi looked up at him. "Who told you?"

"The police called me in the other day. They asked me if I knew Saori was pregnant. I was stunned. I had absolutely no idea."

"And how she died—did they tell you that?"

"The broad strokes." Tomoya looked at the ground. "It's all so staggering. Incredible, really."

"Yes . . . I know what you mean."

"They told you, too?"

"Yes, the head of the investigative team came here and talked us through everything."

"If I'm honest with you, Natsumi, I was of two minds about coming here today. But I had the feeling that if I didn't come today, tomorrow would only be that much harder. When I walk from my house to the station, my route always takes me past Namiki-ya. The idea of trying to live my life while deliberately avoiding this place is a recipe for heartache. I realized that the best thing for me to do is to keep coming here and to build myself a stock of nice, new memories."

Tomoya was clear-eyed and articulate. Natsumi could see why her sister had been attracted to him. Saori must have felt that life with him would be a positive and enjoyable experience, if not a glamorous one. She must have been thrilled when she found out that she was pregnant. It was the sheer joy of that moment that had exploded her dreams of becoming a singer.

Natsumi said nothing.

"Is something wrong?" Tomoya asked timidly.

She shook her head. "No," she replied. "It's good to see you. In you go."

She escorted Tomoya to a table. "We have our first customer," she called in the direction of the kitchen.

Yutaro's face popped up behind the counter. Catching sight of Tomoya, he flinched almost imperceptibly, then came out into the restaurant.

"It's been a long time," Tomoya said.

Yutaro removed his half apron. "We caused you a lot of trouble."

"No, I mean, trouble. That's hardly . . ." Tomoya waved his hand deprecatingly.

"No need to be coy. The police must have called you in quite a few times?"

"Um . . . well . . . yes, they did. Not that many times, really . . . I told them about transporting the liquid nitrogen."

Yutaro clicked his tongue disapprovingly. "Yes, I heard that silly bugger Shusaku got you to do that. Personally, I never wanted to involve you."

"Mr. Tojima was just thinking about how we all felt; how we all wanted revenge. I'd have been more upset if he hadn't approached me."

"The police told Tomoya everything," Natsumi chimed in, "including the fact that Saori was pregnant."

"Oh, really," Yutaro replied. His voice was low.

"Mr. Namiki, I owe you an apology," Tomoya said, rising to his feet and bowing deeply. "I was the one who suggested getting married to Saori. I was completely sincere, but what I said had a terrible impact on her life. I should have been more careful; she was at a crucial stage in her life."

He seemed to be apologizing for having got Saori pregnant.

"Look at me, Tomoya," Yutaro said gently. "We're grateful for you. It's true that had Saori not been pregnant, she probably wouldn't have chosen to abandon her singing career—and perhaps she would still be alive today. But that doesn't take into account her own feelings. She was thrilled to be pregnant with your child. She was thrilled at the prospect of becoming a mother. As a parent, the thought that she was able to enjoy feelings like that, even if it was only for a short time, is a comfort to me. Am I right?" Yutaro looked to Machiko for her support.

The rims of her eyes were red. She nodded emphatically.

"We bear you no ill will, Tomoya. None. If anything, it's ourselves we should be ashamed of. When Saori found out she was pregnant, she must have been happy and anxious in equal measure. But she never came to talk to me, or her mother. She probably didn't want to worry me. It breaks my heart; as a parent, I wasn't there for her."

Unsure how to respond, Tomoya just stood there in silence.

At that moment, there was a clattering sound as somebody pushed open the front door. Glancing at the entrance, Natsumi saw Yukawa poised on the threshold.

The professor was somewhat put-out when he found himself being stared at by the whole group. He caught Natsumi's eye. "It looks like you're busy."

"No, no." Natsumi waved her hand. "Come on in. Sit wherever you like."

"I'm not here for dinner today." Yukawa turned and faced Yutaro. "I've completed my work at the research center here, so I won't be able to come to Namiki-ya for a while. I'm here to say goodbye, for the time being at least."

"Really?" Natsumi exclaimed.

"I'm very sorry to hear that," Yutaro said wistfully. "I was hoping for a good, long chat with you. I have so many questions."

"You do? Well, let's do that when we get the chance."

Bobbing his head to them all, Yukawa left the restaurant.

"What a character!" Tomoya sat back down.

"You're telling me. And I never managed to figure out what his relationship with the police was," said Yutaro, before returning to the kitchen with Machiko.

Natsumi slid open the front door and went outside. She spotted Yukawa walking off down the street and launched herself after him. "Professor!" she yelled.

Yukawa stopped and turned around. He looked rather puzzled.

"Tell me," Natsumi said. "Who are you, really?"

"Who am I?" Yukawa knitted his brows. "I'm just a regular physicist."

"That's not true. You're a detective."

Yukawa recoiled. "What are you talking about?"

"You first came to our restaurant just after Hasunuma had been released. Now the case has been solved, you're leaving. It's a bit too much of a coincidence. We talked about you. We were saying that you must have helped the police solve this case. That you're a modern-day Hercule Poirot."

"Flattering, but you give me too much credit."

"Really?"

"The fact that I've completed my research and can leave Kikuno at this particular moment is purely a coincidence. That's not true for my reasons for coming to your restaurant in the first place."

"What do you mean?"

"I'm the same as Mr. Tojima."

"The same as Tojima? How?"

"I wanted to help a close friend of mine who'd had a difficult experience. I thought that I might get a hint or two by coming to Namiki-ya and getting to know the locals."

"This friend of yours . . . is he by any chance a policeman?"

Yukawa said nothing; he gave her a knowing smile and made as if to walk on.

"I'm sure you'll be back, Professor."

Yukawa looked thoughtful.

"When I do, make sure that your fabulous *takiawase*'s on the menu," he said.

Natsumi nodded vigorously. "That's a promise."

The physicist grinned at her, adjusted his spectacles with the tip of his index finger, then turned on his heel and strode off with a spring in his step.

THOMAS CROMWELL
and the English Reformation

THOMAS CROMWELL
and
the English Reformation

A G DICKENS

*Professor of History in
the University of London*

THE ENGLISH UNIVERSITIES PRESS LTD

ISBN O 340 O9422 2

First published 1959
Fifth impression 1972

The English Universities Press Ltd
St Paul's House, Warwick Lane, London EC4P 4AH

Printed in Great Britain by
Biddles Ltd, Guildford, Surrey

Introduction to the Series

This series has been undertaken in the conviction that no subject is more important than history. For though the conquests of natural science (nuclear fission, the exploration of space, genetic advance, bacteriology, etc.) have given their character to the age, it is actually a greater need to gain control of the forces of nature loosed upon us. The prime urgency, the deepest necessity is in the human field: to understand the nature and condition of man as a pre-condition of better controls, and fewer disasters, in the world of politics and society.

There is no better introduction to this sphere, and the understanding of its problems, than history. *Some* knowledge of history, we feel, ought to prevent some mistakes: at every point we can learn vicariously from the experience of others before us.

To take one point only—the understanding of politics: how can we understand the world of affairs around us, if we do not know how it came to be what it is? How to interpret the United States, or Soviet Russia, France, Germany or Britain without some knowledge of their history?

Some evidence of the growing awareness of this may be seen in the great increase of interest in history among the general public, and in the much larger place the subject has come to take in education.

The most congenial, as well as the most concrete and practical, approach to history is the biographical: through the lives of great men whose careers have been significant in history. Fashions in historical writing have their ups and downs; men's and women's lives have their perennial interest—though in this series we are chiefly concerned to show their historical significance, the contribution they made to their age: *Men and their Times.*

A generation ago historical biographies were rather unfashionable with analytical historians and technicians, like Namier: he ended by writing scores of miniature biographies of M.P.s. The detailed analysis of Civil War and Commonwealth has ended by showing that there were almost as many party-divisions as there were individuals. We are back in the realm of biography and the biographical approach to history, since there is no greater diversity, variety and subtlety than in the lives of individual men and women, particularly those who left a mark on their time.

A. L. Rowse
Oxford

Contents

Acknowledgements

I GRATEFULLY acknowledge advice on many important points from the general editor, Dr. A. L. Rowse. Dr. G. R. Elton and Mr. G. W. O. Woodward both gave much unselfish assistance with a variety of knotty problems, while Professor G. R. Potter at a crucial stage provided a rousing private tutorial on the Reformation. Few scholars can claim intimate knowledge of more than a few aspects of this immense subject, and my numerous debts to other writers are ill-expressed by the brief bibliography. Many years ago, I felt the need for a succinct provisional reassessment of Thomas Cromwell, yet I am glad I did not attempt one until after the appearance of Dr. Elton's stimulating researches. Again, in framing Chapter VII, I made very extensive use of Dr. J. F. Mozley's *Coverdale and his Bibles*, and while operating in the field of political ideas, certain chapters of Dr. W. G. Zeeveld's *Foundations of Tudor Policy* were seldom far from my thoughts. Though my conclusions often differ radically from those of R. B. Merriman, I could not avoid incurring a deep obligation to his labours, especially in matters concerning Cromwell's early life and foreign policy.

This reprint of 1967 has been purged of the several misprints which, through a misunderstanding, survived in the original edition.

King's College, London
    September 1967.

Chapter One

Early Life

BETWEEN the fall of Wolsey and the hapless last years of Henry VIII, there came to power an administrator of tremendous energy, an institutional thinker, a patron of political philosophers, a bold and original statesman who thought of his own work as creative and who cast his shadow centuries forward upon the history of England. No major figure of that history has suffered from so many misconceptions and calumnies as Thomas Cromwell. Some aspects of the tenacious black legend were invited by his real shortcomings; more still arose from the uncritical acceptance of information supplied by his bitterest enemies; yet most derived from those Victorian ecclesiastical animosities, liberal anachronisms and genteel prejudices which even now encumber our thinking and influence our choices within the Tudor world. Of Cromwell's first thirty-five years we know relatively little, yet that little possesses great significance, for it prepares us to witness the advent of a new man to the controls of the State, a man largely emancipated from those ecclesiastical and neo-feudal values which still held the custom-ridden bulk of English society in their grasp.

Thomas Cromwell was born about the year of Bosworth: though not quite a Londoner by birth, he must have been familiar from early years with the many-spired but malodorous city in and around which his years of greatness were to be passed. By a fortunate survival, the court-rolls of the manor of Wimbledon have preserved several facts concerning his family background. His father Walter pursued various business concerns at Putney; brewer, blacksmith and fuller, he also contrived to lead a life of somewhat more than average turbulence. Though apparently related to the rich Nottinghamshire magnate Ralph Lord Cromwell, he inherited few graces. In 1477 he paid a fine for assaulting and drawing blood; he was frequently amerced for drunkenness, for overburdening the common with his cattle, for cutting more than his share of the furze and thorns, and—a normal professional hazard—for selling ale without inspection by the ale-taster. In 1480 he held two virgates of land in Putney and in 1500 received six more by grant from Archbishop Morton. He became a constable of Putney in 1495 and served frequently as a juror. He last appears in 1514, when he had encountered serious trouble, the lord of the manor having evicted him from his copyholds, because he had 'falsely and fraudulently erased the evidences and terrures of the lord to the perturbation and disturbance of the lord and his tenants'. The elder of Walter's two recorded daughters married a substantial Welshman and became mother of Richard Williams, who was knighted, took the name of Cromwell, and is remembered as great-grandfather of Protector Oliver. The younger daughter married a sheepfarmer euphoniously named Wellyfed; their son was ultimately brought up with his cousin Gregory, son of Thomas Cromwell.

As for Thomas himself, he left home under less happy auspices than his sisters. Unlike his friend Latimer, who was born in no higher degree, he never looked back with pride upon his early life or went to the trouble of recording its details. We are thus dependent upon a number of unverifiable or unsatisfactory anecdotes in Foxe's *Acts and Monuments*, upon a short story based on Cromwell's life by the Italian novelist Bandello, and upon some brief reports from his bitter enemies Cardinal Pole and the Imperial ambassador Chapuys. Foxe asserts that Cromwell told Archbishop Cranmer 'what a ruffian he was in his younger days', a remark probably not intended in the self-condemnatory sense assumed by humourless modern critics. He was certainly brought up in a rough school. Pole relates that he became a roving soldier in Italy, and Bandello that he served with the French army at the Battle of the Garigliano in December 1503. Arriving penniless in Florence and sensing a lack of future in the military life, he entered the service of the rich banker Frescobaldo and also worked as an accountant for a Venetian firm. After two years or more of business-life in northern Italy, it may have been at Pisa that he met some English merchants, who persuaded him to join them in the Netherlands. Here, writes Pole, he spent several years as a business consultant, making local reports to the London merchants on the state of trade throughout the Netherlands.

Foxe's story concerning Cromwell's second visit to Italy was derived from the martyrologist's native town of Boston, and despite its novelish detail, it may form one of the more authentic elements in the early biography. The townsmen of Boston sent to Rome a certain Geoffrey Chambers—he figures in later life as one of Cromwell's agents—in order to obtain the renewal of certain pardons. Chambers doubted his own capabilities and, passing through Antwerp, persuaded Cromwell to accompany him to Rome. Desirous of saving time and money, and knowing how Pope Julius liked strange delicacies, Cromwell prepared certain dishes of jelly in the English fashion, hitherto unknown in Rome. Choosing a moment when the pontiff had just returned from hunting, Cromwell brought in the dishes 'with a three man's song, as we call it in the English tongue'. The Pope, marvelling at the strangeness of the music, called them into his presence. With a caution appropriate to the place and period, he commanded a cardinal to try the jelly, then partook himself and ended by sealing the Boston pardons on the spot. Here at least is one of the anecdotes which one most desires to believe, for it seems so completely in character: it displays the Cromwellian directness, the timing, the economy of means and the touch of sardonic humour. This journey is assigned to the year 1510 and Cromwell must soon have returned to the Netherlands trade, since the letter of an English mercer written many years afterwards recalls a favour Cromwell had done in connection with the cloth mart at Middleburgh in 1512. The state-papers also contain suggestions that he was living both in the Netherlands and in England during this same year, which is taken to be the date of his marriage and resettlement in England.

Though we enjoy few reliable glimpses of his *Wanderjahre*, Cromwell's mature character and public policies both testify abundantly to the educational effects of this period. An Englishman could never entirely return to his native simplicities after having spent two years or more in Italy at the time when Cesare Borgia was exhibiting *virtù*, when Machiavelli was learning the ruses of diplomacy, when Raphael was painting, and when, at the court of Urbino, those famed evening conversations were furnishing material for the *Book of the Courtier*. High Renaissance Italy still maintained her poise; she was not yet resigned to expiating her individualism under the whips of foreign oppressors and clad in the penitential garb of the Counter Reformation. Here the facts still tended to outrun the imaginations of modern poets and novelists; here Browning's insidious Duke had his innumerable counterparts in real life. Italian society had devoted itself to aesthetic rather than to moral ideals; it could boast man's highest artistic and intellectual achievements since the decline of Greece, and yet inevitably it had left educated men to spend too much of their lives on the dark side of the moon. It was a society compounded of high aspirations and sordid realities, both of them alternating rapidly in the life of the individual. Too often the afternoon's elegiacs were succeeded by the dagger-thrust in the dark *piazza*. Climate and temperament, the proximity of the cultured infidel, the involved state-system, the corroding temptations of the papal court, the rediscovery of the antique, the enervating breath of ancient grandeurs and corruptions : all these had long made Italy a unique world, one in which many a dazzled barbarian had reeled with horror and delight on descending the mountain barriers from the north.

Its emancipatory effect upon the Italianate Englishman was already greeted with distrust by conservative English society. Just as today a year in America often liberates an Englishman from the more cloying reverences of European Social Democracy, so a period in Renaissance Italy then liberated his predecessor from both the superstitions and the pieties of a priest-dominated and scholastic-minded society north of the Alps. It did not necessarily produce an immoralism, still less an agnosticism, but rather a certain radical detachment, a trick of thinking in terms of efficiency and effectiveness, an ability to abstract problems (whether of physical science or of the State) from their hitherto accepted theological or teleological context, and to submit them to a cold and factual analysis. It helped a man to see through himself and not to rationalize his own misdeeds with that pathetic pseudo-religious cant and self-deception which marked barbarian rulers and politicians. It helped him to avoid acting in hot blood, to dissimulate his passions, to reject unduly rigid systems of ideas, to realize the truth of Guicciardini's words: 'it is a great mistake to talk of things of the world absolutely, without discriminating, and as it were by rule. For in nearly everything there are distinctions and exceptions, due to variety of circumstances. These circumstances you cannot treat by one and the same standard. They are not to be found in books. You must learn them from your own discretion.'

Above all, Italy helped a man to see his northern world with new eyes and, if he aspired to govern its affairs, to propound fresh answers free of hidebound tradition. We shall in due course review the controversy as to whether Cromwell actually took Machiavelli's *Prince* as his textbook, yet the question can claim little more than antiquarian interest. A man who had travelled extensively and worked in Machiavelli's Italy had little to learn from his book, which was scarcely more Machiavellian than the common political practice and conversation of the day. If we saw a business man with years of experience in America introducing American notions into a European firm, we should not attribute his action to some fashionable textbook from the Harvard School of Business Administration.

The spectacle of the young Cromwell working in the Netherlands has an interest equal to that of his Italian experiences. No training-ground could have been more profitable for a future English statesman than the marts and bourse of Antwerp, the greatest commercial capital the world had hitherto seen. It was a uniquely cosmopolitan city, containing large and permanent colonies of businessmen from all the trading nations of Europe. It was the funnel through which English wool and cloth passed to half the Continent, and through which the Portuguese, with their monopoly of the oriental spice-trade, distributed their vital commodity to the unrefrigerated storehouses and larders of the western world. It was soon to become by far the chief money-market of Europe. As an eminent Manchester scholar has written: 'Antwerp was not only the London but the Manchester of the sixteenth century.'

At this time the Merchant Adventurers, backed by the government, were still waging an economic struggle of the first importance to this country: the struggle to convert the export of wool and unfinished cloth into that of the finished article, hence to derive the maximum profit from our resources, while yet creating employment in England. His participation in these affairs brought Cromwell to the heart of our economic problems, which, as the Netherlands fell under unsympathetic Spanish rule and England nevertheless became dependent on the Antwerp money-market, were destined to increase in complexity. When he came to high office, Cromwell naturally showed a most expert grasp of these all-important relationships, and the one other Tudor statesman who can compare with him in this field had likewise received his training in Antwerp. Beside Cromwell and

Sir Thomas Gresham, the products of English country-house and academic life cut many an amateurish caper when they tried to organize the nation's trade and finance.

About 1512 Cromwell made an advantageous match with Elizabeth Wykys, a woman of more refined background than his own. She came of an old family of gentry and, though her father was in the wool trade, her uncle had been gentleman-usher to Henry VII. Romantic marriages were almost unknown in the circles to which she and Cromwell belonged, and Elizabeth seems to have brought him some useful money. Chapuys disparages Cromwell's wife as the daughter of a shearman, but adds the more significant fact that for some time after his marriage Cromwell kept servants in his house to continue the business of his father-in-law. The point finds corroboration in Cromwell's own correspondence, which shows that in 1524, years after he had turned to a legal and official career, he was still trading in cloth and wool. Of his family life we know little, but none of his enemies ever hinted that his morality in this sphere was other than exemplary, either before or after the early death of his wife. His heir, the dull and modest Gregory, was born in 1513, and there followed two daughters, Anne and Grace. In 1525 appears his only surviving letter to his wife, written during a visit to Kent. It is the letter from any Tudor businessman or landowner to his spouse: amiable, partnerly, but with its eye firmly on business matters. 'To my well beloved wife Elizabeth Cromwell against the Friars Augustines in London be this given. Elizabeth, I commend me unto you and have sent by this bearer a fat doe, the one half whereof, I pray you, may be delivered unto my gossip mistress Smyth, and with the rest to use at your pleasure. And further if Richard Swifte be come home or fortune to come shortly, I will that he resort to me at Begham or Tonbridge with all diligence. Such news as you have in those parts I pray you send me part by this bearer. At Begham the 29th day of November. And farther, I pray you send me word in writing who hath resorted unto you since my departure from you, to speak with me. Per your husband, Thomas Cromwell.' Within three years or so Elizabeth had died; perhaps she succumbed to the sweating sickness which ravaged the country in the years 1527–8. At all events, in the will Cromwell wrote in July 1529 she is 'my late wife'. At this time his mother-in-law Mercy Priour was apparently keeping house for him, since it is for her that he then makes elaborate and affectionate provision, including the bequest of much household stuff.

Meantime Cromwell's life had been gradually moving into new paths, though a curious lack of trustworthy records between 1512 and 1520 leaves some important biographical problems unsolved. During these years there occurred in London a violent crisis between clergy and laity, and thence between Church and State. The case of Richard Hunne and its aftermath form in retrospect an important prelude to the crisis of the Reformation Parliament, and it would not be unduly bold to hazard a guess regarding Cromwell's personal sympathies. Hunne was a substantial merchant tailor, but refused on principle to surrender the bearing-cloth which his parish priest claimed, by way of the usual mortuary dues, on the death of Hunne's baby. The priest prosecuted him in the Bishop's consistory court and won, whereupon Hunne foolishly and unsuccessfully brought him into the King's Bench to answer a *praemunire* charge. The churchmen responded by arresting Hunne for heresy and a search of his house yielded some heretical books, including a Wycliffite bible. After examination by Bishop Fitzjames, an unpopular prelate regarded by Erasmus as the worst type of reactionary, Hunne was returned to the Lollards' Tower at St. Paul's.

This took place on Saturday, 2 December 1514, and on the following Monday morning he was found with his neck broken. After an investigation of the cell, the body and various witnesses, a jury found a verdict of wilful murder against the Bishop's Chancellor Dr. Horsey and two of his henchmen. Readers interested to unravel the complex detective-aspects of this crime should begin with Mr. Ogle's book *The Tragedy of the Lollards' Tower*, since Gairdner and other earlier historians strain every probability and wilfully neglect much evidence in order to exculpate Horsey. In fact, as Mr. Ogle has conclusively shown, his guilt may be regarded as all but certain. Bishop Fitzjames did not, however, show any lack of confidence; he pronounced Hunne a heretic, handed over his body to be burned at Smithfield and thereby reduced his wife and children to pauperism. All London was aflame, and when Parliament met in January 1515 it sought to renew an Act of 1513, which stripped benefit of clergy from the troublesome host of clerics in minor orders. There followed a series of disputes between the bishops on the one hand and the King's Franciscan chaplain Dr. Standish, supported by the judges, on the other. The bishops made no secret of their desire to charge Standish with heresy and he ostentatiously appealed for the protection of the King, who, young, inexperienced and orthodox, acted as peacemaker between the angry contestants. Wolsey, too, had ample reason to support him, for Wolsey stood on both sides. At this time Henry had no motives for staging an attack on the privileges and jurisdiction of the Church, but the affair gave him ample information for later use; from this point he knew all too well the weight of lay support he would receive in the event of a clash between Church and State.

During the disputations, Henry had declared that 'Kings of England have never had any superior but God alone', yet such phraseology had been used by his predecessors even in the fourteenth century, and he cannot thereby be credited with any revolutionary plans. Six years later he published his book exalting the primacy of the see of Rome; it also contained a moving passage on the indissolubility of Christian marriage! The prophetic character of the Hunne crisis can indeed be exaggerated. Despite the unique position and growing unpopularity of Wolsey, the period between these disputes and the meeting of the Reformation Parliament in 1529 did not seem to contemporaries one of impending cataclysm for the English Church. Its majestic institutional structure stood inviolate. Buttressed by a formidable range of institutions and laws, it supervised society concurrently with the State. Alongside Parliament, the clergy met in Convocation to debate canons and to vote clerical taxation to the King. The innumerable Church courts, archiepiscopal, episcopal, archidiaconal and peculiar, regulated not merely ecclesiastical administration and clerical conduct, but also the morals of laymen, even to the point of controlling the testamentary disposition of their personal property. Especially were these courts concerned with matrimonial causes and sexual misdemeanours, the staple fare of so many of their act books which have come down to us from the sixteenth century. And while their punishments were milder than those of the lay courts, their procedure was slow and vexatious in the extreme. The canon law they administered was based largely upon papal decrees and the canons of international Councils of the Church. National custom had also its place; our law of tithe, for example, had extensive peculiarities, while the testamentary jurisdiction of the English Church was unique in scope. Yet such details did not fundamentally alter the international character of this code, the living symbol of a great *enclave* in the sovereignty of the English State.

During the Hunne case and its sequels, those old enemies of clerical power, the common lawyers, had figured prominently, and it was into this profession that Thomas Cromwell moved some time during the years in which little is known of him. We know nothing of his legal studies and early practice, but by 1520 he must already have acquired a reputation in London, since in that year he reported to Wolsey as Papal Legate on a suit involving an appeal to Rome. Three years later he drafted a petition to Wolsey as Chancellor for the grammarian John Palsgrave. Other letters of 1520–24 show him at work as a solicitor and, on one occasion, as a trusted arbitrator in a dispute between an alderman of Calais and Lord Mountjoy. In the latter year he became a member of Gray's Inn; he was now mixing with many influential men, and trading activities were taking a less important place in his life. Which of these friends secured him a seat in the Parliament of 1523 we do not know. During this session he framed, and very possibly delivered, a long and able speech which survives in the handwriting of one of his clerks. It suggests that he had not yet entered into Wolsey's service, since his main aim is to protest against the French campaign and the large subsidies which at this moment Wolsey was demanding from the Commons. Cromwell professes himself distressed at the thought that the King may campaign in person, for if the King be lost, the country will face the horrors of civil war. Before entering a Continental war of aggression, let England first ensure her own safety, especially on the side of Scotland. The renewal of an out-of-date strategy may exhaust all the coin of the realm to the point where a leather coinage may become necessary. Let us employ Fabian tactics with the French; let us strike at them by unifying England and Scotland, a feat within our powers and one which will bring the King more glory than any of his predecessors have attained.

Cromwell's detractors have regarded this speech as the adroit attempt of a climber to rise by flattering the King. On the contrary, this is an opposition-speech, which could scarcely commend Cromwell as a willing instrument of the Crown; moreover, it is a transparently sincere criticism of the effete, backward-looking aspects of early Henrician foreign policy and closely foreshadows Cromwell's actual policy when he came to power. Here in fact is revealed an independent, businesslike, modern mind, and if, as seems unlikely, it helped to promote Cromwell, this promotion would have been by the path of honour. And awkwardly for the critics, it was in Wolsey's service, not in that of the King, that Cromwell came to spend the succeeding years.

An even more absurd misrepresentation has clung to the other document proving Cromwell's participation in this Parliament. In a private letter to his friend John Creke, Cromwell says: 'I amongst others have endured a Parliament which continued by the space of seventeen whole weeks, where we communed of war, peace, strife, contention, debate, murmur, grudge, riches, poverty, penury, truth, falsehood, justice, equity, deceit, oppression, magnanimity, activity, force, "attempraunce", treason, murder, felony, conciliation, and also how a commonwealth might be edified and also continued within our realm. Howbeit in conclusion we have done as our predecessors have been wont to do, that is to say, as well as we might, and left where we began.' The solemn scholars who have elevated this Rabelaisian catalogue into a proof of Cromwell's disbelief in parliamentary government —a notion to which his whole official career effectively gives the lie—may safely be left to the judgement of posterity. Can any member of Parliament have felt otherwise at the close of a long session? Whatever the owls of Minerva may suppose, English humour did not altogether perish between Chaucer and Shakespeare; in Cromwell it was reinforced by an admirably sardonic insight, perhaps sharpened by a touch of Italianate sophistication. And readers familiar with Tudor political treatises will at once recognize the sententious pomposity which Cromwell satirizes. He was in all respects a man of the world.

If Cromwell in fact delivered his critical speech, it did not noticeably check the development of his legal and business activities as an agent of the Cardinal. In 1524–5 petitioners for the latter's favour are seen addressing their initial pleas to the 'right worshipful Mr. Cromwell', who is now also spoken of as 'counsellor to my Lord Legate'. In becoming a member of Wolsey's household, Cromwell entered a milieu of the utmost importance to his future career. It was the nursery of the court, the training ground of future administrators and ambassadors; though inevitably it contained many clergymen, its emphasis lay on service to the State rather than to the Church. 'August and happy

20

house', cried Erasmus, 'O truly splendid Cardinal, who has such men in his councils, and whose table is ringed by such luminaries'. As the later correspondence indicates, this household gave Cromwell a unique introduction to the men destined to prominence during the next decade. He who best knew the Cardinal's circle during the twenties was best placed to dominate English public life in the thirties. But the service proved educative in more senses than one. Wolsey's arrogance and wealth, his financial demands, his enormous combination of powers as Chancellor and Legate, his invasion of all men's jurisdictions, these and many other aspects of his career had vastly augmented the trend of the age towards anticlericalism. Wolsey made even clergymen anticlerical. Though the sequel was to show Cromwell's personal loyalty to his master, he obviously did not escape the prevailing mood. A self-made layman who had risen by the hard road, he was now in daily contact and rivalry with the most ambitious and pampered clerics of the day. Inevitably he developed a resentment towards their pretensions and their easy success; doubtless too a businessman's desire to rationalize the hoary anomalies, inefficiencies and inequities of ecclesiastical life. Just as great anticlericals like Lorenzo Valla had flourished in the heart of the papal curia, so there sat at Wolsey's table a man destined in a few years to smash the system which Wolsey had striven to revitalize through his own wonderful career.

Chapter Two

The Way to Power

WHILE Cromwell was serving Wolsey, the English Church lay under attack by forces quite distinct from those we have grouped under the label of anticlericalism. If on a certain day in 1527 Cromwell had walked a few steps from his house and entered a chamber in the Austin Friars, he could have witnessed an historic spectacle: two Essex Lollards visiting Friar Robert Barnes and coming away with a printed copy of Tyndale's forbidden New Testament in English. Going up to the friar's room, the Essex men found several people there, including a merchant reading a book. They related to Barnes how they had begun to convert the curate of their village, Steeple Bumpstead, to the Wycliffite heresy, and they went on to show him a copy of certain books of their old manuscript Lollard Bible. Barnes began to tease them concerning these antiquated exhibits and, after some adroit sales-talk, ended by selling them a copy of Tyndale's new version for 3s. 2d., 'and desired them that they would keep it close'. This scene forms one of several known and fascinating contacts between the old English and the new German heresies. Robert Barnes was a D.D. of Cambridge, who in earlier years had presided at some of the famous discussions in the 'White Horse'. About the year 1518 at this Cambridge tavern—later known as 'Little Germany'—English Lutheranism had begun a mild and academic infancy. By the time when the Essex Lollards called, the bumptious and indiscreet Barnes must already have been known to his neighbour Cromwell, since in the previous year he had been examined by Wolsey and forced to abjure heretical beliefs. In 1528 he was to escape to Antwerp and spend a long period at Luther's feet in Wittenberg. Three years later began his recorded connections with Cromwell, for it was the latter who recalled him and subsequently used him as envoy to the Lutheran princes of Germany. Their lives were henceforth closely connected to the end.

Also during the year 1527 Thomas Garret, the friend and ultimate fellow-martyr of Barnes, underwent perilous adventures in creating the first Lutheran cell at Oxford. He even had the temerity to operate in Wolsey's own new college, then being perfected by Cromwell. Before the end of the year the Bishop of Lincoln's commissary forcibly broke up this Oxford circle. Yet neither Barnes nor Garret was the great man of early English Lutheranism. William Tyndale, whose translation of the New Testament they were both engaged in selling, had left the country for Wittenberg as early as 1524 and, financed in all likelihood by a group of London cloth-merchants, was shipping his first edition into England two years later. It was the work of a harsh and angular Protestant, who used loaded terminology and linked the sacred text with a series of violently controversial prologues and marginal notes. It also happened to be a work of genius, the ancestor and basis of all the early versions in English. So translated, the New Testament needed no partisan embellishments to become an explosive force. Everywhere in England people seem to have been curious about it, and at whatever point one examines the social history of the early Reformation in England, the Tyndale version makes its presence felt. For many a reader it meant a fresh awakening, a new, personal and direct approach to truths long staled by too circuitous a presentation. There can be little doubt that it also meant something to Cromwell, for, as we shall later observe, he was already in 1527 discussing the scriptures with another Augustinian friar, who had already attained some notoriety for defending Barnes. This was Miles Coverdale, a name destined to take second place only to that of Tyndale in the annals of the English Bible.

Having turned aside to glance at Cromwell's neighbour Barnes, we must not allow the Essex Lollards to smuggle out their copy of Tyndale and vanish without further notice into the busy streets of London. Recent research into diocesan archives indicates with increasing clarity what a more careful study of Foxe would earlier have revealed: that Lollardy, so far from being, as Gairdner supposed, a spent force on the eve of the Reformation, survived in some strength to prepare the ground for Protestantism. The beliefs deriving from Wyclif were more radically Protestant than those of Luther himself; they seem the forerunners if not the parents of English Nonconformity. They exalted the Bible as the sole criterion of faith; they attacked the Pope, the episcopal hierarchy, the worship of saints, the doctrine of purgatory and, above all, belief in transubstantiation. If historians still venture to notice conscious motivations in history, they must surely agree that the Reformation centred around the sacrament of the altar, around the validity of belief in the corporal presence of Christ's body in the bread and wine of the eucharist. Constituted an article of faith at the Lateran Council of 1215, transubstantiation had been further elaborated in consonance with the fashionable Aristotelianism of that day, whereby the 'accidents' or outward appearance of the elements remained unchanged, while their 'substance' was transformed. Late Lollardy, going farther than either Wyclif or Luther, denied the real presence in its entirety. Here was the heresy of heresies, for which men continued to be consigned to the flames until the end of the reign of Henry VIII, then once again under Mary Tudor.

Lollardy had undergone several regional persecutions in the early decades of the century. In the diocese of London, mainly in Essex, Bishop Fitzjames prosecuted about 50 Lollards in 1510 and about as many in 1518. Between 1527 and 1532 his successors Tunstall and Stokesley caused well over 200 heretics, mainly Lollards, to abjure. In the Chilterns, especially around Amersham, sizeable attacks were made by the Bishops of Lincoln in 1506–7 and in 1521. Another centre lay in south-west Kent, where Archbishop Warham became very active in 1511; the Chiltern and Kentish groups were connected by a scattering of Lollards up the Thames valley to Newbury, where six or seven score abjurations took place in the early years of the century. During each of these intermittent drives a few Lollards suffered burning, but in general the movement survived by secretiveness and flexibility rather than by heroism. Its importance lay, not merely in these organized communities, but in its ability to permeate even the remoter parts of England wth diffused beliefs of anti-hierarchical and anti-sacramental character. In the incomplete records of the York diocesan courts, the present writer recently found and examined 33 heresy-cases between 1528 and 1543, besides another 45 in the reign of Mary. At both periods the great majority—those on the proletarian level—remained purely Lollard in character, similar, in fact, to scores of pre-

Lutheran cases. It would seem that by the early thirties the influence of Lutheranism in the provinces was still virtually limited to a minority of educated and half-educated persons, and that in the broad psychological preparation of the English people we must now accord a far from minor role to the operations of the old English heresy. This fact in no way implies that people like Cromwell ever entertained warm sympathies with Lollard radicalism. So far as respectable people were concerned, Lollards remained rank outsiders, and before long every moderate Reformer found himself compelled to ward off any suspicion of sympathy with sacramentarian extremism, whether it derived from Lollardy or from Anabaptism, which latter began during the thirties to percolate from the Netherlands into London and the southeastern counties.

While in the service of the Cardinal, Cromwell occasionally rubbed shoulders with men like Coverdale, yet he can have had little time for doctrinal study or speculation, since he soon became one of the busiest administrators in England. From 1525 until the cataclysm of 1529, Wolsey chiefly employed Cromwell on the project nearest his heart: the suppression of some twenty-nine minor monasteries in order to erect two great colleges at Oxford and Ipswich. In surveying the monastic properties, making inventories of goods, transferring lands, meeting the claims of tenants, drawing up foundation-deeds, building and furnishing the new colleges, Cromwell executed with brilliance a task of enormous legal ramifications and administrative complexity. No lease was too petty for close inspection; no consignment of furniture too trivial for personal supervision. That Wolsey's transfer was an act of genuine enlightenment will be denied by few observers. It involved no doctrinal principles and it received active support from Stephen Gardiner and other ecclesiastics noted in later years for their conservative opinions. It was by no means the first transaction of its kind, for many years earlier Bishops Alcock and Fisher had suppressed religious houses in order to found Cambridge colleges. It subtracted extremely little from the wealth of the religious orders: while it may have contributed to Wolsey's unpopularity, he had already become so widely unpopular in both clerical and lay circles that its political importance deserves little emphasis.

Along with the lesser agents of the Cardinal, Cromwell accepted from interested parties numerous gifts, which would be regarded as gross bribes in the case of a modern administrator, but which then, and for long afterwards, formed the normal perquisites of unpaid or underpaid officials. These early gifts were matters of common knowledge, and Wolsey himself must certainly have permitted them; with reason, since as a layman Cromwell could not be rewarded by the shower of lucrative benefices which fell upon less important officials in Holy Orders. Even when he came to enjoy offices under the Crown, Cromwell disdained no present, large or small; he maintained no secrecy and little subtlety in these matters; he continued to behave as the enterprising businessman, intent to ensure that the acceptance of expensive public office did not restrain the mounting profits which had rewarded his earlier career. One who has followed modern research through the mercenary intrigues of the Tudor political scene will end, not by condemning Cromwell as corrupt, but rather by placing amongst the saintly eccentrics of their age those few sensitive consciences he may encounter. It is the misfortune of many Tudor statesmen to be judged by the exceptional criterion of Sir Thomas More. From the viewpoint of his employers, Cromwell gave far more than current value in return for his extensive pickings. At no stage of this or any later negotiation did he spare himself long hours, hard thinking, wearisome journeys, application to dull detail and a life of complete dedication to the task in hand. His was the administrative genius built on a capacity for taking infinite pains, and on this scale such genius proved a great rarity amongst Tudor Englishmen.

From this time onwards, Cromwell succeeded in making himself the chief lay expert upon the English monasteries, and an extensive book on their last stages could be compiled solely from his correspondence. The scene which presented itself to him in the years following 1525 contained some strange anomalies and problems. Its extant records are remarkably voluminous, while the size and romantic appeal of monastic ruins have also helped to inflate the theme to such proportions that many observers have been unable to view Thomas Cromwell in any other context. Yet the splendours of Fountains and Rievaulx form dangerous guides to the realities destroyed by Cromwell, for the architecture was out of all proportion to the religious lives which it housed. After their early triumphs, the English had not shown themselves conspicuously gifted in this vocation, and by the reign of Henry VIII the number of English religious had become pitifully small, both absolutely and by comparison with those on the Continent. Dr. Gasquet computes at the dissolution 4,721 monks and regular canons, 1,800 friars and only 1,560 nuns. The 357 lesser monasteries attacked in 1536 averaged scarcely four religious persons each, a figure which explains at least one important aspect of the disciplinary and educational problem. At the opposite extreme, the bigger establishments tended to be hampered by debt and overheads, especially by the upkeep of their grandiose buildings. Some maintained swollen domestic staffs. Butley Priory in Suffolk had only twelve canons, but it also kept two chaplains, eleven personal servants, a barber, a schoolmaster, seven schoolchildren, three cooks, a slaughterman, a sacristan, a cooper, three bakers and brewers, two horsekeepers, two maltsters, a porter, a gardener, six laundresses and two bedemen; all these quite part from an understeward, a surveyor and 36 workers on the Butley estate.

The disciplinary state of the religious houses holds few mysteries, since considerable reliance may be placed upon innumerable visitation reports compiled by the bishops. Even so, these documents demand cautious treatment; they give little prominence to the many virtuous denizens who were dutifully maintaining their vows; they concentrate on faults; they are confidential reports based on the obligation of each member to divulge all misdemeanours in private interview with the bishop. No other social group has had to confront so fierce a scrutiny. Moreover, as we peruse the records of a house across thirty years, we gain a foreshortened view of its defects; during such a period a few offences and feuds, even serious ones, do not make it a sink of iniquity. Even, however, when due allowance has been made for all these factors, the episcopal visitations reveal many inadequacies which would not for a moment be tolerated in any modern religious order. We should do wrong to concentrate upon the sensational establishments like Dorchester, with its ceaseless quarrels, its openness to the public and its alleged sexual offences; or like Littlemore, where the prioress lived with a former chaplain, endowed her illegitimate daughter with the convent goods and put her nuns in the stocks; or like Walsingham, where the prior was charged with an amazing range of offences, had his faction amongst the deep-drinking canons, and committed management to the lay seneschal's wife, a crony of the heartier canons and reputedly the prior's mistress. In the average place, the occasional misfit may indeed crop up over the years: the canon who wanders off in criminal company, the nun who has a baby. Considering the folly with which most orders accepted immature professions and then attempted at all costs to retain the maladjusted, the wonder is that such cases did not prove far more numerous.

The really characteristic faults of monks and nuns were more venial in character: irregular attendance at the divine offices, addiction to private property and lay dress, uncharity towards their fellows, and disharmony between the heads of houses and their rank-and-file. Much trouble arose from excessive familiarity with the surrounding lay world. For this fault the hypocritical laity deserved a large share of the blame, since their exploitation of monastic amenities, offices and properties had reached intolerable proportions. During the years 1534–6 the correspondence of Thomas Cromwell contains, amongst a mountain of similar material, many letters from the factions in and around Whitby Abbey. At this picturesque but disorderly institution, Abbot Hexham took his cut in the proceeds of piracy, while his servants waged ruffianly battles with the fishermen in the town below. More serious complications arose from the factions of the local gentry, who tried to operate both through Cromwell and by means of local violence. The young puritan magnate Sir Francis Bigod backed the bailiff James Conyers, while the rival family of Eure supported his enemy and kinsman Gregory Conyers. The first of these factions was leagued with a reforming group of monks, who almost succeeded in unseating Hexham; yet at the same time Bigod, desperately in need of ready cash despite his large estates, borrowed money, not only from Cromwell and the London financiers, but also from his adversary Hexham. This story of chicanery and violence, with the scores finally paid off in the Pilgrimage of Grace, might be warmly commended to any historical novelist.

Some of the less dramatic stories are equally illuminating. The chronicle of Butley Priory provides typical examples of lay interference with a well-conducted house. Here the King's gay sister Mary, dowager-Queen of France and Duchess of Suffolk, spent three summer vacations with her train of ladies and gentlemen. Here she hunted the fox in Staverton Park, supped with the flattered canons in their little private gardens, and once, driven indoors by a storm, hastened to finish her supper in the monastic church. On another occasion her husband Suffolk planted the members of his private chapel upon the house, which proceeded to keep them for nine months. And Butley was not the only East Anglian priory used as a cheap hotel by this handsome and popular couple.

As with the secular clergy, the intellectual achievements of the last generation of medieval monks permit of little easy generalization. Centuries ago, the monasteries had ceased to afford cultural leadership; the best had become parasitic upon the universities, while the worst had sunk rather boorishly into their bucolic settings. The two liveliest traditions in early Tudor intellectual life were the humanism of Italy and the Quietist piety of the Lower Rhineland, which latter had its classic in the *Imitatio Christi* and its English parallels in Richard Rolle and his literary successors. In writings and library catalogues emanating from the English monasteries, these two developments are rather sparsely represented, perhaps the brightest exceptions being the maintenance of the humanist tradition at Christ Church, Canterbury, and of the mystical tradition in the small Carthusian Order. Academic education continued to attract monks at least as powerfully as in any earlier period: the houses of studies kept by various orders at the two universities continued well-filled, and many hundreds of monks figure on the university registers during the last thirty years. Though there was little intellectual scope for educated monks when they returned to their houses, the latter nevertheless contained some men of literary talent like Andrew Boorde and Alexander Barclay, as well as a few deservedly popular devotional writers like William Bond and Richard Whitford.

In the field of popular education, religious houses played no more than a minor role. Monastic cathedrals like Norwich and Worcester had small schools; St. Mary's, York, used some of its ample revenues to keep a boarding-house for fifty boys at the neighbouring cathedral school, while certain smaller houses kept schoolmasters for their young monks and for a few children of their officers and neighbours. Despite these and other exceptions, English education suffered extremely little by the dissolution. On the other hand, monastic hospitality was widely if indiscriminately extended to callers ranging from dukes to sturdy beggars: particular houses like Sawley Abbey in the wild Pennine country conferred valuable services on travellers. It is hard to estimate the precise impact of monastic largesse upon social life. Its critics blamed it for the prevalence of vagabondage, but it was probably not large enough to exert major economic influences. The *Valor Ecclesiasticus*, that great survey of ecclesiastical income organized in 1535 by Thomas Cromwell, records monastic charities amounting only to 2½ per cent. of gross income, but this survey is concerned solely with disbursements and doles which the monks were obliged to make by the provisions of pious benefactors. For all we know, the monks may have given as much again out of pure goodwill, but this would seem a large assumption in view of the debts and financial struggles which beset most houses during the last decades.

Similar considerations apply also to monastic landlordism. All the available evidence suggests that the attitude of ecclesiastical lords to tenants, workmen and neighbours closely resembled that of their lay neighbours. The reports of Wolsey's enclosure commissioners show numerous monasteries charged with enclosure and eviction of tenants. Stray allusions continually support this evidence. The chronicler of Butley Priory, for example, records a riot in 1526 by the men of Orford against enclosures made by the Priory on what they claimed as common land, while in 1517 the Abbot of Peterborough became involved in prolonged legal struggles against the townsmen on account of enclosures forcibly made by him upon the Fens. Sir Thomas More included 'certain abbots, holy men no doubt' amongst the people responsible for harsh enclosures. No agrarian Elysium therefore existed on monastic estates, nor did contemporaries make this claim on their behalf. Some slight idealization inevitably occurs in later literature, but it lacks first-hand character and is unimpressive in scope and intensity. In general, monasteries had always been tenacious, sometimes unscrupulous, in asserting all their legal rights, and the immense number of proceedings brought against them in Chancery from the fourteenth century to the dissolution proves this fact to the hilt.

In fairness, it should be recalled that their financial obligations were heavy and that they often needed to protect themselves against neighbours even more unscrupulous and acquisitive. Again, the fact that laymen as stewards and bailiffs had an influential voice in their policy must help to account for its close assimilation to the general pattern. The greatest men in the realm did not disdain these offices. The Earl of Shrewsbury held at least eleven monastic stewardships, the Earl of Derby seven, the Earls of Rutland and Wiltshire six each. By the time of the dissolution Thomas Cromwell's four or five did much less than justice to his now unique position in the monastic world. By then he was appointing the heads of houses; he corresponded with a vast number of them on intimate terms, while accepting their annuities and gifts right and left. His memory was exact and tenacious, his knowledge of monasticism extensive and peculiar. But Cromwell had only just concluded his apprenticeship in this field of administration when Wolsey, having failed to provide the King with his divorce, fell from power.

The momentous change of October 1529 threw the Cardinal's chief administrative agent into profound anxiety. In terms of material possessions he had become a substantial man with much to lose. The text of the will compiled by him in the previous July gives no complete picture of his lands and properties, but he makes over thirty cash bequests amounting to about £1,600, then a large sum and matched only in the wills of the richer London merchants. Had Cromwell died at this moment, he would have gone down, if not to national history, at least to the social antiquities of London as a mundane but considerate character, notable for his family piety and highly practical beneficence. Besides remembering a host of relatives, friends and servants, he leaves £20 to the making of highways, £40 for sixty doweries to poor maidens, £20 to poor house holders to pray for his soul, £10 to poor parishioners, £10 to prisoners in Newgate, Ludgate, the King's Bench and Marshalsea prisons, and £5 to the five orders of friars to pray for him. This last relatively meagre bequest indicates, however, no scepticism concerning masses for the dead, since he also orders his executors to hire an honest *and continent* priest to sing for his soul for seven years at a cost of £46 13s. 4d. Within a few weeks of drafting these provisions, Cromwell must have begun to doubt whether in fact he would manage to retain this fortune; whether at any rate his ambitions for further advancement were not doomed. According to Pole, a rumour circulated in London at this time that Cromwell had been sent to the Tower for execution. His friend and business-associate Stephen Vaughan showed himself deeply perturbed, and Cromwell himself certainly feared to be sucked down with the great ecclesiastical galleon to which he had entrusted his fortunes. Then came the moment of decision which brought him safely out of the vortex. The story of this critical moment cannot be told otherwise than in the words of George Cavendish, who had that power of observation sometimes vouchsafed to good and simple spirits, and whose biography of Wolsey forms so signal a triumph of character over intellect.

On All Hallows day 1529, when Wolsey had been relegated to retirement at Esher, Cavendish chanced to see Cromwell there in the great chamber, 'leaning in the great window with a Primer in his hand, saying our Lady matins: which had been a strange sight in him afore. . . . He prayed no more earnestly than he distilled tears as fast from his eyes. Whom I saluted and bade good-morrow. And with that I perceived his moist cheeks, the which he wiped with his napkin. To whom I said, " Why, Mr. Cromwell, what meaneth this dole? Is my lord in any danger that you do lament for him, or is it for any other loss, that you have sustained by misfortune?" "Nay," quoth he, "it is for my unhappy adventure. For I am like to lose all that I have laboured for, all the days of my life, for doing of my master true and diligent service." "Why sir," quoth I, "I trust that you be too wise to do anything by my lord's commandment otherwise than you might do, whereof you ought to be in doubt or danger for loss of your goods." "Well, well," quoth he, "I cannot tell; but this I see before mine eyes, that everything is as it is taken; and this I know well, that I am disdained withal for my master's sake; and yet I am sure there is no cause, why they should do so. An evil name once gotten will not lightly be put away. I never had promotion by my lord to the increase of my living. But this much I will say to you, that I will this afternoon, when my lord has dined, ride to London, and to the court, when I will either make or mar, ere ever I come again. I will put myself in prease, to see what they will be able to lay to my charge." "Mary," quoth I, "then in so doing you shall do wisely, beseeching God to send you good luck, as I would myself." '

The immediate sequel proved equally revealing of Cromwell's character and outlook. Though in crisis he had turned to conventional devotions, he had a strong partiality for the laymen of the household and a distaste for the priests, who had become the real beneficiaries of their master's worldly success. When the Cardinal had said mass, he dined with Cromwell and his chapplains, and during dinner the former told Wolsey that he ought to assemble his faithful gentlemen and yeomen, and express to them his thanks and commendation, a gesture which would encourage them to sustain the common misfortune. 'Alas, Thomas,' replied Wolsey, 'ye know I have nothing to give them, and words without deeds be not often well taken.' But Cromwell continued with his customary bluntness that Wolsey had made his chaplains rich with benefices, some being now able to spend a thousand marks a year, and none less than three hundred. While these clergymen had got all the profit, the laymen had nothing, 'and yet hath your poor servants taken much more pains for you in one day than all your idle chaplains hath done in a year'. The Cardinal agreed, and so Cromwell ordered Cavendish to assemble the gentlemen along one side of the great chamber, the yeomen along the other. As they all stood there weeping—in the way strong men did not scruple to do in Tudor times—Wolsey conquered his own emotions and made them a long speech of thanks. This done, Cromwell, still intent to champion their interests and to shame the chaplains, suggested that the latter should subscribe money to send off the laymen on a month's holiday, by which time the King's decision and the fate of the household would be known. Surely, the charity of the chaplains was not so void of grace that they would see the Cardinal lack when they might help him! 'And for my part, although I have not received of your Grace's gift one penny towards the increase of my yearly living, yet will I depart [share] with you this towards the dispatch of your servants.' With these words, Cromwell gave Wolsey five pounds in gold. 'And now let us see', he continued, 'what your chaplains will do. I think they will depart with you much more than I have done, who be more able to give you a pound than I one penny.' Turning to the chaplains (whose thoughts cannot by this time have been very charitable) he added sardonically, 'Go to, masters!' They had no alternative but to meet the challenge, some giving ten pounds and some less, but in the end raising enough to send off the servants with a quarter's wages. This done, the Cardinal returned to his chamber, lamenting the departure of his servants, 'making his moan unto Master Cromwell, who comforted him the best he could, and desired my lord to give him leave to go to London, where he he would either make or mar ere he came again, which was always his common saying'. After a long and secret conversation with Wolsey, Cromwell then took horse for London with his clerk Ralph Sadler, bidding Cavendish farewell with the words, 'Ye

33

shall hear shortly of me, and if I speed well, I will not fail to be here again within these two days'.

The adventurer was as good as his word. A few days later he returned 'with a pleasant countenance' and told Cavendish that he had dared 'to put his feet where he would be better regarded, ere ever the Parliament was finished'. He had in fact obtained the approval of the King and the Duke of Norfolk to become a burgess, and through the good offices of Sir William Paulet, a former fellow-servant of Wolsey, he sat in the first session of the Reformation Parliament as member for Taunton. Here, as Cavendish again shows, he defended the fallen Wolsey and ensured that the Bill of Attainder brought against him would be dropped. He also took a hand in organizing the resentment of his fellow-members against the power and privileges of the Church. It has been demonstrated by Dr. Elton that the first drafts of the document known as the Supplication against the Ordinaries not only contain Cromwell's corrections, but date from the year 1529, three years before this powerful attack upon ecclesiastical jurisdiction and the legislative powers of Convocation was actually delivered. It was hence a genuine House of Commons document, and its early history shows that Cromwell's skill as a draftsman had already obtained recognition by the powerful anticlerical group in the House.

In short, within a few weeks he had begun to win good opinions in a new field and to build up a second career upon the ruins of the first. Until shortly before Wolsey's death, Cromwell, even while he gave careful thought to his own ambitions, continued to work hard on the affairs of his former master. If he was gradually disengaging himself during the year 1530, staying longer at court and dancing attendance less and less upon the querulous old prelate, his conduct throughout these exchanges was marked by far more decency and consideration than that of Wolsey's other former supporters, including Stephen Gardiner himself. Some of his letters at this time show a reverence and an affection for Wolsey as obviously heartfelt as anything in Tudor correspondence. On this score Merriman and other modern biographers excel themselves in prejudice. When Cromwell alone speaks up in Parliament for the Cardinal and gains for him a temporary pardon, this can only have been to gain a reputation for faithfulness; if he fails to prevent the seizure of Wolsey's colleges, then he is no true servant. When Cromwell writes Wolsey a long, news-laden and, as it seems to me, polite letter of consolation, this becomes in Merriman's eyes 'empty' and 'almost contemptuous'. By implication at least, Cromwell even incurs blame for not defying the King and Norfolk at the time of the final attack upon the doomed Cardinal. The reader soon begins to realize that nothing short of a Cromwell who vainly offered up his whole career on Wolsey's funeral pyre would have sufficed to satisfy these faithful followers of the black legend.

To prosper in Tudor times, a man needed to get lordship as much as in the previous chaotic century of the Pastons, and the royal service now presented itself to Cromwell as obviously the most desirable. Many of Wolsey's servants had, on the express advice of their master, long preceded him in making the transfer, which usually involved a formal, quasi-feudal oath. It has been shown that Cromwell must have taken this between 17 December 1529, and April 1530, although until Wolsey's death, in the following November, Cromwell's letters refer almost solely to his own and the Cardinal's affairs. At some date before 10 January, 1531, he was sworn of the King's Council; during this and the subsequent year, leading officials and noblemen sought his help and favours in respectful terms. As yet, however, he was no policy-maker, but a mere executive agent for the King's legal and financial affairs; he took grants of land to the King's use, supervised the drafting and sealing of indentures concerning Crown lands, received sums for building the King's tomb, consulted with the law officers on various aspects of royal business, superintended the collection of clerical subsidies and the revenues of vacant sees. Even now, he was not above a little modest business enterprise of his own. As late as February 1532 Stephen Vaughan was selling some spermaceti for him in Antwerp and complaining that it put him to more pain than anything he ever had to sell, since it was rapidly putrifying and 'subtilly packed, being nothing so good within as without'.

We know little of the personal relationships between the King and Cromwell during the years 1531–2, but the outcome shows that he made good use of his frequent access to the presence, and that Henry speedily came to see in him the high-powered executive able to replace the Duke of Norfolk and the other fumbling amateurs who had overthrown Wolsey, yet lacked the professional experience and the application to assume his functions. When there developed in Parliament a new crisis in papal and ecclesiastical affairs, the hand of Cromwell can first be felt in the sphere of high policy. He had at last arrived, and for eight years both Church and State in England received a guidance infinitely more forceful and far-seeing than at any time between the death of Henry VII and the advent of Cecil.

The personality which had emerged at the end of this long and arduous road seems to me somewhat complex. It corresponds all too little with the rash phrases used by Cromwell's simplifying critics. His portraits in the Bodleian, in the Frick and in the National Portrait Gallery do not in themselves carry us far. The second and third of these show someone not unlike the conventional Cromwell: the administrator, thin-lipped, narrow-eyed, astute, responsible, never yielding a point without calculation. Contemporaries add to these characteristics a short heavy build and an uncouth gait; at times the impression of a patient and somewhat wooden character. These were superficial notions. Chapuys, by no means concerned to flatter, remarks that his countenance was extremely mobile, and that when he became engaged in a conversation of interest, his face would suddenly light up, the dull expression yielding to a subtle, cunning and intelligent aspect. At such moments, his conversation became extraordinarily witty and entertaining; he then had a habit of giving a roguish, oblique glance whenever he made a smart remark. The only portrait suggesting this animated Cromwell is that in the Bodleian; here he seems for the moment the serious but sardonic listener, who in a second or two will flash out a piece of repartee.

By this time his career had taught him self-control in its various forms. Each rung of the ladder had been slippery, and as every Tudor courtier and moralist knew, the least reliable rung was the one at the top. In the courts of princes the smooth surfaces of formal address masked rampant jealousy and treachery; for all the bows and titles, men fought like animals for pre-eminence, privilege and wealth. Even those born near the summit had to be cunning, cautious, adaptable. How much more so the rare man who had risen from the bottom and had been entrusted with the least popular tasks of government! Life became infinitely calculating; he must learn when to be humble, when to be hard, when to be sociable, when to take advantage of an opponent's weakness. If such a man had been educated in Italy, he might have developed the explicitly low view of human nature in the manner of Machiavelli or of Guicciardini, and seldom can he have found occasion to take a view more elevated. Cromwell, as the letters of his correspondents show even more clearly than his own, was the precise opposite of the flint-faced automaton of legend. On the contrary, he was infinitely adaptable to human nature, all things to all men. One would say he possessed a genius for friendship, if one did not suspect that too many of his friendships were dedicated to the purpose of his career, his ministry and his mission.

He was a good mixer and even in the days of his power his correspondents do not address him as an ogre, but as a highly approachable magnate, one who preferred to be tackled frankly and who, if he could so act without injuring himself, would readily do them good turns. Surrounded by enterprising suppliants, he can scarcely be blamed for getting services in return for many of these favours, since here was the bond by which Tudor government subsisted. No English minister has ever bound so many men of all sorts and conditions to himself; a great institutional organizer, he also contrived to gain intimate personal relationships with a surprisingly large section of the ruling and middle classes. Satirical, witty, sometimes openly cynical, he must also have known when to avoid the harsh jest, for his friends of longer standing were by no means backward in confiding to him their most intimate problems and aspirations. That early puritan Sir Francis Bigod confessed to him in emotional terms that he felt his mission in life was to preach sermons, and he besought Cromwell to license him to be a married priest, or else something equally sensational: a lay preacher. In a small group of old friends like Stephen Vaughan, Cromwell certainly inspired sentiments which look uncommonly like affection. Conversely, the highly organized life of a first minister with a whole gamut of lesser offices ended by gravely limiting the chance of disinterested friendships. Too much of this type of dedication seems good for nobody: we have all met the eminent public administrator in middle age, gaining in suave precision as he loses the capacity for personal affection, ever in danger of seeing his associates as pawns in the institutional game. Even before he reached this stage, Cromwell sometimes showed the aggressive touch of the sharp businessman. In his *Survey of London* Stow relates how Cromwell built his house in Throgmorton Street near the Austin Friars and, intent to enlarge his garden, took down the pales of the neighbouring gardens, measured twenty-two feet into what they claimed as their land, erected a brick wall along this new line and removed on rollers a shed belonging to Stow's father. Cromwell had no doubt acquired some legal title to this land, but it is evident that he chose to assert it in an arbitrary manner. It is fair to add here that Stow also recalls having seen when a boy more than two hundred poor fed twice a day at Cromwell's gate.

He was certainly loyal and generous towards people who had helped him in his struggling days. Whatever the hostility of public opinion in the remoter provinces, Cromwell enjoyed a certain popularity in London. On his fall in 1540 his arrest was kept secret and sudden, since the government feared trouble in the city. His scaffold was carefully guarded; a war of broadside ballads arose over his death and had to be suppressed by the Council. Foxe tells a whole series of anecdotes to illustrate his liberality and the good turns done by him to people of whom Foxe approved. His enemies alleged that he was unpopular amongst the lords and gentry because he was a 'great taker and briber' like Wolsey, but they admitted that 'he spent it honourably and freely like a gentleman (though he were none) and helped many honest men and preferred his servants well'.

The term Philistine has been levelled too freely against Cromwell, perhaps through mistaken impressions deriving from his cult of efficiency. It is not justified by his habits and cultural attainments. He appears indeed as a man of taste who appreciated the amenities and elegances of his age, while shunning the ostentation which had turned men against Wolsey. He was interested in the substance and purposes of power rather than in its trappings, and his mode of life represented a sensible compromise between his modest origins and his high office. Even when prime minister and among the richest men in England, he continued to live in relatively small houses. That near the Austin Friars, his favourite residence, was sumptuously furnished, and the Venetian Ambassador, who often dined there, praised everything he saw. This house, which he had bought from his friend Anthony Vivaldi, was no palace, but had a gate tower, a large dining-hall and ample kitchens. Cromwell entertained well and went to great trouble about food, having a wet and dry larder built in each of his houses. Coverdale is full of the pleasures of staying with him; even his arch-enemy Chapuys often sat at his table and remarks that on such occasions the most careful politicians were put off their guard by Cromwell's pleasing presence and address, which led them to reveal things they should have kept private.

He seems to have had that passionate love of quality in physical objects which marks many a self-made man who has had to earn them by hard work. He corresponded at length with Stephen Vaughan about an iron chest of elaborate workmanship, which was so expensive that Vaughan hesitated to purchase it for him. He also wanted to buy in Flanders for forty crowns a carved dining-table ' of such size as there are few in England'. A mutilated list of his furniture shows that, at a time when they were not widely collected in England, he had at least twelve pictures. He also purchased a globe with explanatory notes, and the only two copies of the *Cronica Cronicarum* which could be found in Antwerp. As will appear, the claim that he made Machiavelli his Bible cannot be substantiated, yet there can be no doubt that his stay in Italy had given him a love of Italian literature. In April 1530 Edmund Bonner writes to remind Cromwell of a promise to lend him the *Triumphs* of Petrarch and the *Book of the Courtier,* and 'to make him a good Italian'. Stray references suggest that he had read quite widely when time permitted. Amongst his official papers are a poem, 'Amongst all flowers the rose doth excell', a dialogue between Pasquillus and Marforius, and various Italian verses. Both before and during his prominence in public life he had innumerable friendships with literary men such as Miles Coverdale, translator of the Bible, the versatile Lord Morley, who dedicated a work to him, Thomas Elyot, famous author of *The Governor,* the brilliant humanists Richard Morison and Thomas Starkey, and John Palsgrave, who wrote one of our best early French grammars and dictionaries. His personal interest in Biblical translation and political thought will become increasingly apparent. In the days of his power he was an enthusiastic patron of scholars and writers, extremely conscious of their social importance in the swiftly-expanding world of ideas. Ample evidence indicates that such interest was far from being solely limited to the creation of political propaganda. Though his appointment in 1535 as High Steward of the University of Cambridge chiefly reflected his political influence, his relations with that University were not purely formal, since he had been maintaining scholars there as early as October 1530.

His recreations were otherwise typical of contemporary magnates. He spent large sums on singing birds, kept a small orchestra of musicians among his servants and a fool to amuse his guests, played bowls, cards and dice, sometimes losing at court very large sums. He kept nearly a hundred horses in his stables, but habitually rode a mule to and fro between his house and the court. He shot with the long bow and hunted, but his favourite sport was hawking, and he was best pleased by gifts of hawks, spaniels or greyhounds. The Spanish Ambassador went out hawking with him to get private conversation, and reports him as drawing a metaphor from the sport: 'The Emperor and his agents like hawks rise high to come down fast on their prey.'

In considering the suitability of the term Philistine, another consideration may at ths point be deduced. Those who have read the unsavoury reports made by some of his agents concerning the immoralities of monks might leap to the conclusion that Cromwell relished indecent stories. This seems a totally false inference. An English student at Padua once set him a copy of some indecent Italian verses, which he had seen stuck on a church door, but Cromwell waxed furious and the student came very near losing his exhibition. Altogether, a distinctly human being emerges from the personal details, and we shall see that a study of Cromwell's official career, even that side of it relating to his enemies, by no means convicts him of inhumanity. On the other hand, his emotional life remains obscure; its extent and depth might well be questioned, and only a bold partisan would seek to glorify his qualities in this important sphere of human character. His successive environments were all hostile towards delicacy and sensibility; in addition, he became too much the servant of an idea.

Chapter Three

The Opening Moves

SINCE 1527 the royal policy had revolved ever more narrowly around the King's plans to obtain a divorce, marry Anne Boleyn, and obtain a sorely-needed male heir to the throne. His case had from the first been clouded—and has remained so ever since—by his adulterous self-will, by his prior liaison with Anne's own sister, by his rather indecent capacity for moralistic self-deception, by his cruel animosity against a faithful, virtuous and stubborn queen. Judging him solely within the context of private ethics, little can be said in his favour, though he entertained an apparently genuine conviction that Katherine's persistent miscarriages and the deaths in infancy of all his children, save Mary, had been caused by the divine curse pronounced against marriage with a deceased brother's wife. His case in canon law was fairly strong, strong enough at least to convince many learned canonists and more than strong enough to give a veneer of decency to a political divorce based upon national necessity. The dispensation by which Pope Julius II had originally permitted the marriage of Henry and Katherine was declared by the English lawyers to be invalid on five grounds, notably since the King had been only twelve years old at the time, had not sought the dispensation, and had protested against the marriage on reaching the age of fourteen. The dispute afterwards centred upon the query as to whether Katherine and her first husband Arthur had actually cohabited: if so, it was generally held that the papal dispensation would thereby have been invalidated. Katherine herself consistently maintained that cohabitation with Arthur had never taken place, though evidence of sorts to the contrary was also produced. Judged on grounds neither of family-ethics nor of canon law, but on those of *raison d'état*, there remained every argument in favour of the King's divorce and remarriage. And in cases with no stronger legal backing than

41

Henry's, earlier popes had realized that kings are not as other men, and had given them the benefit of the doubt; many men could remember how Louis XII of France had been divorced by the Pope to allow of his politic marriage with the heiress of Brittany.

Pope Clement VII was an irresolute politician, anxious not to offend Henry and most amenable to worldly pressures, yet Rome had just undergone siege and sack, complete with every imaginable brutality, by the troops of Emperor Charles, King of Spain and nephew of Katherine of Aragon. When in the autumn of 1527 the French momentarily recovered power in Italy, Clement relaxed and began to grant Henry some important concessions; they included a dispensation abolishing impediments to the proposed Boleyn marriage, should the union with Katherine turn out to be invalid. In February 1528 Stephen Gardiner the King's secretary and Edward Fox his almoner, both of them formidable canonists, were sent out to augment the attack upon the unfortunate pontiff; they menaced him with the prospects of a General Council and an English schism; for the moment their threats received increasing support from the continued victories of the French. That April Clement granted a bull empowering Cardinals Wolsey and Campeggio jointly and severally to hear the case, declare, if need arose, the nullity of the marriage, license the parties to remarry and legitimize Henry's children. Since Wolsey was the King's man and Campeggio Bishop of Salisbury and Cardinal Protector of England, the prospects seemed fair indeed for the royal cause. Yet from this point everything went amiss. By the end of the year the Spanish armies once again stood in control of Italy, and Clement, relapsing into the grip of Charles, could do no more than play for time. The proceedings before Wolsey and Campeggio dawdled until July 1529, when the consolidation of Imperial control over Rome compelled the Pope to revoke their commission and summon the parties to appear in Rome. The backers of Katherine were triumphant, while to describe the outraged feelings of Henry, the term virtuous indignation would seem quite inadequate. He valued his services to Christendom very highly, and had long felt conscious that neither Providence nor the Roman curia were granting those rewards which merits so substantial might justly claim.

If the resplendent champion of the Papacy were thus fooled by a bogus trial and then called before a foreign tribunal, there could be little justice in the universe, let alone in Rome. At all events, the time had come to appeal elswhere. The resultant fall of Wolsey (who seemed useless to Henry unless he could switch on the fountain of papal jurisdiction) nevertheless accomplished strangely little: he was not succeeded by a mind with a masterplan. Government lapsed into the hands of Norfolk, Suffolk and Anne Boleyn's father Wiltshire—respectively, a soldier with a certain cunning, a handsome façade and a grasping nonentity, none of them showing the slightest claim to original and decisive statesmanship. When Cromwell became chief minister in 1532, the 'great matter' lay substantially where it had lain at Wolsey's fall. The only new step of any interest had been taken on a suggestion made in the autumn of 1529 by Thomas Cranmer, then still a Cambridge don, that the universities of Europe should be consulted on the divorce. This done, loyalty, pressure and bribery produced the predictable series of results. Oxford and Cambridge declared for the King, while Francis I, ever intent to strike a blow at Spain and the Habsburgs, induced the French universities to do likewise. Even Bologna, nominally in papal territory, and Padua followed suit, though after some little largesse had been pressed into the appropriate palms. On the other side, the Spanish universities naturally stood unanimous for Katherine, while Henry did not even trouble to consult those of Germany. Though his successes had some potential value for his propagandists, they failed to stir the Habsburg eagle from its secure nest in the Vatican. The lasting result of the plan lay in the introduction to Henry's notice of the clergyman destined to share with Thomas Cromwell so much of the responsibility for founding a national church in England. In his academic hesitancy, his constantly-developing convictions, his literary sense, at once imaginative and precise, his curious blend of pliability and courage, Thomas Cranmer could scarce have presented a greater contrast with the decisive, resolute and practical Cromwell. Yet at every point these two strange midwives of Anglicanism supplied each other's defects. The harsh logic of history has seldom forced characters so disparate into such complementary roles, but one must not for a moment be tempted to label those roles with the terms 'destructive Cromwell' and 'constructive Cranmer'. The utterly misleading character of such an antithesis will become more apparent as this account advances.

The 'years without a policy' solved few problems, yet they did not lack some notable events. The tension between Church and State mounted amid an atmosphere of foreboding. In 1529 the Reformation Parliament set out along a road the end of which none of its members could have envisaged. It was summoned to deal with a critical situation, and certainly not to stage an ecclesiastical revolution, yet quite empirically, it began to legislate against a few old and obvious abuses. One Act laid down a precise scale of fees to be charged for the probate of wills; another likewise regulated mortuary dues; a third restrained pluralities, forebade clerical trading and debarred beneficed clergy from accepting chantries, the enterprise attacked a century and a half earlier by Chaucer. The fourth of these Acts provided that a criminal taking sanctuary for felony or murder should be branded upon the thumb for future identification, and should lose the benefit of sanctuary if he failed to come forth and abjure the realm on the day appointed by the coroner. These early reforms should also be viewed in conjunction with certain others passed in 1531–2. Ostensibly to prevent able-bodied soldiers and sailors from taking service abroad, one of these later Acts abolished abjuration altogether, confining the criminals to their sanctuaries. Another dealt with the so-called clerics under the lowly order of subdeacon. Should such men be charged with treason, murder, burglary, highway-robbery or arson, they would henceforth forfeit benefit of clergy.

To Gairdner, that paladin of clerical privilege, 'the spirit of the whole legislation was bad, and was clearly intended to punish the only power in the land which could be trusted to denounce wrong in high places with something like authority'. But could it so be trusted? And precisely what moral force derived from the protection of a thug able to stumble through a neck-verse or persuade some incautious bishop to make him an acolyte? Such questions Gairdner does not stop to answer, but he goes on to suggest that these initial reforms could not benefit the poor. If, however, he had studied the scales of probate fees and mortuary dues, he would have seen that in fact they do protect the interests of the poor, and this quite effectively. Then he gives away the game by recalling that these fees had been the subject of complaint in the time of Edward III, but then (when men were sensitive about holy things!) the bishops had merely received notice to amend such abuses.

How long should Parliament and the nation have awaited

these simple reforms? Gairdner might more suitably have reserved his conservative thunders for that other chief episode of the pre-Cromwellian Reformation, the series of events culminating in the Pardon of the Clergy. They began when, in the summer of 1530, writs of *praemunire facias* were issued from the King's Bench against fifteen divines, including eight bishops and three abbots. They were charged with offences under the statutes of *praemunire*, in that they had abetted Wolsey by paying him a portion of their annual revenues. These statutes had culminated in the so-called Great Statute of 1393, the unintentional vagueness of which had left it a formidable if rusty weapon. It had originated in response to the threat of Boniface IX to excommunicate English bishops for implementing obnoxious mandates of the King's courts concerning the patronage of benefices. This Pope had also aroused the wrath of Richard II's Parliament when he threatened to dislocate the work of English government by translating from see to see those bishops who held secular offices. Consequently, the Great Statute had punished with forfeiture of land and goods all persons who should introduce or execute papal bulls injurious to the Crown *in these two particular ways*. It also used high phraseology concerning the independence of the English Crown, 'which hath been so free at all times that it hath been in subjection to no earthly sovereign, but immediately subject to God and no other'. Even so, later attempts to make the Statute exclude *all* papal jurisdiction from the realm lacked historical justification; its text was admittedly ill-drafted and easy to strain, but it neither intended so sweeping an effect nor had made much immediate difference to English practice. After lying dormant for many years, it had been revived by Humphrey Duke of Gloucester as a political weapon against Cardinal Beaufort, while later in the fifteenth century aggressive lay lawyers had used it to stigmatize all ecclesiastical jurisdiction as 'foreign', and had threatened to bring the church courts under the operation of the Great Statute.

The revival of *praemunire* in 1530 and its employment against the fifteen eminent divines obviously sprang from broad political motives. A great many clerics had paid Wolsey these sums, not as an act of submission, but rather to resist him, since, in return for such compositions, the omnipotent Legate could be induced to leave their jurisdictions uncontrolled. 'There is never a poor archdeacon in England', said the Lords in their accusations against Wolsey, 'but that he paid yearly to him a portion of his living.' Several of the defendants may have been selected for this treatment by the government because they had been prominent supporters of Queen Katherine: Fisher of Rochester, West of Ely, Standish of St. Asaph and Clerk of Bath and Wells. Others, however, appear to have supported the King, and seem not to have been chosen on account of governmental rancour. Since some of these men failed to appear in court during the Michaelmas term, a second set of writs summoned them for Hilary term 1531. Before this stage arrived, however, the limited plan was merged into a much larger plan, which involved threatening the whole of the English clergy with a *praemunire* charge. In a message to Wolsey on 21 October, Cromwell himself wrote: 'The prelates shall not appear in the *praemunire*. There is another way devised in place thereof, as your Grace shall further know.' At this moment, Cromwell was about to enter the King's Council, but no evidence can be adduced to prove that it was he who suggested this broadening of the attack.

Quite recently, Mr. Scarisbrick has demonstrated that the new charge against the whole clergy was not, as stated by Hall and consequently by historians ever since, a charge of complicity with Wolsey's usurped jurisdiction. This was merely the accusation against the original fifteen. According to the Act of Pardon subsequently passed, and to other official documents, the charge made against the whole clergy was more sweeping: by merely exercising jurisdiction in their ecclesiastical courts, they had 'fallen and incurred into divers dangers of his [i.e. the King's] laws by things done and perpetrated and committed contrary to the order of his laws and specially contrary to the form of the statutes of provisors, provisions and *praemunire*.' This was a legal fiction of as much crudity as that which had formerly been brought against Wolsey for acting as Papal Legate, though something very similar had long ago been suggested by Crown lawyers. When Convocation met at the end of January 1531, it can scarcely have feared a literal application of the penalties of *praemunire*—loss of property and imprisonment during the King's pleasure—yet it felt justifiable alarm lest its jurisdiction and privileges might suffer arbitrary curtailment by Act of Parliament. Recent debates in the Commons had in fact shown a strong party in favour of such a radical action. Consequently the two Convocations of Canterbury and York agreed without delay to pay the King extraordinary subsidies of £100,000 and £18,840 respectively, in return for a pardon for their alleged offences. The King demanded immediate payment, but the clergy successfully insisted on spreading instalments over five years. They then asked him formally to guarantee their privileges and define the future scope of the *praemunire* act, in order that ecclesiastical judges should know precisely where they stood. It was now Henry's turn to refuse, for the whole advantage of *praemunire* lay in its vagueness: he had everything to lose by stabilizing a situation the very fluidity of which might bring him further sweeping gains.

In February, chief attention turned to a new set of royal demands, two being pre-eminent: that Convocation should acknowledge his sole right to be called 'Protector and Supreme Head of the English Church and Clergy' and that he had the cure of his subjects' souls. The clergy, less subservient during these particular negotiations than has commonly been supposed, refused to agree. They conceded the title of Supreme Head only with the vital saving clause 'so far as the law of Christ allows'; they evaded the royal claim to exercise cure of souls by a clever verbal alteration of the suggested phrase, which rendered it quite innocuous. Altogether, these later attacks did not carry Henry appreciably beyond his previous claims, or indeed beyond the *de facto* powers of previous kings. Here again, the more momentous changes which came after 1532 may well induce us to read into the manoeuvres of 1530–1 more than they were understood at the time to convey. The final plunge had not yet been taken, and ample evidence remains to show that in these years Henry was still hoping against hope for a change of heart in Rome. One can see little more than a formidable campaign of threats intended to remind both the Pope and the English clergy that the King still meant business in the matter of the divorce; this notion makes sense of the somewhat unreal, though not quite unprecedented, crudity of a general attack upon ecclesiastical jurisdiction. The Pardon of the Clergy may thus be regarded as an elaborate essay in brinkmanship rather than a serious first step towards the erection of a national and schismatic Church. Within two years, demands much more precise and irrevocable were to be framed by the Crown and accepted by the English clergy: these demands, not the inconclusive exchanges of 1530–1, mark the entry of Cromwell. Nevertheless, the full length of the front on which the King was prepared to fight now lay revealed. That front covered not merely the whole future of papal jurisdiction and titular headship in England; it covered the independence of the English Church. Irrespective of their attitude towards Rome, the English clergy, their institutions, their jurisdictions, now lay in more danger of legal subjection— whatever in practice that might mean—to the omnicompetent national State.

Within the boundaries of his kingdom, there was little Henry could not accomplish; yet meanwhile in Rome the situation remained static. During the years 1529–32 his advisers lacked any feasible plans either to move the Pope or to dispense altogether with Papal authority. They used one lever after another, and if their levers of 1530–1 were fairly heavy implements, they still lacked the slightest chance of success. By the time of Cromwell's advent, their failure had become all too apparent, and the new minister soon induced the King to abandon the lever in favour of the hammer. Once taken up, the latter instrument rained down its blows with irresistible force; they were timed and placed with great precision, each one just hard enough to achieve its purpose without creating unnecessary havoc. The hammer was statute-law and the striker a Parliament directed by the son of the blacksmith of Putney.

During these same years, the rise of anticlericalism, so far from being restrained by the fall of Wolsey, was fostered by a number of new factors. The burning of Thomas Bilney (a Catholic reformer who held no notable heresies, unless a disbelief in purgatory be so accounted) aroused less excitement than the action of Dr. Parker, chancellor of the Worcester diocese, who in 1531 exhumed and burned the body of a Gloucestershire gentleman for leaving a supposedly heretical will. In this instance laymen had the satisfaction of seeing Parker haled before the King and paying a fine of £300, since no one except the King's officers could legally burn a heretic, dead or alive. It took very few episodes of this type to revive memories of Richard Hunne, since able publicists were now zealously fanning the flames. Chief among these was Christopher St. German, an eminent common lawyer and already in his seventieth year when the Reformation Parliament first met. His theological approach was conservative; in fact, he took little interest in doctrine, the grand passion of his life being the abasement of ecclesiastical jurisdiction. His first book, usually called *Doctor and Student*, had begun its career in 1523 as an academic dialogue in Latin; its more revolutionary suggestions only emerged in 1530–31, when a second dialogue in English was followed by a translation of the first, together with numerous appendices. St. German's other pre-Cromwellian work was his *Division between the Spiritualty and Temporalty*, published in 1532 and inaugurating a famous pamphlet-contest with Sir Thomas More. Then, as the Reformation advanced, the formidable septuagenarian supported it step by step in a further series of writings which acutely discerned its immense implications. His modernity can be overstated, for he drew much upon medieval authors like Marsiglio of Padua, Gerson and Fortescue, yet he grappled with the fundamental problems of law, equity and the relations between Church and State. The claims of St. German are made, not on behalf of any royal despotism, but in favour of a parliamentary absolutism; in several respects this foreshadows the concepts of Cromwell, whom he may well have influenced at a most crucial moment. To the King in Parliament St. German ascribes omnicompetence over all property and temporal things: this mighty organ can control all ecclesiastical exactions, prevent the transfer of land into mortmain, even redistribute property at will between its subjects, clergy and laity alike. Sir Thomas More ridiculed St. German's bland pose as a 'pacifier' in the great controversy, and criticized his habit of reporting dark but unspecific charges against churchmen. But if St. German's tears over clerical sins were hardly sincere, he cannot be blamed for omitting the names, since the bishops would have relished any chance to manhandle so astute an antagonist. St. German admittedly wanted to be in the *avantgarde* and yet avoid the Bishop's consistory court, but More himself was also trying to have it both ways for his episcopal friends. If the latter argued by means of nasty prisons and faggots, they could scarcely expect their opponents to offer them easy chances.

Apart from the fact that its author was also an anticlerical lawyer, Simon Fish's *Supplication for Beggars* has few analogies with the tractates of St. German. Fish was a convinced Protestant making a cruel and wild attack upon the clergy, and exploiting with gross exaggeration the common charges of covetousness and sexual immorality. Though immeasurably their stylistic superior, he surpasses the yellowest elements of the modern press. His pamphlet is couched in the form of a petition by the needy and the sick; they cry out to the King against those holy beggars: bishops, abbots, priests, monks and friars, who have grasped a third of the kingdom's wealth. The Pope is also 'a cruel devilish bloodsupper, drunken with the blood of the saints and martyrs of Christ'; he has held England to ransom since the days of King John. Lured on by their superior wealth, these clergymen corrupt every man's wife, daughter and maid. They have also invented purgatory, that lucrative swindle which enables them to gain money by pretending to release dead souls from pain. No one dare touch them: witness the case of poor Richard Hunne! It is no use founding hospitals for us poor people, since the fat always sticks to the priests' beards. When will the King assert his power, strip away this ill-gotten wealth and force these sturdy lubbers to do some work and keep their own wives? If only this be done, population and wealth will grow, profligacy decrease and the gospel be preached.

Simon Fish was circulating this pamphlet in 1529 and, according to Foxe, Anne Boleyn gave a copy to the King, who kept it in his breast-pocket for several days and protected the author against the wrath of Chancellor More. The story seems over-picturesque, but it does not lack all probability. Although the King must have spotted the cloven hoof of heresy behind these pages, his mood had altered decisively since 1515; in order to marry Anne and have a male heir, he was prepared to use even these savage allies. During the first three years of the Parliament, he came to realize that that there stood behind him not only an anticlerical House of Commons but also, especially in London, an anticlerical public opinion. What he lacked before the year 1532 was a minister with the legal acumen and the resolution to lead these forces towards two clearly-seen objectives: severance from a Roman jurisdiction controlled by his wife's nephew, and the creation of an absolute sovereignty by the Crown in Parliament over all subjects and causes within his realm.

In his work, *The Tudor Revolution in Government*, Dr. Elton has made a detailed survey of the offices held by Cromwell and the use he made of them during the great changes, which, from another angle, we are about to observe. Here a very few salient features will suffice. He began in 1532-3 with three appointments—Master of the King's Jewels, Clerk of the Hanaper and Chancellor of the Exchequer—each then relatively unimportant, but together enabling him to begin the rehabilitation of

Crown finances, a task obviously connected with several aspects of his ecclesiastical policy. In 1534 he became Principal Secretary and Master of the Rolls: it was the secretaryship which mattered, for he proceeded to take it out of its Household context and to set the future pattern by making it a ministry of all affairs. There was henceforth no aspect of Crown administration which he could not and did not touch: in particular his active personal role in the drafting of parliamentary legislation is amply attested in the records. In 1535, Cromwell became Vicegerent in Spirituals: a new and curious minister for Church-affairs. The following year he was appointed Lord Privy Seal and a baron.

As will become all too obvious, Henrician ministers were totally dependent upon the King's personal favour and, however capricious or mistaken Henry might be, the least puff of his displeasure could bring down his mightiest servant. And in relation to ecclesiastical matters, it should from the first be recognized that Cromwell's situation always contained elements of grave weakness. He adhered to one of two schools of thought which arose from the Royal Supremacy: the one which soon proved to have the less secure hold upon Henry's doctrinal sympathies. This Reforming group, led by Cranmer and Cromwell, numbered amongst its members Nicholas Shaxton, Bishop of Salisbury, Hugh Latimer, Bishop of Worcester, and William Barlow, Bishop of St. Asaph and St. Davids. Their theology was in considerable measure Lutheran and never liked by the King, who, having used them to help establish his Supremacy, broke their influence in the reaction of 1539–40. Cranmer apart, the small knot of Reforming bishops and their clerical supporters afforded Cromwell little support; not infrequently they caused him embarrassment. Men like Shaxton and Latimer had all the faults of the academic zealot, while moderate Reformers combining zeal with tact and worldly wisdom failed to emerge. Cranmer alone proved an asset on account of his unique relationship with the King. 'You were born', Cromwell told him, 'in a happy hour, I suppose, for, do or say what you will, the King will always well take it at your hand.' Yet in the longer run, even this influence proved a broken reed; at a moment of crisis Cranmer never managed to protect anything or anyone else from the Wrath of the Prince, which, in a favourite political proverb of the age, was Death.

Chapter Four

The Erastian Revolution

THE statutes which revolutionized both Anglo-Papal and Church-State relations admittedly lack the charm of novelty, yet no aspect of Cromwell's work illustrates to better effect his organizing genius, his grasp of detail, his ability to clinch an issue. Considering their extent, they give rise to few interpretative problems. They were drafted under his close personal supervision and, despite a weakness for grandiloquent preambles which caused one adversary to call them whited sepulchres, he was capable of making his intentions admirably clear.

The initial year 1532 did not show an instant change of method; Cromwell was no doubt concerting his plans and winning over the King and others to full participation. Nevertheless, the destruction of the English Church's legal independence was carried one stage nearer completion. On 18 March the Supplication of the Commons against the Ordinaries, originally drafted by Cromwell himself in 1529, was presented to the King in a revised form. Having admittedly begun its career as a Commons document, did the Supplication derive in 1532 from a still active fund of animosity in the House, or had it now become essentially a 'government measure'? Much rigorous analysis has recently been applied to its extant drafts, yet with divergent results; some aspects of this excessively involved problem still lie *sub judice*, but one may well remain sceptical as to the possibility of any unambiguous verdict. It seems, however, apparent that Cromwell continued in 1532 at least to help draft the Commons' ecclesiastical grievances and that, for their part, the Commons continued to display genuine indignation against the bishops' conduct of heresy-cases at least as late as 1534. The measure was also reintroduced by its sponsors at a moment when the House, irritated by financial demands and by the bills of Wills and Uses, could easily be turned against the Church. The Supplication ascribed the discords of the realm to heretical opinions and to 'the extreme and uncharitable behaviour and dealing of divers ordinaries, who have the right to examine these heresies'. It proceeded thence to enumerate 'certain particular griefs': the power of Convocation to legislate without the assent of King and laity; the vexatious delays and exactions of the church courts; the bestowal of benefices by nepotists upon minors, whereby the poor silly souls of the King's subjects perish for lack of instruction; the excessive number of holy days kept, and 'with small devotion'; the trapping of alleged lay heretics through 'subtle interrogatories concerning the high mysteries of our faith'. This was a cleverly variegated display: on the one hand a justified criticism of abuses, on the other a radical attack upon Convocation's legislative status. The reply of the bishops, probably drafted by Gardiner, was lengthy and less astute. It argued that the Commons grossly exaggerated the discords and that, if those things were really happening, they sprang from the faults of individuals rather than from the system. Where good cause could be shown, reform would be forthcoming, yet the independent legislative power of the clergy had a divine origin, and could not be surrendered. To submit the making of canon laws to the royal assent was beyond the power of the ordinaries. 'We your most humble subjects may not submit the execution of our charge and duty, certainly prescribed by God, to your Highness's assent.'

Henry transmitted the answer of the bishops to the Commons along with the heaviest of hints. 'We think their answer will smally please you, for it seemeth to us very slender. You be a great sort of wise men; I doubt not but you will look circumspectly on the matter, and we shall be indifferent between you.' Had the clergy passionately believed in their legislative independence, they would have resisted at this last ditch, but such convictions as they possessed proved insufficient to disturb their ingrained habit of temporizing with the Crown. Once they knew the King's mind, they offered to delay the operation of new canons pending his approval, and even to revoke old canons found contrary to the laws of the realm, always provided these canons did not touch faith and morals. But the King and his advisers now saw they could play for higher stakes. On 10 May they sent Convocation three articles for its acceptance: that it should pass no new canons unless the King should license it to do so, and supply his assent; that it should submit all canons previously enacted to the King and a commission of 32 clerics and laymen; and that canons thought by a majority of this commission to be repugnant to the laws of God and of the realm should be abrogated, the rest to stand in full power once they received the royal authority. These articles were rapidly followed by a skilful touch of indirect menace. The next day the King sent for the Speaker and twelve of the Commons; to them he explained in plain langugage that he had once thought the clergy wholly his subjects, but now he perceived them to be but half his subjects, since the prelates at their consecration made an oath to the Pope clean contrary to their oath to himself. In modern terms, the long-tolerated division of loyalties seemed to him incompatible with the absolute sovereignty claimed for the State. Precisely what deliberations preceded this meeting we do not know, but Cromwell was supposed by Pole, Foxe and others to have put such ideas into Henry's head. Since the new minister repeatedly expressed similar concepts, he may reasonably be credited with an active and perhaps dominant part in formulating these vital demands, which came so perilously near to abolishing the ancient legislative independence of the Church in England. Nevertheless, could the King have foreseen this as a half-way house towards a lay society liberated altogether from ecclesiastical laws, he would no doubt have experienced profound dismay. This more radical concept lay well outside Tudor possibilities, but if Thomas Cromwell ever envisaged it, one may suspect that he would have been far less shocked than his conventional sovereign. In the event, the Henrician Reformation never looked like taking this second step: ecclesiastical courts and laws continued their losing battle to supervise the nation's faith and morals into and beyond the next century.

Faced by the peremptory royal articles and the menacing talk of the King, the clergy capitulated, and on 16 May they presented him with the document known as the Submission of the Clergy, which granted his demands. And with a fine sense of occasion, Sir Thomas More the next day resigned the Chancellorship, being succeeded by Cromwell's friend Audley.

On the papal front, the year 1532 produced conflicts far less radical and dramatic, but it contributed one enactment of importance, the Conditional Restraint of Annates, which (to revert to our former distinction) falls into the class of levers rather than hammers. Annates were the payments to the Pope for the first year's revenues of bishops, a hoary exaction long resented and under dispute four years previously. The act of 1532 preserved a mild tone: it still spoke respectfully of the Pope, reasserted the Catholic state of the realm, and envisaged the continued appointment of bishops by papal bull. It had two aims. It threatened to deprive Rome of annates, should negotiations to abolish them fail. Equally important, it stipulated that bishops might be consecrated by English authority if the Pope refused bulls of consecration. The immediate purpose of these threats became apparent early the following year, when, with the see of Canterbury at long last vacant by the death of Warham, Henry promoted Thomas Cranmer. Aided by such legislation and by French pressure upon the Pope, he had no difficulty in procuring for his nominee the necessary bulls of consecration.

By this time, however, the moment of revolution was at hand. Of all the Reformation acts, that in Restraint of Appeals, passed in February–March 1533, was at once the most epoch-making, the most clear in its statement of principles, the most central to the Henrician Reformation. It was the banner in Cromwell's hand when he led the nation across the Rubicon. Its immediate purpose may nevertheless be described in terms far less magniloquent: it aimed to free Henry for remarriage, and it is obviously connected with the fact that Anne Boleyn gave birth to the Princess Elizabeth on 7 September, 1533, having been secretly married to Henry in the previous January. It begins with a famous principle obviously borrowed from that fourteenth-century apostle of erastianism, Marsiglio of Padua. England is an Empire, a realm the ruler of which acknowledges no superior human power, governed by one Supreme Head, to whom both spiritual and temporal men are bound to bear next to God a natural and humble obedience. By divine sufferance, the King is endowed with plenary power to give justice to all his people in all causes, without restraint or provocation to any foreign princes or potentates. As for the spiritualty or Church of England, they have always been reputed of sufficient learning and authority to settle matters of divine law without the meddling of any exterior person. Whereas the English Kings, especially Edward I, Edward III, Richard II and Henry IV, made laws to preserve the prerogatives of the imperial crown, and to keep it from the annoyance of the see of Rome and other foreign potentates, nevertheless appeals to Rome in cases of matrimony, testaments, tithes and the like have caused the King and his subjects much vexation and cost, while the great delays resulting from such appeals to this distant tribunal have left the suitors without remedy. Henceforth all these cases shall finally be adjudged within the realm, appeals being carried from the archdeacon to the bishop, and from the bishop to the archbishop, save in matters touching the King, where appeals shall go directly to the Upper House of Convocation.

The successive drafts of this important statute have been submitted to close analysis by Dr. Elton, and with some interesting results. Cromwell emerges throughout as the dominant personality; his clerks drew up most of these drafts, while he personally added some of the most important clauses and constantly corrected others. The theory of the preamble was that set forth under Marsilian inspiration by Cromwell and his pamphleteers. He also called a conference of expert clergy to approve the text before it went to Parliament, and initially he made some concession to clerical views on the course of appeals, for the clergy had a natural anxiety lest the higher ecclesiastical courts should be excluded from this field of business. Once in Parliament, however, Cromwell gained his essential points: he ensured that causes affecting the King should not be dragged through a succession of courts, but go straight to Convocation. And, as will appear, in a later Act he gave ordinary suitors an appeal even beyond the courts of the Archbishop. In general, Cromwell's drafting tended towards the elimination of moral platitudes and towards the stressing of concrete abuses likely to impress Parliament. He also appears to have prevailed upon the King to allow the removal of merely apologetic passages and of uneasy protestations against possible charges of heresy. He had no use for such qualms, such sensitivities which might betray a lack of confidence. So far as can be seen from personal corrections, Henry's direct responsibility for the drafting remained small: at one stage he indeed asserted the high claim that both the temporal and the spiritual jurisdictions in England proceeded 'from the said imperial Crown and none otherwise', but this phrase was not in fact retained. From first to last, the Appeals Act was a government measure, and in the Commons it encountered considerable opposition during the fortnight which followed its first reading on 14 March 1533. Yet according to Chapuys, this resistance was based upon mundane grounds: upon the fear that the Pope might induce other nations to ruin England by refusing to trade with a nation of schismatics. In the event, the bill passed Parliament with only one amendment of substance: that which Henry and Cromwell desired and which affected the course of appeals in the King's cases. The passage of the Act marked the complete winning of the King's confidence by Cromwell, who in the following month was openly acknowleged to be the chief minister of the Crown.

The effectiveness of this Act in relation to the immediate problem of the royal divorce found speedy illustration. In April and May both Convocations were induced to declare that it was against the law of God, and not dispensable even by the Pope, for a man to marry his brother's widow when her previous marriage had been consummated; again, that the consummation of Katherine's marriage with Arthur had been sufficiently proved. A few members of both Convocations ventured to vote against the propositions, but they were carried by heavy majorities. In all these changes, the Convocation of York did not show more signs of resistance than that of Canterbury. The attribution of superior toughness to the northern clerical proctors springs partly from Froude's imagination, partly from the misdating of Bishop Tunstall's protest against the Royal Supremacy, and the false attribution of this personal protest to the whole Convocation of York. At York, as in the Southern Province, the representatives of the clergy were safe, elderly and eminent. Both Convocations were handled by Cromwell's emissaries with tact and skill.

It is a fact of immense significance that some of the ablest clergy in the country had already ranged themselves on his side, and were doing his bidding with zeal and efficiency. On this occasion of the divorce debates, for example, the Dean of York and Archdeacon Magnus (a former diplomat and now a phenomenal pluralist) were reinforced by Dr. Rowland Lee, then Archdeacon of Cornwall, King's chaplain, Master in Chancery and Bishop-elect of Chester. Lee's subsequent letter to Cromwell admirably depicts the lobbying by which Tudor governments furthered their will in Convocation. He first had two lengthy interviews with Tunstall, the leader of the northern conservatives. When Tunstall excused himself, as a former counsel of Queen Katherine, from openly maintaining the King's case, Rowland Lee was not a little shocked. 'I am sorry to see so little stay towards the Prince's, our master's, honour by such. It is no marvel [if] strangers shall strangely censure, when we ourselves so do by him by whom we be supported, specially the thing now done. Thus I write you secretly. Would God we were of one mind, but the diversities of minds in ourselves shall hurt us.' This clerical royalist, sustained by a 'most loving letter' from Cromwell, then arranged for conferences between Dr. Edward Leghton, an Oxford scholar in the King's service, and the hesitant Archdeacon of Nottingham, who had offered to be tractable if he could be convinced by scholarship. Then Lee turned to the chief figures among the northern monks. 'The Abbot of Fountains, I trust, will be good. Now I am towards Byland, Newburgh and Rievaulx. The Abbot of Welbeck will not fail to do the best he can. The Abbot of St. Mary's also, but he is not learned. There shall be as much done as I may.' Here we may see an example of the methods by which the Cromwellian proposals so smoothly traversed the organs of Church and State. We should be wise to think rather less of the dictator with the mailed fist, rather more of the campaign-manager supported by a small but devoted band of constituency-workers. The Restraint of Appeals and the propositions in Convocation ended the legal resistance of Queen Katherine, for Cromwell had now stopped all the loopholes open to her counsel. The facts of the case were prejudged and her appeal to Rome was positively debarred. When Cranmer was licensed by the King to hear the suit, she naturally refused his summons to appear, and on 23 May he declared her marriage *ab initio* null and void.

While the parliamentary session of 1533 thus saw the final severance of the papal nexus and the arrangement of the divorce, the two sessions of 1534 produced a rush of Cromwellian legislation to complete the massive structure of the Royal Supremacy. That of January–March was signalized by four important statutes. The Act in Restraint of Annates covers much more than its title would imply. Besides making absolute the former conditional restraint of annates, it also forbids the procurement from Rome of bulls, briefs, palls, or other things requisite for archbishops and bishops. Moreover, bishops must henceforth be elected by cathedral chapters on receipt of the royal *congé d'élire*, this document being accompanied by letters missive nominating the person chosen by the King. Any member of a chapter who failed to comply became liable to the penalties of *praemunire*, while in the event of a delay of twelve days the King could appoint by letters patent. Under the same penalties, the archbishop must proceed to consecrate. It was in correct interpretation of this act that Lord John Russell wrote in 1848 to a canon of Hereford, who had said he could not conscientiously vote for Queen Victoria's nominee, 'Sir, I have the honour to acknowledge your letter of the 20th instant in which you announce your intention of breaking the law'. At the same time, this dramatic illustration of erastianism did little more than give statutory sanction to the royal control *de facto* operative even at medieval episcopal elections.

The Dispensations Act began by cutting off all payments to Rome, including Peter's pence, the ancient tribute said to date from the time of King Offa, but since the twelfth century commuted by the bishops for a mere £200 per annum. The main purpose of the act was to ensure that dispensations, faculties and other sorts of licences, no longer obtainable from Rome, should be issued by the Archbishop of Canterbury under Crown supervision. This was no academic matter, but one of daily administrative practice. Dispensations were licences either giving authority for some act otherwise illegal in canon law, or remitting the penalty for a breach. In later medieval times they had become largely a papal prerogative; they had in fact occasioned great delays and expenses, as they applied to a wide field of transactions, such as matrimony, ordination, vows, and the translation of bishops from one see to another. In transferring the power to grant such licences to the Archbishop, Cromwell was careful to forestall the possibility that the Canterbury registry might reproduce in miniature the administrative shortcomings of the papal Curia. If henceforth the Archbishop should fail to provide a dispensation upon a reasonable claim, then the Lord Chancellor would direct the King's writ to him, enjoining him under penalty to grant the dispensation, or else to explain his refusal by a certain day to the King in Chancery. This interesting statute also disclaims any intention by the King and his subjects 'to decline or vary from the congregation of Christ's Church in any things concerning the very articles of the Catholic faith of Christendom, or in any other things declared by Holy Scripture and the word of God necessary for your (i.e. the King's) and their salvations, but only to make an ordinance by policies necessary and convenient to repress vice, and for good conservation of this realm in peace, unity and tranquillity, from ravin and spoil'. It ends with the proviso that those religious houses formerly exempt from visitation by the English bishops should not now be transferred to the latter, but should instead be visited by royal commissioners. It forms in short the monument of a layman who boldly identified efficiency with lay control.

The third of these important enactments was the Act for Submission of the Clergy, which put into the statute book the promises given by the Convocations in 1532. It still retains practical force, in that it prohibits Convocation from legislating except by licence of the Crown and with subsequent royal assent—a provision recently invoked to demonstrate the illegality of regulations made by Convocation in 1957 concerning marriage and divorce. The Submission Act also brought Parliament into the foreground, with its obvious implication that the King in Parliament bore an authority superior to that of the King in Convocation. Since Henry in his egotism and theological knowledge took a dangerously personal view of his ecclesiastical supremacy, the Church of England may well owe this element of institutionalism to Cromwell. Fortunately also, Henry's successors were a minor and two women, none of them able and disposed to attempt a quasi-papal role in their own persons. In this broadening of the basis of the Supremacy, Convocation was assigned little part, for Cromwell had every intention of ensuring its subjection to parliamentary controls. Convocation henceforth lacked importance, not merely in English history but in English ecclesiastical history. A further clause of the Submission Act modified the Act of Appeals by providing for a final appeal beyond the Archbishop to the King in Chancery, who would appoint special commissioners, called a Court of Delegates, for each case as it arose.

Finally in this series, the first Succession Act vested the succession to the Crown in the heirs of Henry and Anne, making it high treason to slander the marriage, as many people were doing, or to question the succession 'by writing, print, deed or act'. The spacious generalities of this statute now form an amusing example of royal propaganda, yet its rehearsal of the horrors attendant upon disputed successions do not lack a bitter historical justification; no thoughtful subject of Henry VIII, whatever his creed, can lightly have dismissed such a possibility. Parliament is made to call to its remembrance 'the great divisions which in times past had been in the realm by reason of several titles pretended to the imperial Crown of the same'; when ambiguities allowed 'that men might upon intents expound them to every man's sinister appetite and affection . . . whereof hath ensued great effusion and destruction of man's blood'. Parliament also recalled 'that the good unity, peace and wealth of this realm . . . most specially and principally above all worldly things consisteth and resteth in the certainty and surety of the procreation and posterity of your Highness'. In these terms Cromwell gauged accurately enough the prevalent sense of the nation, the reasoning which, despite the unpopularity of the divorce, carried the people through the crisis behind their ruler. This mood was realistic: any marriage, any undisputed heir, any legal continuity seemed better than the prospect of the abyss. During the century of so-called religious wars, the English nation looked after itself much more effectively than did the French or the Germans. Behind the welter of theological and philosophical rationalization, this instinct for cohesion and social survival must surely be regarded as the recurrent *leit-motif* of the whole Tudor age.

Cromwell saw to it that the Succession Act was far more than a declaration, far more even than a threat. He included a clause to the effect that every subject of full age should take an oath to defend and observe the act. Though he cannot have planned to swear in a whole nation, he soon showed every intention of applying this acid test to eminent or potentially dangerous people. For their refusal to take this oath Sir Thomas More and Bishop Fisher went to the Tower; they accepted that part which acknowledged the right of Parliament to settle the succession upon the heirs of Anne Boleyn, but rejected the parts touching the Royal Supremacy and the unlawfulness of the King's first marriage. The story of their interrogation, imprisonment, trial and ultimate executions (June–July 1535) is marked by a very human heroism, by a cheerful acceptance, by a certain spiritual distinction which make it difficult to subject their standpoints to cold analysis. There are nevertheless some important differences between Fisher and More. In the conduct of the former there was without doubt an element of active disloyalty, justified or unjustified, towards the Crown.

The King already bore Fisher a grudge for his bold championship of Katherine and for his sympathy with the false prophecies of the Nun of Kent. This unfortunate servant-girl had been exploited by a foolish knot of ecclesiastics and taken seriously by many eminent people. By 1533 her utterances turned political to the point of threatening the King with death if he remarried. Moreover, her clerical backers circulated books concerning her revelations and planned to print them. The mildest government could not have allowed the escapade to continue, for political prophecies had always played an important part in sedition and rebellion; they were shortly to have a very large share in provoking the Pilgrimage of Grace. Though More had been relatively discreet, Fisher had on his own admission personally listened to revelations about the King's death, had thought them to be 'threats of God' and failed to report them. A long letter from Cromwell to Fisher rebuts the excuses offered by the Bishop, and urges him to avoid the real risks which in the course of a trial his admissions would present, and frankly to confess his fault to the King. There is nothing sinister about this letter; indeed, it demonstrates that if Cromwell had none of Fisher's holiness, his upbringing had at least emancipated him from such dangerous nonsense. In the end, Fisher was lucky to have his sentence commuted by the angry King to a heavy fine.

If about this same time Henry could have read the correspondence between Chapuys and the Emperor Charles V, his anger would already have reached boiling-point, since Fisher was joining in frequent clandestine conferences with the Imperial ambassador, during which the two concerted measures to thwart the royal policy. Of one such parley Chapuys writes to Charles: 'I see no appearance of these people preparing to yield to the papal censures . . . for as that excellent and holy man the bishop of Rochester told me some time ago, the Pope's weapons become very malleable when directed against the obdurate and pertinacious, and therefore it is incumbent upon your Majesty to interfere in this affair and undertake a work which must be as pleasing in the eyes of God as war upon the Turk.' Chapuys then propounds a plan whereby Reginald Pole should be put upon the throne, though he does not also ascribe the suggestion to Fisher. This was written on 27 September, 1533, and on 10 October, in another secret letter to Charles, the ambassador relates that Bishop Fisher 'advises prompt action on the part of your Majesty, such as I recommended in one of my last despatches. Indeed, not many days ago he sent me word to say that strong measures must now be taken. In the opinion of this good and pious bishop, the majority of the English nation, as I am told, concur; no one doubts but that your Majesty will take the affair in hand.'

Commenting on these passages, Fisher's recent Catholic biographer has written that the Bishop would not have taken this extreme view unless he felt in conscience compelled so to do. 'In his day such an attitude would not seem as disaffected as it would today. Violent changes in dynasties had occurred in his childhood, and the Wars of the Roses were a living memory; the medieval idea that the Emperor of the Holy Roman Empire was the ordained temporal power had been weakened, but it was not completely lifeless.' This is a commendably frank admission, yet we remain at liberty to doubt whether even Fisher framed his actions upon so antiquated a motion as the legality of armed Imperial intervention in the affairs of European kingdoms. In both the good and the bad senses, Fisher had indeed old-fashioned notions, but it is not easy to assign him a role which had seemed antediluvian even in the time of Dante. Whatever be the case, this odd situation *vis à vis* Fisher surely illustrates the strength of the Cromwellian thesis. When a man of such gifts could think about politics as Fisher did; when a Spanish invasion, a civil war, a deposition, and perhaps a Yorkist pretender, were envisaged as the means to save the nation from schism, it was no time to be casual and easygoing. A minister must be prepared either to see all these things happen, or else to strike hard at those who planned them. Fisher could make no pretences to being either a politician or a political prophet, but the imperceptiveness of Chapuys now seems even grosser. His picture of a nation of ardent papalists anxiously awaiting a lead to hurl their heretical rulers from power : this was to become the common dream of Spanish ambassadors and of English *émigrés* for many a long day. And there are writers who still think it true!

Thomas More has been too readily paired off with John Fisher. The ten years' gap between their ages, the marked divergence of their professions and intellectual activities had caused them to approach some of the basic problems from very different angles. More's memory did not hark back to the Wars of the Roses; he had been a child when the first Tudor came to the throne. He was not a theologian of international reputation, but a common lawyer and a great servant of the Crown. He understood the noble aims and solid achievements of the dynasty; in large measure he accepted the rising claims of the State; he parted only with the utmost reluctance from the path upon which Cromwell strove to hold him. If he displayed a shrewd appreciation of Henry's weaknesses, he shared with the rest of Henrician officialdom a reverence for the person of the King as well as a theoretical loyalty to the Crown. Above all, he was not, like most of the prominent oppositionists, a secret frequenter of the Imperial embassy. He had no sympathies with foreign-directed conspiracy, with aristocratic rebellions, with that complex of backward-looking causes, which inevitably exploited and thereby limited the appeal of papalism to Englishmen. On his own showing, his feeling for the Roman primacy had in early life been weak; he claimed—and so solemn a claim cannot in his mouth be regarded as sarcasm—to have been reconverted to this primacy by reading the King's own book written against Luther. Since Henry's change of outlook, More had tried his best by reading and discussion to see the royal case. He offered to swear to the Boleyn succession if he might be released from acknowledging the abolition of papal authority in England. He agreed to accept as heir to the throne anyone Parliament might choose; even Elizabeth, who had been declared illegitimate by the Pope.

Yet while More came near to sharing Cromwell's high view of the omnicompetence of an English Parliament, he felt in the last resort bound to regard it as inferior to the faith of earlier generations, to the laws of the Church, to the accepted tenets of foreign Christian countries. His loud praise of General Councils looked backward to Constance rather than forward to Trent; it seems far from identical with the new papalism of the thirties. On the other hand, his assertion that he had France on his side seemed 'rank malice' to the Duke of Norfolk and many other Englishmen, for France was still the traditional enemy. His recorded utterances make him a clearer martyr for the idea of international Christendom than for that of papal monarchy in the Church. When, however, he took his stand on the unity of Christendom, he passed completely beyond the things which a mind like that of Thomas Cromwell could accept as realities. While acknowledging the grave imperfections of the Church on earth, he yet accorded it his allegiance as a supranational authority in spiritual causes. When at his trial More at last gave up lawyerly attempts to save himself, those in Westminster Hall heard the challenge well and truly made. 'This realm, being but one member and small part of the Church, might not make a particular law dischargeable with the general law of Christ's holy Catholic Church, no more than the City of London, being but one poor member in respect of the whole realm, might make a law against an act of Parliament'. And when the Chancellor asked him if he would be considered wiser and of better conscience than all the bishops and nobles, More answered, 'I am not bounden, my Lord, to conform my conscience to the Council of one realm against the General Council of Christendom. For of the foresaid holy bishops I have, for every bishop of yours, above one hundred; and for one Council or Parliament of yours (God knoweth what manner of one), I have all the Councils made these thousand years. And for this one kingdom, I have all other Christian realms.'

Here was conservatism in its most broad-minded, its most responsible, its most attractive form, yet we may well question the extent to which it could be imposed upon the far less attractive facts of sixteenth-century history. When we pass beyond the strictly theological problems, More's case has obvious weaknesses. Some French Catholic scholars show obvious impatience at this supposed spectacle of heretical England diverging from a United Catholic Europe into an obstinate political and cultural insularity. Few Englishmen of any creed can see this as a true summary of the facts. In the first place, most of northern Europe was diverging and Spain, not England, looks to us the dangerous eccentric of the European family. Had More lived as a nonagenarian to see the Revolt of the Netherlands, whose side would he then have taken? Were Englishmen morally bound to belong to a club, the papal chairman of which was ordered in political and even politico-religious matters by the mighty Habsburg combination, by the famed Spanish infantry, by the Spanish monopoly of Mexican and Peruvian silver? And how could Spain's hold over Rome be shattered, save by transferring it to the older enemy, France? Were rulers like Philip II scrupulous to keep political and religious controls apart? Has not England performed notable services for Europe by resolutely refusing to join all those national hegemonies which have worn the sheep's clothing of international creeds? Had either Fisher or More the least inkling of the way Europe was going, or of the harsh influences which politics were to impose upon religion during the years which lay ahead? What of More's proposition, 'as London's law is to England's, so England's law is to that of Christendom'? How much sense did this make as the century developed? These are not theological questions, but they are questions of broader purport which historians need to ask themselves and others, lest the rousing spectacle of More at his trial may induce the unwary to envisage a far-sighted internationalist confronting a myopic, nationalist and insular Cromwell. If the issues of the sixteenth century were as simple as this, the tasks of its historians could be limited to mere factual research.

In examining these august offenders Cromwell did not, as M. Constant asserts, submit them to needless mental cruelty. He merely performed the functions of a Tudor minister. Extremely little personal bitterness existed between him and More. That during the period of the examinations Cromwell could be both helpful and distressed, we have More's own clear testimony. In a letter to Margaret Roper written from the Tower, More says that when he offered with the King's licence to give his reasons for refusing to answer, Cromwell pointed out to him the legal dangers of this course. 'In this good warning, he showed himself my especial tender friend.' Just as pointedly, More relates that on his final refusal of the oath, Cromwell 'said and sware a great oath, that he had liever that his own son (which is of truth a goodly young gentleman, and shall I trust come to much worship) had lost his head, than that I should thus have refused the oath'. It is an amusing example of M. Constant's handling of Cromwell that he cuts down this quotation to the phrase 'said and sware a great oath', omitting the rest and thus making Cromwell guilty of profanity instead of compassion! And so far as the treatment of the two prisoners is concerned, it was Anthony Bonvisi, an intimate friend of Cromwell, who regularly sent them delicacies, a thing hardly possible if Cromwell were deliberately subjecting them to harsh treatment.

In general it is agreed, even by unfavourable critics like Merriman, that Cromwell did not display that revengeful or passionate attitude towards opponents which so often marked the behaviour of the King. It was the latter who refused Cranmer's merciful suggestion that Fisher and More should be allowed to take a modified oath in accordance with their scruples; when M. Constant says that here Henry was 'influenced possibly by Anne Boleyn and Cromwell', he is simply indulging in unwarranted speculation. And when Rome inadvisedly raised Fisher to the cardinalate, it was Henry's wrath which sealed the fate of the prisoners. If Cromwell had little in common with Fisher, he knew More well. United by devotion to the sovereign, divided by their attitudes towards the international Church, both were fully conscious of the issues at stake, and had apparently been over them together in previous times. But for the indolence of More's biographer Harpsfield, the clash might have been far more graphically illustrated in the extant record. Harpsfield became well acquainted with their common friend Bonvisi, who, says Harpsfield, would often talk of More 'and also of Sir Thomas Cromwell, with whom he was many years familiarly acquainted, and would report many notable and as yet commonly unknown things and of their unlike natures, dispositions, sayings and doings, whereof there is now no place to talk'. There he infuriatingly leaves the matter, and every lover of history will echo the comment of More's modern biographer that Harpsfield almost deserved his sixteen years in the Fleet prison for leaving untold the tempers of these mighty opposites, as related by an intelligent observer with a unique knowledge of both.

Meanwhile, a week before the end of the first parliamentary session of 1534, the Pope had given sentence in favour of Queen Katherine. While fireworks and salvoes of cannon greeted this belated triumph of papal justice, the Roman crowds shouted 'Empire and Spain'. 'Other victories', wrote a simple-minded correspondent of the Emperor, 'have been gained over men; this one is over enemies let loose from hell.' Yet from the viewpoint of Cromwell, the gesture could not have been better timed, for it cemented his work beyond any likelihood of collapse. Unsatisfied, however, with these already remarkable legislative achievements, he elaborated throughout the summer and autumn of 1534 the top floors of the building: three more statutes passed in the session of November–December and leaving the legal edifice of the Henrician Reformation virtually complete.

To the Act of Supremacy the metaphor 'ornamental copingstone' has understandably been applied. It does not confer the Supreme Headship, but merely recognizes it as already existent; it also assigns to the Crown the power of ecclesiastical visitation. The limiting-clause, 'so far as the law of Christ allows', is now dropped. The King has assumed the juridical powers and even, by a species of remote-control, certain of the spiritual powers formerly enjoyed in England by the Papacy. The efforts of Hen-

67

rician publicists to supply theological and philosophical theories of the Royal Supremacy will soon occupy our attention, yet it must immediately be recognized that Henry, Cromwell and Parliament envisaged a Supremacy passing well beyond mere judicial and financial controls. It is true that Henry never asserted a right to administer the sacraments; he did not proclaim himself the personal originator of doctrine; he did not personally preach sermons. Even so, his bishops could not enunciate doctrines or frame liturgies except by his approbation; if he disliked a preacher's opinions, he did not scruple to correct them in public. Even in 1531, he had claimed to be head over the spiritual men of his realm and all their acts, denying any rigid boundaries between *spiritualia* and *temporalia*. In later years he spoke of himself as having committed to him the care of his subjects' souls and bodies. Some Henrician theologians told the King that he could appoint and depose bishops at will. Certainly he soon claimed to administer and confiscate ecclesiastical properties, to reform the canon law, to control ecclesiastical legislation, to try heretics in person and, above all, to visit and discipline the clergy, both regular and secular. At this moment, Henry and Cromwell did not stop to define and thereby to circumscribe the Royal Supremacy by precise definitions. They were more intent to prepare for the next steps. The sting in the tail of the Supremacy Act lay in that mention of visitatorial powers which heralded the dissolution of the smaller monasteries, a process by now certainly envisaged.

Only the simpler of the unfortunate clergy can have supposed that their liberation from the financial exactions of Rome would make them richer. If any were so optimistic, their minds must speedily have been clarified when they perused the Act annexing first-fruits and tenths to the Crown. The conditional restraint of annates had denounced first-fruits as 'intolerable and importable', an almost unique display of incaution in Cromwellian drafting, since the plan to transfer them wholesale and much augmented to the Crown must now involve a measure of embarrassment. Cromwell and his assistants made the best of a bad job and unblushingly launched upon a new preamble of high stylistic quality. In somewhat involved yet mellifluous phrases, it dwells upon the love of a faithful nation for its dread, benign and gracious sovereign lord, 'in whom dwelleth all their joy and weal', its gratitude for the manner in which he has maintained peace and unity, the great, excessive and inestimable charges he has sustained, and so to the inexorable deduction : that he should enjoy, not only the first year's revenue of every ecclesiastical benefice, but also a 'yearly rent or pension' amounting to one-tenth of all its profits, spiritual and temporal. To execute this statute Cromwell prepared in 1535 one of the most technically accomplished of his administrative programmes : that his was the directing mind can readily be seen from the streams of correspondence between him and the commissioners he appointed in each diocese. They were charged to establish the gross income of every ecclesiastical benefice and corporation; alongside this they must place allowances (*allocationes*) such as annual rent-charges, synodals, regular alms distributed under the wills of benefactors, fees of stewards, bailiffs, auditors and receivers. After the deduction of these allowances, the Crown was entitled to the net remainder of one year's income as first-fruits, and thenceforward annually to one-tenth of this remainder. Each incumbent was to pay his annual tenth by Christmas, each bishop to collect the tax for his diocese and transmit it to the Crown by 1 April in the following year.

The commissions themselves are dated 30 January, 1535. Detailed instructions accompanied them showing how the commissioners should divide into sub-commissions, each to its group of rural deaneries, how they should examine incumbents and other officials under oath, inspect registers and account-books. The precise forms to be taken by their returns were also minutely specified. They must miss no sort of benefice, but include episcopal sees, cathedrals, archdeaconries, rural deaneries, colleges, hospitals, monasteries, rectories, vicarages and chapels. In each case, the names of the manors, farms, tenants and other sources of revenue must appear; also the names of the officials whose fees counted as allowances. For the same purpose they took the names of any recipients of rents and pensions, even those of donors for the benefit of whose souls alms had been endowed. Many of these amateur commissioners of inland revenue inevitably plied Cromwell with queries about doubtful cases; he had even to settle quarrels over precedence as between the commissioners themselves. Naturally the chief task was to prevent the taxpayers from submitting underestimates of income, a difficult business, since tithes were paid in kind and a little mild collusion between incumbents and their parishioners could greatly diminish the figures. Cromwell and his henchmen did their best to prevent such evasions. They even ensured that the bishop, though usually chairman of his diocesan commission, should be the only ecclesiastic upon it, since clerical sympathies might lie on the side of the payers. The rest were mayors, sheriffs, justices of the peace, local gentry and professional auditors, all men unlikely to be restrained by excessive tenderness. In the event, the bishops strove like the rest to demonstrate their zeal. Surprisingly enough, in view of the vastness of the undertaking, the slowness of travel and the inexperience of many participants, the valuation-books were in the hands of the Exchequer by the beginning of 1536.

The great collection of returns, known henceforth as the *Valor Ecclesiasticus* or the *King's Books*, is one of the few early national surveys which can be placed without a sense of incongruity alongside Domesday Book, and a student of Cromwellian administration cannot do better than peruse one of the six great folio volumes in which it was printed over a century ago by the Record Commissioners. Contemporary taxpayers regarded Cromwell as a hard-faced fiscal oppressor; as the satirist Brinklow remarked, the Latin Papa had been translated into the English Pay-Pay. The records of the Court of First-Fruits and Tenths show that between 1535 and 1538 these taxes yielded nearly £50,000 a year, a sum not much less than half the previous ordinary revenue of the Crown. Yet for all Cromwell's vigilance, the *Valor* undoubtedly represented an underestimate of clerical incomes in the year 1535. Again, while the great inflation soon increased the nominal values of most benefices, Cromwell's less enterprising successors remained content with the *Valor* assessments. By the latter half of the century the incidence of clerical taxation was thus already far lighter than Cromwell had planned; by the time tenths and first-fruits were assigned to the governors of Queen Anne's Bounty, the burden had become negligible.

Meanwhile, reports of sedition and unrest began to come in, and before the end of the second session of 1534, a Treason Act was passed, making it treasonable to will maliciously, or desire by words or writing, any bodily harm to the King, Queen, or heir-apparent; to deprive them of their dignity, title, name, or royal estates; to publish by writing or words that the King was a heretic, schismatic, tyrant, infidel or usurper; to detain any of the King's ships, ammunition or artillery. It is still commonly maintained that this Act for the first time in English history made high treason of seditious words, yet unquestionable evidence has been adduced to show that, even in the fifteenth century, words could constitute high treason in common law. Nevertheless, members of Parliament, in 1534 not yet scared by rebellion, felt the dangers which lurked within this statute. 'There was never more sticking at the passing of any Act than at the passing of the same,' wrote a contemporary, nor did the adverb 'maliciously', insisted upon by Parliament, go far to protect suspects. Yet the heavy-handedness of the measure lay less in the risk that totally blameless men would fall into traps, than in the fact that it rendered punishable by death any denial of the Royal Supremacy.

A subsequent Act of 1536, 'To extinguish the Authority of the Bishop of Rome', not only indulged in incivilities towards the Pope (who had in the previous year deprived Henry of his kingdom and absolved his subjects from their allegiance) but made it treason on the part of any clerical or lay official, should he refuse an oath renouncing all jurisdiction of the see of Rome and supporting the Royal Supremacy. In 1539 persons going overseas to avoid penalties arising from religious proclamations were also brought within the net of treason. Altogether, these treason laws and some at least of the proceedings taken under them may be regarded as the most genuinely oppressive aspect of the Cromwellian years. Our judgement upon them must, however, depend in part upon the reality of the seditious and rebellious opposition, upon the risks of civil war and invasion, by which England stood threatened. They reflect the fears of an almost unarmed monarchy, aware of the offence it had given to conservative opinion, and anxious to nip actual sedition in the bud. Given the Reformation-policy, the readiness of territorial magnates to play with treason, and the absence of a real police-machinery, this phase of plots and legislative counter-terror was almost bound to develop. In the words of a later Cromwell, 'the necessity was not feigned'. The revolution might be legalist, but it did not know how to remain liberal. For the linking of Catholic dissent with treason the neo-feudal opposition was as responsible as the government, yet the latter had plunged into fundamental changes involving both the consciences and the interests of its subjects, and throughout the rest of the century it found itself faced with a query all too familiar throughout the long aftermaths of historic revolutions. How does a nation stop the sinister pendulum-swing of revolution versus reaction? Tudor and Stuart Englishmen had no ready answer to this question. Violence bred counterviolence, and for a century and a half the ugly dialectic continued to disturb English society.

Cromwell himself was no vengeful persecutor; he has been greatly wronged by the seekers for personal scapegoats. At the same time, one cannot imagine him as ever taking a risk in the treatment of seditious activities: neither he nor any other sixteenth-century statesman would have conceived it possible to experiment with a liberal forbearance towards conspirators and rebels, proved or suspected. Could they return to answer modern criticism, they would no doubt argue that we misunderstand the alternatives which lay before them, and that they would have conferred small benefit upon the people committed to their charge had they allowed sedition to ripen into revolt and civil war. If Sir Thomas More's and Queen Mary's attitude towards heretics cannot be judged in the light of modern western standards, neither can the treason laws of Henry VIII and the penal code of Elizabeth. Both belong equally to the sixteenth century with its mental limitations and its harsh compulsions.

The end of the year 1534 saw the legal revolution in Church and State virtually completed. Whatever be thought of the ethical and theological issues involved, it must be acknowledged a technical triumph in the field of legislation. In our long history, no changes so momentous have ever been accomplished by statute within three years. Never before had a block of legislation so extensive and so closely co-ordinated passed through Parliament. Never had one step led so smoothly to another; never had lobbying been so effectively conducted; never had loopholes for opposition been closed with such remorseless efficiency. Once again the Crown was back under business management. After the gorgeous international advertising of Wolsey and the flounderings of lesser men, the ghosts of Empson and Dudley were enjoying a belated laugh. The new managing director had severed all connection with the big continental combine: he had even presumed to make a subsidiary firm of *ecclesia anglicana*. This severance and this merger had their convenience; indeed, they defined most prophetically some of the main features of English life in the centuries to come. Even so, the spirit of the nation was too ebullient, too emotional, too versatile to tolerate

72

business-management unadorned. And quite apart from the claims of romance, the development of both Reformation and Counter Reformation were destined soon to produce some patterns uncongenial to tidy minds of a Cromwellian stamp.

Chapter Five

Cromwellian Ideas

THOSE who lack admiration for its conduct have naturally claimed that the Reformation Parliament was 'packed', and thus unrepresentative of the nation. It was no more packed, and no less so, than any other Tudor Parliament. Twentieth-century notions concerning fair representation and legitimate influence upon elections are irrelevant to Georgian Parliaments, let alone to those of Tudor times, when a large proportion of the Commons invariably consisted of royal servants and of men linked by special ties with the Crown or the chief ministers, when both ministers and independent magnates quite normally put pressure upon corporations to elect their adherents, when the sheriffs themselves frequently took a forceful hand in county elections. Readers of Sir John Neale's works on the Elizabethan Parliaments will be the first to see the absurdity of the old suggestions that Cromwell was offending against constitutional liberty in writing letters to request the election of certain individuals.

No error could be more fundamental than the notion that Cromwell was an antagonist of parliamentary institutions, the planner of a solitary despotism by the King. Such a plan, if it ever occurred to him, must have been dismissed as totally unrealistic. Under sixteenth-century circumstances, no English statesman worthy of employment would have pursued a scheme so bound to prove ineffective; no king with half the intelligence of Henry VIII would have embarked upon a course so hazardous to his survival. The personal powers of Henry VIII were extensive, yet they looked more extensive than they were. He ruled a tough and turbulent nation, which on grounds of self-interest had turned predominantly royalist, yet had never ceased to think for itself, to protect its legal and representative institutions, and even to be capable of rebellion. His task was to seize upon its prevalent mood and marshal it in the way it was going. The in-

74

ternal tension at this stage of our history did not arise between Crown and Parliament; it arose between the Crown in Parliament and the various *imperia in imperio*: neo-feudal family interests and affinities, jurisdictional liberties, and the Church seen as an independent source of jurisdiction. The monarchy was not conspicuously well equipped with its own instruments: its regular revenues were inadequate to meet any major crisis; it lacked a significant standing army or police-force; outside London it had little by way of a professional civil service. The North alone proved itself, under reactionary leadership, able to raise armed forces far more powerful than those at the ready disposal of the King. The textbook notion that Henry, by some condescending decision, 'took Parliament into partnership', means little to those who understand Tudor government. If he wanted to conduct a policy, the King had no alternative to such a partnership. Clad in the gilded trappings of arrogance and majestic affability, the Tudors had always to play to their public, both inside and outside Parliament; they had to play both to the stalls and to the gallery. When Henry said, 'We at no time stand so highly in our estate royal as in the time of Parliament', he was in part paying a compliment, yet he was also stating a cold fact.

So far as Thomas Cromwell is concerned, Dr. Elton has demonstrated the worthlessness of Reginald Pole's assertion that the minister wished to place the King above the law; he has also displayed the amplitude of the evidence which depicts Cromwell in his true character of common lawyer and parliamentarian. At every stage of his work, Cromwell set forth by precept and practice the legislative supremacy of the King in Parliament. He may be claimed as one of the greatest of our parliamentary statesmen, always provided it be remembered that the character and functions of Parliament in 1532 did not closely resemble those of 1832. It is the deceptive appearance of institutional continuity in English history which has most often lured our historians into confused thinking.

The notion of a despotic and Machiavellian Cromwell derives in very large part from the usual source, but in demonstrating the unreliable character of Pole's testimony, there is no need to vilify the witness himself, for his intentions were not dishonourable. His account of Cromwell's initial schemes was written in 1538, nine years after the chief events it purports to describe, but shortly after Cromwell had taken part in the prosecution of

Pole's relatives in England. In one passage he makes Cromwell conduct as early as 1529 a private interview with the King and with satanic subtlety tell him that kings are above the moral law. Henry is immediately convinced and promotes Cromwell (three years in advance of the actual date) to a place amongst his most intimate counsellors. The interview is not less fictitious than the alleged outcome, while Pole himself admits that he composed Cromwell's speech from sayings he had heard at various times. And while so near the topic, we may briefly review the common statement that Cromwell based his political theories and practices upon a study of Machiavelli. This also derives from Pole's account of 1538, from the passage where the writer describes the only personal interview he ever had with Cromwell. This interview had taken place ten years earlier, during Pole's last visit to England. The two were discussing the duties of counsellors, Pole having expressed the humanist viewpoint that a counsellor's first concern must be the honour and true interest of his Prince. This, alleges Pole, Cromwell ridiculed as an academic dictum of the schools. The counsellor must, in a real world, observe the way in which the Prince's will is inclined, even his unspoken desires. Armed with this knowledge, the counsellor must then find methods to ensure that the prince gets his way, while yet seeming to act with perfect virtue. Pole says he made no comment upon this impiety, but remembered it. Cromwell then belittled book-learning, yet remarked that if Pole wanted to learn from books, he himself had one by a recent author, most clever and subtle, who had not followed his own imaginations (like those of Plato's *Republic*, which after so many centuries still found no place among men) but the things which daily experience proved to be true. Cromwell then offered to lend Pole this book, since he saw 'what great danger I should run into, if I should engage in the conduct of affairs, especially those of princes, instructed only by the works of leisured though learned men, instead of learning from those who had added experience of realities to acuteness of mind'. But Pole never received the book, and he thought this was due to Cromwell's subsequent repentance of his self-revelation. That Cromwell had actually mentioned Machiavelli's *Prince* is not even suggested by Pole, who merely goes on to remark that he had later been informed by people who knew Cromwell's reading that the reference must have been to the *Prince*.

Some heavy doubts have been cast on several aspects of Pole's retrospective account of this interview. Concerning its broad tenor one need not feel totally sceptical, since it is easy to believe that Cromwell, in a characteristic mood of sardonic worldly wisdom, was guilty of baiting the complacent young humanist. Indeed, he may have said many of these things and in some sense have meant them, yet as an accurate and objective account of Cromwell's political sources and principles, the passage cannot claim acceptance. Pole did not leave the actual interview thinking of Cromwell as subject to diabolical inspiration; four years after he had left England, he was still writing to Cromwell in not merely courteous but amicable terms, and even as late as February 1537 his gentleman-usher Michael Throgmorton wrote to Richard Morison, then living in Cromwell's house, that Pole bore Cromwell a hearty affection. But then a dramatic change ensued, and for obvious reasons. By 1538 Pole was calling the minister the devil's emissary and the devil in human form; he doubts whether he should defile his pages with Cromwell's name, yet, as great bandits, murderers and parricides are named in history for everlasting ignominy, as devils are mentioned in the Scriptures, so he will name Cromwell. We also know that, when he himself finally came to read Machiavelli, Pole took the shocked view (which his English contemporaries did not share) and helped to get the book placed on the papal Index of Prohibited Books. What more natural than to deduce, amid the passions of 1538, that the English Satan must have been referring to his Italian counterpart?

The difficulties involved in Pole's story are obvious. The conversation occurred in 1528, but the *Prince* was not published until 1532. It says little or nothing about the duties of counsellors. Again, in or after 1537, Lord Morley presented Cromwell with a copy of the *Prince* and Machiavelli's *History of Florence*, recommending them as books which, even at this date, Cromwell did not know. True, Morley could well have been mistaken: it is even conceivable that Cromwell may have been sent a manuscript-copy of the *Prince* before its publication. Nevertheless, such disharmonies do not enhance our confidence in Pole's story and deductions. The upshot remains that Cromwell cannot be proved either to have read, or not to have read, Machiavelli in 1528, though the odds seem against his having done so. Paul Van Dyke suggested that Cromwell might have been referring to

Castiglione's equally famous *Book of the Courtier*, published in 1528 and certainly possessed by him in 1530. This notion has possibly received too rough a treatment by recent writers, since Castiglione contains at least one passage very close to the discussion. 'The office of a good courtier', he says, 'is to know the prince's character and inclinations, and thus to enter tactfully into his favour according to need and opportunity.' Such a passage comes much nearer the mark than anything in Machiavelli, yet even so, we are entitled to remain unconvinced, since a recommendation to read the *Courtier* as a whole would seem a cumbrous method of administering the lesson in statesmanship intended by Cromwell.

These are amusing detective-problems, yet they remain largely irrelevant to a modern assessment of Cromwell's statecraft. It has already been observed that a man so well versed in affairs in Italy, in the Netherlands and at home had little to learn about 'Machiavellian' methods from reading the *Prince*. Machiavelli might more easily have imparted to Cromwell the converse side of his teaching : the somewhat naïve idealism which inspires him to free his country from anarchy and foreign domination. And the modern readers who are shocked at Cromwell's alleged preference for Machiavelli as against Plato's *Republic* will be those who have not yet read the latter!

One further charge against Cromwell concerns his possible sympathy with the autocratic principles of Roman law. This arises from a self-confessedly vague recollection by another bitter enemy, Bishop Gardiner, who makes Cromwell quote in debate before the King the old civil law maxim *quod principi placuit, legis habet vigorem*. Any minister of the time might in a suitable context have cited this tag. Maitland's contention that England stood in danger of a 'reception' of Roman Law during the period of Cromwell's ministry was satisfactorily demolished by Holdsworth, and no viable evidence suggests a policy of 'reception' on his part or on that of the Henrician government. And whereas such opponents as Gardiner and Tunstall were Roman lawyers by training, no important figure of the Cromwellian group boasted such a background. Its chief lay members, Lord Chancellor Audley and Sir Richard Riche, Solicitor-General and Chancellor of Augmentations, were also common lawyers through and through. Cromwell himself was a parliamentarian of long standing; when his fortunes lay on the knife edge, his solution had been to re-enter the Commons. Once in power, he used statute-law to solve all the problems of the realm and the volume of parliamentary legislation greatly expanded during his ministry.

In this context it may also be remarked that historians have persistently misunderstood the ˙Proclamations Act of 1539. Amongst other things, it is true, this statute enacted that the King might, with the advice of his Council, set forth proclamations as binding upon the subject as an Act of Parliament, provided that they did no damage to estates, liberties or persons, and infringed no laws. No longer, however, can this be assigned a despotic connotation or be used to father autocratic designs upon Thomas Cromwell. No one disputes that proclamations were a common and utterly necessary instrument of day-to-day administration, both before and after the eight years during which the Act stood on the statute book. Cromwell seems, however, to have been one of those uncomfortable about their legal status and anxious to ground them upon the superior basis of statute-law. In July 1535, when Parliament was not sitting, it became necessary to prohibit the export of coin. Before issuing any proclamation, Cromwell consulted the judges, searched the statutes, and found an Act of Richard II upon which it could be based. Moreover, he somewhat nervously asked the law officers of the Crown what would have happened had no such relevant statute existed. He received the reply from the Lord Chief Justice that the King would nevertheless have been free to issue a proclamation 'of as good effect as any law made by Parliament'. Cromwell records that he was 'very glad to hear' this opinion, and the transaction displays him as one of those least attuned to the planning of a personal despotism by royal decree.

Forty years ago Mr. Adair displayed the chief purpose of the Proclamations Act as ultimately passed in 1539. This he found in its fourth clause, which lays down that conviction for breach of a proclamation must take place before a special court, consisting of the Privy Council and the chief judicial officers of the Crown, or at least half of them, while of eight named officials two must always be present. The clause thus set up a court similar to that of the Star Chamber as constituted by the famous act of 1487. If anything, it limited and institutionalized the royal prerogative. Owing, however, to the congestion of business confronting the Privy Council, this enforcement-plan failed to work, and after an attempt at amendment, the whole Act was repealed in

1547. Again, the repeal did not occur because Protector Somerset loved liberty more than Cromwell or Henry VIII; proclamations were in fact used more often and more arbitrarily by Somerset and his successors than by Henry VIII.

The state-papers and the preambles to the Cromwellian statutes also afford no ground for the belief that Cromwell was at any stage attempting to engineer a personal despotism. On the contrary, in the Dispensations Act there stands a very clear acknowledgement of the fact that King, Lords and Commons together exercised legislative supremacy. Cromwell stood in the tradition of Christopher St. German in upholding the omnicompetence of Parliament and statute-law, together with the all-embracing character of state-sovereignty which such law expressed. At his trial Sir Thomas More bravely denied this doctrine, yet the verdict of all subsequent English constitutional history has lain not with him, but with Cromwell. When Lord Burghley said there was nothing that an Act of Parliament could not do in England, he was not merely speaking in the Cromwellian tradition, but foreshadowing the orthodoxy which every modern student of our constitutional history imbibes from the classic pages of Dicey. When Cromwell persuaded the King to solve his problems by national legislation alone, the Papacy and the English clergy found themselves confronting an adversary far more formidable than a wilful autocrat: they stood face to face with what Cromwell called 'Your Royal Majesty and your Lords Spiritual and Temporal, and Commons, representing the whole state of your realm in this your most High Court of Parliament'. The facts corresponded quite closely with this official phraseology, and even the apparently foreign body in this organic structure—the Lords Spiritual—did not in fact behave as such. Almost every one of them swam with the tide, some eager, some uneasy, but only one accepting martyrdom and none embracing exile. With a certain ease and inevitability, Leviathan at last attained his full stature in England.

While the Reformation-statutes bore no resemblance to any previous programme of legislation, the campaign of propaganda which accompanied them was likewise a new and sensational development, for it represents the awakening of government to the political uses of the printing-press. Thanks chiefly to two American scholars, Dr. Baumer and Dr. Zeeveld, much is now known concerning the governmental writers and their books, yet these researches have not yet made the impact upon English histori ography and teaching which their merits demand. They have a special importance for those who seek to understand the genesis of Anglicanism. Copies are extant of nearly 50 books and editions published during Cromwell's ministry with the specific object of defending the new settlement, while in addition the press turned out a stream of proclamations, injunctions and other official material. At least 28 books were printed by the King's printer Berthelet; the rest, with very few exceptions, by London printers easily amenable to Crown influence. Conversely, the government denied the use of the English presses to its opponents. Directed in part by Cromwell himself, this propaganda swiftly responded to events. Within a few weeks of the outbreak of the Pilgrimage of Grace, at least four books were published to denounce the iniquities of rebellion. In the same year, Paul III summoned a General Council of the Church, and the royalists (some of whom had at earlier stages stressed the authority of such a Council) hastily produced tractates denying the Pope's right to make the summons. Likewise, on the overthrow of the Pole family, Richard Morison was immediately set to write a justification.

At the same time, Cromwell's publicists and the Henricians in general were by no means satisfied to write mere *livres de cir-constance* or to produce utilitarian arguments for the Royal Supremacy. They wanted also to place the new policy upon a solid philosophical and scriptural basis; they wanted, moreover, to confer upon it the respectability of tradition and support it by reference to ancient and medieval theory. Like true men of the Renaissance, they grasped for the helping hands of past thinkers, yet they could not reasonably have expected these hands to be numerous: the ancient world showed no closely comparable patterns, while medieval thought in general enshrined the very traditions against which they were revolting. Yet at least one great rebel of earlier times seemed heaven-sent for their purpose, and a lapse of two centuries had conferred upon him, if not respectability, at least a patina of tradition. His thinking could moreover claim to be based upon that of the medieval demigod Aristotle, based as closely as any work of St. Thomas Aquinas or of the upholders of ecclesiastical prerogative. By any criteria Marsiglio of Padua must be accounted one of the portents of medieval scholarship. Theologian, medical doctor and for a time Rector of the University of Paris, he belongs to those Averroist groups of Paris and

Padua which included also the chief medieval ancestors of modern physical science. He completed his work *Defensor Pacis* in 1324 and, when its authorship became known, fled to the Emperor Louis of Bavaria, from whom he accepted high offices and whose excommunication at the hands of Pope John XXII he speedily shared. If Marsiglio's book sprang from a situation analogous to that of Henry VIII, its radicalism was so massive and profound as to make Henry's contemporaries, even Machiavelli himself, look timid. To Marsiglio the nation-state, based upon the legislative capacity of its people, is not only omnipotent but completely self-sufficent for all the purposes of man in this earthly portion of his life. The clergy should be as amenable as other men to the civil courts; they are not by right judges or owners, but merely physicians of the soul, concerned with the welfare of men in the next world. They have no jurisdiction in this one, unless it be specifically derived from the State; if, for example, heresy be punished on earth, it should be punished as a civil offence. Likewise the Church lacks real proprietary rights and merely uses what the State lends it: its property is a gift or subsidy made by the nation to support public worship. If it receives tithes, it does so by kind permission of the lay authority. Ecclesiastical office also lies within the gift of the civil power, which may not only compel ecclesiastics to perform such offices, but also depose them by civil action. The ecclesiastical hierarchy is of purely human institution, bishops and popes having no *spiritual* authority which a simple priest does not also possess. In merely ecclesiastical matters, a General Council, composed of priests and laymen, has the true title to supreme authority. No Pope can claim supremacy as the successor of Peter, who had no pre-eminence over the other apostles. There is, argues Marsiglio, no reliable evidence that Peter was in Rome, still less that he was a bishop; the ecclesiastical primacy of Rome springs from the position of the city as an imperial capital. Canon law itself holds no independent validity, and papal decretals have no legislative force, unless sanctioned by the national community. The Bible, in particular the New Testament, forms the only source of revelation and of divine law; hence only scriptural beliefs are necessary to salvation.

Such doctrines as these, in some places slightly expurgated, in others reinforced by arguments drawn from the *Dialogus inter militem et clericum* (a tract arising from the struggle of Philip le Bel with the Papacy, and englished in 1533) or from later thinkers like Wyclif and the champions of the Conciliar Movement, became formidable weapons in the hands of a government which found itself in conflict with a resurgent papalism. It cannot for a moment be questioned that Cromwell and his publicists were fully abreast of the Marsilian theories and thought themselves to be adapting these concepts of the Church-State relation to the needs of their day and their country. In 1535 Cromwell's henchman William Marshall published the first English translation of the *Defensor Pacis*, and Cromwell personally lent the money for this purpose. In that same year Thomas Starkey, his pamphleteer-in-chief, made liberal use of Marsiglio in *An Exhortation to the People, instructing them to Unity and Obedience*, a book which a recent writer has also called the earliest manifesto of the Anglican *via media*. Richard Sampson and Edward Fox had already in 1533–4 published books using Marsiglio's doctrines to exclude the application of papal law to England. And it would be difficult to depict the Marsilian sovereign state more tersely than did Cromwell himself in that famous preamble to the Act of 1533 which restrained Englishmen from making appeals to the Roman courts. 'Whereas by divers sundry old authentic histories and chronicles, it is manifestly declared and expressed that this realm of England is an Empire ... governed by one Supreme Head and King, having the dignity and royal estate of the imperial Crown of the same, unto whom a body politic, compact of all sorts and degrees of people, divided in terms and by names of spiritualty and temporalty, ben bounden and owen to bear, next to God, a natural and humble obedience'. Yet the Marsilian arguments by no means remained the preserve of Cromwell's circle, for no one used them to more devastating effect than did Stephen Gardiner in his *De Vera Obedientia*.

Of the actual Cromwellian group, perhaps the most interesting was Thomas Starkey, an able humanist and former Fellow of Magdalen, who had spent some congenial years in the household of Reginald Pole at Venice and Padua. At the end of 1534 he returned to serve as chaplain to Pole's mother the Countess of Salisbury, but having approached Cromwell for patronage, soon found himself a royal chaplain. Shortly afterwards Starkey sent Cromwell an essay on the Aristotelian concept of Man and the State, recalling in the preface that it had been written at his patron's specific request. 'It pleased you to demand of me, what thing it is after the sentence of Aristotle and the Peripatetics, that commonly among them is called Policy.' This essay contained the basis of Starkey's *Dialogue between Pole and Lupset*, the book for which Starkey is now best known, but which was not destined to publication until 1871. Even if the author had not made Pole his chief interlocutor, its subject-matter would have made it unpublishable under Henry VIII. Starkey was a forerunner of the liberal 'Commonwealth Party' and entertained trenchant views concerning English social and economic evils. In proposing remedies, the *Dialogue* even went so far as to suggest making the monarchy elective on the King's death. Cromwell can scarcely have encouraged his *protégé* in such daring speculations, yet he conducted further discussions with Starkey, who soon sent him a second essay forming the core of his *Exhortation to the People*. Clear evidence shows that he redrafted the original version of this work in accordance with criticisms expressed by Cromwell and others.

In thinking of Thomas Starkey, one should certainly avoid the impression of a hack-writer paid to bolster authoritarian government and Protestantism, for anyone answering less to this formula could not be imagined. Starkey was a fundamental thinker endeavouring to conduct the controversy upon the highest philosophical level; he was not only the champion of an enlightened social policy, but a would-be reconciler of the warring parties. If anything, he showed more tenderness towards the Catholics than to the Protestants. Henry and Cromwell had placed high hopes in his ability to win over the troublesome Pole, and on the latter's violent defiance in 1536, Starkey fell into disfavour and retired to his benefice in Sussex. Again active in official business the following year, he preached to the King shortly before his early death in August 1538.

A more prolific and successful member of the group was Richard Morison, presumably known to Cromwell since his early days in Wolsey's household. Having gone to Italy to study Greek, he fell into poverty, pawned his books to the Jews and ended as a recipient of Pole's bounty, and wearing a pair of breeches lent by one of Pole's gentlemen. By 1535 he was busily ingratiating himself with Cromwell, who in the following year paid his passage home with the express purpose of utilizing his literary talents. Morison had already written his *Apomaxis*, a counterblast to the attack of the German Catholic controversialist Coch-laeus upon the divorce and the Royal Supremacy, a book which finally appeared in 1537 with a fulsome dedication to Cromwell. Morison's connection with Pole had been much more superficial than that of his friend Starkey, and on Pole's defiance he unhesi-tatingly denounced his former benefactor as 'an evil-willed man'. To Cromwell he wrote, 'I am a graft of your Lordship's own set-ting and will stand in no other's ground. Other men have but tickled the Pope. I have so pricked him that men shall say I know how to anger popes. Would it were the answer to Mr. Traitor Pole's book.' It is hard to assess the sincerity of this amusing and clever humanist. He possibly belongs to that not inconsiderable category of intellectuals whose enthusiasm for a cause finds powerful stimulous from a good salary. Nevertheless, it is easy to underestimate the influence of patriotism on such men. Morison seems thoroughly convinced of his own sincerity and, to do him justice, he continued loudly to proclaim his per-sonal loyalty to Cromwell as late as May 1540, when more pru-dent friends were silent in the face of impending catastrophe. His moment of glory had come during the crisis of 1536–7, when, closely directed by the King and Cromwell, he thundered most loudly of all the pamphleteers upon the theme of loyalty. On this theme Morison also shows himself more than a writer of *livres de circonstance*, for like Starkey he evinces an excellent grasp of the social and economic causes of popular discontent. He was also probably the first Englishman to acquire a close and perceptive knowledge of Machiavelli.

A third member of the circle was the publisher and translator William Marshall, a violent anti-papalist known to have pro-duced books for Cromwell from April 1534. The next year he borrowed the £20 from his patron in order to produce his trans-lation of Marsiglio. The total cost of this edition amounted to £34, and poor sales resulted in an action for debt brought against Marshall and his brother by John Gostwick, Treasurer of First-Fruits. Marshall then appealed to Cromwell to obtain a stay of this action and seemingly remained in business, since he pub-lished an abridgement of *Münster's Chronicle* as late as 1542. Marshall has also been suggested as the possible author of a pro-phetic scheme for a Poor Law made in 1535 at Cromwell's re-quest. More important to the minister's designs was Richard Taverner, a former member of the Protestant cell at Cardinal

College, who returned destitute from a period of study abroad and solicited help from Cromwell. In 1532 the latter persuaded the Duke of Norfolk to give him a small pension, but Taverner is called 'Cromwell's client' in 1533, and three years later he obtained his patron's nomination as Clerk of the Privy Seal. He was meanwhile writing vigorously to further the cause of the Reformation. A full-blooded Protestant, he translated Melanchthon and Sarcerius, and he lived not only to see his books burned at Paul's Cross in 1546, but also to sample peace and prosperity under Elizabeth. His translation of the Bible will shortly meet our attentions. Concerning the precise relations of various other publicists with Cromwell, we should gladly learn more: one of these was Thomas Gibson, the medical doctor who turned to printing and may have been the man warmly recommended in 1537 by Latimer to Cromwell as a cheap and conscientious publisher able to do good service in the cause. Gibson's press appears to have been almost entirely devoted to his own works, both medical and, in the cases of at least three books, anti-papalist in character. Clement Armstrong, an elderly London businessman of obvious sincerity but mediocre literary gifts, took to writing in the last years of his life (1533–6), and sent Cromwell two economic treatises, which have become well known in recent years. But even Armstrong's zeal was probably based on religious enthusiasm, for also among Cromwell's papers are his 'sermons and declarations against popish ceremonies'.

The Cromwellian writers were thus a heterogeneous body, and their leading ideas cannot easily be crystallized in a few sentences. On the doctrinal side, as Dr. Zeeveld has shown, their most fruitful concept was that of *adiaphora*, the category of 'things indifferent' and unnecessary to salvation: for example, fish-eating on Friday, pilgrimage, holy days, prayers to saints and even papal authority, as not expressly commanded in the Scriptures. Like Frith before him, Starkey derived this concept from Melanchthon and gave it classic expression in the *Exhortation*. Those who squabble over *adiaphora*, he urges, are blind children of darkness: keep to the middle path, avoiding irrational superstition on the one hand and arrogant personal opinion on the other. When readers asked whence a ruling between things necessary and things indifferent should come, Starkey told them in effect to leave the problem to Parliament. Cromwell lent his personal adherence to this viewpoint; one imagines it must have attracted him for a variety of reasons; his own cool temperament, his distrust of dogmatic priests, his ambitions to confer peace on the realm and to achieve an understanding with the Lutheran princes. Again, he can hardly have been blind to the likelihood that he and his group would more easily achieve survival in a broad-minded and tolerant climate. Yet the mingled religious and political appeal of adiaphorism was far from being limited to its originators. It appears not only in Starkey, in Morison, in Taverner, in the Ten Articles of 1536, but also in the Thirty Nine Articles (Nos. XX, XXXIV) and in Jewel, Hooker, Whitgift and other Elizabethans. It became one of the pillars of the Anglican *via media* and may reasonably be taken as an early milestone along the thorny path towards religious toleration.

All the Henrician propagandists became .in some measure Marsilians, and like their inspirer sought not merely to free the national state from papal jurisdiction, but also to limit the powers of the clergy to genuinely spiritual spheres. Approaching this latter problem with the terminology of the canon law, they transferred *jurisdictio fori* to the King in Council or the King in Parliament. This term included all the judicial, coercive and legislative functions of the Church, even the power to define doctrine. To the clergy they left *potestas ordinis*, what St. German called 'mere spiritual things': the power to consecrate and to administer the sacraments. Like the rest of the Henricians, Cromwell's group supported the transfer of powers, while specifically rejecting any proposal to ascribe *potestas ordinis* to the King. Neither the latter nor his minister desired to place such spiritual functions in the hands of any layman. Chapuys, it is true, reports that Cromwell summoned certain bishops before the Council to ask them whether the King could not make and unmake bishops, but there is not the slightest reason to suppose that here *faire et refaire* relates to consecration. So long as the King could nominate the bishops, he was not interested in consecrating them; so long as he could say how many sacraments were necessary to salvation, he had no ambition to administer them in person. Whatever the impossibility of secular despotism, once the Royal Supremacy over the English Church came to be discussed, there were inevitably those who tended to envisage it as inherent in the person of the King rather than as a function of the King in Council or in Parliament. The most alarming phraseology of this type is probably to be found in Tyndale, or, at the other extreme, in Gardiner. So far as I have observed, the outlook of the Cromwellians and of St. German is, like that of their leader, more institutional and parliamentarian. In relation to the Church as to the State, they cannot be depicted as propagandists of autocracy. They tend to retain the old, limiting concept of a Natural Law; they are not adulators of Roman law; they proclaim the duties of the monarch as loudly as his privileges, and they reiterate the solemnity of his responsibility before God.

With such canonist concepts as *jurisdictio fori* and *potestas ordinis*, writers like Starkey and Morison are not primarily concerned: these could be left to the technical experts like Gardiner and Fox, who wrote in Latin for the learned of Europe. The Cromwellians were humanists with the background of poor scholars rather than that of great officials; they were charged by their employer to write in English and aim their arguments at the reading-public and even at the masses of the English nation. Their social outlook squares with this approach; also with the bourgeois forces which had come to play an increasing part in English public life under Wolsey and, still more pointedly, under Cromwell. While these publicists denounce the sin of rebellion and urge acceptance of the existing constitutional structure, it must be remembered that in 1536 rebellion was not levelling but aristocratic in character.

Wherever one looks, the emphases of Cromwell and his associates lie upon the opening of careers to men of talent, whatever their birth. Many needy scholars found in Cromwell a benefactor, 'especially', as one put it, 'of poor men, whom you are always glad to help'. Morison appeals to Cromwell by saying that nobility and learning do not go together; later on he staunchly asserts (with Dante!) that ability and character are the true aristocracy. Starkey insists that God does not respect birth; both of them, like Cromwell himself, see the social and the religious problems of their age as demanding above all a scheme of popular education. Similarly Cranmer, another man of the people, opposed in noble words a plan to restrict the King's School, Canterbury, to the sons of gentlemen, while Cromwell, in his Injunctions of 1536, ordered rich clergy to maintain poor scholars at the universities. When the Duke of Norfolk suggested that only noblemen could keep order in the Marches, Cromwell and Cranmer headed the group of councillors who put him in his place: 'If it shall please his Majesty to appoint the meanest man . . . to rule and govern in that place, is not his Grace's authority sufficient to cause all men to serve his Grace under him without respect of the very estate of the personage?' There is obviously nothing surprising in these relatively democratic emphases when *parvenus* were themselves in power, but today, when doctrinaires so often over-stress the contrary aspects of the Reformation, it is important to realize the early strength of this fund of social liberalism on the Protestant side. Unfortunately, its adherents could convert neither Henry nor Norfolk. As for Cromwell, he laid the founda-tions of a social policy in terms of order, legality and adminis-trative institutions, but had not the time, even if he be credited with the will, to move far along the road desired by Starkey and later by the Commonwealth Party. By the reign of Edward VI, this party no longer stood unchallenged in the leadership of English Protestantism, for the more self-interested nobility and gentry had by then cashed in upon the cause and deprived it of any special claims to social idealism. The humanist clerics and bourgeois intellectuals had the best ideas, but their political influence remained as insecure and as vulnerable as that of their patron, Thomas Cromwell.

Chapter Six

Cromwell's Opponents

THE ideals and achievements of the Cromwellian policy cannot be appreciated without some understanding of the complex forces against which the minister was striving. These forces ranged from the highest idealism to the lowest selfishness and irrationalism; so heterogeneous a collection of saints, heroes, politicians, dupes and fools cannot be dismissed with a few labels and generalizations. The conservative opponents of Cromwell, so often lumped together by their admirers and their critics, differed widely on all the significant criteria: the genuineness of their religious motives; their understanding of the causes involved; their loyalties to the Tudor State; their attitudes to the menace of neo-feudalism; their views of the divorce, the Papacy, the plan to dethrone Henry VIII, the prospect of a Spanish-Imperial invasion. At no point can the religious or ecclesiastical history of the Reformation be neatly abstracted from this surrounding *mêlée* of personal, political and economic motives. During Cromwell's ministry there were many opposition-movements, but no co-ordinated opposition-party with a colourable claim to replace the King or even to choose his ministers. A common hatred of the upstart Cromwell must not be confused with a common policy, or even with a common ideal.

Apart from the cases of More and Fisher, the most purely and sincerely religious opposition arose from certain members of the two liveliest religious bodies, the Franciscan friars of the strict Observance and the monks of the Carthusian order. The Observants of Greenwich, founded by the King's father, had been his closest monastic associates, and both his daughters had been baptized in their church. In May 1534 William Peto, one of their most eminent preachers, compared Henry with Ahab, and this to his face. When one of the royal chaplains attempted a counter-sermon, he was attacked from the eminence of the roodloft by Warden Elstow, who called him one of the four hundred prophets into whom the spirit of lying was entered, and who sought to establish the succession by adultery. This again happened in the King's presence and, not very surprisingly, both friars found themselves before the Privy Council. Here they were rebuked by the lords, while, according to Stow, the Earl of Essex told them they deserved to be put in a sack and cast into the Thames. The Earl's name happened incidentally to be Henry Bourchier, not Thomas Cromwell, as Canon Dixon supposed. Elstow, more than equal to the occasion, replied that he should say these things to rich and dainty folk, who had their chief hope in this world; as for the friars, they 'knew the way to heaven to be as ready by water as by land'. At this early stage, the law of verbal treasons had not yet been framed, and the punishment of the Observants proceeded along cumbrous lines. In June the whole order was suppressed, their six houses handed over to the Augustinians, their more obstinate members sent to the Tower, and the rest enclosed in the houses of the unreformed Greyfriars. Some died in prison and many suffered banishment. Of the latter a number, including Peto and Elstow, returned to England under Queen Mary; the superb intrepidity of the former even had its reward in this world, for he survived to become a cardinal, having been suggested for the office of Legate to England.

Though the Carthusian order was more deeply divided, the majority of its members who accepted the Royal Supremacy did so under pressure and with deep misgivings. In April 1535 John Houghton, prior of their London house, together with Robert Lawrence, prior of Beauvale and Augustine Webster, prior of Axholme, denied in the presence of Cromwell that the King as a layman could be Head of the Church. With them stood Dr. Reynolds, a learned Bridgettine of Sion, and John Haile, vicar of Isleworth, who was under the influence of Sion, in its turn a house closely related to those of the Carthusian order. Subsequently tried and condemned, all five followed each other to the gibbet with heroic constancy in May 1535; a few weeks later, three other London Carthusians were similarly condemned and several others distributed to the 'safe' houses of their order. Ten went to Newgate and all died of prison-fever, save one who suffered execution. Like Fisher and More, these Carthusians stand among the most genuine martyrs for Catholicism, 'not less beautiful', wrote Froude with a flash of generosity, 'not less deserving the everlasting remembrance of mankind, than those three hundred who in the summer morning sat combing their golden hair in the passes of Thermopylae'. The details have often been recounted with justifiable horror, but it is a horror which should be directed against the insensitivity of the age rather than against individuals or parties. Protestants, Catholics, politicians and common men were equally hardened to these spectacles and equally guilty of inflicting them. It is hard to say which was the more atrocious: a butchery for treason, a burning for heresy, or the slower torments of Tudor dungeon-life. All were accepted with equanimity by an age inured both to physical pain and to witnessing its infliction upon others. Equally unattractive is the sentiment expressed by Cromwell's assistant Bedyll, when he reported that the Carthusians in Newgate 'be almost despatched by the hand of God'. This curious attitude was also shared by mid-Tudor men of all parties; it was Bishop Gardiner who wrote that by Queen Katherine's death 'God had given sentence' in the divorce-suit.

A very different ecclesiastical oppositionist was Reginald Pole, even more Italianate than Cromwell, living in comfortable exile on the Continent while helping to weave those webs of English conspiracy which strangled so many of his friends and relatives. His mother, Margaret Countess of Salisbury, was a niece of Edward IV and sister of that Earl of Warwick whom Henry VII had executed in 1499, the year before the birth of Reginald. Though the latter and his elder brothers, Lord Montague and Sir Geoffrey Pole, were thus scions of the White Rose, Henry VIII held him in affectionate esteem and paid for his education with the Carthusians of Sheen and at Magdalen College, Oxford. From 1521 to 1526 Reginald Pole continued to cultivate his mind amongst the eminent scholars of Padua; already he was cherished by Bembo and Erasmus alike. A kindly master and patron of scholars, he attracted especial attention by a strict morality and a precise religious observance then unusual in men of his station. Returning to England, he remained a *protégé* of the admiring King, who in 1527 made him Dean of Exeter. And no one grumbled when Pole continued his delightful and scholarly life in the charming house which Colet had built at Sheen. During this period, which saw his famous interview with Cromwell, he disapproved the divorce-plans, honourably refused offers

92

of the sees of York and of Winchester, and tried mildly to dissuade the King without provoking his wrath. In 1530 he took part, however reluctantly, in advancing Henry's cause in the European universities. Two years later he obtained permission to leave England for purposes of study, and spent some months pursuing theology at Avignon. As the winds of France did not suit his health and he longed for his second country, he soon returned to Padua, to his humanist friends Bembo and Flaminio.

He had not, however, slipped from the memory of the King and Cromwell, who pressed him through his former chaplain Thomas Starkey to acknowledge the royal claims. In 1536, however, he ceased to temporize, and in his book *De Unitate Ecclesiae* denounced Henry with a savagery which perhaps only cultivated men in their rare moments of resolution can attain. There lingers about the book and about Pole's mind a strange unreality, enhanced by an academic rhetoric conspicuously febrile even by the standards of the High Renaissance. We have already noted his inconsistencies in regard to Cromwell, but these are minor examples of their type. In his book he at once professes his grieved affection for Henry and accuses him of wholesale murder, sacrilege, robbery, waste, perjury, adultery and lust. Henry is worse than the Tunisian pirates, the Grand Turk, Nero and Domitian; he is worthy to have upon his tomb that epitaph of Sardanapalus, which Aristotle said was fitter for a bull than for a man. Indeed, the King was scarcely worthy of a tomb, but rather, in Isaiah's words, to be cast out from his sepulchre as a useless trunk, and as a putrid corpse to have no fellowship with his forefathers. All this Pole sincerely uttered long before he had any personal reasons for hating the King or the minister, under the absurd impression that it might bring Henry back into the Roman allegiance. More strangely still, he wrote on 16 February 1537, to the Privy Council: 'You say the Pope is the King's enemy, to which I reply thus: I dare to affirm of this Pope, whose acts I see, whose talk I often hear, that I have never heard of a single act or word of his, either concerning the King or concerning those who are in his kingdom, which did not show the affection of a father, and that indeed the most indulgent father towards his son, or the affection of a most loving pastor towards his flock'. This amazing statement he wrote on the eve of his departure to aid the northern insurrection in England, a mission which the Pope himself explained to the Spanish am

93

bassador, and which Pole's own letters show him fully to have understood. Moreover, he was later to write to Edward VI denying that he had in 1539 attempted to induce other kings to take up arms against Henry, and asserting that he had merely intended to persuade the Emperor and the King of France to use the reasoning of love and friendship with Henry. This statement has again been directly disproved by reference to Pole's own writings. We may ironically imagine the terms which certain of Pole's admirers would apply to Henricians or Protestants guilty of such inconsistencies, yet even so, we should be unjust to accuse him of deliberate untruth. He had a bad memory, a retiring and fundamentally unambitious man's distaste for an enforced political role, together, perhaps, with a self-hypnosis accomplished by the instrument of his own rhetoric. Yet this is the writer upon whose testimony, assisted by that of Chapuys, the accepted picture of Thomas Cromwell is to a quite surprising degree based.

Chapuys told the Emperor that if Pole went home, the King would make him a cardinal by the same method as he had made one of Bishop Fisher. Pope Paul III, ignoring this last unfortunate precedent, then overcame Pole's objections and made him both cardinal and Legate to England. By this time, February 1537, the Pilgrimage of Grace had already collapsed. Lack of speed, resolution and nerve had prevented Pole and his backers from leaving English history the romantic spectacle of a White Rose Cardinal Legate riding at the head of an embattled host of north country feudalists. The importance of his defiance, however little personal heroism it involved, should not be underestimated. In view of the drastic nature of the revolution, it is a surprising fact that Pole was the only eminent Englishman, clerical or lay, who took the trouble to escape abroad and raise the standard against the King. Through his known connections with the opposition nobility in England, he became a focus of papal and Spanish enmity towards the kingdom. Like the Elizabethan *émigrés*, he misjudged the situation at home, misled foreigners with his illusory authority, imperilled the lives of his fellow-believers in England, ruined his own family and terminated what little hope existed that the governmental attitude might be liberalized. Unsatisfied with casting him for this over-dramatic role, destiny had also in store for him a brief hour of glory as the spiritual husband of Mary Tudor, this too in an uncongenial world of flames and tears.

So far as concerns effective opposition to Cromwellian policy, the career of Pole has less significance than the Pilgrimage of Grace, the true crisis of the dynasty. In this great northern rising, the opposition did more than resort to arms; it showed itself able, at least in the short run, to muster a force far superior to that at the King's disposal. But for the confused minds of the rebel leaders, the fundamental class-divisions of the movement and the successful duplicity of the professional politicians, the kingdom would at this stage have fallen into bloodshed, perhaps into prolonged anarchy. The detailed events of the Pilgrimage have often been told, and they cannot become our present concern. It engulfed Lincolnshire early in October 1536, but there it died out within the month. Meanwhile, almost the whole of the northern counties had risen under the lawyer Robert Aske, had occupied York and received the surrender of Pontefract Castle, the key to the North: this at the hands of its keeper Lord Darcy, who joined the leaders. After prolonged negotiations with the Duke of Norfolk at Doncaster, the rebels dispersed early in December upon promises of reform and the offer of a free pardon. In January 1537 new risings in Cumberland and in Yorkshire— the latter led by Cromwell's former associate Sir Francis Bigod— gave Henry the excuse he had been awaiting and resulted in a total of some 200 executions, including those of Darcy, Aske and several other leaders of the main revolt. When causes are sought, the extremely voluminous records give rise to severe problems. In particular, the manifestoes of the educated leaders have been elaborately analysed, under the impression that here if anywhere the true causes of the trouble would become apparent. Yet these documents hardly begin to explain why the masses had become inflammable. As so often with mass-revolts, the major task of interpretation is to discover how far the material discontents of the people were guided into political and religious channels by doctrinaire leaders.

In the case of the Pilgrimage, economic troubles play an enormous rôle both inside and outside the 'official' lists of grievances. So far as concerns Cumberland and Westmorland, no one has ever denied that the rising was almost solely economic and social in its motives and manifestations: it was directed from first to last against enclosures and against the increased fines imposed by lords upon tenants entering upon their lands. Elsewhere in the North the same factors achieved much prominence on the eve of the Pilgrimage. In Craven in June 1535 and at York in May 1536 enclosure-riots had caused severe apprehension. Much evidence also attests the bad crops and high grain-prices current in the North in 1534–6. At York and Beverley the ancient group-cónflicts between the close oligarchies of the councils and the unprivileged townsmen had again become rampant, while the clothiers of the West Riding joined the Pilgrimage because Parliament had just laid fierce penalties upon their fraudulent practices. The North suffered from lack of coin; its towns were few and small, its middle-classes relatively unimportant, its potential resources undeveloped. The gentry, though divided by faction, had their own range of grievances. The Statute of Uses prevented their settling portions upon younger sons and crippled their power to borrow by making mortgages illegal. They disliked the treason laws and resented the under-representation of the North in Parliament. Desiring a scapegoat for every grievance, all social classes simplified the issue by blaming Cromwell; they believed in that comic caricature : bluff, good-hearted King Hal, misled by a lowborn, heretical minister.

To do them justice, Cromwell had not handled northern opinion with outstanding tact. While he had recently put the Grand Jury of Yorkshire into the Star Chamber for acquitting an alleged murderer, he had also protected a servant of his nephew from the consequences of slaying a servant of Sir Ralph Eure. But in that world of seething, unpredictable faction, the Eures became the chief champions of the Crown in East Yorkshire, while Cromwell's own friend, the puritan Sir Francis Bigod, was the chief rival of the Eures, and turned rebel. The affair of the jury certainly seems to have been by far the chief reason for Cromwell's extreme local unpopularity. Robert Aske wrote that 'the Lord Cromwell . . . for the extreme assessment of their fines, was and yet is, in such horror and hatred with the people of those parts, that in manner they would eat him, and esteem their griefs only to arise by him and his counsel.' He had also incurred hatred for the disinheritance of Sir Thomas Percy, whose brother Northumberland, the ailing and wretched ex-lover of Anne Boleyn, had just made the King his heir. The Pilgrimage was certainly a Percy rising, despite the non-participation of the Earl. Most of its leaders were Percy-adherents and the name of

were fulfilled with great expedition. Prompted by Cromwell, the King handed the translation to Gardiner and other bishops. According to a not improbable anecdote related by William Fulke in 1583, the prelates answered that it contained many faults. Well, replied Henry, but are there any heresies maintained thereby? When the bishops replied that they could find none, the royal order was immediately given. 'If there be no heresies, then in God's name let it go abroad among our people.'

Why did Henry, so bitter a critic of Tyndale, fall so readily to the blandishments of a translation made by another of his exiled Lutheran subjects? A considerable number of facts and statements combine to show the strength of the influence brought to bear by Anne Boleyn, who maintained during the brief period of her ascendancy a more genuinely personal interest in the vernacular Bible than her detractors have allowed. Again, the Coverdale version presented a proposition very different from those of Tyndale, since it contained a flattering dedication to the King and was not loaded with overt and trenchant Lutheran propaganda. As for Cromwell, he had become deeply implicated in the plan from the time he received Nicholson's letter. As Vicegerent he issued two sets of ecclesiastical injunctions in September 1536 and September 1538; while everyone knows that the latter caused English bibles to be set up in churches, it is seldom realized that the first version of the 1536 injunctions already made this command. There survive three copies of this version by the royal printer Berthelet; it orders that every parson must provide by the following 1 August a book of the whole Bible, both in Latin and also in English, 'and lay the same in the choir for every man that will to look and read thereon'. The clergy shall discourage no man from reading any part of the Bible, 'but rather comfort, exhort and admonish every man to read the same as the very word of God and the spiritual food of man's soul'. On the other hand, the laity must be gently and charitably exhorted that 'they do in no wise stiffly or eagerly contend or strive one with another about the same', but refer controversial points to the judgement of those better learned. These copies of the injunctions were printed about the middle of July 1536, but seem to have been conceived much earlier. In the previous May, Queen Anne had been executed, and by the summer Cromwell perhaps thought it unwise to press on with a scheme she had been supporting. Whatever his motives, he withdrew this particular injunction and left Coverdale's Bible to be sold privately. It evidently met with immediate success, since in 1537 the enterprising James Nicholson himself reprinted it in two revised editions.

By this time Nicholson was confronted by a formidable competitor in the so-called Matthew Bible, edited in reality by John Rogers, then chaplain to the English House at Antwerp, who prudently adapted the pseudonym Thomas Matthew. This version was first read by Cranmer and brought by him on 4 August 1537 to Cromwell's notice. With his usual promptitude, Cromwell took a copy to the King, who permitted it to be bought and read in the kingdom. By 13 August Cranmer wrote to thank Cromwell for his pains. 'You have showed me more pleasure herein than if you had given me a thousand pound, and I doubt not but that hereby such fruit of good knowledge shall ensue, that it shall well appear hereafter, what high and acceptable service you have done unto God and the King, which shall so much redound to your honour that, besides God's reward, you shall attain perpetual memory for the same within this realm. And as for me, you may reckon me your bondman for the same, and I dare be bold to say, so may ye do my lord of Worcester' (i.e. Latimer). Needless to insist, the version which commanded such phrases was also a distinctly Protestant presentation. Rogers had worked intimately with both Tyndale and Coverdale; he afterwards became a close associate of Melanchthon and held office as superintendent of the Lutheran church at Dietmarsch. In course of time, he was to become one of the first martyrs of the Marian persecution. Though a fine stylist and a sound scholar with a knowledge of Greek and Hebrew, he closely followed his predecessors, especially Tyndale, whom he preferred wherever possible to Coverdale. In the Old Testament particularly, Rogers made considerable use of two French translators. One of them was the elderly and eminent Lefèvre of Etaples, who had followed and even anticipated many Lutheran teachings, yet never broke with Rome. The other was Olivetan of Noyon, Calvin's kinsman and early inspirer, whose French translation had appeared in 1535 under Waldensian patronage. To the text Rogers added over two thousand notes, more peaceable and moderate in tone than those of Tyndale, yet owing a substantial debt to Oecolampadius and other Lutheran scholars.

Cromwell's connections with the Matthew Bible did not cease with its arrival upon the market. Its publisher was that characteristic figure of our early Reformation, Richard Grafton, a grocer of London and a merchant adventurer of Antwerp. Knowing whence favours might come, he sent Cromwell six copies and received the payment of ten pounds. Fearing piracy by his rivals, he then pestered Cromwell to licence the version under his privy seal, and to forbid any other publisher to reprint it for three years. Failing this support, he continued, would Cromwell please order every parish priest to buy a copy and every abbey six copies? His business letters, their acumen plentifully interlarded with godly phrases, read little to our modern taste, but we need not for a moment doubt Grafton's evangelical sincerity. Biblical publishers were then understandably worried men; they were compelled to invest large sums in risky enterprises beset both by powerful conservative enemies and by trade-rivals uninhibited by modern laws of copyright. The hard facts of the situation ensured that their motives must be mixed. The *naïveté* of these early Protestants appears more pointedly in Grafton's argument that the dissemination of bibles would put a stop to the religious disputes then rife in the realm!

Placed between the rivals Nicholson and Grafton, Cromwell did the fair thing by both of them. He gratified the former by licensing his Coverdale Bible, as he had now licensed Grafton's Matthew Bible. Yet the fact that no private edition of the Matthew Bible appeared may well be due to prohibitory hints or orders issued by Cromwell to other publishers. While he did not, as Grafton urged, force the clergy and the monasteries to purchase the Matthew Bible, he spurred on the bishops to force some sort of Bible upon the parishes, hence benefiting both Nicholson and Grafton, who were now competing on even terms within an enlarged official market. Already in the autumn of 1537 Latimer ordered every clerk in his diocese to obtain by Christmas a bible, or at least a New Testament, in Latin and English, and to read a chapter a day. At the beginning of 1538 a royal proclamation commanded the justices of the peace to see that the clergy preached the word of God sincerely and truly, and that they suffered the people to have the English Bible. In the subsequent months several bishops, even some of known conservative views, like Vesey of Exeter and Lee of York, issued corresponding injunctions. Alongside Cranmer and Latimer, Bishop Shaxton of Salisbury led the Reforming group and gave especially detailed directions. In this diocese, clerics with benefices valued at ten pounds or more were commanded to buy the whole Bible, while the poorer ones might rest content with a New Testament. All must read a chapter a day and learn by heart a chapter a fortnight. Shaxton urged, though he could not yet order, every parish to buy an English bible from its church funds, or from money formerly given to maintain lights before images; this copy must be chained to a desk in the nave, 'where he that is lettered may read, and other unlearned may hear wholesome doctrine and comfort to their souls'. A circular letter written by Cromwell to some or all of the bishops about the spring of 1538 indicates the degree of pressure he was bringing to bear in this same direction. He hears that the King's ordinances are being remissly observed in the dioceses and commands the bishops to lay forth the English Bible openly in their houses. The parsons and vicars must be made to provide copies at their own cost for the parish churches, so that every man by free access to them may be the more apt to understand sermons or scripture and to instruct his family at home. In addition, the bishops must make their clergy exhort the laity to read the Bible in the spirit of an instruction which Cromwell is enclosing: this instruction is to be sent out to every parish priest, together with a date, appointed by the bishop, before which the English Bible must be laid forth in every church. No particular edition was prescribed, and hence, under this purposeful directive, the existing editions of both the cheaper Coverdale Bible and the dearer but better Matthew Bible were no doubt rapidly exhausted. Immediate and general compliance with this order should not, of course, be assumed. It is known, for example, from visitation records of the Lincoln diocese that in the autumn of 1539 many churches still lacked bibles, either because copies had become unobtainable, or because of slackness, apathy and distaste on the lower levels.

For some time, Cromwell had been planning an authoritative edition of the English Bible. Early in 1538 he decided to entrust the revision to the safe, moderate Coverdale, and the printing to Grafton and his partner Whitchurch. These latter were men of standing, and may have been known to control more capital than Nicholson, or other possible publishers. In the event, the making of this Great Bible was attended by some sensational developments. On technical grounds, the Vicegerent chose Paris as the place of printing, since, in his own words to the French ambassador, 'printing is finer there than elsewhere, and with the great number of printers and abundance of paper, books are dispatched sooner than in any other country'. As he was to learn, there were also circumstances of a less favourable sort. At the request of Henry VIII, King Francis licensed Grafton and Whitchurch to print the Bible both in Latin and in English with any printer in France, and to transport it to England, provided it contained no 'private or unlawful opinions'. The partners consequently transferred to Paris, where they lodged with their printer Regnault, and on 23 June 1538, they wrote to tell Cromwell that they were 'entered into your work of the Bible' and to send him the first printed sheets. They intended to print two copies on vellum, one for the King, one for Cromwell: they are probably the two now surviving at St. John's College, Cambridge, and in the National Library of Wales. Already at this date, Grafton and Whitchurch asked for any financial help Cromwell could give them; they also feared danger from the papists and begged Cromwell to defend them by sending letters to the English ambassador in Paris. Ironically enough, the latter was Bishop Gardiner. In August and September further letters report steady progress. In October Edmund Bonner had replaced Gardiner at the embassy and reported 'a stay made at Paris touching the printing of the Bible in English'. On 13 December the publishers were trying to send Cromwell some of the printed sheets through Bonner, but four days later the blow fell when the Inquisitor-General of France forbade the continuance of the work and summoned Regnault before him. Grafton and Whitchurch, glad to escape, fled to England. On 31 December Cromwell told the French ambassador that he had personally sunk £400 in the enterprise. The book, he argued, could not possibly spread heresy in France, since its text was a mere word-for-word translation to help Englishmen who knew no Latin. He besought the King of France to allow the printing to continue, or at least to agree that the unfinished books should be sent into England. After much delay and palaver, the presses, type and workmen of Regnault were permitted in February 1539 to be transferred to England, where the work was duly completed. On his return to Paris, Grafton succeeded in salvaging four great vats of printed sheets, which a corrupt French official had quietly sold to a haberdasher for lining caps, instead of obeying the Inquisitor and consigning them to the flames in the Place Maubert.

The suggestion was made by A. W. Pollard that the French

intervention was political rather than theological in purpose, but this notion is thoroughly disproved by contemporary evidence, which also reveals pressure arising from Rome and from English conservatives anxious to interrupt the printing in Paris. Foxe blames Gardiner for secretly backing the attempt to destroy the Great Bible, but here one expects violent prejudice and fails to find any solid support for the assertion. After Cromwell's time, it is true, Gardiner tried to get the Great Bible rescinded. As for Bonner, he apparently did all in his power to help Grafton recover what he could from the *débâcle*. Whatever Bonner's reactionary zeal in later years, Foxe's jaundiced view that he was guilty of duplicity during these exchanges cannot be maintained, for he was at this time a zealous Cromwellian who freely acknowledged that he owed everything to the minister. Not only did he show himself the dutiful ambassador, but as bishop of London he hastened to place six copies of the Great Bible in St. Paul's, and was among the first bishops to order that the Epistle and Gospel should be read at high mass in English. On the other hand, it is difficult to comprehend the minds of those ecclesiasts who attempt to depict the conservative majority of the bishops as burning with zeal to translate the Bible, yet mysteriously prevented by sinister forces. Occupied by heavy duties, deterred by a perfectly intelligible caution and worldly wisdom, anxious to wrap up explosive controversial words in Latinized wadding derived from the Vulgate, they were the last agents to undertake the task. For good or ill, the early history of the English Bible derives from the militant Protestants and from their political backer Cromwell. We cannot at once blame them for the controversies they aroused and deny them the initiative in a great experiment. Even the role played by Cranmer in this act of the drama seems a little ambiguous and confused. His sense of the urgent desirability of a good translation and his active support for the Matthew Bible cannot be questioned, but even here he seemed curiously unaware that it derived overwhelmingly from Tyndale, who had been condemned as a heretic after Cranmer's own promotion to the see of Canterbury. Again, his plan to divide out the translating of the New Testament between ten bishops of uneven scholarship, and still more uneven doctrinal partisanship, would generally be described as unintelligent had it come from a lesser man. This point was granted even by Canon Maynard Smith, whose reverence for the bishops and dislike of

Cromwell led him into some inaccuracies and underestimates regarding Cromwell's share in the Great Bible.

The first edition of the latter was completed in April 1539, but some substantial changes appear in that of April 1540, which, furnished with a preface by Cranmer, became the standard. Before the end of 1541 no less than seven editions had been published. Cromwell's own further dealings with the project were highly necessary to maintain the just interests of the publishers. In November 1539 Cranmer wrote that Berthelet and Whitchurch had paid him a visit and stressed the heavy cost of publication. Berthelet was not a partner of the firm, but probably attended as an independent expert to advise Cranmer. On his advice, the Archbishop wished to fix the selling price at 13s. 4d., but Whitchurch had told him that Cromwell would prefer ten shillings. The publishers thought this latter price low, but would accept it, provided Cromwell would grant them a monopoly. The minister did the next best thing and immediately obtained a patent from the King forbidding any printer to print an English Bible for the next five years, unless deputed by himself. There is no evidence that he used this monopoly for personal profit: in fact, in April 1540 he allowed Berthelet to print an edition independently of Grafton.

The character of the Great Bible certainly justified Cromwell's choice of his former associate Coverdale. As his basis, the latter took the Matthew Bible, which was a compound of his own earlier work and, to a larger extent, that of Tyndale. This he corrected with the aid of two very sound guides: Sebastian Münster's edition of the Hebrew Old Testament, published along with a Latin translation in 1535; and the New Testament of Erasmus. The chief innovation was intended to placate the Catholic addiction to the Vulgate. Where the latter added anything to the Hebrew or Greek text, Coverdale now inserted the addition in smaller type and in brackets. This very significant step cannot have been taken except by Cromwell's consent: it may well represent an original suggestion from the minister, since Coverdale himself was well aware of the small authority possessed by these additions and cannot have welcomed them, either as a Protestant or as a scholar. Cromwell himself had a statesman's awareness of the gratuitous offence given by Tyndale's and Rogers' presentations of the Scriptures. Their prologues and notes were calculated to alienate conservative opinion, and a Bible which repelled a section of the nation could not possibly play the exalted part within the State-Church for which he had cast it. In the event, the mature methods of Coverdale were admirably adapted to an 'official' version. Though he continued in the Great Bible to reject such words as 'church', 'priest' (for a Christian minister), 'charity' and 'penance', he also avoided some of the expressions which had aroused Catholic feeling. In general, his work is sober, exact and restrained, toning down at some sacrifice of vividness the asperities and inconsistencies of Tyndale.

To assess the ultimate results of all these versions would lead us far beyond our present subject. No English Bible, however carefully presented, led to any immediate or easily-won spirit of charity. On the one hand, we soon encounter fanatical Protestants who would not stop reading the Bible aloud in church, even during service-time. On the other, we find Queen Mary's government burning copies of the Great Bible, trying to roll back the years and withdraw the English scriptures from the laity. Again, according to that able but noisy Protestant Thomas Becon, in many parishes the laity remained quite apathetic in these matters, 'so little pleasure have these filthy swine and currish dogs in that most sweet and singular treasure'. Yet it is of the nature of all such stories to represent the exceptional: concerning the quiet and steady mental processes at work throughout England during the two decades which followed official acceptance of the English Bible, records are largely and inevitably silent. In view of the outcome, there can be little doubt that the Great Bible played a major part in the gradual permeation of English society by scriptural habits of mind. What Cromwell persuaded the King to give could not be effectively withdrawn by any successor, even by Church and State acting in conjunction. Of the rivers which England crossed during the momentous years of Cromwell's ministry, this one seems in retrospect the widest and deepest of all.

The remainder of Cromwell's biblical activities may be briefly recounted. Some time in the year 1539 there appeared yet another translation: that of the barrister Richard Taverner. Details regarding its backers are unknown, yet since the translator was among the most vigorous of Cromwell's team of pamphleteers, and since the publisher Thomas Berthelet was the King's printer, the work must have proceeded with the full allowance, and probably with the active support, of the Vicegerent. Like the Great Bible, Taverner's version provides a revision of Matthew, though one of a much less painstaking character. Taverner knew no Hebrew, but he was a good Greek scholar, adhering so literally to the Greek text that he sometimes fell into obscurities. He did not, however, lack literary initiative and often invented expressions which found their way at last into the Authorized Version. Taverner himself was a thoroughgoing Lutheran, and it may have been at Cromwell's request that he omitted Tyndale's prologue to *Romans* and other ultra-radical embellishments which had remained in the Matthew version.

Though Archbishop Cranmer's contributions cannot be regarded as of pre-eminent importance, a preface by him was submitted for Cromwell's approval and then placed in the various editions of the Great Bible from April 1540 onwards. In consequence, the latter often received, absurdly enough, the title 'Cranmer's Bible'. Yet the musical English and charitable spirit of this preface earned the many commendations since bestowed upon them. With a grace of style beyond the reach of his English contemporaries and a liberal foresight greater than that of his episcopal colleagues, the Archbishop takes a characteristically Anglican view of the function of the Bible. Most of the Scriptures, he urges, may be understood by simple men, since their authors wrote to instruct and not to indulge their own vainglory. Nevertheless, they contain hard passages, and from these the plain man is more likely to derive enlightenment by consulting his parish priest, or a preacher, than by propounding them for the subject of an ale-house wrangle. The popularity of this latter primrose path to scriptural knowledge had already attracted the attention of the government. By a proclamation of April 1539 no one except a beneficed man or university graduate was allowed to expound the Bible or to read it aloud in church. This month saw in fact the beginning of a strong conservative reaction unpalatable to Cromwell, but there is no proof of his own hostility to this not very oppressive safeguard. He cannot have shared the King's doctrinal alarm, but as a statesman he feared the internal disunity which arose from doctrinal strife and faction. In opening his last parliamentary session on 12 April 1540, he made a moving plea for a concord which should triumph on the one hand over the 'temerity and carnal liberty' of the gospellers and on the other over the 'inveterate corruption and superstitious obstinacy' of the conservatives. Hence arose quarrels and commotions most detestable to all good Christians. They called one another papist and heretic, miserably abusing the Holy Word of God which the King had permitted them to read in the vulgar tongue. They turned God's gift, now into heresy, now into superstition. The King favoured neither side, but professed the true faith of Christ. He desired to establish the rule of the Gospel, to separate pious from impious ceremonies and to eradicate disunity by enforcing penal laws. Cromwell then went on to announce Henry's plan to draw up the *Institution of a Christian Man*. This speech foreshadows in striking degree Henry's own much-vaunted last speech to Parliament. It had already become painfully obvious that, whatever its future advantages, free access to the Scriptures had failed to produce any immediate foretaste of Isaiah's millennium, when the wolf should dwell with the lamb and the lion eat straw like the ox.

Why did Cromwell show this pertinacious and creative furtherance of the vernacular Scriptures? His critics are as usual ready with their simple answers. 'His main object', writes an eminent clerical historian 'was to destroy the power of the clergy, and thought that the best way for doing so [*sic*] was to concentrate on the Bible rather than on the altar. Anyone could read an open Bible for himself, but no one but a priest could celebrate Mass.' This may well be a boomerang likely to hit the champions of medieval ecclesiasticism hardest. If mere Bible-reading helped to destroy certain types of clerical power, perhaps they were best destroyed. Even so, to the Church as understood in the later Middle Ages, the Bible presented two challenges. It pointed obvious contrasts between the intricate legal, coercive, liturgical, economic and architectural apparatus which the Church had developed, and, on the other hand, the unaffected simplicity which marked the lives of Jesus of Nazareth and the Apostles. Again, the Bible had much to say about the controls exercised by kings over a national religion, but it said extremely little about the Papacy and the bishops.

All this admitted, I find the merely secular and destructive Cromwell, the Biblical *saboteur*, a little too simple for the known facts. Must the unfortunate man never be allowed a motive outside the straight role assigned him by Gairdner's Tudor saga? One whose Biblical interests long antedated his power to turn them to political ends need not be denied a belief in the educative power of the Scriptures for a new type of Christian society. And if he really believed that the English Bible would finally destroy the influence of the priesthood, this must have been the greatest of all his miscalculations! Even in Cromwell's circle there were not wanting men like Sir Francis Bigod, who foresaw the new type of clergy which the Bible and the pulpit would produce. Evidence exists in plenty to show Cromwell's real dislike for the unscriptural accretions which had become so prominent in the medieval church; for men of his stamp this attitude was presumably based upon logic rather than upon sensibility. To change the basis of clerical authority, to maintain the momentum of reform and rationalization, to render impossible a reversal of the statutory changes: these ideas, or some very like them, must have occurred to so intelligent and incisive a mind, but it seems to me difficult to relegate them all to a purely political sphere. The whole essence of the situation lay in its lack of these neat 'religious' and 'political' categories. Cromwell was no theological innovator; despite his reputation as arch-heretic, he made no spectacular departures from orthodox doctrine. Even so, his sympathies lay with the near-Protestant Henricians such as Cranmer and Latimer, who stood decisively and disinterestedly for the policy of the open Bible. In Cromwell's mind, if I conjecture aright, the policy had some individual connotations. It was most likely related to his notions of efficiency in Church and State. And since Erasmus had come to dominate the educated minds of Europe, an 'efficient' Church could not be wholly divorced from the concept of the Bible as educator of the common man.

Chapter Eight

The Dissolution

IN January 1535 a grandiloquent commission appointed Thomas Cromwell Vicegerent, Vicar General and Special Commissary to exercise all jurisdiction inherent in the Supreme Head of the English Church. It permitted him to appoint deputy-commissioners at will, gave him and them power to visit all ecclesiastical institutions, and make enquiry concerning the conduct of the clergy, 'even if they shine in archiepiscopal or episcopal splendours'. They might punish the culpable by deprivation, suspension or sequestration, control all synods, chapters and convocations, preside over the elections of prelates, cite and coerce all subjects of the realm in causes ecclesiastical, receive the surrenders of churches, and in general exercise the full plenitude of ecclesiastical power. This is an astonishing document; it enlarges even upon those grandiose papal commissions to Wolsey which seem to form its model. Cromwell's new titles, themselves borrowed from ecclesiastical usage, are employed rather loosely and interchangeably in subsequent documents; sometimes he is simply called Vicegerent.

The most immediate purpose of the commission was to empower its recipient to visit the religious houses, a partial suppreson of which had been for some time adumbrated. As early as February 1532 a new-style secularization had been executed when the canons of Christ Church Aldgate, their finances in a hopeless muddle, surrendered to the King. The latter assumed their properties by statute and, unlike Wolsey in former years, made no pretence of devoting them to charitable and educational purposes. In March 1533 Chapuys understood Henry to say that he was determined, and bound by his coronation oath, to unite to the Crown all the goods which churchmen held of it. At this stage also, the small but reputable Observant Order defied the King and suffered dissolution. During 1534 Chapuys twice suggested the imminence of a more general attack; he even credited Cromwell with a plan for distributing ecclesiastical revenues amongst the gentry in order to gain their support. In the autumn parliamentary session, a scheme of unparalleled radicalism became the subject of memoranda now among the state-papers. It suggested a system of salaried bishops with their former temporalities transferred to the State; the King to have first-fruits, half the incomes of cathedrals and collegiate churches, and a third of every archdeaconry. Monasteries with less than thirteen inmates were scheduled for confiscation, while from the larger houses sums proportionate to the number of religious would be assigned to their upkeep, the surplus being presented to the King. The authors of the plan are unknown, but it was probably one of those accorded serious thought by Cromwell. Whatever its obvious merits as compared with that ultimately adopted, its political implications must have been considered too dangerous. It contravened the principle *divide et impera*. In particular, Cromwell cannot have relished the prospect of driving the hitherto compliant bishops into opposition, and thus introducing rancour into Parliament, where episcopal influence and voting-power retained importance. So far as the secular clergy were concerned, the safe step was not such a confiscation, but rather the exploitation of their large taxable capacity.

One cannot seriously question that the monastic dissolutions were primarily based upon the financial ambitions of the government. Those who thought more sentimentally than Cromwell may indeed have felt many other motives. To make other kings envy, admire and conceivably imitate England; these were thoughts which seem to have suggested themselves to Henry's mind. Cromwell himself had no love for monasticism. Here he typified both the merchant classes and the civil service: while we cannot, despite his dislike for incontinent priests, credit him with sensitive moral repulsions, his tidy, efficient mind was doubtless repelled by the ample measure of disciplinary and administrative chaos which struck all observers of the monastic scene and which had occupied so large a share of his own energies. In his version of Utopia, there can have been no place for monasticism. However elaborate the injunctions he issued on the eve of dissolution, he cannot have entertained serious schemes of monastic reform. The absence of any such schemes emanating from either clerics or laymen remains a striking feature of the last phase of English monastic history: it betokens a general discouragement extending far beyond men of Cromwellian outlook. Yet even in 1534, the new Royal Supremacy did not in itself necessarily demand a general dissolution of the monasteries. Whatever Romish inclinations were attributed by greedy or prejudiced enemies to the religious orders, they did not undergo suppression because of any special devotion or loyalty to the Holy See. Apart from the attitude of a few Carthusians and Observants, this was the last charge which could justly be brought against English monks as a whole. It is again tempting to detect in the dissolution a far-seeing plan to bind a great body of aristocratic and middle-class purchasers to the Crown, the Royal Supremacy and the new régime in Church and State. This notion, which certainly suggested itself not only to Chapuys but to some of the purchasers, cannot have escaped the mind of Thomas Cromwell. The latter stood in no position to forecast, even in his own mind, the amount of property which the Crown would need to alienate over future years in order to meet current necessities. Nevertheless, he allowed the alienation of an extremely small part of the monastic lands between 1536 and his fall, despite the unprecedented government-expenditure of those years. Nothing seems less likely than that he would have approved the reckless sales which marked the years 1543-7 and which may have accounted for almost two-thirds of the monastic lands.

From the time of Cromwell's entry, there existed every inducement to undertake a capital levy of heroic proportions in order both to meet short-term needs and to endow the Crown in permanency with the financial keys to strong government. Cromwell provided good management and began to acquire some departmental surpluses, but the economical days of Henry VII had gone beyond recall. The Reformation Parliament proved stingy with hard cash; the customs revenues were declining; military equipment was becoming more elaborate; inflation steadily increased the cost of fortifications, ships and palaces. In the year 1533 the northern marches cost the Crown nearly £25,000; in 1534 the Geraldine rebellion cost £38,000 more than the Irish Government could produce; in 1536 the Pilgrimage of Grace cost £50,000 to suppress, and in the following years the constant threat of invasion forced Cromwell to find very large sums for levies, fortifications and the Navy. In Tudor times the price of security was always higher than Englishmen were prepared to admit and never more so than in the later years of Henry VIII. If in the event the monasteries made the supreme sacrifice, many other interests in the realm, especially the secular clergy, had since 1531 been subjected to unprecedented grants and taxes. After Cromwell's time the bishops' lands were to be noticeably diminished by a series of one-sided deals with the Crown. Insofar as it seemed politic, even the laity were by no means neglected. Numerous gentle families were gouged by the system of wardships; profitable attainders crowded in from treasons, real or alleged; the ample Percy lands were assured to the King. Yet all these sources could not be made to yield a windfall of the size demanded for current problems and for endowment. For such a levy, where else could one turn than to the rich, defenceless, not very popular and—as it seemed to men like Cromwell—useless, decadent religious houses? The financial and political reasoning involved a simple process of *reductio ad absurdum* familiar to our own social-democratic minds. Englishmen have seldom proved slow to discover moral reasons for policies of material expediency, and the moral reason for regarding the political lightweight as the social irrelevance suggested themselves to Tudor minds as readily as to ours, and with even less conscious hypocrisy.

The general visitation of the monasteries began in July 1535 and lasted into the early months of the following year. Both by modern and even perhaps by contemporary standards of fairness, its conduct lies open to grave criticisms, and these, unlike so many others, may quite justifiably be levelled at Cromwell in person. He chose the visitors, supervised their work and was obviously concerned to produce a condemnatory document. On the other hand, enraged observers have too frequently applied the standards of modern royal commissions to a world where neither royal officials nor monks bore much resemblance to their present counterparts. A manuscript of the 86 articles of enquiry given to the visitors exists, with corrections in Cromwell's own hand. He no doubt also drew up the 25 injunctions to be given to the monks and nuns, though here he allowed additions at the discretion of the visitors themselves. These two documents have been denounced as a plan to make monastic life intolerable and to break the whole system by demanding impossible standards of loyalty and discipline. Yet apart from the injunction confining the religious to the precincts of their houses and forbidding them to receive visitors (one which, at least as a temporary measure, should not have worried those of genuine vocation), there is little or nothing in the injunctions which cannot be paralleled in those of innumerable episcopal visitations. While Cromwell can be credited with no serious scheme to reform monasticism, he cannot justly be charged with seeking to crush it by excessive disciplinary demands.

The visitors employed by him were all lawyers, either clerical or lay, with no admiration for the religious life. Dr. Richard Layton, Archdeacon of Buckingham and later Dean of York, was a garrulous cleric from whom the grosser tales mainly derive, but who nevertheless proved somewhat lax in imposing the injunctions upon the monks. His colleague Dr. Thomas Legh, a narrow-minded, legalist Cambridge don, would have none of this leniency and reported it to Cromwell, whereupon Layton countercharged Legh with arbitrary methods. With his 'satrapic countenance' and an arrogance of manner which offended his own cousin, the famous Bishop of Lichfield, Dr. Legh seems the least likeable of the visitors. He preserved, however, a certain reputation for impartiality and took trouble to obtain good pensions for certain prominent monks. A third visitor, Dr. John London, had in former times figured as a staunchly conservative Warden of New College, active in suppressing early Protestantism at Oxford. In later years he displayed equal zeal in enforcing the reactionary Six Articles. While he offended the Protestants by such actions, his disbelief in relics irritated old-fashioned opinion. Dr. London thus earned a bad press from both sides, and gave both a splendid theme for moralization by dying a few years later in the Fleet prison. Nevertheless, his letters to Cromwell show more signs of genuine concern for the expropriated religious than do those of his associates. One of his fellows at New College, Dr. Bedyll, also took part, as did Dr. John Tregonwell, another conservative in religion and destined to enjoy high favour in the days of Queen Mary. Dr. John ap Rice has been rightly described as 'a milder version of Dr. Legh', and should not be confused with his colleague Dr. Ellis Price, who operated only inside Wales and who, with that liberality of outlook which had long marked the Welsh clergy, took his mistress with him on progress. The houses of friars were visited separately by compliant members of their own orders like Richard Ingworth, suffragan Bishop of Dover, and Dr. Edward

Baskerville, yet another conservative, who under Elizabeth fell into trouble by refusing the Oath of Supremacy. In general, however, the unlucky fates alleged by Spelman to have befallen the buyers of monastic properties did not extend to Cromwell's monastic visitors, all of whom, except Dr. London, ended their lives in prosperity.

All these men must have been well aware that Cromwell expected their reports to give Parliament and public opinion an unfavourable picture of monastic life, and any visitors with moderately elastic consciences could easily satisfy this expectation. Without burdening their souls with gross fabrications and falsehoods, they could accept every accusation or piece of gossip. If tongues had wagged readily at any normal episcopal visitation, they could well be expected on this special occasion to wag with even greater malice. The monastic world was already disintegrating fast; morale was low, and every temptation existed for the less worthy to curry favour with the visitors. And even one or two monks with strong grudges could provide sufficient material for a damning report upon a house. Again, the too familiar mixing of monastic with lay society now had its nemesis. Unlike the bishops in the past, the Cromwellian visitors took notice of accusations from persons not members of the community concerned, and in the immediate neighbourhood there were always lay people who could be relied upon to supplement, accurately or inaccurately, the element of scandal. For visitors who had no wish to present a balanced picture, it was all too simple: one had merely to select the shade of grey which seemed acceptable. The haste with which these agents operated was admittedly often no greater than that displayed by many bishops in normal visitations, yet in neither case can a real sifting of alleged offences have been possible. The smaller monasteries of southern England having been visited by October 1535, Layton wrote to Cromwell that 'there is neither monastery, cell, priory, nor any other religious house in the north, but Dr. Legh and I have familiar acquaintance within ten or twelve miles of it, so that no knavery can be hid from us in the country'. They were consequently sent into the northern counties and perambulated them with such amazing expedition as to raise doubts whether they could even have been present at all the places claimed. Whatever their physical movements, they knew that Cromwell wanted the report by

February 1536, so that a dissolution-bill could be duly supported on the assembly of Parliament.

In passing judgement upon this cheap and nasty visitation, it seems reasonable to mention one or two slightly mitigating factors usually omitted amid the vociferous condemnations levelled against Cromwell and his hirelings. In matters of politics, justice, administration and religion, the age lacked that measure of balance and fair play which has more recently come to mark liberal western thought and behaviour. Just as controversialists, even naturally generous men like Thomas More, heaped un-measured contumely upon their opponents and could admit no ounce of good in them, so juries convicted unpopular defendants upon flimsy evidence, so litigants ascribed every subtle malice to their opponents, and so officialdom took the blackest possible view of individuals or of institutions it proposed to attack. If Legh and Layton were by our standards grossly unfair to monasteries, so were the bishops to Lutheran or Lollard groups. Again, the reports are not all unfavourable; Layton, for example, reported well on Durham, and Ap Rice upon Lacock. Likewise, in the very few cases where we can place a recent episcopal visitation along-side the *comperta* of the Cromwellian visitors, at least some of the latter's charges are shown to have been quite accurate. This is true of certain Yorkshire houses, where Archbishop Lee had recently exposed various of the offenders noted during their lightning tour by Legh and Layton. As already suggested, independent evidence shows that a number of houses deserved lurid reports, nor do these impressions rely solely upon episcopal en-quiries. A contemporary letter of the Abbot of Warden about ignorance, violence and vice amongst his own monks does not, for example, make pretty reading. Again, the many charges of homosexuality made (especially in the North) by Legh and Layton may well be multiplied through malice, yet a number of such cases do occur in bishops' visitations and other respectable sources. That such offences sometimes arose in celibate but poorly-disciplined and ill-selected communities may surprise mid-twentieth century observers a trifle less violently than they used to surprise our Edwardian antiquaries. As for the superstitious relics preserved in monasteries, these were in fact very numerous, if on the whole very harmless. The women at Arden, for example, made offerings to the image of St. Bridget for their sick cows; others venerated the Virgin's milk at Clementhorpe or thought the girdle of St. Bernard at Newburgh helped those in labour. Such white magic was offensive to people who wanted a Christ-centred Christianity, yet it must have comforted many a poor creature and in many cases might well have been left to wither slowly in the sun.

The text of the Act of 1536, which dissolved religious houses with incomes under £200, displays some questionable features, notably the assumption that the line between 'vicious, carnal and abominable living' and adequate performance in religion could be drawn at this particular financial level. On the other hand, its provisions did no great violence to men and women of genuine vocation, and had it come twenty years earlier, it might have formed a prelude to genuine reform. The abbots and priors received very adequate pensions, especially in view of the fact that, on the average, they had only been presiding over miniature establishments of four or five persons. Some went to study at the university; some took benefices in addition to their pensions. As for the male rank and file, they were offered alternatives: either to receive 'capacities' allowing them to leave religion and serve as secular priests, or else to accept transfer to one of the greater houses of their respective orders. No complete statistics survive to indicate the proportion of those with weak vocations who took the former course. It was undoubtedly large. Of the 42 monks and canons in seven Sussex houses, no less than 38 took capacities. The Augustinian canons, the largest group in England, had even in normal times commonly served the parishes appropriated to their houses and so tended easily to assume the status of secular priests. On the other side, the majority of the Cistercians appear to have taken the opposite line: at Stanley all the monks desired to remain in religion, being transferred to Beaulieu and other Cistercian houses of the region. The prospect of transfer provided in itself a test of vocation.

As may be seen from their surnames, a large proportion of religious were drawn from the close vicinity of their houses; they might now be compelled to a radical change of background. With that small-mindedness characteristic of ingrowing academic or religious communities, the monks at the receiving house sometimes failed to make their guests welcome. When four Sawley monks arrived at Furness, the Abbot himself found excuses to repudiate them. Conversely, some of the newcomers refused to settle under new discipline: the former Abbot of Quarr chose to go to Beaulieu, but only to prove a quarrelsome member of this house. Yet in these respects we doubtless hear of the trying exceptions, not of the many who took the change in their stride. In making their choice, some shrewder monks and canons must have anticipated the ultimate fall of the greater houses, and have judged it wise to make their exit to a benefice before the flooding of the market by unemployed priests. Those of the rank-and-file who returned to the world at this first stage received gratuities, but no pensions: with these some expressed discontent, and the ill-fated Abbot of Barlings illegally sold the abbey plate to increase the rewards of his grumbling canons. When the final dissolution came, those who had stayed in religion were naturally pensioned along with their colleagues at the greater houses.

A feature of the interval between this first upheaval and the final act of 1539 was the sparing of numerous houses prepared to pay a heavy fine for the privilege. Of the 372 houses recorded by the *Valor* as having incomes under £200, only about 220 fell immediately. The whole Gilbertine order temporarily survived, thanks to the influence of its Master, Robert Holgate, a staunch Cromwellian, a future Lord President of the North and first Protestant Archbishop of York. Also during this interval, several prominent monks fell foul of the government and some, though by no means all, met the end of traitors. Adam Sedbergh, Abbot of Jervaulx, previously a supporter of the King, was precipitated into trouble by ex-Abbot Thirsk of Fountains, a bad ruler in his time of office and a busy intriguer in retirement. These two suffered execution, and Sedbergh's name, with the date 1537, may still be seen where he inscribed it in his prison in the Tower. Another semi-innocent victim was Abbot Paslew of Whalley, who pleaded guilty to a charge of treason, but had probably been implicated by ill-luck rather than by intention. Prior Wood of Bridlington, along with half-a-dozen other East Riding religious, was condemned on account of his part in Bigod's revolt. Mackerell of Barlings was an armed leader of the Lincolnshire Pilgrimage and paid the price. Through the attainder of their heads, the houses of Jervaulx, Whalley, Barlings, Bridlington and Kirkstead were deemed, by a dubious interpretation of the treason laws, to be dissolved.

Nevertheless, several of the prominent monks often assumed to have suffered with this group did in fact escape. One of these was Edward Kirkby, the former Abbot of Rievaulx, who spent six weeks in the Tower after the Pilgrimage and whose execution was rumoured. He is nevertheless known to have survived as a parish priest until 1557. The case of this man has recently been shown to contain none of the ingredients of martyrdom. Owing to violent internal quarrels at Rievaulx, its founder, the Earl of Rutland, had approached Cromwell to secure Kirkby's resignation. After protracted negotiations, he was induced to resign, and in 1534 received a handsome pension of £44 per annum. Kirkby then unsuccessfully tried to bribe Cromwell to reinstate him. When an Act of Parliament allowed his successor to halve the pension, Kirkby again engaged in prolonged efforts to get Cromwell's support and then tried to use the Pilgrimage of Grace to recover what he conceived his rights. Throughout the whole story, no political or religious principles were involved; Cromwell and numerous other people were put to enormous trouble because the Cistercian Order could not settle an internal quarrel. Another non-martyr was Lawrence Cooke, Prior of the Doncaster Carmelites, who, though specially excepted from the royal pardon and attainted, ended by receiving a pardon. Abbot Bolton of Sawley, though deeply implicated in the rebellion and condemned, may also belong to this group: there is no evidence that he was executed, and his name does not appear with the rest in the list of attainders for treason drawn up in 1540. Some other heads—Stonywell of Pershore, Love of Coggeshall and Peryn of Tavistock—were also accused of treasonable speeches, yet survived to enjoy their pensions.

Of these treason-actions brought against prominent monks, the most unjust were probably those of 1539 involving the three Benedictine abbots of Glastonbury, Reading and Colchester, who had all originally accepted the Royal Supremacy. Our knowledge of the charges brought against them remains imperfect, though the first two were regarded as implicated in the treason of the Poles and had supplied the northern rebels with money. In December 1539 Abbot Marshall of Colchester was reported by his servants and physician to have denounced the King's avarice, wished success to the Pilgrimage and asserted the unlawfulness of the dissolution of the greater monasteries. He denied to the last that he had ever asserted the Roman primacy. In the previous year, Abbot Hobbes of Woburn had been found by a local jury (including some staunch religious conservatives like John Gostwick) guilty of upholding the Pope's authority and condemning the royal divorce. Duly sentenced and executed, he may have stronger claims to be regarded as a Catholic martyr than the rest of this group. A few months later, Nicholas Heath, Prior of Lenton, also suffered for an attack on the King similar to that of Marshall.

In the examinations of some of these unfortunate suspects Cromwell was personally involved, and a note remaining in a list of his memoranda reads: 'The abbot of Reading to be sent down to be tried and executed at Reading with his complices, similarly the abbot of Glaston at Glaston'. Such a note truly represents one of the shadows upon Cromwell's reputation, yet M. Constant misunderstands its nature when he writes: 'Even before the trial, Cromwell had already, of his own authority, condemned the abbots to death.' Cromwell did not personally try these men, find them guilty and condemn them: he had no authority to do so. Therefore, if M. Constant's sentence means anything, it must mean that Cromwell suborned, bribed or threatened the juries at Reading and Glastonbury. But no evidence supports the suggestion, and this for a very good reason. In 1538–9 juries very readily convicted treason-suspects on flimsy evidence. Rebellions, plots, fear of foreign invasion, the burning and torture of English merchants in Spain, had produced their result: an exaggerated anxiety to appear ultra-loyal to an exacerbated monarch and an angry nation. Lord Russell, one of the more upright notables of the day, was among the commissioners who tried the Abbot of Glastonbury; however mistakenly, Russell thought the accused to have been justly condemned in a fair trial. The atmosphere was unhealthy and all too apt to produce harsh injustices, yet it was an atmosphere common to a large part of the nation and in no sense peculiar to the mind of the King's first minister. That overworked personage, compiling multitudinous memoranda for his private use, and knowing the facts of these cases, obviously assumed it a foregone conclusion that the abbots would be convicted of treason and executed. The spectacle remains unpleasant, and it is hard not to think of these cold phrases as throwing light upon the blunted, mechanical and calculating state of Cromwell's mind near the end of his career. Nevertheless, this is a vastly different matter from making him the sole author of judicial murders. Of this situation he was a victim as well as a partaker in a widely-shared responsibility. The national and international crisis had already developed when he took power: its embitterment cannot uniquely or even chiefly be blamed upon him or even upon the King. And if he could return to argue his case in retrospect, Cromwell would doubtless point out the fact that a major historical crisis was surmounted with little bloodshed precisely because, at the earliest sign of trouble, his government struck ruthlessly at the heart of the resistance. Weak and vacillating rulers, he would perhaps urge, ended by causing large-scale revolution, repression and slaughter. The abysses underlying this argument remain all too familiar from innumerable recent examples and the dilemma of power will remain as long as politics exists: it is the factor which must exclude men of sensibility from joining the unclean game in troubled times.

In 1536 Cromwell can scarcely have envisaged any immediate likelihood of a general dissolution of the greater monasteries, since the act of that year is allowed to describe the latter as 'divers and great solemn monasteries of this realm, wherein (thanks be to God) religion is right well kept and observed.' Nevertheless, the way was soon being smoothed for those greater houses prepared to make a voluntary surrender. The important abbey of Furness, which had narrowly avoided the treason-charges brought against its neighbour Whalley, took this line of least resistance early in 1537, and apparently with the genuine concurrence of the monks. In November the Cluniac priory of Lewes did likewise, closely followed by the Cistercians at Warden. Some heads were pressed into surrender by government agents; others hastened to London with seeming alacrity. Equally prominent during these years is an increase in the practice of collusive leases between religious houses and the local gentry. Even at the otherwise model house of Lacock, Abbess Temmes showered offices and long leases upon at least five of her male relatives, who continued to occupy a large part of the estates and to enjoy their various pensions long after the dissolution. A larger operator was Prior Munday of Bodmin, who issued very long leases to various of his kin and bribed his canons to permit the use of the convent seal for this purpose. It might further be added that Munday, formerly a canon of Merton, had recently been pushed into his office by the influence of his friends with Cromwell. Of the heads of the various houses at the surrender, a large number were Cromwell's recent appointees. They were safe men, prepared to accept the view that English monasticism was dead, to surrender without fuss when desired, to co-operate with the commissioners in an orderly and businesslike handover.

Between 1537 and 1540 surrenders were obtained from 158 male and 30 female houses. Meanwhile the orders of friars received separate treatment. They did not surrender house by house, but within the year 1538 underwent a systematic suppression. In this transaction Cromwell's chief agent was Richard Ingworth, formerly Dominican prior of King's Langley and now suffragan Bishop of Dover. His letters reflect to perfection that curious combination of intimacy and subservience which marked the attitude of so many subordinates towards Cromwell. The latter stimulated his zeal by the reproach that, though he had changed his habit, he had not yet changed his friar's heart. Ingworth vociferously replied, "Good, my lord, judge me not so, for God shall be my judge, my friar's heart was gone two years before my habit, saving only my living; but the favour [i.e. to the friars] that I have showed hath not been for my friar's heart, but to bring all things with the most quiet to pass'. He went on to describe the brethren as mostly anxious to cast off their religion and their habits, though as yet they lacked money to buy new suits. Other prominent friars took a similar view. 'We all long for a dispensation', wrote the Warden of the London Franciscans to Cromwell, and he proceeded to elaborate the theory that God has moved princes to take away their 'papistical and slanderous apparel', just as he once corrected the children of Israel through the Chaldeans and the Babylonians. The friars had become the most deeply divided section of the regular clergy. Not only had they developed a faction of extremist Protestants, but in many places they had stirred up major local quarrels by their contentious preaching against each other. Cromwell apparently regarded them with impatience. Foxe, partially supported by the London diarist Wriothesley, preserves an anecdote illustrating this attitude. Friar Gilbert Berkeley, a well-known Franciscan of Lincoln, Nottingham and York, became notorious for continuing to wear his friar's cowl after the dissolution. Cromwell, walking through St. Paul's churchyard, spied him in a shop. 'Yea', said he, 'will not that cowl of yours be left off yet? And if I hear by one o'clock that this apparel be not changed, thou shalt be hanged immediately, for example to all others.' This harsh warning Berkeley took to heart with great profit. He not only put aside his cowl but accepted a living in Norfolk, married a masterful wife, and ended as the henpecked Elizabethan Bishop of Bath and Wells.

The Dissolution Act of 1539 was primarily framed to grant full recognition to the long series of surrenders and to prevent any doubt about legal titles. It rehearses how many houses 'without constraint, coaction or compulsion of any manner of person or persons' had since 1536 surrendered to the King. It vests all their properties in the King, his heirs and successors, and then does likewise with those of all other monasteries 'which hereafter shall happen to be dissolved, suppressed, renounced, relinquished, forfeited, given up or by any other means come to his Highness'. One of this comprehensive list of fates had befallen every house by 23 March 1540, when last of all the Augustinian abbey of Waltham made its surrender. By this time Cromwell must have made Henry the richest ruler in Christendom, since for a brief space the King held nearly one-half of the wealth of the national Church which had voted him its Supreme Head.

Throughout these last months of Cromwell's career, the King and his ministers still maintained pious intentions to utilize a substantial proportion of the windfall in schemes for the rehabilitation of the Church. In particular, the insufficiency of bishops had already attracted their concern. As early as 1534 an Act of Parliament had named 26 towns for the sees of suffragan bishops, who could be appointed at the request of the appropriate diocesan. The offer was accepted in over half the possible cases during Cromwell's ministry, and it represents a useful extension of the former system, whereby suffragans with titles *in partibus infidelium* had been assisting the diocesan bishops. The dissolution of the monasteries now enabled the King to plan a much more important step: the creation and endowment of new dioceses. A manuscript in Henry's own hand sketches a plan for thirteen new sees based on monastic buildings and lands: for Essex at Waltham; for Buckinghamshire at Newnham; for Oxford, by joining Osney and Thame; for Nottingham, from Welbeck, Worksop and Thurgarton; for Cornwall, by uniting Launceston, Bodmin and some third house; for Lancashire and Richmondshire, by joining Fountains with the Archdeaconry of Richmond. The others proposed were Westminster, Peterborough, Gloucester, St. Albans, Dunstable, Leicester and Shrewsbury. Yet in the event, only six new bishoprics materialized: those of Peterborough, Gloucester, Oxford, Chester, Bristol and Westminster, the last-named only to be dissolved in 1550. The monastic chapters of Coventry, Rochester, Winchester, Ely, Durham, Carlisle and Norwich were abolished and replaced by deans and secular canons. To each a new code of statutes was presented, and together with the six entirely new sees, they henceforth became known as Cathedrals of the New Foundation. In addition, professorships of Greek, Hebrew, Theology, Law and Medicine were founded at Oxford and Cambridge. For this meagre settlement, with its tragically missed chances in the field of education and its curious disposition of sees, Cromwell cannot be blamed, since at the time of his fall the whole plan remained merely under discussion. The efficiency he displayed in other branches of Church-reform disposes one to think that he would have been dissatisfied with such piecemeal and lop-sided schemes.

Concerning monastic pensions, much is known from the voluminous records of the Court of Augmentations, the department which Cromwell erected to manage the new acquisitions of the Crown. Yet in the view of the present writer, the evidence is not quite satisfactorily set forth by Mr. Baskerville in his remarkable work *English Monks and the Dissolution of the Monasteries*. Here the abbots and priors, better documented than their inferiors, occupy too great a share of the picture. Nobody doubts their idyllic fate. Their pensions were liberal—often surprisingly so—and a fair proportion gravitated to bishoprics and other lucrative benefices. What, however, of the rank-and-file? it would seem that here the optimism of Mr. Baskerville has sometimes carried him a shade too far. The friars were turned out unpensioned, though it is true that many soon obtained clerical employment. When, for example, the Gloucester Dominicans were dissolved, they numbered a prior and six friars. Two years later, and again eight years later, espiscopal visitations were held: they show all the seven men serving as stipendiary priests in and around Gloucester, while at least two of these subsequently obtained actual benefices. Nuns were poorly pensioned, yet even so, like all incumbents and pensioners, had to pay their tenths to the King: I have before me, for example, a list of 1573 which shows several aged nuns paying tenths of 4s. on annual pensions of only £2 6s. 8d. The friars, whose houses had little or no property, and the nuns, who came mostly from poor houses, cannot by any stretch of imagination be regarded as handsomely provided for, and together these groups numbered at least three-eighths of the total body of ex-religious. The great majority of monks and canons received pensions in the close vicinity of five or six pounds per annum, which by the decade 1540–50 represents no more than the earnings of an unskilled labourer or the income of a very poor priest living on one chantry.

This situation—characteristically qualified by the fact that denizens of rich houses got larger pensions—suggests bare decency rather than generosity. Considerable numbers of male religious have been observed occupying benefices during the years succeeding the dissolution. To begin with, there were over 9,000 parishes, probably over 3,000 chantries, and an unknown number of private chaplaincies. Consequently a fair proportion of the 7,000 ex-religious priests may within a very few years have been absorbed as vacancies arose. Those unlucky during the first decade then presumably found things more difficult, since in 1549 the dissolution of the chantries threw a fresh group of priests upon the ecclesiastical labour-market, while greatly decreasing the number of emoluments available. Again, in 1552–3 the actual payment of pensions fell into serious arrears owing to the financial straits of Edward VI's government. Few monks and nuns traded their pensions, and the intrinsically improbable picture of astute pensioners outwitting innocent Augmentations officials (who were notoriously hardbitten) is disproved by the enquiries made at various times into the administration of pensions. Yet however many modifications should be imposed upon the optimism of Mr. Baskerville, there can be no return to the heroics of Gasquet or even to the more subdued lamentations of M. Constant. Mr. Baskerville was not entirely unfair or irrelevant when he implied that such people should first have studied the brutality with which both Catholic and liberal governments in Spain, France and Austria suppressed religious orders in the eighteenth and nineteenth centuries. The story of the dispossessed cannot be made into one of the great tragedies of English history. We should be even more misguided to shed many tears over the fate of monastic servants. The great majority, who worked out of doors, must have been readily employable by the new owners; at worst, they were in the position of other husbandmen of the time. Indoor servants, like the yeomen waiters and the barber at Butley Priory, would often have to seek employment elsewhere, but in some cases they are known to have been generously paid off with 'rewards' amounting to a year's wages. Both monastic stewards and corrodians were compensated or pensioned, and on every pension-list their names appear along with those of the monks and nuns. Altogether, we may safely scrap the old picture of an avalanche of sturdy beggars discharged from the closing gates of monasteries upon the highways of England; it is one of those many which may be relegated to the pages of the romancers and the propagandists.

Chapter Nine

Vicegerent in Spirituals

IN all seven editions of the Great Bible, an illustrated title-page illustrates Cromwell's pre-eminence as the direct intermediary between King and nation. Across the top of the page the King sits in state, delivering bibles with one hand to Cranmer and with the other to Cromwell. These recipients stand bareheaded, with expressions of great piety and accompanied by ecclesiastics and noblemen. Below this tableau the two dignitaries re-appear in a second scene; now wearing appropriate headgear, they hand out bibles respectively to the clergy and the laity. At the bottom a large and picturesquely attired crowd of men and women are crying *Vivat Rex* and *God Save the King*. In the first three editions Cromwell's personal arms appear below his figure, but in the fourth and later ones, the effect is somewhat marred by the omission of these arms in favour of a blank space. These were the editions published after his fall and execution! Even though the plate was not, as often supposed, the work of Holbein, no doubt it seemed a pity to waste one so fine and so expensive.

Striking though it be, this picture tends to underestimate the functions of Cromwell as officially envisaged during his period of rule. In the field of ecclesiastical administration, as distinct from that of spiritual functions, the Archbishop was not in fact permitted a co-ordinate role with Cromwell. And in all matters affecting clerical discipline, The Vicegerent could and did issue orders directly to the clergy. The scope of his office was also vividly illustrated when Convocation opened on 16 June 1536, and Dr. William Petre not only appeared as Cromwell's deputy, but successfully asserted his own claim to take the chair, a tangible illustration of the Royal Supremacy which must have startled—and was presumably intended to startle—the bishops. On 21 June Cromwell attended in person to introduce the sentence of nullity of marriage between the King and Anne Boleyn, a document which both Houses obediently approved. The great list of heresies known as the *mala dogmata* and presented to the Lower House on 23 June was not, as some writers have supposed, an act of defiance against Cromwell or even against his Lutheran allies. Practically every item it contains can be found in purely Lollard or Anabaptist cases of heresy; the document constitutes a denunciation of popular extremism which was admittedly widespread, but which Cromwell had taken no deliberate part in encouraging. On 11 July Cromwell attended Convocation once more in order to sign the Ten Articles, the first of the Henrician formularies of the Faith. These were presented by Edward Fox, Bishop of Hereford, one of the prelates closest to Cromwell and who had recently been in Germany negotiating with the Lutherans. On these grounds and because they show some superficial similarities to the Wittenberg Articles, the Ten Articles have often been taken as marking a close *rapprochement* between the government and the Lutherans; but on closer examination, as M. Constant and others have made clear, the resemblance largely vanishes. Though the Ten Articles adopt Melancthon's formulae on questions not in dispute with the Catholics, their divergence from Lutheran doctrine is in many places obvious. They do not, as often supposed, reduce the seven sacraments to three : they merely define the sacraments of baptism, penance and the eucharist without giving any total number. On penance, they contradict the Lutherans by retaining auricular confession and by asserting that penance is a sacrament of divine institution and necessary for salvation. On ceremonies they do similarly, by praising the veneration of images and virtually the whole range of Catholic observances. They also retain prayers for the dead. Needless to stress, their eucharistic position remains staunchly orthodox. Altogether, they were clearly dominated by the personal outlook of the King, who, even when Cromwell most desired to encourage the Lutheran princes, would make no more than a series of minor diplomatic gestures. The ugly consequences for Cromwell of this insular, self-confident and conservative attitude will soon become apparent.

A most interesting illustration of his official relationship with the bishops derives from the tract *Of the Authority of the Word of God against the Bishop of London*, published about 1540 by the Scottish Reformer Alexander Alesius, whom Cromwell and Cranmer had called from exile in Antwerp and who, rebuffed by theological conservatives in Cambridge, had come to study and practise medicine in London. Alesius describes in detail a debate held early in 1537 by Cromwell and the bishops concerning the number of the sacraments. This meeting he places 'in the Parliament House', and though Foxe, who borrows his account almost verbatim, arbitrarily alters this to 'the Convocation House', it was not a formal meeting of the Upper House of Convocation. However prejudiced, Alesius is a first-hand authority, since Cromwell happened to encounter him in the street and took him along to the conference. On their arrival, the Scotsman noticed that the bishops did obeisance to Cromwell and that he sat in the highest place. Opening the proceedings, he thanked his hearers on behalf of the King for their assembly to determine the controversies surrounding the Christian religion. The King, he continued, studied night and day 'to set a quietness in the church'. His desire was 'to set a stay for the unlearned people, whose consciences are in doubt what they may believe'. Although the King 'by his excellent learning knoweth these controversies well enough', he will allow no alterations save by consent of Convocation and his whole Parliament. He desired them to set aside malice and obstinacy, to debate 'friendly and lovingly', without brawling and scolding. The King would not suffer Scripture to be defaced with glosses and papistical laws, or by the mere authority of doctors and Councils of the Church. Much less would he admit doctrines not contained in Scripture but approved only by continuance of time and old custom, and by unwritten verities, 'as ye were wont to do'. His Majesty would give them high thanks if they could attain a godly and perfect unity, 'whereunto this is the only way and mean, if ye will determine all things by the Scripture, as God commandeth you in Deuteronomy; which thing His Majesty exhorteth and desireth you to do'.

Our observer Alesius then provides a long, interesting, but doubtless unfair and self-centred account of the debate which ensued. The Catholic view of the sacraments was most earnestly defended by Stokesley, Bishop of London, whom Cromwell reproved by name for defending mere 'unwritten verities'. After a speech by Cranmer, Cromwell turned to Alesius and commanded him to declare his opinion, introducing him to the bishops as 'the King's scholar' and desiring them to hear him impartially. Alesius, no doubt elated by this chance opportunity, cited the Scriptures and St. Augustine to prove that only two sacraments, Baptism and the Lord's Supper, could claim divine institution. Edward Fox, just back from Germany, gave him general support. Thanks to the diligence of the Germans, said the Bishop of Hereford, the gospel was now shining before the world, and Truth the daughter of Time would triumph. So encouraged, Alesius made another plea that the sacraments should be limited to those two instituted by Christ.

In his reply Bishop Stokesley continued to maintain the authority of the Councils and old doctors of the church, to the polite amusement of the enlightened. 'Now when the right noble Lord Cromwell, the Archbishop, with other bishops who did defend the pure doctrine of the gospel, heard this, they smiled a little one upon another, forasmuch as they saw him flee, even in the very beginning of the disputation unto his old rusty sophistry and unwritten verities.' Alesius would then have proceeded further to confute what Foxe calls 'this blasphemous lie', but the Vicegerent bade him to be content, 'for the time began to go away, and it was twelve o'clock'. On the next day, Alesius again attended Cromwell, but a message from Cranmer warned them of the hostility of the conservative bishops and caused Cromwell to keep his champion from harm by excluding him from the debate. Instead, he bade Alesius give him his notes to show the bishops at some future opportunity. 'Thus', concludes Foxe, 'through the industry of Cromwell, the colloquies were brought to this end, that albeit religion could not wholly be reformed, yet at that time there was some reformation had throughout all England.'

This account of the conference provides, despite its partisan character, a valuable glimpse of Cromwell's official role as moderator in the great controversy. He is first of all deputy and spokesman for a king with strong theological views, yet he is also the well-informed layman capable of understanding the tenor of the disputations. He does not personally bandy the texts and the dogmas, yet he is no merely neutral chairman. While avoiding any suspicion of sacramentarian heresy, he distinctly backs the advanced party and brings to the conference a theologian of foreign background, one who stood as far to the left as any man could safely stand in Henrician England. Moreover he introduces this controversial outsider as one enjoying royal patronage, and deliberately uses him to confound the conservative bishops, a far stronger element on the bench than the account of Alesius would suggest. As might be expected from his championship of the vernacular Bible, Cromwell strongly supported those who wanted a doctrinal settlement based closely upon the Scriptures and excluding the unwritten traditions, medieval doctors and General Councils of the Church. That some measure of social and even religious idealism was probably involved in this attitude, we have already suggested. Yet Cromwell was no doubt also astute enough to realize the very considerable flexibility of action allowed by the Bible to princes and governors, astute enough to foresee that if a quietness should be successfully imposed upon warring consciences and factions, it would owe more to politic power than to the intrinsic simplicities of holy writ.

In the August of 1536 Cromwell had issued to the clergy his first set of injunctions, a characteristic and mundane programme of decent, practical reforms. It is a fundamentally secular document, not closely modelled upon episcopal injunctions, yet constructive and enlightened in its social and educational emphases. The clergy are ordered to instil into the young, both by admonition to parents and by direct teaching, their *pater noster*, articles of the faith and ten commandments in the mother tongue. In their sermons they must teach these clause by clause, till the whole be known. They must urge upon parents the need to place their children to learning, or to some honest occupation or husbandry, lest the young fall into begging and stealing. Daily we see valiant men descending into these courses, says Cromwell, because their parents suffered them to be nurtured in idleness, whereas, 'if they had been well educated and brought up in some good literature, occupation or mystery, they should, being rulers of their own family, have profited as well themselves as divers other persons, to the great commodity and ornament of the common weal'. Rich clergymen, he continues, shall give exhibitions to scholars at Oxford, Cambridge, or in some grammar school, one for every hundred pounds of annual income. A miscellany of precepts follows. The people must not be allured into superstitious devotions to images and relics; the clergy must avoid card-playing and alehouses. All non-resident incumbents with £20 a year or more are ordered to distribute before the churchwardens a fortieth part of their incomes to the poor inhabitants. Incumbents must also be prepared to bestow the fifth part of their benefices towards the repairs of chancels, when these are their legal responsibility.

If few ecclesiastical historians have praised these injunctions, this is presumably because of their source. But they represent precisely what any sensible, educated, middle-class layman had to say to the mid-Tudor English Church. Few forward-looking churchmen can have quarrelled with such principles, even though the Church itself was powerless to enforce them. It is perhaps the uneasy feeling that Cromwell was the only authority capable of imposing simple and obvious reforms upon the Church which has earned him so much hostility from ecclesiasts. They have always found it easier to harp on the fact that Cromwell destroyed the monasteries than to recall that he strove to make the clergy perform a more positive and humane function in society, one which they have in fact come to exercise.

The work was continued by a second set of injunctions dated September 1538, the most important provision of which has already been described. Yet this placing of bibles in the churches, planned in 1536 but now enforced, should also be seen within the context of the educational proposals which distinguish both sets of injunctions. By those of 1538 the clergy are bound not merely to set up bibles and refrain from discouraging readers, but even 'expressly provoke, stir and exhort every person to read the same, as that which is the very lively word of God, that every Christian person is bound to embrace, believe and follow if they look to be saved, admonishing them nevertheless to avoid all contention and altercation therein, but to use an honest sobriety in the inquisition of the true sense of the same, and to refer the explication of obscure places to men of higher judgement in scripture'. Every Sunday and holy day the clergy are required to recite to their parishioners twice, thrice or oftener if need be, a sentence of the *pater noster* or creed in English, so that all may learn them by heart. These essentials once learned, the parishioners may then be taught to understand them. Parents and householders must be exhorted to pass on this teaching to their children and servants. Likewise the people must be taught the ten commandments by heart. At confessions every Lent, the clergy must examine every person as to whether he can recite the articles of their faith and the *pater noster* in English. Those who are not perfect should be told that every Christian person should know these things before receiving the blessed sacrament; they may even be threatened with possible future injunctions debarring the ignorant from communion. Sermons must be provided by incumbents at least quarterly; these shall purely and sincerely declare the gospel of Christ and exhort the hearers to works of charity, mercy and faith—especially those prescribed by Scripture—and to avoid reposing their trust in works devised by men's unscriptural fantasy, as in wandering on pilgrimages, offering money, candles or tapers to images and relics, 'kissing or licking the same', or saying over a number of beads 'not understanded nor minded on'. Images thus abused must be removed; no candles, tapers or waxen figures must be set before any image or picture; parishioners must be admonished that 'images serve for no other purpose but as to be books of unlearned men, that can no letters'. Non-resident parsons must appoint curates able to execute these injunctions and stand responsible for any default. Incumbents shall admit no unlicensed preachers, yet they shall offer no resistance to those who are duly licensed by the King, the archbishop or the bishop of the diocese.

More firmly than any of their contemporaries, Cromwell and his party had grasped the point that it was upon instruction in the elements of the faith, rather than upon ecclesiastical courts and legal coercion, that the future position of the Church in society must depend. This conviction was by no means the prerogative of Englishmen or of Protestants; in these same years the Jesuits were working their way to the same basic conclusions.

On a less exalted level, but also in accordance with these injunctions, Cromwell's agents proceeded in 1538 to a general assault upon images and saints' shrines to which pilgrimage was made. Especially prominent among these agents was the former Dominican Dr. John Hilsey, who had succeeded Fisher in the see of Rochester, and who exposed the Blood of Hales, the Rood of Boxley and other time-honoured frauds. His early death in the same year removed one of the ablest minds in the Cromwellian group. To this episode there are obviously two sides. The destruction of important works of art and the predatory confiscation of the rich treasures at the shrines of Winchester, Chichester and Canterbury have been quite justifiably deplored. On the other side, there can be no question but that gross superstition and even fraudulent rascality surrounded some of these places: later generations, in which light-headed materialism of this type no longer forms a burning issue, have all too easily invested it with picturesque romanticism. There occurred in the middle thirties a very real revulsion against these abuses. Its coarse, plebeian side can be seen in the ballad *The Fantasy of Idolatry*, printed by Foxe. A more educated and naïvely idealist aspect can be seen in *The Fall and Evil Success of Rebellion*, written in 1537 by the Yorkshire gentleman Wilfrid Holme, who exultantly sees the New Learning sweeping away the cobwebs of monkery, magic, idolatry, ungodly pseudo-science and the hair-splitting metaphysics of the schoolmen, while the nation marches forward to a glorious future, led by a devout monarch and guided by a Christocentric religion based on the Gospels. In short, the story belongs to the Erasmian Renaissance as well as to the English Reformation. The most spectacular victim of this eikonoclasm, the shrine of Becket at Canterbury, had also important political connotations; in reply to the papal threats which followed its destruction, the King issued a manifesto denouncing Becket as a 'rebel who fled into the realm of France and to the Bishop of Rome to procure the abrogation of wholesome laws'. Cromwell stood amongst the prime movers as well as the executors of this campaign. Foxe states that the 'fresh and quick wits pertaining to his family' were responsible for 'divers excellent both ballads and books . . . concerning the suppression of the Pope and all popish idolatry'. Foxe's tastes were admittedly not ours, but the evidence was badly abused by the eminent Victorian clericals who used this passage to make Cromwell 'the great patron of ribaldry, and the protector of the ribalds, of the low jesters, the filthy ballad-mongers, the ale-house singers . . . in short, of all the blasphemous mocking and scoffing which disgraced the Protestant party'. The one example cited by Foxe was not written by a member of Cromwell's household, nor was ballad-writing limited to the Protestant faction.

From our examination of the injunctions of 1538 we have omitted the best known, which reads as follows: 'Item that you and every parson, vicar or curate . . . shall for every church keep one book or register wherein ye shall write the day and year of every wedding, christening and burying made within your parish for your time, and so every man succeeding you likewise.' To provide for the safe keeping of the register, the parish shall provide 'one sure coffer with two locks and keys', the one to remain with the incumbent, the other with the churchwardens.

Every Sunday the book must be duly entered up in the presence of at least one of the wardens. For every omission the guilty party shall forfeit 3s. 4d. *to* the church repair fund. Even this valuable innovation was greeted by Victorian ecclesiastical back-biting. Canon Dixon, who calls it 'but an inadequate attempt to supply the loss of the registers of various kinds which had been kept by the monks', should have known better. No medieval monk ever kept anything remotely resembling a parish register: the occasional note in a monastic register concerning the death of some notability or some aristocratic patron of the house does not give it even a distant family resemblance to the record under discussion. Cardinal Ximenes is said first to have introduced parish registers in his province of Toledo in 1497; they were ordered in France the year after Cromwell began them in England, but they became general throughout Catholic countries only after the Council of Trent. It is possible, but unproven, that Cromwell may have encountered such records during his travels on the Continent. There can certainly be no question regarding the necessity of the reform. To the laity parish registers were infinitely more useful than they are today. No parallel records then existed, and in the small communities of the period, marriages within the prohibited degrees were all too likely to occur. Conversely, divorces disguised as decrees of nullity were often sought not merely on grounds of blood-relationship, but on the absurd ground of spiritual affinity contracted between a baptised person and his kin on the one hand, and his sponsors and their kin on the other. A case is cited in England where a man was punished for incest because he had married as his second wife the god-daughter of his first. A hierarchy which could evolve these legal fantasies and yet fail to organize any systematic records of marriages, baptisms and deaths was indeed inviting forcible reform at the hands of the State. The need was obvious enough to a number of humble parish clergymen in various parts of early sixteenth-century England. If we wish to observe the pre-history of parish registers, we must make a mighty effort, dismiss monks from our minds, and look at the few surviving parish registers kept before the date of Cromwell's order. At Tipton in Staffordshire a register was maintained, if somewhat scrappily, from 1513. Altham, Lancashire, has one with many entries ranging from 1518 to 1533, while at Perlethorpe and Carburton, both in Nottinghamshire, there are entries as early as 1528. Some dozen· others beginning between 1530 and 1538 are still in existence. No doubt all these represent the efforts of a small minority of exceptionally conscientious priests, yet there must have been more of these primeval registers which have since perished: at this period there existed among the parish clergy a good deal of spontaneous commonsense waiting to be organized.

At the same time, suspicious people in the remoter provinces assumed, apparently without the slightest grounds, that the plan contained a trap; that Cromwell entertained unpleasant fiscal motives. As early as 1536 rumours of such intentions were already current among the northern rebels. Among the many false reports which contributed to the Pilgrimage of Grace, there came the rumour that christenings, marriages and burials would now be taxed. In 1538 again, Sir Piers Edgecombe reported to Cromwell that in Devon and Cornwall the people feared lest the King and his Council should cause parsons to 'make a book wherein is to be specified the names of as many as be wedded and buried and christened. Their mistrust is, that some charges more than hath been in times past shall grow to them by this occasion of registering.' Despite these prejudices, the decree speedily took effect. At first the registers were kept in paper books, or even on loose sheets, but in 1598 incumbents received orders to have their early registers transcribed into parchment books. Not all did so, but of the 800 surviving registers which date back to 1538–9, the great majority are preserved in the form of these later copies: only in a few cases have the paper originals survived. Today, when our early parochial archives have merely historical and genealogical interest, we need a new Cromwell to ensure their safe keeping, perhaps in regional repositaries where they could be cared for and readily consulted by scholars. Meanwhile, a still superb if somewhat depleted treasury of parochial records should occasionally remind us of Cromwell's contribution to the cause of order and efficiency in Church and State.

The protection extended by Cromwell to Protestant heretics does not depend on the several anecdotes retailed by Foxe: it appears in the Act of Attainder and could easily be deduced from several of the state-papers. It therefore comes as a surprise to be told by at least two well-known historians that the heretic John Lambert 'was condemned to death by Cromwell'. How much truth lies in this statement can easily be verified by anyone who troubles to read the only source of importance: Foxe's vivid narrative of this *cause célèbre*. Lambert, a former Fellow of Queen's College, Cambridge, and chaplain to the Merchant Adventurers at Antwerp, had been in trouble for heresy on many occasions, not only with More and Warham in earlier years, but recently before the Reforming bishops, Cranmer, Shaxton and Latimer. Even Robert Barnes, terrified lest the Lutherans should be tarred with the brush of extremism, joined in reporting it to authority when Lambert took the extremist Zwinglian line on the eucharist. Undeterred, Lambert also denied the right of bishops to jurisdiction, and then made the mistake of appealing from them to the King. His appeal came at a moment when Henry was seeking not only to placate conservative English opinion, but also to achieve agreement with one or both of the great Catholic powers. He therefore saw in Lambert's case a splendid opportunity to demonstrate the orthodoxy and majesty of caesaro-papalism in England, and on 16 November 1538, he staged a magnificent heresy-trial at Whitehall. Arrayed in pure white to symbolize high ecclesiastical jurisdiction, and surrounded by his bishops and peers, Henry personally subjected the unfortunate Lambert to one of the most terrifying judicial ordeals of history. The vulgar and easy process of browbeating to which the Supreme Head descended has too often been described to warrant full repetition. Having brushed aside Lambert's nervous qualifications, Henry caused him to deny the Real presence and then retorted, 'Mark well, for now thou shalt be condemned by Christ's own words, *Hoc est corpus meum*'. After this brilliant dialectical triumph, he gave Lambert five hours of disputation with successive bishops in the face of a hostile, noisy audience. At first the victim put up a gallant performance, but in the last stages he relapsed into a daze, broken by a few spasmodic interjections. Torches were brought, and when the last bishop had finished, the King asked Lambert whether he would live or die. 'My soul I commend to God', replied the exhausted heretic, 'my body I submit to your clemency'. But Henry's patience was also exhausted: 'If you do submit yourself unto my judgement, you must die, for I will be no patron of heretics. Cromwell, read the sentence of condemnation against him.' The Vicegerent, who had not yet opened his mouth, obeyed. How could he do otherwise? Only in this nominal sense did Cromwell condemn Lambert to death.

Protestant opinion held that Gardiner had engineered the

whole affair, so as to put Cromwell in a dilemma: either he must openly read the sentence against a heretic or be suspected by the King of heresy. In some degree this was Cromwell's situation, but the intrigue attributed to Gardiner may well be a hostile fabrication, whereby later Protestants like Foxe tried to cover their embarrassment. By blaming the *bête noire* of Winchester, one withdrew attention from the spectacle of Barnes and óther Lutherans helping to get a sacramentarian heretic into trouble. If Cranmer and Cromwell felt hostile eyes directed upon themselves, they do not seem to have behaved with conspicuous nervousness. At the trial Cranmer dealt charitably with 'brother Lambert'. As for Cromwell, he sent for the condemned man on the morning of his execution and held a secret interview with him in his private room, after which Lambert breakfasted with the gentlemen in Cromwell's hall. When Foxe wrote, these were verifiable facts which he is unlikely to have invented. When, however, he continues, 'it is reported of many that Cromwell desired [Lambert] of forgiveness for that he had done', he was merely repeating the rumour which would naturally arise after a secret interview and an especially revolting execution. On the other side, those who have cited one of Cromwell's official letters as representing his real view of the trial have offended against the probabilities. In writing to Sir Thomas Wyatt in Paris, Cromwell lauded the King's excellent gravity, the inestimable majesty with which he exercised the office of Supreme Head, the benignity with which he essayed to convert the miserable man. 'I wished the princes and potentates of Christendom to have had a mete place for them there to have seen it. Undoubtedly they should have much marvelled at his Majesty's most high wisdom and judgement, and reputed him none otherwise after the same than in manner the mirror and light of all other kings and princes in Christendom.' This passage need not and probably does not represent Cromwell's own thoughts, nor does it throw doubt upon Foxe's less edifying account of the King's performance. The French court was one of the chief targets of Lambert's propaganda-trial, while here was the lesson which Henry expected Cromwell to disseminate in Paris and throughout Europe. And when it came to such flatteries, even the trowel advocated by Disraeli was no adequate implement for the needs of Henry VIII.

Chapter Ten

Foreign Policy and the Reaction

FROM the moment of England's rupture with the Papacy in 1533, foreign relations exerted little effect upon the internal Reformation. They nevertheless form one substantial strand of the rope which dragged Cromwell to disaster, and we cannot end the story without a glance in their direction. In his speech of 1523 Cromwell had already shown himself the holder of hard-headed views on English foreign policy. It seems likely enough that he shared the anti-French prejudices of his generation, yet he had fully emancipated himself from the romantic Agincourt-mentality which survived at every level of English society into the reign of Henry VIII. He had not, however, enjoyed the training which makes a great foreign minister. While his earlier career had helped him to a consummate grasp of the economic aspects of international relations, Wolsey had not given him diplomatic experience, and from his rise to power he became so deeply immersed in administrative reform, ecclesiastical policy and the overwhelming detail of current administration that he can scarcely have perfected his knowledge, or devoted much basic thinking to foreign affairs. More important, he never held un-disputed control of the field.

On Wolsey's fall Henry had personally assumed the super-vision of external relations, and during the period 1532-40 we seldom or never witness a truly Cromwellian negotiation. The King's trenchant if spasmodic intelligence had brought him to a viewpoint which events were destined in large part to justify. The costly and disappointing entanglements into which Wolsey had led the nation disposed Henry to seek a position of friendly neutrality between the two great Continental rivals, Francis I and Charles V, and to avoid alliances which might involve war. It must be admitted that during the early thirties he did not show conspicuous ability in his efforts to attain this ideal.

Though at first he needed the help of Francis towards the obtaining of his divorce at the hands of the Pope, he needlessly alienated that King in 1533 by his rudeness in sending an independent embassy to Pope Clement while the latter was the guest of Francis upon French soil. There are no strong reasons for accepting the supposition that this insult sprang from the advice of Cromwell, though it seems certain that the latter, his eye on the supreme economic importance of the Netherlands, was already leaning towards an understanding with their ruler Charles V. Doubtless he was also completely sceptical concerning these last-minute hopes of wringing a divorce from the Pope. So long, however, as Katherine of Aragon lived and her nephew Charles retained a sense of family duty, any *modus vivendi* between England and Charles proved too difficult to achieve; moreover, during the years between the divorce and Katherine's death. Henry showed a lack of decency in his shabby treatment of Katherine and her daughter, treatment duly reported by Chapuys to Charles and the reverse of conciliatory in its effects. Having thus lacerated both great powers, Henry did not scruple to rub salt in the wounds by such actions as the execution of Fisher and More, which, unlike the burning of obscure Anabaptists or the hanging of humble rebels, had an immense notoriety-value throughout the courts of Europe. Assuming that Henry's broad objective was sensible, nothing can appear less effective than his methods during these years, and the contrast so strongly implied by Merriman between the all-wise Henry and the blundering Cromwell would seem by no means applicable to the facts of the case. Indeed, the consistency with which Henry desired a policy of detachment may always be questioned, the more so because after Cromwell's death he himself departed from it so disastrously as to furnish the supreme example of its wisdom.

Under the circumstances obtaining in the early years of his ministry, Cromwell's cautious mind inevitably turned towards the notion of discovering allies, and as he surveyed the European scene, few potentially useful suggestions presented themselves. But one new constellation was in the ascendant and—for all an observer could tell at this moment—might soon dominate the heavens. The Lutheran princes of Germany, led by the Elector of Saxony and the Landgrave of Hesse, had in 1530–31 banded together in self-defence against the Emperor and formed the League of Schmalkalde. While the future extension of Lutheranism could not be predicted, it was obvious both to France and to England that the multifarious difficulties of Charles would most likely prevent him from crushing these princes, whose military and diplomatic weight might, in a world so delicately balanced, be manipulated with decisive effect. It is certain that Cromwell had already decided to explore this field by the summer of 1533, when his close friend Stephen Vaughan was one of two agents sent to tour Germany and report on the state of politics and religion in that troubled country. And from the first it was obvious that an ideological banner could be flaunted to attract the Lutherans. In January 1534 Nicholas Heath and Christopher Mont were despatched to tell them that the King of England had also become an enemy to the Pope and would willingly join with them to extirpate false doctrine. Their response proved frigid, for the princes were not fools; they took religion with deadly seriousness and perhaps already suspected the authenticity of Henry's Protestantism.

While nothing arose for the moment from this first overture, another interesting Protestant connection soon came under review. Under the guidance of violent Reformers led by the demagogue Georg Wullenwever, the great Hanseatic city of Lübeck was seeking to dispose of the vacant throne of its neighbour and rival Denmark. These Lübeckers were people genuinely in need of English help, and they had the means to flatter Henry's egotism. In August 1534 he signed a treaty with the city whereby, in return for an English loan of 50,000 gulden, Lübeck promised to support his divorce and denial of Roman authority, and also (should he decide to accept) help him to the throne of Denmark. Visions of Scandinavian hegemony floated before Henry's eyes, and the plan at least offered a means to deflate the pretensions of the Emperor, since the latter had proposed his own candidate for the Danish crown. By the signing of the treaty, however, the enterprise had already begun to go astray. The mercurial Wullenwever had also approached the nearby Duke of Holstein with an offer of the crown. On his refusal, the Lübeckers had angrily invaded Holstein, but had been shocked to find themselves driven back and their city besieged. At this stage the Danes had themselves taken a hand by offering their throne to the Duke, who had thus in July 1534 become Christian III. This event destroyed the contention of Lübeck that it desired to introduce pure religion into Denmark, since the new King was himself a Rutheran. At this time, Robert Barnes, the former friar and Lutheran missionary, had embarked upon a fresh phase of his stormy career by crossing to Hamburg and acting as an official emissary to the Lutheran states. In the summer of 1534 Barnes was advising the King to extricate himself from the Lübeck alliance and to ally with King Christian. As yet, Henry's pride forbade this rational course, and he gave ships and two skilled engineers to assist the Lübeckers. When Christian sent over an embassy to demand an explanation, Cromwell was assigned the task of bluffing and lying, though he had assisted in these negotiations only in a subordinate capacity. After further victories by Christian and the loss of some English ships, Wullenwever fell from power and suffered execution; hence the summer of 1535 saw Henry's withdrawal from the unlucky and ill-judged scheme. Its cost admittedly did not begin to compare with that of a campaign in France, yet Henry had succeeded in alienating the very power which he desired to attract: that of Lutheran princes, to several of whom Christian was related. Only in February 1536 was England able to make a treaty with Denmark which mitigated this unfortunate situation.

Meanwhile in 1534-5 French relations at first promised to improve, but then deteriorated still further. King Francis took the initiative by sending two embassies to arrange dynastic marriages: first that of the Princess Mary, then that of her baby step-sister Elizabeth, to a French prince. It was on the former of these occasions that the ambassador Admiral de Brion tried to frighten Cromwell by the suggestion of an alliance between Charles and Francis, directed against England. Cromwell had done his best to cater for French tastes by sending for beautiful young ladies to come to court and entertain the visitors. Finally he appeared with a parting gift for de Brion, but the latter approached Chapuys with ostentatious civility and declared that if they two could only bring their masters to accord, all would go well. Henry and Cromwell doubtless understood the element of bluff in such a demonstration, but from about this time a Catholic alliance against heretical England loomed amongst the more fearsome possibilities. The threat might also present opportunities to either power if it wished to cajole or blackmail England into helping it against the other. In 1535 Francis, encouraged by the temporary absence of Charles in Tunis, brusquely demanded financial support from England to help him attack Milan; he then seized English ships at Bordeaux, causing Cromwell and Gardiner to make repeated efforts to obtain their release.

With both great powers thus unfriendly, if not as yet united against England, it now seemed appropriate to bid once more for the support of the Lutheran princes, whose influence and beliefs were rapidly gaining ground throughout the German states. After Barnes had exercised some preliminary blandishments, Edward Fox, Bishop of Hereford, went on an embassy late in the year and obtained a conditional offer from the Lutherans to recognize Henry VIII as Defender and Protector of their League. Their condition was a hard one for Henry: he must first accept the Confession of Augsburg, make it a basis for the Reformation in England and defend it at any future General Council of the Church. His reply showed the firmness of his intention never to become a Lutheran or to import a religion made in Germany. He answered that he had long been minded to set forth true doctrine, but being a King reckoned somewhat learned (a conscious understatement), and having learned men in his kingdom, he could not accept from anyone the faith of the realm, which was grounded in the Scriptures. His attitude towards the Lutherans showed no significant variations. He saw no harm in allowing Barnes, Fox and Heath to argue theology at Wittenberg, so long as he remained uncommitted and very much master in his own house.

At this moment, in January 1536, when both France and the Germans seemed broken reeds, Queen Katherine died and thus opened the way for a new *rapprochement* with the Emperor. The very next day Cromwell instructed Gardiner to assure the French Government that this event had removed 'the only matter of unkindness' between Henry and Charles, and to remain 'the more aloof and be the more "froyt" and cold in relenting' to any French overtures or requests. He felt that the blackmail-weapon had now changed hands. Francis took the hint and began efforts to regain Henry's support. Meanwhile Cromwell also saw Chapuys, urging upon him that no reason now remained for hostility. The Emperor was nothing if not hardheaded; his relations with France were still strained and formed but one of the many problems which beset his vast Empire. Thus it was not long before Henry enjoyed the delicious spectacle of both great powers bidding for his support. At this stage, however, Cromwell seems for the first time to have pressed a policy of his own, for he went to Henry along with Chapuys to propose an Anglo-Imperial alliance. The request again makes one wonder whether Henry had hitherto been very decisive about his policy of disengagement: certainly he cannot have explained such purposes with clarity to his chief minister.

At all events, his mind was now resolved and, according to Chapuys, a piquant scene ensued in the Privy Chamber. After the Imperial Ambassador had offered terms for negotiation, the King took Cromwell and Audley out of earshot and seemed to be angrily disputing with the former. 'After a considerable time, Cromwell grumbling left the conference in the window where the King was, excusing himself that he was so very thirsty that he was quite exhausted—as he really was with pure vexation—and sat down on a coffer out of sight of the King, where he sent for something to drink.' Henry then came across to Chapuys and closed the interview with various rude remarks against the Emperor. Later that day Chapuys called on Cromwell, whom he found so upset 'that he was hardly able to speak for sorrow, and had never been more mortified in his life than with the said reply'. We do not know the precise proposals and arguments used during this altercation between Henry and Cromwell; it is extremely improbable that the latter could have favoured an offensive alliance likely to involve large-scale Continental warfare. Nevertheless, Henry appears justified in his refusal of any Imperial alliance, since extensive hostilities between Francis and Charles soon broke out again and continued throughout most of the years 1536-7. During this period—the cleverest phase of Henry's foreign policy—the King pretended he would gladly arbitrate 'for the peace and weal of Christendom', while in actual fact seeking to embroil the contestants still further. In accordance with such a directive, Cromwell ordered our ambassadors at both courts to give 'an answer so general that it doth neither refuse their alliance, nor much encourage them to conceive that they may without difficulty obtain their desire'.

This fortunate conjuncture of foreign affairs left the government unimpeded to crush the Pilgrimage of Grace, but by the autumn of 1537 the exhausted contestants on the Continent arrived at a truce, one destined soon to strengthen in a manner sinister to the interest of England. The subsequent year saw Henry, once more without a wife and engaged in collecting portraits of the Duchess of Milan and other noble dames, with a view to strengthening his position by a foreign marriage-alliance. He even suggested through his agent at the French court that a number of possibles should be brought to Calais to undergo his personal inspection, and altogether made himself so ridiculous as to invite a taunt from the French ambassador Castillon which drew a blush even to his own cheek. Making no progress in this enterprise, he then transparently sought to embroil the Emperor and France by dangling the prospect of marriage alliances between his daughter Mary and princes of both these powers. While such overtures were in progress, Cromwell once again displayed his preference for an Imperial alliance and Castillon complained to Henry of his minister's 'great Spanish passion', thus attracting upon Cromwell's head renewed reproofs from the King. In a revealing phrase, the latter told Cromwell that he was a good manager, but not fit to intermeddle in the affairs of kings.

This time, however, the situation did not develop in such a manner as immediately to justify the royal policy of detachment, since in the summer of 1538 Francis and Charles made the Truce of Nice and met in unaccustomed friendship at Aigues Mortes. Marshal de Montmorency, the leading soldier of France, was known to be urging his master to ally with Charles in a joint invasion of England. While Henry continued to anticipate that the two would soon drift apart, Cromwell, who had the task of preparing the country against possible invasion, did not share this optimism. He was ever the tidy-minded administrator, highly responsible, anxious to tame the future, determined to leave nothing to chance. His genius operated most effectively in the field of domestic affairs, where the willed and calculated effect could often be secured, but in that of foreign policy, then as now, gambles had to be taken and hunches obeyed. Masterly inactivity often rewarded England, however dark the reports, for the complexion of Europe changed swiftly enough to make a short-term and opportunist policy the wisest. So often may we observe this antithesis between opportunism and doctrinairism in the chequered story of Tudor diplomacy. Always the opportunists like Henry VII and Elizabeth emerge unscathed, while the doctrinaires, the would-be builders of systems like Wolsey and Mary Tudor, end in confusion. Henry VIII and Cromwell both stood somewhere between the extremes, but the latter leaned somewhat towards the doctrinaires. He had to organize insular defence, but he found it difficult to conceive of a purely insular policy, whereby England would neglect foreign alliances, even one with the ruler of the Netherlands, that integral part of our economy.

Debarred again from an effort to re-establish this old connection by an alliance with the Emperor, he now proceeded to revive the plan for a closer understanding with the Lutheran princes. There was nothing inconsistent in turning from a union with Charles to a union with the enemies of Charles. In Merriman's words, 'As he had always considered the friendship of the Emperor more valuable than that of Francis, so he considered his enmity, which he now regarded as inevitable, as more to be feared'. This being so, what could serve better than an alliance with the princes who, especially with English help, could check the Emperor and prevent his using military or economic weapons against England? Like Walsingham and others after his time, Cromwell wanted to see English battles fought by foreigners on the Continent; indeed, it is not purely fanciful to draw an analogy between him and Pitt, with the German princes cast for the role of Frederick the Great. But in so dignifying Cromwell, we should also give similar credit to his master, who was also a forward-looker, plainly conscious of the protection conferred upon us by control of the Narrow Seas, and an active planner of our growing naval power. Between King and minister we see in embryo the subject of many a future debate, the debate forced upon successive generation of Englishmen until, in our own day, the rise of air-power has revolutionized the major conditions, hitherto prescribed by physical geography and the mobility of armed forces.

Early in 1538 Cromwell prevailed on Henry to send Christopher Mont back to Germany, with the result that by May a Lutheran embassy arrived in England headed by Franz Burckhard, Vice-Chancellor of Saxony. The negotiations were nevertheless speedily bogged down again in theological discussion. It seems likely enough that Cromwell, left to his own plan, would have been quite satisfied with a doctrinal treaty close to the Lutheran position, trusting to uphold it at home through the enhanced strength of the Crown and the harsh lessons recently administered to rebellious conservatives. Henry, on the contrary, was only too relieved when he discovered that the armed preparations of the Emperor were to be directed not against himself but against the Turks. Seeing hence no immediate need of the stubborn Lutherans, he sent the embassy home again in October with the message that an alliance needed maturer deliberation, and that to accomplish it a second embassy would be required. Cromwell, who had merely managed to prevent him from breaking off negotiations altogether, should at this new rebuff have left the King to his own devices in the field of foreign affairs. Instead, he prepared to revive his pressures at the earliest opportunity, and new events soon conspired to provide one. In January 1539 Charles and Francis met at Toledo and agreed not to make any new alliance or marriage-compact with Henry, unless by each other's consent. Cromwell, who had been using the interval to amuse himself with a somewhat chimerical plan for a league of Italian princes against the Pope, once again persuaded Henry to send off the indefatigable Mont on a fresh visit to John Frederick of Saxony, Philip of Hesse and other Schmalkaldic leaders. The supplementary instructions given by Cromwell to Mont make it clear that he was now striving to lift the discussion out of its sterile theological channels and to concentrate upon two proposed dynastic marriages, one between the young Duke William of Cleves and the Princess Mary, the other between Henry himself and Anne, the elder of the same Duke's unmarried sisters.

The choice of the Cleves family supplies an important hint as to the limitations of the Protestant element in Cromwell's foreign policy, for its members were as yet Catholics and not, as so often stated, professed Lutherans. Whatever the desire of the minister to hold the King to a continuing forward policy in religion, his chief interest lay in the political aspects of the alliance rather than in luring the King towards a public display of Protestant sympathies. But if the Catholic allegiance of the House of Cleves made it more acceptable to Henry, the proposed marriages would certainly form a bridge between England and the Schmalkaldic League, since the Duke of Saxony, who had himself married Sybilla, elder sister of Duke William and Anne, stood on intimate terms with the family and had even promised to supply the doweries of his wife's younger sisters. Circumstances had conspired in other ways to confer a considerable diplomatic and strategic lustre upon Cleves. Its late Duke, who died just as these negotiations opened, had built up a centralized administration in his three provinces of Cleves, Jülich and Berg. Moreover, his son and successor William had recently been left the neighbouring province of Gelderland by its childless ruler; at which point the Emperor, reasserting his own claims to that province, had driven Cleves to the protection of Saxony and the Schmalkaldic League. Again, the Cleves lands lay between Charles in the Netherlands and the Lutheran princes whom he wished to attack. For a minister who wanted Henry to operate a North German alliance so as to gain a close grip upon the Netherlands and upon Imperial policy, the Cleves matches must have seemed a heaven-sent opportunity.

The mental calculations of Cromwell beyond this point remain somewhat obscure. He must clearly have foreseen the reverse of these advantages: the danger that England might be committing herself to armed intervention, or at least to squander that immense treasure which he was even now pouring into the royal coffers. We do not know precisely how he planned to steer clear of these abysses. The fact remains that at this stage of his career he thrust ahead, pulling his reluctant master behind him. Did he for once lose his habitual caution and experience a measure of *hubris*? Did he become doctrinaire to the extent of wanting to make his policy look consistent and homogeneous by means of a Lutheran alliance? Did he want the satisfaction of forcing Henry to take medicine which he, Cromwell, thought so obviously good for Henry? Was he applying the old proverb make or mar to new and chancier fields? Had he by now absorbed the Machiavellian concept of *virtù*, the idea that Fortune like a woman gives herself to the bold, that by a superior resolution the great man can control at least that half of his future which does not lie in the lap of Destiny? Whatever the correct answers to these questions, the negotiations for the Cleves match represent a major turning-point of Cromwell's career.

It was naturally to the family friend and protector John Frederick of Saxony that Christopher Mont was ordered to address his first enquiries. Cromwell's further instructions were most circumspect. Having discreetly enquired regarding the shape, stature, proportion, complexion, learning, activity, behaviour and honest qualities of the Lady Anne, Mont should not then crudely demand her, but merely stir the Saxons to 'offer her, as the noblest and highest honour that could come into that noble house of Cleves, if they could bring it to pass'. That Henry himself took pains to preserve a personal loophole becomes ob-

162

vious from the fact that all the material parts of the negotiation were conducted solely in Cromwell's name. Nevertheless, a further worsening of our relations with France and with the Empire encouraged the over-confident minister to press on with the scheme. At this time he was working with immense industry to put the ever-rusting defences of England into some sort of order: his state-papers become littered with muster rolls, weapons, ammunition, provisions and reports on coast-defence. Throughout the country, general musters were held and beacons prepared. Cromwell even took the French ambassador on a tour of the royal armoury and let fall the staggering aside that the King had twenty others as good and better, 'whereat he wondered and said that he thought your Grace the prince the best furnished thereof in Christendom'.

This tension relaxed somewhat in March 1539 when Francis sent his new ambassador Marillac, but the rejoicings at the English court seem childish enough, and Cromwell himself no doubt guessed what we now know: that Francis had not relaxed his hostile intentions and was merely playing for time. So far as the Germans were concerned, the new overtures began with a repetition of the old story. In April Henry cordially received the Saxon ambassadors Burckhard and Baumbach, but still they came intent to discuss a theological understanding and with very limited powers to negotiate any political alliance. When in May it was heard that the Emperor Charles had signed a truce with the Lutheran princes, the King once again sent home the ambassadors. Not least downcast by the news was Robert Barnes in Hamburg, for he had been successfully working to conciliate that intimate ally of the Lutheran princes, Christian of Denmark, whom he had brought to the point of sending to the English court a joint embassy with Saxony to discuss a political league. By what mysterious access of grace did Barnes, at home the embodiment of indiscretion, make an effective diplomat? This possible embryo of a North European Protestant alliance —the dream of so many generations during the long crisis of Reformation and Counter-Reformation—may be placed amongst the larger concepts of Cromwellian diplomacy, but Cromwell is unlikely ever to have felt it so near his grasp as did the sanguine Barnes, who was now heading for a clash with people much bigger than himself. At this stage came the passing of the reactionary Six Articles, the report of which dismayed not only the Lutheran princes but the House of Cleves..

In the summer of 1539 the ever-fluctuating scene brought both sides a fresh motive for renewing contact. Henry discovered that Francis and Charles were again likely to meet and discuss a coalition against him. The former had invited the Emperor to pass through France in order to repress the rebellious city of Ghent, and his consequent appearance in the Netherlands naturally tormented the Duke of Cleves with fears lest Charles should proceed to deprive him of Gelderland. While Henry had dropped the unpopular plan to marry his daughter Mary to the Duke, he maintained a mild interest in Anne of Cleves. It is far from certain that Cromwell even allowed him to see the unexciting personal reports which were coming through. Nicholas Wotton depicted a gentle but utterly unaccomplished female, 'for they take it here in Germany for a rebuke and an occasion of lightness that great ladies should be learned or have any knowledge of music . . . your Grace's servant Hans Holbein hath taken the effigies of my lady Anne and the lady Amelye and hath expressed their images very lively.' Unfortunately for Cromwell, Christopher Mont accorded Anne indiscriminate praise, and while the famous Holbein portrait now in the Louvre is no aphrodisiac, it does at least omit the traces of smallpox which less respectful eyes were quick to observe. When Henry at last saw the original and married her in January 1540, he had good reason to regret his failure to arrange a parade of suitable candidates in Calais. When, months later, Cromwell was in the Tower and hoping to save his skin by helping Henry to a divorce, he wrote a long and curious report of conversations between himself and the King, in which the latter, with much more frankness than taste, had reported his aversion from Anne and his consequent failure to consummate the match. Cromwell had obvious motives for exaggerating these stories, but the details are precise and are partially supported by a letter from Anne to her brother.

In any event, the King did not visit the fallen minister in prison and is not very likely to have dictated details so intimate through a third person. Whatever the case, the failure of Cromwell's political scheme became apparent almost as swiftly as the King's personal aversion. Even amid the continuing hostility of the great powers, the Lutherans staunchly demanded a doctrinal understanding and Henry as staunchly rejected it. On 12 January, 1540, Cromwell summoned Burckhard and Baumbach, who were both again in London, and demanded point-blank a political alliance. The Lutherans were again compelled by their orders to stress the impossibility of such a step in the absence of theological agreement. Cromwell at this point observed that, wherever his personal sympathies might lie, he must hold to his King's belief even to the point of death. Before the end of the month, Henry politely dismissed Baumbach, boasting that he stood in no danger from Charles and Francis, and that in any case his naval strength was more than adequate to meet any opposition it would be likely to encounter. And what use would German soldiers be to him, for they would always be seasick?

This touch of heavy humour did not make the King's mood less dangerous, and Cromwell now realized the necessity of dropping the Lutherans. But he could not spirit away the all-too-solid form of Anne, or escape from the menacing fact that, like Wolsey before him, he had jockeyed the King along a path with a dead end. It is certainly untrue that in January 1540 his death-warrant was sealed, or that an ill-fated foreign policy was solely responsible for his downfall. Even so, the ultimate significance of these events cannot be minimized: not only did they profoundly annoy the irascible King, but they also identified Cromwell ever more clearly with the Lutheran cause and made it far easier for his enemies to press those charges of heresy which proved their sharpest weapons in the final assault. From this point, no further threatening developments on the Continent furnished Cromwell with an excuse for his actions. By February the need to achieve a German alliance had quite plainly receded, since after crushing Ghent Charles repudiated his promise to invest the son of Francis with the Duchy of Milan. Not only did the Emperor thus re-open the old quarrel with France; he also reasserted his claim to Gelderland, hence making it all too likely that Cleves and the Lutherans would call upon Henry for practical support, a prospect from which the King recoiled in dismay. Shortly before Cromwell's arrest in June, Henry sent an emissary to Charles in Brussels, assuring him that Cromwell had exceeded his instructions and placing upon Cromwell's shoulders the blame for negotiating with the Lutheran princes.

It is now high time to take up the threads in domestic affairs which also led to the Reaction and to the fall of Cromwell. They are no less complex than those we have traced in the sphere of foreign policy. The likelihood had always existed that, when the policy of Reformation reached a certain climax, it would receive a violent check. The intrinsic weakness of the Cromwell-Cranmer group amongst the nobility and the bishops, even amongst the predominantly conservative squirearchy and the agrarian masses, need not again be stressed. But the timing and the severity of such a reaction depended upon the King, whose personal friendship towards Cranmer and whose reliance upon Cromwell's administrative genius were props he could not and would not lightly discard. In the summer of 1539, certain observers thought the moment had already arrived, for it was then that the first gaps were torn in the Cromwellian front by the Duke of Norfolk and the conservative bishops. But the sequel indicated that the King was not nearly prepared for a change of ministry.

When the new Parliament assembled on 28 April, Cromwell had on his list of impending measures 'a devise for the unity in religion', but the King had evidently given him no precise indication of its form. The committee set up in the Lords at Henry's request was headed by the Vicegerent, but it consisted of four Reformers (Cranmer, Latimer, Goodrich of Ely and Capon of Bangor) and four conservatives (Lee of York, Tunstall, Clerk of Bath and Wells and Aldridge of Carlisle); the King may even have intended the inevitable deadlock, which enabled him to assume personal control as *deus ex machina*. On 16 May he authorized the Duke of Norfolk to offer six articles to Parliament for discussion: as yet they stood in the form of questions, but they were questions to which Henry now knew the answers. It may be that while Cromwell was immersed in committee-business, Norfolk and Gardiner had captured the King's ear, but Henry's own grasp and enthusiasm cannot be doubted. Not only did he revise the first extant draft of the Six Articles Act in his own hand, but he soon came down in person to the debate and, as a conservative lord put it, 'confounded them all with God's learning'. The very exclusion of the Vicegerent from the task of introducing an important religious measure boded no good to Cromwell and his policy. When Parliament reassembled after a week's prorogation, Gardiner emerged from the wings and joined one of the committees formed to draft the Act, which during June passed through all its stages. Cromwell naturally submitted to the strong lead of the King, while doing what he could to mitigate some of the harsher provisions. Even so, the final terms of the Act proved wholeheartedly conservative and its penalties violent in the extreme. It asserted transubstantiation and condemned those who denied this doctrine to burning and to forfeiture of all property, without possibility of escape by abjuration. The other five articles stated that communion in both kinds for the laity was unnecessary, since the whole Christ was present in both bread and wine; that the law of God prevented priests from marriage and demanded the continued observance of vows of chastity; that private masses should continue and that auricular confession was expedient and necessary. For obstinate denial of any of these five, a man should be judged a felon and so suffer death and forfeiture, but in the event of abjuration, he should be imprisoned at the King's pleasure, and suffer death only if twice convicted.

At this stage, Cromwell stood face to face with something more formidable than a mere clerical reaction. The lay lords headed by Norfolk had played a predominant part in the passage of this fierce Act, while a considerable section of the lower orders, their normal conservatism reinforced by the spectacle of religious disunity in the realm, did not hesitate to rejoice at the strong line taken by King and Parliament. In London itself, according to Hall, five hundred persons were speedily presented for heresy under the Act. At the same time, the outcome showed that the Six Articles were intended—like most Tudor penal legislation—to operate as a deterrent rather than as basis for a close inquisition into the nation's conscience. So far as Foxe's information went, only about 25 persons were actually burned under the Act during the last eight years of the reign. The immediate political consequences likewise proved undramatic. Only two of the Reforming bishops—Shaxton and Latimer—resigned their sees, and Latimer afterwards alleged that he did so at Cromwell's own request. And distressed as Cromwell himself must have been at this triumph of reaction, he soon found that Henry still valued his services. During the second half of 1539 he recovered his influence and, as already observed, went ahead with the Cleves match. The Act also failed to put Gardiner into a significantly more powerful position. Cromwell continued to hold him at a distance from the King, while the new appointments to the episcopal bench did not come from Gardiner's faction. Capon and Bell, who succeeded Shaxton and Latimer, were moderates, while Bonner, who became Bishop of London on Stokesley's death in the autumn, remained a bitter personal enemy of Gardiner and a Cromwellian up to the time of the minister's fall.

So matters substantially remained until the early months of 1540 saw a further shift of the front. Norfolk's special embassy to France in February provides an interesting link between foreign affairs and the intrigue for power at home: Norfolk had everything to gain by staging a reconciliation with France, since this diminished the need for Cromwell's German alliance and increased the impatience of the King with the match he had just been led to make. But again, Norfolk's success in March did not in itself entail Cromwell's fall, an event which cannot closely be synchronized with the foreign situation. At home threats more dangerous were developing. In this same month the minister suffered grave embarrassment from the behaviour of Barnes, who, home again and flushed with his diplomatic successes, lost touch with life's stern realities and made a violent attack upon Gardiner in a sermon at Paul's Cross. On the Bishop's protest, the King called the disputants before him and ordered Barnes to confer with his adversary. The Reformer at first professed himself convinced, and was even offered a fat benefice by the elated Gardiner. Yet within two days Barnes rushed in disillusion from the bishop's palace, only to be summoned again before the King, together with his two chief associates William Jerome and Thomas Garret, that early hero of Oxford Protestantism. Ordered by Henry to preach sermons of recantation, they complied in so unsatisfactory a manner as to gain for themselves cells in the Tower. Their defiance culminated on 30 March, when Barnes withdrew his recantation.

These events delighted Norfolk and no doubt correspondingly depressed Cromwell, yet the latter took care to avoid any gesture of sympathy for Barnes and his friends. On the day of Barnes's fatal sermon, Cromwell was in fact dining with Gardiner in a supreme effort to come to terms with that insidious enemy, whom the King was about to recall to the Council. Gardiner allowed Cromwell to think the dinner and discussion a success, yet he implacably awaited the moment to strike. On 10 April the French ambassador Marillac was already prophesying Cromwell's imminent fall: he had noted the imprisonment of the three Protestant divines and the appearance upon the Council of the three conservative bishops, Gardiner, Tunstall and Clerk. Once again the prophecy was premature, for on 12 April Cromwell opened the parliamentary session with a nobly-worded plea for mutual toleration and charity, while six days later he was created Earl of Essex and Great Chamberlain, with substantial grants to maintain his dignities. Even the common suggestion that the King was merely preserving him until he had negotiated the subsidy bill and the confiscation of the properties of the order of St. John does not agree with the dates, since he survived some little time after these measures had safely passed through Parliament. Meanwhile ecclesiastical affairs were again slipping from his grasp, since the committee appointed to define doctrine was heavily loaded with conservatives.

In May the trap was gradually closing; faced by the task of delivering Henry from Anne of Cleves, he was now confronted with the certainty that, as soon as he succeeded, Henry would marry Katherine Howard, Norfolk's niece, whom the wily Duke had carefully planted under the roving eye of the King. Before the end of the month Cromwell had abandoned his restraint to the extent of arresting on his own responsibility Gardiner's lieutenants, Sampson Bishop of Chichester and Dr. Nicholas Wilson. It was rumoured that he planned to seize five more conservative bishops, but while he was again immersed in parliamentary routine, Norfolk and Gardiner succeeded in convincing the suspicious King that he was guilty of heresy and treason. The long intrigue ended on 10 June, when the captain of the guard came to arrest him in the Council Chamber. Taken by surprise, and doubtless filled by the furious thought that he had not completed his task, the victim hurled his bonnet to the ground in rage, called on his enemies to say if he were a traitor, and then urged them to dispose of him quickly and not leave him to linger. Norfolk snatched the George from his neck and Southampton the Garter from his knee; the councillors, a few moments ago conformable to his leadership, joined in the storm of vituperation as the fallen statesman was taken by boat to the Tower. No one save Cranmer, and he very cautiously, dared express regret or recall past friendship with Cromwell in the presence of the King. By the evening, archers guarded the door of his house, while inside men packed his plate and money for the King's use. This was the accepted sign that a man would die.

The last scene in the Council Chamber serves to remind us of another important influence behind the triumph of reaction. Dr. Elton has recently shown that the development and complexion of the Privy Council itself were important factors in the downfall of Cromwell. The Council had now become a compact and efficient body which rendered a single super-minister no longer essential. It contained, however, no Cromwellian group of ministers likely to support their leader in time of crisis; he had never manned it with his personal adherents and it was united only by loyalty and subservience to the King. Such colleagues as Tunstall, Southampton, Browne and Kingston were unconcealed conservatives in religion. Lord Russell and Chancellor Audley, ostensibly close friends of the minister, were Cromwellian only by self-interest and prepared to drop their leader at the slightest breath of royal disfavour. His own former servant Ralph Sadler naturally concentrated upon self-preservation when Cromwell's power began to totter. In April Cromwell had relinquished the secretaryship to Sadler and Wriothesley, but if his motive was to bring more of his own associates to the Council, he did not in fact receive any appreciable access of strength at these hands. Grounds in fact exist for the supposition that Wriothesley worked behind Cromwell's back for his overthrow; certainly this un-pleasing character became on Cromwell's fall an eminent mem-ber of the Norfolk–Gardiner reactionary group. This being the case, Cromwell's situation bore little resemblance to that of a modern Prime Minister. To avert or mitigate the disfavour of the King he had not even a phalanx of sympathetic officers of state, let alone a parliamentary party, behind him. The service of a suspicious monarch had created in the governing group an atmosphere devoid of generosity, fair play, friendship and any loyalty except to Sovereign and to self. When Cromwell fell, it suited his critics to depict him as the creator of this merciless atmosphere, and many a historian has foolishly accepted the charge at its face-value. Indeed, from the viewpoint of self-preservation he had woefully lacked ruthlessness. Unmoved, he had watched subservient juries condemn more or less harmless monks, but he had not sought, while he had the chance, to lay those elaborate traps which would have destroyed his real enemies. With the powerful he had preferred hospitality and per-suasion. When their turn came, Norfolk and Gardiner knew bet-ter; they knew that 'stone dead hath no fellow', and they dis-dained to utilize no lie, however fantastic, if it served the pur-pose of his destruction.

The Attainder originally introduced in the Lords on 17 June

was afterwards dropped in favour of another version drawn up in the Commons, the one finally passed by the end of the month. The charges rehearsed against Cromwell seem at least as monstrous as those brought in former years against the most innocent of the conservatives. The methods of his accusers are best illustrated by their initial search for someone who would swear that in 1538 Cromwell had announced he would make himself King and marry the Princess Mary. Some of the accusations actually retained seem little less amazing. As the Act stands, the chief author seems to be Norfolk, since it dwells so repeatedly on the fact that Cromwell had been of poor and low degree, 'as few be within this your realm', and relates that, when reminded of these low origins, he had replied that 'if the lords would handle him so, that he would give them such a breakfast as never was made in England, and that the proudest should know'. We are powerfully reminded of Lord Darcy's prophecy. Hall ascribed Cromwell's fall chiefly to his offence against the 'snoffing pride of some prelates', but he also fell because in the service of the State he had never taken blue blood at more than its intrinsic worth. Of the major charges, the less serious relate to an alleged misuse of powers by acting without the King's consent; the more serious are charges of heresy. The first group was wisely kept vague: he had set at liberty people suspected of treason or attainted of misprision; he had sold licences to aliens to export money and goods; he had set up commissions without the King's knowledge; he had pretended to have power over the King; he had given passports to aliens without the King's consent. Such charges proved easy to make against a minister with such a range of powers and duties. As Cromwell himself readily admitted, 'I have meddled in so many matters under your Highness that I am not able to answer them all'.

The heresy-charges were only a shade more precise. Being a detestable heretic and utterly disposed to sow common sedition and variance amongst the King's true and loving subjects (perhaps the most astonishing phrase in the document!), Cromwell had spread heretical literature, caused heretical writings to be translated, and had asserted it lawful for every Christian man to minister the sacrament. As Vicegerent he had licensed heretics to preach and teach, had set them at liberty, refused to listen to accusations against them, and in order more firmly to establish heresies, had drawn to himself 'by retainours' many whom he infected. Finally, someone was found to swear that on 31 March 1539, he had said in the parish of St. Peter the Poor that the teaching of Barnes and other heretics was good and that, even if the King would turn from it, he himself would not, but would fight in the field sword-in-hand against the King and all others. Bishop Burnet later remarked with justice that had Cromwell really uttered such sentiments, Bedlam would have been a fitter place for his restraint than the Tower.

No wonder his enemies resolved to proceed by Act of Attainder, since this precluded court-proceedings in which the most incompetent defendant could have revealed the absurdity of such charges. Judging by Cromwell's letter to the King, the men who testified to verbal treasons were Sir George Throgmorton and Sir Richard Riche, Chancellor of the Augmentations. These names, as Dr. Elton has remarked, destroy any lingering belief that the charges were true. Throgmorton had been a prominent critic of the divorce; he was the brother of Pole's chief lieutenant and a well-known enemy of Cromwell. Riche was the witness who had already perjured himself to produce evidence of verbal treason against Sir Thomas More. In his letter of 12 June to the King, Cromwell protested that he never remembered speaking to these two together and that, 'if I did, I am sure I spake never of any such matter: and your Grace knoweth what manner of man Throgmorton hath ever been towards your Grace and your proceedings; and what Master Chancellor (Riche) hath been towards me, God and he best knoweth'. If Henry stopped to read these words, he might well have hesitated before executing a minister on such testimony; perhaps he remembered its character when, so soon afterwards, he came to see how he had been deceived.

This first letter of Cromwell is full of outraged and transparent declarations of loyalty, somewhat lost in the pedantically unpunctuated edition of Merriman. 'For as I ever', he exclaims, 'have had love to your honour, person, life, prosperity, health, wealth, joy and comfort, and also your most dear and most entirely beloved son the Prince his Grace, and your proceedings, God so help me in this mine adversity, and confound me if ever I thought the contrary! What labours, pains and travails I have taken according to my most bounden duty, God also knoweth; for if it were in my power, as it is God's, to make your Majesty to live ever young and prosperous, God knoweth I would. If it had been or were in my power to make you so rich as ye might enrich all men, God help me as I would do it. If it had been or were in my power to make your Majesty so puissant as all the world should be compelled to obey you, Christ he knoweth I would, for so am I of all other most bound, for your Majesty hath been the most bountiful prince to me that ever was King to his subject; yea, and more like a dear father (your Majesty not offended) than a master.'

The second letter from the Tower, that of 30 June, is much less dignified and moving, for it is the one in which he reports the evidence concerning the King's early relations with Anne of Cleves. The interval had also emboldened him to think there might be a remote chance of playing upon Henry's sentiments. While he professes himself 'ready to take the death when it shall please God and your Majesty', he continues, 'and yet the frail flesh inciteth me continually to call to your Grace for mercy and pardon for mine offences'. And at the end of his letter he adds: 'Most gracious prince, I cry for mercy, mercy, mercy'. This ejaculation has inevitably been taken out of its context to show that Cromwell made a squalid end, which he did not. Most political prisoners of the period used these tactics, and Tudor manners did not inculcate the concealment of natural emotions. Moreover, quite unlike Sir Thomas More, Cromwell had every reason to think of his death as senseless, for it vindicated no principle and seemed to leave a task manifestly incomplete. When the last hour arrived, it was likewise in keeping with contemporary manners that on the scaffold the condemned offender should make an improving, loyal, resigned and religious oration. Not infrequently its sense was remembered, written up and embellished by admirers. On 28 July, his long wait ended, Cromwell made such a speech and apparently made it well, though the beautiful oration and prayer put by Hall and Foxe into the mouth of 'this valiant soldier and captain of Christ' are no more verbally authentic than those assigned to their heroes by the great historians of Antiquity and of the Renaissance. So, concludes Foxe, 'he patiently suffered the stroke of the axe, by a ragged, butcherly miser, which very ungodly performed the office'. And so, he might justly have added, there passed from the scene the most devoted, laborious and efficient servant of the Crown in the long history of England.

Chapter Eleven

Modern Perspectives

HISTORIANS have commonly overestimated the states-manship and originality of Henry VIII, and in consequence have underrated those of Thomas Cromwell. Even so, the King's services to the nation may still in retrospect be considered great. When the dangers of relapse into anarchy had by no means sub-sided, one cannot regret that a great and masterful personality came to occupy the throne. Despite his fits of inhumanity against individuals, he bestowed upon the short and troubled lives of Tudor men and women the incalculable blessing of a long in-ternal peace, and upon his work was founded the even longer Elizabethan peace. Bearing in mind the too often hideous fate of Continental common men in the age of the so-called wars of religion, it would be no exaggeration to call Henry a true friend of the common Englishman. Yet this stabilizing and restraining role of the King can scarcely be dubbed creative. Ever in ultim-ate control, Henry prescribed the conditions and boundaries within which more original and industrious minds might operate, yet he himself neither generated nor consistently released the forces of change. It seems a matter of demonstrable fact that all the great constructive and destructive achievements of his long reign were crowded into the brief eight years of Thomas Crom-well's ministry. Even if we knew nothing in detail concerning the minister's personal responsibilities, it would be impossible to regard the phenomenon as pure coincidence. In comparison with this concentrated series of decisive actions, the rest of the reign looks at best a holding-operation, so much of its spectacular effort being in the last resort sterile. Henry's personal creative-ness may be fairly judged by the achievements of his last six years, when he held his ministers and subjects in a grip of un-precedented firmness, yet dissipated quite inconclusively the im-mense resources which Cromwell had placed in his hands. No part of his reign comes so near to deserving the reproach of failure.

Within the Cromwellian years, the spectacle is marvellous even where it is unattractive. It abounds in new ideas, still more in sheer political and administrative energy. The dead weight of ancient routines and ideas is hurled aside with a radicalism all the more remarkable in that Cromwell, unlike his namesake and unlike Napoleon, had to hand no rich stock of revolutionary doctrines. The statesman we have just glimpsed in a Reformation context was also the director of innumerable activities external or peripheral to our subject. Few administrative schemes, for example, have exerted more interesting effects upon the religious and intellectual history of Britain than the new *régime* established by Cromwell in Wales. His statutes culminated in the dissolution of the turbulent Marcher lordships, the complete shiring of the country, the reception of English law, conciliar government, justices of the peace and parliamentary representation. Alongside these steps went Rowland Lee's ruthless campaign against crime and disorder. The wisdom of this policy, in which Cromwell persisted when even Lee feared it might be premature, is in no way impugned by those evils which sprang from the neglect of Welsh problems by later governments. Though Cromwell cannot have foreseen the less direct results of his measures, he showed a firm and conscious grasp of the creative nature of social order, a principle never demonstrated to greater advantage than in Wales. The criticisms of Welsh parochialists, ever oblivious to the true achievements of their own expansive nation, should not be directed against the reformer who set free a small yet highly gifted nation to influence, enliven and diversify far larger societies. In particular, the subsequent history of British religion, both at home and abroad, would be as unthinkable without its Welsh components as without those which in later generations emanated from the Scots.

That the experience of Wales was no accident of history may be seen in the parallel experience of northern England, where Cromwell refashioned the King's Council in the North and made it function effectively for the first time in its history. Here Robert Holgate (another able ecclesiastic dubbed by the romantics 'a creature of Cromwell') began to change another lawless and faction-ridden people into one of the most energetic and purposeful sections of English society. When a worthy life of Cromwell comes to be written, it will devote many pages to the statesman-ship which broke the feudal liberties and the sanctuaries, re-pressed the family factions, maintained peace and even co-opera-tion with the Scots, promoted the overthrow of the Geraldines in Ireland, began the series of national poor-laws and removed the focus of the cloth-trade from Antwerp to London. It may devote even more to the Cromwell who stopped the debasement and export of the coinage, solved by one statute the old problem of Uses, remoulded and expanded the national system of finan-cial courts, made the Principal Secretary chief minister in place of the Chancellor, and perfected the development of the small and workmanlike Privy Council. In the field of the State, he was indeed a true 'universal man' of the Renaissance. That there existed a personal and opportunist element in some of these changes cannot be denied; it could not be otherwise when so much of the drive and the supervision came from a single man surrounded by rivals, and never permitted a pause for the con-solidation and delegation of authority. Yet unlike Wolsey, Crom-well was a Pygmalion whose creations had a strange power to develop a vitality of their own, one which in many cases long outlasted the brief rule of their author. Not all his labours were proof against the incapacity of his successors, yet in general their survival-value proved high, because they possessed administra-tive logic and corresponded with the needs of that day and the next.

Behind the complexities of detail, Cromwell's policy looks highly coherent: his work is all of a piece and bears a personal signature. In his Reformation-policy, just as in all other spheres, he was first and foremost a state-builder. The significance of the English Reformation is very far from being limited to religious or even to ecclesiastical history: it is a crisis and a resolution of crisis in the history of the English State and people. It forms a crucial chapter in the story of our sovereignty, of our national law and institutions, of our psychological responses to the claims of authority. The main result of the Cromwellian phase was the transfer of the great ecclesiastical sector of English society and law to the sovereignty of the King in Parliament. And if this transfer belongs to the rise of Leviathan, the fact should be judged neither in our present-day context nor even in a Hob-besian context, since in mid-Tudor times the need to strengthen the State was far stronger than at any later phase of English history. Oliver Cromwell was chiefly concerned to wrest the helm of the ship from incompetent steersmen, but Thomas Cromwell had to repair the rotten timbers of the ship itself. In his day, Englishmen were not choosing between autocracy and democracy; they were choosing between a powerful State and intermittent anarchy. By no means every detailed step of the Cromwellian Reformation can be justified by reference to such needs, yet the whole transaction belongs to the story of the nation in its broadest aspects: it can never be understood by narrowly ecclesiastical historians.

In the international sphere, Cromwell has obvious significance as a leading agent in the severance of Englishmen from the ancient papal bond and from the ideal of an international Christendom. The strictly doctrinal aspects of this step must be left to theologians. Regarding its political and cultural implications, we have already recorded the view that these have been commonly exaggerated, that More's idealism meant little in terms of international peace, justice, brotherhood and freedom, that the revolt of the northern nations against a Mediterranean-centred Church had now—irrespective of mere personalities—become practically inevitable. Cromwell's intellectual limitations appear less in his rejection of a dubious internationalism than in the *naïveté* which made him see in Rome, rather than in Spain, the detested centre of a system in which English interests must always suffer betrayal. Yet he was neither the creator of the English insular tradition nor the inventor of a radically new foreign policy. While opposed to wasteful jingoism, he retained the anti-French prejudices of his generation. Again in an established medieval tradition, he strove hard to maintain peace with the ruler of the Netherlands. Failing this, he sought to organize alliances in Germany. Personally well-travelled and highly cautious, he represents the less insular of the two moods of subsequent English foreign policy.

Greater ultimate significance attaches to Cromwell's part in the evolution of erastian principles; in the emergence at home of a lay-dominated society with its mind firmly fixed upon moderation, good sense and security in this world. Not for Englishmen the superb follies of Spain's self-martyrdom to a fanatic ideal. Even less did they want to see other-worldly aspirations used to justify internal anarchy and bloodshed. Before the harsh experience of civil war had impressed similar lessons upon Bodin and the *Politiques* in France, Englishmen, clerical and lay alike, rejected the primacy of doctrinal allegiances, preferred peace to a sword and embraced the vision of a paternal state, harsh against traitors yet mild towards heretics. The early stages of this process may with all the greater confidence be ascribed to Cromwell and his group, since the King himself seems to have understood its implications none too clearly. If from one angle Cromwell was a careerist who sold the King a revolutionary plan to gain his divorce, his far-seeing mind obviously penetrated beyond these mere occasons and implements of change to the concept of a more efficiently and rationally organized nation, one based not merely upon administrative and judicial reforms, but upon a new triangular relationship between Church, State and Society. Worldly security is not an ideal which can be freely impugned by our own generation. Those who criticize the erastian programme as earthy and mundane would not themselves prefer to have lived in an England torn by pseudo-religious strife. Such critics should reflect that Tudor men and women were no mere stepping-stones towards our noble selves, that they did not exist to provide us with colourful spectacles, or even with the prototypes of modern liberal democracy. Unavoidable circumstance made their lives harsh and short; their small share of ease and amenity depended in large part upon royal justice and the peace of the commonwealth. Here they had emphatically no reason to envy either foreigners or their own forebears.

In retrospect Cromwell stands out as the leader of an invasion of our public affairs by laymen and the lay spirit. He and his like show a vivid consciousness of the shortcomings of ecclesiastical administration and jurisdiction; behind the thin facade of courteous reverence, they entertained a strong resentment against the professional *esprit de corps*, the easily-won wealth, the hauteur and fundamental worldliness of their prelatical associates. No fair-minded observer would deny that much hypocrisy marked this lay invasion. It was accompanied by too much greed and self-interest. Given a juster vision, its exponents might also have concentrated a part of their reforming zeal against the penal ferocity, the inequities, the corruptions from which even lay justice had yet by no means liberated itself. Too few of them showed either Cromwell's penchant for rationalization, or the ardour of the Commonwealth Party for economic and social reform. Yet though the lay invasion was not executed by angels of

light, some of its results might now be reasonably defended—
—even by churchmen! Throughout its long history the Christian Church has often been corrupted by worldly power, and as often, to its ultimate benefit, been struck down in judgement. By the reign of Henry VIII, the incapacity of the English Church to achieve self-reform had too long invited interference by its lay members and by their clerical allies. Yet the radicalism of the changes they thrust upon it has commonly been exaggerated. Cromwell did not, for example, seek to destroy ecclesiastical jurisdiction. As the records of any diocesan registry prove, the church courts survived his ministry intact; their methods underwent no significant modifications; their control over the lives of both clergy and laity showed no sudden or dramatic decline throughout the Tudor age. It was an evolutionary process which turned the national Church from judicial and coercive into persuasive and missionary habits of mind. Again, the lay revolution was to a surprising extent executed by clergymen. They were critical rather than Protestant, and they provided Cromwell with some of his ablest agents. Such men as Rowland Lee, Robert Holgate, Edward Fox and Thomas Starkey have inevitably been castigated as renegades—inevitably, but in general unjustly, for they believed in what they were doing, and grasped the simple point that ecclesiastical and social reforms were unlikely to be initiated by any other agency save the State. Cromwell spent a large part of his career working with clergymen; he never allowed his anticlericalism to interfere with his use of the best available talent and conviction. It might indeed be more accurate to describe the Cromwellian movement as anti-prelatical rather than anticlerical, for while the lower clergy took his reforms as they came, the bishops never looked quite the same again.

In this story of Cromwell's alliance with the critical forces of society, the Protestants play a somewhat dubious role. He became notorious as the protector of numerous individual Reformers; despite his apparent lack of spiritual ardour, it looks as if previous historians have not taken his religious convictions with nearly enough seriousness, He showed both temperamental and logical affinities with the Lutherans; he collapsed partly because he had laid himself open to charges of heresy, and had taken risks to build a Protestant confederation; he emerged somewhat startlingly in literature as John Foxe's 'valiant soldier and captain of Christ'. Far more significantly, he ensured the extension of Protestant ideas by giving the English Bible to the people, an action which alone assures him a curious yet conspicuous place in the history of religion proper. For all that, he proffered the Bible to the public in a spirit very different from that which animated men like Foxe. We have already glimpsed a likelihood that the biblical policy was related not only to the anticlerical but to the constructive and educational aspects of his social policy. Between the Bible and erastianism in general, the logical connections seem also obvious. A religion based on scriptural research and exegesis logically demanded a measure of mutual forbearance between the differing schools of interpretation, but where else could this forbearance be ensured save within the framework of State-supremacy? The return of Protestantism to persecuting, conformist and would-be oecumenical notions proceeded to obscure this logic—both inside and outside the Anglican communion—until the nineteenth century. It remains nevertheless a logic explicit enough in the settlement envisaged by Cromwell, who in matters of religion saw the State less as formulating the rules of the game than as a referee duly empowered to keep the players in order. His secular awareness of the limitations of dogmatism, together with the liberal concepts of Melancthon, caused him to stand much nearer to modern tolerationist concepts than did either Henry VIII or Calvin.

Quite apart from these concepts, it is also difficult to exaggerate the importance for English Protestantism of that breathing-space which his ministry provided. These years saw the old orthodoxy lose its last chances of pursuing inquisitorial tactics with a reasonable hope of success. The fact received tacit admission even from Henry VIII, whose political commonsense forbade him to follow Cromwell's death by a Catholic persecution of any great intensity and scope. Yet if Cromwell did much for Protestantism, it was yet neither strong enough nor sufficiently well-led to repay his services. Emphatically, he did not ride to power upon a wave of Protestant sentiment, and if he ever anticipated massive political support from a fast-growing Protestant body, he must have been sorely disappointed. The English Bible apart, his ecclesiastical enterprises might have been pursued with equal success had Lutheranism never reached England. And could he have foreseen the theocracy about to emerge from Geneva, he might have admired its cult of efficiency, yet he might also have exclaimed, more vociferously than any, that new presbyter was but old priest writ large.

With the origins of Anglicanism his connections appear somewhat more clear-cut. Unspiritual by nature and background, he obviously contributed little to its devotional ethos, but more than any man he supplied it with the less ethereal rudiments of its character: its notion of the *via media*, its institutionalized Supremacy of King in Parliament, its adiaphorist attempt to comprehend divergent doctrinal trends, its valiant effort to be scriptural, its emphases upon patriotism, service to the State, sound learning, public education and good sense, as opposed to strict logic. Throughout the last hundred years, the Anglo-Catholic viewpoint has been predominant in Anglican historiography, and the antipathy of its adherents towards a hard-boiled lay Vicegerent can well be understood. They wanted almost all the results of the Reformation, while detesting the process itself. At the same time, emotion should not have blinded these historians to the creative influences of Thomas Cromwell and of his humanist-clerical assistants, who began to formulate the medial position of the national Church. Even strong doctrinal partisans within the Anglican communion need nowadays feel no shame concerning this early branch of their family tree. If the Cromwellians were neither saints nor martyrs, they did not much resemble the villains of neo-Tractarian melodrama. The growing realization that even Cromwell had his special brand of idealism may help to make him a shade more acceptable even to those who, inspired directly or indirectly by Dixon and Gairdner (if not by Gasquet and Belloc), have hitherto averted their eyes in pained rejection. Cromwell bore an important share in defining the terms upon which a national and imperial Church was to be linked with the State. These inhibiting links have naturally been regarded with impatience by many of its most devoted members. Too often in their warring convictions they have overlooked the corresponding advantages. A Church based upon relatively comprehensive and liberal lines would otherwise soon have been fractured through the efforts of zealots to capture it for their respective schools of thought. Precisely because of its mundane detachment from dogmatic zeal, the State has always tended to enforce this experiment in active toleration which forms the peculiar appeal of Anglicanism. And the greatest spiritual achievements of the Church of England have generally been attained in conjunction with the State and with national secular enterprise.

Amongst the major ecclesiastical schemes of Cromwell, I take the dissolution of the monasteries to have less historical importance than has commonly been supposed. It may be deposed from its former pre-eminence for many reasons: because the monasteries had already ceased to be an influential force in English life; because monasticism could not in any case have survived in Elizabethan England; because Cromwell's attempt to endow the Crown with monastic revenues was thwarted by the squandermania of Henry's last years; because it now seems impossible to elevate the social and economic results of the dissolution to the status of a cataclysm in our history. Today no informed students of the period can be impressed by the worthless quotations from Fuller, Spelman, Cobbett and various later sentimentalists, which Gasquet and others have utilized to produce that familiar cataclysmic picture: the wealthy Protestant gentry rack-renting the peasantry and driving men from the land by enclosures; the poor made ever poorer, the monks themselves driven to 'a deplorable life of vagrancy and poverty'. The literary evidence of contemporaries lays an almost negligible emphasis upon the dissolution as a cause of poverty, but even if it had taken the dramatic line, most of it would be worthless, because pamphleteers and pulpit-moralists who did not understand such elementary background-factors at the great inflation cannot claim acceptance as serious economic analysts. At no stage of the Tudor period was the extent of enclosures very large, but they had been a problem recognized by legislation many years before the monastic suppression, while religious houses themselves had not infrequently enclosed to the hurt of their tenants and neighbours. Again, on the present evidence, no spate of rack-renting can be shown to have arisen from the dissolution. In any case, why should tenant-farmers have prospered by the immense mid-Tudor rise in food-prices, while their landlords contented themselves with low, pre-inflationary rents? The silvermines of Peru destroyed long in advance the extremist legends beloved alike by Fabian and Catholic propagandists. And even supposing the monasteries had survived and had suddenly switched to a quixotic policy, by what financial wizardry could they have kept their rents static in an inflationary world?

In one respect, at least, the significance of the dissolution seems little diminished by modern research. It continues to occupy an important place among the factors which, as the Tudor age advanced, rendered the landed gentry a more numerous and a more potent section of English society. From this time a thriving market in land became a continuous feature of the nation's economic life, and over the years land was to prove an excellent investment for most of its purchasers. In any sizeable shire, one may point to several clear examples of families which based a new or a growing prosperity upon wise purchases of monastic and other church lands. Many of these so-called 'new men' were certainly younger sons of established families, though often they attained independent estates through the profits of an official or legal career. Less commonly, it would seem, the newcomers were substantial yeomen, already achieving economic equality with the class they were destined to enter. Less commonly still, in my experience, they were genuinely newcomers with little previous background save that of business or the professions. When we seek to check these broad impressions by detailed reference to regional and local history, the surviving records demand slow and painstaking analysis. It was easy for Savine and Liljegren to make a list of the original grantees of monastic lands drawn from the Patent Rolls; easy, but almost in vain, since little interest attaches to the many transient first buyers who held these lands for very brief periods during the years immediately following the dissolution. With far greater significance, the Particulars for Grants can be made, in the light of local knowledge, to establish the prevalent types of ownership into which the lands fell during the two or three decades between 1540 and the early years of Elizabeth. Such information 'in depth' is well worth having, but as yet it has been presented in full detail only in the case of the county of Devon. Here Dr. Youings has shown that these lands did not pass to a handful of rich men but increased the number of moderate-sized estates. More important, they did not create a new class of profiteer-merchant-landlords, but by 1558 were widely distributed amongst members of established local families, less than 10 per cent. being owned by people who came in from outside Devon. This unsensational picture is in general supported by Mr. Hodgett's researches on the Lincolnshire monastic lands. The groups of London speculators who here initially bought parcels with a view to profitable resale were ephemeral owner. Professor Habakkuk has recently given strong reasons for the belief that many so-called speculators were mere humble agents from whom the real purchasers took over the lands within a short space of time. There seems nowhere evidence to indicate the rise of a novel type of landlord emancipated from the decent usages of rural society. Again, the purchase of monastic lands had nothing to do with doctrinal allegiances, and many of the greatest purchasers were known religious conservatives. Even the widespread notion that the sale of monastic lands guaranteed England against the revival of Catholic doctrine has little to recommend it: not for a moment was Mary's reaction seriously threatened by nervous owners of ex-monastic lands, nor did even this injudicious ruler attempt to make such owners disgorge their unholy purchases. Further research will need to produce many surprises before we can make the dissolution a general scapegoat for pauperism and other social evils, the causes of which can be seen plainly enough in quite different fields of the national economy. All in all, Cromwell's dissolution-policy doubtless represents an injustice towards the monastic ideal; it was certainly a failure, in that it brought no lasting financial stability to the Crown; yet it cannot, on the evidence now available, be supposed to have exerted catastrophic or permanent effects upon the material lives of Englishmen. For the neglect of the Crown to make better use of monastic revenues in the ecclesiastical and educational fields we have already seen the absurdity of blaming Cromwell, who was destroyed when he had scarcely completed the dissolution itself. By a curious irony, so many of the financial plans by which he set such store were fated to be nullified through unforeseen circumstance or by incapable successors.

With such considerations in mind, we should do belated justice to the memory of a great English statesman and patriot by devoting more attention to those fields in which he received some opportunity to follow up his initial reforms and exercise some control over their sequels. In the light of modern knowledge, such elements of his work seem likely to bulk much larger than in the past. To those whose ideals still centre around an international Church, a papal headship and a powerful clerical order, the destructive elements must continue to bulk larger still. Rightly or wrongly, many nations in the western tradition have refused to revert to such ideals, and it is across their histories that the influence of Thomas Cromwell and of his Elizabethan legatees stands most patently inscribed. On some other aspects of his story a growing measure of agreement between Catholics and non-Catholics may remain within the bounds of possibility. I like to presume, for example, that the merely sordid, selfish, cruel careerist has returned for ever into the realm of legend where it belongs, and that Thomas Cromwell's revolutionary conviction, the breadth and bigness of his ideas, are now being reasonably demonstrated. A reader who still doubted his ultimate sincerity, his zeal to 'edify' or create, might turn with profit to that long, heartfelt, even emotional letter which he wrote to Bishop Shaxton during their disagreements in March 1538. It has a strangely convincing ring when the writer declares that he, just as much as any priest, feels himself engaged upon God's work, and that he aims solely at constructive results. 'I do not cease to give thanks that it has pleased His goodness to use me as an instrument and to work somewhat by me, so I trust I am as ready to serve Him in my calling as you are. . . . My prayer is that God give me no longer life than I shall be glad to use mine office in edification and not in destruction.'

Select Bibliography

A. *Thomas Cromwell*

The **Bibliography** *of British History*, ed C. **Read** (2nd edn., 1959), obviates the need for extended reference to older works. Most of the extant documents concerning Cromwell's general and ecclesiastical policies are calendared in the 21 volumes of the *Letters and Papers of Henry VIII*, ed. J. S. Brewer, J. Gairdner and R. H. Brodie (1864–1929). R. B. Merriman, *The Life and Letters of Thomas Cromwell* (2 vols., 1902), prints in full a tiny proportion of these documents: those written by Cromwell himself. Merriman's introduction, especially the section on foreign policy, remains very valuable, yet he is curiously hostile and anxious to believe the worst. He even evolves an irresponsible fantasy to the effect that Cromwell may have poisoned Queen Katherine: Cromwell had, after all, spent time in Italy and she was in his way!

Of the earlier writers, almost the only one to emancipate himself from the prevalent spirit was P. Van Dyke in his *Renascence Portraits* (1906). The most important recent contributions to the study of Cromwell's ministry are those of Dr. G. R. Elton. His major work, *The Tudor Revolution in Government* (1953), lies farther outside the Reformation-theme than a number of his articles, which afford a balanced interpretation of Cromwell's personality, aims and outlook. The following are especially relevant: "King or Minister? The man behind the Henrician Reformation," in *History*, xxxix (1954); "The Political Creed of Thomas Cromwell," in *Trans. Royal Hist. Soc.*, 5 ser., vi (1956); "The Evolution of a Reformation Statute," in *English Hist. Review*, lxix (1949); "Parliamentary Drafts, 1529–1540," in *Bulletin of the Institute of Hist. Research*, xxv (1952); cf. also *ibid.*, xxvii (1954); "Thomas Cromwell's Decline and Fall," in *Cambridge Historical Journal*, x (1951); "The Commons' Supplication of 1532," in *English Hist. Review*, lxvi (1951). For a rival interpretation of this last, see J. P. Cooper in *ibid.*, lxxii (1957). Dr. Elton's recent *Star Chamber Stories* (1958) throws some fresh sidelights on Cromwell's policy and outlook: with the exception of the reprinted chapter on the Quondam of Rievaulx, I have not used this material, but it will be found entirely in accordance with the present interpretation.

B. Political Thought

On the political theory of the Cromwellian circle, two important books are available: W. G. Zeeveld, *Foundations of Tudor Policy* (1948), and F. L. Van Baumer, *The Early Tudor Theory of Kingship* (1940). Both contain valuable bibliographies. Dr. Baumer has also written on Thomas Starkey and Marsiglio in *Politica*, ii (1936–7), and on St. German in *American Hist. Review*, xlii (1937). On the Cromwell-Machiavelli problem, see Elton, "The Political Creed of Thomas Cromwell," above, and T. M. Parker, "Was Thomas Cromwell a Machiavellian?" in *Journal of Ecclesiastical Hist.*, i (1950). On Clement Armstrong, see S. T. Bindoff in *Economic History Review*, xiv (1944–5), and on Wilfrid Holme, A. G. Dickens in *Yorks. Archaeological Journal*, xxxix (1956). For the political writings of Stephen Gardiner, see P. Janelle, *Obedience in Church and State* (1930). There are valuable general accounts in J. W. Allen, *History of Political Thought in the Sixteenth Century* (1928), and in C. Morris, *Political Thought in England. Tyndale to Hooker* (1953).

C. The Monasteries and their Dissolution

The *Bibliography of British History* (above) has a section on this topic. Some recent contributions are:

Visitations in the Diocese of Lincoln, 1517-1531, ed. A. Hamilton Thompson (Lincoln Record Soc., xxxiii, xxxv, xxxvii, 1940–44–47); *Monastic Chancery Proceedings*, ed. J. S. Purvis (Yorks.

Archaeol. Soc., Record Series, lxxxviii); *The Register or Chronicle of Butley Priory*, ed. A. G. Dickens (1951); E. M. Thompson, *The Carthusian Order in England* (1930); G. Baskerville, *English Monks and the Suppression of the Monasteries* (1937). On the devolution of monastic lands, see *Devon Monastic Lands: Calendar of Particulars for Grants*, ed. J. Youings (Devon and Cornwall Record Soc., new series, i). Dr. Youings' conclusions are summarized in *Bulletin of the Institute of Hist. Research*, xxiv (1951). See also her article, "The Terms of the Disposal of the Devon Monastic Lands" in *English Hist. Review*, lxix (1954). H. J. Habakkuk, "The Market for Monastic Property 1539–1603," in *Economic History Review*, x (1958), deals with a variety of problems concerning the sale of the monastic lands. G. A. J. Hodgett's unpublished London M.A. thesis (1947) *The Dissolution of the Monasteries in Lincolnshire* has also much information on sales and speculation. See also the same writer's "The Dissolution of Religious Houses in Lincolnshire and the Changing Structure of Society" in *Lincs. Architectural and Archaeological Soc. Reports*, iv. (i) (1951). On monastic pensions, see A. G. Dickens in *English Hist. Review*, lv (1940), which modifies Mr. Baskerville's conclusions. The standard volumes of D. Knowles on medieval monasticism will shortly be followed by another, bringing the story to the Reformation. The best short survey of the monasteries on the eve of the dissolution is in P. Hughes (below). A. Savine, *English Monasteries on the Eve of the Dissolution* (1909), remains indispensable for the economic side and for the *Valor Ecclesiasticus*. S. B. Liljegren, *The Fall of the Monasteries* (Lund, 1924), prints a list of the original grants to 1547.

D. *The English Reformation*

The best brief account is T. M. Parker, *The English Reformation to 1558* (1950). F. M. Powicke, *The Reformation in England* (1941) is also a distinguished outline. Of the more extended works, P. Hughes, *The Reformation in England*, vol. i, is capacious, scholarly and seldom suppresses inconvenient facts; viewpoint, moderate Roman Catholic. The two volumes by H. Maynard Smith, *Pre-Reformation England* (1938) and *Henry VIII and the Reformation* (1948), are widely read and brightly written; viewpoint, clerical-Anglican. G. Constant, *The Reformation in England* (2 vols., 1934, 1942), is a selective Romanist partisan, but his references are valuable. The well-known general works on the Tudor period by S. T. Bindoff (1950), J. D. Mackie (1952) and G. R. Elton (1955) naturally contain much useful material on the Reformation and its periphery.

The following deal with special topics: J. F. Mozley, *Coverdale and his Bibles* (1953) is much the best account: viewpoint, strongly pro-Reformer. The same author's *William Tyndale* (1937) is a useful but somewhat idealized biography. On *praemunire*, see W. T. Waugh in *English Hist. Review*, xxxvii (1922); this is more lucidly summarized in *History*, viii (1923–4). On the state of the late medieval Church, A. Hamilton Thompson, *The English Clergy* (1947), is excellent. The crisis of 1514–15 and its aftermath are treated by A. Ogle, *The Tragedy of the Lollards' Tower* (1949). On early Lutherans, see E. G. Rupp, *The English Protestant Tradition* (1947). C. W. Dugmore, *The Mass and the English Reformers* (1958) is an important work on the central doctrinal dispute. On the Pardon of the Clergy, J. Scarisbrick, in *Cambridge Historical Journal*, xii (1956); on the Proclamations Act, E. R. Adair in *English Hist. Review*, xxxii (1917); on Treason by Words, I. D. Thornley in *ibid.*; on the Northern Convocation, A. G. Dickens in *Church Quarterly Review*, Oct.–Dec. 1938. On the Henrician bishops, see L. B. Smith, *Tudor Prelates and Politics* (1953); apart from A. F. Pollard's classic *Wolsey* (1929, 1953), perhaps the best individual biography is C. Sturge, *Cuthbert Tunstall* (1938). For Robert Holgate, see *St. Anthony's Hall Publications*, no. viii (1955). W. Schenck, *Reginald Pole* (1950), is a sympathetic but rather uncritical study, and G. Mattingly, *Catherine of Aragon* (1950), an able biography; both take the Catholic standpoint.

E. Regional History

The social, economic and religious history of the Reformation, written on a regional basis, offers a promising field for research. A. L. Rowse, *Tudor Cornwall* (1941), is a learned and attractive survey of society, very informative on the Henrician Reformation. A. G. Dickens, *Lollards and Protestants in the Diocese of York* (1959), deals with the merging of these heresies from 1509 to 1558 and has a full account of Sir Francis Bigod. An outstanding regional study of another type is R. R. Reid, *The King's Council in the North* (1921), which contains much else besides institutional history; e.g. the best short account of the causes of the Pilgrimage of Grace, pp. 121 *seqq.* Note also Youings and Hodgett above.

Index

192